ZOGARTH

THE
PRIMAL HUNTER
BOOK TWELVE

THE PRIMAL HUNTER 12
©2025 ZOGARTH

Aethon Books
www.aethonbooks.com

Print and eBook design and formatting by Kevin G. Summers. Artwork provided by Antti Hakosaari.

Published by Aethon Books LLC.

Aethon Books is not responsible for websites (or their content) that are not owned by the publisher.

ALSO BY ZOGARTH

———

Want to discuss our books with other readers and even the authors?

JOIN THE AETHON DISCORD!

Calling all LitRPG fans: be the first to discover groundbreaking new releases, access incredible deals, and participate in thrilling giveaways by subscribing to our exclusive LitRPG Newsletter.

https://aethonbooks.com/litrpg-newsletter/

Previously in The Primal Hunter

Oh, we're still Nevermore, huh? Well, it's with great sadness I must inform you, dear reader, that the Nevermore arc will end in this book. I know, I know, it could (and should) totally have been at least two books longer, so I apologize to all those who wished that Nevermore would indeed be forevermore.

Anyhow, Book 11 begins as we – together with the Wyrmgod of Nevermore, Villy, and Minaga, who are all having a little streaming party watching Jake's adventures - join our party of five Nevermore Attendees after a thirty-year time skip where they've been clearing floors and getting levels, all growing in power as they make it all the way to floor 70.

I could include the full stat sheet here... but I'll show mercy to the audiobook listeners and not do that.

During these few decades, Jake had gained roughly thirty levels, putting him at level 253, and thus in mid-tier C-grade. Not to mention, his skills had all grown significantly, something a couple of decades tend to result in. His other party members experienced similar growth, with Sylphie – the best and fluffiest murder bird in the multiverse – having gained the most, putting her at level 267.

The Fallen King, Unique Lifeform, and former Tutorial boss now turned ally, as well as Dina and Sword Saint, dryad druid, and swordsman, respectively, all kept up with their levels, making the entire party far more powerful. Seeing as they've all hit a bit of a plateau with their leveling, they decide to move onto another aspect of Nevermore they had to do sooner rather than later:

Challenge Dungeons.

Which was, yes, all of Book 11. And the start of Book 12. I do love my dungeons.

These Challenge Dungeons all had to be completed individually, and each would take roughly two years. With five available, the party decided to split up and meet back up in approximately a decade.

As a reminder (which is kind of the point of a recap), the reason why all these Challenge Dungeons are important is due to the final Nevermore Leaderboards. Every Nevermore Attendee part of this Leaderboards competition gained Nevermore Points as they climbed the floors, with the occasional small percentage modifier that would add extra points at the final calculation also gained.

The Challenge Dungeons are the most significant sources of these percentage amplifiers, with each of them providing one based on the performance of the challenger. The Challenge Dungeons also naturally added points, making them overall the most efficient section of Nevermore time-wise to gain points in, with the general consensus being that the true winner of the Leaderboards contest would be found in the Challenge Dungeons.

Seeing as the order in which one does these five Challenge Dungeons doesn't matter, Jake ends up picking the one with a name that appeals the most to him first: the Colosseum of Mortals.

After saying farewell for now to his party members, Jake entered this first Challenge Dungeon, and the instant he was inside, it became clear these Challenge Dungeons were different from anything Jake had experienced before.

Inside the Colosseum of Mortals, Jake's stats were reduced to an even 10 across the board (besides what was increased by his percentage amplifiers, making him still decently stronger), all his skills besides a few basic ones were gone, and all his equipment was taken away.

The objective of this Challenge Dungeon is to fight in the Colosseum of Mortals and win as many matches as one can to advance through the grades. There are a bunch of more rules but for the sake of brevity, those shall be swiftly skipped over.

Entering his first fight in the arena, Jake quickly makes work of his foe. And the next one after that... and for a good while, Jake is just smashing everyone he encounters effortlessly, as none of them stand a chance. Slowly, Jake Thayne morphs into the feared Doomfoot, the persona of a bored hunter who started kicking stuff to try and at least introduce some level of entertainment to the fights.

However, this casualness ends when he encounters his first actual foe: the Benevolent Monk. Someone he would later come to learn was an image (read: a cloned version that isn't actually a clone) of a god known as the Soulfist Daolord.

Jake, still cocky from having easily won everything so far, ends up getting his ass handed to him and only winning due to the Benevolent Monk implementing a rule that the winner will be the one who first lands ten hits. Jake, walking away feeling like a loser with a technical victory goes and finally gets some proper weapons for the upcoming fights that only get harder...

Well, they would get more challenging, after Jake advances higher in the ranks. For now, most were still opponents he could beat easily.

Lots of kicking and stabbing later, Jake soon makes it to where the true fighting begins. In order to not make this recap me just going over every single fight again, here's a highlight of opponents selected because I decided to:

The Necromancer, who's actually a god from the Risen known as the Undying General, and a Transcendent with the ability to be really good at not dying. Something Jake was not prepared for, as in this fight, Jake ends up losing his first life (Jake had 10 lives within this Challenge Dungeon). He wins the rematch, though.

Another god, the Dark Mistress, who's an image of Umbra, someone Jake beats relatively easily through the power of his Bloodline making him a nightmare to someone relying on stealth and assassination tactics.

Rematch with the Benevolent Monk, Jake getting a proper fight this time around, ending with a cryptic message about how they would definitely encounter him and his "lord" again after Jake wins.

Warrior of Valhal, the wife of Valdemar, and the de-facto leader of the Primordial faction, also known as Gudrun. Through relying on tools and guile, she put up a good fight, but Jake still comes out the winner, as no tool is better than a good bow.

The Lord of the Hunt, a hunter from the Pantheon of Life known as Artemis in the outside world. Using a combination of nature magic and archery, she instantly catches Jake's attention as the two of them face off in a duel of bowmanship, Jake eventually winning the bout, though not without taking his fair share of injuries.

Luckily, the Lord of the Hunt also enjoyed the duel and invited Jake to use a healing pool in her residence within the Challenge Dungeon, and as an economically-minded person, who was Jake to reject such a cost-effective proposal?

This is where another important aspect of the Colosseum of Mortals has to be pointed out. The images used of gods had the ability to regain all of their memories as gods after their defeat, allowing them to interact with the challenger if they so desired. They remained images, and their memories were from the time they were created – sometime before the integration of Jake's universe – but they were essentially the same people as on the outside.

This is quite crucial as it adds to the surprise and creates quite a bit of future drama when the image of Artemis - fully aware it's a god - and Jake decide to perhaps get a bit closer than anyone had expected.

Not that Jake cares in the moment as he enjoys spending time with Artemis. Between his fights, the two of them have fun together in various ways, some of them archery-related and some of them only suitable for adult audiences. Oh, and before anyone asks (and I know a lot of people have asked), no, never gonna write anything downright explicit. Use your damn imagination... and don't link me your smut fanfiction if you decide to make one... because, yes, that has also happened. I'm not gonna tell you which two characters that one was about...

Moving on, Jake soon climbs to the top to become the Grand Champion of the Colosseum of Mortals. With that, he only had one fight left against the toughest foe yet. A simple warrior wielding an axe, who also happens to be the leader of Valhal and a being many recognize as the most powerful entity in the multiverse: Valdemar.

At this point, Jake had nine lives remaining. With confidence, he walked into the arena, only for a few things to be clear. First of which was that, contrary to every other image of gods in the Challenge Dungeon, Valdemar had full memories of who he truly was. Secondly... Valdemar was an absolute monster compared to any opponent prior.

Nine lives soon became eight, then seven, six, and as Jake lost them one by one, he learned more about his opponent. It also quickly became apparent that the goal wasn't necessarily for the challenger to defeat Valdemar but merely to earn his recognition.

Jake naturally wanted to win and spent every life he had learning more about his opponent. This continued until, finally, he walked into the arena with one life and a plan in mind...

Funny fact, on Patreon, the chapter Jake entered the arena for the final fight was also the chapter I went on a 1-month break. Good times, man, good times.

Jake's final battle with Valdemar is a hard-fought one that ends with Jake getting the recognition of Valdemar for his power, meaning he'd completed the Challenge Dungeon. As a sign of respect, Valdemar stopped holding any of his power back as his Transcendent ability fully activated, making him several times stronger as he lifted his axe for the killing blow.

That's also when Jake realized that his opponent hadn't ever fully taken him seriously during the fight, and as the axe descended upon him, he decided to finally stop suppressing his survival instinct but fully let it loose.

Entering a state of absolute clarity, Jake eventually does stuff and kills Valdemar (yeah, not gonna elaborate more on it than that; go reread the full fight if you want a complete recap :P).

This victory comes with a lot of extra Nevermore Points and even a cool title, giving some extra stats. Oh, and a mythical item to put in his spatial storage where it can sit snuggly with all the other stuff Jake throws in there and forgets.

However, perhaps the most impactful effect of Jake's victory wasn't inside the Challenge Dungeon but what it caused on the outside.

Nevermore wasn't only a massive mega-dungeon but one of the premier information brokers of the multiverse, using all the data they gathered on those who did the dungeon. A base requirement of the many gods who gave their images to the World Wonder was also to be made aware of what happened within. This is to say that Artemis was informed of what happened with her image there, but so was Valdemar, making them both quite interested in our little hunter.

During Jake's fun time within the Challenge Dungeons, the world outside also moved as Meira — Jake's former slave and now Chosen of Duskleaf — in a display of her newfound status, returns to her home village for the first time since she was kidnapped by the Order of the Malefic Viper after the fall of the Brimstone Hegemon.

There, she reunites with her family and effectively claims the clan's entire area as her own dominion, making use of the clout afforded to her by Duskleaf. So, yeah, things are going quite well on her end.

Back with Jake, he begins his second Challenge Dungeon, a place known as the Test of Character. As the name implies, this is a Challenge Dungeon that tests the character of the Nevermore Attendees by having them take on the identity of people within different scenarios and seeing how they handle it. Out of all the dungeons, this was by far Jake's least favorite, and the only thing he really got out of it was time to upgrade his Gaze of the Apex Hunter to mythical grade. His percentage amplifier and points from this one were certifiably mid.

Things did get interesting after the Challenge Dungeon, though.

During his time there, a lot of gods from all over the multiverse had gathered at Nevermore, and after Valdemar, Nature's Attendant, Artemis, and several other gods went, other Primordial also noticed, which led to both the Holy Mother and Blightfather – another two Primordials – paying a visit to the World Wonder.

The streaming party put on by the Wyrmgod of Nevermore quickly got crowded as this Leaderboards competition turned into an impromptu get-together for some of the pinnacle beings of the multiverse. Many of them showed great interest in Jake, so great that right as he was about to exit the Test of Character Challenge Dungeon, he was invited to instead visit the gods observing him, and how could Jake possibly say no to that?

It could be argued if this was a good or bad decision, as Jake soon found himself in front of half of the Primordials in the universe, all scrutinizing him. Even Eversmile was present, hiding in the back with all the gods not able to sit with the cool kids, and after a few threats, Jake definitely wasn't going to reveal his presence. Anyway, with Jake present, Valdemar definitely didn't beat around the bush but shamelessly approached Jake with an offer to make Jake his Chosen, with Villy telling Jake not to make the rejection too harsh due to sneaky plans related to Yip of Yore (not gonna elaborate here either).

After the rejection, Valdemar wasn't dejected in the slightest but decided to have a bit of fun as he challenged Jake directly to an aura-measuring contest, one Jake gladly met head-on as their auras clashed within the streaming room. Most of the gods at the cool kids' table could handle it pretty effortlessly, but Artemis, the odd one out as she wasn't a pinnacle god, found herself heavily pressured, making Jake shield her during the competition.

Once Valdemar was pleased, he laughed out loud and reiterated his interest in Jake while giving him an open invitation to visit Valhal at any time – one Jake was definitely going to take him up on one day.

Following his little side adventure, Jake gets a lot of profession levels from having acted like Jake acts before it's time to head into his third Challenge Dungeon. In this Challenge Dungeon, we finally reunite with Minaga as Jake enters Minaga's Endless Labyrinth.

From there, Minaga's nightmare once more began as Jake began to go through his labyrinth like a world-record speedrunner, exploiting any and all mechanics possible to go fast while the developer wallows in tears, unable to deploy a patch to fix any of the exploits. Jake didn't even bother engaging with the actual labyrinth challenges to find the right path but just stormed through using his Sphere to guide him.

The only thing limiting Jake's progress was his speed and the time limit for completing each section of the labyrinth. Eventually, after Jake had already shattered every record of the Challenge Dungeon, Jake decided to go out with a bang as he faced off against his very first B-grade. While the fight did eventually result in his death, Jake was proud he'd held on as long as he did and had renewed confidence in facing one sooner rather than later.

Through the power of cheese, Jake walked out of Minaga's Endless Labyrinth with another massive batch of Nevermore Points and a peak-level achievement, providing him an even larger percentage bonus to all his points.

With the third Challenge Dungeon down, Jake only had two remaining. Sadly for me as the author, the book was already getting pretty freaking long at this point, and any hopes of including all the Challenge Dungeons in the same book were quickly squashed. I could fit in at least one more, though.

House of the Architect was a Challenge Dungeon all about creating things. The actual creations could be nearly anything, and even the process behind every creation was judged. With ten creations in total to submit, there was a lot of room for variance – and seeing as variance in submitted creations was also rewarded – Jake got working on many different things.

Rather than go over every creation, let's just mention the most important parts of this Challenge Dungeon. The first was who judged these creations. Jake came to learn that it wasn't the Wyrmgod or even some mechanism designed for the job but the Bound God of Nevermore. That's to say, the original and part-owner of the World Wonder, forever bound to the place. Hence, the name Bound God, one sharing a name with the place itself, calling herself Nevermore.

The second impactful creation Jake submitted was an upgrade to his stealth skill. During his time with Artemis in the Colosseum of Mortals, she helped inspire him in ways to upgrade the skill by relying on his high Perception, and Jake finally succeeds and creates an incredibly powerful skill that allows him to effectively shift himself out of the realm of perception others could see.

The third and final important creation covered in this recap wasn't a thing but a person. Jake wanted to improve his abilities with curses, and during a visit to a planet that was part of the Challenge Dungeon, Jake made the impromptu decision to adopt a student who he taught how to use curse energy. Well, the word taught wasn't really accurate. It was more right to say he gave the young man called Temlat full access to information regarding whatever subject he wanted to study.

Jake willingly taking this incredible hands-off teaching method proved to be quite the mistake. The world Temlat came from was a pretty messed up one, and Jake failed to realize how consumed with revenge his first student was that he didn't stop him before it was too late. He didn't even properly question why Temlat also felt interested in plagues...

In the end, all Jake could do was watch as Temlat transformed himself into a being with no purpose other than to exert his revenge, only for Jake to ultimately end his first student's existence in an act of mercy. Having killed his first student, Jake, needless to say, isn't keen on having another any time soon as he realizes he isn't suited to teaching others. Definitely a bummer all around.

Jake ended up finishing the House of the Architect Challenge Dungeon with a pretty damn good score, primarily due to the diversity and quality of all the different items he submitted, including ones heavily affected by his Bloodline's abilities. His Path as an alchemist really came in handy there, and exiting the Challenge Dungeon, Jake has a damn good average performance in the Challenge Dungeons so far with four completed.

Which isn't to say he's without competition. As Jake completes his Challenge Dungeons, so do all the others he competes with on the Leaderboards, as well as his friends and allies. Each shows the areas they specialize in, with examples such as Arnold – resident void scientist mate of Jake - performing incredibly well in the House of the Architect, and Sylphie performing far above expectations in Minaga's Labyrinth due to her ability to still hear the wind giving her hints where to go.

However, it also quickly became clear that few are good everywhere. Some perform incredibly well in one Challenge Dungeon, only to flunk out entirely in another. To be at the top, one needs to do well in all the Challenge Dungeons. While Jake did phenomenally so far in the eyes of most, he still had the Test of Character dungeon where he performed pretty poorly, at least in his own opinion.

That's to say that if he wants to dramatically increase his chances of winning the entire competition, he needs to do well in the fifth and final Challenge Dungeon. Luckily for him, the challenge there isn't an entirely unfamiliar one as we're about to join Jake as he begins his journey as a package delivery worker!

And even more luckily for Jake, he won't even have to pee in bottles while doing it, which does perhaps make it a bit unrealistic I guess. Funny how even the vast multiverse filled with evil snake gods has its proper standards for acceptable work environments.

Anyway, let the final Challenge Dungeon begin as the Nevermore arc nears its end, and it's finally soon back to Earth!

CHAPTER 1

TO BE A PACKAGE DELIVERY WORKER

Delivery jobs were definitely one of the most vital functions of modern society. Before the system, who could even live without getting stuff delivered to their house within a day of ordering it online? It was truly an impossibility, and the hard-working delivery workers were the ones who made that a reality.

Jake had spent a while in university working as a delivery driver to make some money... and let's just say he hadn't particularly enjoyed the job. True, there was something zen and relaxing about having a route and a set number of packages to deliver entirely on his own. Yet it had only been zen until the quotas became more and more unrealistic to the point where they began to interfere with Jake's studies, making him quit.

All of this is to say that Jake entered the Neverending Journey with a clear advantage over most other Nevermore Attendees, as he had experience in the field. Surely, working as a package delivery driver for less than a year over a century ago would have led to translatable skills in a Challenge Dungeon within a World Wonder, right?

Jake's thoughts on the description of the Challenge Dungeon were also pretty simple. The entire thing seemed straightforward from an initial assessment, but he got the feeling that wasn't the case. Why did the Wyrmgod feel the need to issue so many warnings about people trying to take advantage of him? The note about trusting no one, in particular, set a kind of ominous tone for what was to come. One thing was for sure: this wasn't just going to be about going fast from A to B. Definitely still a part of it, but far from everything.

Still standing outside of the city, watching the crowd enter, he tried to get a better feeling for the people he would be dealing with. A few quick uses of Identify showed that the guards at the checkpoint were all around high to peak D-grade, with a single C-grade captain of sorts sitting inside of the guard building, reading something.

Seeing this, and considering he was meant to be a Courier, Jake got in the queue to enter rather than sneaking in. He even went as far as removing his mask, pulling down his hood, and lowering his level to just over 200 using Shroud of the Primordial. At this early juncture, he saw no need to attract unnecessary attention.

After about ten minutes of queuing, it was Jake's turn. He went up to the small booth and found a bored-looking elven guard sitting on a stool. "Name, level, and occupation."

"Jake, level 212, no formal work, but looking to become a Courier."

The guard looked up and quickly gave Jake a scan. "New around these parts? Where do you hail from?"

"Never been in this area before," Jake answered, not answering the last part on purpose.

Noticing this, the guard narrowed his eyes. "I asked you where you're from?"

"Nowhere," Jake answered kind of truthfully. "I'm a hunter. I just went wherever I wanted and always traveled before this."

The man let out a *hmph* sound as he shook his head. Using some device that looked a bit like a typewriter, he wrote a few things before printing out a small credit card-looking thing and handing it to Jake.

"Here, hold onto that. It's an identification card. If you are looking for Courier Jobs, check out the local Guild Hall. Oh, yeah, and don't cause any trouble."

"Thank you. I'll be on my best behavior." Jake smiled and nodded as he headed into the city.

Checking out the small card on the way, he quickly read what was on it. It was as basic as could be, just saying he was an early-tier level 212 C-grade, had an occupation of *blank*, and the name of Jake. Besides that, there was a small magical seal down in the corner, probably functioning the same as a pre-system chip or watermark.

He had arrived during the day, and the city was positively buzzing. The streets were filled, and Jake guessed this place alone housed a few hundred thousand. Race-wise, he saw a lot of humans, but there were also plenty of other enlightened races. He even saw his fair share of beasts both in and out of humanoid form. Among them, the highest-leveled one he saw was level 234, so still a bit low, but a good start considering he was currently in the easiest part of the Challenge Dungeon.

Walking down the well-paved streets with actual streetlights lining it, Jake didn't at all feel like he was in a dungeon. The people there also weren't merely window-dressing; they acted entirely normal, so that was a good thing.

With his Pulse, he quickly managed to locate the Guild Hall that the guard had mentioned. It was a massive building toward the center of the city, about six stories tall. It was also filled with people, with dozens exiting and entering every minute—some from the doors and some flying off the roof.

On that note, this city had sky-lanes. Marked areas in the air for people to fly, much akin to usual roads, just in the third dimension. It wasn't something Jake hadn't seen before, but in this city, it seemed especially well-managed, with colored beams of light directing people.

Entering the Guild building, Jake quickly took in the atmosphere. It reminded him a bit of an old bar mixed with a bank, if that made sense. It didn't quite give off the Adventure Guild vibe, but it seemed a lot more professionally organized. You even had to take a number while waiting your turn to talk to the employees.

Something Jake promptly did as he found an empty seat to wait. As he was sitting there, he began to scan the room more, including the people in it. There were very few present not in C-grade, with most organized into parties ranging between three and ten members. What did genuinely surprise him was the composition of these teams.

They were mixes of all races, even more extreme than on the streets. These parties included beasts and other kinds of monsters, many of which weren't even in humanoid form, and no one batted an eye. Jake wasn't really one to talk, considering he was often seen with Sylphie, but he still thought it was weird to see a large wolf sitting at a table, eating from a plate with excellent table manners.

After waiting for a good ten minutes, Jake was called to one of the tills staffed by a dwarf with a massive beard. "So, how can I help you today? Oh, and can I have your identification card, please?"

"Looking for work," Jake said as he handed the dwarf the card.

The dwarf quickly took the card and scanned it under the desk before handing it back. After seeing the result, it was Jake's turn to get a scan. He felt the use of Identify on him, and then the dwarf nodded. "You're new around here, aren't you? No affiliations? You give off that kind of vibe."

"Right," Jake confirmed, pretty damn sure this was scripted by the Wyrmgod. "Heard you may be looking for a Courier?"

Jake hadn't actually heard that; he just felt like this was how the conversation was going to go. This entire scenario currently reminded him of that damn Test of Character, as he had to play a role... but at least he could make that role entirely his own.

"Couldn't be more right." The dwarf gave him a big smile. "Got a few jobs available. Check them out."

Just like that, three floating system messages appeared between Jake and the dwarf.

Courier Job 1 (Easy): Deliver a letter to the Merchant's Union within the city.

Courier Job 1 (Medium): Transport a small shipment of ores to the Firesteel Blacksmith within the city.

Courier Job 1 (Hard): Deliver a Darkeye Diamond to Polsted in Polsted's Jewelry Shop within the city.

Quickly skimming the three options, they all just seemed too damn easy. What's more, they were all within the city. If he had to guess, this was just some kind of tutorial job.

"Can I accept all of them at once?" Jake asked.

"Hah, only one at a time," the dwarf said. "It's unlikely the client wants to keep waiting forever for you to finish other deliveries before getting to theirs."

"I'll take the job to deliver the Darkeye Diamond, then," Jake said, naturally choosing the "hard" option.

"Good—had trouble finding anyone to deliver that for the entire day," the dwarf said with a smile as he quickly reached below the desk and took out a token before handing it to Jake. "As you said you were looking for work, I assume you don't have a Courier Medallion yet?"

Jake nodded. "And you would be right."

"Take this, then," the dwarf said as he handed a small metal token that looked like a big coin to Jake. "Infuse some energy into it and bind it to you."

Jake looked at the Courier Medallion for a bit as he used Identify, scanning its properties.

[Courier Medallion (Inferior)] – The lowest rarity of Courier Medallion for a novice in the field. This Medallion will hold information related to jobs and can give general directions to your destination if those are provided (may not be entirely reliable). Will automatically upgrade as Courier Jobs are completed and your reputation grows.
Requirements: Soulbound.

Seeing no reason not to do as asked—and feeling pretty sure getting this Medallion was mandatory anyway—Jake infused some energy into the item, making it his own. As he did, the dwarf took out a piece of paper that turned into energy and flew into the token.

Courier Job accepted.

"Right, everything should be in the Medallion now," the dwarf said with a courteous smile. "Just two seconds while I go grab the diamond."

Jake nodded as the dwarf headed to a back room, where he then unlocked what looked like a magical safe. After doing some magic stuff, a small jewelry box appeared in his hand, wrapped in some kind of cloth with runes on it. Likely a protective measure.

Returning to Jake with the box held carefully in both hands, he stopped right before he put it down on the table. "Just to make sure, you do have a spatial storage item yourself, right? Or will you need to borrow one?"

"I got my own," Jake confirmed.

"Excellent!" the dwarf said as he put down the box. Jake instantly put it in his necklace, keeping it away from prying eyes. The dwarf suddenly turned serious. "Also... before you go, just a bit of a warning. This diamond is quite valuable, and I heard there might be others out to get it themselves. So be careful, alright? Only give it to old Polsted personally. When the job is done, we will know, but still come back here if you need more work afterwards."

"I'll be careful and definitely come back later," Jake said, matching the solemn energy of the dwarf.

"You know, I am getting a good feeling about you," he said encouragingly. "With some good jobs under your belt, your Courier Medallion should upgrade quickly, and I can see you becoming a real known name in the game."

"I bet you say that to every new Courier," Jake said with a wink as he turned to leave. He wasn't joking either; he was pretty sure the dwarf did indeed say that to everyone who entered this Challenge Dungeon. At least, everyone who didn't somehow fuck up this early introductory part.

The dwarf just shook his head as Jake walked out of the Guild Hall. He still had the Courier Medallion in his hand and quickly infused some energy according to the faint instinctive knowledge he'd gotten when first binding it. As he did, what looked like a compass appeared on its face, pointing toward what he assumed was his destination.

With a direction set, Jake made his way over there. The city was pretty big, yes, but it wasn't *that* big, and with a brisk pace and maybe a few One Steps thrown in there, Jake reached the street where the jeweler was located within minutes. Using the Medallion, he quickly confirmed which shop was this Polsted's... not that the massive sign above the entrance didn't also help.

Going toward the store, Jake saw that it looked closed. However, there was a man standing behind a desk inside, so Jake decided to knock on the door. The young-looking guy quickly ran over and opened the door.

"Yes, how can I help you?" he asked carefully. On his way over to the door, Jake had noticed quite a few curious gazes at his back, primarily from two beastfolk across the street.

"Courier here," Jake said, ignoring the onlookers. "I am meant to deliver a package to Polsted."

"Ah, the diamond arrived!" the man said happily as he opened the door fully. "Please come in right away."

Jake entered the jewelry shop after the young man and followed him toward the large display case. It was filled with expensive-looking jewelry, most of it enchanted but with what Jake would consider pretty low-quality enchantments. It was also made for D-grades, with the properties all being shit. It was probably to avoid any incentive for those doing the Challenge Dungeon to try and rob the store or something.

"Now, can I confirm the goods?" the young man said as he stood behind the counter with a big smile on his lips. "I assume you have it with you."

Giving him a look, Jake raised an eyebrow. "Supposed to deliver it to the owner of this shop. A guy called Polsted."

"It's fine," the young man smoothly explained. "Polsted isn't in today; that's why we're closed."

"Oh, how come?" Jake asked. It wasn't like sick days were a thing after the system arrived.

"He is working hard on a project at home, and I'm honestly not sure when he will be back," the young man said, sighing.

Jake shrugged. "Guess I'll have to stop by his place and deliver it, then."

"Polsted's gonna be pissed if you disturb him," the young man said with a slight hint of panic. Then he quickly gathered himself. "Please, man, don't make this hard for me. The boss is gonna be up my ass if I let you go interrupt him, and even more pissed if he comes back and the Darkeye Diamond still isn't here."

"Sorry, got my orders," Jake said. "Now, where does Polsted live?"

The young man seemed to realize Jake wasn't going to give up the goods and threw a look over Jake's shoulder to someone outside. He clearly tried to do it subtly, but with Jake's Perception, how could he possibly hide anything?

"Look, how about I send someone to try and get him?" the young man asked.

Jake sighed internally rather than answering. Behind him, the two beastfolk he had seen looking at him curiously entered the store, clearly trying to be stealthy, considering they both had stealth skills active.

"I think we both know that isn't going to happen," Jake said with a sigh.

The young man's animated smile faded as he sneered. Right as he did so, one of the beastfolk appeared right behind Jake and raised a spear before holding it to Jake's throat.

"How about you just be a good little Courier and leave the damn diamond here and fuck off?" the young man said in a pretty threatening tone.

Jake identified the beastfolk holding the spear, and honestly, the level impressed him a bit. Level 243 was pretty high compared to most others around; that was for sure.

"Well, isn't this fun?" Jake commented, ignoring the spear. "How about doing this instead: you tell me where to find Polsted, and I don't kill your two friends here? Alternatively, you can tell me after I kill them."

The young man looked at Jake as if he was an idiot—and fair enough; he did look like a level 212 human who had just threatened two people over level 240. So, to make his threat look less dumb, he unleashed some of his aura from his true level.

He did so with the intent to intimidate, but it got an instant reaction from the beastkin threatening him. The spear instantly went for Jake's throat, prompting him to sprout a small layer of scales that blocked the tip of the spear. The weapon utterly failed to penetrate.

"Bad move," Jake said as he turned his head and looked at the spear wielder, his eyes glowing for a second as Primal Gaze activated. The man collapsed without a sound, and Jake turned back to the young man behind the counter trying to rob him. *Trying* being the key word. The other beast-folk rushed Jake full of bloodlust, also earning him a quick look with Gaze. He, too, fell down like a marionette with its strings cut.

"Now, where were we?" Jake asked with a smile. "Oh, yeah, where's Polsted at?"

"You... They're dead... How..."

"Chop, chop," Jake said, hurrying him along. "Polsted. Location. Now."

"Al... Alright, just please don't..." the young man stuttered before quickly gathering himself and giving Jake some actual directions.

"See, that wasn't so hard," Jake said casually. "Now, clean up this place so poor old Polsted doesn't come into work with two corpses in his store. Can't be good for business, now, can it?" He then turned and left the store.

As he headed toward Polsted's place, Jake couldn't help but think how this whole Courier thing was indeed incredibly similar to the job he'd had in university. Except this time around, he had a far better way of handling scammers.

CHAPTER 2

ODD JOBS GALORE

It turned out that poor old Polsted had been held up at home by a fourth accomplice from the crew trying to rob his store. Everything had been part of some big conspiracy: The young man had been a new employee who was just there to scope out the place, and after learning where the jeweler lived, they'd followed him home one day and held him at swordpoint. From there, they would spend the next day robbing the store. The reason the young man had been the only one in the store was to inspect the magical seals on the display cases and eventually dismantle them.

The Darkeye Diamond hadn't even been part of the expected haul. It was pure coincidence Jake had come by that day, and the thieves had assumed they could just rob the stupid Courier along with the rest of the store. That, or Jake's insistence on seeking out Polsted had put a target on his head.

Of course, Jake knew there weren't actually any coincidences going on, but rather a carefully crafted scenario that tested the Courier and kind of set the stage from the get-go for how these jobs would work. Jake wouldn't be surprised if the easy option involved simply delivering a letter in a mailbox, with the medium option being something in between that and what Jake had to do.

Jake's takeaway from the first job was that he had to be careful while delivering stuff, as it was pretty damn easy to mess it up and fail the delivery. It also made a lot more sense why he wouldn't lose one of the three lives if he did mess up, as it would have been so easy. In fact, Jake guessed quite a few would have just given the package to the young man who appeared to be working in the jewelry store. The only reason Jake had been suspicious was because of the very minor clues the young man had given off. That, and the dwarf's insistence that the package be delivered to "old man Polsted."

Unless calling the "employee" an old man was some weird inside joke between the dwarf and Polsted, it was highly likely that something shady was going on.

After finishing with the job of delivering the diamond to Polsted and teaching another robber the literal definition of the phrase "if looks could kill," Jake headed back toward the Guild Hall for another job. On the way, he also took the time to reflect a bit on the newly upgraded mythical-rarity Primal Gaze. He hadn't really had a good opportunity to test it since the upgrade, and he had to admit it had gotten a lot stronger than before, especially when it came to the soul-killing part.

In truth, he hadn't thought it would actually work. He had just hoped to either do some serious damage or knock them out, but the skill turned out to do a bit more than that. True, he had used it with the intent to kill, so it wasn't like he felt bad about the outcome. Quite the opposite, in fact.

Killing someone around twenty levels below him with a single look was damn good. Before, killing any C-grade outright hadn't been easy, but now it had worked effortlessly, and he got the feeling it would still have been lethal even if they had been a few levels higher. They were pretty weak for their levels, yes, but they were also enlightened and tended to have somewhat stronger souls than the average monster.

Then again, it wasn't like killing them without Gaze would have been hard. A single well-landed stab with Eternal Hunger on each would have gotten the job done just as well. An arrow from a few dozen kilometers away, too. But Primal Gaze was definitely the best way to kill them for a few reasons, one being more important than the others.

First of all, it was as fast as a kill could be, making it by far the most efficient. Second, killing someone with a look had a damn great intimidation factor, and convincing the young man to not only tell him where Polsted was but even turn himself in for his crimes to the guards had been easy as pie after seeing his two friends each die from a glance. It also helped that Jake had very much implied the young man could share the same fate as his friends if he didn't go to the guards.

Third, and most importantly, with the way Primal Gaze worked, Jake would effectively pit his own soul against someone else's when using the skill. This was actually pretty good exposure training for his own soul to potentially experience a bit of growth simply due to the practice, though he wasn't sure how much it would help, especially when the targets were so weak.

Oh... and finally, one incredibly vital reason: killing with weapons was messy, and Jake was a good Courier who didn't leave the client with an extra, unnecessary cleanup fee.

Jake was still deep in thought when he arrived back at the Guild Hall. It had only been a few hours since he left the first time around, with much of that time devoted to dealing with guards who'd come to Polsted's place for a statement after everything was done.

After entering and grabbing a number, the same dwarf he had talked with the first time called him over. "Hey, new Courier, over here!"

Jake didn't need to be told twice that he could cut the line as he hurried over. Surprisingly, nobody gave him any nasty stares. The dwarf seemed to notice Jake's surprise and explained things once he stood in front of the desk.

"People give some extra respect for Couriers; it's a dangerous job, after all, and few want to walk down that road. They prefer to just do other odd jobs—something I am sure I don't need to tell you after that last job of yours. Things got nasty, eh?"

"Definitely did," Jake confirmed. "Say, can you tell me a bit more about this odd treatment of Couriers? I also noticed how the guards seemed weirdly... I almost wanna say *hands-off* with me. They just told me that you guys at the Guild would handle it."

"Because they are hands-off," the dwarf said. "For someone who entered the Courier industry, you sure know little about it. Oh, well. You are promising, so let me give you a quick rundown. Couriers are neutral, unaffiliated individuals who do not answer to or work for any specific faction outside of the Guild. This means you have some level of diplomatic immunity, dependent on the rank of your Medallion, and the Guild is in charge of taking care of any potential trouble you get into. Of course, there are limits, so do control yourself, but in a case like this, you acted in the interest of your client and didn't go overboard, so things are fine. Just know that if you do go too far, the Guild itself may send an enforcer... You don't want the Guild to send an enforcer."

"I'll be careful... but I've also been wondering, what exactly is the Guild?" Jake also asked, knowing full well that if he'd been a native to this world, he would have just outed himself as a complete moron who had lived under a rock his entire life. Or maybe it would have outed him as a transdimensional traveler. Or, well, you know, someone just doing a Challenge Dungeon inside of a World Wonder.

Luckily for him, the dwarf didn't at all comment on Jake's lack of any common knowledge. "The Guild is a massive organization that operates on every single continent, has affiliates in every major city, and has managed to remain entirely neutral despite the political turmoil. Not to say there aren't internal problems, but those aren't for you to deal with. Suffice to say, the Guild has enough power to rival any faction, and we are quite respected."

"This is a somewhat cheeky question, but who is the strongest in the Guild?" Jake asked for fun, wondering if he could take them.

"The Founder," the dwarf said with a sense of respect. "An absolutely legendary adventurer. Rose to power about forty thousand years ago after he managed to singlehandedly beat back the dragon tribes, even slaying the Dragon King in the process. He made the Guild after retiring and still rules it today. One of only five known S-grades in the world."

Jake was nodding along mentally to the explanation until he got to the end. There were fucking S-grades in this world. That meant there were also plenty of A-grades and B-grades around. All of this is to say that fucking around could quickly lead to finding out if he somehow managed to piss off the wrong people. This was definitely good to know.

It also left him with one other important question.

"Any gods?"

"Gods?" the dwarf repeated. "Well, some people do refer to the Founder as a godlike entity, but I am not sure if calling him a god is right despite his overwhelming power."

"I see," Jake said, nodding as he conducted a minor test. Purposefully, he began to let out a bit of aura from his Shroud of the Primordial. It was the part that signified his Blessing as the Chosen of the Malefic Viper. The aura with divine quality slowly seeped out, but the dwarf didn't at all react as he just looked at Jake, who stood there quietly.

"So... any more questions?" he asked after Jake hadn't said anything for several seconds. "I've got some more clients waiting if you wanna take another job, or do you perhaps want to take a rest first?"

Jake fully retracted his aura and smiled. "Yeah, let me look at the jobs available."

His small test had naturally been regarding Blessings. He wanted to see if others could feel his Blessing, as that could potentially have allowed him to use it to mess with people at some point. However, it seemed not a single soul could detect it, making Jake believe the Wyrmgod had prevented the use of divine auras from being a thing. This restriction was probably for the best. Otherwise, it would be an absolutely massive advantage for those with Blessings, as they could use the aura to intimidate practically everyone, especially in a world with no actual gods. Jake could only begin to imagine the ways one could exploit Blessings... and he wasn't even that crafty compared to others who could have no doubt found far more ways to take advantage.

"Here ya go—three more jobs available," the dwarf said as he took out three papers. Right as he did so, three system messages also popped up in front of Jake's eyes.

Courier Job 2 (Easy): Deliver five letters to their respective destinations within the city.

Courier Job 2 (Medium): Deliver the shipment of Minor Vitae Ruby to the Merchant's Union within the city.

Courier Job 2 (Hard): Go to the Firesteel Blacksmith and pick up the Governor Blade. Then deliver the Governor Blade to the Governor's office. Both locations are within the city.

After skimming them all, still working on getting a better idea of how this entire Challenge Dungeon worked, he naturally picked the hard option again. The only revelations here were that old jobs would disappear if he didn't pick them, and that a Courier Job could be chained. That is to say, have multiple steps and not just a point A to point B delivery.

The dwarf once more infused Jake's Medallion before the newly appointed Courier got to work. The second job turned out to be a tad easier than the first one, with the only added difficulty coming from Jake having to enter the Governor's Office, which was well-defended. The defenses were at least a lot better than elsewhere, with guards around level 250, and they gave off decently strong vibes for their levels. The magical formation protecting the office was even better, likely laid down by a high-tier C-grade.

This job took a bit of socializing, but not enough to put Jake off. If he had to guess, this entire mission was to hammer home the concept that Couriers had a unique political position in this world. Just flashing the Medallion was enough for the suspicion of most to fall away, and while Jake didn't get to meet the Governor directly, he was attended by a direct aide and seen immediately.

With another job done, Jake saw no reason to stop. He headed back to the Guild Hall and accepted a third hard job that required him to deliver items to three different people across the city. That seemed easy enough... except this one was on a timer, as it was an urgent job.

Alright, it was still easy as hell, not requiring Jake to hurry at all as he completed the rush delivery to all three clients. This Courier Job did teach Jake that Couriers were allowed to fly freely, even within cities. So that was a nice snippet of information.

The Courier Jobs continued in this fashion for several days, keeping Jake within the starting city for all of them. Every job introduced minor elements or twists to add to the difficulty or teach him new job concepts. One of the Courier Jobs was even to deliver a person. No, not some fucked-up slavery shit, but an escort mission for someone who had to enter the slums and didn't feel safe going there. Mind you, there wasn't anything in the slums that was actually dangerous. The client was just a posh lady who acted entitled throughout, with the biggest difficulty during this job coming from resisting just punching her in the face and leaving.

Besides that, he faced a lot of small, interesting twists. In one job, he had to find a delivery client who had gone into hiding. In another, he had to deliver a letter without being seen by any of the neighbors of the client, but Jake's favorite one was a job where he was attacked by a dog in a yard.

That one sure brought back memories from his old delivery job days, and the same solution he'd used back before the system also worked wonders here. Needless to say, Jake couldn't and wouldn't hurt a dog that was just protecting its territory as it was supposed to; he just made dogs back off by staring them down.

Sure, Jake did know staring into the eyes of a stranger's dog was heavily advised against, but in Jake's case, it had always been a great way to make the dog go away. His Bloodline was truly versatile, and had been even back then.

By now, Jake had completed nineteen jobs, and he was honestly beginning to feel more than a little bored despite the new elements introduced. It just felt like a normal job, which made him suspect that the initial Courier Jobs being this mind-numbing was also part of the experience somehow.

However, when he returned for job number twenty, something finally changed.

"Back again, I see," the dwarf said with a big smile. "You are definitely the most hard-working Courier I've seen in a good while! Listen, the third job this time around is a bit different from those prior... It will require you to leave the city for a while."

That's right—Jake was finally allowed to act as more than a small-time, in-city delivery man. He had graduated to become a... not-in-city delivery man? Jake wasn't sure there was a term for it, but damn, did it feel good to finally be let outside.

CHAPTER 3

SPECIAL DELIVERY

Actual traveling.

Who would have thought that a Courier job would include traveling? Sure had Jake fooled after running around the same city for several days. Sure, it hadn't been the worst, and there'd been plenty of diversity thrown in there to make it entertaining.

Nevertheless, Jake was glad that phase of the Challenge Dungeon was over as he proceeded with Courier Job 20. It wasn't like he had to go far, but it did feel good to finally be out in the open. He had traveled around a bit in the House of the Architect's worlds, but he hadn't gone full speed most of the time, as he'd had to actively scout out the environment.

Now, speed was the only thing that mattered. With Jake using One Step repeatedly, the city had long since turned into a blip on the horizon. Every single step cleared around a kilometer of distance, having improved quite a lot during all his time in Nevermore. He was still a ways from passing a thousand miles like the name indicated it technically could, but considering the sheer speed with which he could trigger the skill, that wasn't really a problem.

Jake had experimented a bit with actually trying to increase the distance a lot, and it was possible. His record was about a hundred and thirty kilometers—eighty miles or so—with a single step. However, that step had taken him well over a minute to perform and had been done under perfect circumstances with nothing in between him and his target destination. This is to say that if Jake just wanted to travel quickly, smaller but faster steps were far more effective. Also a lot more efficient, as a One Step taking him a hundred and thirty kilometers consumed way more than a hundred and thirty times the stamina of those taking him only a single kilometer.

With his speed, Jake was the fastest in his Nevermore party when it came to purely traveling, though Sylphie beat him thoroughly in shorter distances. His relatively high stamina pool and constant supply of potions also meant he wouldn't really ever run out of energy as long as he didn't push himself too hard.

For his very first job outside of the city, the Challenge Dungeon had even picked something super exciting, too. Jake had been tasked with— wait for it—delivering a tax form for a local mayor to fill out. He even had to bring it back again once it had been filled, making it twice as exciting!

Alright, yeah, the Courier Job sucked ass, and it was clear the entire intent of this was for Jake to travel a longer distance than usual. Jake wouldn't really call it long-distance travel, though, as it only took him a bit over five hours to reach the small town in question. It would probably have taken longer if any of the local wildlife had dared get in his way, but luckily, they were all on their best behavior, as blasting his aura pretty much worked like a mass repellent.

Reaching the small town in question, Jake saw that there were two guards at the entrance, both barely in C-grade. They looked tired and wore slightly damaged armor, and observing the area, it looked like they had been struggling quite a bit with monster attacks recently.

I can almost smell it...

Entering the town by flashing his Medallion, Jake headed to the mayor's office straight away without any problems and delivered the tax form to a secretary there. Right as he did so, the mayor himself exited his office and saw Jake, and it looked almost as if a wave of relief washed over him.

"Ah, you're the Courier—am I right?" the man said with a bright smile. "Thank you for the delivery. Tax papers, right? I will get to it immediately so you can bring it back, but..."

Here it comes...

"... we have recently been dealing with excessive monster attacks from a nearby monster nest, which have put a strain on the guards. Seeing as you made it all the way here safely, you look like you can handle yourself, so would it be possible to look into it while I do the form?"

A side quest!

Right as he thought this, a system prompt appeared before his eyes.

Courier Side Job: Eliminate the nearby monster nest.

Objective: Monster nest eliminated (0/1)
Accept Side Job?

Jake nodded, having no reason to refuse. "I'll take a look at it in the meantime. Do you know where this nest is located?"

Courier Side Job Accepted.

"Thank you!" the mayor said, relieved. "I believe the guards mentioned all the attacks usually come from the north, so I reckon it is in that direction. As for any details, I couldn't possibly tell you the exact situation; we simply haven't had the resources to send out a scouting party."

"It's all good; I'll find it," Jake said reassuringly. "Just have those forms ready by the time I return!"

"Most certainly," the mayor said with a small bow as Jake headed out of the office again.

On the way, he released a Pulse of Perception. About a hundred and fifty kilometers to the northeast, he saw a big collection of monsters gathered around a few small hills and rock formations. The monsters all looked to be of the insect type, but with their small number, they definitely weren't of the eusocial type. If they had been, Jake doubted the town would still be around.

It definitely looked like a monster nest, and Jake decided to make this an express delivery of death to the monsters.

Jumping and summoning his wings, Jake shot into the air and flew up a few dozen kilometers. Once he reached a good height, he slowed down and pulled out his bow. He could see the monsters quite well from this high up, and using a few quick Identifies, he saw they were all in the 210-220 range. This made Jake feel like one wasn't necessarily meant to fight the robbers in the first Courier Job if this was supposed to be the first job with semi-mandatory combat.

Not that it mattered to Jake either way. Nocking an arrow, he took aim and let loose, firing a quickly charged Arcane Powershot. Right as the arrow was released, Jake nocked another, which he charged ever so slightly longer before letting go of the string.

He did this with five more arrows before he felt like it was good enough. Jake didn't see a need to wait before he began flying downwards, and as he did, the first arrow arrived and split into dozens right before it hit the monster nest. Due to the difference in charge between each Powershot, the next arrow arrived nearly at the same time, followed by the remaining five.

A few seconds later, as Jake was flying downward, he got a system notification along with all the other kill messages.

Objective: Nest eliminated (1/1)

With a smile, Jake quickly made it down to the ground again and reentered the mayor's building, having only been gone for a handful of minutes. He did so fully expecting the mayor to still be busy filling out paperwork, but to his surprise, he met the man in front of his office, the signed form in hand.

"Thank you so much for the assistance!" the mayor said with a bright smile. "Here is the form, all filled out! Once again, I cannot express the depth of my and the town's gratitude for your help, and I wish you luck on your way back. Of course, should you wish to rest after dealing with the nest, you are more than free to stay at the local inn."

Side Job Completed!
Side Jobs Completed: 1

Jake stared at the guy and notification a bit before just nodding. "I only did as I should, and thanks for the offer, but I will head back immediately."

"Of course, of course," the mayor said with a sense of admiration. "Truly a man of duty! Even after a grueling fight, he does not delay a job."

"Yeah, sure." Jake said his goodbyes and headed out, successfully suppressing a laugh from the comments on his harrowing battle with the local monsters. Right as Jake exited the office, a few local townsfolk thanked him, and even the guards at the gate gave him words of gratitude as he began heading back to the city.

Jake had so many questions, even if he knew the true answer to all of them was probably dungeon fuckery.

How the hell had the mayor known the nest was eliminated minutes after it had happened? How had he filled out the form so fast? How had everyone else in town also instantly known? What were these Side Jobs actually for? What did they give? Actually, to extrapolate on that point... what did any of these jobs give?

Jake had carried out twenty Courier Jobs now and had yet to earn a dime. No one had even mentioned any payment. Was he doing charity work or something without knowing? How the hell did the Courier industry even work? Wait... maybe he was meant to be an independent contractor who had to send his own invoices?

Of course, the ultimate answer was just that none of this mattered. Side Jobs and Courier Jobs most certainly just gave more Nevermore Points and a better achievement at the end of the Challenge Dungeon. Simple as that. But Jake still liked to imagine the utter lunacy of a world like this existing where society was only held together by unpaid Couriers.

Making it back to the city again took a bit less time than the way to the town as Jake hurried. Turning in the tax records to the dwarf, Jake picked up another quest to go visit a town, and from there, Jake became the dedicated Courier for the local area, visiting most of the cities one by one.

By the time he had done thirty jobs, even the easy-difficulty Courier Jobs required him to leave the city. The difficulty also went up a tiny bit monster-wise as he went to more and more dangerous territories. There were a few cases of trickery here and there, such as someone claiming he had already sent payment and thus didn't need to write a check right then and there—despite Jake's job making it pretty clear he had to return with the aforementioned check.

Instances like these were honestly pretty normal, and in most cases, it didn't end in violence. Just a bit of pressure was enough to make most people crack in this early part of the Challenge Dungeon, and the slightest mention of the guards would have the merchants suddenly talking about everything being a misunderstanding.

In regard to Side Jobs, Jake didn't always get one, but they were becoming more numerous. From what he gathered, these Side Jobs were auxiliary tasks not directly related to delivery. Many could even be completed during the Courier Job, such as one time where Jake was asked to kill a certain number of monsters on his way to a town, or another where it was requested that he check out a certain area to see if a new powerful beast had made the place its home. All while running to a town anyway, making them pretty much free.

Nothing so far had been difficult for Jake at all. Even the timed missions were just a joke. Giving Jake three days to get somewhere he could reach in three hours was honestly just sad. Alas, he was in the easy part of the Challenge Dungeon right now, and hopefully, the difficulty would step up soon.

A bit less than two weeks after arriving in the Challenge Dungeon, Jake had completed Courier Job 35 and returned to the same Guild Hall as always to speak to the dwarf he had gotten pretty damn friendly with by now.

Walking in, Jake gave the man a smile, not even bothering to take a number.

"Job's done," Jake said.

"I saw." The dwarf gave Jake a big smile. "Here, let me have your Medallion."

"Huh, why?" Jake nevertheless placed it on the table. The dwarf didn't even try to pick up but just pointed at the item.

"Now take a look at it."

Jake instantly realized what the dwarf was getting at, and a quick Identify confirmed it.

[Courier Medallion (Common)] – The second-lowest rarity of Courier Medallion for a relative newcomer to the field who has begun to get some experience under his belt. This Medallion will hold information related to jobs and can give general directions to your destination if those are provided (may not be entirely reliable). Will automatically upgrade as Courier Jobs are completed and your reputation grows.
Requirements: Soulbound.

Finally, Jake was no longer running around with an inferior-rarity Medallion! Alright, it wasn't that big an achievement, but Jake was happy for it. It had "only" taken 35 Courier Jobs. This made Jake wonder if he would have had to do more easy jobs to upgrade it... Maybe 50 easy Courier Jobs and 40-something medium jobs? It didn't really matter, but Jake liked to tell himself he had saved time.

"Congratulations are in order," the dwarf said, clearly happy for Jake. "Less than two weeks, and you're already beginning to no longer be a complete novice. If you keep this up, you may just become a real top-tier Courier who can take on the truly dangerous and rewarding jobs!"

Jake wasn't sure about the rewarding part, considering he was an unpaid worker, but he still smiled in response. "Thanks, mate. Now, just because I went up in rank doesn't mean I'll stop my momentum. So hit me with the next round of jobs!"

"Yeah... about that," the dwarf said, his mood fading a bit. "I have good news and bad news. What do you want first?"

"Alright... hit me with the bad news, I guess."

"After getting promoted, you can go to one of the small-sized cities to do jobs—rather than here, which is rated as a smallest-sized one. Usually, you would do this through the teleportation gateway... but... there was an accident." The dwarf let out a big sigh. "So now it is no longer operational, as the space locator or something has been broken."

Yeah, this is one hundred percent a scripted event, Jake very quickly concluded, as he already knew where this was going.

"And the good news?"

"In order to get the teleportation gateway up and running again, we have two options. Either we can call a space mage to come to fix it here, which will take about a month... or someone has to bring the currently broken space-locator thing to the mages in the small-sized city, and they can fix it remotely from there to get the network up and running again." The dwarf looked at Jake. "I don't think I have to tell you who this someone would be?"

"Not sure how this is considered the good news."

"It's a Special Courier Job," the dwarf said in a serious tone. "The trip there will be a lot more dangerous and take a lot longer than the jobs you have done so far, but if you succeed, you will already be well on your way to upgrading your Medallion again. I also need to warn you that since your Medallion has been upgraded, I can't give you any properly challenging jobs if you stay in this city, which may delay your next upgrade, but the choice is naturally yours."

As the dwarf finished his sentence, a system prompt expectedly popped up.

Choose your next action:
Accept Special Courier Job 1: Transport the Space Magic Locator to the small-sized city.
Or
Continue doing regular Courier Jobs in the smallest-sized city for 1 month (30 days).

Needless to say, Jake was going on a cross-country road trip... because there was no fucking way he would stay back and do regular, boring Courier Jobs for another full month.

CHAPTER 4

TO MAKE WORK INTERESTING

The Courier Dungeon, as Jake had dubbed it, had an extremely simplified and straightforward societal structure. Everything was split into tiers, it seemed, with even the cities being very distinctly separated. The first city Jake arrived in was a smallest-sized city, which meant it was below a certain population threshold. Half a million, based on what Jake gathered.

Ranked just above the smallest-sized cities in the hierarchy were the small-sized ones, which had between half a million and five million. Above these were mid-sized cities with between five and twenty-five million, then large-sized with twenty-five million to a hundred million. Cities above a hundred million were pretty rare and were classified as giant-sized cities. There was no upper limit to these, and the only giant-sized cities Jake soon learned about were the capital cities of some of the many different factions.

Below cities were towns and villages. Anything below fifty thousand was a town, and below five thousand a village. Towns and villages did not have any teleportation circles in them and weren't connected to the network. Jake found this incredibly dumb, considering the relatively low investment needed to connect them and how it would make life for everyone so much easier, but the in-world reason was one of safety, as anything that wasn't a city couldn't protect the teleportation circle adequately.

It was a pretty dumb reason, as they could just have the circle self-destruct or something if they ever got invaded. Then again, if the infrastructure had been that immaculate, Couriers would have way less work and could just teleport everywhere, so it made sense for the theme of the place.

Back on topic, these towns and villages were all tied to the nearest city, which held governance over them and responsibilities such as tax collection and whatnot.

Now, having this kind of structure within a single faction kind of made sense. If it was organized from the top down and enforced, Jake could see it appearing even outside of Nevermore at the hands of someone with a management fetish.

However, it made no bloody sense why every single faction in the entire Challenge Dungeon world had decided on the exact same structure. Shit, even if it was just the enlightened factions, Jake could get it, but even the monster-focused factions had the exact same city-town-village structure, even down to the numbers.

On that note, yes, Jake did come to learn there were far more factions than he first expected. Jake had appeared in the human-focused enlightened faction, but several more existed, all in conflict with one another. Other factions included the dwarves, elves, Risen, scalekin, demons, one more with a mix of enlightened races, and finally, three different monster-focused ones. If there was a common race in the multiverse, Jake was pretty damn certain it could be found in this Challenge Dungeon within one of the ten factions.

Jake also had a theory that other Nevermore Attendees would appear elsewhere based on their race. Someone like Sylphie would likely appear in one of the monster-focused factions, while someone like Irin would appear in the demon faction. Now, where the Fallen King and someone like Dina would appear was a bit of mystery, as neither of them had a race with a faction directly related to them, but Jake reckoned it didn't really matter either way. As a Courier, race no longer mattered, and from what Jake saw, despite these factions being primarily race-based, there was plenty of diversity everywhere with no discrimination going on.

Jake had learned all of this shortly after he completed the first Special Courier Job and arrived at the small-sized city with the Space Magic Locator. The trip to the city had taken Jake just a bit over a day and a half, and honestly, it was as uneventful as could be. A few times, Jake encountered what he believed to be pre-scripted ambushes and whatnot, but in every instance, the monsters abandoned their attack the second they detected Jake's aura. Ah, but he was attacked by bandits once, all of whom ran away after he killed their leader.

In the small-sized city, Jake had gone to the next Guild Hall and met an elven woman who became his next go-to attendant. He quickly began taking on new jobs, one of which required him to collect a number of books and return them to a library. The twist with this job was that—just like in the real world—people sucked ass at returning books. Worst of all, one of the people who had to return a book was a guy who had accidentally placed it in his own personal library and needed Jake to help look for the damn thing. Sphere helped a bit, but sadly, as he could only see the shape of the book and not read the cover with just spatial perception, he had to actually look at the books himself.

After Jake had returned all the books, he stayed with the librarian for a while and learned some world history and about how the Challenge Dungeon worked. That is where he learned about the cities, got some tidbits about every faction, and was told that as a Courier, he wouldn't need to worry about anything, as he would be welcomed with open arms wherever he went... depending on the job, that is. If he was transporting something for an enemy faction, he could very easily have a target on his back.

After his talk with the librarian, Jake had gone back to the Guild Hall for another job, which he promptly accepted. Even the hard jobs sometimes took place within the far larger, small-sized city. Yes, it was a bit dumb to call it small, considering it was pretty damn big in Jake's mind, but in-world, it probably made sense, considering the city was several times larger than the smallest-sized one. Many of the jobs naturally also required him to head outside of it to the towns and villages, and these tended to take longer simply due to the travel time.

The small-sized city turned out to not be that much different from the smallest-sized one. The difficulty still wasn't really there. The social challenges he faced were also easy enough for someone like Jake to handle. Even if Jake wasn't the most socially adept person, in a multiversal context, he was actually pretty damn good. He wasn't overly naive and trusting, which would definitely be a huge weakness in this Challenge Dungeon. Not being very precise when listening to the language of jobs could also get you in trouble, and a lack of patience with shitty clients was pretty much a death sentence for an aspiring Courier.

For this reason, Jake could easily see many so-called geniuses struggling. An ultra-talented fighter, groomed and trained from an early age by experts, always viewed and recognized as someone with high status and genius intellect, definitely wasn't trained in dealing with a guy arguing that half of the metal in a shipment being the wrong kind shouldn't be a problem, as they were "pretty much the same anyway."

Yep, Jake could definitely see a few of them losing their cool here and there. This was part of the Challenge Dungeon test, too, and truthfully, the most overpowered thing one could have in this dungeon was experience in retail or other customer-facing, low-wage jobs at some point.

It wouldn't be an exaggeration to say that the young geniuses never really had to deal with stuff like this and would find themselves completely out of their comfort zone. They didn't ever have to deal with being an employee, as they were always the ones giving commands. One would think that Jake also wasn't very good at dealing with entitled and arrogant assholes, but surprisingly enough... he found it kind of fun.

In Jake's opinion, the worst part about work before the system had been the monotony of it all. Its sheer predictability and lack of challenge in everyday tasks as he got used to them. The lack of anything truly interesting happening to shake up the monotony... The lack of anything memorable on a given day.

However, despite work sucking most of the time, there were also good days. The days with something exciting happening. It didn't even always have to be something major, but just something exciting to shake up the usual routine.

Jake fondly remembered a day when the sprinklers in the office had gone off unexpectedly, and Casper had been asked if he could figure out how to turn them off temporarily until the company responsible for maintenance got there. Jake had been dragged along, and together, they had gotten completely drenched before finally finding a way to turn off everything. The office had, of course, already been turned into an utter mess at that point, and the rest of the day was spent cleaning up, figuring out which electronics had been saved in time, and listening to Jacob's frustrated call with the maintenance company, which had claimed that missing three consecutive inspections definitely couldn't have been a factor in the malfunction.

That day had been so unpredictable. It had been one twist after another, and even so many years later, Jake remembered the day so clearly. Especially the end, with Casper and Jake sitting on the rooftop, drinking soda while claiming they were trying to dry and save some keyboards. It had been a good and memorable day.

In some ways, this entire Challenge Dungeon reminded Jake of that day. Being a Courier was like work, yes, but rather than monotonous tasks, it was more like a job where no task was ever straightforward. It wasn't just delivering a box and leaving for the next house again, day in and day out.

Instead, it was more like those special delivery jobs you only had once in a blue moon, but every single time.

It was that one memorable work day, over and over again. Jake didn't doubt that the unpredictability of what you would face at every job was frustrating to many, but for Jake, it just made it more engaging and kept him interested. Definitely far more interested than the Test of Character, where Jake had just been a passive observer most of the time. At least here, Jake could work on his movement skills while traveling and meet a bunch of insane and interesting characters when talking to the people there.

Finally... compared to all his prior jobs, there was one core difference in this world. Here, you were allowed to bitch-slap the people trying to scam you. It was the most cathartic experience for anyone who had ever had to deal with customers like that, and based on what Jake saw, it had no negative influence on his performance. Which kind of made sense. What could they even do about it? Stop hiring free Couriers? Yeah, fat chance.

All of this is to say that Jake quite enjoyed this Challenge Dungeon, and that was reflected in his speed when doing jobs. He felt excited to get to the point where the jobs weren't only interesting but also offered a genuine challenge when he had to fight stuff, so while he didn't recklessly rush through the jobs, he did very much speedrun them.

Only three weeks after arriving in the small-sized city, Jake completed Courier Job 65, which surprisingly enough was sufficient to earn him yet another upgrade. Standing within the even larger Guild Hall in the small-sized city, the elven attendant flashed a huge smile as she congratulated him.

"I read your file right as you first came here, and in truth, I believed your evaluation was highly exaggerated, but seeing your work ethic, I believe it was just the opposite," the elf said with a bow. "It was definitely a conservative estimation; that's for sure! I cannot remember having ever worked with a Courier who has been promoted this fast."

That's right—Jake's Medallion had rapidly gone up yet another rank.

[Courier Medallion (Uncommon)] – A Courier Medallion of a respectable rarity for a relatively experienced Courier. This Medallion will hold information related to jobs and can give general directions to your destination if those are provided (may not be entirely reliable). Will automatically upgrade as Courier Jobs are completed and your reputation grows.
Requirements: Soulbound.

The description change was slight, but it was there. And, hey, it was nice to be recognized as a relatively experienced Courier after only about a month on the job. It was definitely a faster promotion rate than any prior job Jake had ever had, and if he kept working hard, he was sure he could earn a senior position within a year.

"So, what happens now?" Jake asked. "Got more jobs for me, or...?"

As predicted, the elf's mood shifted a bit as she took out a piece of paper from below the desk. For some reason, this paper had a golden outline and wasn't anything Jake had seen before. She looked almost nervous as she handled it, glancing to both sides before speaking.

"Listen... we got a Special Courier Job in just today. It isn't anything you have to do, and it's a pretty risky one... so before I even present it to you, I need to know if you are interested?" she said with a low voice.

Jake mimicked her serious mood as he leaned in slightly. "What are the details of the job?"

"I'll take that as you showing interest. Alright, so about five years ago, the Infernal Baron—a powerful B-grade—created a bounty reward for anyone who could capture a certain kind of elemental he needed. I didn't think something like that would ever become relevant here, but just a few hours ago, a band of adventurers returned with the exact elemental he had requested. Now we need someone to deliver it to him in the closest medium-sized city."

"Alright, pretty straightforward so far," Jake said, nodding. "But I guess there is a twist."

The elf nodded. "Three problems. First of all, the elemental is currently sealed within a containment device, but as it is still very much alive, and due to the nature of the containment device, it cannot be put into any spatial storage. This brings us to the next problem: It needs to be delivered covertly, because his enemies cannot know he obtained the elemental, and as the teleportation gateway scans any living being that passes through, it will need to be delivered directly without the use of gates."

"Alright, so I would have to travel there on my own. What's the final problem?"

"The adventurers who captured the elemental... Well, they weren't the best. The containment device they used was poorly made, and the seals on it are less than stellar, so by our expert's evaluation, it won't last more than a week. So it needs to be delivered directly within a week while making sure no one finds out what is being transported. I know it is a lot to ask of someone who just got promoted, but your progress so far—and the fact you could make your way to this city by yourself that quickly—makes me believe you are up to the task and have the required travel speed."

As she finished, a system message popped up in front of Jake.

Accept Special Courier Job 2: Transport the Sealed Elemental to the Infernal Baron in the mid-sized city without your cargo being discovered. Time limit: 7 days.
Or
Use the Teleportation Gateway to travel to the mid-sized city and forfeit the Special Courier Job.

"Can't keep the Baron waiting for long, now, can we?" Jake promptly answered with a smile. "I naturally accept the job."

"Great!" the elf said with relief as she took out a table-tennis-sized metal ball and placed it in front of Jake. He used Identify on it quickly before taking it and hiding it away.

[Sealed Elemental (Unique)] – A sealed elemental of the fire affinity can be found within. Due to the shoddy work of the ones who sealed it, this item is slowly deteriorating and will reach critical failure in a week (7 days). Any attempt to interfere with this item may result in the seal breaking prematurely.

"Remember, be careful," the elf insisted. "Even if we have hidden the fact we obtained the elemental well, I am not sure the adventurers were as good at keeping their mouths shut, so it may have spread, and enemies of the Baron may attempt to impede you in your travels. While they will not know what exactly you are transporting, as even the adventurers have no idea as to its value, they will be more than keen to find out, and I doubt their methods to do so will be peaceful."

"I'll be wary." Jake nodded seriously as he turned to leave. "I'd better get going. Thanks for everything so far."

"It has been my pleasure." She smiled and bowed once more as Jake exited the Guild Hall... and instantly felt a few hidden gazes on him.

Yep, this job is definitely not gonna be a peaceful one.

CHAPTER 5

PACKAGE POLICE

J ake felt like this would perhaps be the first "real" job. It gave him a different feeling compared to all the ones he had done prior, and after accepting it, he was more sure than ever these Special Courier Jobs were a bit like those special fights in the Colosseum. In more ways than one.

Based on the words of the Guild attendant, Jake suspected that all of these Special Courier Jobs were linked. A part of a longer quest chain of sorts. He believed he had only been offered this job because he had made the run with that Space Magic Locator, and it was even probable that his speed in that task had been factored in. In fact, Jake wouldn't be surprised at all if these jobs changed based on how a person performed beforehand, meaning he would have gotten an entirely different—or maybe just slightly easier—job if he hadn't been as fast as he was.

If all of this was true, it made sense the difficulty had a big spike with this job. He even had to potentially interact with a B-grade. Of course, Jake didn't believe for a single second he would have to fight one, as that would just be insanity, but he could see himself being thrown into a situation where he had to avoid the wrong dialogue choice.

Returning to the job at hand, Jake found himself standing outside the Guild Hall, four sets of eyes on him. That in itself wasn't out of the ordinary, but the fact two of them followed him even after he walked away from the Guild Hall proved they weren't just the usual observers who kept track of all the adventurers and Couriers coming and going.

Not wanting to have a few tails, Jake sped up and quickly weaved in between the many buildings and streets. Within only a few minutes, he felt that no one was keeping track of him anymore, so he ducked into the upper floor of a house with an open window no one was currently in. Yes, this was most definitely trespassing, but if someone broke into your house and trespassed, but you never noticed anyone had ever been there, had it really happened?

Inside the house, Jake started out by making his mask visible, hiding his face. So far, he hadn't worn it a single time throughout the entire Challenge Dungeon. It tended to have a negative effect when making conversation, so he had purposefully gone without. However, things were a bit different now, and he was totally fine with coming off as intimidating, as he doubted anyone who wanted to talk to him during this trip did so with kind intentions.

Next up, he altered Shroud of the Primordial so it once more hid his level and didn't just tell everyone he was 211. As a final touch, he infused a bit of mana into his cloak, making the shadowy thing almost seem alive as it began to ripple a bit, like a flickering shadow. He also considered using his stealth skill but decided against it. It may sound weird, but he wanted people to know he was leaving.

With all his preparations done, Jake checked himself over and confirmed everything was as it should be.

Definitely looking a lot less approachable now, he thought happily as he exited the house he had trespassed into once more, making sure to remove any traces he had ever been there.

Checking the compass on the Medallion, Jake noted the direction to the mid-sized city and got going. He wasn't going to relax at all with this job, as he quite frankly didn't have the leeway to do so. While checking out the library, he'd also studied the local geography and memorized a few maps, so he knew the distance to the mid-sized city was a bit over twice what he'd covered to reach the small-sized one. With the first trip taking him one and a half days, this one would take at least three.

This was another reason Jake felt confident this Special Courier Job was the first mission with some real difficulty. He seriously doubted someone like the Fallen King could even make the trip within the required seven days. He simply wasn't fast enough. The Sword Saint would also struggle, but Jake believed he would be able to make it quite comfortably if he wasn't disturbed too much on the way. Whether Dina could do it or not was a total toss-up. Sylphie could naturally do it easily, being the fast little bird she was... assuming she didn't get scammed by someone.

Flying through the air, Jake quickly exited the city limits, feeling a few new curious eyes on him during the flight. Those who were just curious about the hooded figure flying around weren't what bothered him, as gawking was a pretty normal reaction, but a few lingered for a bit too long. He even felt two skills reminiscent of his own Hunter's Mark attempting to land on him, but he rebuffed both. One of them tried again, but Jake once more defended as he sped up and seemingly got out of range.

This was definitely the most attention that had been placed on Jake for any job thus far. Far behind him, using his Pulse, he even saw the two who had tried to mark him fly into the air and look after him, both holding some devices in their hands... likely for communication.

That about confirms it... This flight is gonna have some turbulence.

Alas, there wasn't much Jake could do about it right now. As he flew, he took out the Sealed Elemental from beneath his clothes and observed it a bit more closely. As mentioned, it was about the size of a table tennis ball and pretty smooth. Inspecting the magic circles on it, Jake confirmed what the Guild attendant had said. He had no way to extend the duration of the seal. In fact, the entire structure of it was almost made to collapse. Whether that was on purpose or not, Jake didn't know, but he wouldn't rule it out... though the ones he suspected of being behind this faulty seal weren't necessarily any bad actors; it was just as likely to be the Wyrmgod, who'd designed the job.

Jake considered for a moment where best to hide the item if a fight did break out. He decided that the safest place would be somewhere it couldn't fall from, and with a way smaller chance of accidentally getting hit. Using his arcane mana, he covered it in a thin but firm layer of protection before popping it into his mouth and swallowing hard. Using internal muscles that weren't really something normal humans had access to, Jake stopped it before it even fully entered his stomach, where it could sit nicely for the duration of his travels.

Sure, eating it was a risk, and he even considered using Palate on it, but the stomach was a bit too close to a spatial storage. Besides, he was busy nurturing one of the ten legendary-rarity Blightroots in there. A natural treasure filled with death-affinity energy he had gotten as a present from the Risen during his Chosen Ceremony. It had been in there ever since the stomach healed from the whole Dark Witch debacle and had been a great help when making all his necrotic poison. He still didn't feel confident working with the root, but there was definitely much to be gained from it... especially since it seemed to contain traces of the Blight affinity created by the Viper's fellow Primordial, the Blightfather.

Back on topic, Jake had eaten the Sealed Elemental for a few reasons despite the risk. Having it inside of him would shield it from most detection and divination magic capable of specifically searching for it, and if someone was nearby, they would have a much harder time sensing it. It also just made Jake feel safer knowing where it was and that he didn't have to think about it falling out while fighting. Yep, he definitely ate it solely for logical reasons... and no, he didn't want to think about what would happen if the seal broke while he had the thing inside him.

With the Sealed Elemental in his stomach, Jake continued his journey by summoning his wings and using One Step in between wing flaps. This was his fastest method of movement, allowing him to truly build up momentum as he flew and teleported through the air while flaring his aura to keep any monsters who got too curious at bay.

After about half a day of travel, Jake spotted something in the distance. It was a village, from the looks of it, and for a moment Jake considered making a pit stop there, as he doubted its placement right on the path to the mid-sized city was an accident. He ultimately decided against it. Besides, as he got closer, he got the feeling he wouldn't even have to go greet the village. In fact, it looked like the village would be more than happy to fly out to greet him! With quite a few people, too, for a wonderful, unwanted welcome party to a village Jake didn't even plan on visiting. How nice of them.

For a second, he thought about flying around and avoiding them, but then he stopped himself and just continued flying toward them. He wasn't sure what they had up their sleeve, but he got a feeling he would regret it if he didn't go to them directly.

As he got closer, the group of about thirty people fanned out, clearly to block his path. Getting the message, Jake stopped as a human man with a large beard and full, heavy armor flew slightly forward to greet him. Using Identify, he saw the man wasn't dangerous in the slightest, though he was one of the higher-level individuals in the group.

[Human – lvl 249]

"Hello there!" the man said with a reassuring smile as he projected his voice to Jake while still keeping over a hundred meters of distance between them. "Real sorry to bother you, but we have had reports that smugglers carrying illegal substances have recently been through this area and have been tasked with putting a stop to it. Due to the crackdown, they have even begun to use Couriers... You wouldn't happen to be a Courier recently out of Hillspring City, would you?"

"Drugs? Really? Damn, that sucks. Luckily for me, I am not carrying any drugs, so no reason to bother me." Jake smiled as he felt the use of a skill on him. It didn't work, but Jake recognized it as similar to the one Silas from Neil's party had that was capable of detecting lies.

"Ah, you must have missed me asking... but I need to confirm if you are a Courier or not," the man insisted.

This was probably a crucial moment where one could attempt trickery... but Jake didn't feel the need to. "Yep, Courier here, straight out of Hillspring less than a day ago."

The plate-wearing man likely expected some kind of information from the person detecting lies, but even if he wasn't told anything, he didn't miss a beat. "Is that so? I am really sorry to bother you, but were you tasked by the Guild to deliver an item to the Infernal Baron? That is the cover currently used by the smugglers to trick Couriers, and the Baron himself isn't involved at all. They are even sophisticated enough to change item descriptions and make the delivery look like something it isn't."

Jake, acting shocked, gasped in an exaggerated way. "Shit, really? I am transporting something to that Baron!"

A big smile crept onto the man's lips. "Good thing we caught you, then, or you could have gotten in real trouble once you arrived at Infernal City with your delivery! The Baron would have had your head, even if you are a Courier! Tell you what... I do know this seems fishy, but let me share this... The crackdown on this particular substance is so pervasive that every gateway scans for it. That's also the reason you were forced to make the trip by yourself and not just take the gate. What's more, due to the nature of the substance, I even heard it cannot enter spatial storage."

"You're describing exactly what I was asked to transport," Jake confirmed enthusiastically.

What Jake was doing could seem risky, as the Special Courier Job required the cargo to remain undiscovered... but Jake felt very confident discovery wasn't just them knowing he had cargo for the Baron or even what it was. They clearly already knew. No, it was to ensure no one could Identify exactly what he was transporting. Shit, he even felt confident that should someone discover it and die before they could report it to anyone, he still wouldn't fail the job. In conclusion... it was probably only these "enemies" of the Baron that couldn't discover the Sealed Elemental.

"I see," the plated man said with a sigh. As Jake wondered what the man's next response would be, he smiled. "I know this is a lot to ask, but could you show me the goods in question? I would hate for this to be a false positive and to have made false accusations. Of course, if it is as we suspect, we would more than gladly take the illicit goods off your hands.

Naturally, we will make sure the Guild is properly notified of everything, too, and we have the express permission of the Infernal Baron to produce a letter of annulment for the Courier Job."

Honestly, the more the guy spoke, the more believable he sounded. Not even necessarily because of what he said but because of the powerful mental manipulation skill he was applying. This was likely why he had been the one to walk forward and speak.

"That all sounds great, Mister Package Police!" Jake answered with a big smile behind his mask. "Sadly, I got my orders, and even if everything you said is correct, I got a reputation for being reliable, you know? Besides, everything you just said is total bullshit, so it isn't like there is much to consider."

The man's smile faded instantly when he heard Jake's response. Yet he didn't outright attack. "Look, this is a far more complicated matter than you want to get involved in... There are people you do not want to make your enemies. So just hand over whatever you need to deliver to the Infernal Baron and be on your way... or things could get tricky for you."

As he said this, an aura erupted from down in the village as a figure flew up. Jake had noticed this person long ago, throwing them a glance and an Identify as they joined their mates.

[Scalekin – lvl 311]

Jake smiled, now finally knowing why he got the feeling he would regret not clashing with this group directly.

Seeing the lack of a response, the bearded man seemed to assume that Jake was shocked or something. "We have nothing against you and would prefer to settle this without unnecessary bloodshed. Yes, this is very much a threat, but we are under orders, same as you. So just make the easiest choice for everyone involved and live to see another day."

"Thank you," Jake said, entirely ignoring the man as he looked at the scalekin in the back. "You know, it feels like it's been so long... probably because it has."

"What the hell are you going on about?"

Rather than answering, Jake held out his hand, and a bow appeared in it. Between the many Challenge Dungeons he had done, he had truly missed something like this... especially after having just done the House of the Architect.

"Can I ask you to do me a favor, too?" Jake asked the scalekin directly.

In response to Jake's words, and probably also the fact he had pulled out a bow, the scalekin released their aura as a wand appeared in one of their hands. Jake felt the aura and grinned even more than before. *Not weak... not weak at all.*

"I was gonna ask you to put up a proper fight, as it's been so long since I had one... but it looks like that's freely included already."

CHAPTER 6

"PRETTY GOOD FIGHT."

J ake didn't relax for even a moment before immediately activating Arcane Awakening at its stable 30%. A level 311 humanoid was simply not anyone he could take lightly, and if he let his guard down, things could quickly get hairy.

In response, the bearded man and all of the lower-leveled people did something surprising. Rather than attack, they all turned on their heels and backed away at impressive speeds. The scalekin was the only one who slowly floated toward Jake.

At least they have a proper sense of when fighting is a bad idea.

Looking at the scalekin, Jake tilted his head. "You gonna remain silent and mysterious?"

The scalekin pointed their wand at Jake in reply, and magic began to gather. Jake quickly nocked an arrow and prepared to shoot when a white flash erupted from the wand. It wasn't an attempt to blind him; instead, the air around the scalekin mage became bathed in mana as what looked like fragments of silvery metal began floating around them.

With Sense of the Malefic Viper, he quickly identified the affinity. *Some kind of metal affinity... with... Oh, fu—*

Jake released the string of his bow right before he had to dodge to the side. A loud explosion sounded as a silvery bolt of lightning flew past him. Before Jake had time to try and nock another arrow, a second thunderclap sounded as another bolt was released.

Dodging this one, too, Jake kept flying upwards to get some distance. The range of the lightning was limited, and Jake believed he had an advantage at longer range. As he began flying upwards, the arrow he had loosed during their initial exchange also arrived, but the mage summoned a large tower shield and blocked it, only getting pushed back slightly when the arrow exploded.

However, the blast did do something. It made the hood of the scalekin fly back, revealing what looked like an albino lizard of some kind with what Jake recognized as clear male traits of this particular species. Did it matter that Jake figured out whether it was a male or female scalekin? No, not at all.

Continuing his upward flight, the mage below made another move. The air around him shimmered as the metal fragments began collecting into dozens of spears, and at the same time, a magic circle of some kind appeared below him. A few of the metal spears were shot toward Jake, but he dodged all of them. They flew past him and into the clouds above, the attacks thrown haphazardly as the scalekin focused his attention on the magic circle.

Jake didn't want to see what the scalekin was cooking up if he could avoid it and thus began to pelt his opponent with arrows. Likely because he knew he had a low chance of hitting Jake, the scalekin decided that rather than using all the metal spears to attack, he could use them as counters to Jake's arrows to buy him some time. At least, he tried to.

Shooting a series of arrows in quick succession, Jake controlled each of them and made their flight patterns unpredictable. The scalekin seemed surprised, blocking one side with a shield and using the spears on the other. Sadly for him, Jake wasn't playing around. Right before the arrows hit, they each split into dozens, exploding before they even hit him or the shield. The resulting explosion sent the scalekin staggering back, and the magic circle began to flicker as its caster lost focus.

Taking advantage, Jake released a Powershot he had begun charging when he shot the Splitting Arrows before. With the scalekin not entirely focused, he failed to react fast enough. The arrow hit him and blasted him down through his own magic circle, breaking it apart in the process.

Jake was prepared to follow up as he nocked another arrow, but his danger sense suddenly warned him. Turning around, Jake summoned a barrier of stable arcane mana. A white bolt of lightning struck him from within one of the clouds. With his sphere, he noted that the spears he had dodged earlier had all stopped in mid-air behind him, and one by one, they began to transform into bolts of pure energy.

Below him, the mage had also gathered himself, and it seemed like he was done playing around. The robe covering his body was already mostly ruined due to Jake's attacks, and through the mage's own power began to slowly disintegrate to reveal pristine silvery armor beneath, covering everything besides the scalekin's face. For a brief moment, at least. Then a helmet began to grow out of the armor, covering his face and leaving no obvious openings.

Dealing with the final lightning bolt from above, Jake turned to look at the mage. He looked like a full-plate warrior tank, and Jake didn't doubt he was one tough bastard, considering the armor hadn't taken any noticeable damage yet. To make matters more annoying, the mage had overcome one of the usual weaknesses of heavy armor—low speed—by firing incredibly fast lightning bolts.

Spreading out his arms, the scalekin summoned even more mana and conjured what looked like metal blades. Jake's response was to nock another arrow, having also decided to take things up a notch. Arcane Awakening intensified as he activated the offensive 50%, aiming to dodge every blow and focus on dealing damage for now.

When he fired an Arcane Powershot, the mage responded by holding up an open palm. A spearhead emerged from it before getting blasted out. It hit Jake's arrow, and both exploded mid-air. As a follow-up, the mage shot dozens of blades toward Jake, all crackling with lightning energy.

As they met a barrage of arcane arrows in their path, the air filled with explosions of arcane energy and lightning. The mage kept summoning blades, and Jake kept shooting arrows, both refusing to back down and controlling their attacks to hit each other when they didn't try to have an arrow or blade sneak by. Occasionally, an attack on either side would make it through, but Jake easily dodged those while the mage blocked.

The attack speed on both sides slowly picked up. Jake shot faster and faster, and he felt the strain. He also got the feeling this status quo was not good for him, as he was burning through resources faster than he was comfortable with. One also had to remember that his foe was more than fifty levels higher, resulting in him likely having a deeper mana pool, especially since he was a dedicated mage and not a hybrid like Jake.

Not all was bad, though, as Jake was also cooking something up. However, rather than relying on an obvious magic circle, Jake had a Protean Arrow getting slow-cooked within his quiver. Still, Jake would prefer to change things up, so he did just that.

Rather than continue their duel of blades versus arrows, Jake stopped shooting and instead began charging an Arcane Powershot. Without anything to impede their path, the blades reached him in less than a second, ready to slice him apart, but Jake was ready with his best counter to every attack.

With light movements, Jake dodged and swayed as the many blades flew by him. Some of them left lightning trails that tried to singe him, but his cloak and armor took the brunt of whatever got through, allowing Jake to keep charging.

He had gambled that the mage had stopped controlling every blade manually and was just firing them in his direction, and he had been right. The scalekin mage quickly realized his strategy wasn't working and stopped summoning them, but didn't seem particularly bothered.

Jake was ready for some other form of attack, but the scalekin just stood there as Jake charged his attack. Even if Jake was confused about why the scalekin was doing that, he wouldn't abandon his attack. He kept charging the Powershot to its full potential before releasing the string.

A shockwave of energy erupted as what little lightning energy clung to Jake was pushed away. The arrow descended, surrounded by a dense wave of pure destructive arcane energy. As it went downwards, Jake saw the scalekin merely raise a hand. The silvery metal mana began to gather into a shield, which was when Jake realized why the mage had stopped attacking.

The arrogant asshole was confident he could just block whatever attack I was charging... Yeah, fuck that.

Just before the silvery mana had formed a solid shield to block the arrow, all the mana suddenly stopped moving. Up above, Jake stared down, two glowing eyes visible through his mask as he unleashed a Primal Gaze that froze not only the scalekin's body, but also his energy.

The freeze only lasted for a fraction of a second, but it had entirely thrown off the scalekin's timing. The unfinished shield shattered instantly when the arrow hit it, and even if the scalekin became able to move again, there simply wasn't enough time to react.

Jake blinked rapidly to remove the blood dripping from his eyes after using Primal Gaze on a far higher-leveled foe. The scalekin was blasted downward at impressive speed as the arrow hit him. From his Hunter's Mark and Sense of the Malefic Viper, Jake felt that the attack had done some damage. Not wanting to lose his advantage, he nocked another arrow and released an Arrow Rain that filled the sky.

The rain of destructive arcane arrows hit the ground soon after, and everything exploded. Staring down at the hundreds of craters, Jake was happy they were pretty far away from the village, because if not, there wouldn't have been much left of it.

Despite the devastation, Jake clearly saw the silvery figure below stand back up, now sporting a nice hole in his otherwise pristine armor. He looked more annoyed than anything as he took to the air. Seeing no reason to let the scalekin do so in a relaxed manner, Jake decided to give him a few arrows along the way, but the scalekin still had his shield and managed to deflect them as he tried to get closer to Jake.

Jake felt the energy within his opponent building up, the air around him quivering. Audible cracks could be heard as the mage pointed at Jake. Small sparks of lightning appeared and then released a barrage of exploding metal fragments. Jake retreated as he saw the mage use one hand to raise his shield toward the air, and the other to lift his wand.

Not wanting to let him do his weird mage stuff, Jake chose to take a few scratches from metal fragments and shoot a quickly charged Arcane Powershot. He did this fully expecting the scalekin to dodge, but his opponent didn't move at all. The arrow hit the same hole in the armor as last time, piercing the scalekin square in his chest and making him flinch... but he also managed to finish casting his spell.

Jake's follow-up arrow was blasted to pieces when the mage shot a humongous lightning bolt into the air. As an absolute pillar of pure power burned into the sky and even the ground below, Jake felt like something happened within it... which turned out to be kind of true.

When the light faded, what appeared wasn't the mage but a massive pillar of pure metal in his place. It soared kilometers into the sky and even deep into the ground, and Jake wondered what the hell was happening until the entire thing started moving slightly.

Parts of it turned into cubes and fall off, but mid-fall, they started to warp even more, forming spikes or other sharp metal objects. Soon, the entire pillar began to crumble. Metal weapons rained down and covered the ground below, and the mage's form was soon revealed, now sporting an entire cube of pure metal that surrounded and shielded him.

Well, isn't this guy one tough nut to crack, Jake thought with a smile.

On the ground below, the many metal weapons began to stir as faint crackles of electricity surrounded them. Jake looked down and then at the mage in the cube, sighing. He had a plan, but it would take a bit to modify a certain arrow, so for now, he really only had one choice.

The very next second, weapons shot into the air, flying straight for Jake. Thousands of swords, axes, spears, arrows, and all sorts of other spiky things either went straight for Jake or formed a maelstrom of metal around him, restricting his movements.

Knowing there was no room to hold back, Jake went all-out with Arcane Awakening finally at its full power. The weapons came from all sides, but Jake was ready as he entered super-dodging mode. It reminded him of some of Minaga's trap rooms; the attacks came from everywhere, but with a few well-placed barriers, arcane explosions, and two katars to deflect blows, he found the openings he needed to remain relatively unharmed even as the attacks intensified.

Lightning bolts began to jump between all the weapons, sometimes also shooting for Jake, forcing him to summon his scales to handle the constant attacks. However, even with his scales and passive arcane barrier from Awakening, he still took some damage, as avoiding every attack simply wasn't feasible, and the lightning bolts were pretty damn strong, especially considering how many there were.

This continued for nearly a minute as the pressure kept mounting. Jake didn't doubt this was some killer attack the scalekin mage saved for a tricky situation, hiding inside his metal cube while controlling everything. The mana cost for the assault had to be extreme, but Jake didn't bet on his opponent running out of mana. Besides, he was a Courier on a job and couldn't drag out the fight too long... and by now, he was ready to finish it.

It took some extra time due to the focus he had to dedicate to not losing a limb, but soon, Jake's preparations were ready. After dodging and finding a small opening, Jake released a large blast of arcane mana to give him a moment to act. He reached out and touched the metal cube, which began to glow dark green as Touch of the Malefic Viper activated and awakened the poison within the scalekin.

His opponent had been hit by two arrows, with the second one especially delivering a good dose. Sadly, Jake hadn't had time to make any of his Heartrot Poison quite yet—okay, he had kind of just forgotten to—but it wasn't a problem, as he would most likely have used his Sleeping Night Toxin anyway.

While the scalekin had some impressive defenses, his pure Vitality didn't strike Jake as very high, which was proven true when the poison was activated. Within the cube of metal, the scalekin coughed up blood and lost concentration. All the weapons flying around Jake stopped moving.

A large Protean Arrow appeared in Jake's hand as he began flying toward the metal cube and charging a Powershot. The scalekin within was still struggling with the poison and its explosive activation, but he quickly noticed Jake approaching and gathered himself, setting the many weapons in motion again.

His reaction was commendably quick... but not quick enough. Shadowy energy surrounded Jake's body as a second version of himself flew out of him toward the metal cube. His Eternal Shadow, with katar in hand, delivered a Piercing Cursed Arcane Fang into the metal cube. A blast of lightning was released from the cube in response, dispersing the shadow, but the attack had gone through.

The piercing effect made a hole rather than fully breaching, but it left just the opening Jake needed. Right before all the weapons reached him again, Jake released the string. His Protean Arrow flew forward and struck the same hole just made by his shadow, further amplified by Jake pouring in what little Hunting Momentum he had been able to build up.

When the Protean Arrow hit, the attack activated in two stages. First, a large blast of arcane energy shot forward, blowing a hole in the cube for the rest of the arrow to pass through. The mage was partly hit by this arcane energy and moved to defend himself within as the second part—the arrow itself—struck him.

Within the cube, the arrow pierced straight through the mage and pinned him to the back side of his own cube. After barely having to dodge a few weapons coming for him, Jake triggered the arrow with a mental command, and the entire thing exploded, the cube serving only to amplify the power of the explosion.

It also turned out the cube was a lot more vulnerable to attacks from the inside. The large arcane explosion left cracks all over the cube as it began to crumble and fall apart. Fragments dropped to the ground, along with the many weapons and the mage himself.

Jake raised his bow and took aim again. The mage was badly injured and had even lost one of his arms in an attempt to contain the explosion, but he still tried to block Jake's arrow by summoning his shield again. The first arrow curved slightly just before it hit, striking the shield at a weird angle and making the mage spin in the air. To throw him further off, Jake even activated the Arcane Charge from his Mark, making the mage's entire body flash with destructive arcane energy and utterly unable to respond to the next attack. The second arrow hit the spinning mage in the back, sending him reeling even more, while the third struck him square through the thin gap in the armor at his neck, piercing straight through.

Five more arrows followed as the scalekin remained in freefall, every one of them coated in poison. Jake had kind of expected the mage to have one more card to pull out, but before the scalekin even hit the ground, all signs of life faded, and he got a system message.

You have slain [Scalekin - lvl 311 / Aluminum Magister - lvl 334 / Luxmetal Alchemist – lvl 288]

Jake read the notification quickly and was a bit disappointed at the confirmation that he indeed hadn't gotten any experience in this Challenge Dungeon either.

It wasn't all bad, though.

"Pretty good fight," Jake mumbled to himself as he turned to look toward the village.

Right before the bearded man had left, Jake had thrown a subtle Hunter's Mark on him. He was hiding away in the village, or at least he had been, as Jake now saw him getting a move on, likely after seeing the result of the fight.

After quickly flying down and depositing the body of the scalekin in his storage in case it would come in handy later, he began flying toward the village, ready for a second conversation with the fake package police.

CHAPTER 7

BRANCHING PATHS

The scalekin sure hadn't been the most talkative, so Jake hoped to get some information out of the bearded man who'd originally greeted him. He and all his friends were trying to run away now that the mage had died, knowing that they didn't stand a chance even if they got involved.

Power differences, especially at higher grades, weren't just a simple math equation. Two people with half of Jake's stats wouldn't be equal to one Jake, and even if a few hundred of them came at him, Jake was confident in smacking them all down. There were certain conceptual gaps caused by higher stats and grades, resulting in far less damage being dealt by those who were a lot weaker.

Jake had ways to close the gap between himself and someone at a higher level, but such a thing was generally considered quite rare based on what Jake had seen, likely because, in order to get stronger against higher-leveled opponents, you had to get used to *only* getting anything out of higher-leveled opponents.

All of this is to say that despite there being around thirty of them, the fact Jake could fight, let alone kill the scalekin mage meant they wouldn't be able to even touch him. Assuming he was in any condition to fight, of course. Jake did have the minor problem of being on a timer as he flew toward the village.

Arcane Awakening had been suppressed down to the more stable 30%, but he had to keep it going or he would enter a period of weakness. While he could re-trigger Arcane Awakening even while in this period of weakness, it would lead to an even worse backlash afterward, so he would very much prefer to avoid that.

Chasing down the bearded man didn't end up taking long, especially with the stat boost active. On the way, he also manipulated his cloak to entirely cover his body, and after a bit of quick cleaning up, he looked like he hadn't even taken minor wounds during the fight. That should add a bit to his intimidation factor.

The man and his companions had fled through an underground tunnel to a hideout disguised as a small hill about ten kilometers from the village. From a distance, it looked entirely normal, as the ones who'd crafted it had transformed an actual hill and then placed all magic formations on the inside. Quite clever and a lot harder to spot that way, and most C-grades would definitely miss it.

Reaching the hill, Jake pulled out his bow again, nocked an arrow, and drew the string as he yelled, his voice infused with mana and Willpower, **"I will count down from ten. When I reach zero... well, you can guess what happens. Ten, ni—"**

Before Jake could even say nine, the bearded man and two others flew out from within the hill, their bodies phasing through it seamlessly. They all had their hands up above their heads, and Jake didn't feel the slightest threat from any of them.

"Don't shoot!"

Jake slightly relaxed the string but didn't lower his bow immediately. "See, that wasn't so hard. Now, I believe we have some things to discuss, including why you decided that attacking a Courier who is just trying to do his damn job was a good idea."

"We... We got a job... I am not sure about the details, so—"

"So you're gonna tell me everything you do know? Great!" Jake said in a cheerful tone as he kept his eyes on the three of them. He also looked inside the hill, wondering if they were maybe trying to set up an ambush, but they were all just hiding... potentially hoping Jake thought only the bearded man and the two who'd exited with him were hiding there.

"We're just middlemen. Adventurers," the man hurriedly explained. "I don't even know who the job is from! That mage was the one who brought everything and hired us for his bosses. He had a letter with instructions, part of the payment, and everything like that. We were just here to make the presence of the Silenced less suspicious."

Jake took in what he said. One word toward the end stuck out due to the emphasis the man put on it. "Silenced what? I know the scalekin wasn't a big conversationalist, and I didn't get anything out of him besides the occasional small grunt, but I'm not sure making his lack of talking his defining trait is polite."

The bearded adventurer looked a bit confused for a moment, then stammered, "Do... Do you not know what a Silenced is?"

It sounded like Jake was really meant to, so he tried—and failed—to play it off cool. "Remind me."

"Someone from the Silenced Order. Slaves who have had their ability to speak or even properly communicate entirely sealed away, primarily used by those who want them to accomplish tasks they really don't want anyone to talk about or track back to them. Rare to see any C-grades of the Silenced Order, though. Mainly due to how expensive they are and their limited availability. Especially a late-tier C-grade, as after becoming Silenced, progress pretty much stops. Their Paths are ruined."

The explanation almost felt too long and thorough, making Jake think he had hit some intended dialogue option. Especially the last part, which struck Jake as unnecessary added information. Alas, it told him everything he needed to know.

"So, in summary, someone unable to communicate came to you with a letter telling you to stop me in my path, and you did so without thinking that maybe, just maybe, the Courier wasn't just some pushover?"

"Not just stop you—stop any Courier coming out of Hillspring and going this way—and yes, the fact the Silenced couldn't handle you was not part of the calculations... but we were never necessarily meant to kill you! Just incapacitate and intimidate. Look, all I know is that you are transporting something someone really doesn't want the Infernal Baron to have, or at least come into possession of, without this employer of ours knowing what it is. We didn't even necessarily have to obtain what you are transporting, but just confirm what it is and report it." Once again, the adventurer was saying more than Jake thought any good contractor should about a clearly confidential job. Also, for someone just meant to incapacitate, the scalekin mage had sure liked going for his vitals.

"And how exactly were you supposed to contact this employer?" Jake questioned, feeling this was the good dialogue tree to go down.

"The Silenced knew a ritual to contact the employer..." the man said, afraid that Jake wouldn't like the answer. Then he suddenly remembered something. "Ah! But we can contact the broker who put us in contact with the Silenced! He should be able to at least find a representative of the employer! I have a token to do it that should work even at this distance."

"See, that sounds like a workable solution," Jake said with a smile beneath his mask as he decided to put his bow away and, with a single step, teleport down in front of the bearded man, making him flinch. "Do it. Now."

Without missing a beat, the man did as asked, pulling out a token that looked like a metal slate of some kind. He infused some energy into it, and a semi-transparent screen appeared in mid-air. Seconds passed, the bearded adventurer looking more and more nervous, hoping the broker on the other side would pick up.

After half a minute, there was finally a response. The screen warped and grew big enough to show an entire person as a figure appeared. The person was hooded, and when the bearded adventurer saw the person, his eyes opened wide.

"Who are you!? Where is Elmin!?"

The figure barely reacted to his outburst, but Jake felt them turn and look him over on the other side.

"The Courier, I presume. I see you failed. How unfortunate."

Jake couldn't discern whether the voice was male or female, and the hood hid any clues as to the answer.

The bearded man seemed even more agitated than before as he yelled, "What the fuck did you do with—"

"He had served his purpose... and so have you served yours."

Without any warning or even time for Jake to react, some energy came alive within the bearded man, and he exploded like a popped balloon. The two at his side followed suit, and Jake even saw the people in the hideout suffer the same fate. Within three seconds, all of them had died, and in the environment, Jake felt a faintly familiar concept.

Karmic magic... Well, fuck me.

"Now, as for you, Courier..." the figure said, keeping their attention on Jake, who had just been standing there even as the blood splashed over him.

He hadn't flinched for even a second, and he wasn't going to do so now as he stared at the figure on the other end. Even if he couldn't feel their actual aura, he didn't doubt they were, at the very least, well into B-grade, if not higher.

"What?" Jake asked, trying to sound almost annoyed. He took this attitude very much on purpose for one simple reason... They couldn't feel how powerful Jake was through the token either. Same as Jake couldn't feel their power. So he would prefer to front that he was maybe stronger than he actually was. Seeing as the token also only relayed sound and visual information, he slowly prepared for his escape, the stealth skill beginning to activate.

"Taking an antagonistic attitude will earn you nothing, Courier. Our quarrel is not with you, and we are not your enemies."

"Oh, really? Tell that to the little lizard you put in my way." Jake scoffed. "Seemed pretty damn antagonistic to me when he began to throw his metal sticks."

"The Silenced was merely following orders and was perhaps a bit... overzealous in their approach. Capture was ordered as a preferential resolution, but it seems like that was far beyond the capabilities of the Silenced. However, that matter has already concluded. Rather than dragging out this needless topic, let us proceed with something more productive. Business. You are delivering something we want, and we are willing to compensate you for it."

That they wanted to strike a deal instead of just issuing threats was a good start. Jake crossed his arms. "What exactly are you proposing?"

"Continue your journey as normal. None of our agents shall get in your way, but when you arrive, do not seek out the Infernal Baron. Instead, go to the Guild and inform them you lost the delivery on the way. We will then send someone to find you and, once the item is confirmed, post a Courier Job you are to accept. It shall be ensured that there will be no negative impact on your reputation. If you do this, there will also be a substantial reward waiting, along with new and highly valuable allies."

"Hm," Jake said, looking deep in thought. "I will need to think about it, so give me a few days. I planned on making a small detour on the way, so I wouldn't arrive in the city within ten days anyway. I assume this is all good on your end? That should also help sell the story if I do wanna go with saying I lost the delivery."

The figure took a brief pause, almost as if consulting with someone. "Very well. You are to take this token and use it to contact us once you have an answer. We will give you five days to respond, or you will come to regret your—"

"You know what? I thought we were doing business, not you suddenly deciding you're my boss and can order me around. With that attitude, I guess you'll know when I arrive in the city what I want to do." Jake scoffed. "I'll be in touch."

"Wait, take the—"

Jake's attempt to front himself as someone more powerful than he actually was had entered its final stage. He waved the figure off as he turned around and began walking away while at the same time triggering two skills.

Eternal Shadow of the Primal Hunter activated first, a shadowy version of himself casually continuing his walk. The real Jake stopped mid-walk as he fully activated his stealth skill, and instantly, he knew it had worked. The projected figure lost sight of the real Jake as the shadow perfectly replaced him, only to disappear into cursed smoke a few steps later.

Jake stood completely still, looking at the projected figure for a few seconds. He couldn't read anything concrete from the person, but it looked like they were discussing something with someone. The figure took a final look around, and five seconds later, the projection disappeared, the token cracking down the middle. A second or so later, the entire token crumbled into dust and was scattered by the wind. The only remaining evidence of their interaction was the splatters of blood covering the ground.

Not wanting to take any chances, Jake flew a good distance away. There was a small forest of sorts nearby, consisting of just a few thousand trees total, but it was a nice spot for Jake to lay low for a while. After he got there, he found a nice hidden spot, sat down, and deactivated his boosting skill, letting the period of weakness wash over him. He could have held on for a while more, but doing so would only have extended the time he would have to wait.

Entering meditation, Jake reflected on his conversation with the projected figure. Through it, he had confirmed a few things. First of all, they didn't seem like they had any information on Jake as a person at all. If they did, there should have been some surprise that someone registered as barely in C-grade had killed a late-tier C-grade. None of that had happened, making Jake pretty sure the Guild didn't have any information leaks on him, at least.

Secondly, they genuinely had no idea what he was transporting, for if they did, there was no way they would have agreed to him waiting ten days to arrive. The Sealed Elemental would get out of its seal in less than a week, and while it was a possibility this organization or whatever just didn't want the Infernal Baron to have the item, they clearly also wanted it.

Finally, this organization was powerful. Based on how the figure had acted, Jake got the impression he hadn't spoken to the big boss but just a subordinate, and if a subordinate was capable of applying karmic magic to trigger some remote bombs placed inside all of the adventurers, the ones actually in charge were definitely not people Jake could mess with.

At least, not directly. Right now, one of his big advantages was that they also didn't know how strong Jake was. With Shroud of the Primordial, he could hide everything about himself, and even if he showed himself to be in C-grade, many stronger people could hide their grades like that. The mere fact that anyone, even an S-grade, would only see three question marks when trying to Identify him would definitely help.

Adding on the fact they were clearly careful in regard to anything involving the Guild, Jake believed he had a legit shot at bluffing them. Assuming he wanted to bluff them, that is. There was also one more thing. Jake wasn't even sure if this second path to the Special Courier Job wasn't actually a legitimate option... especially since he had gotten a system message right after talking to the projected figure.

Special Courier Job 2 updated.
Special Courier Job 2: Transport the Sealed Elemental to the Infernal Baron in the mid-sized city without your cargo being discovered OR Transport the Sealed Elemental to the mid-sized city and instead deliver the Sealed Elemental according to the plans of [Unknown]. Time limit: 7 days.

That's right... a branching quest with multiple outcomes. Actual decision-making was required.

CHAPTER 8

INFERNAL BARON

After recovering from using Arcane Awakening, Jake didn't continue his journey right away. Instead, he took a small break inside the miniature forest to prepare some things. During the House of the Architect, he had learned to craft both a better poison and acid, but since exiting, he had made neither.

Both of those would honestly have been useful in the last fight, especially the acid. With a good amount, Jake could have tossed it on the cube or even put some of it into the Protean Arrow he created to more efficiently destroy the scalekin mage's defenses. Whether he would have used the Heartrot Poison was a bit more of a toss-up, as the Sleeping Night Toxin was still damn effective.

Either way, Jake wanted to at least have the option. Besides, he had improved his general crafting skills and wanted to make a new batch of Sleeping Night Toxin to ensure he had the best poison possible for what was to come. There was no doubt in his mind that this wouldn't be his only combat encounter with a powerful foe in this Challenge Dungeon.

With regard to the decision Jake had to make about his delivery spot, he didn't really see it as a choice. In Jake's mind, he had been hired to do a job, and he was going to do that job. It wasn't really about doing what was right or wrong in his head, nor choosing what was most beneficial to him. Jake just felt like one should stick to an agreement already made, and he wasn't the kind of person to be bought off by someone else.

That isn't to say there was nothing that could make Jake change his mind. If he arrived in this mid-sized city and found out that the Infernal Baron was some psycho who liked to roast and eat children or some other fucked-up shit like that, he could totally see himself going to this other organization merely out of spite. Not that he thought the organization was much better, considering they had a propensity to kill everyone Jake had seen them working with so far. Not to mention that they also used slaves based on what Jake had heard about this Silenced Order, making him less than positive toward them.

When Jake was done crafting all his poison and two full barrels of acid, he continued his journey. Jake also decided that for the rest of the trip, he would keep his stealth skill active. Due to the main cost coming from activating it, he could have it up pretty much indefinitely. Doing so should also help him appear more mysterious, as the organization wouldn't know how he had gotten to the city even if they had scouts placed on the path. Assuming none of those scouts were high-tier, Perception-focused C-grades or B-grades, that is.

The entire encounter with the scalekin mage, the projection, and his crafting session had put him back ten or so hours, but Jake believed it would be worth it down the line. He did hope that he wouldn't have any more interruptions for the rest of the way, and with luck, the stealth skill would help with that.

As the days passed uneventfully, Jake got some good practice with using his stealth skill while also moving quickly and employing both One Step and his wings. The system assistance did most of the job for sure, but in just a few days, Jake managed to remove some very minor clues betraying his presence when using One Step. Mainly, these were tiny ripples created by space effectively compressing around him whenever he used the skill, but with some slight tweaks, he also hid those far better. A talented space mage would probably be able to feel them, but the average person definitely wouldn't. Or perhaps couldn't, based on how the beasts didn't react at all despite Jake stepping down practically right next to them.

After a bit over three days of total travel, the mid-sized city appeared in the distance as a small blip. It still took him another seven hours to actually reach it—one of the downsides of extremely high Perception and flying high up in the air—meaning he had used a bit less than half of his allotted time when he finally arrived.

This city was a lot bigger than the small-sized Hillspring, and Jake doubted there were only a few million people living there. Assuming one counted the thousands of farmsteads and buzzing villages surrounding the large city itself, at least.

Checking his compass, Jake saw it was pointing toward the very center of the city. From a distance, Jake could see a castle atop what looked like it had once been a volcano, with buildings constructed up its cliffside. While it was a bit on the nose, it definitely looked like the kind of place someone known as the Infernal Baron would call home.

However, Jake didn't go there immediately. He stopped a bit outside the city and landed close to the gate entrance so as to not fly inside. If this organization had powerful scouts waiting, flying into the city was a lot more suspicious than using the gates, as according to the laws, only influential and powerful figures could fly into the city. Well, them and Couriers, of course.

That didn't mean Jake would enter officially, though. He kept his stealth skill up as he went through the checkpoint, easily spoofing the magic circle of detection covering the entire city with Shroud of the Primordial. The guards at the gate were all around level 250, which was another decent step up, but none of them looked particularly strong. Jake did sense a far more powerful C-grade inside one of the offices close to the official entrance, though.

Once inside the city, Jake considered whether he should go to the Infernal Baron immediately or check out the Guild Hall first. Both things seemed risky, though. If the organization had placed people capable of detecting him, they would definitely be at both of those places. Ultimately, he settled on going to the Baron directly.

I need to enter the Baron's place without raising suspicion... Jake thought to himself as he walked casually through the city streets. Just going there directly would definitely be suspicious. As it was on a mountain, he could easily observe from down on the streets how many took the winding path up to the castle gates, and so far, he had seen no one take that route. As for those flying to the castle, he only saw a single beast do it.

Jake considered what to do until he got an idea. The problem wasn't anyone knowing he'd entered the Baron's castle... it was that they knew it was him entering it. As of this moment, the organization only knew a few things about Jake. They knew how he generally looked, and they knew he was a human, so Jake was thinking... what if he just changed both of those things?

Shroud of the Primordial was a borderline cheat, and with it, he could easily change how he was Identified. As for his looks, while simply wearing a mask would hide any skin, Jake decided that he would be far more suspicious if he tried to fully conceal his identity. So, he had a far better plan.

Finding a building close to the path leading to the Infernal Baron's castle, Jake made sure he wasn't followed before dipping in and getting to work. First, he changed his race and level to display him as a level 270 scalekin. The level was chosen to show that he was pretty strong, but probably not strong enough to have been the one to beat the mage.

As a final touch, Jake switched his clothes to something a bit more casual, shamelessly stealing from whoever lived in the house he'd broken into. Once he was fully clothed, he activated the final part of his disguise. Dark green scales covered his body, courtesy of Scales of the Malefic Viper.

Granted, Jake still looked pretty human due to his features, but it wasn't anything egregious. There were many scalekin who just looked like humans with scales covering them, primarily those who were children of a human and a scalekin.

Finding his new looks adequate, Jake exited the building again. Before, he had told himself he wouldn't just fly to the castle, as that would be far too bold if there were scouts looking for him... which was exactly why that was exactly what he would be doing.

Taking to the air, Jake did not summon his wings but just flew using regular energy manipulation. The instant he went into the air and began to make his way toward the castle, dozens of eyes were upon him. Most disappeared a few seconds later, but a good few remained. Some of them even felt pretty damn powerful, but even so, they didn't stand a chance at piercing his Shroud.

Luckily, there was no killing intent within any of them either. Soon enough, Jake also felt some attention land on him from within the castle. Jake was ready for someone to fly out and greet him, especially when he entered the range of a large magic circle covering the entire castle.

His prediction of someone flying out turned out to be slightly off as his senses warned him something was coming. The air around Jake slowly solidified until space itself froze, and Jake felt the presence of a powerful space mage. Choosing not to fight it, he stopped flying as a voice spoke in his head.

"This is the Infernal Baron's personal residence. State your business or turn around." Through the mana and the presence in the voice, Jake felt pretty darn certain he was dealing with a B-grade.

"I come for an audience with the Infernal Baron," Jake answered, kind of hoping he wouldn't have to say more. While he doubted that was how it worked, the job explicitly stated Jake had to deliver the Sealed Elemental without others finding out what it was, and this could also include some mage working under the Baron. Well, it was also possible this space mage was a plant from the organization, but Jake wouldn't really bet on it.

"For what purpose?" the voice answered, making Jake curse internally.

Saying he was a Courier could give the gig away, especially if the mage demanded to see the delivery. Ultimately, Jake decided that he would try and stay as professional and tight-lipped as possible. *"A matter concerning only the Baron himself. I cannot say anything more than that, but I can swear that should you not allow me this audience, the Infernal Baron will be greatly inconvenienced."*

This was another place where choosing a level of 270 could come in handy. The Infernal Baron was in B-grade, and no matter what tricks the space mage believed Jake could have up his sleeve, he simply wouldn't be able to pose any danger.

A few seconds passed, Jake really hoping he would be allowed through, before he finally got an answer. *"The Baron has agreed to meet you, with the condition that should you be wasting his time, this will be the last audience you will have with anyone."*

"He will not be disappointed," Jake quickly answered.

A bit childish with the death threat, if Jake was just a fanboy trying to waste the man's time, but alas. He was the client, and as the saying goes, the customer is always right. Unless the customer is a fucking idiot, in which case they are probably rarely right about anything.

The space around Jake loosened as a portal appeared right in front of him. Jake took the cue and entered, finding himself standing in what looked a bit like the throne room soon after. There was no throne, however, just a cozy-looking set of armchairs with a small table between them. On one of these chairs sat a woman who still gave off some space mana, making him certain she had been the one to summon the portal.

On the other was a human who looked to be in his twenties, a bit younger than Jake expected. He had a thin red beard and deep red hair, and just being in the room with him, Jake felt the temperature increase. Both of them also gave off B-grade auras—and not just early B-grade, either.

"So, you wanted an audience?" the man said, leaning back and raising an eyebrow. "I sincerely hope—for you—that this is not a waste of my time."

Jake looked at the man and woman. "I believe it would be best if this matter is only discussed with the Baron."

"Oh?" The Baron smiled and turned to the woman. "Heard that? He wants you gone."

Before the woman could even respond, Jake sent a telepathic message to the Baron—one the B-grade luckily didn't reject. *"I am a Courier, and I believe I have something for you."*

The Baron's facial expression didn't change in the slightest as he kept looking at the space mage, who answered with a small scoff, "Quite rude to come in here and begin to make demands."

"But also ballsy," the Baron pointed out. "Look, let's play along, eh? I will be sure to tell you all the funny details later."

The woman looked at the man, somewhat perplexed, but eventually nodded. "As you will."

Standing up, she gave Jake one more glance before she disappeared from the room in a ripple of space magic. Then the Baron waved his hand, and a barrier encased the entire room, hiding their conversation from any curious listeners. At least, that was what the Baron probably believed it would do.

"So, what do you—"

"There is still a third party capable of hearing us," Jake warned the man telepathically.

The Baron had stopped himself mid-sentence and stared at Jake before asking out loud, "How do you know that?"

At this point, Jake had to assume the man was trying to be unsubtle on purpose, as he just answered normally. "I have my ways."

Narrowing his eyes, the Baron stared deeply at Jake. "I know who is listening, and it is fine. However, do tell me..."

Without Jake reacting in the slightest, a magic circle appeared below him. The Baron let out a bit of power and used his presence to try and partly suppress Jake. It was just intimidation, really.

"Who exactly are you?"

"A Courier here to make a delivery," Jake answered in a calm tone.

The Baron scoffed. "Are you daft? I know the information on the Courier I hired. Early-tier C-grade human male. The only one of those things you are is a guy, so do not make me repeat myself a third time... Who are you?"

Sighing internally, Jake had to confess he hadn't expected the man in front of him to be so careful. He had wanted to hide who he was from others, but hiding from the client hadn't been part of the plan.

"I am exactly the one you hired," Jake responded as he took out his Courier Medallion. "Look, the job is infused into this Medallion by the Guild itself. Currently, I am just in disguise, as I met some... trouble along the way."

To prove his point, Jake had the scales slowly recede and disappear on his face.

Staring at the Medallion, the Infernal Baron seemed to be capable of realizing Jake was at least telling the truth about that. "Assuming I believe you, do you have the goods?"

"Before that, I believe it pertinent to know who this third-party observer is," Jake answered, not showing the slightest sense of fear despite the magic circle still beneath his feet, ready to erupt in flames that would burn him to a crisp. "The job was very clear about the fact that I was not to allow anyone to know of this delivery besides the Baron."

Narrowing his eyes, the Baron waved his concerns off. "I already told you it's fine."

"The order was clear," Jake insisted.

"Do not test my patie—"

"Enough," a voice cut through the room, and Jake had to hide a small smile as the third person finally revealed himself, at least in part.

Between Jake and the Baron, a figure made out of pure flames appeared. He was not there in person, but instead using some form of projection skill. The moment he showed up, the Baron hurriedly stood and fell to his knees, not even looking up. Jake naturally remained standing.

The man who had appeared looked just like the Baron in front of him, except a bit older. His aura was also different, and not just in power. Jake felt the man's innate authority. It stemmed from something Jake hadn't really cared a lot about or dedicated much attention to... The nobility system. Something pretty rare, considering many who claimed themselves kings or nobles did not have the actual system title to back it up.

"Let us not bother a man simply sticking to unparalleled professional ethics," the figure of flames said in a playful, scolding tone as he kept his eyes on Jake. Instantly, Jake knew the man in front of him was on a whole other level compared to the Baron.

A-grade... close to S-grade, probably...

"Allow me to introduce myself, Courier. I am known as the Duke of Flames, the father of the one who hired you, and the true client of this job." The Duke flashed a big smile. **"And I believe you might just be what we've been looking for."**

CHAPTER 9

SPECIAL SIDE JOB

Jake definitely felt like he had unlocked some secret quest chain or something. Delivering to a B-grade through a Special Courier Job this early on was already a pretty big achievement, but now even an A-grade had appeared before him. Plus, because Jake knew a bit about the world he found himself in, he understood how important someone like a duke was.

The country Jake found himself in had only three dukes and one king. All the dukes and the king were A-grade, with the strongest fighting force of the entire kingdom being part of the duke factions or directly under the king. This is to say, someone with the Duke title was pretty much at the top of the Challenge Dungeon world in both power and influence.

There were also some S-grades out there, but they were few and far between. Some were hidden Lord Protectors, some were like the Founder of the Guild and did their own stuff, and others were in isolation or had left the world for the stars, with no one knowing where they were.

However, despite all this, there was still one tiny problem with the Duke showing up.

"It is a pleasure to meet you," Jake said with a nod. "But I still have to make my delivery first... and despite you being his father and the true client, my job doesn't specify any of that. Would it be possible for you to give us a moment alone? I am certain we can discuss things afterwards."

The Duke seemed taken aback as he looked Jake up and down for a few moments. The Baron also stared daggers at Jake and looked like he wanted to blow up the magic circle beneath him any second. There was definitely tension rising... until the Duke let out a slight chuckle that turned into a full-on laugh.

"**Good! Even before me, you refuse to compromise in the slightest! Very good! I shall do as asked and give you a moment. My son here will signal me when we can return to the true discussion at hand.**" The Duke's flaming figure faded away, and a second later, Jake confirmed he was no longer peeking, actually sticking to his word.

"You are lucky you weren't reduced to a mere pile of ash," the Baron said with a scoff. "To dare show such disrespect toward the Duke..."

"I showed no disrespect, merely the professionalism I was hired to display," Jake said in the most professional voice he could muster. "Now that it is just the two of us, let us confirm the delivery." Waving his hand, Jake took out Eternal Hunger. "Let me just retrieve it right quick."

Considering Jake had eaten the item, he also needed a way to get it out again. While forcing himself to throw it up was certainly one possibility, he felt like it was a bit too nasty to show in front of a client. Stabbing himself in the stomach and pulling out the Sealed Elemental directly was definitely more polite, right?

The Infernal Baron looked on as Jake gutted himself, frowning a bit when Jake pulled out the orb. Jake assumed he was just nervous that the item had been ruined, which was almost offensive. He was no amateur Courier who would ruin the delivery in such a reckless manner. Shit, Jake even made sure not to spill a single drop of blood on the Baron's floor. He kept it all inside, and what little did drip out was burned away with destructive arcane mana before it ever reached the ground.

With the item successfully extracted, Jake quickly removed the stable layer of arcane mana around the Sealed Elemental and used Identify on it just for good measure... because the result definitely took him by surprise.

[Sealed Elemental (Unique)] – A sealed elemental of the fire affinity can be found within. Due to the shoddy work of the ones who sealed it, this item is slowly deteriorating and will reach critical failure in less than a week (6 days). Any attempt to interfere with this item may result in the seal breaking prematurely.

The seal on the item was meant to last seven days in total. However, despite around three and a half days passing, it said the seal would still last another six days. Jake suppressed a frown to avoid outwardly displaying any of his surprise. Internally, though, he did wonder what was going on.

Wait... maybe it's a bit like those items the Nalkar vampires tried to preserve back in the Order? he considered after a bit, and the more he thought about it, the more right he thought he was.

Every item decayed with time. Even equipment would lose its enchantments if long enough passed, just turning into an inert object worth less than the raw materials it was made up of. It would take a long time, with equipment pretty much always outlasting the lifespan of whoever originally wore it, but it was inevitable. With maintenance, an item could be kept active for an even longer period, if not nearly indefinitely, by replacing the enchantments with identical new ones, using the same framework set by the original creator. If one could find an equally skilled crafter with a Path similar to the original creator, of course.

Some items were a bit harder or complicated to maintain. In the case of the Nalkar vampires, they didn't want to re-enchant anything, as that would effectively destroy the original items as it was, while other items simply couldn't be maintained. This mainly happened with items of legendary rarity or above. Finding someone capable of re-enchanting these items was often borderline impossible due to the Records in the item and the difficulty of finding a crafter with a similar enough Path. Luckily, they would last a long time by themselves anyway, but even they would lose their power with time. In these cases, the best way to preserve them was to simply make sure they didn't degrade as fast.

The vampires used complicated formations to make this possible, each creating a beneficial environment for every individual item, but for some, all they could do was isolate it from all outside influences... which was exactly what Jake had done with the Sealed Elemental.

Jake's stable arcane affinity was really fucking good at isolating things. In all honesty, Jake hadn't expected it to work, as he assumed the item was breaking down primarily due to system fuckery, but seeing it work was a pleasant surprise nevertheless. He knew that even with total isolation, deterioration would still exist, but to see how effective his stable arcane affinity was with just a simple barrier was nice.

"Let me see it," the Infernal Baron said as he waved his hand, and the ping-pong-ball-sized item flew toward the B-grade. Once he had the item in his hand, he made a small hand motion. Sparks flew, and a big smile appeared on his face.

"Great, and it's in an even better condition than I expected," the man said, looking incredibly pleased. "And now that I have the item, I presume you have no more complaints if the Duke rejoins us?"

"My job here is done," Jake said, shrugging.

Snapping his fingers, the Baron released a faint pulse of mana, and less than a second later, the flaming figure of the Duke of Flames flared back to life. **"I assume all is well now?"**

"Yes, Father," the Baron said as he held up the item. "An early C-grade fire elemental variant."

The flaming figure nodded as he turned his attention back to Jake. **"Now for you, Courier. I remember you saying you met some challenges along your journey. Would you enlighten me as to the details?"**

Jake considered for a moment whether he should explain everything, and in the end, he saw no good reason not to. Plus, based on the words the Duke of Flames had said about Jake being what they had been looking for, he was pretty damn sure this was the start of a major quest chain, and withholding information could potentially lead to him missing out.

"Very well…" Jake said as he briefly explained what had happened. He included how he had met the adventurers, fought and killed the Silent scalekin mage, and encountered the shadowy figure that used—or had someone use—karmic magic to kill every witness. To finish, he informed the Duke of Flames and the Baron of their offer to give the elemental to them instead, also noting that these people did not seem to know what Jake was actually delivering.

"I see… Things were much as we had expected," the Duke of Flames said after Jake was done talking. With a serious gaze, he looked directly at Jake. **"Let me ask you first, Courier… are you willing to take on work that may be riskier than anything you have encountered prior? Jobs that may very well prove lethal if the slightest mistake or slipup is made?"**

Jake was more sure than ever that he had just stumbled across a special quest chain and quickly nodded. "If the job is worth doing, I see no reason to reject it. Of course, I will need to know the details first."

The Baron glared at Jake again, clearly not happy he would even insinuate he wouldn't downright agree to anything his father wanted. The man in question, on the other hand, didn't seem offended in the slightest.

"I expect nothing less from a Courier of your level," the man said with a smile. **"Do not worry. Everything I will ever ask you will naturally go through the Guild. You are a Courier, after all."**

"In that case, I will temporarily agree," Jake said.

"Good. Now, allow me to get you up to date as to why I may need your assistance." Jake felt a big lore dump and quest description incoming. **"The elemental you have just brought us is not for me or my son, but my daughter. Our Legacy revolves around consuming**

elementals to progress and refine the powers of our flames, and the more powerful and higher-tiered the variant of the elemental, the better. Many do not agree with this Path, some of whom you encountered on your way here."

Jake nodded along. He did know such things existed, and there were even quite a few alchemists who consumed numerous Soulflames. Actually, wasn't Jake a bit like this? Only instead of eating elementals to progress, he could eat poisons.

"This organization, as they call themselves, has been hounding my household for the last century or so. In the beginning, they were just a minor nuisance, creating some ultimately inconsequential challenges, but in the recent decade, they have grown in power at a frightening speed. The last year especially has resulted in more trouble than ever before. I believe powerful forces have gotten involved, but I cannot prove anything or uncover any evidence... I need someone like you to help me with just that."

Jake considered this to be good background for the upcoming quest chain. He did have one burning question, though. "I fail to understand why you would need a C-grade Courier that badly. Are there not more powerful and skilled people available already working under you?"

"I cannot make any moves myself. As a Duke, everything I do is closely monitored. I cannot even leave my residence in peace without potentially causing a conflict with another faction, and as you come to learn more details of what I need your help with, my limited abilities to act will become even clearer. My family, for the most part, also suffers the same fate of inability to assist, as do all those officially part of the dukedom. While I do have some hidden cards, their affiliation with this kingdom is impossible to hide. You, however, I have looked into. You are related to no one and nowhere. A clean slate that neither my best spymaster nor the Guild could find a single detail about before you appeared and signed up to be a Courier. That is exactly why I need someone like you."

"I take it this organization causing you trouble is based in another country?" Jake guessed after hearing what the Duke had to say. It made sense based on everything else the man said, especially when he mentioned his inability to act directly.

The Duke smiled. "That is correct, but alas, things are not that simple. If it was just a faction from another country, I would have been able to make some moves, but the last time I tried to, I found myself blocked by an unknown power. Coupled with the recent rise in power of this organization, I can only reach one conclusion. Someone from this kingdom has gotten involved with them, and if I am right, it is one of the other dukedoms, if not the royal family themselves."

"Assuming you are correct, why would they choose to ally with an organization actively trying to sabotage one of their fellow nobles, especially one from a different country? Purely internal politics?"

"Some politics, yes, but primarily fear. The other dukes and even the king himself have stagnated. The Lord Protector is peak A-grade but has failed to evolve even after so long, and his lifespan is running out. If the Lord Protector dies, I will take the top spot as the most powerful person in the kingdom—something a lot of people don't want. My problem is that all of them are publicly supporting me, and there are even talks of naming me Grand Duke. Meanwhile, behind the scenes, I already know many of them are subtly trying to keep me in check, as I am the only one remaining who has a legitimate chance at reaching S-grade."

Listening to the story, Jake honestly thought all these other nobles were either shortsighted or just downright dumb. Sure, if they were talking about the kingdom in isolation, it was more understandable to try and keep the competition down, but if everything the Duke of Flames said was true—and Jake got the feeling it was—wouldn't they just leave themselves in a vulnerable situation after the Lord Protector died if they had no one to take their place?

Jake also didn't like the entire notion of keeping others down to remain strong in comparison. In his opinion, those dukes and the king should just get their shit together and stop being wussies who had "stagnated."

Stagnation was just a bad excuse for having stopped trying to progress. It was something people who had taken the "easy" route said when they stopped being able to pick the low-hanging fruits and didn't dare to try and climb the tree itself. Any of these A-grades could stand up right now and seek out whatever powerful beings lived in this world, or maybe just fly into the starry sky and look for the monsters roaming in space.

"I am still not entirely certain what exactly you want to hire me for," Jake said after hearing everything the Duke of Flames had to say and better understanding the situation.

"It is a lot to ask... but I need you to get an in with this organization, and you have already been presented with a golden opportu-

nity," the Duke of Flames answered as he threw the Infernal Baron a glance. The Baron nodded and tossed the Sealed Elemental back to Jake.

"Take the delivery and give it to them, just as they asked," he explained. **"In truth, we don't really need this particular variant much. Getting a Courier into the organization is far more valuable, at least. Of course, we have to ensure they do not know you are doing this with my knowledge, so you need to find a way to hide it before meeting them in order to not raise any suspicion. Are you up to the task?"**

As the man asked this, it finally appeared. The kind of system message Jake had been waiting for.

Special Courier Side Job: Assist the Duke of Flames in delivering the Sealed Elemental to [Unknown] without letting them know you have met with the Infernal Baron yet.
Objective: Package delivered (0/1)
Accept Side Job?

With a nod to the Duke, Jake accepted the system prompt. Jake had many thoughts about what this Challenge Dungeon would be about, but in all honesty, he had never expected to get a job as a double agent in a political game while working for a late-tier A-grade Duke.

It was definitely a novel experience, and Jake was all for it.

CHAPTER 10

INFINITE LOOP AGENT

Mission: Mysterious Organization Double-Agent Infiltration went much more smoothly than Jake had expected. After he left the Baron's place, Jake just relaxed in the city for a day and did a bit more crafting. After this day, he left the city again, still disguised as a scalekin.

Once a good distance away, and when he was sure no one was watching, he changed himself back to looking like—and Identifying as—a human before flying back toward the city with his stealth skill active while also wearing his usual getup. Once he got close to the mid-sized city again, Jake dispelled his stealth skill while still flying up in the air, instantly feeling many gazes upon him.

This time, he showed no subtlety and just flew into the city. During the conversation with the mysterious hooded figure, the person had told him to go to the Guild Hall and say that he had lost the package during transportation, and while Jake wasn't a fan of doing that, the Baron and Duke assured him they would still report the job as completed successfully to avoid negatively impacting Jake's reputation.

However, as it turned out, this wasn't even necessary...

Shortly after Jake entered the Guild Hall, and before he even had a chance to approach one of the employees, a regular-looking guy sitting off to the side of the room sent him a telepathic message.

"Excuse me, you're a Courier, right? Might you be coming out of Hillspring City? I have an aunt living there, and I heard some bad news..." Disregarding how weird it was to send a telepathic message to say something like that, Jake knew this was just a probing question.

"I am indeed," Jake replied. *"The trip was long, but when you have an important delivery to an even more important client, you cannot slack off too much. One in high places, both figuratively and literally."*

"You have arrived earlier than I expected," the person said when he affirmed Jake was the one. *"I am here representing a mutual friend. Please play along."*

Due to the speed of telepathy, Jake had barely entered the Guild Hall when the man sitting close to the door stood up and opened his arms wide. "Bloody hell, you're finally here! Lizzy has been on my ass since she heard you were coming. Good to see you, buddy."

The man went over and dragged Jake into a hug, Jake naturally playing along. "You know how it is with work and everything. Can't always know my schedule ahead of time, but hey, I'm here, aren't I?"

"That you are! Now, let's get going before she rips both of us a new one!"

Jake did as asked and nodded, and the two walked out together while making idle chatter. Since no one seemed to care about the reunion of two old friends, Jake and the other guy quickly got away from the Guild Hall and headed toward a large mansion close to the outer walls, no one following them.

The man Jake had met was barely C-grade, and someone Jake later came to learn was pretty much just a middleman who worked for a wealthy lady—Lizzy—in the mansion. However, in order to appear less suspicious, the two of them acted as if they were in a relationship. These were the first two people Jake met and confirmed to be part of this organization, even if they were auxiliary members who pretty much carried out direct orders without questions despite knowing pretty much nothing about the organization that employed them.

Once in the mansion, Lizzy and the man introduced themselves and, after some probing questions, fully confirmed Jake was who he said he was. Jake was subsequently led into a cellar beneath the mansion, where he was left alone with a token and surrounded by quite a powerful barrier. One definitely not made by the two C-grades living there.

Down in the cellar, Jake activated the small token the pretend-couple had given him, and soon after, a familiar hooded figure appeared.

"I am glad to see you are reasonable—not only in your decision to take us up on the offer, but by not delaying your arrival needlessly," the figure said right away, not even saying hello or anything.

Jake had already taken out a chair before he used the token and was currently sitting in a relaxed pose. Very purposefully, mind you. He had been fronting as a powerful individual with this organization before, and he was going to keep doing so.

Jake shrugged. "Eh, I thought I might as well get things done quicker this way."

"Nevertheless... it was a wise choice, and I hope you continue to make wise choices," the figure answered. **"Now, could you confirm the nature of the item the Infernal Baron wanted you to deliver? Show it to me?"**

"Patience, patience. Before all that, let me just explain things a bit from my viewpoint." Jake leaned forward and looked directly into where he suspected the eyes of the hooded figure would be. "Right now, I am stuck between two factions. Some nobleman Baron, and a shadowy organization that has been semi-threatening me from the get-go. I am entirely neutral toward this Baron, as I, quite frankly, don't know shit about him. Meanwhile, you have made a less-than-stellar first impression, which I would heavily advise you to address. Especially since I also get a strong impression you want more than just to buy a delivery from me. So, how about we start with some honesty before we proceed? Who exactly are you?"

The figure was silent for a few moments, Jake getting the feeling the person was consulting with someone. After a few seconds, they spoke again. **"Very well... how much do you know of the Infernal Baron and the family he belongs to?"**

"Fuck all," Jake said, shrugging.

"Then allow me to enlighten you..."

Jake got his second lore dump in two days as the figure explained most of the same things the Duke of Flames had. They mentioned how it was a big family, how their patriarch was a duke and near the peak of A-grade, and how their Path included consuming—thus killing—elementals as part of their Path. Of course, the tone of the explanation was a lot different from the Duke's.

While the Duke of Flames had presented everything matter-of-factly with a sense of pride, this figure had a lot more emotion. It was clear they didn't like the family at all. Fact-wise, things were pretty much the same, though, and Jake got the impression neither party was lying about anything. They just had their own spin on things.

"As for our organization... we oppose the Duke of Flames and the actions of his vile spawn. They are a scourge upon this world, and cleansing it of their presence would be a blessing. As for details... I will need to see if you truly have the delivery in question before saying more."

By now, Jake thought he had done enough to not appear like a pushover. He hadn't been entirely subservient, which was exactly how he wanted things to be. Same as with the Duke of Flames. Jake was a contractor, not an employee, so the person who hired him wasn't allowed to say jack-shit about how Jake did things, and he wanted to make it very clear he always had the option of giving them the middle finger and quitting, if only out of pure spite if they tried to fuck him over.

"Alright, fine," Jake said as he dug into a pocket in his cloak and took out the Sealed Elemental, which he had re-cast a stable arcane barrier on.

After quickly erasing the barrier, the shadowy figure used Identify on the item, confirming its authenticity but making no moves for Jake to hand it over. **"The genuine delivery indeed,"** the figure said with a nod. **"Thank you for trusting us with this... but before we continue, may I ask you... If you were to choose between supporting the dukedom that I told you about or an organization you knew borderline nothing of beyond it opposing this dukedom, who would you support?"**

The question sounded genuine, but Jake didn't really appreciate the fact that the barrier he was standing within apparently also had the ability to discern lies. At least, the figure tried to find out if Jake was lying using it, naturally failing upon encountering Shroud. Well, under usual circumstances it would have, but this time around, Jake let it go through, as his honest answer was one he was fine with the organization knowing.

"I would support whoever offers me the most. I became a Courier to challenge myself and to gain as much recognition as possible as I grow my reputation and rank. Who I work for doesn't matter in the grand scheme of things as long as I benefit." Of course, he didn't include the part about doing all this to get a lot of Nevermore Points and a great Grand Achievement, but hey, they didn't ask.

"A purely selfish approach where pragmatism takes precedence, I see... but let me ask. What do you think of elementals? How do you see them?"

"With my eyes?" Jake said with a smirk. "But in all seriousness, I can't tell you how I feel about an elemental before meeting them, now, can I? People are different, and I am sure some of them are assholes."

Once more, Jake allowed the lie-detector skill to fully work. Based on all the context clues, Jake was pretty damn sure this organization was very pro-elemental and cared a lot about them, so making himself appear sympathetic toward them would prove beneficial. Also, it was pretty easy to say he didn't have anything against elementals, considering he didn't.

"You referred to elementals as people... I hope you realize how rare that is," the figure said.

Shrugging, Jake kept up his casual demeanor. "I mean, considering I have a niece of sorts who is an elemental, it would be very weird for me not to consider them people."

Alright, technically, Sylphie wasn't just an elemental but a weird mix between beast and elemental, but that did make her at least partly elemental, which made Jake's statement not a lie.

"I see... I believe I can explain a bit more about who we are and what we stand for, and with this explanation, you will understand who you should truly support..."

Once again, it was lore-dump time. As expected, the group that hated the Duke of Flames could be summed up as a hardcore elemental-rights organization. Not the peaceful protest kind, either, but the type to actively try and kill every single member of the dukedom in what they felt was a justified position. The figure even explained how killing anyone who helped the dukedom in any way was the right thing to do. Even if that help only came in the form of being a poor E-grade farmer.

That was when Jake learned that the "inconsequential challenges" the Duke of Flames had talked about encountering for nearly a century were things like this elemental-rights organization slaughtering thousands of E- and even some D-grades in the Duke's territory. Terrorist attacks, effectively.

Something the Duke evidently didn't give a shit about. He'd only started to care when the organization began to mess with his ability to collect rare elemental variants. Oh, by the way, rare variants tended to also be the sapient sort and not the regular mindless elementals, so... yeah.

After listening and assuming everything he had learned about this scenario was true, Jake reached a conclusion:

They both fucking sucked.

Alas, Jake was not in the Challenge Dungeon to pass judgment, nor was he in any position to. At least, not yet...

Luckily, the shadowy figure was finally finishing their lengthy explanation of the organization's goals, and just in time, as Jake soon decided the Grand Achievement wasn't worth listening to the extremist speech.

"... and once the elemental race can once more roam freely, fearless of the monstrous Duke and his spawn, only then will our quest be complete. Only when the Path is driven to utter ruin, every single person of that horrible Lineage dead, is it time to celebrate.

When their legacy is nothing but a bad memory! So let me ask you, Courier... are you willing to be on the side of justice?"

"If justice is the one who offers the best terms, then yes," Jake said, not buying into the extremism. "But hey, if it's also fighting the good fight, that's just a nice bonus."

"I understand you do not share our conviction, but not to worry —that is no requirement. As a Courier, let your actions speak. So, let me request of you your first mission. We need information on the Duke of Flames from an insider, and we believe that you could become that insider. Be our agent at his side who will assist us. Of course, to do that, sacrifices must be made, and while it is a shame that a young Soothfire Elemental will meet its end in such a horrific way, the Sealed Elemental must be delivered in order to not raise suspicion. So, are you willing to assist us?"

As the figure said this, not one but two notifications popped up. One saying he had completed a side job, and one giving him another.

Special Courier Side Job Completed.
Special Courier Side Job: Deliver the Sealed Elemental to the
Infernal Baron.
Objective: Package delivered (0/1)
Accept Side Job?

So... yeah, Jake had to head back to the Infernal Baron again to deliver the Sealed Elemental for the second time to the same person. It was a bit silly, but Jake was pretty sure he had just gone from being a potential double agent to now potentially being a triple agent.

Also, Jake learned that the organization somehow knew the name of the elemental within the Sealed Elemental item... which made him suspect they'd perhaps somehow known all along? In either case, shit was getting complicated, and Jake hoped he would be able to keep up with all the nonsense.

After Jake left the mansion, he headed straight for the Infernal Baron's place again. He still went through the trouble of disguising himself and whatnot, pretty much just putting on a show since he felt people keeping an eye on him—clearly, the organization still wasn't super trusting quite yet—as he made his way to the Baron.

Of course, the Baron also knew that Jake could be under surveillance, so everyone acted as if it was Jake's first time arriving. Once he was finally in front of the Baron and re-delivered the Sealed Elemental, the questioning began.

Jake only gave half-truths as he explained his meeting, ending with the organization asking him to potentially join. He purposefully didn't mention anything about them wanting Jake to infiltrate the Duke's faction, though he did throw in his belief that this was something they could want down the line.

So, to summarize, Jake was now working with the dukedom to infiltrate the elemental-rights organization that wanted Jake to work with the dukedom, who wanted Jake to infiltrate the organization, who wanted Jake with the dukedom... and both sides believed they were the smart cookies who had thought up this wonderful plan, not knowing the other party had the exact same idea.

Where did this leave Jake? Well, from an outside perspective, he could now openly associate with the dukedom faction. He also didn't need to be careful if he ever met with the organization, as that was what the Duke expected Jake to do. Yep, things were definitely a mess, and Jake was looking forward to the kind of high-octane missions he might receive as what he would describe as an infinite-loop agent.

"The first step has been taken, but we still need to work through the Guild, seeing as you are a Courier," the Duke of Flames said as their meeting finished. **"We will need some time to organize things, and we will contact you soon. However, to ensure that you qualify for the next task, it would be pertinent to work on improving your reputation as a Courier and upgrade your Medallion."**

This last sentence poured water all over Jake's hopes and dreams. That's right—it was back to grinding regular old Courier Jobs, showing that even when one moved up in the world to become an infinite-loop agent, one still couldn't quit the grind.

CHAPTER 11

NEVERMORE: ON THE GRINDSET

"You two had a lot of fun with this one, huh?" the Viper commented as he watched Jake perform Courier Job after Courier Job. Despite it not being outright confirmed yet, he had the strong impression that both Minaga and the Wyrmgod had been heavily involved with this particular Challenge Dungeon.

"Fun? Do you have any idea how much work it was?" Minaga said with a sigh. "Out of every Challenge Dungeon, this one took by far the longest. Well, besides the Test of Character, but I wasn't much involved with that, so it doesn't count."

"I take it Nevermore itself also got quite involved with the balancing?" Vilastromoz further inquired.

"The sheer complexity of having so many starting points, all the quest paths, and keeping it all dynamic and adapting to the Nevermore Attendee required far more work than initially estimated," the Wyrmgod explained, offering some insights into the World Wonder for the many gods capable of listening in. "The original plan was to have this Challenge Dungeon ready last era, but we had to delay it primarily due to Nevermore and the system not accepting the balancing."

"Not certain I would call this balanced," the Blightfather decided to chime in. "Seeing Azal also doing the Challenge Dungeon pretty much confirmed the lack of critical thinking from many of the characters. They are either too trusting or, in certain cases, too easily fooled, while in other instances, getting any kind of advantage is borderline impossible."

"We are well aware," the Wyrmgod said, sighing. "However, it was necessary to do it like this. If we tried to adhere to realism too much, the time required to unlock any high-level quest path would simply take far too long, so we had to tweak the logic of the world quite a lot. With the aim of the Challenge Dungeon taking around two years on average for the high-level performers, this is the solution we settled on.

"Also, you cannot argue that some individuals aren't simply this trusting, even among the higher grades. People can get blinded by their goals, considering what they do so important and justified that they automatically assume everyone else will share their opinion, thus seeing no need to be critical. Having the ability to identify these people and distinguish them from the less fanatical is most definitely a skill worth learning."

"Even so, it teaches many unrealistic lessons along with the healthy ones," the Blightfather insisted. "Additionally, it makes little sense to remove all status from everyone. As a variant Risen of the highest echelon, Azal should have been recognized, yet the denizens of the Challenge Dungeon seem incapable of doing so, even daring to treat him like a lesser. It goes against their very Records to act like that."

"Race isn't something that should give an advantage in this dungeon, same as Blessings, and even the status as a Bloodline Patriarch or Transcendent also won't offer any notable advantages," the Wyrmgod argued back.

"Such a fundamental change to social dynamics for certain races shouldn't be taken that lightly. How would you view it if..."

Vilastromoz remained quiet, not really having much to add as the two Primordials discussed openly for all to hear. It was rare for such a lively discussion to appear, and while both of them went at each other, the Viper also knew both enjoyed it. As sad as it sounds, it was rare to find people even willing to argue back instead of just taking anything you said as gospel, so to get pushback was almost novel.

The Viper considered getting involved just for the fun of it but decided against it, as the topic didn't overly interest him. The only thing he really cared about was the information that the Challenge Dungeon was new, and it being new meant one thing:

It was exploitable.

All the Challenge Dungeons had obvious exploits that got fixed with every new iteration. Minaga's Labyrinth and how he improved his special mist was a prime example of this, with every one of the Challenge Dungeons having similar improvements and "nerfs" to certain Paths every new era. Seeing as this was the first, it meant many things had yet to be fully ironed out, as it was simply impossible to account for every Path without some live testing. The only reason the system accepted it despite the flaws that would be revealed was that every attendant who competed had the same circumstances and the same opportunities to take advantage.

As for what specific exploits were to be found... well, Vilastromoz already had one minor oversight in mind. One he was certain Jake would be able to take full advantage of, even if he did so unknowingly. In fact, he had already been exploiting it despite not realizing it yet.

No one else seemed to have really noticed either, making the Viper smile to himself. *This should be a good one...*

———

Time quickly passed with Jake back on the job, on that grindset. The Courier Jobs were similar to the ones he had done before, but there was a slight twist. After Jake had done exactly twenty, he was contacted by the Infernal Baron, who informed him that an important upcoming job would require his Medallion to be upgraded within three months if he wished to accept it. So, he had some more pressure on him to get promoted in time... Alright, not really. Jake had plenty of time.

He completed the jobs incredibly quickly and efficiently, not once running into any real problems. It was to the level where Jake questioned what was actually being tested, as the scams he was exposed to all seemed way too obvious.

Then again, maybe it was just because Jake had grown up on Earth, where one could—for some inexplicable reason—sell through social media with little oversight or regulation, with every second seller just being a straight-up scammer. From that, Jake had learned some basic lessons about making deals like this and been taught some damn common sense.

His number-one rule was to always stick to the agreement, almost to a fault. Oh, did the client want to change the delivery location last minute? Nope, Jake would go to the original place. Someone else was sent to pick up the delivery? Not gonna happen; only the client would get it. While this did make people mad, Jake wasn't going to risk things needlessly. Sticking to just a few basic principles like this seemed to serve him very well, and in the instances where he did have to show some flexibility, he believed he managed well and showed proper caution.

Indeed, in the end, the time limit didn't prove to be an issue; he got his Medallion upgraded well ahead of time along with yet another promotion at work.

[Courier Medallion (Rare)] – A Courier Medallion belonging to an

experienced Courier who is beginning to build up quite the renown. This Medallion will hold information related to jobs and can give general directions to your destination if those are provided (may not be entirely reliable). Will automatically upgrade as Courier Jobs are completed and your reputation grows.
Requirements: Soulbound.

With his promotion, Jake could finally get Special Courier Job 3. As for this one... well, things just liked to get more complicated, as the Duke of Flames was the first to give Jake a task.

"There is a political conference taking place in the Phoenix Wing Empire. We of the Human Kingdom will naturally send a delegation. I need you to deliver something to someone I have working in an outpost in the Empire before the delegation arrives and work with my subordinate there to uncover any potential people related to this organization who may attend the conference. But for now, go to the organization and see if you can discover more, then report to my subordinate once you arrive in the city of the conference. We will post an official job tomorrow morning for a Courier to deliver a package of important documents to the outpost, so make sure to accept it."

Right after Jake had gotten this task, he naturally went straight to the elemental-rights organization, which he had decided to rename as the People for the Ethical Treatment of Elementals organization for no particular reason. PETE for short. Yes, it was a very original name that Jake had thought up entirely on his own without any inspiration whatsoever.

Anyway, Jake naturally informed PETE of what the Duke wanted him to do, and they, of course, also had a task for him.

"Some of our core members will also attend this conference, just as he suspects, and we will need you to ensure they are not discovered by the Duke of Flames. Go to the Phoenix Wing Empire as the Duke wants, and once there, make contact with one of the members and work with them to keep them safe. While you're there, attempt to discover if the Duke has any allies within the Phoenix Wing Empire. Also, we believe the Duke may suspect some of the plants within his dukedom of working with us. Try to find out who he suspects so we can extract them in time."

The two tasks weren't mutually exclusive, and Jake naturally decided to kind of do both.

He kept up his act as an infinite-loop agent by making executive decisions about what information he would share, giving just enough to keep both sides happy. PETE wanted Jake to help extract those the Duke suspected? Alright, Jake would help the majority of them get away, not telling them that he was the reason the Duke had located them in the first place.

By the way, the city Jake had gone to for this conference was another mid-sized city, though slightly larger than the one that hosted the Infernal Baron, showing Jake was truly moving up in the world. For this entire conference, only C-grades were present, likely because no country wanted a bunch of B-grades and above to be in their lands due to how big of a security risk it was. They would still communicate using projections, but all of the powerful people worked from home.

This second mid-sized city in the Phoenix Wing Empire differed vastly from what could be found in the Human Kingdom. The architecture was much more vertical and heavily inspired by nature, with large, hollowed-out trees sometimes serving as buildings. Population-wise, it was still a mix, but it was clear this empire had a lot more beasts and beastfolk compared to the Human Kingdom.

What they also had were elementals in human form, all of which were more than antagonistic toward the Duke's people. They were oddly fine with Jake, even when he was with the Duke's people, showing how over-powered the status of a Courier was.

When it came to the job at hand, the entire conference was a bit of a mess, if Jake was being honest, but he did discover many exciting things he disclosed to both PETE and the dukedom, making them trust him even more than before. During the conference, he even completed four entire Side Jobs by sneaking around and discovering stuff others wanted to keep hidden... Oh, and one job where he had to convince a noblewoman not to get married by finding evidence that some guy was only after her because of her family. It had fuck-all to do with anything else he was doing, but Jake had done it for some bloody reason anyway.

After the conference was done, Jake remained in the Phoenix Wing Empire, with the Duke thinking he had successfully infiltrated PETE further, while PETE believed Jake was working with foreign agents of the dukedom to get them more information, both of which were one hundred percent true.

Seeing as Guild Halls were in every major city and that both sides said he should wait until the next time they needed him, Jake returned to doing regular Courier Jobs. Weeks turned to months, Jake completing jobs all the while, before the next Special Courier Job came in. He promptly completed this, too, and through it, he finally met one of the higher-ups in PETE for the first time. It was the shadowy figure he had spoken to many times, and she turned out to be a B-grade Marquise from the Phoenix Wing Empire.

As more and more snippets of information were revealed, Jake got further ammunition to use on either side, only letting a bit spill here and there to keep both happy with his work. Jake still wasn't certain what his endgame would be, but the more he learned about both sides, the less and less he liked them.

After about two months in this mid-sized city, Jake had done around a hundred jobs there, and with them came yet another promotion.

[Courier Medallion (Epic)] – A Courier Medallion belonging to a highly experienced Courier with a strong reputation. This Medallion will hold information related to jobs and can give general directions to your destination if those are provided (may not be entirely reliable). Will automatically upgrade as Courier Jobs are completed and your reputation grows.
Requirements: Soulbound.

Jake had now worked for several months, and even if he was rapidly getting promoted, he had yet to see a single paystub. He was definitely being exploited, even if things were a bit... weird. PETE kept talking about rewarding Jake handsomely for his help, and the Duke of Flames said the same thing, but nothing ever came of it. This was despite even the Guild attendants occasionally noting how some jobs "gave quite a lot!"... but when Jake turned in a completed job... nothing.

So, yeah, dungeon fuckery galore. He sure as hell hoped the final reward would set things right, or he would have to sue for unpaid wages.

When Jake was done in the mid-sized city, he got a Special Courier Job to go to a large-sized one in yet another country. This job wasn't directly linked to the Duke of Flames or even PETE, but when he got to this new city, Jake discovered both had a presence there, primarily because PETE just followed the dukedom wherever they had any people.

More Courier Jobs followed as Jake worked his ass off, not even taking lunch breaks or accounting for unpaid overtime. He was definitely also breaking a lot of work safety rules with the way he did the Courier Jobs, but so far, he had luckily avoided a fine.

A few more Special Courier Jobs came in while Jake had an epic-rarity Medallion, each Courier promotion taking longer than the last. Jake also kept learning more about his two biggest clients until he finally discovered a *very* juicy piece of information that also kind of answered something he had been wondering about.

Despite Jake having thought it impossible, PETE had already known what was inside the initial Sealed Elemental delivery. This elemental was meant to be delivered to the Infernal Baron, who would then send it back to his little sister to assist her in her Path. What Jake didn't know was that the one who had requested this specific elemental was the daughter of the Duke... and that she had made the request at the behest of PETE.

In this large-sized city, Jake even came to meet with the girl, where she spilled her heart out about how she hated her family's Legacy and didn't want to consume elementals to progress, which was also why she was still only in early C-grade despite not being much younger than the Infernal Baron. Quite the plot twist that she was working with PETE, and definitely not something her family knew about.

Except, it turned out she wasn't really working with them, just being taken advantage of. Despite her assisting them, PETE still hated her guts just because of her family and wanted her dead alongside everyone else in the dukedom. So she was pretty much just an idiot being fooled.

But wait! That wasn't actually true either! She had figured out they were trying to take advantage of her a long time ago and was now working with a third party, which was where Jake came into play. Soon enough, she offered him jobs to destroy both the dukedom and PETE.

In another huge plot twist, the daughter of the Duke was the one who had gotten another dukedom of the Human Kingdom involved to take down the "Dukedom of Flames," as they called it. In the process, they also wanted to eliminate PETE using the Duke of Flames, weakening him in the process.

The mess had turned even messier, and Jake was smack in the middle, now effectively working for three factions at once. Was he still an infinite-loop agent? Jake wasn't sure at this point... In fact, he even considered if perhaps a fourth party should get involved.

Nevertheless, Jake kept chugging along, and soon, over nine months had passed since he entered the Challenge Dungeon. Hundreds of regular Courier Jobs had been completed, along with eleven total Special Courier Jobs, and who even knows how many Side Jobs and Special Side Jobs. The plot was also thicker with intrigue than ever, and Jake finally began to get a clear picture of everything. With all these jobs done, the Guild naturally also recognized his efforts.

**[Courier Medallion (Ancient)] – A Courier Medallion belonging to
an extremely experienced Courier with an excellent reputation.
This Medallion will hold information related to jobs and can give
general directions to your destination if those are provided (may
not be entirely reliable). Will automatically upgrade as Courier Jobs
are completed and your reputation grows.
Requirements: Soulbound.**

With another upgrade under his belt, Jake got a Special Courier Job to
return to the capital of the Human Kingdom. He knew the leader of
PETE—an early A-grade—would also be there, along with every other
dukedom in the country and the royal family. Powerful people from other
factions had also snuck in, and Jake felt a final showdown would soon
occur.

As for Jake's role in this final showdown... well, that was yet to be
decided, but considering he hated every faction he had met so far, he
reckoned things were about to get even messier, and he would gladly be
there to take advantage.

CHAPTER 12

A TWIST TO THE TWIST

The lines were drawn as the palace in the Human Kingdom capital rapidly filled up. The three dukes would be in attendance, and not just with projections. Just about every noble of any influence had shown up, and when the king entered along with his wife—a mid-tier A-grade—things got even more intense. Especially when the old man following the two of them appeared. He was slightly hunched over and had a frizzled beard and no hair, with an overall weak-looking demeanor, but his aura told a whole other story.

Jake, who was also taking part in this "party," if one could really call it that, stood on a balcony and watched as these people entered. His gaze temporarily landed on the Lord Protector, as he was called. While he was no Snappy, in the context of this world, he was definitely one of the strongest. A peak A-grade existence that even the otherwise arrogant Duke of Flames approached respectfully as he bowed to the old man.

Now, while attending this party was wholly expected based on the trajectory of all the special missions he had done thus far, the way he had gotten his invite was a bit... off. Not because he had gotten one, but because he had ended up getting four separate invites. One from the Duke of Flames' daughter and her associated dukedom, another one from PETE, a third from the Duke of Flames, and the final one from the Guild itself, which had given Jake a Special Courier Job to attend the party. It didn't specify what Jake had to do once there, just to attend it.

He wondered if the Special Courier Job was a failsafe if someone failed to get invited or if it was something everyone who had gone down this same quest path received. Then again, the party revolved around the Side

Jobs from all the different factions. So maybe he'd always been fated to get this Special Courier Job? In either case, Jake found it pretty funny to get all those invites, especially since he'd had to go through a complex "vetting process" for each one, as every faction wanted to ensure Jake was truly on their side.

How the hell he had passed every single one of them, Jake had no idea. All of them had used lie detectors, and Jake had even ended up meeting the person who had killed those adventurers with the scalekin mage. It was the Duchess of the dukedom that the Duke of Flames' daughter had allied with, and an A-grade in her own right. She was a powerful karmic mage, and she'd used her magic to scan Jake throughout their entire vetting process, ending up walking away with the conclusion that Jake didn't have any positive karmic relations with the other factions. She had pointed out how Jake didn't have a particularly good connection with her and her husband's dukedom either, but Jake had easily excused that by saying he was being a professional and just working with them. They were still a bit suspicious, but after he passed a lie detector confirming he wasn't "working for the benefit" of any of the other factions, they approved him and gave him an invite.

This process was pretty much the same with all of the factions, though their means to confirm Jake was, at the very least, not working with the enemy varied a bit. Jake was honestly kind of lucky in this entire process because he could truthfully say he held no positive feelings toward any of the other factions and that he didn't work to support them. They couldn't ask if he was working with them outright, because as an infinite-loop agent, he naturally was, so as long as he didn't support them, that had to be good enough, right?

Jake also came to learn that Couriers were apparently even respected in royal courts. Alright, the low-ranked Couriers probably weren't, but Jake was considered a highly respected professional by now with lots of experience. Never mind the fact Jake hadn't even had the job for a year.

As he was standing and observing all the guests arriving, Jake considered what his next move would be. The king had organized this party, but at the request of two of the three dukedoms, both of whom wanted to use it to "expose" their enemies. As for how they would expose them? Well, they all had the exact same plan that could be summed up in one word:

Jake.

Not only was he their star witness, but he was also the guy with all the evidence. All of them had asked him to get an ancient-rarity Medallion before this meeting, as with it, his trustworthiness would be even higher.

Who wouldn't give a high-ranking Courier with an impeccable track record at least some trust and hear him out?

The problem was that Jake still didn't like any of them. Exposing PETE's leader, as well as the fact they worked with another dukedom that hated the Duke of Flames, seemed like the easiest solution to causing a big conflict. Of course, he could also expose the fact that the Duke of Flames was running an illegal drug and weapon trade in collusion with an enemy country to fund his endless hunger for elementals... or maybe that the daughter of the Duke of Flames liked to "punish" those who helped her father for fun behind his back.

PETE was the easiest to deal with. They were the weakest standalone faction by far, and Jake had a hard time not seeing them burn to the ground no matter what he did to expose them. He had learned that nobody, not even their allied dukedom, knew the true identity of their leader, so that was something Jake could expose to get rid of them.

However, Jake had begun to form another plan.

What if he just exposed all of them at once to the king and sat back to watch the world burn? What if he made some false statements to involve the third dukedom that otherwise wasn't part of anything? Or maybe even a foreign country?

Jake was still deep in thought, noting that the final guest had just about arrived, when he noticed someone walking up beside him. Jake was leaning on the railing of the balcony, and this person joined him in looking at all the esteemed guests below.

"Quite the gathering," the man said with a smile.

"It is indeed," Jake said as he glanced at the newcomer. He gave off the aura of an early B-grade and looked on the younger side. He had long, combed-back hair and a confident demeanor, and while Jake didn't recognize him, he already knew who it was as he picked up the presence the man was disguising.

Ah... there it is... Jake thought to himself. He had been waiting for the final twist to reveal itself, and here it was. Throughout Jake's work with all of these different factions, there'd been one place that *did* know everything Jake was up to. Not his thoughts or plots, but that he did work for all of them at the same time.

He was naturally speaking of the Guild itself.

"I heard you are quite the distinguished guest today," the man stated as Jake subtly felt the area around them shift, a sound-isolation barrier appearing without anyone else noticing. "Many friends in high places."

"Not sure I would call them friends, but my work indeed takes me around, and I am here for work today as well," Jake said with a shrug. "I am a Courier, after all. Completing jobs is what I'm meant to be doing."

"And quite a Courier you are. Within a year, you went from a total newcomer to someone so highly respected." The man gave him a big smile. "I even heard that you have a borderline perfect track record, never really messing up any jobs, despite what hiccups you may have encountered."

"Just doing my best," Jake said as he kept leaning and looking down at the crowd while talking to the man who did the same.

"That, I believe... The question is, what will you do now?"

Jake turned and looked at the man. "I don't know quite yet... Does the Guild Founder have any suggestions?"

That's right—the plot twist was that the Guild Founder was also going to be at this party and approach Jake! Had he kind of predicted this would be the case? Not fully, but he had suspected there would be one more twist, and the Guild Founder revealing himself during this party would be entirely on-brand for the Challenge Dungeon.

However, Jake didn't want to lose his agency and momentum by having the Founder reveal himself at an inopportune time. Besides, Jake being able to recognize the S-grade despite his technique to hide who he was, even from the peak A-grade, had to impress him, right?

The Founder frowned at Jake's question. "Guild Founder? I apologize if I gave you the wrong impression, but I have no idea what you are talking about."

Jake smiled a bit as he turned back to look down at the crowd, which was far too busy socializing to notice the two of them. "You know, none of those people down there can recognize you, so I understand why you question how I could. It wasn't anything you messed up; I just have a little something that is also part of the reason I am a good Courier: good intuition."

"So you believe I am this Guild Founder just because of some gut feeling?" the man who was totally the Founder questioned.

"No, I *know* you are the Guild Founder because of my gut feeling," Jake answered in a confident tone. "You have hidden your S-grade aura well. Well enough to fool pretty much everyone in this world... but not me."

"Quite loose reasoning for such an impactful statement," the man said with a light smile, seemingly not really trying to hide who he was anymore.

"My instincts are more trustworthy than anything anyone can ever tell me," Jake shot back.

"In that case, what are your instincts telling you to do in this situation as you look down upon the people gathered here, knowing you hold the power to upend the entire political landscape with nothing but words?" the Founder asked in a serious tone, having dropped the act.

"They aren't telling me to do anything, but they do make me fully aware that things are, for lack of a better word, fucked. Powerful nobles are fighting while the uninvolved people just living in their territories suffer, and everyone is doing shit under the table, trying to get one over on each other all the time, never daring to openly confront anyone." Jake finished with a sigh.

The Guild Founder slowly nodded as he spoke, "It is shameful, but yes, things are indeed a mess. Tell me, do you know why the Guild was initially established?"

"Enlighten me," Jake offered as he felt another option to resolve this entire mess of a storyline slowly materialize. He remembered the dwarf attendant in the very first Guild Hall he'd ever entered telling him the Founder had made the Guild around forty thousand years ago, but never the reason, so he was also a bit interested.

"Back in the day, before the Guild, all of the enlightened races were united to some extent to fight back the monster factions led by the dragon tribe. The borders were open, there was free travel and trade, and friendly meetings between monarchs were frequent. Despite the constant conflict with an enemy faction, it was a more peaceful time for the regular citizens living far from the battlefield.

"It was a tough time for those of us who did live close to the frontlines, though, and I grew up right on those borders. I found out at an early age I had potential and quickly rose to power with the sole intent of finally bringing peace by defeating the Dragon King and ending the war. When I made it to S-grade, I challenged the Dragon King and managed to come out on top. The dragon tribe crumbled after that, and the monsters united under the tribe scattered, some forming their own factions that stand to this day. I genuinely believed my actions would be the end of conflict... but in the world of politics, there always needs to be an enemy, it appears."

Jake nodded along. Having an enemy meant you had something to unite against. In fact, Jacob's father, Arthur, had used this strategy to gather the United Cities Alliance against Jake and those with divine factions, making a boogieman out of them.

"The once peaceful alliance between the enlightened races fractured, and the lines were drawn. Borders closed, wars began to brew, and things were looking more dire than ever. No one talked. Everyone expected others to plot against them, as they, too, were plotting against someone else. I at first tried to calm everyone, but I was treated with nothing but fear and heard nothing but false promises and platitudes. Something had to be done, and in the end, I settled on making the Guild."

"You did it to create a neutral faction that could operate across borders to get people talking?" Jake questioned.

"Precisely," the man said, smiling. "At least... at first. The scope of the Guild's dealings only expanded from there until it became the organization you see today, but the original plan was for Couriers to be wholly neutral parties whose primary job was to travel between countries to lessen the information gap. This did help, as some line of communication was opened up between the different factions... but that was then. Things have changed yet again, and it seems like the idea of what a Courier is has faded from memory. Or at least, what the status of a Courier used to mean."

Jake remained silent, but he was beginning to get a good idea as to where this entire thing was going, and he wasn't sure he liked it.

"And you... you are a prime example of this change," the Founder said with a hint of disappointment in his voice. "The intent was for Couriers to remain neutral, not getting too involved in politics, but now, nearly every force with any influence actively exploits the Courier system for their own gain. They make Couriers work with them despite that being contrary to what they should be doing. I was truthfully disappointed when I looked into you. Your track record was so brilliant, your work ethic impeccable, and I believed you were one of the most promising Couriers I had ever seen... yet you have chosen to work with these factions and gotten yourself so deeply embroiled in their factions, supporting them and—"

"Wrong on that one," Jake quickly cut him off.

"Hm?" the Founder exclaimed with a frown. "Are you claiming you haven't completed Special Courier Jobs for these factions in droves, each Courier Job submitted to further their goals?"

"That isn't what you said. You said I supported them. Have I worked with them? Yes, but supporting would mean I helped them more than I hurt them, and right now, I think I'm pretty even on that one with all of them."

The frown on the Founder's brow deepened. "What are you saying?"

Jake turned to look at him directly again. "That I don't support any of them. Also, don't get it twisted; I wasn't the one who chose to work with them. The Guild did. The Guild accepted all these Special Courier Jobs. Shit, I got involved in this entire mess because of one such job, and now here we are. Or are you going to fault me for accepting jobs offered to me?"

In all honesty, Jake was a bit offended at what the Founder said, and he got the feeling he had to dispute it. He also just didn't like the insinuation he was allied with any of the assholes in the hall... but from the looks of it, this Founder didn't believe him at all.

"Have you truly deluded yourself that much, or are you simply trying to fool me for whomever you support?" the Founder said, shaking his head. "I know why you are here today, and I know of this internal conflict in the Human Kingdom. I also know you have come to assist one of the factions present in this hall."

Before Jake had a chance to react, the man placed a hand on Jake's shoulder. Some form of magic activated as the man infused a smidgen of power into Jake's body, and Jake felt it searching for something. "Even if you attempt to deceive me, I am far from new to this game. Your clear karmic connection with... with..."

The Founder just stared at Jake for a second before he cleared his throat. He lifted his hand slightly and placed it down again as another bit of energy was infused. "As I was trying to say, karma cannot be hidden even if... if..."

His words trailed off as he stared at Jake with wide eyes. "How is this possible? There is... nothing... What's going on?"

Jake was also confused for a moment until he understood what had happened, and a lot of things suddenly fell into place. Without even thinking about it, he checked out a certain skill... and there it was in the description of Shroud of the Primordial.

"The karmic threads in your wake, an endless web impossible to unravel..."

So... well... it turned out that no one being able to detect his karmic connection was pretty damn good when trying to hide who he had any connections to.

————

The Malefic Viper smiled at the horrified look on the Wyrmgod's face as he realized what was going on at the same time as Jake.

Minaga only flashed a giant grin filled with schadenfreude as he pointed at the Wyrmgod. "I told you using karmic magic to detect faction allegiances was going to be a problem!"

"It is the most reliable way a person could detect something like that... and with them being A-grades and above, no C-grade should be able to block or avoid it..." the Wyrmgod answered in a defeated voice.

That's right... In truth, what Jake had been doing throughout this entire Challenge Dungeon was a horrible fucking idea for anyone normal. Fence-sitting and trying to get one up on everyone would have been discovered a long time ago by any of the many A-grade karmic mages working for all of the larger factions. Simply lying wouldn't be enough, and the second they detected Jake sowing good karma with any of the factions through efforts that helped them in any way beyond his express orders, he would have been discovered.

But with Shroud of the Primordial, they simply couldn't see anything. Mind you, Jake formed karma just like everyone else; Shroud did nothing to block any of that. But it sure as hell did make it impossible for a bunch of mortals to see jack-shit, and coupled with their simplistic and over-tuned level of trust... Yeah, it was a recipe for disaster, and the Malefic Viper was all for it.

"Wait..." Minaga suddenly said. "Won't this also mess up the—"

"No spoilers," the Viper interrupted, enjoying this more than he probably should. "Let us all just enjoy the show as you take notes for fixes in the next iteration."

CHAPTER 13

NEVERMORE: BEST COURIER EVER

Jake, of course, knew about Shroud of the Primordial. He'd used it all the time during this Challenge Dungeon so people couldn't tell when he was lying while manipulating it, so it didn't block whatever truth-telling ability was being used when he told the truth. He didn't know how to make Shroud display his lies as true answers, only how to block it from giving any response at all... but he did have a feeling this was something he could learn to do at some future time. Considering it had taken him many decades to learn how to manipulate the responses from Identify, however, this definitely wasn't the time or place to try and teach himself that ability.

However, one part of the Shroud he had borderline forgotten was its ability to block anyone's ability to detect karma-related stuff. One had to remember that Shroud's primary function was to hide Jake so people couldn't find him unless he allowed them to. It was a counter to divination first and foremost, but in the process of blocking that, many other things were also included. Like karma.

In many ways, it had to be, considering karmic magic was a huge part of most forms of divination. Plus, if someone could track Jake's karmic threads, they would be able to track him simply by following them. While the phrase "karmic thread" was very much used as an analogy, many karmic mages actually saw literal threads of karma while using their skills. It was simply the conceptual understanding they'd reached, likely because of this common phrase and the way others taught the concept of karma. That being the case, it would be pretty easy to just follow a thread from someone related to Jake straight back to him, so of course, Shroud had to block that. It had to tangle these threads into a web that no one could make any sense of, and the karmic threads never truly led back to Jake.

All of this is to say that while Jake did form karmic connections with everyone he encountered, to any karmic mage trying to analyze these threads, nothing made sense. These threads were very much conceptual in nature, and most karmic mages—the Guild Founder included—only comprehended them by looking for something particular.

As everyone had endless karmic threads leading out from them, karmic mages pretty much had to look for a specific thread or connection in mind. If they didn't, they would just see every single karmic thread a person had. In Jake's case, that would include every single person he had ever met or influenced, both directly or indirectly... In other words, billions of people at the very least. The Founder was an S-grade and could search Jake for karmic connections within the limited scope of the room they were in, which was why he was so confused when he didn't see what he had expected. He had likely assumed Jake had a powerful karmic connection with one of the factions while having an antagonistic one with others... Instead, his skill had concluded that Jake had no positive or negative karmic connections with any of them at all.

The only way for this to be the case was if Jake truly didn't have any strong connections with any of them, either good or bad, period. Well, that, or if Jake, a mere C-grade, was capable of blocking the skill of the Founder, an S-grade and one of the strongest people in the entire world. One of these was definitely more believable than the other, and the Founder looked at Jake with genuine astonishment.

"You... are truly telling the truth. No, even so, how is this possible? Some karmic connections should have been formed no matter what, yet I can't find anything." The man frowned deeply as he considered matters further. "What exactly are you? How did you accomplish this?"

"Beats me—I don't know anything about karmic magic," Jake said truthfully, shrugging. He only knew what little he had read here or there about karma, which was enough to make him decide that it definitely wasn't a school of magic for him. "Have you considered that I was telling the truth regarding my actions? That I heavily considered the implications behind everything I did?"

The Founder was silent for a moment before nodding slowly. "Now that I think about it... it's true that your deceit would have been discovered a long time ago by one of the many other karmic mages working for these factions if you did try to trick them. Due to their incredible abilities in the areas of counterespionage and scouting, the Path has flourished in the last many millennia, and every faction has plenty of A-grades who would have been able to see straight through the actions of a C-grade Courier no matter how smart he tried to be..."

Jake kept silent along with the Founder as he considered these words, yet internally, he had a minor panic attack. *Fucking hell, I got lucky with Shroud, or things could have ended very badly...*

While everything Jake had done seemed like it could work out on the surface, especially considering how dumb the natives of the Challenge Dungeon were, in reality, it should never have gone as far as it had. Under normal circumstances, Jake would probably have been discovered the very first time he became an infinite-loop agent, if not in the very next job.

Shroud was the only reason Jake was still alive and could continue as he did. It wasn't just a matter of Shroud of the Primordial being a skill capable of hiding karma, either. Jake was sure many other factions also had abilities to hide karma-related stuff, especially those like the Court of Shadows... but their skills wouldn't work for shit in this Challenge Dungeon. The skills could hide karma, yes, but if the one searching for it was an A-grade? Even if they walked around with mythic-rarity karma-hiding skills, it would be seen through simply due to the sheer difference in power.

The only reason Jake was fine was due to how Shroud worked. When someone tried to pierce Shroud, they didn't merely try to pierce the hiding abilities of a C-grade. They competed directly with the Records and power of the Malefic Viper. That was why it could hide him from all but the most powerful of gods in the multiverse... and why a bunch of A- and even S-grades didn't stand the shadow of a chance. Even if the Founder had been a Godking, he would have been unable to see anything.

Of course, this wasn't anything the Founder would ever reasonably conclude. So he'd gone with the most reasonable conclusion he could: Jake had somehow managed to avoid any kind of strong karmic connection with any faction, meaning he hadn't chosen to side with anyone and had remained one hundred percent neutral, even to the concept of karma.

A few seconds passed, the Founder just standing there, before he finally smiled, lowered his head a bit, and nodded to himself. "I see... I see..."

He then looked up at Jake with a bright smile on his lips, the entire mood changed. He even went as far as bowing slightly. "I apologize for my offensive statements, and I hope you can forgive me. For me, as the Founder of the Guild, to offend one who truly walks the purest of Paths as a Courier... It's truly shameful."

Jake just stared at the man for a second before he mentally shrugged. *Yeah, sure, I can roll with this.*

"I simply did what had to be done and acted as I saw fit of a Courier," Jake responded, trying to sound as genuine as he possibly could.

"And you have exceeded all expectations anyone could ever have of you," the Founder said, looking somewhere between relieved and happy. "However, things are still not as they should be. Do you know why I came here today?"

"How could I possibly read the thoughts of the Founder?" Jake responded. "But if I had to guess, it has something to do with me and the way the Guild has been used and abused by many of the factions present."

"Your guess is correct for the most part," the Founder said, nodding. "I originally wanted to expose them, using you as the showcase of what they had done wrong, and set an example of what happens to Couriers who willingly assist factions, along with punishing the factions who used you... but I now realize my wrongs. You truly never had any interest in politics, merely carrying out the Courier Jobs that the Guild gave you. How can I possibly blame you for that?"

Jake felt a bit of cold sweat on his back as he couldn't help but ask, "Say... when you say you would have punished the Courier who did what you thought they did, what do you mean by that?"

"I planned on stripping you of your title as a Courier, taking your Courier Medallion, and, depending on your actions and whether you refused to truly repent and see your wrongs, ending your life right then and there. With repentance, perhaps you would have even been allowed to become a Courier once more, but you would have naturally started from the beginning."

Jake very much didn't like the sound of that potential scenario.

One had to remember that the objective of this Challenge Dungeon was to complete Courier Jobs, so if Jake was stripped of his rank, he would no longer be able to progress. Starting from the beginning would also suck major ass, as based on what Jake guessed and what would just be logical, the higher-ranked Courier Jobs would give more Nevermore Points for a better final score and Grand Achievement.

"Heh," Jake slightly laughed as he scratched the back of his head. "I guess it's good I am not the kind of person who would get involved politically with different factions, and definitely not the type to have my own plots and plans."

Yep, Jake would never do any of that. How could he? He was the best and most genuine Courier ever!

"It is indeed fortunate," the Founder said, nodding. "And perhaps this outcome is even better. I was the one who made the Guild invite you today, ensuring you would attend so I could enact my original plan. However, with what I know now, I am even happier you are here. So, let me ask you, Courier... would you be willing to assist me in exposing this corruption and punishing those who abused the Courier system and Guild?"

"Before I answer, could you elaborate a bit more on what exactly these factions did wrong in your mind?" Jake had to ask; it was the one thing that had been bothering him a bit. "Every Special Courier Job I was given by them went through the Guild. Isn't the Guild also to blame for all this happening? The Guild accepted all these jobs and gave them to me, making everything appear official. If what the factions did was truly against the rules, wouldn't the Guild have rejected the jobs?"

The Founder sighed loudly at Jake's question and looked down. "They should have, if everything was working as it is supposed to. It is normal to vet every job, but that simply hasn't been done in any of these cases. The nobles used the Guild as an arm of their own factions and threatened the employees into accepting any job they wished to assign them. To make matters even worse, I even have records of them manipulating the documentation behind the jobs and falsifying reports regarding completed jobs. Let me just confirm... have you been promised that they would 'ensure' you wouldn't suffer reputational damages even if you failed a job, as long as your failure benefited them?"

Jake recalled quite a few instances as he nodded. "More than once."

"As I expected," the Founder said, nodding back. "Perhaps it is all my fault. I have been hands-off for too long, and their respect for the Guild and what we stand for has deteriorated with the generations that have passed. Few remember who I am, and even the executives of the Guild have fallen into corruption. I plan on doing a heavy cleanup, but to start properly, we need to remind everyone what the Guild truly stands for and why we used to be so respected."

"Alright, I'm in," Jake agreed.

He wasn't sure if this was the best quest path, but it seemed like a good idea to ally with one of only a few S-grades he had ever heard of in this world. Plus, the guy didn't seem all that horrible compared to the others he had met. His biggest crime, as far as Jake knew, was inaction and laziness in regard to addressing the problems the Guild faced, and who was Jake to blame someone for not watching their own faction properly? He sure as hell was guilty of the same crime.

While it wasn't necessarily a flaw, the Founder was also a bit of a softie, considering how he'd said he wouldn't have killed Jake even if he had been a willing pawn of one of the factions and willingly repented.

"Thank you," the Founder said with a pleased nod.

"So, what's the plan?" Jake questioned.

"I believe there have been enough plans and plots already," the Founder said as he and Jake remained looking down on the mass of people mulling about in the hall. "Rather than continue down this track, we shall be direct and forthcoming with our objective."

Despite them standing on the balcony and talking for so long, no one had approached them. Everyone just kept socializing below, almost as if they were waiting for Jake and the Founder to be done with their conversation before doing anything. Jake saw all of the big players already there, and he counted more than fifty total A-grades present in the room. It was an overwhelming force, and Jake doubted many regular C-grades could ever feel comfortable in a situation like this, but he felt pretty calm.

The strongest person present was the peak A-grade Lord Protector. At least, that was what people believed. The old man was swarmed with nobles—nearly as many as the king and queen, who had taken seats on two slightly elevated chairs that looked a bit like thrones.

Jake looked over and saw the Duke of Flames standing confidently off to the side, chatting with some lesser nobles. He saw the Duke's daughter talking with others, including the A-grade who led PETE. The two other dukes were naturally also there, along with nobles from a bunch of other countries there as diplomats. Based on what Jake had heard, this was the biggest political conference in decades, so it was definitely a good spot to reveal nefarious actions taken by others to a significant and influential audience.

Of course, that was exactly what several factions in the room wanted to do... none of them knowing they'd be the ones having their actions revealed that day.

"Come... it's time," the Founder said as he stood up straight, Jake doing the same. "Let us remind them what the Guild is and what it stands for."

As he said this, Jake had a system window appear in front of him.

All Special Courier Side Jobs Failed.
Special Courier Job 10 Updated.
Special Courier Job 10: Attend the Royal Conference in the capital of the Human Kingdom. While there, assist the Guild Founder in

revealing the corruption of the noble factions and their abuse of the Guild and Courier System.

He had failed all the quests to assist the factions and been left with only one objective remaining... and he couldn't wait to see the chaos that was about to unfold.

Chapter 14

Miscalculation

J ake wondered what all the nobles he had been working with were thinking when they saw him walk down the stairs. He had just failed all of their Side Jobs, though they clearly didn't know this. These jobs had all been about exposing the other factions and had been mutually exclusive, as each required him to betray everyone else... Of course, Jake didn't view anything he had done as a betrayal, as he'd never held any loyalty in the first place.

The Duke of Flames had wanted Jake to expose another dukedom for working with PETE and even another country, as PETE was based there. This other dukedom, which the daughter of the Duke of Flames worked with, wanted Jake to expose the Duke of Flames' illegal activities and the damage caused by his incessant desire to consume more elementals. At the same time, they would also expose PETE to make themselves look like they would never have worked with such an organization in the first place.

Lastly, PETE also wanted Jake to expose the Duke of Flames alongside this other dukedom for working with the Duke of Flames' daughter, as they had heard she would join this dukedom and thus continue the Lineage of the Duke of Flames. They didn't want to see that happen, and instead wanted them utterly eliminated.

The person they all wanted Jake to do his exposing to was the king of the Human Kingdom. He had the full backing of the third dukedom, the Lord Protector, and the entire royal army behind him, making him the most influential and powerful person in the kingdom... which shouldn't come as a surprise, considering he was the king.

From what Jake had gathered, he guessed the king already had a good idea about some of the stuff going on and kind of just wanted everything to be swept under the rug to avoid any open internal conflicts in the Human Kingdom. Any dukedom falling would be bad for the Human Kingdom, as their overall power would fall, and with enemy countries on all sides, civil war wasn't recommended.

However, even if the king wanted things to be resolved behind closed doors, the second things were brought forth to the public, he would have to act openly and decisively or risk losing influence, thus looking like he could be walked all over. That was what all the factions who wanted Jake to expose shit banked on anyway.

Based on the words the Founder sent to Jake as they walked down the stairs, he was willing to give the king a chance to right the wrongs in his own kingdom, primarily on account of the Lord Protector. The royal family had never abused the Guild, and what jobs they had commissioned had all been above board. Perhaps because the royal family still held respect for what the Guild stood for... or because the Lord Protector had been one of the people fighting alongside the Founder back in the war against the dragon tribe and knew that risking making the Founder an enemy was a horrible idea.

As he and the Founder walked down to the main floor, they naturally attracted some attention. Jake had many friendly gazes land on him from the many factions, all preparing for him to carry out their wishes. Probably because he was the only one who publicly worked with Jake, the Duke of Flames stepped forward without any surprise from the other factions.

"Ah, it's great of you to finally join us," the Duke of Flames said, entirely ignoring the Founder beside Jake, who was presenting as an early-tier B-grade.

"Of course," Jake responded a bit curtly but still keeping it professional. "I was hired to carry out a job here, after all."

"Indeed you were." The Duke smiled as he turned to address the king and queen sitting on their throne, along with everyone else present. "Allow me to introduce someone. This is a Courier I have been working with recently, and I am certain many of you have also come to know of him in recent times. A true rising star of the Guild, and a man with an impeccable record."

Jake remained quiet, not saying no to flattery when offered.

"I originally hired him with the intent of sniffing out those who have been targeting me recently," the Duke of Flames continued in a very holier-than-thou tone. "You have all heard of them—the terrorist organization that has been wreaking havoc in my dukedom and threatened the stability of this very kingdom with their actions. This hiring was made with little hope... but I had underestimated the expertise and abilities of this Courier, and in less than a year, he managed to uncover those behind the plot targeting our blessed country."

Muttering filled the room, all attention now on Jake. Many scanned him using different means, with the Founder continually getting ignored despite standing right next to him. Jake especially felt the gazes of a few people present, one of whom walked forward to speak with a magnanimous smile.

"The Duke of Flames speaks the truth. Those who have taken actions to hurt this kingdom and its reputation must be punished, no matter who they are!" He was the Duke who opposed the Duke of Flames, and another person who believed Jake was actually there as his ally.

He also got a telepathic message from the leader of PETE. *"Now is the time to strike... Topple both of these monsters from their high peaks and be the arbiter of justice. Be the harbinger of a new age where elementals can live free from the Dukedom of Flames and all those who dared allow their vile existence."*

Jake would've been lying if he said he felt comfortable. As he carefully considered his next words, he briefly threw a glance at the Founder, who nodded at him. Jake then turned to the king and bowed slightly. "Your majesty, I have indeed made some discoveries during my work as a Courier I believe are pertinent to share with the court."

"Before you proceed, I need to clarify something..." the king said. "Who are you here working for? Where do your loyalties lie?"

Jake detected a truth-telling skill from the queen sitting at his side. Those skills were pretty damn common in this world, huh?

The king's question also communicated that he did indeed know some internal conflict was going on. Luckily, Jake had an easy answer to his question.

"I am here as a Courier representing the Guild. As for loyalties... I have none but the loyalty I hold toward myself and my dignity. As a Courier, loyalty as a concept isn't something I see the need to consider. I am merely here to carry out a Special Courier Job—nothing less, nothing more." Usually, giving long answers with details and absolutes when faced with a lie-detector skill wasn't recommended... unless you were capable of fully telling the truth when doing so. In these cases, it only served to strengthen your voice.

After a second or two, the queen nodded to the king, who looked genuinely surprised at the confirmation of Jake being truthful.

"So, you are not here at the behest of any of the nobles of the Human Kingdom?" the Lord Protector, who was sitting a bit off to the side, asked as he directed a sharp gaze at Jake.

Yep, he definitely also knows something. Fuck, I am happy I didn't try this shit all by myself without any backing...

"I was given side jobs by three people present to attend and carry out their will," Jake answered truthfully. "However, I was also given a Special Courier Job by the Guild, which is the one I am here to carry out."

Who knew that things were a lot easier when you could just tell the truth while knowing you had an S-grade at your side, willing to defend you should anything bad happen? Because damn, was something bad about to happen as Jake began to reveal a bit too much—in the eyes of those who had hired him, at least.

Jake felt three gazes on him filled with hidden bloodlust. All of them A-grades, with the Duke of Flames the most powerful of them. They were warnings—no, threats—to carry out what they wanted him to do and not say more than he had to.

"Oh?" the Lord Protector said, continuing the conversation in place of the king. "And what did these three people want you to do here tonight?"

"To reveal underhanded dealings while exposing the organization that has made moves against the Duke of Flames in recent times, including the hidden backers of this organization," Jake said, feeling the threatening gaze of the Duke of Flames lessen slightly... only for it to return stronger than ever with his next sentence. "This includes the illegal activities undertaken by the Duke of Flames in his attempt to continually acquire elementals he can consume to fuel his own Path."

As Jake finished speaking, the telepathic messages began rolling in.

"What the hell are you—"

"Shut your mouth, or—"

"Why would you—"

Jake ignored all of them and focused only on the Lord Protector and two royals.

The eyes of the Lord Protector narrowed as he gave the king a look. Seemingly suppressing a sigh, the king's face turned a lot more serious. "These are very heavy accusations... Are you sure you can handle what may come from you making them? The consequences if anything you say is revealed to be a lie?"

"As I said, I am merely here carrying out a Special Courier Job and representing the Guild," Jake answered. "I am only to share the truth according to the wishes of my client."

The king didn't look all that happy with Jake's answer, yet he motioned with his hand. "Then proceed... Let us hear what you claim to have uncovered."

And hear it, they did. Jake held nothing back as he explained everything he had done for these different factions. How he had worked for all of them at once, effectively infiltrating them while doing all his Courier Jobs. He even sprinkled in some of the physical evidence he had swiped during his many interactions with them, everything he said continually checked by lie-detector skills.

Some of his revelations sent shockwaves through the crowd. Especially when he revealed the Duke of Flames' daughter had worked with another dukedom to take him down and even supported PETE. Jake felt pretty sure a good portion of the room would already have made moves to kill him if the faint presence of the Lord Protector didn't already cover his body, signaling none was to make a move, lest they suffer the consequences.

The only real strategy Jake had in his big revelation was saving the identity of PETE's leader for last, as he felt pretty damn sure she would make a move the moment he did. Once revealed, her chances of escaping unscathed were nil, so to at the very least get revenge and kill the Courier who exposed her was only to be expected.

A prediction that turned out to be entirely accurate... as the moment Jake turned and pointed out the leader of PETE, without any warning, her aura exploded and she flew straight for Jake. The Founder stood between Jake and the woman, but he didn't even need to make a move.

Without Jake being able to detect any movement, the old man appeared right above the A-grade woman. She didn't even manage to scream before her entire body imploded, and Jake felt powerful ripples of space mana from the old man as he squished her entire body into a small red ball of flesh no larger than a golf ball faster than Jake could even react to her movements. The entire debacle barely even affected the throne room, given that the magic used by the Lord Protector was so limited in scope, but it definitely set the mood to see an A-grade dying.

With everyone looking, the Lord Protector waved his hand, and what looked like a spatial ring appeared in it. He then infused some energy into it. Jake watched the enchantments begin to break apart, and after a second or two, the old man fished out a few items, including a notebook and some odd crystals.

"This journal lays out plans made by this terrorist organization to sabotage the Duke of Flames... and the crystals are those uniquely found in the Dukedom of Blades," the Lord Protector said in a matter-of-fact voice.

Wait... did that dukedom seriously pay PETE in crystals only found in their territory? Jake questioned, though he kept his mouth shut. Things were going his way already, and there was no reason to ruin it. *Wait... maybe the PETE leader has these on purpose? So if she did die, she would at least take down some people with her using the evidence she was carrying?*

"That woman was also from the Phoenix Wing Empire," the Lord Protector continued as he glared at the Duke of Blades. "Do you have any explanations for yourself?"

Surprisingly enough, the Duke of Blades remained calm despite the accusations as he shook his head. "I truthfully do not... for I have never worked with any such organizations."

"Are you saying the accusations of this Courier are false, despite his testimony already having been confirmed as true?" the king questioned in a sharp tone.

"I am not denying he believes they are true... but I fear he has been led behind the light." The Duke of Blades sighed. "All the truth-detecting skills can see is whether the person speaking believes they are telling the truth, not what the actual truth is. I fear that the Courier may have been fooled into believing we were working with this daughter of the Duke of Flames."

"And you're saying you're not?" the king continued questioning.

"Most definitely not," the Duke of Blades said in an offended tone. "Neither would we work with some horrific terrorist organization who targets the innocents. I believe this may all be a plot by the Duke of Flames to undermine my dukedom using his daughter... or, looking at the Duke, perhaps even his own daughter tricked him?"

"I... What are you talking about!?" the Duke of Flames' daughter said in an outburst. "You promised that—"

"Silence!" the king yelled as he slammed his fist into his chair, sending out a shockwave of energy. The room became even more tense than before, and while Jake remained silent, he was honestly pretty confused about something...

Why are they not just using lie-detector skills on this Duke of Blades?

It made no sense to avoid doing so... unless...

"Duke of Flames... do you have any defense against these accusations?" the king asked, looking at the Duke.

"Are you seriously claiming I would have hired a terrorist organization to target my own family and dukedom?" the Duke of Flames said. "That I would willingly commit all sorts of criminal activity simply to acquire some more elementals? Perhaps I have been too zealous in my pursuits, and my subordinates may have taken things too far, and I may even have been blind to the rebellious actions of my daughter, but I am fully willing to submit everything for review. I want us to remember I am the injured party..."

Jake watched the Lord Protector frown deeply, while the king looked like he was deep in thought. "Hm... this certainly is a matter that must be investigated further..."

"Perhaps, Your Majesty, this is all a plot by this terrorist organization to cause internal strife within the kingdom?" the Duke of Blades chimed in as he looked at the Duke of Flames. "While the Duke of Flames and I most definitely have our differences, I am certain they are nothing we cannot solve behind closed doors with the royal family as mediators."

Without any hesitation, the Duke of Flames nodded. "No one has any interest in seeing us split more than an enemy country, and I, too, am certain we can reach a satisfactory conclusion through negotiation and following proper legal procedures to find out who is truly behind this plot."

What the fuck is going on? Jake questioned as the entire mood in the hall shifted once more. However, Jake soon realized why things were going so wrong... The king was resolute in sweeping things under the rug, and the two dukes had given him a golden opportunity to do so. They just had to play theater, and some faux investigation could discover some fall guys to be arrested and executed while maintaining order.

The two dukes also knew this, Jake confirmed after receiving a message from each.

"What a pathetic attempt... I had high hopes for you, but it seems you are dumber than I thought," the Duke of Flames said. *"Did you truly think your word was enough? That a mere C-grade could lead to my downfall? You overestimate yourself. Ah, but I must thank you for exposing that I had a snake of a daughter, and for getting rid of this annoying pest of an organization that has been bothering me. You have proven most useful despite your idiocy. I would recommend that you stay and enjoy the rest of the party... for this will be your last."*

"You have proven yourself most unwise," the Duke of Blades also sent. *"It is sad to see someone I was told was so promising invite his own death through sheer arrogance."*

Jake had no idea what to say... but he realized his plan had been fucked from the beginning. Even if he had truth and facts on his side, it didn't matter in the grand scheme of things, and his strategy of targeting everyone would end with nothing but the death of a C-grade Courier after some fake investigations were carried out, with no one remembering anything about the Courier in a few years.

The king turned to Jake and nodded after the two dukes had spoken. "Thank you for bringing all of this to light, and we will be sure to carry out thorough investigations to uncover the whole truth."

And that was that... The king had swept things under the rug. From the looks of it, this didn't sit well with the Lord Protector, but he didn't speak up. They had all made a decision, and Jake could do nothing about it. His protests would be viewed as nothing but contempt toward the king's decision and land him in even more trouble. Jake had entirely miscalculated how all of this would go, perhaps only highlighting his political ignorance...

"Now," the king said, "let us not see the day ruined, but continue to enjoy oursel—"

"Is this truly your decision?" the man who had been standing next to Jake this entire time asked.

As the king frowned at the interruption, the Duke of Flames stepped forward. "Who are you to question His Majesty's decision!?"

His aura rolled out of him, increasing the temperature in the room, and he attempted to pressure the man he believed was an early-tier B-grade... only to find his aura rebuffed. He coughed up blood from the backlash and stumbled back as the Founder's aura exploded.

Jake, not missing a beat, smiled. "Allow me to introduce my client for this job... the Guild Founder."

CHAPTER 15

LEGENDARY COURIER

Considering there was only a handful of S-grades in the entire world, it didn't take long for the people present to identify the man Jake had arrived with. His overwhelming aura suppressed every single one of them, his power simply at a whole other level, even compared to the peak A-grade Lord Protector.

"Ge... General..." the Lord Protector stuttered as the Founder's form also changed. Jake already knew he had transformed his body, so it didn't really come as a surprise when he turned into a slightly older-looking human man. It did surprise everyone else, though.

Jake did, however, learn that the Founder had apparently been a general back in the day.

"I must admit I find myself disappointed," the Founder spoke as no one else dared open their mouth. "I truly, for a brief moment, believed this could be resolved without my involvement. Alas, I was proven wrong. Despite all the evidence and the testimony of a high-ranking Courier with a borderline-perfect track record, your response is to do... nothing."

"We... We will conduct a thorough investi—" the Duke of Blades tried to say, yet he was silenced with a single glance.

"Do you think me a child? That I could not see through such an obvious attempt to suppress the truth by all parties involved?" The Founder shook his head as he looked at the Lord Protector. "Are you also going to tell me I'm an idiot, Colonel?"

"No... No, sir," the formerly awe-inspiring Lord Protector said as he bowed. "It is just as the General observed."

"At least someone besides this Courier is capable of telling the truth," the Founder said, scoffing as he turned his attention back to the king. "You, too, lived during the war. Many of those here today did... yet you all seem to have forgotten what happened then—and the aftermath. Why I made the Guild in the first place. Do I need to remind you, little king? Remind you of the oath your kingdom swore? The promise you made!?"

The king looked down, almost ashamed. By now, the tides had truly turned, and things were not looking good for the dukes. The Duke of Flames, who had wiped the blood off his lips, clearly also noticed this, fighting to avoid being fully suppressed.

"Lord Founder..." the Duke of Flames began as he tried to get his bearings. "I truly apologize for how things turned out... but... is the Guild not also breaking protocol by getting directly involved in an internal conflict of the Human Kingdom? While it is true we were partly to blame, we were also fooled by this Courier as he plotted against us all, and he was the one who initiated today's conflict with his widespread accusations. I can admit I hired him through the Guild for use against my political foes and to get rid of the terrorist organization harassing me... but is that truly so wrong? Is that truly a crime deserving of the Guild Founder's wrath?"

The Founder let out a loud sigh as he looked directly at the Duke of Flames. "You just admitted to your biggest crime... how you used the Guild," the Founder said in a loud voice with an undertone of anger. "In truth, I do not care for the internal conflicts of the Human Kingdom. The internal disputes of any country, for that matter. But this entire thing has been made possible by exploiting the nature and good reputation of the Guild. For years, the Dukedom of Flames has pressured the Guild into accepting Courier Jobs to hide its dirty dealings, and the other dukedoms are no different. You have viewed the Guild as nothing more than a tool for you to abuse without ever considering the consequences or when things would reach a breaking point... so let me just make it clear. That breaking point was well and truly reached today when you tried to make such an exemplary Courier into your accomplice." Jake saw a few of the people present shiver as a bit of bloodlust emanated from the S-grade.

Jake had to do his utmost to hold himself back from grinning. The people who had been calling him a fucking moron only minutes ago were now shivering because the Founder had shown up. He alone was strong enough to utterly suppress every single person in the room, and in truth, his actual words barely mattered. His arguments were meaningless in the grand scheme of things.

It was the same as when Jake had spoken up. It didn't matter if everything Jake said was the truth. Before a bunch of A-grades, his words simply didn't matter, as he was only some C-grade whelp in their eyes. Perhaps this wasn't the lesson one was meant to learn from this Challenge Dungeon, or maybe it was... but it reaffirmed something Jake already knew but had foolishly disregarded during this dungeon. Power still came first and foremost before everything else.

As the Viper had said a long time ago, if you were strong enough, your word became truth. Your interpretation of a situation became the correct one. As a Chosen, Jake was usually capable of borrowing the influence of the Malefic Viper, and in many cases, people even believed his opinion mirrored that of the Viper, making them take him more seriously. In cases where he interacted with peers who didn't necessarily care about his status or had an equally high status, Jake was still considered one of the stronger people, so he could still be part of the conversation as an equal.

In this Challenge Dungeon, Jake was no equal to the dukes he had tried to call out, and it had been shown when everyone sided with the A-grades to just sweep everything under the rug. Power meant everything, which was once again demonstrated when everything Jake had said was suddenly given a new level of legitimacy and taken far more seriously because the Founder popped up to tell them to take Jake seriously.

"I..." the Duke of Flames began, looking like he was trying to come up with a counterargument, only to have the Lord Protector stop him.

"Do not sully the reputation of the Human Kingdom further with your stupidity," the old man said, scoffing as he looked at the Founder and kneeled. "I am ashamed that something like this could have happened under my watch... I have been blind to what is happening for too long."

"No, this is ultimately my responsibility," the king spoke as he, too, promptly kneeled. "I knew many of these crimes of the dukedoms were taking place, yet I did nothing. I even knew they abused and threatened the Guild to do their bidding and used the Guild Founder's institution as if they owned it. I reneged on my responsibilities and can only be ashamed of my own incompetence and failure to do what I must. For this, I can only beg for forgiveness and, if the magnanimity of the Guild Founder allows it, try to better myself and this country."

Jake was honestly impressed at how the king handled the shit that was all the way up to his neck. He didn't make any excuses, just taking responsibility while admitting things that had otherwise not come to light already. Finally, he'd promised to better himself and the Human Kingdom as a whole. Overall, a pretty good apology.

"And how will you take responsibility?" the Founder questioned.

Without any hesitation, the king stood up and spoke loudly, "Detain the Duke of Flames and the Duke of Blades along with their immediate family and close collaborators."

"Your Majesty, this is—" the Duke of Flames began to argue before the king threw him a sharp gaze and spoke even louder than before.

"Lethal force is permitted should they resist."

For a moment, Jake thought the Duke of Flames was going to fight it out, but he ultimately didn't. Jake had a feeling that had the Founder not been present, the power-hungry Duke would have escaped, leaving behind everything to save his own hide. Even if the Lord Protector was stronger than him, the Duke of Flames was still a close second and more than capable of getting away, even from a space mage. Of course, with the Founder also there, his chances of escape were nonexistent, so he'd wisely decided to surrender.

"Your actions were sufficiently swift... Alright, I shall give you a chance," the Founder said, and it looked as if an almost physical weight had been lifted from the king and Lord Protector. "However, I shall remain in the Human Kingdom for now to ensure everything proceeds in a satisfactory fashion. I take it there are no complaints?"

"Having you as a guest would be a great honor," the king said, bowing as the royal guards and Lord Protector began to escort out the two dukes along with a bunch of other nobles.

All of them already had pretty bleak facial expressions, and when the Founder proclaimed he would stay in the kingdom for a while, things only got worse for them. That pretty much killed all escape plans, and the Duke of Flames especially looked like a plan he was beginning to form in his head had already fallen apart.

Throughout this entire debacle, Jake had just been standing next to the Founder. He was pretty much the only person present who hadn't bowed or full-on kneeled at some point, nor carried an unmistakable sense of reverence for one of only five known S-grades. Jake hadn't needed to say anything after doing his assignment and laying out the evidence, and that honestly felt pretty good.

He wondered if someone more skilled in the political arena could have handled things better and not necessarily needed the Founder's help. Perhaps it was possible, especially since the Lord Protector wasn't happy with the status quo... but Jake sure as hell had no idea how to make it happen. Alas, it didn't matter, because Jake had managed to make a good impression on the S-grade Founder and gotten super fucking lucky the guy was even there in the first place. If not, he would have probably lost one of his lives on this day.

"Thank you for your help on this day, Courier," the Founder said after a bit more discussion with the king. He said this with many nobles and the king still present as everyone looked at them. "Without you, this would have been much more difficult, and your actions helped uncover the depths of this corruption. You truly are an exemplary Courier and fully deserving of the reputation you have built for yourself. An example for all other Couriers."

"No, I should be the one thanking you for trusting me with this job." Jake bowed, keeping up his persona as the perfect employee. "And I am just happy when the client is happy."

"I believe you," the Founder said, laughing as he patted Jake on the shoulder. "I truly do."

Jake smiled in return. This definitely felt like some kind of climax to the story. He had met the Guild Founder himself and worked with him, upended the political landscape in one of the countries, and even had an A-grade killed and several imprisoned. However... for some reason, Jake didn't feel like this was the end, and a note of dread began to worm its way into his mind as the Founder spoke once more.

"Ah, but I shouldn't hold you up for too long... You have completed this Special Courier Job flawlessly, and I must thank you once more, but I also know you must be eager to continue following your calling. I am certain many others out there need such an exemplary Courier... and who knows, perhaps you can even reach the realm of Legendary Couriers."

You gotta be kidding me...

Special Courier Job 15 Completed.

"If you go to the Guild Hall, I am sure they have many Courier Jobs available, even for someone of your skill, and as I work to restore order and remove corruption, I may even need the help of a skilled Courier once more. If I ever do need you again... can I trust in your assistance?"

Jake really wanted to tell the guy to just fuck off, but instead he smiled. "As long as there is a Courier Job worth doing, and I am capable, of course I'll be there to help."

"In that case... I truly thank you once more. Now, I need to remain here and speak to these fools a bit longer, but you are free to do whatever you wish." The Founder smiled as he gave Jake another pat on the shoulder.

"I shall be heading straight to the Guild Hall, then... Work awaits," Jake said respectfully as he gave the Founder a small bow and left the royal palace. On the surface, he was smiling, but on the inside, he was cursing loudly. He'd just thought, for the briefest of moments, he had "beaten" the Challenge Dungeon in less than a year, but it turned out he had just finished one of the goddamn story arcs.

Relax, Jake... Just keep going at it, and at some point, you'll run out of jobs or become unable to finish them.

––––––

"That could have gone worse," Minaga said with a grin. "A lot worse. Jake is really freaking lucky his strategy worked out somehow... or maybe it's that weird instinct or intuition or whatever that helped him along. Who knows? For my own sanity, I will just call it pure luck."

Valdemar, who usually didn't bother saying much, actually spoke for once. "Luck is also kind of a skill."

Vilastromoz wanted to call that out as bullshit but held his tongue. He didn't deny luck was a thing, but to call it a skill was going overboard... even if Valdemar was known as someone notoriously lucky.

"Luck is just when preparation meets opportunity," the Blightfather chimed in. "Many of those who dare claim others *just got lucky* are incapable of even taking advantage of the opportunities they gain."

"But isn't someone who gets more potential opportunities considered luckier, then?" the Holy Mother asked, also deciding to get involved... likely just to take a jab at the Blightfather.

"Opportunities are more often taken rather than given," the Blightfather said, shaking his head. "And the definition of an opportunity varies widely. For the talented, they can turn every day into a few opportunities. A powerful beast nearby may be viewed as nothing but a danger to the common person, but for the strong, they are an opportunity to test themselves and claim Records. Still, none will claim someone is lucky for choosing to face a beast they have a high chance of dying against."

"Why are we even discussing the definition of luck?" Minaga questioned.

"You started it," the Wyrmgod simply added.

"And now I'm finishing it," Minaga said with a grin. "Anyway, back to Jake. Man, am I looking forward to when he unlocks the final arc. Gonna be so funny."

The Wyrmgod sighed but didn't say anything. The Viper wondered what would happen... but seeing as Minaga looked so amused, he had a feeling something really interesting... or stupid... was about to occur. After Jake had done a load of more average Courier Jobs, of course.

———

Jake remembered always finding it incredibly funny in video games how none of your prior accomplishments were properly acknowledged. One could be the divine archmage and emperor of a nation, but some random farmer would still give you a quest to kill rats, and the recruiter of a new faction would still call you "new blood" and act as if you were a total novice.

It was a nice joke and something to laugh about when it happened, even if it could take you a bit out of the story, but surely, this kind of thing wouldn't happen in the "real" world, now, would it? Well...

Jake Thayne, Courier extraordinaire and the man who had personally worked with the Founder to expose the corruption of many nobles of the highest rank. A man who had led to the death and arrest of many A-grades. A man even the king and Lord Protector would show respect to, and a true benefactor of the Guild itself, soon found himself busy trying to convince a bunch of children who had "stolen" his package that the toys inside weren't for them, but his client.

After Special Courier Job 15, Jake had gone to the Guild Hall, where, despite all the kind words they had for him, they still gave him regular-ass jobs to do. Was the difficulty higher now, and did he even get into a few fights during some of them? Yes, but it was clear combat wasn't really the core of this Challenge Dungeon. It was instead just the ability to handle different annoying situations while not losing your cool or getting tricked.

Jake had hoped he would only need to do a few more Courier Jobs for something interesting to happen, and he was kind of right? After he had done "only" 50 jobs in the capital city of the Human Kingdom, he was contacted by a Guild employee on behalf of the Founder. He was then given a Special Courier Job to go to a different capital city and work there for a while to "audit" the Guild, doing another fifty to seven Courier Jobs before reporting back.

This pattern continued, weeks turning to months, with Jake traveling all over the world inside the Challenge Dungeon. Every new country had unique challenges and different cultures to navigate, but Jake thought he did pretty well as he really got into the groove. Soon enough, over half a year had passed since getting his ancient-rarity medallion, and Jake had been to nearly every capital city. Things were a bit stale by now, but he kept up his work ethic, as he knew things were bound to end at some point.

Finally, after around eight months as an ancient-rarity Courier, Jake met the Founder once more and attended a ceremony where he was given the highest honors as a Courier. His Medallion was upgraded for what he believed was the final time as he stepped into the ranks of Legendary Couriers.

[Courier Medallion (Legendary)] – A Courier Medallion belonging to a Legendary Courier, a title that has only been seen a few times through history and can only be given by the Guild Founder himself. This Medallion will hold information related to jobs and can give general directions to your destination if those are provided (may not be entirely reliable). This is the highest-known rank of the Courier Medallion.
Requirements: Soulbound.

As even the description of the Medallion said, this was the highest-known rank, and after getting it, Jake felt as if he was well and truly done with the Challenge Dungeon... but no message appeared. Perhaps it had been silly of him to expect something known as the Endless Journey to have an end, but it had to end at some point, right?

After the ceremony where he got promoted, Jake was given a week off to relax. However... just two days later, as Jake was chilling and doing a bit of alchemy—he had run out of potions again—a Guild employee suddenly stormed into the room.

"Hurry, you must come!" the attendant said in a panicked voice.

"What happened?" Jake asked.

"Somehow, the dragon tribe returned!"

CHAPTER 16

NEVER EASY

So... dragons. Dragons were scary, and in all honesty, there was no way in fucking hell Jake was going to be dealing with one. Any True Dragon was B-grade and a high-tier variant, meaning even the weakest of them could blast Jake to pieces without him ever really standing a chance.

This begged the question... with dragons suddenly returning, what the hell was Jake to do? Well, he learned that only half an hour after the Guild employee had come to fetch him. The dwarven woman had led Jake to a meeting room where Jake saw quite a few influential figures already gathered. Royals from many different countries had shown up, as well as high-ranking people not part of any country. Jake even felt the aura of a second S-grade at the Founder's side.

When Jake entered the room, he only got a few glances from the roughly seventy people present. Every single person was at least A-grade and either a duke, royal, or leader of some organization. He instantly questioned why he was there, but seeing as no one else did, he decided to just bow slightly and find a seat off to the side.

A dozen or so more people arrived over the next half an hour, all of them also A-grade. Apart from the Founder and a woman Jake recognized from a poster he had seen in the Phoenix Wing Empire, no other S-grades appeared. The Phoenix Wing Empire was the only empire in the world, solely because they were the only faction with an S-grade ruler, and the Phoenix Empress proudly stood side by side with the Founder, giving off an aura that, while inferior to his, still outshined everyone else present.

Alright, Jake could also try and enter the race, but he didn't really feel like attracting any attention.

"Good, we are all here," the Founder said after a few more minutes passed and everyone had gotten settled. "I believe you are all aware why we are here, so let us not delay needlessly. Our world faces a crisis, and we will need the help of everyone present to weather this storm."

Murmurs filled the room, but no one asked any questions. From the looks of it, everyone indeed knew what this was about as the Founder began to elaborate with lore and details of what exactly they were dealing with.

"Forty thousand years ago, I killed the Dragon King, yes... but the Queen still managed to flee along with her whelplings and other survivors. No one knew where they went, and despite searching everywhere on the planet and all the local solar systems, not a single trace was discovered. We believed they were gone forever or had perhaps died... but as of a few hours ago, a group of dragons was confirmed in a neighboring solar system, rapidly heading this way. They are led by the Dragon Queen, the now S-grade Dragon Prince, and three other S-grades, with hundreds of A-grades and over ten thousand B-grade True Dragons. The numbers of C-grade dragon spawn, wyverns, and dragonkin are impossible to count, as they are all being transported in secured barges."

"Moreover," the Phoenix Empress added, "we have reason to believe that some dragonkin and dragon tribe sympathizers have already arrived on the planet and been here for a while, preparing for the return of the dragon tribe. Now, many of them have begun to make their moves, and we have strong reason to believe even some nobles are supporting them."

The Founder suddenly turned to Jake and motioned toward him. "Recently, as I am sure you all know, there was an internal struggle in the Human Kingdom after some nobles went too far and exploited the Guild. This was all discovered through the valiant efforts of this Legendary Courier. During the following interrogations with the Duke of Flames, we discovered that the Duke had not only been committing many crimes and exploited the Guild... Two centuries ago, he also entered an alliance with the dragon tribe who offered him an S-grade Dragon Flame Elemental for his cooperation in toppling the Human Kingdom and weakening the Guild. It was only due to the efforts of this Courier that we were able to learn this and even get an early warning, giving us more time to prepare."

Jake just sat in the corner as all the A-grades and even two S-grades gave him respectful looks for his contribution to the war efforts. He tried to look humble but honestly had no idea what to do or say, so he just nodded solemnly, which the Founder luckily took as an opportunity to continue.

What followed was a long explanation of their war efforts, and to sum it up, things weren't looking good. The plan was for all of the B-, A- and S-grades that could possibly be gathered to come together and face the dragon tribe in space before they even reached the planet. However, even if they gathered a powerful army, the dragon tribe still simply had more powerhouses. From what the Founder said, this Dragon Prince was also more powerful than the Dragon King had been, so even if the Founder had continued to make some progress in the last forty thousand years, he was unsure if he could win. If the other four S-grades were factored in, things were bleak for sure, with their side only having two S-grades.

I wonder... if I had sided with the Duke of Flames completely and continued to assist him, could I have ended up on the side of this dragon tribe? Jake considered as all the talks continued. They still had a while before the dragons arrived—the early warning courtesy of Jake uncovering the crimes of the Duke of Flames—and during this time, all the preparations that could be made would be made.

As the meeting began to wind to a close, the Founder asked Jake to follow him to a private office. Jake could already feel another Special Courier Job coming as he closed the door behind him, and he saw the Founder activate some magic to seal off the room.

"Courier... things are even worse than I presented them out there," the Founder began as he sighed. "If things continue as they are, we don't stand a chance. While we may be able to defend for a while, we simply do not have the power to beat them in a straight-on fight... unless we get more allies."

Oh... this trope, Jake thought, already knowing what was coming next.

"The Phoenix Queen and I are the only ones who can fight the S-grades among the ranks of the dragons, but there are also others from our world who can. Two old comrades from back during the war, known as the Blademaster and the Nine Seals Demon. The problem is, I am not entirely sure where they are; all I heard was that both went off to train many, many years ago."

"You need me to help find them?" Jake asked, presenting the obvious question.

"Yes," the Founder said with a nod. "While I do not know where either of them are, I do know someone who at least is aware of the location of one: the Blademaster. He sealed himself away for isolated training about ten thousand years ago, but his wife should still be living in the Elven

Kingdom, and if anyone knows where my old friend went, it's her. Seek her out, and ask… and try to do this without raising any suspicions. I am certain that I am currently being tracked, the same as the A-grades, and I have to head to the frontlines soon to establish our defenses. As a C-grade Courier, you should be mostly inconspicuous, but be warned there will likely be many pursuers anyway."

"Alright," Jake said, nodding as he got yet another Special Courier Job.

Special Courier Job 20: Locate and recruit the Blademaster.

Sweet, short, and simple. With a mission that just had to be the start of the final arc of this Challenge Dungeon, Jake headed off to find the wife and convince her to tell him where the Blademaster was. He expected a lot of difficulty during the journey, as he found out that the woman lived far away from any of the major cities on a small farmstead, meaning he had to travel a lot on foot without any teleportation circles available. At least he could get to the closest city pretty easily.

As Jake left the city, he saw that things were really busy. Everyone knew an attack was incoming, and while the normal citizens couldn't do much, they helped those with power as much as they could. Powerful defensive formations were set up, and people charged what looked like big mana batteries they would send to the frontlines to power massive defensive barriers and assist the fighters up in space. No one even tried to flee, as they knew doing so wouldn't help with anything… If the dragons returned, their living in a city or hiding out would mean nothing.

Jake was certainly noticed as he left the city, but surprisingly, no one followed him. As he kept flying, Jake wondered when the people the Founder had warned him about would show up, but he didn't see anyone. Well, not with his eyes, anyway. He did spot a group of people roaming around with a Pulse of Perception a few hours from the city and promptly made sure to employ stealth as he flew around them. He did the same with whatever else he got the feeling could be an enemy on the way. He honestly didn't want to meet or talk to anyone but this wife, so he stayed clear of everything possible. This was not a combat-focused Challenge Dungeon, so he had no reason to fight when unnecessary, right?

Now, if he could've gotten experience, things might have been different… but alas.

Due to his careful and stealthy approach, Jake reached the farmstead about a week after leaving the elven city without meeting any trouble on the way. As he got closer, he saw many powerful formations already defending the place, so he stopped right outside and he yelled as loud as he could, **"Excuse me, but I'm looking for someone known as the Blademaster! Asking for a mutual ally! I was hoping you could give me a moment of your ti—"**

Before Jake was even done yelling, he was rudely interrupted by his entire body turning into an ice statue, and even the air itself froze all around him. He was physically unable to let out any sound or even move a muscle as his insides were entirely frozen over. Yet despite the less-than-pleasant sensation of being a popsicle, he didn't feel any danger at all, suggesting the one who had frozen him wasn't aiming to kill but simply capture him.

An A-grade elven woman appeared in front of Jake a second later and observed him closely. With a wave of her hand, she unfroze his head. "Speak. Who are you?"

"Courier here on a job directly from the Guild Founder to ask you for the location of, or a method to find, the Blademaster," Jake answered in his usual polite tone. Even if the woman was being a bit rude by freezing him, he wouldn't lose his professional attitude.

The woman looked surprised as she narrowed her eyes. A bit carefully, she melted all the ice on Jake's upper body, allowing him to move freely. Just as she did, Jake took out his Courier Medallion and showed her before she could demand for him to prove his identity.

She looked at the Medallion carefully for a second. "A Legendary Courier... This must not be a small matter... Why do you need the Blademaster?"

"I take it you are pretty isolated out here and don't get news that often?" Jake questioned.

The woman scoffed as if offended by the question. "I enjoy the solitude when my husband is not here."

"Well, to bring you up to speed..." Jake said, offering a completely complimentary news-delivery service, "the dragon tribe is back, currently fighting the Guild Founder, Phoenix Queen, and many others in the neighboring solar system. Things are not looking good, and they need the help of the Blademaster."

"This is..." she muttered. "Alright, I'll take you to him."

"Great."

Jake smiled as the woman entirely unfroze him and dragged him along for a flight to a nearby mountain range. Once inside, Jake felt that they'd entered a vast system of formations, likely set up by the S-grade to defend himself during his isolated training. Looking around, there were hundreds of caves spread around the mountains.

"He is here, with one of these caves leading to his location... However, I am unsure which one, and seeing as each has defensive formations, we will need to carefully search each of—"

"That one." Jake pointed after he was done scanning the result of his Pulse of Perception.

The A-grade woman looked at him. "You speak with such certainty... How would you possibly know which one it is?"

Now, it was Jake's turn to scoff and look offended. "What do you mean how do I know? I'm a professional Courier."

Half an hour later, Jake and the wife stood in front of a huge gate leading into a sealed chamber as they knocked a few times. With the wife by Jake's side, the Blademaster soon noticed her and opened up. After a brief talk where Jake flashed his token and said he was working for the Founder, they had a second S-grade in the bag. Power-wise, he was somewhere between the Phoenix Queen and the Founder, so he was definitely a good addition.

When Jake asked if he knew where any of the other S-grades were, the Blademaster frowned. "The Phoenix Queen sure knows where the Nine Seals Demon is. Last time I checked, those two were an item."

For a moment, Jake considered whether this was yet another plot twist —whether the Phoenix Queen had actually been with the dragons all along, and that was why she had kept hidden that she knew where this Nine Seals Demon was. That didn't feel quite right, though, so he would have to confirm.

With the Blademaster recruited, the S-grade quickly helped Jake get back to a major city, where he promptly went to the Guild and reported his success. Meanwhile, the Blademaster and his wife headed toward the frontlines. In the Guild, the employee gave him a token from the Phoenix Queen.

Seeing no reason to delay, he headed to a nearby room and infused some energy into it.

The projection of the Phoenix Queen appeared in front of Jake a few seconds later and spoke in a grave tone, "I heard you found the Blademaster... Good. You have proven your skills are indeed worthy of respect, and if anyone can do this, you can. I did not hide the location of the Nine Seals Demon maliciously; I just had to make sure you were skilled enough to find her. While I do not know where the Nine Seals Demon is, I know a way to get her to come to us. She left the planet a long time ago, but before she left, she set up a trial to find any prospective students worth teaching, meaning it can only be entered by C-grades. Inside this trial, I also know, she placed a teleportation circle for her to return from borderline anywhere in the galaxy. Pass her trial and tell her we need help... and we need it fast. The location of the trial is already known by the Guild, so get it from them."

"I will head there straight away," Jake confirmed as he received yet another Special Courier Job.

"Good, but be warned: The Nine Seals Demon is a master of traps and formations, and her trial will be filled with them. I wish you luck for the sake of us all... This task will not be easy."

To make a long story short, Jake would put this "trial" at the difficulty level of a moderately hard Minaga's Endless Labyrinth Section. Far below the best Jake could do for sure, which made for an easy Special Courier Job.

At the end of the trial, Jake indeed found a large chamber with a massive teleportation circle in the middle, as well as an orb that one could infuse power into. Jake didn't really think much as he went and did just that. A projection appeared soon after.

A woman with red skin, barely wearing any clothes and covered in tattoo-like markings, soon stood before him. The Nine Seals Demon looked down at Jake for a moment. **"Ten thousand years, and someone has finally passed my trial... and it turns out to be a mid-tier C-grade. A bit unexpected, but not unwelcome. Now tell me, why did you pass my trial?"**

Oh, yeah—Jake had decided to display his actual level a while ago. He also didn't wear his mask anywhere, as he came to learn that it only had a detrimental effect when dealing with clients. Not that he could blame them.

"Greetings," Jake said, bowing. "I apologize, but I am not here for anything strictly to do with the trial. I am a Courier here to inform you that your homeworld is getting invaded, and I was tasked by the Phoenix Empress to contact you. She told me this place houses a teleportation circle to bring you back from wherever you are."

The Nine Seals Demon was quiet for a while before she sighed. **"Tell me... has the Phoenix Empress gone to the frontlines to fight?"**

"Yes," Jake quickly answered, getting an odd feeling from her question.

"I see," the Nine Seals Demon said, sounding a bit concerned. **"Very well. To activate the magic circle, take the crystals in the adjacent**

room and place them in the four focal points of the formation, and I shall return promptly to meet her."

Jake looked at the projection for a moment, then nodded. "Alright, but one question first... Since when did you side with the dragon tribe?"

The projection stopped and stared down at him. **"What do you mean?"**

"Yeah, that being your response pretty much confirms it." Jake shook his head. "Seriously... you didn't ask any questions, didn't ask me to elaborate about anything, and instantly asked about the frontlines despite knowing nothing of what's going on. That's suspicious as hell. If you didn't already know what was happening, that is."

Her projected image sighed and kept looking down at him. **"Too clever for your own good, huh? Tell me... if you are so clever, how much do you truly know about this entire conflict? Why there ever was a war, to begin with? You are on the wrong side of history. The planet you stand on was originally inhabited by the dragons and beasts. We who dare call ourselves enlightened arrived much later as nothing more than refugees, but the dragons took us in. Helped us rise to power... and once we did, we turned around and betrayed them. Killed their leader and forced them from their own home while rewriting history to make us look like the victims. All the dragon tribe is doing is setting things right, and—"**

"Ma'am, I don't care," Jake interrupted, truly not giving a shit. "Just here on a job, and seeing as you aren't an ally, I'll be taking my leave."

"And here I thought you would see sense... Very well. If that is your choice, so be it. But don't think for a second you are leaving here alive."

With those words, her projection exploded. Magic formations on the walls activated, and everything around him rumbled as a collapse became imminent. Seeing as he was over a hundred kilometers below the ground in a heavily fortified trial, this could definitely be a problem. What's more, in the distance, he heard several explosions as all the traps he had passed began going off, and from the sounds of it, these explosions were getting closer.

Bloody hell... Why can't this shit ever be easy? And I don't even get hazard pay.

CHAPTER 17

"WHAT A TWIST."

As the entire trial threatened to promptly come down on his head, Jake sighed. Usually, a collapsing cave wouldn't really be a problem, and it would, at most, annoyingly trap him for a while, but this place was a bit different. It was clearly rigged to explode and kill whoever was inside, and upon releasing a Pulse, Jake saw that the pathways he had taken to enter the chamber were rapidly collapsing. If he really hurried, there was a chance he could still make it out the way he came, though it would be far more dangerous than the way down there. Even then, it was a risk, and he predicted he would get trapped at quite a few points, requiring his fair share of digging.

He could do all that... or he could just go straight up and not waste any more time than he needed to. Summoning his wings, Jake rapidly infused energy into them before he had an enchanted rock fall on his head. A green mist began to emerge, which he then manipulated to slowly surround him. Jake's body soon enough began to turn a dark green color as he took a deep breath before activating the emergency escape ability of Wings of the Malefic Viper.

Shooting upwards, Jake had little control of his movements, so he just focused on going up. He felt himself pass through solid matter as if nothing could stop him. Even the enchantments placed on the chamber didn't manage to impede his ascent, as they were ultimately made to strengthen the material, not stop someone using a skill like Jake's to travel straight through.

As everything warped, Jake wasn't sure exactly where he would end up. After a few seconds more, Jake figured it was good enough. He deactivated the skill and appeared in the real world once more. Once his eyes and body refocused, he found himself standing in mid-air, above the clouds, with the ground far beneath him.

The wings on his back slowly withered away, and Jake felt the backlash. He could no longer activate the skill, and probably wouldn't be able to for a good while... at least a few days. Jake had purposefully not kept the skill going for longer than necessary to avoid the cooldown being too long, even if he could have continued for a good while.

"Well, the Nine Seals Demon was a dud," Jake said, sighing again.

He had honestly been lucky to discover she was a secret ally of the dragon tribe, because that had definitely been a risky gamble. Had Jake known for sure she was an ally of theirs? No, he'd just felt things were a bit off with her responses and lack of surprise when he'd mentioned the world getting invaded. Almost as if she had expected it to happen. Her concern had also felt completely fake.

When he'd then accused her of being an ally, her response had also seemed off. She had frozen and just looked at him before asking what he meant. Had she truly been an ally of the Founder who had fought the dragon tribe, wouldn't she have been extremely offended that some C-grade accused her of working with her hated enemy?

Nothing was definitive proof, but Jake had risked big and won. The fact she had crumbled so quickly and confessed everything had been very lucky for sure. As for her explanation about how the dragon tribe was actually the wronged party and the entire "you're actually working with the baddies" spiel... yeah, Jake honestly didn't care. He was the Chosen of an evil snake cult. If he cared about being associated with the "bad guys," he would have had a faction change a long time ago.

The conversation did bring up one more annoying question he had to ask himself, though... Was the Phoenix Queen an ally? The Founder had mentioned this Nine Seals Demon as an ally before, so there was a chance she had switched sides recently, and the Phoenix Queen had no idea. It could also be that the Phoenix Queen was also an enemy who would stab them in the back, which could be disastrous if the Founder trusted her. At this point, there was no way to determine her allegiance, and Jake had no idea how he would go about things.

Either way, shit was messy, and Jake was definitely not equipped to handle it. He considered what to do but ultimately decided to return to the Guild. Whenever in doubt, he returned to the core objective of this Challenge Dungeon: to complete Courier Jobs. So, if he could "trust" anyone, it had to be the Founder who'd made the Guild.

Luckily, the trial hadn't been that far from a major city, and a few hours of using One Step later, he was back in one. After a few more teleports, Jake arrived in the capital city of the Human Kingdom, where he headed to the Guild Hall to hopefully contact the Founder directly.

He ended up having to wait half an hour inside there before he could finally talk with the S-grade.

A projection appeared, and Jake saw the form of the Founder. He looked a bit worse for wear and was sitting with his legs crossed, likely also using this conversation to restore some energy. **"Courier, thank you for helping get the Blademaster here. I heard from the Phoenix Queen you went to recruit the Nine Seals Demon? Her abilities would be a great help in fortifying our defenses."**

"Yeah, about that... Turns out the Nine Seals Demon is on the side of the dragon tribe," Jake said with an apologetic look. "I luckily discovered this before summoning her here, so a crisis was temporarily averted."

"What?" the Founder asked, confused. **"Impossible... She was... No, I believe you; you have yet to lie to me. What exactly happened when you contacted her?"**

Jake explained everything about their conversation and how he'd had to escape the collapsing cave, sprinkling that in to make it clear she had tried to kill him, likely to bury what he knew. The Founder frowned even more deeply than before when Jake told him about her describing the dragon tribe as the planet's original inhabitants, and the enlightened races as nothing more than refugees who took over. His interpretation of history was a bit different, though.

"Refugees? While it is true some were, many were brought here by the dragons as slaves after their homeworlds were destroyed by the tribe. It was no rebellion toward a benevolent ruler, but a revolution against a tyrannical one that took place over centuries. We did also get some help from other enlightened who arrived, but to paint us as the aggressors and not us simply defending ourselves... Either the Nine Seals Demon has been utterly fooled, or she tried to fool you."

Jake wanted to tell him that he still didn't give a shit about the history of the world, and that he kind of assumed both of them were full of crap when it came to telling him what actually went down, but he held his tongue. Instead, he waited for the Founder to give him some time to think. As this happened, Jake also saw he had completed the Special Courier Job to find the Nine Seals Demon, so that was nice.

"You have once more done us a huge service. If the Nine Seals

Demon had been summoned to the planet and attacked from behind, dismantling our defenses, the consequences would have been disastrous. I also understand your concerns about the Phoenix Queen, and I will make sure to confirm if she is also a spy... but I doubt it. For now, do keep what happened with the Nine Seals Demon hidden, though. I will tell her if I believe that best while subtly investigating."

That was definitely a flag of some sort, and Jake quickly interjected. "I believe it would be best to tell her now. There is a good chance the Nine Seals Demon joins the invasion force at some point, and if the Phoenix Queen is actually on our side right now, the shock of seeing someone she was once close with may turn her to the side of the dragons. If, on the other hand, you discuss this with her first, she will not be shocked, and far more likely to refuse to listen to anything the Nine Seals Demon says."

It was pretty common knowledge that people were incredibly biased toward the first side of any story they heard. If the Phoenix Queen already had the interpretation that the Nine Seals Demon had either gone insane or been tricked, she was far less likely to be convinced. This all assumed she wasn't a traitor right now, of course.

"Hm, perhaps you are right," the Founder agreed. "Very well; I shall discuss it with her as soon as possible."

One potential disaster avoided there... or I accelerated her betrayal, Jake thought to himself. "How are things going at the frontlines? And is there anything more I can do to assist?"

"Our defenses are holding for now, but it is only a matter of time... The Blademaster has been a massive help and bought us a lot of extra leeway. However, nothing has truly changed. We need more allies... and..."

The Founder looked like he was hesitating a lot, unsure if he wanted to continue.

Jake felt like he had to press him. "Please, if there is any way, it is my responsibility to try and assist. So if there are any jobs, never hesitate to give them to me."

Still clearly unsure, the Founder considered for a bit before finally sighing. "Very well—you have yet to fail so far. There is one person you could approach, but it is no ally or old friend. What I am about to tell you is not something many know, and not even the Phoenix Queen is aware. Around twenty thousand years ago, I discovered an unknown aura. I noticed as the sole S-grade and went to investigate. It was another S-grade, and I foolishly got in a fight. I barely held on for a few minutes and nearly lost my life, but I was spared in the end. That is when I came to learn who I had been fighting... the brother of the Dragon King, who had been thrown out, as his mother was a human."

Yep, Jake had definitely unlocked some more hidden lore and a very special job. More special than the regular Special Courier Jobs.

"Back in the big war, he was not involved, as while he despised his brother, he still didn't want to kill his own kin. The reason I am hesitant to try and make contact is that, truthfully, I do not know what his intentions are now. I do not even know if he will side with us... or perhaps choose his own kin and be our end. All I know is that without him, our chances are slim, while with him on our side, our victory is assured. Of course, our destruction is also unquestionable if he joins the enemy side, but at this point, it is simply a risk we have to take."

"I understand," Jake said, nodding. "A huge risk with a potentially enormous reward. How am I to find this dragonkin?"

"Once more, I must be truthful... I am not entirely sure. All I know is that he is either on this planet or one of the inhabited moons. When it comes to his exact location, all I have is a runic horn he left me with when I encountered him back then. He claimed that the runes on it could be deciphered to find his exact location, but I never really even considered messing with it, as I feared he would know if I did, and admittedly, I fear this dragonkin. Now, my fear is no longer a consideration. Also, while I respect your skills, you won't be able to decipher it, as you are ultimately still only C-grade."

Jake felt a bit disrespected, but the Founder was probably right. Jake's chances of deciphering something made by an S-grade were borderline nonexistent, especially if he was on a bit of a timer.

"Instead, you must find experts capable of doing so. I have a few names in mind and shall include their locations when I transfer the Special Courier Job. Pick up the horn from my vault before you leave, and guard it with your life. Oh, and finally... due to the nature of the runes on the horn, it cannot be put in spatial storage, and with its draconic traits, I do not doubt for a second it will release an aura recognizable to dragons and their allies... so be careful as you travel, alright? There is a good chance the dragon tribe is also aware of their lost prince, so I doubt this will be a smooth journey. I would ask someone else to do it, but you are the only one I trust this task with. Now, hurry. I must go; time is not on our side... May you succeed and win us this war."

As the projection disappeared again, Jake got yet another Special Courier Job. At least, he thought it was just another Special Courier Job, but he was proven wrong as he read it.

Final Special Courier Job: While carrying the Horn of the Forsaken Dragonkin, seek out different experts capable of deciphering the runes on it. Once the runes are fully deciphered, meet the Lost Dragonkin and convince him to join the war against the dragon tribe. While carrying the horn, you will be repeatedly pursued by allies of the dragon tribe. This Special Courier Job must be completed before the frontline falls.

That's right—the final Special Courier Job of them all. Just one more left and Jake would be done... though he got the feeling this one wouldn't be all that easy or fast. Without hesitation, he went by the Founder's Vault. Using his legendary Medallion with the Final Special Courier Job inside, he unlocked it, finding only the horn within.

The horn was about the size of a goat's and slightly curved. It had a brownish color but was covered in golden runes all over. Picking it up, Jake tried to analyze the runes, but after just a brief scan, he shook his head. *Fuck... No, I can't solve that... Shit, I doubt even Arnold could.*

Using Identify on the horn, he quickly confirmed it was at least also the real item.

[Horn of the Forsaken Dragonkin (Legendary)] – The horn of the ousted son of the deceased Dragon King. This horn is covered in runes that must be deciphered in order to unlock its true function. Cannot be put in any kind of spatial storage. Gives off powerful draconic Records, making it an item easily tracked by the dragon tribe.

"Oh well," Jake muttered as he took the horn, and on the way out of the Guild Hall, he took a small over-the-shoulder bag to carry it in. It was a bit too big to eat, so this would at least make it not too annoying to carry around.

Checking the location of the first expert, Jake frowned a bit. Of fucking course they were located in the middle of nowhere. With no reason to delay, Jake hurried out of the Guild Hall and went on his way, not wasting any time to get this final job done. He just hoped that whatever the dragon tribe and their allies were cooking up wouldn't be too annoying.

———

Within a hidden mansion, ten figures sat. Nine of them were C-grade, all giving off auras of the late-tier, while the final one was a true A-grade powerhouse. They were positioned at a round table with a large crystal ball in the middle.

"The C-grade Courier is on the move," one of the C-grades, a human, said. "He has the horn."

These people were all of different races, each representing different countries on the planet, except for the A-grade, who showed strong draconic traits. Unsurprising, considering he was a dragon in human form.

With a large smile, the A-grade spoke, "Good... the royal prince was right. In their desperation, they will lead us straight to him. Now, we just need to capture this Courier, and victory shall be ours. My movements are sealed, but you all should be able to act freely, so this task falls to you. Mobilize your forces and track him down."

Waving his hand, the crystal ball began to glow. Nine smaller crystal balls emerged from it as the A-grade did his magic. "The horn is linked to the Dragon Prince, and using it, we shall track this Courier easily. These artifacts will all show you the location of... Wait a moment."

The A-grade frowned a bit as he cast his magic again. He tried two more times, then sneered and looked at the C-grade who had spoken earlier. "You said a C-grade had taken the horn from the vault!"

"He... He did," the human confirmed. "I have an insider in the Guild who confirmed it..."

"Well, then tell me, you bloody moron—why the hell is the tracking spell not working on the horn!? No... wait... Ah, I see. Clever of them." The A-grade nodded confidently. "There is no way a mere C-grade could hide both himself and the horn from me... which can only mean one thing. He is a decoy meant to throw us off while the real horn remains in the vault. That, or someone powerful enough to hide it from me has taken it for transport."

Everyone around the table nodded in recognition. "Truly a brilliant deduction," a beastfolk chimed in.

The dragon nodded, satisfied. "Seeing as he is nothing more than a decoy, don't bother with the Courier carrying the fake horn. If you have any agents that are in his path anyway, feel free to try and detain him and interrogate him for information, but there is a big chance that even he believes he is carrying the real horn, so I am not sure there is much to be gained."

Once more, everyone nodded at the brilliant analysis from their leader. Truly, he had seen through the ploys of the Founder and Guild.

———

Minaga just grinned as he looked at the Wyrmgod.

The Primordial didn't say anything, just watching the livestream quietly with a stoic expression on his face.

Vilastromoz also smiled to himself as he watched Jake running around, wondering why the hell no one was bothering him.

Minaga leaned slightly forward and looked at the Viper with the subtlety of a rampaging behemoth. "Psst... Did you know Jake actually does have the real horn, but due to his totally fair Divine skill, they falsely believe he doesn't?"

"Wow," the Viper responded with totally genuine shock. "What a twist."

CHAPTER 18

FORSAKEN DRAGONKIN

Maybe it was Jake's fault for expecting too much, but he had very much assumed he would meet some kind of opposition during his travels. He had set out to find people to decipher the runes, but on the way to the first one, he didn't get intercepted by a single enemy. Were there times when something looking like an ambush was hidden in the most obvious flight path? Yes, but Jake just easily avoided those or kept his stealth skill active to pass by unnoticed.

After his visit to the first rune-reading person, he was told that she alone couldn't decipher everything, but she managed to make some progress before sending him off to the next person with her notes. At this second person's place, he had a bit more deciphered, and at the third, a bit more than that.

Days turned to weeks, and soon Jake had spent over a month traveling between these rune decipherers. Each of them, for some fucking reason, liked to live in bum-fuck nowhere, meaning Jake had to travel a lot to get to them. With time, he did notice the search parties looking for him increasing, but with a mixture of Pulse of Perception, a legendary stealth skill, and probably also Shroud of the Primordial doing its stuff, Jake remained undisturbed for the most part.

It did annoy him that some of the rune decipherers were stereotypical shitty-quest NPCs that would only help Jake if he helped them first by doing some dumb side job, but Jake didn't really have a choice. In total, Jake spent nearly three months before he finally met the last rune decipherer. The old man looked at the notes made by the others who had looked at the horn, and after about an hour, he succeeded in solving the final rune.

Right as he did so, all the golden runes covering the horn gave off strong light as they warped and changed. Jake quickly reached out and took hold of the horn, and the moment he did, two things happened. First, he suddenly knew exactly where he could find the Forsaken Dragonkin... and second, a giant beam of light shot into the sky as the full aura of an S-grade dragonkin blasted out.

Jake was pushed back slightly as he watched the old decipherer fall to the ground, knocked out by the blast. This wave of aura spread further than Jake could see, and with how big it was, they could likely feel it all the way at the frontline far up in space. Quickly running outside, Jake stared up as the sky rumbled, and he didn't doubt for a second that many powerful beings were approaching. What's more, he got a feeling things had suddenly turned for the worse elsewhere, too, which was confirmed by his next notification.

Final Special Courier Job Updated: While carrying the Horn of the Forsaken Dragonkin, meet the Forsaken Dragonkin and convince him to join the war against the dragon tribe. While carrying the horn, you will be repeatedly pursued by allies of the dragon tribe, who are now aware of your location. The frontline is rapidly falling, and time is not on your side.

Yep... things were definitely a lot worse now than before, and Jake didn't delay for a second as he headed straight to the teleporter in the city. He was lucky that the horn had only given off that one giant blast of aura and didn't continue to emanate, but it had still pinged this location to every single person on the planet.

However, Jake soon met another problem... The second he activated the teleporter to a new city and went through to the other side, a whole new blast of aura shot out of the horn. Due to how many people were near the teleportation gate, Jake knocked out over ten thousand people with his first teleport alone.

Fucking hell, Jake cursed, but he didn't stop as he teleported three more times to get as close to his destination as possible. Tens of thousands, if not far more, were knocked out in Jake's wake as he sent off a sequence of pings to whoever was pursuing him, informing them of which direction he was heading.

When Jake had finished his final teleport, he stormed off immediately. His wings were naturally available once more after his prior use of the escape skill, and he quickly summoned them and used One Step for maximum speed. He rapidly got away from the city, found a quiet place, and went down to activate his stealth skill. With it active, Jake continued his journey, using Pulse of Perception every thirty seconds or so for the first period of travel despite the headache it induced, as he was feeling pretty damn paranoid.

And for good reason. Powerful beings were coming his way, and no longer limited to just C-grades, either. With the fall of the frontlines rapidly approaching, those on the planet who had been lying in wait were now moving far more openly. Through Pulse, he did spot some people also fighting against them, as the war had pretty much broken out everywhere, and shockwaves of energy from B-grades fighting could be felt in the distance.

Jake had to fly more carefully than ever as he slowly approached a mountain range in the middle of nowhere. There were no towns anywhere close to it, and he had to cross a desert-like plain with nothing living there just to reach it. Even the mountains were entirely bare rock, with not a single plant growing anywhere.

Yet the horn responded as he got closer and closer to his destination. When Jake entered the mountain range, yet another blast of aura was released, making Jake grit his teeth, as he knew everyone was coming his way now. Things were really out of hand, and before anyone had a chance to catch up, Jake reached a small cave at the foot of one of the mountains.

Entering, Jake walked through it for a while until he reached its end. There, he found a heavily enchanted stone gate with a slot in it that looked very similar to the horn he had been carrying around all this time. Briefly inspecting the cave walls and the gate, Jake quickly recognized everything here had been fortified to such a degree that he doubted even the Founder could break through with force. Taking out the horn, Jake slotted it in, and all the runes activated. Jake felt like he was on some treasure-hunting expedition as the golden runes spread to the rest of the door, which then slowly sank into the ground and allowed him passage.

Walking through the open gate, Jake entered a long, brick hallway where torches lit up on both sides. He had already scouted ahead and knew he was in the right place and that there were no traps, so after walking calmly for a few minutes, he reached a large chamber unimpeded.

There, right in the middle of the large chamber, was a single figure. The floor was covered in a large magic circle that seemed to be feeding this person power, and they didn't even react when Jake made his entrance. Yet

Jake felt the attention of this being upon him... and he knew it was the strongest creature he had met in this Challenge Dungeon so far, and not by a little. He didn't even dare use Identify, as he was pretty damn confident the being would be aware if he tried it.

Probably at the level of Viridia... and I heard she is close to the peak of S-grade...

"Greetings," Jake said with a polite bow as he stopped a good distance away, not entering the range of the magic circle.

The dragonkin slowly opened his eyes, and two red irises looked Jake up and down. "That horn... I had nearly forgotten I even gave it out. Tell me, what is a mere C-grade doing here, interrupting me? It wouldn't have anything to do with the little scuffle outside, now, would it?"

"You are correct." Jake nodded, seeing no need to hide anything. "The planet is facing a crisis, and I was tasked by the Guild Founder—the man to whom you gave the horn—to seek you out and request your assistance."

Right as Jake said this, a notification appeared in front of him. The Final Special Courier Job had changed once more.

Final Special Courier Job Updated: Successfully convince the Forsaken Dragonkin to assist you.

As Jake read the objective, he cursed internally. He had a bad feeling about this one.

"You are asking me to help the man who killed my father?" the Forsaken Dragonkin asked as he tilted his head. "What's more, he wants my help to kill my half-brother and other family members?" He flashed a toothy grin. "Now, why would I ever want to do that?"

Alright, it was clear the dragonkin already had full knowledge of what was going on, which did make his opening line kind of weird. However, it meant that simply explaining the situation in detail wouldn't get him on Jake's side, so he had to actually do some convincing. The problem with that was... Jake had no idea what to say. Doing all he could to not show his uncertainty, Jake simply nodded as he kept up his professional demeanor.

"Yes, that is exactly what the Founder and I are asking of you," Jake answered. He had to gamble on the Forsaken Dragonkin having a somewhat positive view of the Founder. If not, why had he left him alive back then and even given him a horn to find him with? It wouldn't make any sense if he actually gave a shit about his "family," so Jake would gamble on the Forsaken Dragonkin not liking them, considering them forsaking him and all. "As for why... I would ask why not. You are clearly no ally of the dragon tribe nor your so-called family."

The Forsaken Dragonkin looked at Jake with some amusement as he chuckled. "You're not wrong, but why would that make me want to help you? The dragon tribe doesn't matter to me much anymore. If I wish to see them wiped out, I may as well do so after they have exhausted some of their strength in this war. Wouldn't that be more efficient and just make more sense?"

As the dragonkin talked, Jake got more and more confused. *Why are we even having this conversation?*

It sounded like the dragonkin wanted Jake to convince him or something. Like he needed convincing. As an S-grade, why else would he bother talking to some random C-grade? If he had already made up his mind on not helping, he could just be doing this for his own amusement, but Jake really hoped a high-tier S-grade wasn't that bored. Plus, the Courier Job had to mean convincing him was possible somehow.

"If that is what you want, then surely no one could stop you," Jake answered. "But I would still try and do my utmost to convince you to assist us, so please, is there anything I can do to sway your mind? I am most certain the Guild Founder and all those who oppose the dragon tribe would be more than willing to compensate you in any way they can if you save them."

Hey, if Jake had no idea how to convince the guy, why not ask him how to? Who knows, maybe it could even work.

The Forsaken Dragonkin smiled and tilted his head before standing up. "Now that you mention it, there may just be one thing you could do to convince me." Without any warning, the dragonkin appeared beside Jake. "You know, I've been watching the happenings of this world for a while. Ever since my dear brother contacted me a few centuries ago and informed me of his return while asking for my help, I kept an eye on things. Considered if this world even stood a chance, and, if either side would rule, who I would be able to tolerate the most. I do not care about ruling anything... I am merely pursuing whatever lies beyond my current level of power. What comes after S-grade: the mythical realm of godhood."

"Understandable," Jake answered as the dragonkin stood beside him with an amused look.

"That is to say, I need whatever side wins to stay out of my way when I want them gone, and to support me when I want anything."

"As I mentioned, I am sure that can be arranged, and that the Guild Founder and all other factions would be more than willing to do whatever they can for the one who saved them. Even if that includes doing your every bidding until the day you ascend." Hey, no one said he couldn't make unrealistic promises as long as they beat the dragon tribe, right?

"Ah, but wouldn't the dragon tribe do the same? In fact, that is exactly what they offered already when I spoke to my dear brother. The thing is, my impression of them isn't the best, so if both sides are equally subservient, I see no reason not to side with this Guild Founder of yours and choose the side you represent."

Wait, things are actually going kind of well? Jake asked himself as he smiled and nodded.

"While I am unable to make any definitive promises on behalf of everyone, I can swear I will do my utmost to convince them to assist you in attempting to reach godhood, and with the authority and trust given to me by the Guild Founder, I am highly confident in my success." In fact, he felt like a deal was pretty much struck.

"Oh, I believe you," the Forsaken Dragonkin said as he stood right in front of Jake. "You have made quite the impact ever since you appeared out of nowhere in this world. You weeded out corruption, became chummy with the most powerful people, and rose to a position second only to the Guild Founder within his little Guild, as far as I can tell... Impressive for a C-grade. Almost too impressive."

"I am merely doing my best as a Courier and carrying out all jobs given as perfectly as I possibly can," Jake answered, hoping that being professional would be enough. Still, his bad gut feeling only kept getting worse.

"Now, that... that is where I begin to question things." The dragonkin smiled. "Why? Why are you carrying out these jobs as best as you can? Why are you seemingly so loyal to the Guild? Why do you risk your own life carrying out their bidding? To this point, I have yet to figure out what *you* get out of it. You are clearly competent, yet if I go purely by your actions, you seem like nothing but a thoughtless slave doing as his master wants."

Jake narrowed his eyes as he looked directly at the S-grade. "I have my own reasons for doing what I'm doing."

"I think this is the first time you've been wholly honest with me," the dragonkin said. "You just keep making me more and more curious. You stand before me now, yet I sense no fear. No reverence. Nothing. Are you truly only a C-grade?"

"Does it matter?" Jake questioned. "What would anything regarding me as a person matter when it comes to your choice of who to support?"

"Oh, it matters a lot. You have influence. Your voice matters, and as I said, I can't quite figure you out. There are few things I actively dislike, but at the top of that list is doubt... uncertainty. Elements I cannot, with confidence, control. You are an uncertainty, and I am not sure if I can control you... so I have an offer. A task you can do for me, and if you accomplish it, I will help the Guild Founder and his allies wipe out the dragon tribe for good."

Jake really didn't like where this was going. "What do you want?"

"It's simple... Prove to me your professionalism and dedication to your job as a Courier. Prove to me you will truly do everything in your power to carry out your duties."

The Forsaken Dragonkin looked entirely serious as his smile faded and he pulled out a dagger, pointing the handle toward Jake.

"Kill yourself."

CHAPTER 19

THE ART OF THE DEAL (AKA LYING)

J ake stared at the Forsaken Dragonkin, wanting more than anything to yell, "*What the fuck did you just say to me?*" but he managed to hold himself back. However, his face did reveal his distaste for the question, showing that he should have maybe worn his mask for this entire thing.

"Oh? Did the question offend you?" the dragonkin asked in an amused tone.

"I merely fail to see how my death would change anything," Jake answered.

"It would convince me to help. You don't need to know anything more than that. Now, why the hesitation? With every passing second, more people die, and the chance of the Guild Founder falling only increases. You can end it all by simply ending yourself... A small sacrifice, if I say so myself."

Jake's eyes narrowed as he seriously considered the proposition for a moment. Not because he actually considered doing it, but more to try and understand why it was even offered within this Challenge Dungeon.

One had to remember that Jake had three lives, so that could make one think that Jake killing himself would just be the smart thing to do. However, the rules of the Challenge Dungeon made things a bit messier. He remembered the text clearly:

Should you die, you will return back to where you originally accepted the most recent Courier Job. The Courier Job you died in the midst of will no longer be available. You have three total lives.

There were a few things here. It only said Courier Job in the description, not specifying anything about Special Courier Jobs. Jake had just assumed that since Courier Job was in both names, both counted. There was also the part about returning to where he'd accepted the Courier Job after failing it. Did this mean Jake was just teleported and revived there? Or did it turn back time to the moment he accepted the job? Jake once more assumed it meant turning back time, but he would fail in either case.

Unless... the Special Courier Job was completed *before* Jake was returned. In that case, what would happen? Would Jake just die and exit the Challenge Dungeon while also completing it at the same time? Would he see a nice epilogue slideshow as if he had just finished an RPG?

There were many interpretations, and there was even a chance that killing himself would actually lead to a "good" ending for the world. Of course, there was also the chance that it just fucked Jake over completely and sent him back without having done the Special Courier Job at all.

Finally, this could also simply be a test. The kind of thing where Jake would take the dagger, but just before he actually killed himself, the S-grade would stop him and say he had proven his determination simply by showing he was willing to do it.

Now, no matter the case, Jake's answer would still be a solid "fuck no."

It wasn't even a question of whether this would work to complete the Challenge Dungeon. The dragonkin had simply asked Jake to do something he wouldn't ever do. To kill himself would go as directly against his Path as anything could, and even if it probably wouldn't really matter, Jake didn't want Records of him choosing to kill himself like this associated with him.

Also, Jake didn't even think he could try to genuinely do it. Chances were the S-grade could detect if Jake was faking it, so the "he will stop me at the very last moment" option wasn't even valid. If it required Jake to truly be willing to kill himself, how was it different from actually killing himself? Truthfully, Jake simply valued his life too much to even fake it. He wouldn't even willingly kill himself to save all of Earth, so why the hell would he ever do it for some random world in a Challenge Dungeon?

Last but not least, this simply couldn't be the solution. To even get to this stage of the Challenge Dungeon, one had to be pretty damn good. One had to be a multiversally recognized talent, and someone often called a genius, and while Jake could see the logic in teaching these young geniuses how not to be assholes to others by using their status, he didn't see a world where the Wyrmgod thought teaching them to be doormats willing to kill themselves was a good idea.

"You are awfully quiet for someone on a timer," the dragonkin said, as Jake hadn't said anything for a while. "Are you truly in a position to be considering the offer that deeply? Why do you even need to consider it when I thought you were such a loyal and dedicated Courier, willing to do anything to get the job done?"

Jake clearly heard the mockery in the dragonkin's tone, making him lose his cool for a brief moment and reply with a snarky, "Oh, I'm sorry. I was thinking the joke had already run its course and was waiting for you to stop fucking around."

The Forsaken Dragonkin's smile only grew as Jake said this. "And there he is. The one hiding beneath the mask. Are you now going to tell me now what you really are and what you're doing here? Because I don't believe for a second you just appeared out of nowhere and suddenly found your passion by being a Courier."

"I think I already told you my matters are my own, but true, I'm not just doing this work out of the goodness of my heart," Jake said, having already decided.

Clearly, any typical strategies for convincing the dragonkin wouldn't work, so he tried to switch up the tactic a bit and act more like he usually did.

"But you do genuinely need my help," the Forsaken Dragonkin pointed out.

"Need your help? No, not really; it would just make things easier for me." Jake shrugged. "The people fighting up there do need you, though. If not, they're fucked for sure."

"And what would happen to you if they all die?"

"I would probably just leave," Jake said honestly. "No reason to stick around if everything is just a burning mess. But don't misunderstand—I do want to complete my current job, which is to have you help the Guild Founder and the others, so how do I make you do that? And no, I'm not fucking killing myself."

"I see... So, what if I just kill you instead?" the Forsaken Dragonkin asked as his aura was released. It pressed down on Jake with actual energy, making his knees slightly buckle, but Jake quickly responded by infusing stable arcane energy into them... meaning that rather than bend, they would get squashed like they were under a hydraulic press if the pressure got high enough.

"That would also be highly annoying," Jake said as his lips tore just from moving while under the pressure.

"Annoying? What an insignificant word to describe the end of your

Path." The Forsaken Dragonkin scoffed as he kept up the pressure. "You're telling me you won't kill yourself, but dying to me barely matters?"

"You can't kill me... At least, not for good..." Jake kept staring the dragonkin in the eyes despite his own body repeatedly taking damage.

The Forsaken Dragonkin tilted his head, and the pressure severely lessened. "Now you got me curious. I don't need a lie-detector skill to know you truly believe that... What gives you such confidence?"

"Tell you what..." Jake said as he popped both his shoulders back in place, undoing the aura's dislocation. "I'll tell you after you've dealt with that dragon tribe."

"Heh..." The dragonkin shook his head. "I may be curious, but at this point, I am inclined to believe you are just insane rather than there being any actual reason."

"Fair, fair," Jake said, nodding as he took out and drank a health potion. "But isn't it worth the gamble? From how I see it, you have four choices: You wipe out the dragons and side with the Guild Founder, you help the dragon tribe and kill the Founder, you wait for both to fight it out and swoop in to beat down the winner and have them serve you—the winning side very likely being the dragon tribe—or... fourth, you just kill all of them and don't bother with any factions."

The dragonkin kept looking at Jake as if he were some interesting specimen, and he seemed more and more amused. "And now you talk about wiping out everyone with such casualness..."

Jake shrugged, partly to roll his shoulders and make sure they were correctly popped into place, and partly to, well, shrug. "Not my first time seeing a world be destroyed. But I can't recommend it unless you really hate everyone here."

"If your goal is to intrigue me more, you are doing a good job," the Forsaken Dragonkin said with interest. "I already had the belief you didn't originally come from this planet or even any of the nearby solar systems, and seeing as I believe you have seen the fall of a world and that I am aware of any planets falling nearby, that only enforces it. So, where do you actually come from?"

"If I told you, it would stop being such an intriguing mystery, now, wouldn't it?" Jake answered with a smile.

"Alright... then how about this. Have you ever met a god before?"

Jake raised an eyebrow, somewhat surprised by that question—in part because it felt like people with connections to gods would have an advantage with this one. Alas, Jake saw no reason not to tell the truth. "Obviously."

"So a god sent you here?"

"In a roundabout way, you can say that." Jake nodded. "Now, not going to answer more, but I am kind of getting a feeling regarding what you wanna ask about... You want to know how to achieve godhood, don't you?"

"We all do, don't we?" The Forsaken Dragonkin asked without an ounce of seriousness, shrugging. "Why? Got any tips or tricks?"

"No, of course not," Jake said with a deadpan expression. "But I may be able to help you... after you help me."

"And how exactly will you help me?" the dragonkin said, looking even more amused than before, and from the look in his eyes, Jake knew the path he was going down was correct... because he saw a small smidgen of hope.

"I cannot tell you directly how... but I can show you instead," Jake said as he took a deep breath. "Please stand back a bit; this isn't something I can easily do."

The thing Jake was about to do had come to him as they spoke, and in all honesty, it was a huge gamble. Even if things seemed to be going well, Jake had the feeling the dragonkin still wasn't going to actually help him. He was beginning to realize he truly didn't care what happened, and Jake's guess that he was just fucking around in this conversation was actually mostly correct.

Would he have still helped if Jake had killed himself? Maybe, maybe not. Again, it didn't matter, as Jake firmly believed it hadn't been a real choice unless one was maybe on their last life or something. So Jake had cooked up this little ploy instead. He would, for a moment, convince the dragonkin in front of him that he was actually the avatar of a god, just long enough to get him to help Jake. *Genuinely* help Jake.

The Courier Job involved convincing the Forsaken Dragonkin. Jake believed there probably were things you could say to make him side with you, and maybe someone like Miranda could have done it by offering him things or making good arguments about why assisting the Founder would be wisest... but Jake wasn't able to do that. He had kind of tried but failed badly. So, he would just go with something only he was capable of by lying and deceiving using his special abilities.

"Alright, I'll bite," the dragonkin said as he raised both hands and backed away a bit. "But let's make this your last chance. If you fail to be convincing, I'll kindly throw you out of here... because, honestly... that fourth option of wiping out everyone does actually sound quite appealing."

Jake didn't say anything, as the words of the dragonkin pretty much served as confirmation. That had probably been his plan all along. To have the two sides fight it out, and then, rather than make the winners his servants, just kill them all. It made sense... He was Forsaken, after all. He hadn't bothered making anyone his servants before now, despite being capable of all this, so why would he even bother now? Plus, the dragon tribe had clearly betrayed him and thrown him out, while the human side, even if they served him for a while, would all despise him simply for his heritage. Simply put, he had no love for either side, but Jake still believed he could be convinced to at least tolerate the enlightened races.

Sitting down, Jake crossed his legs and took a deep breath, and the S-grade observed him with interest. Entering Soul Meditation, Jake dove into his Soulspace. There, he saw the shadowy figure that looked a bit like himself representing Eternal Shadow, some other collections of energy here and there and a shitload of arcane energy covering the skies.

However, right in the middle of the world floated a small, black object. A single droplet of dark blood. Jake approached this blood drop, sensing the intense aura of the Malefic Viper it emanated. This was the blood Jake had absorbed all the way back in the Trial of Myriad Poisons just following the tutorial. It wasn't just regular blood, either, but blood containing Records and energy from the Malefic Viper. A fragment of his power.

Jake hadn't really messed with it much, even if he did study it when using Sagacity of the Malefic Viper. It was still filled with knowledge for him to unlock, but forcibly doing anything with it simply wasn't possible. The only reason it was even dormant and didn't kill him outright despite being inside of him was his Bloodline's suppression ability—and the Viper never actively trying to take it back.

Over time, Jake had crafted many theories as to how he might use this small droplet but never dared to test them. Jake had no idea what messing with it could even help him with, so there had been little reason to try before. He was already slowly absorbing it, and with time, he would make all the Records inside truly his, so trying to mess with it directly was high-risk, borderline zero reward.

Now, things were different, so Jake was going to try one of the things he had theorized was maybe possible. Something that, even if possible for him to do, would be utterly useless outside of this particular Challenge Dungeon. Besides, with it being a Challenge Dungeon, even if Jake messed up, he wouldn't actually die.

Approaching the drop of blood, Jake carefully reached out and stopped just before touching it. Controlling himself as best he could, Jake lessened the suppression of the drop ever so slightly. It passively began to fight back, and its Records began to run rampant, not unlike the time he had absorbed all the cursed energy from the Root of Eternal Resentment.

A dark green aura spread from the drop of blood as it mixed with Jake's Bloodline, and with full focus, he projected it outwards. At the same time, he released his Bloodline aura fully and opened his eyes out in the real world.

His aura exploded with the presence of his Bloodline as it blanketed the entire room. However, his presence was different than usual, faintly infused with that of the Malefic Viper's from the drop of blood, giving it a mildly divine quality.

For the very first time, the Forsaken Dragonkin looked at Jake with genuine shock. Jake saw his legs slightly shake from the mixed presence, but before anything more happened, Jake had to pull it all back and fully suppress the drop of blood once more. As everything returned to normal, Jake coughed. Blood filled his glove, and he made damn sure the dragonkin saw it.

"What was..." the dragonkin muttered.

"A preview," Jake said as he wiped the blood away and looked at the dragonkin.

"A preview of what exactly?" the Forsaken Dragonkin said with intense interest.

Jake just smiled. "Godhood. And if you want to learn more... you know what to do. Help me to succeed in my task, and I'll be sure to help you afterward."

The Forsaken Dragonkin looked at Jake for a moment. Jake knew he had deployed plenty of magic to see if he was telling the truth. Perhaps he detected some of Jake's words were half-truths, but he had never really outright lied, so in the end, the dragonkin simply nodded.

"Very well... you have a deal."

Final Special Courier Job Updated: Await the outcome of the war.

"Pleasure doing business," Jake said, smiling. "You can find me back here when you return."

"I'll make sure of it," the dragonkin said as he teleported to the entrance of the hall, and as he did, Jake felt the entire place seal off.

Jake just shook his head and released a Pulse of Perception. He saw that outside of the mountain he was in, hordes of people had gathered, ready to strike at any moment. With a second Pulse, he saw the Forsaken

Dragonkin appear in the air outside. The third showed not one of his pursuers left alive, with only wayward ashes falling.

Pretty scary.

Leaning back, Jake lay down, put his hands behind his head, and looked toward the ceiling of the cave. Now, all he had to do was wait for the outcome of the war, just as the quest said. As he was lying there, Jake felt pretty satisfied. He had pulled off the damn bluff of a century.

Jake had initially considered trying to bluff using his Bloodline alone, but he knew that wouldn't have worked. The dragonkin knew about him, and nothing Jake did would make sense if he was actually some godlike being already. Sure, there was a minuscule chance Jake was just some immortal monster playing a delivery man with self-imposed rules for fun, but Jake wouldn't bet on the dragonkin reaching that conclusion.

However, by mixing in the aura from the drop of blood, Jake had changed his presence slightly, and the divine quality it added was unquestionable. He knew any S-grade could sense it, as well as the sheer difference in grade between that energy and their own. Plus, the aura of the Viper clearly wasn't the same as Jake's, communicating that there indeed was some god backing him.

Now, one may ask why Jake had never tried this kind of bluff before, and the reason was pretty obvious... This shit would only work on anyone who had never actually met a god before, much less the Malefic Viper. If Jake tried to blast the aura from the blood in the wider multiverse, it would easily be detected as "off," and Jake would get bitch-slapped for trying to fake it, while probably catching a heresy charge on top.

Plus... why the hell would Jake need to do this kind of bluff when he had a True Blessing to blast people with if he wanted to intimidate them using his connection to the Malefic Viper? It wasn't like blasting the aura from a fragment of Records from the Viper made Jake's connection to the Primordial any less recognizable.

No, the only reason it had worked here was because of the rules of the Challenge Dungeon. Jake had effectively found a way to still flaunt his Blessing despite being unable to, which felt pretty damn good. Now, he just had one minor problem.

I hope I don't actually have to give that dragonkin tips on how to become a god...

CHAPTER 20

THE TRUE PATH TO GODHOOD

The gods watched the screen as Jake just relaxed on the floor while yawning lazily. In space, the Forsaken Dragonkin was rampaging, truly motivated by a promise of a potential Path to godhood. No one in the room really said anything, simply observing events unfold until, finally, Minaga chimed up.

"So... another note in the development log?"

"Yes," the Wyrmgod responded flatly.

"Alrighty then." Minaga smiled, clearly not upset with the situation. Looking at Vilastromoz, he couldn't help but give a big thumbs-up.

"I fail to understand... How did your Chosen even do that?" the Blightfather questioned the Viper after a bit. The Wyrmgod had shown the screen to everyone in the inner circle—the Primordials, Nature's Attendant, and Artemis—so he was fully aware of the shenanigans Jake had been up to. This was naturally with the Viper's permission, as he found their reactions very amusing, and what was better than bragging to old acquaintances?

"Do what?" the Viper asked, feigning confusion.

"Project your aura... or at least a cheap imitation of it."

"Oh, that... Yeah, Jake ate a drop of my blood infused with my Records and power a while back and has thus far not volunteered to give it back," Vilastromoz answered nonchalantly.

There were a few raised eyebrows around the room as the Holy Mother also joined the conversation for once. "Impressive. To be able to handle such Records without seeing his own Path broken is not something you see often, and it truly shows his dedication. It isn't something I would expect many mortals to be capable of, much less a C-grade."

"C-grade? No, he ate it in E-grade, and my guy didn't even ask." The Viper sighed as he shook his head.

Eyebrows raised even higher than before at the revelation. The only one that seemed entirely undisturbed was Valdemar. Unsurprising. He and Jake had many similarities in this regard, as Valdemar had also been known for eating stuff he really shouldn't be capable of while he was still a mortal. Even now, as a god, he would just casually gobble down natural treasures other Primordials were wary of.

"In any case, Jake did pretty damn well," Minaga said, carrying along the conversation. "He even gave us so much good feedback on the Challenge Dungeon, outlining many things to address for the next era. Of course, I wouldn't really expect many others to be capable of most of the stuff he pulled off, but there were some good data points anyway."

Minaga was in a great mood, and the Viper couldn't help but take a jab. "Feels good to see another Challenge Dungeon be utterly exploited after your labyrinth, eh?"

"I have no idea what you are talking about, and such accusations are utterly unfounded and unwelcome," Minaga said, trying to shut him down with a deadpan face. "Minaga's Endless Labyrinth is a marvel of dungeon engineering that is perfectly balanced with no exploits."

"Right, right." The Viper nodded and kept smiling.

"You speak as if the Endless Journey Challenge Dungeon was an utter mess, but I believe its self-correcting mechanisms did well," the Wyrmgod said after a while. "The Viper's Chosen also adequately adapted to the situations he was in, and even if he had unique advantages, he also faced some extra challenges due to them. Ones he overcame, mostly due to these same unique advantages, true, but if one can say one thing, it is that he is good at exploiting said advantages."

"There were a lot of problems, though," Minaga pointed out. "Admit it—this entire Challenge Dungeon was a bit of a mess and not the most successful launch."

"Some would argue that nothing truly scenario-breaking happened, and the overall performance was fully acceptable. A few individuals being able to exploit a Challenge Dungeon does not make the entire project a failure. If it did, we would have had to decommission your labyrinth many eras ago." The Wyrmgod said all of this in his usual dry tone as he verbally murdered Minaga.

"No need to bully the poor Unique Lifeform," the Viper said, shaking his head. "But hearing you talk about how it isn't a total failure... I wonder, how are Jake's team members doing in this Challenge Dungeon? Or if they've already completed it, how did they do?"

The Wyrmgod briefly threw a glance at Nature's Attendant, and after the god nodded, the Wyrmgod turned back to the Viper. "Three of them have already completed it, with only the Unique Lifeform yet to be done. As for how they all did or are doing... see for yourself."

With a wave of his hand, the Primordial summoned four new screens. Each showed one of Jake's party members inside the Endless Journey in a highly sped-up fashion, presenting their entire runs in mere seconds in Realtime, which was more than slow enough for the gods there.

Now, let's see how they did, the Viper thought as he looked at the four screens one by one.

———

The first screen showed the Sword Saint standing on a podium in what looked like a conference hall, talking to the many figures present. Among them were dragons in human form, the Founder, and a few other S-grades, including beings Jake had never encountered or even knew existed. This was clearly the end of his run, and the mere fact he had gathered all these individuals was impressive in its own right.

After days of debate and division of land, an accord had been struck, and peace—at least temporarily—had been established. A clear political victory, achieved in an entirely intended way by a man who had been ruling a massive clan and navigated politics for close to a century before the system.

Even if the swordsman had repeatedly said he wanted to distance himself from politics and focus on his Path of swordsmanship, that didn't mean he had to throw away the political abilities he already had. Skills that were borderline second to none.

Needless to say, the Sword Saint's performance was considered exemplary. He ended his Endless Journey run with a Legendary Medallion, still a good distance away from getting a mythical one. Perhaps he could have done slightly better if he had not lost two lives trying to set up this political meeting, and if he hadn't had to make as many concessions in the final negotiations as he did.

———

On a second screen, Sylphie chased around an entitled customer while pecking him on the head until guards came to arrest her. She then proceeded to peck them, too, until more powerful people came, and she had to run away and flee from the very first starting city in the Phoenix Wing Empire.

Her first Endless Journey Challenge Dungeon life ended with her getting fired as a Courier on her second job with a lengthy criminal record —something she didn't like, which got her killed after she tried to fight an entire city's worth of guards.

With her second life, she managed to do a bit better but still got mad when a woman tried to scam her, making her retaliate by having a tornado rip a small village to pieces. In the Courier World, this was considered bad business, and Sylphie failed her job. This, she did not like, and she raised a ruckus in the Guild and ended up getting chased away from the city again. Having decided to just explore a bit, Sylphie eventually ended up in a too-dangerous area while searching for something tasty to eat, which got her killed.

After these two deaths, she got a tad more serious and even did a number of jobs, but she barely did one a week, mostly just getting bored and flying around. Until she got a Special Courier Job, that is, which ended up getting her in contact with the son of the Infernal Baron. The difference here was that this man didn't want to recruit Sylphie; he had detected her elemental heritage and thus wanted to consume her. This was how Sylphie ended up joining what Jake had called PETE, and Sylphie ultimately ended her Endless Journey by taking down the Duke of Flames in a political act of mutual destruction that also got the hawk burned to a crisp.

Sylphie's overall performance in this entire Challenge Dungeon was pretty damn substandard for what one would expect of a "genius." Sylphie was happy enough, though, as she did manage to scam some natural treasures out of PETE before she left. She ended up with only a Rare Medallion despite having spent quite a while in the dungeon, mainly just messing around.

———

A third screen showed Dina walking through vast grasslands, the plants swaying with her steps. The entire land was alive, pulsing with power, reaching the very peak of S-grade as the living planet allowed her presence. All across the massive planet, portals had opened for the arriving enlightened races, the Guild Founder and many others among them as they prepared to establish themselves anew, knowing they could not meet the dragon tribe in combat without facing total destruction.

Things had been especially bleak after the Nine Seals Demon returned and managed to get the Forsaken Dragonkin on their side with promises of a place in the universe that could give him the final push to godhood. Luckily for them all, Dina had managed to work with a seed sent out from this new planet that had landed on the main Courier World one and made a deal, relying on her Bloodline.

Her Endless Journey had been far from a conventional one, as she had relied on her Bloodline perhaps more than Jake and used plenty of summons to carry out tasks. Annoying customers and those trying to scam her had also been easily dealt with, mainly through a few compliance-enhancing spores in the air.

As for the larger political issues she faced... well, all the conversations she'd had with the Sword Saint about the art of leadership had really come in handy there. This all led to an ultimately great performance, even if she did make a lot of mistakes, netting her an Ancient Medallion, just shy of a legendary one.

———

On the fourth and final of these new screens, the Fallen King was still doing the Challenge Dungeon, as he had done the same as Jake and saved this one for last. He had struggled a bit with being treated like a mere Courier in the early parts, but he had quickly suppressed his own pride to simply follow the objective and focus on getting a good reward.

Using his soul magic, he did better than most would expect from someone who rarely had to use words to get their way. Also, while it was a skill he rarely used, being able to detect lies from those a lot weaker than him was no difficult feat, and liars and scammers utterly failed to get one over him. When it came to the Special Courier Jobs, he also performed great. In fact, he even had many advantages, as he managed to leverage his identity as a system-recognized king to get his way in certain situations. One had to remember that while Jake was also a noble, he didn't really integrate this fact into his Path, nor did he openly project his nobility rank.

The Fallen King, on the other hand, did this openly, acting as if he were some high-level diplomat working for another massive faction far away. This did seem to get the job done for the most part, as he progressed steadily and kept everyone on their toes while making them hesitant to make aggressive moves toward him. This status as a king would also have its very own note in the Endless Journey Exploits Log, but ultimately deemed a non-issue, as C-grades with the system-recognized title of king wasn't really a thing, and making changes just to address the uniqueness of a Unique Lifeform wasn't worth it in any way.

One big weakness the Fallen King did have in this Challenge Dungeon was his lack of speed when delivering goods during the regular Courier Jobs, and while he did alleviate this a bit through different means, this was ultimately still his big limiter as he continued his Endless Journey. However, even with this, his final result should be more than acceptable.

————

In the final Challenge Dungeon the gods observed, Jake soon enough had visitors. The Forsaken Dragonkin was returning, but he was not alone. With him were several others, including the Guild Founder, the Phoenix Queen, and even the Nine Seals Demon, who looked a bit worse for wear while leaning on the Phoenix Queen.

Jake stood up as these figures approached the chamber. When the barrier sealing him in naturally faded, Jake stepped forward and saw the S-grades. "I take it matters have been settled?"

"They have," the Guild Founder said with an exhausted but happy smile. "It will take a long time to rebuild... but with the dragon tribe no longer lurking as a threat, I have hope our future will be a bright one... Now, let us return to the Human Capital. While there are many losses to mourn, there is also your unquestionable achievement to celebrate, and—
"

"Before any of that... you have a promise to keep," the Forsaken Dragonkin interrupted as he looked at Jake with narrowed eyes. "Or did things change?"

The Forsaken Dragonkin did not hold back as he used a skill to make completely sure Jake was telling the truth. It was certain that should he try and bullshit his way out or lie, the situation would not turn out well, especially considering Jake had yet to be told he could leave the Challenge Dungeon. So he did the only thing he could... and told the truth.

"I am still a bit spent from the preview I gave you earlier," Jake said with full honesty. "But I swear to you that I will share with you the true Path to godhood soon. The method every single one of the dozens of gods I am aware of have in common."

Jake had had some time to think as he was waiting, and he had gone over what all these gods had in common. He had considered their Paths and what they had done to reach godhood, and he'd realized one universal truth about them all that he would share with the Forsaken Dragonkin when he was ready.

There were some amusing reactions from the Guild Founder and other S-grades when Jake mentioned gods, but none of them said anything. The Forsaken Dragonkin had looked skeptical, but at Jake's reassurance, he simply nodded. He did seem like he planned on staying close to Jake for the time being, though.

"In that case... let us return and celebrate as the Courier recovers," the Guild Founder said, and together they all departed back toward the city.

Once there, they held a nice celebration and ceremony. The deaths of those who'd fought were honored, the Forsaken Dragonkin was called a hero that all of the nations would support, and the fighters who'd stood their ground were rewarded. However, despite all the S-grades, Jake was the main character being celebrated in a big ceremony put on by the Guild Founder.

Jake was praised, and in the end, the Guild Founder decided to do something unprecedented, crowning the first-ever Mythical Courier. Throughout this all, Jake just smiled and waved, seriously hoping the system message would appear before he had to fulfill his promise to the Forsaken Dragonkin... Luckily, it did so as soon as Jake had his Medallion upgraded and officially got his final promotion.

Congratulations! You have completed the Endless Journey Challenge Dungeon!
You have risen to an otherwise unknown realm of Mythical Courier. A Courier rank that only you possess, granted to someone recognized by all in the land. As a Mythical Courier, you can choose to stay in the Endless Journey and continue completing regular Courier Jobs, or you can choose to retire and end your journey for good.
Exit the Endless Journey?

Seeing this message, Jake smiled... but he still had one more thing to do. After the ceremony was over, Jake and the Forsaken Dragonkin went to a chamber by themselves, as it was time for Jake to teach the S-grade how to become a god. He wouldn't be bullshitting, either, because he had truly figured it out.

"You should be fully aware of what will happen if you have attempted to fool me," the Forsaken Dragonkin said as Jake took a seat across from him.

"I know, so I'm not going to bullshit you," Jake said as he took a deep breath. "Do you know what godhood is?"

"Surprise me," the dragonkin said with narrowed eyes.

"While you may see godhood as your ultimate goal, in reality, it is just another step on your Endless Path. It's the hardest one by far, but far from the end. From what I've heard, some call it the moment you truly realize your Path and 'prove' it, so to say, but in the end, it all boils down to simply staying true to yourself and dedicated to your Path."

He spoke only truths, and the Forsaken Dragonkin seemed more receptive than before. "But the question is how...What tangible methods can one deploy to reach godhood?"

Jake took another deep breath as he looked upwards. "The how... is simpler than you think. From all the gods I have observed, and how they followed their Paths, I realized they all did one thing that those who failed to reach godhood didn't."

"What is it? What do I need to do?"

With a serious look on his face, Jake quickly prepared himself to leave the dungeon.

"Get good."

CHAPTER 21

THE ALL-STARS OF THE CHALLENGE DUNGEONS

J ake had never wanted to leave a dungeon more. He promptly exited the Endless Journey before the Forsaken Dragonkin could properly understand what he had just said. He kind of snickered to himself as the chamber was replaced by a white void similar to the ones he had seen before fully leaving other Challenge Dungeons.

Speaking of the Challenge Dungeon... Jake had done pretty well, hadn't he? While doing the Endless Journey, Jake had honestly had a hard time getting a feeling for his level of performance, but considering he'd gotten a Mythical Medallion and even done so without losing a single one of his three lives, he had to have done pretty damn well. He wouldn't say it was at the "impossible" tier, though... which was why he was honestly a bit surprised when he read the Grand Achievement.

Grand Achievement earned: Successfully completed the Endless Journey while proving yourself a truly Mythical Courier. With minimal errors during Courier Jobs, a persistently near-perfect performance, and fast deliveries, your performance as a normal Courier was unquestionable. During Special Courier Jobs, you showed great skill to get yourself out of perilous situations, and with the aid of your vastly overqualified stealth abilities, you managed to operate nearly unimpeded during all your jobs. Your Journey may not have been Endless, but it seems your talent is.
100,509 Nevermore Points earned. Due to earning a Grand Achievement, you will receive a 25% multiplier to all Nevermore Points at the final calculation.

Jake smiled a bit as he read the description... and for some bloody reason, it finally now clicked why the Endless Journey had seemed to be "off" and easier than it probably should have been. It mentioned his stealth skills were vastly overqualified, and while his Unseen Hunter was a great skill, he wouldn't say it made him overqualified... but Shroud of the Primordial sure did.

It explained a lot. Jake had only gotten attacked when he went straight into an ambush or approached enemies by himself. No one ever tracked him down and attacked despite several Courier Jobs saying he would be hunted. So, it seemed like the skill had been far more of a cheat than Jake already knew, and coupled with the cheats Jake used knowingly, he could see how he had gotten the 25% bonus. It was just on the margins, though, if his theory about needing at least 100,000 Nevermore Points was true.

Jake wasn't going to feel bad about "cheating," though. Everyone who was talented was a bit of a cheat in their own right. His own party made that clear enough, as it contained another Bloodline, a Transcendent, a weird borderline-never-seen-before hawk-elemental hybrid, and finally, a Unique Lifeform, who were literally born cheaters.

What especially didn't make him feel bad about cheating was the reward he got from it... because he had succeeded. Even before seeing all his system notifications, he'd felt in his body he had succeeded and, more importantly, that his little theory had been right.

Back when Jake cleared his first Nevermore Challenge Dungeon and gained the 25% multiplier, it had come with a title reward. It was the only title he had gained from any of the Challenge Dungeons, as the title specified he could only have one at a time. The title itself had been good but not overly exciting.

Colosseum of Mortals: True Grand Champion – You have proven yourself the one true Grand Champion of the Colosseum of Mortals, defeating beings that stand at the apex of the multiverse, and exited the Colosseum of Mortals with more than 10,000,000 Colosseum Points. Even a Primordial was slain on your path, making you truly worthy of the title. Only one Nevermore Challenge Dungeon title can be held at a time. +200 to all stats.

Jake had theorized that there was more to it, though. He believed that if one did *really* well, there would be some kind of meta-achievement for doing so in all Challenge Dungeons. And, as always, his intuition that was the case proved true.

Reward gained: Nevermore All-Star Challenger Title.

Being right felt awesome, especially when being right also meant you got an even more awesome title.

Nevermore All-Star Challenger – You have proven that you stand at the apex of not one, but multiple disciplines. Achieve at least a 100% Nevermore Points multiplier through Grand Achievements from the five Challenge Dungeons available in the C-grade version of Nevermore. This must be done while actively competing on the Nevermore Leaderboards. Only one Nevermore Challenge Dungeon title can be held at a time. +300 to all stats. +5% to all stats.

Comparing this title to the one just giving +200 to all stats wasn't even fair. It now being +300 to all stats was nice for sure, and for someone like Jake, it was a few full levels' worth of stats, but the 5% was where the real meat was at. Percentage titles weren't easy to get and were considered pretty rare—even if Jake had his fair share already. Their impact throughout one's entire Path simply made them invaluable, as they would give massive benefits even when one reached S-grade... potentially even in godhood.

One also had to remember one more thing... Jake was kind of double-dipping with this title. He had gained a title for getting a big multiplier that could likely help him get yet another title once Nevermore was over. He at least expected there to be another title, as that only made sense... The big question was whether there was potentially more than one. Oh, well. He would find out eventually.

Taking stock of his Nevermore Points multiplier, Jake smiled. He had gained 5% twice—once from the Dark Witch, and another time during the climb—along with the 25% from Minaga's Labyrinth. Adding that to the current 105% from the Challenge Dungeons, Jake was sitting on a comfortable 140% Nevermore Points multiplier. And it wasn't as if he didn't have a lot of those.

Nevermore Points: 1,242,425

With the multiplier, Jake had just shy of three million. For now, that is. There was still time to clear some more floors, and who knows, maybe he could even reach above four million total points if things went well.

As he had completed a Challenge Dungeon, Jake naturally also gained one more thing: his item reward. He hadn't really considered what he would get, as most of the rewards so far had been kind of novel or things that were only really useful circumstantially. So, with little expectations, he checked out the reward... which turned out to be a bit of a mistake.

What appeared before him was an odd, sculpture-looking thing. It looked a bit like a crystalized splashing wave or something, but from it, Jake felt an intense aura... and when he saw the name in the system notification, his eyes opened wide. They opened even wider when he used Identify.

[Wyrm's Breath of Akashic Awakening (Mythical)] – Infuse a piece of equipment with additional Records while also attempting to awaken or amplify existing Records within, upgrading the item to a maximum of mythical rarity. If the item is already at mythical rarity, all existing Records will still be empowered. Contains faint Records related to the Wyrmgod of Nevermore, making this item especially suited to upgrading items related to the space affinity. WARNING: Touching directly upon the Records of an item may make others related to the associated Records aware. Additionally, some items do not have enough innate Records to amplify or awaken, lessening the effect significantly.
Requirements: C-grade. Soulbound.

Sometimes, you go in with zero expectations and end up incredibly pleasantly surprised. This was one of those moments. Jake hadn't given much thought to what this Challenge Dungeon might offer as a reward, so that only made the surprise even better.

When it came to the Wyrm's Breath, Jake recalled an item he had bought a long time ago, all the way back in E-grade: the Token of Akashic Awakening he'd purchased during his first meeting with Sultan, which could upgrade an item to epic rarity. Needless to say, this one was far, far more valuable. Epic items were a dime a dozen, while mythical equipment was incredibly rare. Something that could potentially upgrade a piece of equipment to mythical rarity even more so.

Jake had used the first Token of Akashic Awakening on his Boots of the Wandering Alchemist, and looking at the description of this item—especially the part about the item he wanted to upgrade needing good enough innate Records—Jake had a feeling he would use it once more on the boots. Jake had already upgraded them two times, most recently at the beginning of C-grade when he made them ancient rarity, but he felt pretty damn confident they had more than enough innate Records to become mythical too.

Smiling with satisfaction, Jake put the Wyrm's Breath away and exited the white void entirely, leaving the fifth and final Challenge Dungeon for good. His vision flashed for a moment before he appeared outside of the entrance to all the Challenge Dungeons. Perhaps he shouldn't have been surprised, but there were even more people than usual there, and he was kind of happy he had remembered to put his mask and cloak back on.

Jake released a Pulse of Perception right away to feel for any of his party members. He frowned a bit when it didn't pick up any of them, making him wonder if he was really the first. Or at least, he wondered about that until he returned to the Order of the Malefic Viper's very small base of operations on the city floor.

There, he learned that both Sylphie and the Sword Saint had already finished their five Challenge Dungeons and returned to a prior floor to do their own thing for a while. Jake also remembered the weird time-painting he had been given by the Sword Saint before he entered the first Challenge Dungeon. It was made to track time, allotting a total of ten years to do the dungeons and ten more to make a final push for some additional floors and levels.

Taking out his painting, Jake confirmed that he was actually well ahead of schedule. All of them seemed to be. Despite having done all five Challenge Dungeons, only around eight and a half years had passed. Seeing as Jake was the third to be done, he also reckoned the Fallen King and Dina would finish before all ten years were up, so there was a chance they would have more than ten years to grind.

Jake considered for a moment whether he should do the same thing as the Sword Saint and Sylphie by going to a prior floor—probably the one just before this city floor—but after a bit of thinking, he decided not to. Instead, he went to one of the private rooms in the Order of the Malefic Viper base.

During the last many years, Jake hadn't really ever taken a break to properly go through stuff, and he decided now was a better time than ever. He had just gained the Wyrm's Breath that he could use to upgrade an item, and he also had another Challenge Dungeon reward saved—namely, the High-Quality Storybook Page.

[High-Quality Storybook Page (Unique] – The page of an unknown storybook containing empty Records of a tale yet untold. Allows you to infuse the Records of a skill into the storybook page.

Ripping a page infused with the Records of a skill will grant you an opportunity to upgrade the skill. The effect is lowered as the rarity of the skill increases, and the page will not accept Records of certain skills. It will have no effect if used on skills at or above legendary rarity. Skill upgrades are not guaranteed.
Requirements: C-grade. Soulbound.

With this, Jake would be able to upgrade a skill, and while he hadn't quite decided on one, he saw no reason to delay using it any longer. Plus, he wanted to be at his best when it was time to begin doing floors once more.

There was also the Cradle to check for his Soulflame growth... and some alchemy to get done, especially considering his party members would probably want more potions and elixirs and such for when they continued. So much to do, and *hopefully* so little time; he really hoped the Fallen King and Dina would also arrive soon so they could get going.

————

Jake was far from the only one who was finishing up the Challenge Dungeons. Many powerful parties were getting them done, though Jake's was one of the first of the Leaderboards teams to do so, as they'd been quick in reaching the city floor where all the Challenge Dungeons became fully available.

However, some other teams did match Jake and company's speed. What's more, as these people finished up the Challenge Dungeons, they didn't do so quietly. Instead, their results were announced and spread throughout the city floors and quickly picked up by the different factions. Davion from Valhal did all five, ending with a multiplier of 70%, with his best performances in the Colosseum of Mortals and the House of the Architect, proving himself a diverse fighter. 70% was around the point where one had bragging rights, and it was impressive, especially for someone like Davion, who'd been a very focused fighter to get it.

With time, more scores were shared. Dozens more came out with a 70% score, including people from the Court of Shadows, Holy Church, Altmar Empire, Pantheon of Life, Dao Sect, and pretty much every other faction. Soon, a few with 75% scores also reared their heads.

Not long after, the Holy Church made a big deal out of a member of theirs who'd gained an 80% multiplier. It was a member of Jacob's party, but naturally not Jacob himself. Much praise was levied, but it was short-lived.

He was soon overtaken when Azal the Ghost King exited the five Challenge Dungeons with an overall multiplier of 85%. This was the kind of score that proved he truly was a multifaceted genius, and his existing popularity skyrocketed.

Of course, there were also many who didn't share any details about their performances and kept it all a secret. Many were simply disciples of powerful individuals and saw no reason to publicize anything, while others didn't want to draw unwanted attention. They would showcase their true talent on the final Leaderboards instead. A great example of someone who just didn't care about attention was Arnold. He had ended with a total multiplier of 75%, but he didn't tell anyone... and he wasn't even the one with the highest score on his team.

Some also performed below expectations. There had been much hype about Eron, the new Chosen of the Lifesoul Daolord, but his score was never publicized—in part because he ended with a mere 50% multiplier. He was simply too lopsided. He'd earned a 25% multiplier in House of the Architect and 15% in Minaga's Endless Labyrinth, but those were his only good performances, with the Test of Character being the only other Challenge Dungeon where he'd earned a multiplier.

Time passed, and soon an announcement made waves. A dragonkin from the Regalflight—the golden dragons—had achieved a multiplier of 90%. She was the daughter of one of the Grand Elders within the Dragonflights, and they proudly flaunted their achievement.

Not too long after, a previously unknown figure matched this performance. A Demon Prince from one of the hells that few had their eyes on made this shocking announcement, giving the oft-forgotten demon faction some buzz.

More scores were published for a while, as all the big factions had big performers, but very few reached their mythical 90% multiplier. It had to be noted that these multipliers mattered beyond simple clout. If one reached 70% after doing all five, there would be a title that improved at 80% and 90%, too. At 90%, it would even give 5% to one's three highest stats, making it incredibly impactful and one many people aimed for—and failed to hit.

As the era was long, someone would definitely get more than that at some point... but none of them had expected it to have already happened a while ago, as the announcement had merely been delayed to a better time. Definitely intentional, with the aim of generating the most attention.

It was naturally made by someone who cared a lot about his reputation and one of the people most had their eyes on... Ell'Hakan, the Chosen of Yip of Yore. His score sent a new shockwave through Nevermore, as he didn't just announce the final score but what he got in each Challenge Dungeon.

20% in the Colosseum of Mortals, succeeding in gaining the recognition of Valdemar with his final life. Proving his ability to fight, even without all his skills.

25% in the Test of Character, never once taking control but exploiting the situation by never having to, and instead guiding the person he was inhabiting to always choose the outcome he wanted. This proved his strong character and unshakeable will in the eyes of many.

10% in Minaga's Endless Labyrinth. The first true stumble on his journey, but still a very respectable score.

20% in the House of the Architect, showing his ingenious creative mind. Nobody needed to know he had exploited much within this Challenge Dungeon.

20% in the Endless Journey, proving that even if he was a Chosen, he could also show humility and adapt... assuming that was what he had actually done, not merely making use of his Bloodline to sway things in the directions he wanted, exploiting the prone-to-be-exploited natives of the dungeon.

With a score of 95%, it was difficult to imagine anyone could beat him. While getting a 100% multiplier was possible, it was simply so rare and often didn't happen more than a dozen or so times in every era. At least, that was how many openly stated they had gotten the score, though there may have been more who kept it hidden. In either case, it was simply that hard to find someone talented in so many different areas at once. As for getting above 100%... that sounded like a pipedream to most.

As for Jake publicizing his score... well, he was frankly too busy doing alchemy to decide if he wanted to rain on everyone's parade.

CHAPTER 22

MYSTERIOUS BETTER BOOTS

P erhaps it shouldn't come as a surprise, but having the strongest people all leave their planets for Nevermore at roughly the same time could cause some... troubles, especially for those who had usually ruled with an iron fist. In the absence of a tyrant, a tyrannical regime could easily collapse, and this happened all across the 93rd Universe as uprisings took place, even if the revolutionaries would more likely than not be utterly crushed once the tyrant returned from the World Wonder.

One also had to remember that many places were still struggling with battles against beasts and monsters. This forced the stronger ones there to make a choice: Use the token provided by the Wyrmgod to leave for Nevermore, or remain and fight for your faction, family, and friends. To many, this wasn't even a choice, as they wouldn't abandon those they cared for, but for others, it wasn't a choice simply because their own power was the most important.

As for who was right, it could honestly be difficult to tell. Even if they fought against the beasts and monsters now, what about the future? What would be the plan for facing the Prima Guardian when that descended? It was clear to many that Nevermore wasn't simply an optional World Wonder for people to go visit if they felt like it, but a borderline mandatory power boost to make the world capable of facing the Prima Guardian.

This difficult choice of sacrificing the now for the future or risking the entire planet with the hope that they would be capable of facing the Prima Guardian haunted many. Especially those who had managed to become World Leaders, who now had to figure out how to strike a balance between their strongest fighters going to Nevermore or remaining to fight.

Of course, some planets didn't face this issue. Since only C-grades monsters that hadn't consumed the special unique treasures provided during the integration could enter the areas designated for the enlightened races, the risk of C-grades hordes invading simply wasn't there. Only the weaker worlds with a handful of C-grades faced this, and they were at least lucky that beasts could also go to Nevermore, making many of these potential threats leave... which kind of added another threat down the line. How would those who didn't go to Nevermore compete with those who did?

Honestly, in many places, it was a mess. However, one place that appeared entirely unaffected was a certain little planet called Earth. There, things were very much running as usual, even with nearly all of the most influential people gone. One would think that with the massive influx of freed slaves and other individuals sent by the many factions who wanted closer relations with Jake, things would get a bit chaotic, but things remained calm.

There had been some fear that after Miranda left, issues would crop up with no one to handle them. Especially when Lillian also went to Nevermore, along with several others who were part of the leadership. The only ones from the World Council who remained were the Sky Whale, who saw no rush to go to Nevermore, and Arthur, who wouldn't go at all.

This pretty much left Arthur as the only one in charge at the very top when it came to governing the enlightened races, and his presence was a big reason for the calmness. While he wasn't powerful in the traditional sense, he was a man who had more than enough knowhow when it came to management, and with the influence he had been given by being part of the World Council, he easily governed when everyone else was gone by continuing all the policies he, Miranda, and others had enacted.

The factions that still remained on Earth, such as the Court of Shadows and the Sword Saint's clan, also didn't start anything during this period. Even if they wanted to, the risk was simply too big. And not just because of what would happen when Jake and the others returned, but due to the many people who had arrived vehemently supporting any establishment Jake was part of.

The freed slaves especially had a high level of loyalty, more so to Miranda than Jake. She had put a lot of effort into integrating the influential former slaves, giving many of them official positions of leadership, and even if many of these influential ones had now also left for Nevermore, those loyal to their former fellow slaves kept carrying out their wills.

The beasts and monsters were also very much averse to starting anything. Some because of the Sky Whale, but others due to the over-whelming presence of the Fallen King, who many saw as the true leader of the monster factions on Earth. Even if the King ruled as a tyrant through power, this was one of the instances where even in the absence of the tyrant, stability remained... for they all knew he would come back one day. Even if they tried to take control of things, none had confidence that they wouldn't lose it immediately upon his return. Along with their lives, of course.

All of this is to say that Jake had, very much unknowingly, been the impetus behind establishing one of the most stable planets when it came to internal conflict in the 93rd Universe. And he didn't even need to use his arcane affinity.

———

Jake didn't really listen to much of the buzz about people getting big Nevermore Points multipliers and all that other noise. In all honesty, even when he heard some mutters from others in the small Order base, he didn't care. Despite people probably being curious, he also didn't see any reason to publish his own results.

While it was likely others had worked hard partly for their factions to gain recognition, Jake wasn't like that. The only person Jake needed to recognize he had done well was Jake himself. His pursuit of power and rewards was as selfish as could be. Not to say that Jake wouldn't go out and tell everyone; he just wouldn't take the initiative to do so.

If the Viper asked him to go out and flex, Jake would do it. If Ell'Hakan or some other asshat tried to taunt Jake with their super cool score, Jake would gladly smack down their ego. Going out to brag on his own just seemed a bit too tacky, in his opinion. Besides, they would all know how well he had done when Nevermore ended and they saw the Leaderboards. That was the score that truly mattered, not this small mile-stone of Challenge Dungeons.

No, rather than waste his time on all this flexing, Jake focused on far more important stuff. Alchemy-wise, Jake had spent a good amount of time just crafting stuff. He even felt he was very close to gaining a level, though he didn't get one right away, as he had only been going for a week, making a few potions and elixirs while also stocking up on poison.

As for why he had just done alchemy so far... well, he was kind of stalling.

Jake would be lying if he said he didn't second-guess himself quite a few times when it came to using his newest mythical reward. He hadn't really doubted himself at first when he decided to upgrade his boots, but a small sliver of uncertainty did begin to creep in as he considered it further. Not because he didn't want to upgrade the boots, but because of something in the Wyrm's Breath description...

"Contains faint Records related to the Wyrmgod of Nevermore, making this item especially suited to upgrading items related to the space affinity."

This little part of the description made Jake question if it would even be a good idea to use it on the boots. Not just because of this space-affinity thing, but because Jake wondered if perhaps he should actually use it on one of his existing mythical items... or maybe even the Mask of the Fallen King. However, without even needing to try it, he understood that the item would have no effect on the mask, likely due to its unique origins.

Improving Eternal Hunger could be big, though. Or maybe even turn his bow into a mythical one. The bow had been given directly by the system, and even if he had upgraded it once, it should still have enough innate Records, right?

There were honestly so many good options. Shit, there was even his necklace... Alright, that one would be a waste, as it was one of the easier items to upgrade. But maybe his creepy cloak could be good to upgrade? At least that would help him find out why that damn merchant had been so happy to get rid of it when Jake bought it.

At this point, Jake fully recognized he was stalling, and rather than keep doing alchemy, which would no doubt lead to another level and thus a skill selection that would inflict him with even more decision paralysis, Jake stopped fucking around.

After taking off his boots and putting them on top of a small table, Jake also took out the Wyrm's Breath. He looked at both items a bit before using the Wyrm's Breath. Doing so was pretty easy, as Jake just had to hold it while willing for it to affect the boots in front of him. He really hoped things would end well as the Breath began to shine brightly and let out a torrent of energy. A moment later, it looked as if the sculpture-like item came alive as it began to burn, releasing a bright white flame that seemed to distort space itself.

The flames soon flew toward the boots, setting them aflame. Jake felt a bit worried as the torrent of fire grew until it reached the ceiling, the boots just sitting there, seemingly unaffected. Then, just as fast as everything began, the flames dispersed unceremoniously.

Jake stared at the table and boots, both of which appeared utterly untouched. The boots themselves were also the same old leather boots that looked like they couldn't even be given away for free at a thrift shop. As for feeling an aura from them... well, Jake had never really felt much from the old things.

However, he did get a system notification, and as he used Identify on the boots and saw the change, he knew it had been a success.

[Boots of the Wandering Alchemist (Ancient)] – Boots once offered to an alchemist before setting out on a journey to experience the world outside at the behest of his master. Despite being made of simple leather, the Records of the ancient alchemist have left a deep mark on this item, allowing it to transcend many ranks. With every awakening, the Records within grow in power, the item improving in tandem to reflect its growth, even if many secrets within still elude you. Enchantments: +350 Endurance, +250 Agility, +200 Perception. Reduces energy expenditure from all movement-related skills by a moderate amount. Increases sensitivity towards earthbound plants and natural treasures.
Requirements: Lvl 200+ in any humanoid race.
-->
[Boots of the Wandering Sage (Mythical)] – Boots once offered to an alchemist before setting out on a journey to experience the world outside at the behest of his master. With time, this wanderer became recognized as a Sage, the same as his master who once wandered in them, too. This has left a deep mark on this item, allowing it to transcend many ranks despite being made of nothing but simple leather. With every awakening, the Records within grow in power, the item improving in tandem as they reconnect with their Origin.

Enchantments: +1500 Endurance, +1000 Agility, +500 Perception, +500 Willpower, +500 Wisdom, +500 Intelligence. Reduces energy expenditure from all movement-related skills while also increasing their effectiveness by a substantial amount. Increases sensitivity towards earthbound plants and natural treasures. While wearing the Boots of the Wandering Sage, never let difficult terrain impede you, as you shall always find a solid foothold.
Requirements: Soulbound.

First of all... that was a lot of stats. Secondly, a lot had changed, first and foremost being the name. Boots of the Wandering Sage. However, it still confused him a bit... Who was the sage? The First Sage? Villy was also considered a Sage, right? Or was it a third person altogether? Yeah, alright, Jake would definitely have to ask Villy about this.

When it came to the effects beyond the stats, the natural-treasure detector seemed the same. He also quickly spotted that the energy-cost reduction on movement-related skills had changed to also increase the effectiveness of movement-related skills. Such a change was quite frankly massive, and he very much looked forward to seeing how much it did.

The final effect was a tad weird. It said difficult terrain would never impede Jake and that he would always find a solid foothold. This effect could both be extremely powerful but also kind of useful... Honestly, there was no way to tell before he put on the boots and did some testing.

Now, did this item truly look like a mythical piece of equipment? Fuck no—it was a pair of old, worn-out leather boots... Alright, effect-wise, they probably did. Jake didn't really have a great frame of reference, but he felt like the boots did qualify; it was just that many of their effects were hard to quantify. Also, it was quite shocking to see that even after becoming mythical, they still apparently had room for improvement. This was also part of the reason why Jake was so sure these boots had either belonged to Villy or the First Sage at some point. Who else would have Records that powerful?

He had questioned if they belonged to Villy before and kind of written that theory off, but now he wasn't sure. As he looked at the boots, he also remembered something. He leaned forward and grabbed them, then quickly checked the lining of the leather boots. He saw that the message about looking forward to meeting him was still there, and for a moment, he was worried... until he found another message etched into the other pair. A new one. This one was a lot shorter than the first but perhaps even more impactful.

When two becomes five, reunite with one.
- A Sage

While it wasn't definitive... Jake was pretty damn certain this was related to the First Sage. It had to be. Also, when it came to the riddle of sorts, Jake instantly solved it. He currently had two charges of Path of the Heretic-Chosen, and this message was telling him to save up five. As for reuniting with one, well, he was called the *First* Sage.

Jake didn't really need to think much before he decided to try and reach out to the Viper, as he felt like a conversation about his old boots was long overdue. He had barely reached out when he felt the Malefic Viper respond, surprising Jake a bit, as he thought he couldn't normally talk to Villy while inside Nevermore, but things were quickly cleared up.

"Alright, got a closed and secure connection," the Viper said. *"See it as an extra reward for your performance and for your great bug-finding efforts during the Challenge Dungeons. Now, I already have a good idea why you want to talk... It's about those boots, right?"*

"It is indeed about the boots," Jake responded. *"So... what's up with them?"*

"Eh, alright, I'll give you some lore on the old things. Yeah, they belonged to me. For a while, at least. As a beast in humanoid form, my equipment didn't give me any stats, so it didn't really matter what I wore. So, for a long time, I didn't care much and just took whatever I could get here and there. But honestly, everything just kept getting torn, as nothing was enchanted. After I met the First Sage, he gave me these boots when he sent me out to do stuff, and even after his death, I kept them. Even back then, they were always a bit... special. Believe it or not, they haven't changed at all from how they looked when I first got them. While I won't say they are indestructible, I sure never encountered anything that could ruin them for good. I don't really know much about them besides that, only that they belonged to the First Sage before me."

"If they are so precious... why give them out as a dungeon reward?" Jake questioned.

He knew how much the Malefic Viper cared about and respected the First Sage, so to give his boots to some E-grade in a Challenge Dungeon really didn't seem like something the Viper would do. Even if Jake was his Chosen, it was still a massive risk to just hand out an item like that. If Jake had died or lost them, they would've been gone for good.

"Oh... well, I guess I didn't include the part where I lost them in A-grade when I had to escape a collapsing minor dimension," the Viper said nonchalantly. *"So I was a bit surprised when I saw them again... because the only reward I had designated to be given for that Challenge Dungeon was the spatial storage necklace. That's why I was so insistent on you upgrading them—because they sure aren't the exact same boots I used to have. Those weren't even real pieces of equipment with a rarity attached to them."*

"Wait... so the system just decided to randomly reward them after modifying them as a reward suitable for someone in early E-grade?" Jake asked, even more confused. *"Why? Isn't this all a bit too much of a coincidence*

when I also happen to have met the First Sage in a vision? That I suddenly end up with an old pair of his boots?"

Jake still hadn't shared the thing about the etched messages. Not the first one, and not this new one, as he got a weird feeling that he probably shouldn't share it. The implications behind these messages appearing were simply too impactful, and Jake wanted to figure out more before he would talk about it. And so far, he only had some vague theories. Was the First Sage communicating with him from beyond the grave? Did he have some weird Transcendence that allowed him to somehow know Jake would one day get them? Some kind of future-prediction stuff? Or maybe he really had somehow merged with part of the system or something? There were so many possibilities, and Jake felt equally unsure about all of them. If this was all just some weird coincidence or something, Jake didn't want to give Villy false hope that he could somehow communicate with the First Sage directly.

The Viper took a bit and sighed before he answered Jake's question. *"With the system, coincidences are rarely just coincidences,"* he said in a thoughtful tone. *"As for why you got the boots... now, that's the big mystery, isn't it?"*

CHAPTER 23

STORY TIME

J ake still felt extreme confusion when he thought about the First Sage. All Jake really knew was that he was a man from the First Universe who'd died in C-grade while also being the teacher of Villy. Well, and the fact he had apparently been so ridiculously talented it beggared belief, and that he also had a Bloodline, which the Viper had gained many years after his teacher's death.

However, even taking into consideration his extreme talent, things didn't really make any sense. How was he capable of leaving messages on boots he had owned trillions of years ago? How was a C-grade even capable of doing that in the first place?

"Do you think all this boots-business could have been orchestrated by the First Sage?" Jake said after a brief pause, but he instantly felt a bit dumb for even asking. *"No, never mind, that's—"*

"He could have," the Viper cut in." *One thing I learned while spending time with him was that he truly encapsulated the meaning of the phrase 'never say never.' He did things as a C-grade that I would think impossible for anyone who wasn't a god... or even above that. And that was just what he showed me. I am sure there was far more I never saw."*

Jake frowned as he listened to what the Viper said. *"But... how? He was just a C-grade. Aren't there certain rules about equivalent exchange and one having to pay with energy for things? Unalterable rules set by the system that even Transcendent Skills cannot ignore?"*

"There are, but where there are rules, there are also ways to bend them, and the First Sage was a master of bending the rules. Never once did I hear him say something wasn't possible when I asked, just that I

hadn't found the right method to do it yet. Moreover, when I pressed enough, he often revealed clues, making it clear he had already found a solution to my inquiry. That is the kind of monster he was... someone truly limitless."

Jake was once again silent for a moment, then began somewhat tentatively, *"If I had a way to meet him..."*

"You should do it," the Viper said. *"Even if the notion sounds silly... but I guess you are a bit of a silly existence yourself in the first place. I think he would have found you interesting if the two of you had ever met. Or, from the way you asked your question, it appears he does indeed find you interesting. Let me take a stab—you're going to try and use Path of the Heretic-Chosen?"*

"Yeah," Jake said, nodding. He still wasn't sure how much he wanted to share with Villy about what he knew about the man. Not for any insidious reasons; he just didn't feel like anything he could say would help the Viper. But he did still ask one thing. *"Also... if I could ask him a question for you, what would it be?"*

"If it was me meeting him, I would ask a question I am not willing to share... but if it's you, I guess I would have you ask him... how come he never found a solution to the one problem that caused his death? Why did someone I do not doubt would have become the first god just... give up? Or... if he even did give up in the first place, or had some higher goal in mind..." The Viper's voice was filled with more emotion than usual. The kind of emotion Jake only ever heard when Villy talked about the family he once had as well as the First Sage.

"Alright," Jake said as the conversation naturally died out. Which made it the perfect chance to change the topic. *"What are your thoughts on all this Nevermore Challenge Dungeon stuff? Mainly the multiplier scores. Should I go out and advertise my score to smack down some fools, or...?"*

"That's up to you," the Viper answered, clearly not opposed to the change of topic. *"But if you want me to decide, I wouldn't share it. Doing so won't really do you any good, especially if you wanted to do so with the intent of harming Yip of Yore's Chosen. In fact, you may just end up aiding him. He is writing a story where he is the underdog, so if you come out in a clear attempt to suppress his reputation, I am certain he would spin it as you showing fear toward his growth. That you felt the need to come out and show off how much better than him you were. No, if you really want to mess him up, the best thing you can do is nothing. Don't acknowledge him—just do your thing and regard him as nothing more than an afterthought. You will end up clashing on the Leaderboards whether you want to or not, and you*

will end up clashing more in the future, so try not to get caught up in his tempo. Walk to your own beat."

Jake listened to the Viper's words and sighed. *"Why couldn't you have made enemies and begun some conflict with someone like Valdemar so I could fight his Chosen instead? You know, someone who would actually want to fight me and not all this complicated meta-story bullshit."*

"Boohoo, this is a good lesson for you! And as I said, you will have your epic showdown someday. Every great story ends with a final battle at the climax... You just have to make sure this turns out to be one of those stories where the villain wins in the end."

"Wait, why am I the villain? He's the guy who attacked me first."

"Because he's the self-insert author, so you are a villain automatically simply because you are antagonistic toward him... Ah, but do watch out. With your growing reputation as a Harbinger of Primeval Origins, they may change up their tactics and try to make you into a redeemed villain who ends up joining the good guys to take down the big bad. You know... me."

"And I repeat: please choose a normal enemy next time. Someone with a big sword or something."

"How is Yip's Chosen that different?" the Viper very helpfully pointed out. *"He uses a halberd that's got three blades."*

"Small blades."

"Very villain-like of you to insult another man's weapon for being too small..."

"You know what? Maybe I should join him as a valiant hero who helped take down the evil Malefic Viper once and for all."

"Now that would be a plot twist I didn't see coming," the Viper answered in a similarly joking manner. *"Anyway, the Wyrmgod is giving me nasty looks, probably afraid I am trying to give tips or share things I shouldn't, and I am sure he is mighty uncomfortable with having no idea what we are talking about. So when I cut the connection, do something mysterious that makes him question if I broke the rules, alright? See ya!"*

Right as Villy cut the connection, Jake frowned deeply and muttered out loud, "To think it worked like that..."

To really play his part, Jake kept looking thoughtful—until he genuinely did get thinking about everything they had talked about, especially the First Sage. Villy clearly suspected things with his teacher weren't as they seemed, and he hadn't at all seemed surprised when Jake said he could potentially interact with him. As if nothing the C-grade could do would ever surprise him. He'd even recommended that Jake meet him if he could... which Jake most assuredly would.

I just need to reach level 300 in my profession first, Jake thought. It seemed far away, but Jake believed it wouldn't be that bad.

Refocusing on the task at hand, Jake took his mind off all those thoughts of the future and turned his attention toward the now. Taking the mythical boots off the table, Jake quickly put them on. As his foot slid into the first boot, his eyes opened wide.

This... This is... the peak of comfort-wear.

It was perhaps the most magical aspect of the boots: how damn good they felt to wear. It was truly out of this world, and Jake couldn't help but smile as he put both on. Oh, yeah, the stats and other effects from the mythical item were also good, but if comfort was an enchantment, that would definitely have been their best one by far.

Sadly, Jake couldn't really test them here and now. He instinctively had some idea about how they had improved, but seeing as the room he was in was sealed off from the outside, he couldn't even test out the treasure-detecting abilities.

However, he did feel one change. It was incredibly subtle, but when Jake stood up to revel in the feeling of the best boots in the multiverse, it was as if he stood more... stably than before. He tried to move a bit, but nothing really seemed different besides this minor odd feeling. It was as if he would have a harder time slipping and falling or something.

Shrugging, Jake shifted his attention to the second thing he wanted to get done before his party gathered. Taking out the Storybook Page from his inventory, Jake studied it a bit as he considered what skill to use it with. He already had a few in mind, but the nature of the item made things a bit more complicated than just selecting a skill below legendary rarity that he wanted to upgrade.

The problem was that the item didn't give a skill upgrade, just the opportunity to get one. As per the description:

"Ripping a page infused with the Records of a skill will grant you an opportunity to upgrade the skill. The effect is lowered as the rarity of the skill increases, and the page will not accept Records of certain skills... Skill upgrades are not guaranteed."

Had this not been the case, Jake would have used the page on Big Game Hunter without any hesitation. While he couldn't confirm it, Jake felt pretty damn certain that the skill was included in the "will not accept Records of certain skills" part. Another thing he felt sure was included was the archery skill, as well as any of his basic crafting skills, as those kinds of skills were always considered a bit special. That being the case, Fang of Man was more likely than not also restricted.

Jake also pretty quickly decided he wanted to upgrade a class skill, as he wanted another boost in combat capabilities. While sitting there, Jake began going through his skills one by one. As this was just an opportunity to upgrade a skill, and seeing as the effectiveness lowered as the skill rarity increased, he decided to go with one of his epic-rarity ones.

He also wanted the skill to be one he would find difficult to upgrade on his own without any new inspiration. This meant a skill like Piercing Cursed Arcane Fang was ruled out, along with something like Splitting Arcane Arrow Rain. Jake felt pretty confident about upgrading those on his own if he just worked on them actively.

Eventually, he ended up with two skills worth heavy consideration. The first was Avaricious Arcane Hunter's Arrows. It was the epic skill Jake used to generate his regular arrows, and seeing this upgraded would lead to a significant damage increase. It was also a skill that was kind of difficult to upgrade, as it had the avaricious tag alongside its ability to instantly summon arcane arrows. Both of these added quite a lot of complexity, and he really didn't want to lose either effect if he tried to upgrade it himself.

The second skill Jake considered also had the avaricious tag, and was even more complicated. It was one of the core skills Jake used all the time to do more damage than usual, and was, in some ways, one of the reasons his amazingly high Perception allowed him to do as much damage as he did. It was naturally Mark of the Avaricious Arcane Hunter.

As he considered these two skills, Jake brought up both their descriptions and studied them closely. However, after a while, he closed the Arcane Hunter's Arrows one. He looked closer at Mark, kind of impressed by the many things it did despite only being in epic rarity.

[Mark of the Avaricious Arcane Hunter (Epic)] – Your prey is chosen; the hunt is on. Covertly mark targets, making you aware of their positions at all times until the marks expire or are dispelled. All damage done to marked targets is increased. Arcane damage has its damage amplified further. The extra arcane damage inflicted while the marks are active will be built up in the form of an arcane charge that you can detonate to release all the stored-up energy. Additional bonus experience earned for slaying a marked target above your level (this effect remains even if your target dies to the mark detonating or within a short duration of the detonation). Adds a bonus to the damage inflicted, the duration of the marks, and the subtlety and number of marks available based on Perception.

The skill did a whopping four things at once. It allowed him to mark and track creatures, deal extra damage to those tracked, store up an arcane charge to explode, and gain even more experience from kills. What's more, everything scaled solely with Perception. While Jake wasn't all clear on the math, he was pretty certain the damage amplification of Mark was responsible for a good percentage of his total damage output due to this Perception scaling.

Moreover, this was a skill so complicated Jake didn't really have any good ideas on how to upgrade it while at the same time being "only" epic rarity, meaning the Storybook Page should have a good effect. It was a bit of a gamble, but unless Jake wanted to rely on another skill selection to get a system-given upgrade, he felt this was the best way.

He could spend a long time thinking up more reasons... but after only a few more justifications for this being the best choice, Jake decided to stop delaying. He held the page and began to infuse it with the Records of the skill. He did this simply by thinking about wanting to do it while holding the page, and he subtly felt energy leaving his body as the page began to glow and fill with runes he couldn't at all recognize.

Once the runes were complete, Jake tore the page in two, and a flash of energy was released as his consciousness shifted.

———

While Jake was busy being knocked out by the Storybook Page, his party members closed in on finishing their Challenge Dungeons. This included the Sword Saint and Sylphie, who had already finished theirs and returned to the prior floor to do some minor practice by hunting down monsters and sparring a bit.

During their joint hunting efforts, they naturally shared how they had done over the last few years—even if communication was a bit strained due to the Sword Saint still not being fluent in the language of Ree.

In the Challenge Dungeons, Sylphie ended up with a pretty good total multiplier of 45%. Her best performance had been Minaga's Labyrinth, where she got 25%, being the little cheat of a bird she was. The second best was the Colosseum of Mortals, where she had ended up with a 10% multiplier, though admittedly, many would come to claim the version she did was easier. Instead of level 0, she'd been set at level 200. The opponents had mostly been the same—even if there were some monster opponents thrown in there—and the arenas had changed to accommodate the fights of larger scope. Also, even if skills were still removed from everyone,

Sylphie was pretty lucky in that much of her magic was just innate manipulation, which was how she had done as well as she had. She'd also done okay in the Test of Character, where she had ended up with only a 5% multiplier, a feat she repeated in the House of the Architect.

Her personality was simply too flighty, and her Creations had come mainly in the form of skill upgrades she decided to work super hard at, along with some other small things she'd tried to create. These Creations included a nest the size of a small city, created entirely from the many trees and plants occupying a huge part of the jungle world. Finally, to finish out the list of Challenge Dungeons, there was the Endless Journey, where Sylphie hadn't even gotten a Grand Achievement, meaning she got some Nevermore Points but no multiplier.

She didn't care much, though. Sylphie had never wanted to compete on those silly Leaderboards when she knew Uncle was going to be the best there anyway. However, Sylphie did notice her current fighting partner seemed less than pleased with the Leaderboards and big score stuff. Even if Sylphie was not the smartest bird when it came to seeing when others felt sad, she could see that the old swordsman she was training with seemed frustrated. Sylphie had gone to this floor because she was bored and wanted to fly around and fight, but the swordsman had come after all of those big announcements of performances in the Challenge Dungeons. As if he felt he couldn't delay his progress for even a second lest he fall behind.

Again, Sylphie didn't care about all those scores... but the old swordsman sure seemed like he cared a lot.

CHAPTER 24

PROMISE & MARK

To be strong... was something that truly didn't matter in the world before the system. One could be the best swordsman in the world or the best martial artist, but the difference between the bottom and the top was never that significant. Even the greatest fighter would lose against a few average men who teamed up on him. If they had weapons, even fewer. If they had a gun... a single shot could end the journey of a martial artist who had trained his body and skills to perfection over decades of struggle and hard work.

Due to this, and the peace of society as a whole, being able to fight rarely mattered. It was more done for sports or to stay in shape rather than any practical applications. Sure, the army did also teach hand-to-hand, and being able to stand your ground could come in handy when situations got tricky, but that was about it.

Yet Miyamoto had dedicated much of his life to training with a sword. Despite how many people told him he was wasting his time, he'd kept training whenever he could and only laid down his sword the day his body no longer allowed him to lift it.

It had simply been a passion of his, pursued for no other reason than the fact he enjoyed it. He'd worked most of his life, and it became his one selfish pastime where he could just be himself and ponder. His one childish pursuit...

And when the system arrived, he realized indulging in this childish pursuit was no longer that childish. Instead, it became a true Path to power, and no one looked down on him or questioned if he was wasting his time whenever he trained. One other thing did change, though, and that was the reason for his training.

Miyamoto had always been ambitious. It was simply an innate trait of his. During the tutorial, he had simply fought, doing his best alongside the allies he gathered as he struggled to survive. His body was weak in the beginning, but as time passed, he got stronger and stronger, and he still remembered that one fateful day.

It was a rather large fight, and one of the youngsters was struggling. Miyamoto had a breakthrough as he hurried over and managed to kill the opponent in the nick of time. The young woman who had been lying on the ground had called him something then. Something reminding him of a rather childish concept. She'd said he was like the Sword Saint of history...

The title stuck with him, as others also began to call him it, and Miyamoto never corrected anyone. Instead, he took this new title as a promise. To be the Sword Saint was to be at the peak of swordsmanship. To be the strongest...

And as of this moment, Miyamoto didn't feel like he lived up to that promise. He hadn't for quite a while, especially after he returned from the Challenge Dungeons and heard how others had done. Even if others said he hadn't done badly, he was still far from satisfied.

The Sword Saint had done quite a lot better overall than Sylphie and finished with a final multiplier of 70%. His 10% in the Colosseum of Mortals had very much been a disappointment to him, as it turned out to be one of his worst despite, on the surface, looking like one he should have done well at. However, he had also gotten very unlucky. His "basic state" was that of an old man who had been a single step away from death before the system. When he'd entered the Colosseum and had his stats reduced, he was far more negatively affected than someone like Jake. His brittle bones had made him take more damage every time he tried to block. His old muscles had made him slower, and his striking power especially had been negatively affected by his aging physique. He simply didn't have a body that could make full use of his stats.

This wasn't a problem when he had his full stats... but in the Colosseum, it became a severe limiter, in many ways making it impressive that he even managed to get 10%. He did feel sad about having had to use his Transcendence to beat Umbra, though, as it meant he could barely walk when he faced Valdemar for the final fight... but at least the backlash had been minimal due to the special circumstances of the Challenge Dungeon. By the time he had finished the Test of Character afterward, he was all good.

Speaking of the Test of Character, the Sword Saint did a lot better there. In fact, it ended up being one of his best-performing Challenge Dungeons, netting a 20% multiplier. Despite still being "young" in the context of the system, he felt like an old man, and he was very much set in who he was. He was good at judging situations and adapting when necessary, no matter what story he experienced.

A place he did a lot better in than expected was the House of the Architect, where he got a 10% multiplier. He had not expected to get much here, but he had ended up surprising himself. In many ways, it had been a good respite, as he had done this one last and had spent longer in it than any of the others. This allowed him to spend plenty of time working on his painting skills while naturally also upgrading some class-based skills, making it a very pleasant experience.

Endless Journey had turned into a tie for his best, yielding a 20% multiplier. It had also been another Challenge Dungeon he had very much enjoyed. Doing the menial jobs as a Courier had reminded him of the jobs he had when he was young, especially while in the military. The later happenings and dealing with the political turmoil had reminded him of what he had to deal with in his later years. Except, the political arena was too... simple. Easy. Simplified. There were a lot of twists and turns, but in the end, nothing ever felt too complicated, and he'd ended up challenging himself by aiming to broker a peace agreement between the dragon tribe and the Guild, as well as all the other nations. He was quite proud he'd succeeded in that, even if he knew peace would be short-lived in a realistic setting.

Finally, he got 10% in Minaga's Endless Labyrinth. There was not much to say there. He was fast and had managed to decipher many of the clues given, even deploying some tricks of his own to go faster. All in all, the Sword Saint had performed as a peak-tier genius... but he still felt disappointment in himself.

For to "only" be a genius was far below the promise he had made and the burden of the title he had taken upon himself. He felt far below the realm of monstrous existences like Jake and even Ell'Hakan, whom he had faced in combat once to score a minor victory. Yet even then, he knew there was more to the Chosen than what he had shown... Far more, which was clearly proven true by how well he was doing in Nevermore.

Sitting on a small hill on the sixty-ninth floor, Miyamoto simply observed as Sylphie ravaged the land in front of him, showing that she had also improved. A figure sat beside him, made up of pure energy that only he could see and interact with.

"You are too harsh on yourself," Iskar, the former Monarch of Blood, said.

In Nevermore, he could not fully materialize his body and thus occupied an intangible form only the Sword Saint could see as the owner of the divine item.

"I do not believe I am," the Sword Saint said as he sat meditatively with his sword across his legs. "Look at the young hawk. Her personality is utterly whimsical; she never seems to take any situation seriously, and she appears to only be playing around... yet her rate of improvement is unquestionable. Despite it looking like she isn't trying, you can see she is innately pushing herself to improve with every fight. Instinctively, she is driven to improve. She needs no motivation or purpose for doing so; it's merely in her nature."

"You speak as if you aren't also improving by the day," the Monarch of Blood said. "Every entity has different rates of improvement, coming at different intervals, but more importantly, in different spurts. Remember, the Path to power is not a sprint but a marathon toward the peak."

The Sword Saint didn't comment on the cliché words he had listened to so many times before. He just kept watching Sylphie as she battled the pack of beasts while considering if he truly was going about things the right way.

"You know..." Iskar added after a while, "one of the things that's holding you back is your profession."

"I will not become a vampire," the Sword Saint said with a sigh.

"I'm not saying you have to," Iskar said. "I'm just saying that maybe there is something to look at there. You have a lot of untapped potential you never truly dove into, especially in regard to certain affinities... because I do not believe that the Primordial of Time chose to give you a Divine Blessing for your swordsmanship alone."

The Sword Saint sighed as he closed his eyes. He feared his Path becoming murky again if he tried to diversify himself too much... but perhaps the former Monarch of Blood had a point. His Patron, Aeon, had told him that his time affinity was quite impressive, after all.

———

The hunter stalked his way through the forest as his prey moved a few kilometers ahead of him. It was a small group of scaled, deer-like creatures, all moving in a defensive formation. Even so, the hunter wasn't worried. He knew he would find his time to strike as he felt for all their locations, and as he peered through the trees, the outline of every beast was clear as day.

Time passed as the hunter kept up his tracking while making sure to mark any potential future prey along the way. Every time he marked one, he became able to see them even through solid matter, as they were highlighted in his vision.

After only a few more hours, the hunter spotted his chance. The creatures had all split up slightly, slacking on their defensive formation as they consumed herbs in a small clearing. Without missing his chance, the hunter took out his bow. Not once did he get close or enter their line of sight as he secured a high position to shoot from.

As the hunter moved to draw the bow, arcane energy appeared and formed an arrow. Pulling back the string, more arcane power appeared as an Arcane Powershot was slowly charged, the hunter still a few dozen kilometers away from his prey.

Releasing the string, the first arrow flew forth. It slightly curved around all the trees in the way and slammed into the side of the first beast's head before it could even react, making it fall to the ground, bleeding heavily.

Rather than assist their comrade, the other beasts didn't hesitate to take off in four different directions. However, sadly for them, they were all already marked. The hunter didn't even care to pursue; he sprouted wings and flew further up into the air, where he nocked another arrow.

Another Arcane Powershot blasted out and hit one of the fleeing deer, which was now over thirty kilometers away. The damage it suffered was even greater than that of the first deer the hunter had hit. He nocked and released a second Powershot in rapid succession, hitting a third deer for more damage yet again. It wasn't an extreme amount, and the reason for the extra damage was the distance between him and the marks.

With a few more arrows, all of the deer were soon taken down—except for one. The hunter looked at it closely, the outline of its Soulshape revealing the damage done. The outline was slightly damaged, letting the hunter know the injury was significant and would potentially lead to death on its own. Not that he would leave that up to chance; he shot one more arrow to finish off the final beast.

Right as the last deer died, everything warped. In the very next second, the hunter found himself standing atop a watchtower. He narrowed his eyes and spotted a scout in the distance. Instantly, he marked the target. The scout tried to use his stealth skill, yet the hunter maintained tracking, as the scout failed to dispel the mark completely; its resistance to any form of dispel mechanics was simply too strong.

After the scout was successfully hunted down, things warped again into a third scenario.

This hunter using Mark in different ways was quite an odd character... because it wasn't really Jake. Not to misunderstand, Jake was along for the ride, reminiscent of the Test of Character—though without the ability to take control—but even if the hunter used skills Jake had, it clearly wasn't him.

The Storybook Page seemed to trigger a miniature version of a mix between the Test of Character Challenge Dungeon and Jake's Path of the Heretic-Chosen, though compared to Path, it was a lot worse. It didn't have the time-rewind stuff and the ability to allow Jake to hyperfocus during the most important moments, but it did allow Jake to experience the use of a slightly different version of Mark than his own a few times.

A total of nine visions ended up playing out, each of them using a variant. One of them allowed Jake to kind of "see" the area all around the target, another allowed him to use Mark in an area to hit everything there, and a third changed Mark from a solo-hunting skill to one that grew more effective as more people targeted the marked prey.

Nine different versions, but Jake was stuck on the first one, as it had the effects he wanted the most. The outline of the Soulshape was something he could see being very useful for a very particular reason that would be clear in the future, and the bonus damage based on distance was definitely a great addition. Ah, not that the part about dealing more damage based on distance was unique, as that was present in all the different skill upgrade Paths, likely due to influence from his class.

After what felt like several days to Jake, but was in reality only a few seconds in the real world, the effect of the Storybook Page ended. Jake awoke back in the Order, but he didn't hesitate to enter meditation as he reflected on the visions. He remembered the feeling of using the skill, and he began to integrate it into the skill.

After about a full day of focused meditation, Jake opened his eyes to a system notification, putting a smile on his face. *Success.*

Without further ado, he opened up the description of the improved skill.

[Mark of the Horizon-Chasing Arcane Hunter (Ancient)] – Your prey is chosen; the hunt is on. Covertly mark targets, making you aware of their positions while allowing you to see an outline of

**their Soulshape at all times until the marks expire or are dispelled.
All damage done to marked targets is increased. This extra damage
is amplified further based on your distance from the target. All
effects increase for arcane damage done. The extra arcane damage
inflicted while the marks are active will be built up in the form of
an arcane charge that you can detonate to release all the stored-up
energy. Additional bonus experience earned for slaying a marked
target above your level (this effect remains even if your target dies
to the mark detonating or within a short duration of the
detonation). Adds a bonus to the damage inflicted, the duration of
the marks, the maximum effective distance, and the subtlety and
number of marks available based on Perception.**

The description had naturally gotten longer since Jake had added two
extra wonderful features. The first one was the ability to see an outline of
his foe, while the second was increasing his damage with distance. Yet
another skill that did so, which was naturally only good.

Stacking similar or identical effects that worked together was the best
way to get extremely powerful attacks. Jake stacked skills dealing more
damage to higher-leveled foes and opponents he was far away from, while
someone like the Sword Saint stacked skills and effects that increased the
sharpness of his katana. At least, Jake was pretty damn sure he did that.

The final improvement to Mark was something Jake had added on as a
bit of a bonus. During one of the visions, he'd noted that the marks had a
limited range before they would automatically be dispelled, so he'd worked
on alleviating that, which had materialized in the form of the effective
distance now also scaling with Perception. Jake had been pretty sure it
already did that, but hey, it was good to have it in system text.

Along with all of the new effects, all existing effects had naturally also
increased. With how much the skill did, it wasn't a massive amount, but
Jake was pretty sure that this one skill upgrade alone increased his effective
damage output per arrow by a few percent, and that would be amplified if
his target was very far away.

Jake felt more than satisfied with the upgrade, and it sure put him in a
good mood. His mood only got better a few minutes later when an attendant came and knocked on the door to his chamber, informing him that
Dina was also done with her Challenge Dungeons. Now, they just needed
the Fallen King, and it would be time to do some live testing as they
continued their Nevermore journey.

CHAPTER 25

THE GANG BACK TOGETHER

It ended up only taking two weeks more before the whole gang was back together. Jake spent this time primarily working on some of the things he had been putting off a bit, like making sure everything was still running smoothly in the Cradle for his budding Soulflame and then doing the very important work of briefly checking out his Puzzle Box of the Seeker. He'd planned to play with it for just a day or two, so it was very understandable that Jake felt slight annoyance when he was interrupted after a couple of weeks.

Sylphie and the Sword Saint had already returned to the Order compound at this point and were doing their own thing until it was time to meet back up, well ahead of schedule. Jake ended up being the last to arrive at their reunion, as he just needed to get in one more attempt for his current puzzle, which he was certain everyone would understand.

Walking through the small compound, Jake saw the four of them gathered in a sealed-off meeting room. He enjoyed the feeling of the walk due to his even more comfortable boots, as he couldn't help himself from feeling for natural treasures using the boots' function. He detected a few, and he quickly realized their range covered the entire damn city floor.

Arriving in the meeting room, Jake checked out the situation just before entering. Sylphie was sitting on a small nest she had made on a table from what looked like tablecloths, looking very comfortable. Meanwhile, the Sword Saint and Dina were both sitting in chairs, while the Fallen King floated menacingly in a corner. None of them looked different compared to the last time they met, though that wasn't really a surprise.

But that didn't mean they hadn't changed. When Jake entered the room, he instantly took in their auras. Compared to roughly eight and a half years ago, everyone had gotten quite a lot stronger. Even if their levels hadn't grown due to the nature of Challenge Dungeons—besides Sylphie and the Sword Saint, who had gained one on the sixty-ninth floor—that didn't mean they hadn't gotten stronger. Everyone had gained at least one title netting a few more stat points, but what mattered most were the skill upgrades and conceptual improvements and such that had sharpened their overall abilities.

Jake himself had also gotten quite a lot stronger. He was the one who had gained the most levels due to his little meeting with the gods and his aura-measuring contest with Valdemar, along with the All-Star title. Not to mention all the skill upgrades he had gained, as well as overall improvements across the board.

"Ree!" Sylphie instantly greeted Jake as she zoomed over and sat down on her usual spot atop his head. Jake just smiled and scratched her head, making her flap her wings happily. He had to admit he had missed the little featherball.

"The last to arrive, as expected," the Fallen King commented.

"Says the person who was the last to get done with all the Challenge Dungeons," Jake shot back.

"Yet I still finished within the agreed-upon deadline. Also, I thought it was viewed as impolite for humans to finish prematurely? Especially for you male versions."

"Pretty mean of you to insult an old man like that," Jake muttered as he shook his head with disappointment, throwing glances at the old man in the room.

"Good to see you too, Jake," the Sword Saint said with a light smile. "Now, rather than sit around and take jabs, let us get everyone up to speed. We will have plenty of time for banter when we continue our descent."

The Fallen King didn't argue, and Jake also knew when to shut up. He kept scratching Sylphie, who was also being a polite little hawk. For now, at least.

"To begin with... let us get a mutual idea of our shared growth during this period, as I am certain it has been most fruitful for us all. Let me begin with how I did in the Challenge Dungeons." The Sword Saint then volunteered a brief summary of his Challenge Dungeons. When he was done, he gave the floor to the dryad of their party, and she did the same.

Dina had done pretty damn well, with a total multiplier of 70% from all the Challenge Dungeons, tying with the Sword Saint perfectly. Broken down, she had gained 15% from the Colosseum of Mortals, 15% in the

House of the Architect, 10% in Minaga's Endless Labyrinth, 20% in the Endless Journey, and 10% in the Test of Character. Jake had to admit this was actually pretty good from her, considering she was a healer, and healers tended to struggle in places like the Colosseum of Mortals.

Jake thought so, at least... until she shared how she'd won pretty much all her fights by spreading poison spores in the arena to slowly kill her opponents. She'd done this by getting around the rules of the Colosseum, which stated one could only bring weapons and tools bought for the arena to a fight. Using her skills and innate talent, she'd spread spores from outside the entire Colosseum before any fighting even began. She'd done this through a special flower she grafted by combining different herbs, generating spores that she could control in flight using her Bloodline. Overall, her tactics had been pretty damn gruesome, yet effective for someone who wasn't the best in a regular fight. The mental image of her just delaying as her opponents slowly coughed up blood and died was a pretty dark mental image, though.

The Fallen King was next to summarize his last many years, and it turned out he had done quite a bit worse, with a final multiplier of 45%. In the Colosseum of Mortals, he'd ended with a respectable multiplier of 15%, and in the Endless Journey, he'd repeated that feat, earning another 15%. However, things only went downhill from there, as he'd only gotten 5% in the House of the Architect, the Test of Character, and Minaga's Endless Labyrinth. Jake saw the clear dissatisfaction from the Unique Lifeform, even if he understood why the Fallen King had faced so many problems... These Challenge Dungeons truly weren't made for something like a Unique Lifeform.

He didn't have the diversity for the House of the Architect due to his Path, and he wasn't overly fast for Minaga's Labyrinth. Additionally, he wasn't as good at deciphering the runes, as all his magic was purely instinctive and not something he had studied to learn the required skills. As for why he had done badly in the Test of Character, though... Well, Jake wasn't going to pry too much there.

Sylphie shared her results next, and Jake saw the Fallen King looking a bit grumpy that she had gained the same level of multiplier as him. Sylphie clearly also noticed this, as she very proudly screeched at her great accomplishment.

"All you did was find an exploit within a Challenge Dungeon and use that to your advantage," the Fallen King argued to make himself feel better. *"That is not a true representation of power, and a Unique Lifeform such as myself is merely disadvantaged due to the bogus rules."*

"Ree!"

"Having a unique skill does not make you a Unique Lifeform."

"Ree!" Sylphie refused to back down, even jumping on the table to look more defiant.

"She's got a point," Jake added. "As she is probably the only Sylphian Hawk in existence, calling Sylphie a lifeform that is unique isn't entirely inaccurate."

"That does not make it the same," the Fallen King said, trying to shut Jake down. *"Unique Lifeforms are clearly defined by the system, not by a bunch of C-grades that think they know better."*

"Ree."

"There is no agreeing to disagree here; we are discussing indisputable facts," the Unique Lifeform, who everyone was bullying into feeling a little bit less unique, argued. *"Unless you have a title quite literally proclaiming you a Unique Lifeform, you are not a Unique Lifeform."*

"Ree, ree."

Now it was Jake's turn to look confused as he stared at the hawk. "Wait, you do have such a title?"

"She does not; I can detect other Unique Lifeforms, and she isn't one," the Fallen King said dismissively.

"Ree!" Sylphie said madly as she screeched a few more times.

Jake's eyes opened wide, and everyone looked surprised. He and Villy had talked about Sylphie probably being unique, but they didn't really have any way to truly know. Turns out they could have just asked the little hawk to get a definitive answer.

Sylphie apparently had a title called Lineage Progenitor, which said Sylphie was one of a kind and the first in a new Lineage of powerful beasts. It quite literally called her unique and the first of the Sylphian Hawks. As for the effects of the title, Sylphie didn't share anything, as her parents had told her not to share such things. A diplomatic move, making Jake happy that Hawkie and Mystie had at least taught her some responsible things... even if they'd pawned Sylphie off to Jake for most of her life.

However, even if Sylphie didn't give many details, they did have someone in their party who knew a bit more.

"Lineage Progenitor... I heard about that title before," Dina added, sharing some of her precious knowledge of the multiverse. "It usually appears when a regular beast or monster mutates or has a particularly impactful evolution into a powerful variant that differs a lot from any others, effectively creating an entirely new Lineage of races... sometimes even entirely new species. Naturally, the level of change has to reach certain thresholds, and the Lineage Progenitor is always particularly powerful. To think Sylphie was one... I will have to tell Grandpa about this."

"Pretty sure he already knows, considering a whole bunch of gods are having a fun-time streaming party with the Wyrmgod watching us right now, your grandfather among them," Jake added casually with a shrug.

Everyone turned to look at Jake with confusion, at which point he realized, *Oh... Oh, yeah, they definitely didn't know that.*

"Alright, things will make a bit more sense with context, so I guess it's my turn to summarize my time doing stuff?" Jake said. "Let's start with the Endless Journey and work backward."

After Jake was done describing the Endless Journey, the Fallen King called him a cheater, while everyone else congratulated him for his great performance. After the House of the Architect, they remained impressed, though Sylphie had to get the jab in that Jake had already reached a tie with both her and the Fallen King for multiplier score with only two Challenge Dungeons. The small bird truly went for the jugular, gladly accepting mutual destruction.

Jake talked about Minaga's Endless Labyrinth next, where he shared how many Sections he did... and... well, alright, he had probably overdone it a bit. He had done sixty Sections more than Sylphie, who had also gotten 25%. At this point, the Fallen King was truly looking salty over how much of a cheat Jake was. Especially since he had already matched the record holders of their party with two Challenge Dungeons left to go.

When it came to the Test of Character, Jake had naturally done the worst out of all his Challenge Dungeons, but the nonexistent face of the Fallen King fell when Jake told them about the end of the Colosseum of Mortals.

"So, one thing led to another, and I ended up killing the image of Valdemar, which sure raised quite the ruckus," Jake shared. "I am not going to give any details, but man, it was one hell of a fight."

"You... *killed that thing?*" the Fallen King questioned. "*I faced a level 100 version... and I find it difficult to imagine any being I can remember, even in mid-tier D-grade, ever facing that creature without any skills...*"

"I used my spores and reached Valdemar without any deaths at all, even if it got really close against both Umbra and the Undying General... but I couldn't do anything against him, as he was entirely immune to my spores," Dina muttered. "I died ten times in a row without ever even standing a chance, no matter how many preparations I made. I even tried filling the entire arena with seeds, and he just cut everything down."

"Ree," Sylphie also said, a bit depressed that Valdemar had apparently just said he "really liked her wind and found it refreshing" before cutting it apart. Sylphie had also been quickly torn apart despite her semi-elemental wind form. Valdemar's Transcendent skill simply didn't care if something could be cut physically—he would cut it anyway.

"Well, as you all noted, it sure as fuck wasn't easy, and apparently, killing the image is so rare that Valdemar himself decided to come by... followed by a few others, including Dina's grandpa, who came along with Artemis," Jake shared.

"Why would Artemis come?" Dina said, confused. "I know she had an image in the Challenge Dungeon, but..."

"Eh, private reasons." Jake just waved that off, not wanting to share more than he had to. In order to not get questioned, he decided to add something he knew would surely shift everyone's attention. "Oh, yeah, the Blightfather and Holy Mother also stopped by, and when they came, a whole lot of other gods also arrived... By now, it's a whole party up there."

"You... talk as if you've been there," Dina said a bit tentatively.

"I have," Jake confirmed, seeing no reason to deny it. "Was an experience for sure. Even got a few levels from it. Anyway, let's get a move on already. No time for banter, right?"

"No, I am actually very interested in what happened," the Sword Saint commented, not letting Jake get away that easy. "For you to have gained levels must mean you did something, right?"

"Just a small presence competition with Valdemar for the fun of it," Jake said, once more trying to wave it off.

"Why would you ever openly oppose a god like that!? Much less a Primordial!?" Dina said in a very critical tone. "That was just so needlessly reckless."

"In my defense, we both had a good time," Jake said, defending himself excellently.

"Ree?"

"Oh, no, Valdemar is way fucking scarier in real life than just his image," Jake answered, still able to vividly remember the presence of the man. The sheer bloodlust he had built up, and the overwhelming power that would have crushed Jake into paste if the Primordial had poured in the slightest energy.

"Are we just going to ignore how this living cheat also got 25% in the Colosseum of Mortals?" the Fallen King said, finally steering the conversation back on topic. *"If my math is correct... that puts you at a total multiplier of 105%."*

Jake smiled. "Truly a math genius."

"That is... impressive," Dina muttered. "With that, you can really compete..."

"You're not going public with it?" the Sword Saint asked.

"No." Jake shook his head. "Everyone will know when it matters anyway."

"Fair," the Sword Saint said, nodding as he smiled. "While it saddens me to know that my own chances are slim on these Leaderboards, there is one thing we can all still do: prove we are the best party. Also, while Jake can indeed compete, his final score is still reliant on everyone here... so let's show them."

Jake smiled at the small pep-talk as he stood up. "I assume that means no more fucking around?"

The old man nodded. "Let's get back in gear and see how far we can truly go. Even if I cannot find my own name atop the Leaderboards... I guess it's acceptable to be known as one of the four party members of the top record holder."

CHAPTER 26

FLOOR SEVENTY-ONE

Welcome to the seventy-first floor of Nevermore: The Nine Towers
You have arrived on a planet long abandoned by those who once
lived there. Yet artifacts are left behind. Nine massive towers are
scattered across the planet, once part of a greater purpose, each
holding secrets and power of the civilization that once was.

Your goal is to explore each tower and then ultimately decide if you
wish to activate or destroy them. But be warned, for even if much
time has passed, the defensive systems of the towers still remain,
and who knows what entering them might lead to, much less the
outcome of their activations.

Main objective: Activate or destroy the Nine Towers.
Bonus objectives: Discover the true nature of the Nine Towers.
Current progress: Towers activated (0/9), Towers Destroyed (0/9)
Note: More hidden events, achievements, or objectives may be
hidden on the floor.
Current Nevermore Points: 1,242,425

It was almost nostalgic to read the long system message about the floor
they had just arrived on. Jake would rate it to be about as nostalgic as
the feeling of the Golden Mark left by the Fallen King, allowing them
all to stay in communication even when far apart.

The five of them had appeared on top of a small hill, giving them a
pretty bad view of what they were dealing with. Jake, taking the job of

scout as usual, quickly flew into the sky and scanned the area before he made a rough calculation of the curvature of the planet, ultimately concluding it was pretty fucking big. It was not as big as post-system Earth, but maybe about two-thirds the size.

"You see anything?" the Sword Saint asked when Jake landed back on the ground.

"Bunch of beasts, but they are all weak and barely in C-grade," Jake said. "Ah, but there are quite a few elementals here and there, their levels all around 280. I also spot two towers, one over there and one over there." He pointed in two directions. The others could see one of the towers far off in the distance, but only Jake had the Perception to see the tip of the second.

These towers were all roughly ten kilometers tall, looking like huge skyscrapers. One of the two Jake saw had a red crystalline color, while the second looked more yellowish. So, it appeared that the towers had been nicely color-coded, which made it a lot easier to communicate about what towers people were at.

Jake also shared the size of the planet and other characteristics as the others listened. Once he was done with his explanation, Dina briefly shared that the local plants told her that this planet was rather special: It had absolutely nothing underground, nor any bodies of water larger than lakes. It was definitely a weird place, but confirming those two things was helpful, as it meant they wouldn't waste any time looking for hidden achievements underground or underwater.

"So, I guess we all know what we're doing?" Jake asked after they were done talking.

"Split up," the Fallen King answered without any hesitation.

Dina nodded. "That does seem like the best way."

"Ree!" Sylphie agreed.

"Alright, and if anyone is in trouble... well, better make it on your own and get the fuck away, because no one will be nearby," Jake added with a grin. "Then we can all group back up and take down whatever may be the issue."

"Sounds like a plan," the Sword Saint said, seeming almost giddy to set off on his own. They all were.

After a brief division of where to go, they moved out. Dina would take the second-closest tower, while the Fallen King would take the closest. Jake, the Sword Saint, and Sylphie would head off in three other directions to try and find a tower each. The Sword Saint did stay behind for a second, though, as he took out a canvas and began to paint one of his teleportation paintings so he could return to the hilltop if needed.

Setting off, Jake quickly used One Step—

Everything warped for a second, and Jake suddenly found himself far beyond where he had wanted to step down, temporarily disorientating him. *What was... Oh.*

Jake had formed some estimates of his newly upgraded boots, concluding they were good but not overly impactful. His very first step disproved that. One Step had taken him nearly twice as far as usual and consumed even less stamina than before... and that wasn't even the crazy part.

The crazy part was that when Jake felt space warp around him, he remained utterly stable within this warped reality. It was like he was an untouchable entity within the fluid and shifting space. Only now did he truly realize the meaning of "always finding a solid foothold." What also surprised him was the concept behind this effect. It was pure stability. It was a slightly different concept from his arcane affinity, but definitely similar in many ways.

Taking a few more steps, Jake picked up speed as he continued to feel space warp. The reason space warped as it did was because the skill was getting pushed beyond what it normally allowed Jake to do forcibly... which introduced the easy fix of just following the advice he had given the Forsaken Dragonkin in regard to using the skill:

Get good.

It wasn't as if the boots actually made movement skills twice as effective and barely cost anything. No, Jake had just been horrible at using One Step, according to the standards of the mythical boots, which made the baseline improvement from the boots incredibly effective. Which was fair enough. One Step was just an ancient skill, after all.

Hours quickly passed as Jake zoomed forward, pretty damn proud of his speed. He had improved a lot, but as he felt the Golden Marks and the locations of his other party members, he realized he was definitely not the one who had improved the most. The Sword Saint, Dina, and Fallen King were also certainly moving faster, but Sylphie? Sylphie was on a whole other level as she zoomed about.

At first, he wondered if she was using her sprinting skill and would soon run out of gas. But she kept up her utterly ridiculous speed for hours as she moved far faster than Jake... No, not just Jake. The four other members of the party put together.

"*Hey, Sylphie,*" Jake said through the Golden Mark, "*you sure got a lot faster, eh?*"

"*Ree! Ree ree ree,*" she responded, gladly explaining how she had managed to drastically improve her ability to move incredibly swiftly while at the same time remaining ridiculously efficient.

"*I am not entirely sure what 'riding the wind super swooshily' means, but if it works, it works, I guess,*" Jake responded, realizing no Sylphie explanation would ever help him.

Not long after, the Fallen King became the first to reach his destination since he had gone to the closest tower. Right as he arrived, he contacted the group.

"*Allow me to send you some mental images of what I see,*" he communicated to all of them. It appeared he had made an upgrade to his Golden Mark skill, allowing him to now also send pictures. What the Fallen King sent couldn't really be called a picture, though.

Jake received an odd mental image of sorts that, while clearly visual in nature, just looked off in every way. He saw a strong outline of the tower, but the color of the tower was an odd shade of gray with weird lines going across it. He also saw what looked like veins running through the entire tower, as well as small wisps of energy in the ground and even floating in the air all around the Fallen King. Because oh, yeah—the picture wasn't exactly a two-dimensional one, but more of a semi-three-dimensional snapshot where what appeared in front of the Fallen King was far clearer than what was behind and to his sides.

"*Is... Is this how you see the world?*" Dina asked pretty quickly after the message was sent.

"*I tried to make it more interpretable to your minds,*" the Fallen King answered.

"*Imagine not having eyes,*" Jake joked, even if the lack of eyes was the reason the King's sight was so odd. He viewed everything through some weird soul-sight or something at all times, which definitely had some advantages but also many disadvantages, as his view distance was quite limited.

The King didn't say more as he entered the tower through a gate. Inside, the tower was clearly spatially expanded, and from what Jake saw in the limited "pictures" the Unique Lifeform repeatedly sent, everything was a mess inside. Nevertheless, he began exploring by looking over the lobby, trying to find any clues for the bonus objective.

After searching and not finding anything, he began to climb the stairs of the tower. There was also what looked like an elevator there, but it was clearly broken, and the Fallen King also quickly confirmed that breaking walls and ceilings wasn't feasible, as everything was incredibly strengthened. That wasn't to say it was impossible, just way too time-consuming.

Reaching the second tower floor, the challenges began to appear as they got their first clue as to what kind of creatures had built these towers in the first place. Robot-like golems were stationed as guards on the second tower floor. Eight in total, with four of them patrolling and four others in sealed-off side rooms. Their levels were all 275 to 280, making them relatively strong... but far from strong enough. This was also where the King's vision was good, as things like walls didn't matter when it came to detecting living beings nearby... which kind of made Jake feel dumb for having tried to hide from the King behind trees back in the tutorial.

The Fallen King didn't hesitate to simply float into the room with the four guards. He was instantly noticed by the guards, who quickly proved to be aggressive as they attacked on sight. When the four of them charged at once, the Fallen King raised one of his ivory claws, which began to glow with golden power.

A wave of golden force was blasted out the very next second, hitting all the guards. They all stumbled back, seemingly unhurt, but through the vision of the Fallen King, Jake could see it definitely wasn't so. Golden cracks had formed on their Soulshapes, signifying some significant soul damage.

Before they had a chance to attack again, the Fallen King continued forward and released a second golden wave. The four guards fell back further when a third wave came soon after. One of the four Soulshapes shattered on impact like it was made of glass, and the golem fell to the ground dead. A fourth wave spelled the end of the other three, the King keeping up his casual demeanor all the while.

Gotten a lot stronger, Jake mentally noted as the Unique Lifeform continued exploring the floor. However, it quickly became clear this wasn't going to be a fast endeavor. On a wall, he found a floor plan that depicted around a hundred floors in total for the tower, with the lower levels being residential and the higher ones research-based. The ones at the very top had no information on them at all, but just looking at the floor plans, Jake already had a good idea of what they were dealing with.

"Each of these towers are probably mini-dungeons of sorts that get progressively harder as you ascend," Jake communicated through the Golden Mark. *"Expect a boss of some kind towards the top. Also, since there are nine... if you get the chance to activate the tower, don't do so right away, alright? Getting a feeling we shouldn't just activate these towers willy-nilly."*

"As you will," the Fallen King responded, not trying to argue. The other three also quickly agreed. They had learned over many years that questioning Jake's gut feeling led to nothing good.

While the Fallen King continued his tower climb, the others continued exploring the planet. Dina soon reached her tower and began to climb it, and not long after, Sylphie also discovered one, which she promptly entered.

Jake peered down as he flew very high up in the sky, trying to get a proper lay of the land. Most of the planet was wide-open plains with a few lakes here and there, with intermittent large deserts in between. There were barely any mountains or hills. The only tall things were the towers.

What really surprised him was that he saw no buildings anywhere. No traces of any civilization having ever lived there at all, despite the floor descriptions. The roaming beasts were also surprisingly low in number. There were far fewer than Jake assumed there would be on a planet this big.

His big clue as to what was going on came when he saw what looked like a small forest. All the trees still looked young, making Jake frown and send a message to Dina. *"Hey, Dina, can you ask some of the plants you encounter how old they are?"*

"You also noticed?" she quickly responded. *"Something is wrong for sure. Meadows of grass can often be extremely old, yet I didn't meet any that were more than fifty years old. Actually, I have yet to encounter any plants older than a few decades at most..."*

Frowning at the revelation, an idea began to form in Jake's head. After a week or so, they had all reached towers and started exploring them. The Fallen King had taken nearly half a day just clearing one tower floor, and finding the way to the next one proved challenging simply due to how big they were while also being filled with enemies.

Jake was quite a lot faster, and despite reaching a tower just three days after their arrival, he had already overtaken the Fallen King by doing something very cheat-like. Rather than fight all the guards, Jake used Unseen Hunter to sneak through the tower, using his sphere to navigate.

Only on tower floor fifteen did Jake encounter the need to fight, as there were methods of detection he couldn't avoid... such as golems blocking doorways he had to pass through. Jake was making rapid progress, but he was not the only one, as all of them were breezing through the towers.

When they had finished Nevermore floor sixty-nine, they'd still done well, but things had begun to get hard toward the end, and getting good achievements had started to prove difficult. Now, it was as if they had been given a second wind from the Challenge Dungeons. They had gotten stronger, refined their skills, and refocused. However, that wasn't the only thing that had happened.

After just reaching C-grade, one would have a lot of momentum for gaining levels. They came fast and easy, at least for a little while. But soon, one began to run out of momentum as experience accumulated faster than quality Records, resulting in lower leveling speed. This was inescapable, even for someone like Jake, who had insane Records due to his Bloodline and Path as a whole.

Jake and all the others had leveled slowly for the last many years of doing floors... but that too had changed now. The Challenge Dungeons had given jack-shit when it came to experience but had instead refueled them all with new Records. It had filled up their momentum tanks, and now...

You have slain [Tower Golem Enforcer – lvl 287] – Bonus experience earned for killing an enemy above your level
'DING!' Class: [Arcane Hunter of Horizon's Edge] has reached level 257 - Stat points allocated, +50 Free Points
'DING!' Race: [Human (C)] has reached level 258 - Stat points allocated, +45 Free Points

The fast levels were now back on the menu as Jake slaughtered his way up the tower with excitement, feeling the same glee from the rest of his party. A second growth spurt was underway.

CHAPTER 27

CHIEF OVERSEER

Jake sat atop a pile of metal as he quickly deciphered the magical seal on the cube he had looted from the Tower Guardian lying destroyed beneath him. Once he got the cube open, he quickly checked its contents and nodded.

"Yep, I can confirm these towers are all made to terraform the planet in some crazy experiment," Jake sent through the Golden Mark. They had already kind of known it from other clues, but this was confirmation, which was good enough for the system.

Bonus Objective Completed: Discover the true nature of the Nine Towers. 3500 Nevermore Points earned.
Bonus Objective Gained: Locate the ones behind the construction of the Nine Towers.

Jake put the cube away as he jumped off the pile of metal and prepared to head to the top room of the tower, which he'd spotted through his sphere. As he walked toward the hidden stairs, he threw the large golem a final look with a smile. *Pretty fun fight, even if it was quite a bit weaker than the scalekin metal mage.*

His satisfaction with the fight was improved by the fact that he'd gained yet another level, and far faster than he had expected.

You have slain [White Tower Guardian – lvl 305] – Bonus experience earned for killing an enemy above your level

***'DING!' Class: [Arcane Hunter of Horizon's Edge] has reached
level 258 - Stat points allocated, +50 Free Points***

Jake was the first to reach the top of a tower due to the power of
stealth. The others were also doing their thing with swiftness, and it
wouldn't be that long before five of nine towers were conquered. He felt
confident all of his party members could beat the Guardian on their own,
assuming it was only as strong as the one he had just taken down.

Reaching the hidden staircase, Jake summoned his Alchemical Flame
and burned a hole in the wall, as he couldn't be arsed to try and find the
opening mechanism. Jake had already scanned the hidden room while
walking up the stairs, and while there was no one there, it was bloody filled
with electronic stuff.

The room below did have a few computer-like things, but Jake had the
feeling that it was just a front of sorts, while the real deal was to be found
on this hidden top floor. As he reached the top of the stairs, a new achievement popped up for all of them.

**Achievement earned: Reach the top of one of the Nine Towers and
uncover the hidden control room. 2000 Nevermore Points earned.**

They were pretty easy points, and Jake sure wouldn't complain. None
of the others did, either, as Jake found another cube with information and
deciphered it. This hidden control room was for advanced forms of
terraforming and managing the autonomous experiment still in progress.
In fact, it was revealed that should anyone mess with the control panels on
the floor below, the ones who had set up the experiment in the first place
would be alerted.

On this top floor, Jake also found a deactivated teleportation circle,
and while he didn't have a good grasp of how these kinds of things
worked, he could luckily do the same as the Fallen King and temporarily
share his vision. Using that, he learned from Dina that it was a special
closed-circuit teleportation circle. Collectively, they guessed that this circle
connected to corresponding circles in other towers.

Jake spent the next full day or so deciphering all the information he
could in the tower, primarily to figure out how to activate the teleportation circle. The magical puzzles to unlock stuff weren't that complicated,
and soon enough, Jake also came to learn that activating any one tower
would start a chain reaction in the others, the end result being the death of
anyone outside a tower. As for what would kill them...

"*So... not to scare anyone, but there seems to be a total of four space stations in orbit around this planet, as well as a few thousand satellites, all aimed to scorch the surface of the planet on command,*" Jake warned everyone. "*The good news is that we are in what's called a hibernation period right now, where only a few people are awake on the space stations, so as long as we don't activate something haphazardly, they probably shouldn't notice what we're doing.*"

At least, that was what Jake believed... but it quickly became clear that whoever was controlling these towers had already detected Jake and company and what they were doing, as they quickly deployed countermeasures. Luckily, they couldn't activate the extermination protocol without entering the towers, but transport ships were sent down, filled with even more C-grade golems.

It was a great time all around. Jake had initially been a bit disappointed with the number of enemies, but now they were practically being delivered on a silver platter. After Jake left the tower, he was attacked by a few dozen golems who seemed intent on capturing rather than killing, but he was having none of that. He destroyed all of them—after getting agreement from his party that this was the right course of action, of course.

This seemed to get the message across, as every subsequent attack was made with deadly intent. Jake kept exploring the planet with intermittent fights, all the while sensing the observation of the satellites far above. About a week later, the Fallen King finished exploring his tower, too, followed by the three others, who completed theirs within a few days. As predicted, every time a tower was cleared, they could activate the teleportation circles and travel between them freely.

This was a necessity, as the annoying space golems kept coming down and entering the towers, trying to take back control—or worse, activate the towers and kill everything on the planet. This forced their party to keep two people on defense at all times, teleporting between towers when necessary to fend off attacks. This task was assigned to the Fallen King and Dina, who was especially well-suited to defense since she could—quite literally—take root and plant flowers to both forewarn and defend. The Fallen King was just a menace in the smallish hallways, and his soul attacks were especially effective against larger crowds of golems. Oh, yeah, and he was pretty damn slow anyway.

Meanwhile, Jake, Sylphie, and the Sword Saint acted on their own to get the final four towers. Due to the size of the planet, they had to travel a lot while getting harassed by the damn space golems, who seemed to have endless numbers.

After an additional month, the second batch of towers had been taken over, bringing their total number of captures to eight of the nine towers. However, the final tower turned out to be quite a bit more difficult to capture than the others, as the researchers had decided to fortify the location. The attacks on the other towers didn't stop, though, and ultimately, they decided on just having Jake and Sylphie attack the final one, the Sword Saint also staying back to defend while researching more of what these towers could do. When they finally conquered the last tower, the ability to teleport to one of the four space stations was also unlocked, and... well...

One thing led to another, and around a year later, Jake and company crashed through the atmosphere on a mothership while fighting a horde of five-meter-tall mechs with miniguns. The end of floor seventy-one was close at hand.

Only a final fight awaited them, as they needed an access code to start something called the Revitalization Protocol, which would begin restoring the planet to its former state while putting an end to the experiment that had periodically killed all life on the planet. The entire point of this experiment had been manipulation of the planet's innate affinities, and from the looks of it, the researchers had failed horribly despite keeping the experiment going for so long.

Now, Jake, Sylphie, Dina, the Fallen King, and the Sword Saint found themselves standing in front of the burning wreckage of what had once been a kilometer-wide mothership. The vessel had served to coordinate with the four space stations that they had naturally also destroyed.

From the wreckage, a single figure rose, having been awakened from hibernation by the crash. It remained entirely undamaged, as it had been in a sealed-off control room. Standing over ten meters tall, the robot-like creature reminded Jake of those car-transforming robots from movies and TV, and when it pulled out a sword, Jake feared copyright infringement was taking place right in front of his eyes. Things got a bit better when it activated what was clearly some kind of astral magic, which Jake definitely hadn't seen in the movies. Oh, yeah, it was also definitely a lot stronger than the movie robots... by far the strongest thing on this floor, at least.

[Chief Overseer – lvl 320]

The party didn't even have to communicate as they made their move. The Fallen King and Sword Saint moved toward the robot as Sylphie circled around and Jake created some distance. Dina was the only one who remained roughly in place as she took out her staff and cast supportive magic on their two frontliners.

Mana gathered as a large discharge of astral energy was released from the boss, bathing the surrounding area. The old power generators of the mothership served to amplify this mana, effectively creating a massive domain that helped empower the boss.

With swift movement, especially for such a large creature, the Chief Overseer charged at the Sword Saint, who was closest. The old man didn't react as the huge blade bathed in starlight descended, and two barriers overlapped right before he was hit—one green and one golden.

Not having to block, the old man drew his blade and released a large crescent cut that sent sparks and small metal fragments flying, pushing the robot back. At the very same time, an arrow also arrived, but in an impressive display of dexterity, the boss managed to barely block using its blade.

Sadly, this made it unable to defend itself when a green whirlwind struck from behind, throwing it entirely off balance. The Fallen King didn't sit idly, either; while he had made a barrier with one claw, he used his second to blast a shockwave of force into the robot's leg. A second barrage of Arrow Rain struck the boss soon after, with the Sword Saint also following up.

The Chief Overseer wasn't weak enough to fall to this pressure, though. Its entire form turned into light as it teleported right behind Dina, evading another barrage of attacks. It swung its blade down toward the dryad, only to find itself blocked by Bobo, her living armor, which was already ready to defend as Dina turned and slammed her staff down.

A torrent of vines erupted from the ground, entangling the boss and launching it airborne just as another Arcane Powershot blasted it to the side, sending even more metal parts flying. The other three struck again, forcing the robot to turn into a beam of light once more, this time going after Jake.

However, right as it appeared behind Jake, he just smiled and took a step that teleported him nearly five kilometers away. With a second step, he was back with his party, almost ten kilometers from the boss. This was when they learned the big robot also had some solid ranged-weapon options, as light erupted from its back and shot toward the five of them in dozens of warping beams.

The boss moved and arrived at the same time as the attack, but its sword found little purchase as a vine erupted from the ground and stopped its swinging arm. A shockwave of force sent the robot flying as the Sword Saint, Jake, and Sylphie all unleashed ranged attacks, resulting in the Chief Overseer getting pushed further and further back while trying to defend itself, revealing several other weapons that all proved mostly useless.

One could say many things about this boss, but it was definitely durable. Despite all of them attacking repeatedly, they had managed to do little noticeable damage, and whenever they did cut or blast off large chunks of metal, the Chief Overseer used some kind of self-repair magic. Alas, even if it looked like the robot was barely being damaged, its energy resources were drained at a rapid rate. The large astral domain did help the robot, but honestly, it barely seemed to do anything, as the Fallen King and Dina both messed with it in between attacks.

What the boss also severely lacked were adequate offensive tools. The sword strikes seemed strong, but against the double barriers, it simply didn't stand a chance. While it did have a lot of offensive options, none of them were truly powerful. Minutes passed, the boss slowly getting whittled down until they finally reached the second phase of the fight.

Turning into a beam of light, the Chief Overseer returned to the wreckage of the mothership. It floated just above the pile of metal and stopped, then raised its sword toward the sky. The sword rapidly began to transform into an umbrella-looking thing, and at the same time, the astral domain also reacted.

It imploded in an instant, draining all the energy that remained in the batteries of the mothership. A dense barrier of powerful mana surrounded the boss. The umbrella-like thing was revealed to be some kind of satellite dish when, a moment later, it shot a beam of light toward the sky.

"Kill it quickly!" Jake sent through the Golden Mark, as he got the feeling things would get annoying if they didn't hurry. It didn't take a genius to figure out the Chief Overseer was communicating with the many satellites still floating in orbit far above them.

In response to Jake's words, no one held back.

A giant golden beam erupted from the Fallen King, shearing away much of the barrier, followed by a pillar of pure vines that burst up right below the boss, physically piercing the barrier and forming cracks all over it. Jake's Protean Arrow arrived next, shattering the entire barrier and bathing the Chief Overseer in an explosion of powerful arcane energy. Yet even so, it didn't stop what it was doing, even if it did move the arm, not holding the transformed sword to form a shield... which ended up doing very little.

The Sword Saint stood right in front of the giant robot as he drew his blade. His entire aura changed when he did, and his entire body seemed to turn younger for a second as he executed what was still the single most powerful attack anyone in their party was capable of.

"Glimpse of Spring: Stormcut."

As if a new crescent moon of water was born on the surface of the planet, the swing released a massive wave that cut through the large robot. The arm it tried to defend with was severed, and half of its body was also sliced, doing extreme damage as several parts began falling to the ground. Yet the Chief Overseer had barely survived. For half a second longer, that is.

A loud boom echoed out as a green gust passed, serving as the calm before the storm. The Chief Overseer barely managed to turn its head before Sylphie arrived in the form of a massive green tornado that had taken the rough form of a drill, Sylphie herself serving as the pointed end.

The weakened robot was blasted entirely apart, the beam of light from the sword fading away. Yet as it did, Jake's danger sense also warned him, so he quickly called through the Golden Mark, *"Self-destruct!"*

Without needing any further prompts, everyone arrived at Dina's location almost instantly, as she was already casting her magic. Everyone helped form their own barriers, and just as they did, the boss's body lit up, went supernova, and exploded, sending out a wave of powerful, destructive astral light.

Several defensive barriers were burned away, but in the end, the death explosion failed to get through Dina's final barrier. It soon faded, leaving the party standing in an utterly massive crater, the wreckage of the mothership entirely obliterated. The only trace that remained was a large sword now stuck in the ground in the middle of the crater. It wasn't far-fetched to assume that was where the access codes could be found.

Also, it wasn't some bait-and-switch, as the boss was indeed very much dead.

You have slain [Chief Overseer – lvl 320] – Bonus experience earned for killing an enemy above your level
'DING!' Class: [Arcane Hunter of Horizon's Edge] has reached level 259 - Stat points allocated, +50 Free Points
'DING!' Race: [Human (C)] has reached level 259 - Stat points allocated, +45 Free Points

"Well done, everyone," the Sword Saint said, looking a bit tired as he usually did after pulling off his Transcendent mini-version skill.

Jake nodded as he smiled. It sure was good to have the whole gang together, and they had all gotten substantially stronger, not to mention the second wind of levels that would just make them all grow even faster. It honestly made him feel bad for the poor enemies on the floors to come...

Alas, sacrifices were inevitable in the glorious pursuit of making numbers go up.

CHAPTER 28

LEVEL 260 CLASS SKILL SELECTION

I t didn't take long before they used the access code to finish off the seventy-first floor, having done so quite a lot faster than floor seventy. Also, while it was true these floors were quite a lot bigger than those before, everyone in the party had also gotten quite a bit faster, and when fighting didn't slow them down as much, it added up.

Activating the Revitalization Protocol took place within one of the towers, all five of them standing together as Jake pressed the big red button. When he did, all of the towers hummed to life, sending beams of light into the sky and releasing waves of mana that washed over the landscape. All of the satellites in orbit also began to shoot down beams that infused the world with mana and different affinities, doing just as the protocol said it would. Soon, the satellites would run out of energy and shut down, and the towers were also quickly emptying themselves, putting an end to the experiment once and for all.

With time, the planet would recover, and the towers would become empty relics that would eventually break down due to environmental factors. Jake and company naturally had no intention of sticking around for that long, as they saw that, behind them, a door had appeared right beside the teleporter taking them to various towers.

"Well, this floor could have gone worse," Jake muttered as they all entered the door to the in-between room. Sadly, this one was as boring as the prior ones, with only Minaga having had interesting variants. It had the same features, such as one door to the latest city floor, one to the next floor, and, naturally, the one they had just entered through.

"The Nevermore Points are adequate, if fewer than I expected," the Fallen King said.

"I just think our sense of what we should get was warped by the Challenge Dungeons rewarding so many," the Sword Saint responded as Jake also checked over all the Nevermore Points they had gained from the floor —minus the two bonus objectives Jake had completed early on.

**Seventy-first floor completed. 14,200 Nevermore Points earned.
Achievement earned: Activate five tower teleporters within a
month (30 days) of each other. 3000 Nevermore Points earned.
Achievement Earned: Never once allow any of the Researchers to
enter the top floor of a tower. 3000 Nevermore Points earned.
Achievement earned: Defeat the entire command structure of the
Researchers. 5000 Nevermore Points earned.
Achievement earned: Defeat the Chief Overseer without ever
allowing it to trigger any of the satellites. 5000 Nevermore Points
earned.
Achievement Earned: Do not cause needless destruction or kill
unnecessary wildlife. 1000 Nevermore Points gained.
Achievement earned: Activate the Revitalization Protocol. 10,000
Nevermore Points earned.
Achievement earned: Complete the seventy-first floor within 500
days while triggering the Revitalization Protocol. 7000 Nevermore
Points earned.
Current Nevermore Points: 1,296,125**

Overall, the floor had given just a bit over 50,000 Nevermore Points, making it quite good. Less efficient than the Challenge Dungeons, yes, but those had honestly been overpowered when it came to getting points, just as the Sword Saint said. Speaking of points from the Challenge Dungeons, Jake wondered...

"So, I need to ask... do I have the most Nevermore Points with—"

"Yes, you do, Jake," the Sword Saint cut in before Jake had a chance to unsubtly humble-brag. "Now, do we need a recovery period, or should we proceed immediately?"

Jake was a bit bummed, but with the others wanting to get a move on, he agreed, and they went to floor seventy-two.

Right as they entered the door, they found themselves in the middle of what looked like a hastily constructed city square, and the floor description popped up.

Welcome to the seventy-second floor of Nevermore: Settlers of Kantaan

Jake quickly skimmed the rest of the description, and to sum it up... this was a city-defense floor, at least for the most part. The story was that a faction of different enlightened species had sent people to this faraway planet using some special teleportation measure to set up a city in preparation for the rest of the citizens, who would arrive in a big ark at a later date. The problem was that they had kind of fucked up when measuring what kind of beings already lived on the planet and how receptive they would be to these new settlers.

Because the natives were not happy with these unwelcome guests.

Their job was to defend this city from rampaging beasts belonging to different monster factions present on the planet while also expanding and placing two new settlements for when help arrived. This help would come in the form of the ark that would arrive after five years, based on the description, but through different means, they could help them speed up and come faster.

There was probably more to it, but Jake and company didn't have much time to think, as soon after arriving, an attack came from a horde of rampaging monsters. They were a mix of dinosaur-looking beasts, and based on what Jake and the others later learned, the beasts generally came in four flavors: lizards, mammals, elementals, and even undead.

"There is probably some moral question here regarding settlers just coming to a new planet and trying to take it over unceremoniously," Jake said, the Sword Saint nodding.

"It's effectively a form of colonialism," the old man added, "though the matter is complicated by these settlers having been forced to go here by their faction. They don't have much of a choice, effectively making them refugees."

Dina looked a bit confused as they talked. "Why is it complicated? Isn't it normal to want to spread out and expand even if you are not forced to? This faction merely wishes to grow and has sent a seed to sprout on this planet."

"On our homeworld, the act of expanding and forcing out the natives already living there has a very negative history, and for good reason," the Sword Saint answered calmly.

"But if any living being needs to keep expanding to realize their Path, it's natural that others will be pushed away. A tree's growing crown steals sunlight from those in its shade, and there is limited mana for all to share in the ground below." Dina didn't sound like she was trying to argue, but was simply confused about why Jake and the Sword Saint even discussed morals in this case.

"*Humans from Earth are always keen on discussing the rights and wrongs of a situation,*" the Fallen King chimed in. "*I learned that plenty by attending the World Council we established. Yet they are also utter hypocrites in many matters, including happily encroaching on nature to expand their settlements and industries. As long as they don't hurt other humans, they tend to show little care.*"

"Isn't that fine?" Dina said. "Humans are a social species who live together, and their Path is to grow through working in unison and sharing Legacies and whatnot. To care about the preservation of humans over the lives of others is just natural."

"You know what?" Jake said. "Now we're getting all philosophical again, which we frankly don't have the time to do, as the attack arrives in... like thirty seconds. So, quick vote, do we do the objective and defend the city, or try to look for an alternative solution?"

Jake wanted to put things to a vote to finish up quickly, but... well, it turned out no one really wanted to vote, as they simply didn't have any strong feelings either way, making everyone abstain in case someone did have an opinion. Jake also didn't particularly care if these settlers were evil colonialists or desperate refugees; he was just there for the levels, and if defending the budding city gave more levels, he was all for it.

On a side note, Jake did think his leveling had been a bit slow on the prior floor, even if he had admittedly avoided combat when he could, as the hunting teams and whatnot weren't that interesting of opponents. Also, the Path Jake walked was one where he wanted to be challenged, so he wanted to avoid easy fights, but still, levels had come slow.

Well, it turned out part of the reason Jake had leveled slowly was that he'd been on the edge of a level-up when they killed the Chief Overseer... which translated to Jake also getting a level within an hour of arriving on floor seventy-two.

'DING!' Class: [Arcane Hunter of Horizon's Edge] has reached level 260 - Stat points allocated, +50 Free Points

Jake got the level, and after only a bit more fighting, all the attackers were dead. At this point, he had already informed his party of his level-up. Everyone gave him knowing looks as he retreated from the frontlines and found a little spot to sit and chill. There, he smiled and opened the system menu. That's right—it was time for an old tradition.

Arcane Hunter of Horizon's Edge class skills available

It had been quite a while since Jake had his last new class skill. Back then, he had selected Arcane Supremacy, which had been a great boon, and he was definitely looking forward to what was on offer this time around. With all the Challenge Dungeons, there had to be traces of Records from those in the skills available.

With great expectations, he proceeded as usual and went through his options one by one.

[Superior Arcane Kick (Rare)] – You have shown yourself an experienced martial artist, allowing you to—

Jake kept smiling, even if he was saddened to see there were only four new skills available... because fuck that shit. So, he moved on to the first real option, even if it wasn't that much better.

[Cursed Arcane Bolt of Hunger (Rare)] - Allows the Hunter to summon bolts of arcane mana containing curse energy to defeat your foes. Two kinds of bolts can be summoned: a stable and a destructive version. The destructive bolts will explode upon impact, and the stable version will be tough and piercing. Stable cursed arcane bolts will have slow-acting curse energy, while destructive cursed arcane bolts will act aggressively. Due to the Sin Curse of Hunger, the overall damage of the Cursed Arcane Bolt is reduced in exchange for all damage dealt, now stealing a slight amount of energy. Adds a small bonus to the effect of Intelligence when using Cursed Arcane Bolt of Hunger.

This was one of those skills Jake had no intention of ever selecting but still valued, as it gave him some insight into what was possible. It had clearly been gained due to his research and improvement of his control of curse energy during the House of the Architect, and was an interesting merging of curse energy and Jake's arcane affinity. Having life-stealing arcane bolts definitely did seem intriguing, even if he wasn't sure how useful it would actually be if it came at the cost of overall damage done.

Either way, cool skill to look at, but not really an option. Especially not with such a low rarity. Not that the next skill was *that* much of an improvement either, even if the rarity at least went up.

[Destabilizing Arcane Explosion (Epic)] – Remain unimpeded as you destabilize the world and all that seeks to harm you. Allows you to erupt in a destructive arcane explosion with the aim of disrupting all energy constructs and the concept of stability itself in your immediate surroundings. This arcane explosion will significantly weaken all environmental mana and objects, and is incredibly effective at dismantling enemy energy constructs. Adds a bonus to the effects of Wisdom, Willpower, and Intelligence when using Destabilizing Arcane Explosion.

He wasn't quite sure what to think about this one. Was he going to pick it? No, definitely not, but the concepts in play were a bit surprising. The description told him that it was possible to directly attack the concept of stability itself using his arcane mana, which was... well, wasn't that pretty much what the acid Jake had made also did? It kind of was.

Definitely another one of those skills to keep in mind for future freeform magic and when considering other upgrades. He was a bit surprised at one thing, though. This was the third skill, and it was only epic rarity. He had kind of expected better with his high-tier class. Then again, he probably shouldn't be that surprised.

Jake had read something a good while back that made him theorize the skills weren't that awesome due to him having already improved some himself. Seeing an upgraded version of Mark was definitely something he could have imagined, along with a better stealth skill. So it seemed like the system had to make skills more from things Jake had done rather than the innate Records of the class itself. Not to say there weren't any skills like that... the next one available being one such example.

[Barrier of the Arcane Hunter of Horizon's Edge (Ancient)] – Embrace stability as you become impervious. Allows the Arcane Hunter of Horizon's Edge to summon a barrier of pure, stable arcane energy, blocking out any kinds of direct attacks that attempt to pass through—both physical and magical alike. This effect is further improved when blocking attacks from long distances and higher-leveled foes. All affinities not of your creation will be significantly suppressed within the barrier and a slight area around it. Mana or stamina will be consumed depending on the

nature of the blocked attacks. Adds a bonus to the effects of
Wisdom and Endurance when using Arcane Barrier of the Arcane
Hunter of Horizon's Edge.

Definitely the first "real" skill to consider. It was very similar to the barrier skill that had been offered back in D-grade, even having the same concept-suppressing effects. This one was quite a bit better, though. He especially liked the part about its effectiveness increasing based on enemy power and distance.

Admittedly, Jake did kind of lack a good defensive skill. Right now, he relied on freeform stable barriers and Scales of the Malefic Viper whenever he had to block an attack he couldn't simply avoid. Then again, that was also the biggest reason why he maybe didn't need the skill: Jake would rather just dodge. So this skill would only be useful when there was no other choice.

That led to the question of how much better it was than just a few layers of freeform stable barriers coupled with Scales. Jake naturally had no way to determine that, but it was a valid concern, in his mind.

Ultimately, Jake wasn't *that* keen on the skill, even if it could be useful in some cases. He was more interested in just improving his freeform arcane magic instead, perhaps taking some inspiration from this skill. He had taken inspiration from the last barrier skill offered, too, partly in his Unseen Hunter skill, where the barrier he could create when not moving was capable of suppressing concepts.

Moving on, Jake honestly felt a bit disappointed so far. However, when he saw the final skill... yeah, he still wasn't sure how to feel. The rarity looked great, at least.

[Brave Presence of the Emerging War God (Mythical)] – As you set
foot upon the battlefield, let none hold doubt that a god of war has
appeared. Having proven yourself and received the personal
recognition of Valdemar, you have shown yourself to truly have the
bravery and presence required to one day be recognized as a true
War God. Allows you to emanate a Presence of Bravery by infusing
it with inner energy, increasing the physical stats of all allies
nearby while putting mental pressure on your opponents. Any
allies fighting in the presence of the Emerging War God will be
nearly impervious to all forms of mental attacks. As bravery fills
their spirits, retreat is no option, as even when resources are
lacking, bravery remains. All effects of Brave Presence of the

Emerging War God scale with Willpower and Endurance, as well
as your overall level of power.

There was no need to try and theorize how Jake had unlocked this skill choice. It said why right there in the description. This had been born from the Records of Jake clashing directly with Valdemar, probably coupled with the Primordial's genuine intentions of having Jake join Valhal. Records recognizing Jake could be an Emerging War God.

Jake wasn't sure how to feel about that.

Ignoring everything else and just looking at the skill, Jake had to recognize it was a damn powerful one. It would allow him to make everyone around him more powerful simply by proximity, put pressure on enemies, and even make all allies borderline immune to certain forms of magic. Based on that thing about bravery and lacking resources, Jake also read it as allowing those influenced by him to keep fighting despite not having stamina and mana left. All in all, it was a mythical skill through and through… but not one fitting Jake's Path at all.

The skill never once mentioned making Jake himself stronger. Even if it did, the skill still had a stamina cost Jake didn't doubt would be high. He didn't need all the mental resistance stuff, either. This skill was, without a shadow of a doubt, absolutely incredible for someone leading an army or even a party leader, but Jake was neither of those. He was a hunter who was solo most of the time. He was no god of war, and quite frankly, he didn't want to become one.

In the short term, this skill would probably still be useful since he was fighting in Nevermore with his party, but what about when they were out? Jake was going to be alone for the most part again, out hunting more and more powerful foes. This skill would be nearly useless in that case.

Not to mention how Jake felt it would "pollute" his Path as a hunter to have a skill like this. He feared it could end up unlocking a bunch of other commander-like skills in the future, which Jake definitely didn't want.

No… no, while the skill was interesting and even a bit flattering, it wasn't one Jake wanted. It didn't fit him, no matter how powerful it was.

This left Jake with a bit of a problem when the usual strategy of just picking the highest-rarity skill at the end of the list didn't work. It didn't help that he didn't like any of the other skills on offer, either.

However, where one sees challenges, there can also be opportunities. Because while none of these five options were any good, they weren't the only ones he had to choose between. Jake still vividly remembered the skill he had skipped for Arcane Supremacy when he reached 230, and when he checked the list, it was still there, just as he had hoped.

He was naturally talking about Penetrating Arcane Arrow of Horizon's Edge.

> *[Penetrating Arcane Arrow of Horizon's Edge (Ancient)] – No defenses shall stop your arrows as they pierce the foes that dare impede your Path toward the horizon. Allows the Hunter to create a Penetrating Arcane Arrow that will pierce through nearly any natural barriers and have a far higher penetrative effect on any defenses made by the target. Will temporarily lower the defenses of the foe if they are struck successfully. These effects scale in power with the enemy's defenses and the level disparity between you and higher-level opponents. On an internal cooldown, the Horizon-Chasing Hunter can push himself beyond his usual abilities and infuse the concepts of the Penetrating Arrow of Horizon's Edge into another self-created arcane arrow. Doing this will temporarily make the skill unavailable, with this period dependent on the power of the arrow you infused. Due to their conceptual synergy, Penetrating Arcane Arrow of Horizon's Edge receives significantly increased bonuses from Unblemished Arrows of the Horizon. Adds a bonus to the effectiveness of Agility, Strength, Wisdom, Intelligence, and Perception when using Penetrating Arcane Arrow of Horizon's Edge.*

Reading this skill once more, Jake felt certain. He had wanted it back then and had only skipped it because Arcane Supremacy was just too good in comparison. Now, there was no clearly superior other choice, and Jake was more than pleased with selecting this one, as it would finally give him proper armor-penetrating attacks. The ability to infuse the skill into another self-created arrow was of particular interest, as he looked forward to seeing it mesh with Protean Arrow.

After barely any more thinking, Jake selected the skill. Instinctual knowledge entered his mind as he closed his eyes and took everything in. Once he had fully internalized all the knowledge, he opened his eyes again to find that the Sword Saint had come over to check in as they waited for the next attack to arrive.

"Got a good new skill?" the old man asked with a smile. He still had a couple more levels to go before it was his turn, but it wouldn't be long.

"Yeah," Jake said, nodding as he stood up.

The Sword Saint smiled even more as he raised an eyebrow. "You know, while you were selecting a skill, the others and I discussed this floor, and we agreed that perhaps it would be wise to send one of us out to scout the area and see if we could slay any leaders or commanders in charge of—"

"Yes," Jake interrupted as he grinned. He wasn't going to say no to a chance like that.

"How lucky you agreed; I was just thinking you would be suitable for the job." The old man chuckled. "Now, get going as we hold down the fort. Stay in touch and keep us informed of what you find."

Jake didn't need to be told twice that he could go play. He took to the air, briefly exchanging a glance with his party members as he passed. As they all waved him off, he heard the Sword Saint's voice through the Golden Mark.

"Happy hunting."

CHAPTER 29

SOME PROPER BLOODY HUNTING

A vast grassland filled with flowing hills, some of which were kilometers tall, stretching as far as the eye could see. Large piles of dirt were stacked atop many of the tallest hills as monsters sat there, watching the horizon.

The grasslands themselves were filled with beasts of all sorts. They populated the area, many having made small nests or caves to call their own as they took in the dense natural mana filling the environment. In some of the deep valleys between the hills, forests could be found, creating natural barriers to defend the beasts within while also serving as focal points of natural mana gathering. These small forests were where the strongest beasts were gathered, absorbing the environmental mana to grow stronger while at the same time allowing their kin to function as meat shields should there ever be an invasion.

Within the deepest of all these forests, a powerful being sat in a clearing, munching on fruit that could only be classified as valuable natural treasures. It was a large beast, about four meters tall, with two arms and legs, incredibly thick fur, and two curved horns growing on each side of its head. It was incredibly bulky, and the long hair and hide looked more suited for a cold environment, which wasn't overly surprising when one saw its race.

[Woodland Yeti Lord – lvl 310]

It was a creature that had likely left the cold northern pole of the planet and evolved with time to become the local lord. With its power, it had become an overlord of these vast plains, leading and commanding its forces to attack the newcomers who had come and begun to encroach on its domain. So far, it had only sent the weaker of its kin, but with time, it would no doubt send more, perhaps even joining the assault on this new settlement itself. Naturally, it would also have to consider the movements of the other lords first so as to not weaken itself needlessly.

For now, there didn't seem to be any rush as the yeti ate the fruit and absorbed the energy within. The plains were peaceful, and the guards hadn't reported anything wrong. Not that the Yeti Lord wouldn't know if something was wrong even without those weak guards. This was its domain, after all. It had skills that made it impossible for anything to strike it unnoticed from any—

The warning from its danger sense arrived too late, and even when it tried to move... it couldn't. Its very soul shook with fear as some powerful apex predator's eyes landed on it.

The Woodland Yeti Lord barely had time to move its neck before an object struck the top of its skull. A passive skill of the yeti activated to make its hide and long hair significantly more durable, but the sharp object still easily pierced through, hardly meeting any resistance.

Blood flew out but was annihilated by the purplish destructive energy surrounding the attack as the sharp projectile went into the yeti's skull and continued its descent through its entire body before striking the ground beneath, sending up an explosion of soil, rock, blood, and flesh. It was all embraced by destructive energies as hundreds of trees all around the clearing fell over from the impact's shockwave.

The Woodland Yeti Lord tried to fight back against its certain death, but as if to rub salt in the wound, a powerful toxin had quite literally been rubbed into all of its wounds, making the situation more than a little bleak.

Still, a late-tier C-grade lord was not to be trifled with. A powerful skill activated, enlarging and empowering the yeti's body as it used its ultimate boosting skill in a last-ditch effort to—

A second attack arrived, and a second explosion rang out within the forest. The yeti, who was already almost dead, fell over on the soil that pulsed with powerful veins of destructive energy, never to get up again. In such a fashion, one of the powerful lords of the planet fell in the midst of its own domain. Slain without anyone ever even noticing that a hunter had chosen it as prey.

———

*You have slain [Woodland Yeti Lord – lvl 310] – Bonus
experience earned for killing an enemy above your level*

Jake stood in mid-air, staring down at the scene far below and the carnage
he had wrought. Several hundred kilometers beneath him, a clearing had
been destroyed, leaving a crater with a dead yeti in the middle; all the trees
around this clearing had been tipped over away from the crater. Four more
arrows fell atop the corpse in the following second or two—unnecessary, in
the grand scheme of things, but Jake had shot them just to make sure. It
took a while for his arrows to arrive, after all, so he couldn't wait to see the
results before deciding if he had to shoot more.

At that moment, Jake felt both happiness and a small tinge of annoyance. Happy that he had killed a boss monster of the Nevermore floor so
easily, but a tad annoyed he hadn't done so in a single shot. It was the peak
of first-world problems, and Jake knew it, but he had still hoped to kill the
yeti in one shot. Things were only made worse by how bloody close he'd
come with that single arrow.

I'll get the next boss in one shot, Jake assured himself as he reentered
stealth and moved on in another direction. Using a mix of ridiculously
high Perception, his tracking skill, and just looking at where monsters
tended to gather, Jake sought out the next lord for him to test his newly
empowered most powerful arrow on.

It ended up only taking him a few more days before he arrived at a big
lake with a few smaller islands in the middle, the largest of which had a big
lizard on it, just chilling there in its home. When Jake saw it, he was happy;
it had really thick scales, which was helpful when testing his new Penetrating Arrow. Or at least, more useful as a test target than the yeti had
been.

[Targehide Lizard Lord – lvl 308]

This lord looked a lot like an ankylosaurus. Why did Jake know what
an ankylosaurus looked like? Well, he, like many others, had also had a
period in his life where he liked to read online wikis for far too long, giving
him more knowledge about ancient dinosaurs than he could possibly ever
need.

Anyway, the ankylosaurus was known for its incredibly thick armor,
especially on its back. This Targehide Lizard was exactly the same, with a
back covered in thick plates of tough hide and studded with gem-looking

dots. Despite being two levels lower than the yeti, this one was definitely stronger and far more durable.

Floating far up in the air, Jake began his setup for the one-hit kill attempt. First of all, before he even flew up to his attack location, he'd marked the lizard, revealing the outline of its Soulshape and naturally increasing all the damage he would do to it. As he observed it closely, Hunting Momentum was also building up just a little bit. Not much, but everything counted.

While Jake didn't have full knowledge of his opponent, he did have a good enough general idea of what he needed as he began to construct his Protean Arrow. Far up in the sky and within his Unseen Hunter stealth field, Jake wove countless strings into an arrow made to pierce the thick natural armor of the dinosaur.

Once the arrow was fully assembled, Jake observed the one-and-a-half-meter-long, spear-like arrow and nodded, satisfied. Usually, he would have created the arrowhead with a payload at the front to explode and break apart some of the armor to get through, but from the last arrow, he felt certain that wasn't needed. Within this one, he could hide another surprise.

Taking out a bottle of Heartrot Poison, he coated the arrowhead fully, making sure there was plenty for the big body of the dinosaur far below. Lastly, he moved on to the new step in his preparation phase that had been introduced by the Penetrating Arrow skill.

Holding the shaft, Jake channeled energy into the Protean Arrow. There was no visual effect except for a brief moment where a small gleam of energy ran across the entire arrow. It didn't feel any different either, but Jake smiled as he felt the effect, took out his bow, and drew a deep breath.

Arcane Awakening activated fully at 60% in the very next second, making his body erupt with arcane energy. As a reminder, using the boosting skill during preparations didn't really have any effects and often made things harder, as his energy was more volatile due to the boosting skill.

Nocking the arrow, Jake took aim at the dinosaur below. It was relaxing, hidden within a small cave on the island, but with the Mark, Jake could easily see through the rock. The eight or so meters of rock the arrow would have to pierce through before hitting the dinosaur didn't really matter, courtesy of Penetrating Arrow. Due to its increased bonus from Unblemished Arrows, the destructive arcane energy surrounding the arrow would be enough to easily shear away a few dozen meters of un-reinforced rock.

Energy began to spike around him as he charged Arcane Powershot. Seconds passed, and the energy kept building. Several skills were working in tandem, reinforcing and stacking on top of one another. Big Game Hunter, Unblemished Arrows, his archery skill, Mark, Steady Aim, Arcane Supremacy, Stealth Attack, and several others... all to unleash one devastating strike few C-grades his level would ever have a chance of matching.

While it was true that the Sword Saint had the strongest attack in their party with his Glimpse of Spring—not counting the Fallen King's unique skill—that was only during normal combat. In circumstances like this, the old man simply didn't stand a chance against Jake's sheer offensive might, and they all knew it, which was why Jake had been given this task.

Jake continued charging his arrow for a dozen more seconds before he felt his body straining to hold on. His skin flayed, but as always, he pushed himself just to the very edge before he released the string. A massive explosion of arcane energy rocked the sky, all of it concealed within the domain he'd created with Unseen Hunter, resulting in no one noticing.

What they did have a slight chance of noticing was the rapidly descending arrow, but even that was mostly hidden by his stealth skill.

Right after shooting his first arrow, Jake shot another, followed by several more in quick succession, all using Arcane Powershot. He only stopped when he felt like something in his shoulder would break if he shot one more. Besides, it was also time for the final nail in the coffin.

Within the cave, the dinosaur noticed the first attack a few moments before it arrived, warned by its instincts. However, right as it tried to mobilize its energy to defend, it found itself fully incapacitated due to the orange glow of Primal Gaze in Jake's eyes. This was one of the hidden bonuses from Mark... Despite the physical barrier, Jake still had clear visual contact that allowed him to see the Soulshape, which was more than good enough for Primal Gaze.

Effortlessly, the arrow penetrated the eight meters of rock before striking the Targehide Lizard Lord in the back, right where the armor was strongest. The sheer impact created a crater and destroyed the entire cave, sending out a shockwave that rocked the small island as the beast slammed into the ground. Jake would be lying if he said it didn't face resistance, but it still managed to pierce through, which the lizard lord had clearly not expected. Its eyes opened wide just as it regained movement.

The arrow pierced deep into the beast, but its sheer resilience ultimately proved too much; the arrow only got about halfway before stopping. Luckily, Jake had partly expected this to happen. He unleashed his little surprise hidden in the Protean Arrow. Still deeply embedded within the dinosaur, the large arrowhead exploded, leading to a devastating result. Fragments of sharp, stable arcane mana coated in Heartrot Poison blasted out from the exploding arrowhead, filling the inside of the beast with what was effectively poison-coated shrapnel. The beast roared in pain, heavily damaged but not quite dead yet.

Once more, Jake had failed to kill in a single strike, and the dinosaur responded as best it could. The gem-like objects on its armored back began to glow and emit powerful white light... only to be instantly suppressed when Jake's follow-up attack arrived.

Dozens of arrows rained down and exploded the entire immediate area, doing little damage due to the high durability of the beast but still managing to momentarily halt its actions. The next many follow-up stable arcane arrows hit the lord directly, penetrating the hide that was significantly weakened and cracked from the first arrow. Coupled with the reduced overall resilience from the "debuff" left by the arrow, Jake's attacks all did some real damage.

Yet even when the final arrow landed, the beast still lived, though not for long if a certain hunter had anything to say about it. Jake, still standing far up in the air, extended his hand, which began to glow dark green. From afar, he used Touch of the Malefic Viper to further amplify the Heartrot Poison he'd inflicted upon the boss and continue ravaging its body. As a final touch, he exploded all the arcane shrapnel within the dinosaur.

It struggled, and Jake knew that no matter what, the boss was already doomed. Activating the arcane charge from Mark, the beast below flashed with energy for a second before it finally went still, breathing its last a few seconds later.

You have slain [Targehide Lizard Lord – lvl 308] – Bonus experience earned for killing an enemy above your level

Jake nodded as he deactivated Arcane Awakening and let the weakness wash over him. The arcane platform beneath him was long gone, but even without pouring in any energy, Jake still stood solidly on the ground... because, yeah, that was another benefit of his newly upgraded boots. When they said he would always find solid ground, they meant it, even if that solid ground wasn't ground at all but rather air.

After recovering, Jake continued his hunt by tracking down boss after boss. They were all roughly at the same level, and Jake killed them one by one, even having a happy moment when the ninth boss truly did die from a single arrow. Primarily because it had been a lich belonging to the undead natives on the planet, making it a caster with pretty bad defenses.

There were only a few cases where Jake got into a real fight, having to do more than just bombard with arrows from what was probably the stratosphere. He still handled all these pretty smoothly and got away before he was overwhelmed by hordes of monsters coming to the aid of their lord.

As he killed more and more, the other lords did become more cautious, placing more sentries and bolstering defenses. Alas, they couldn't act cowardly, as it would undermine their authority, meaning most still had solo domains. It didn't help that Jake purposefully tried to avoid going in a predictable pattern, even skipping some lords on purpose to attack some further away from the settlements. Because oh, yeah, there were now more settlements, he'd come to learn from the others through the Golden Mark. In fact, a second city had been established only a month after Jake left... and the reason for this happening so quickly was quite apparent.

"The settler's leader has shown surprise at the decrease in the frequency of the attacks, almost as if someone had been going around killing the ones in charge of leading these attacks, resulting in the unity between these beast hordes breaking down and creating internal strife as they fight to select a new leader among them," the Fallen King shared with Jake, obviously amused.

What few attacks did come were easily handled by the four others, who also actively worked to make the settlements grow faster and speed up the ark's arrival—and thus, the completion of the floor. Something that came a lot sooner than usual... at least from their perspective.

When Jake had killed so many leaders of these beast and monster factions that the attacks had pretty much stopped, Jake made his way back to the settlements, where the Sword Saint had already made his preparations. Dina had also created quite a few plant soldiers to defend and act as sentries should anything happen. Once he'd arrived, Jake saw what the old man had cooked up.

One had to remember that the time they had in Nevermore was based on how much time the party spent there from their perspective. Waiting for an ark to arrive wasn't something they wanted, which was why Jake felt pretty happy they had a guy blessed by the Primordial of Time on their team.

Inside one of the settlement houses, the Sword Saint had used his skills to paint odd murals on the walls. Jake was unsure what it was when he first arrived but soon learned it was a damn time dilation chamber. A pretty simple one at that, but it was actually pretty damn effective: When inside it, every two hours represented the passage of an entire day in the outside world.

Using that, they passed the seventy-second floor after only eight and a half months. For the settlers, it was more like fifteen months, but time dilation was overpowered. They did still have to go out once in a while when some attacks arrived, but Dina's summons made them aware every time with ample warning.

Moving on to the next floor, Jake hoped he could repeat the one they had just done... because hot damn, had it been effective in the leveling department. He'd finally done some proper bloody hunting, fully following his Path.

'DING!' Class: [Arcane Hunter of Horizon's Edge] has reached level 261 - Stat points allocated, +50 Free Points

...

'DING!' Class: [Arcane Hunter of Horizon's Edge] has reached level 265 - Stat points allocated, +50 Free Points

'DING!' Race: [Human (C)] has reached level 260 - Stat points allocated, +45 Free Points

...

'DING!' Race: [Human (C)] has reached level 262 - Stat points allocated, +45 Free Points

Luckily for him and all the others, the ensuing floors had far fewer gimmicks and were all pretty much just pure combat and leveling galore.

CHAPTER 30

APPROACHING THE END

Time passed swiftly within Nevermore as the final sprint to complete as many floors as possible to rack up points continued. As the end gradually approached, the gods naturally got more active while monitoring all the important groups. At ten years remaining, there had been approximately a few hundred individuals who were fighting for the top spots of the Leaderboards, with this number only decreasing as the months went by.

The gods chilling in the streaming room couldn't hold themselves back from commenting on all the developments, especially when they viewed the ones associated with their own factions. Yet one person kept being brought up—not just because of himself, but the party he had. It was rare to see a single group with close relations to four Primordials after all, and with Valdemar getting quite invested, too, the demand for Jake clips was through the roof.

"You still aren't sad Jake didn't want a skill based on your Records?" Minaga asked after they'd finished watching a highlight from a fight involving Jake and his party. "I think he and that Runemaiden of yours could make a good team if you brought him to your side. One wielding a bow with devastating arrows in the back while the other keeps the foe at bay and is nearly impervious to damage..."

They all knew Jake had rejected a skill related to Valdemar. Not because they knew what kind of skill had been offered, but because they knew he had to have been offered one. The Primordials were the gods that had been around the longest and knew the most about the system, so for them to deduce Jake would have to be offered some skill because of his clash with Valdemar was only to be expected.

"Heh, if it didn't suit his Path, it didn't suit his Path," Valdemar said, shrugging. "Isn't it only more exciting that he rejected me? Actually, isn't it better? For someone powerful like him to join Valhal while not really having any skills from Valhal will only expand our Legacies! Gudrun is gonna be more than on board to recruit him."

"Openly talking about stealing someone's Chosen isn't proper etiquette, now, is it?" the Holy Mother chimed in, her tone more playful than scolding.

"Bah, Jake is his own person; he can do whatever he wants." Valdemar waved her off. "I'll just make sure we give him the best offer to join us. I might even throw in a case of my personal brew to really convince him."

"That one's gonna be tough," Minaga said, shaking his head. "The Endless Empire is already willing to—no, wait, never mind. That was confidential. Ignore that I said anything; the source is unreliable anyway, and I've never even met the guy in person. What I am saying is, if Jake ever appears open to recruitment, there's gonna be competition."

Vilastromoz, who had remained quiet, finally joined the conversation. "You talk as if you stand a chance... Don't you think his current Patron may have something to say?"

"Sure he might"—Valdemar grinned as he leaned forward—"but whether he can hold onto my fellow human is entirely dependent on if he's powerful enough to, now, isn't it?"

Valdemar and Vilastromoz both spiked their auras, but the Wyrmgod interfered instantly. His own presence washed over theirs before they could cause too much of a ruckus. It pushed both of theirs back, suppressing them slightly with a clearly superior aura.

"Behave when you are in my domain," the Wyrmgod said with a sigh.

Vilastromoz and Valdemar both did as told, though the human Primordial muttered, dissatisfied. No matter how powerful they were, they were still within the domain of the Wyrmgod. In Nevermore, he was the most powerful being beside the Bound God of the World Wonder itself. Considering the limitations of Nevermore and the contract that she and the Primordial had made, the Wyrmgod was definitely more capable of displaying his powers.

That was obviously part of the reason no one had shown up with their real bodies. Now, chances were they would be able to escape Nevermore if they were truly there and got into a conflict with the Wyrmgod, but it certainly wouldn't come cheap, not even for Valdemar.

The mood had turned a bit sour, but an unexpected savior of the vibe entered.

"It's almost disgustingly simplistic," the Blightfather commented as he studied a clip of Jake slaying a mini-boss on floor seventy-eight with a single arrow. An expert change in subject, and done rather easily, as he hadn't really been paying much attention to the bickering. "The hunter's Path, that is. There are certainly many complicated concepts infused into his blows, but all the applications are so minimalistic in execution. Complexities are sheared away for pure useability when he fights. There is little thought, yet his actions are rarely ever something that could be considered questionable. Indeed, I understand why Minaga described him as a natural fighter; his adaptability when facing any opponent is remarkable."

"Don't tell me you are also trying to steal another Primordial's Chosen?" the Holy Mother prodded. "It shouldn't surprise me, yet I still find myself disappointed."

"I never said I wanted to recruit him. One can admire something impressive without coveting it—a concept I understand you find difficult to comprehend." The Blightfather shook his head. "Besides, even if I did want him to join the Risen, I am uncertain how well his Path would mix with changing his race, especially as I sense his soul is altered, likely by a skill of some kind. His Bloodline certainly also complicates things. No, I wouldn't want him to be one of the Risen, but I would certainly welcome him to come for a visit. Perhaps to see an old friend of his."

Vilastromoz wasn't surprised the Blightfather had already seen through some aspects of Jake's soul, even the part where his Truesoul had slightly changed when he got the Anomalous Soul skill. The Viper had few he would say could match him when it came to the study of the soul, but the Blightfather was definitely one of them. If not, he wouldn't have been able to create a race like the Risen and the entire ecosystem required for this new undead race to not only survive but thrive.

"Speaking of old friends, how is that cursed trapper Jake knows doing?" Vilastromoz asked.

"Adequately," the Blightfather responded. "Better than I expected, honestly. Which perhaps shouldn't be that surprising, considering his talent in dungeon engineering. The knowledge he had before the initiation has led to some interesting insights those who were born into the system simply cannot possess due to the fundamental change in natural laws. Not that he is a contender for any Leaderboards. But he is worth nurturing, I guess, if for nothing other than his connection to your Chosen."

"Hey, Casper is a great guy all on his own, and I will hear nothing to the contrary," Minaga cut in as he crossed his arms.

"I never said he wasn't," the Risen Primordial said as he glanced at the Wyrmgod. "Now, how are those Void God fanatics doing? Are they a threat to the Leaderboards?"

"You know I am not going to share any details," the Wyrmgod said, shaking his head. "But if you are asking if I expect to see any beings with close connections to the Void Gods on top of the Leaderboards, I would have to say no."

"A bit disappointing," the Viper added with a sigh. "I thought we could have a first."

The Wyrmgod shook his head. "The Path related to the void is simply too limiting in nature."

It was similar to the case of Unique Lifeforms. Using void energy limited you to *only* having void energy, as it simply consumed every other trace of energy within the body. This meant there were many things one couldn't do that could make some floors or Challenge Dungeons harder than usual, much like the Unique Lifeforms, who also had very limited Paths. This was also why Unique Lifeforms barely ever placed top ten on the Leaderboards despite their many innate advantages as pinnacle beings of the multiverse.

"Any news from the Dao Sect who has the Chosen of the Lifesoul Daolord participating?" Nature's Attendant finally also asked, the man rarely speaking. He just focused on making sure Artemis wasn't overwhelmed while being forced to be in the presence of the five Primordials, who sometimes got into arguments and flared their auras. Most of his time outside of that was spent watching Dina and her adventures, along with some other promising groups from the Pantheon of Life.

The fact he was interested in the Bloodline Patriarch from Earth didn't surprise Vilastromoz either. The man was an absolute anomaly with magic clearly based on his Bloodline, making it almost transcendent in nature. The sheer absurdity of his existence simply went a bit under the radar due to the other overshadowing anomaly from the same homeworld.

Given his use of life magic, it was only natural that the Pantheon of Life was interested in what he did, even if the Viper knew Nature's Attendant wasn't a big fan of the C-grade. Because what he did was far from something that followed the natural order.

"While the Chosen of the Daolord isn't a contender for the Leaderboards, a party member of his is," the Wyrmgod answered. "She is the disciple of the Heartsoul Daolord, and while she only carries a Divine

Blessing, chances are high that she will be made a Chosen when she reaches A or maybe even B-grade."

They proceeded to discuss a few more candidates, some of whom had only really made themselves known during the Challenge Dungeon period and truly grown into their power over the last decade. The multiverse was a big place with no lack of talent. Some young, promising geniuses from the United Tribes proved themselves, and others from the demon factions showed their skills alongside people from many different powerful factions. Not to mention those who were just personal disciples of powerful beings in the multiverse or standalone talents, many of whom had not been known at all before Nevermore despite every Primordial faction's extensive information network.

Some geniuses were also looked at and then forgotten if they disappointed expectations. Others were just somewhere in the middle, where the gods could look at them, nod in unison and agree they were talented and had a good chance to reach a high grade, and then move on without thinking about that person again. People like Draskil fell into this camp, as well as, quite frankly, ninety-nine-point-nine percent of the geniuses of the many factions. Because here, towards the end, they only focused on those at the very top. Those who truly stood a chance to grab a top spot on the Leaderboards.

Yet even as all the promising young talents showed themselves, and no matter how many rising stars proved their worth, two names were always mentioned. Two geniuses from the new universe who had already proven themselves as apex beings of this generation, both the Chosen of gods recognized as also standing at the pinnacle.

It was naturally Jake Thayne, the Chosen of the Malefic Viper, and Ell'Hakan, Chosen of Yip of Yore. These were the two people the gods agreed would more likely than not claim first and second... The only question was who would take the number-one slot... and how their presence would shake up the All-Time Leaderboards.

———

While many competed for the top spots on the Nevermore Leaderboards, one must remember that the vast majority of those who did the World Wonder had nothing to do with this competition. There were many limitations as to who could compete on the Leaderboards, and most—especially those who knew it wasn't like they were competing with the top geniuses—just ignored that entire feature.

Instead, they used Nevermore for all its other merits. They used it for the same reason nearly everyone went back to Nevermore in all grades and even into godhood: It was simply one of the best leveling spots in the entire multiverse.

Dungeons, in general, were a borderline requirement to facilitate progress. The natural ecosystem of planets couldn't support the growth of everyone at once, especially when more powerful beings appeared. A single monster going from C- to B-grade would lead to the deaths of numerous creatures with roughly equal levels. This was obviously unsustainable, so a proper source of creatures to fight was required... which was where dungeons came in.

A single dungeon could be used over and over again to progress, removing the need to hunt other forms of life, thus preserving the planet at least a little bit.

This naturally became less of a problem when one reached higher grades and could explore space. Based on estimates, less than one in a thousand planets were fully integrated into the wider social system of the multiverse. Most were just planets that had never truly made contact with any other factions, or perhaps just filled with monsters who never developed sapience.

Even more planets were just empty, save for elementals who spawned simply due to the mana density. These areas of "wilderness" in space were great hunting spots, even if they did have the challenge of powerful foes often being few and far between, a problem dungeons didn't tend to have. So, dungeons were still a better option.

And ultimately, Nevermore was just the biggest dungeon in the entire multiverse. It was somewhere people went to get levels, and with the special time dilation of the World Wonder that didn't result in a negative impact on Records, the place just got even better.

On top of that, as a World Wonder, Nevermore had special titles associated with it. These went beyond the Leaderboards and Challenge Dungeon variants, as both those things were only available to C-grades and weren't present in later versions of Nevermore.

Outside of these special C-grade titles, everyone would gain a title based simply on floors cleared and overall performance, granting Records and sometimes even a few stats. Most people did it for the Records, though, as the stats were often inconsequential.

One such person who was just in Nevermore for the levels was Miranda. She wasn't someone who cared much about the fifty-year limit or trying to optimize how many floors she could clear. She was just there for the experience and nothing else. If possible, she didn't even want to engage with anything that had to do with the Leaderboards and Jake because, as she put it... this was her only damn holiday in years.

The group the Court Witch had gone with wasn't what one might expect, though. She had ended up going with some individuals from the Order of the Malefic Viper, both to get a good party going and because she wanted to disconnect a bit from her usual daily life. She wanted to fully dedicate herself to her Path as a witch, at least for a little while. Besides, it wasn't as if her decision not to go with other people from Earth was out of the ordinary.

Sultan had teamed up with a group of mercenaries working for the Golden Road Emporium, who were pretty much hired to help him gain more levels than he usually would. Based on what the merchant had said, this was apparently partly a reward for his great performance in preparations for Jake's Chosen Ceremony.

Many other groups from Earth had also teamed up with people outside of the planet. Needless to say, quite a few also teamed up with fellow Earthlings or some of the newly integrated slaves. Earth as a whole was getting a huge power-up during this period in preparation for the Prima Guardian, as quite a large portion of Earth's C-grades had gone.

As mentioned, none of these people were there to compete on any Leaderboards. They were not there to engage in the competition... yet many still paid attention to the Leaderboards. Not to see their own names anywhere, but with hope and expectations of seeing their World Leaders there.

CHAPTER 31

ONE LAST FLOOR

Jake had no idea how many of the damn imps he had killed before they stopped coming. The demon captains who had once led the army of small-winged casters had long been slain, but that didn't mean the swarm didn't prove a challenge simply due to its sheer numbers.

His body was covered in burns and wounds by the time they were all dead, as it had simply been impossible to avoid every attack. His party members weren't in much better condition, as they had been fighting at other entrances to the large cavern they found themselves within.

Luckily, before more demons could arrive, Dina made her way over. A soothing green aura washed over him as several small plants grew in his vicinity, making Jake nod at her in recognition. "Thanks."

"No problem," she responded with a smile. "Are there more coming from this way?"

"Doesn't look like it," Jake responded as he released a Pulse of Perception. "Not from any of the other tunnels, either."

"Alright, we should be safe to regroup, then," Dina said. "You may also need to have your Golden Mark reapplied in case something does happen."

"True," Jake said, nodding with a sigh. These demons had been a bloody nightmare in that regard. They'd kept using dispelling magic and disrupting mana, which had resulted in them removing the Golden Marks over and over again.

When they made it back to the center of the cavern, Jake finally dropped his boosting skill to sit down in exhaustion. The other three were already there, also recovering from the ongoing fight. Entering meditation, Jake felt Dina reestablish her restorative domain around them. This not only helped Jake's resources and injured body recover faster, but also shortened the period of weakness.

Which was needed in case more demons came back. Jake had quite a few complaints about floor seventy-nine, but a lack of enemies most certainly wasn't one of them. In fact, it was nearly the opposite, as there were pretty much only enemies who stuck together in huge swarms.

The fact that the last objective of this floor was to defend the giant crystal within this particular mountain didn't help either, as it just resulted in all the enemies funneling to them. The only semi-good part was that the long and narrow tunnels allowed their party to avoid being surrounded.

While meditating, Jake checked his system notifications, pleased to see he had gained another level from the fight. The first in a while, as the period of faster leveling from the Challenge Dungeons was well and truly done already, at least when it came to his class. Not that Jake was complaining. The gains had been pretty damn good over the last few years, and he was even getting close to yet another skill selection.

'DING!' Class: [Arcane Hunter of Horizon's Edge] has reached level 284 - Stat points allocated, +50 Free Points
'DING!' Race: [Human (C)] has reached level 273 - Stat points allocated, +45 Free Points

It had been a bit over ten years since they finished with their Challenge Dungeons, and Jake had evidently gained quite a few levels during this period. In fact, it had been even faster than just after reaching C-grade. The reason for this was primarily the fact that they had met rather strong enemies on every single floor, unlike when they first entered and had to grind through a lot of easy floors. The bosses had been especially tough, and on floor seventy-five, they had faced one of those event bosses. That was the strongest opponent they'd encountered in Nevermore thus far, being a level 325 variant with respectable power.

The fight had been pretty damn long, but it did help that Jake had significantly weakened it with his opening shot from stealth. In the end, the Sword Saint had ended up using two Glimpses of Spring, leaving him weakened for a while, with both Sylphie and Jake also overusing their boosting skills. Dina and the Fallen King had been a bit better off, but that was mainly because the fucker had ignored the Fallen King for the most part, as it had been borderline immune to soul attacks, making the Unique Lifeform the smallest threat.

Dina had been fine solely because of her many defensive means. She was naturally still tired afterward, having used her most powerful skills too, but as a healer, she was naturally good at making sure she wouldn't be the one in most need of healing and recovery after a long fight.

In summary, the event boss on floor seventy-five had been strong enough to warrant the use of everything in their arsenal, save for their most powerful trump cards that would leave them incapacitated for a longer period, potentially with permanent consequences. That is to say, the Sword Saint didn't have to fully use his transcendence, the Fallen King didn't have to use his unique skill, and Jake didn't have to pull some weird Bloodline bullshit out of his ass. But it had gotten a bit close for comfort.

Anyway, from there, the next few floors had been pretty straightforward, with a lot of fighting and a lot of levels.

Having cleared nine floors—he counted this one as pretty much already completed—in around ten years was pretty fucking good, if Jake said so himself. But it had come at the cost of some things. They had taken no breaks and even purposefully avoided the city floor after floor seventy-five. For some reason, Jake had a feeling going there wouldn't be a good idea, and his party had no reason to disagree as they hurried onwards.

The lack of breaks had resulted in a lack of focus on professions. While keeping up their tempo over the last decade, Jake had barely done any alchemy. Sure, he'd crafted sometimes to keep them restocked on potions, elixirs, and his own poisons, but a lot of it had taken place within time dilation, as the Sword Saint sometimes set up small time chambers for them to get through timed events more quickly.

Due to this, despite the boost in momentum from the Challenge Dungeons, Jake had only gained a total of three levels in his profession in an entire decade. That was less than one every three years, and just around a third of the levels he had gained from popping in and saying hello to a bunch of Primordials having a streaming party. Looking back at his notifications, it wasn't even as if he was close to another level, as his last one had come half a year ago.

'DING!' Profession: [Heretic-Chosen Alchemist of the Malefic Viper] has reached level 262 - Stat points allocated, +35 Free Points

Still, levels were levels. And at level 260, Jake had naturally unlocked another skill selection. All in all, it had actually been a pretty damn interesting selection, if utterly inconsequential for now; the reason for this would become clear when one knew of the skill he'd selected. Ah, but the first two offerings had been just a bit too basic, to put it nicely.

[Fortifying Curse Toxin Theory (Uncommon)]
[Acid Chemistry Theory (Rare)]

To clarify, these skills were purely related to knowledge, and they didn't really have any effects when crafting. At least, nothing Jake didn't feel confident doing with freeform magic or, more importantly, through Sagacity of the Malefic Viper. Sagacity already had Records related to these two knowledge skills he just hadn't fully unlocked yet, so selecting either would only be done with the intent of merging it with Sagacity down the line. Jake thought that was a waste of a skill selection. Not to say the third skill offered was that much better.

[Advanced Arcane Sealing (Ancient)] – Protect what is yours, and should anyone try to rob you, leave them with nothing. Allows the alchemist to create a seal of arcane magic to cover an object or several objects at once. While the object is sealed, energy leakage is nearly entirely eliminated due to the stable arcane mana. The sealed object will be hidden from nearly all senses and unaffected by all outside sources. Should anyone try to forcibly destroy the seal, the arcane mana will turn destructive and damage or destroy the sealed object as well as itself. Sealed items can only be unsealed by those possessing the arcane affinity of the hunter. The effectiveness of Advanced Arcane Sealing is improved by Wisdom, Intelligence, and Willpower.

Jake still liked this one, though—not because he wanted it as a skill, but because of what it represented. This skill, much like the prior two, was clearly based on what he had done in the House of the Architect. For Jake to be offered an ancient-rarity skill just for sealing an item in his arcane mana was honestly bonkers. Sure, some of the obscuration features in the skill probably weren't fully innate concepts spawned from just placing a barrier around an object, but he reckoned some of them were.

This told him that the simple act of sealing something in mana was roughly equivalent to, at the very least, an epic skill through pure conceptual power from his arcane affinity. So, yeah, this skill offering was damn great to see, but he didn't select it because the two next ones were more... interesting.

Jake had naturally looked at them individually back during the actual skill selection, but in truth, it made a lot more sense to see them as a set, considering the two skills were effectively identical.

[Chosen's Offering of the Malefic Viper (Legendary)] – To deliver an offering to your Patron and gain recognition in kind is the greatest honor. Allows the alchemist to make an offer to the Malefic Viper and be granted an Offering Fragment. Based on the value of the Records and energy in the offering, you will be rewarded with a better Offering Fragment. The Offering Fragment contains Records and energy related to the Malefic Viper and can help empower other sources of Records and energy related to the Malefic Viper. All offerings must surpass a certain threshold to be submittable, and out of respect to the Malefic One, there is an internal cooldown for the skill dependent on the value of the Offering Fragment received. Whenever an offering is made, your connection to the Malefic Viper as his Chosen grows.

[Heretic's Offering of the Malefic Viper (Legendary)] – To infringe upon the domain of the Malefic Viper and rob the Primordial's Records is a great achievement. Allows the alchemist to make an offer to the Malefic Viper and be granted an Offering Fragment. Based on the value of the Records and energy in the offering, you will be rewarded with a better Offering Fragment. The Offering Fragment contains Records and energy related to the Malefic Viper and can help empower other sources of Records and energy related to the Malefic Viper. All offerings must surpass a certain threshold to be submittable, and to hide your heretical actions from the Malefic One, there is an internal cooldown for the skill dependent on the value of the Offering Fragment received. Whenever an offering is made, your status as a Heretic of the Malefic Viper grows.

These two skills, as mentioned, did effectively the exact same thing. They allowed Jake to make an offering and get an Offering Fragment in return. An Offering Fragment that could then be used while crafting to infuse Records from the Malefic Viper into the creation, functioning a bit like a light version of when Malefic Viper's Poison activated. Jake sure as hell didn't doubt that using an Offering Fragment as a catalyst during crafting would prove highly effective.

In addition to this, each of the skills also served to push Jake further down either the Path of a Heretic or the Path of a Chosen. This was just a small note at the end of each skill, and it probably wasn't something that would bother most of those who received these options. Why would a heretic care about becoming more heretical, or a Chosen care about being closer to his Patron? They naturally wouldn't. In fact, walking further down either Path was just purely positive, as it would solidify their Path.

However... Jake wasn't either of those. He was the Heretic-Chosen, walking straight down the middle between being a Chosen and a heretic. He was both at once. A living paradox. That was why alarm bells instantly went off when Jake read the last part of the two skills.

For the system to directly push him down either Path couldn't end well. Jake's instincts also warned him about both of them, yet the longer he looked at them, the more he also got the feeling they could be really good... which was when Jake had a little thought.

See, Jake felt pretty confident using either of those skills would prove detrimental, but what if, ya know... he just picked both? If he could offer both Heretical and Chosen offerings at once, wasn't that a Heretic-Chosen offering right there? At least, that was Jake's logic.

And now for the real genius: In order to avoid triggering this effect, Jake would just never use the legendary skill... ever.

The only downside to this ingenious plan was that Jake would select a legendary skill he would purposefully avoid using or even thinking about for the next thirty levels. Then there was also the slight risk that picking one of them would lock him out of the other, making Jake end up pretty damn screwed. Oh, yeah, and then there was also the fact that skills innately contained Records, so would he fuck up just by picking one? Who knows? But hey, nothing ventured, nothing gained.

So, with that in mind, Jake had asked the Sword Saint to flip a coin for him to determine which one he would go with first. It had resulted in Jake picking Chosen's Offering, so worst-case scenario, he would just have to fully lean into being a subservient and ass-licking Chosen... or just never use the skill until he one day found a way to get rid of it or merge it with something else.

Returning his attention to the present, Jake opened his eyes and stretched a bit, having meditated for a bit over two hours to heal up. Drinking a potion, he also used a Pulse of Perception and saw that the attacks were pretty much over. Sylphie was down one of the tunnels, shredding a few stragglers, but that was it. The other large entrance was guarded by a floating Unique Lifeform on lookout duty while Jake recovered.

Dina had gone over to the crystal and infused the small domain she had established around it to make it mature faster. The Sword Saint had also joined her, and while he couldn't use time magic, as that would screw up the maturation process, he could at least help provide some mana and even water the dryad's plants, assuming that even did anything.

Soon enough, the crystal fully matured and shot a beam of light into the air. The entire mountain began to break apart as all its mana was sucked in, and they witnessed the birth of a powerful natural treasure. It was an impressive one for sure—not that their party was sticking around to admire it. They couldn't even steal it, so what was the point?

A few seconds passed before two elementals teleported down to them, both of them powerful B-grade variants with sapience. They thanked the party for defending the crystal before taking it away, and with that done and dusted, a few notifications popped up.

Seventy-ninth floor completed. 15,800 Nevermore Points earned.

With the notifications also came a door, standing right where the crystal had been. There was no need to delay as they all entered the in-between room, and just as they did, Jake turned to the old man.

"How long do we have left?" Jake asked him. As someone Blessed by Aeon, he was surely the best at keeping track of time, right?

The Sword Saint considered the question for a moment. "Can you allow me to fully Identify you?"

"Sure?" Jake said.

The old man did just that, then clearly used it on all the others, too, answering, "Ten months, twenty-three days, and twenty-two hours. That is when Sylphie will be forced out of Nevermore. The rest of us are all within a day of that. This discrepancy is likely caused by the Challenge Dungeons and how the time distortion in those may vary slightly."

Jake stared at the old man, wondering how the hell he hadn't known the old man could see time stuff when using Identify. Then again, maybe it was something new? In either case, Jake decided to do as the Sword Saint had done and Identify everyone in the party. Jake himself was level 273, which was pretty good, in his opinion, but his leveling speed looked horrible compared to both the Fallen King and Sylphie.

[Fallen King – lvl 281]

[Juvenile Sylphian Hawk – lvl 287]

As monsters, they were natural cheats and tended to level faster than enlightened races. Sylphie was even more of a special case since she was still growing naturally. Still, it sucked to lose to them. But hey, at least Jake did beat both Dina and the Sword Saint when it came to leveling.

[Dryad – lvl 270]
[Human – lvl 272]

Alright, the margin with the Sword Saint was a bit low with only one level, but a level was a level. Dina was the slowest of them, which wasn't that surprising. Her race levels were slow because she was a dryad, a long-lived creature who also grew naturally, albeit at a far slower pace. One of her racial skills literally allowed her to merge with a powerful tree and sleep within it for potentially thousands of years to get a few levels. It wasn't something she planned on doing, but that it was an option at all felt silly to Jake, even if Dina was half-plant.

"Ten months and change is not a long time…" the Fallen King commented.

"Neither is it a little," the Sword Saint said.

"It should be enough," Dina said with confidence.

"Ree!" Sylphie agreed.

Jake also nodded. They should have enough for one more floor, though that would definitely be their last. Jake's mission wouldn't just be to beat it, though.

"We're going for the event boss, right?" Jake asked, just wanting to make sure. His party looked at him as if his question wasn't even worth answering, making him smile. "Then let's get a move on already. One more floor of Nevermore to go… so let's make it a real banger."

CHAPTER 32

FLOOR EIGHTY

J ake and company appeared on what would more likely than not be the final floor of Nevermore. Their spawning location was the top of a large, ruined tower, giving them a clear view of the surrounding area. However, before Jake had a good chance to look around, he noticed the mana in the air and how it was filled with death.

Luckily, he didn't have to speculate about its cause for long, as the floor description popped up right then.

Welcome to the eightieth floor of Nevermore: Plateau of the Twin Emperors
In a vast land ruled by two tyrants, you are tasked with ending the constant war. The armies of these two tyrants clash in war zones between the two empires of the land known simply as the Vast Plateau. You find yourself standing in a long-abandoned war zone where remnants of battle still remain. Due to the nature of these wars, cursed lands and vast areas have appeared that are considered inaccessible due to the accumulation of death-affinity mana, resulting in the appearance of many undead. The land you now find yourselves in is one such place.
To end the deterioration of the Vast Plateau, the war must come to an end. Decide your next course of action. Will you join either side of the conflict? Will you attempt to negotiate peace by making them realize the doomed Path they are walking down? Or will you be the enemy of both, as you become a danger so significant you

force the two warring emperors to come together? Another option
altogether?
The choice is yours.
Main objective: End the conflict.
Bonus objectives: Join either side of the conflict or choose to remain
a third party.
Current progress: Conflict ended (0/1)
Note: More hidden events, achievements, or objectives may be
hidden on the floor.
Current Nevermore Points: 1,953,950

As Jake and the others read the long description of the floor, they got the gist of the place. It was a pretty basic setup giving them an excuse to fight in a war if they wanted. There was probably more to it, but their goal wasn't to figure out who was right or wrong, only which decision would give them the most excuses to fight and gain levels while unlocking the event boss.

Addressing the Nevermore Points, Jake did feel pretty fucking good about how many he had racked up in the last ten years or so after the Challenge Dungeons. It was just about seven hundred thousand, with every floor giving more than the last—except for floor seventy-five, which was a bit of an outlier due to the event boss.

For reference, floor seventy-nine had rewarded just under a hundred thousand Nevermore Points, which was a tad less than double what floor seventy-one had rewarded. It was a big increase, but not that out of pocket, especially when one considered how much the difficulty also spiked. Jake and his party, straight out of the Challenge Dungeons, would have gotten their asses handed to them against the event boss on floor seventy-five, and also had serious trouble with the floors after that.

Jake sure as hell doubted many, if any, of the Leaderboard groups were capable of challenging anything above the lower floors in the eighties, assuming they even had the time. That was still a lot of potential Nevermore Points one could earn. He knew Ell'Hakan had been ahead of him timewise with all the Challenge Dungeons, granting approximately a full year extra to do floors, so assuming they matched Jake and company's speed, they would end up doing one more floor than them. It wasn't a lot, but it was something.

All of this is to say that things could get a bit hairy here toward the end. Alas, the only thing Jake should focus on was himself and clearing this floor. He would disappoint himself if he didn't at least beat that orange fucker, but beating him still wasn't the primary objective.

"You notice anything?" the Sword Saint asked. "Outside of the environmental mana clearly communicating that we are in undead territory..."

Asking Jake about his thoughts at the beginning of every floor was pretty much standard by now, as he often could either see something with his adequate Perception stat or had some gut feeling. In other cases, primarily in worlds filled with nature, they also asked Dina for some insight from the local fauna. Here, however, there weren't any living things for her to ask.

Jake looked around and saw dead land spreading in all directions. The ground was gray and dry, with some movement here and there from undead. Skeleton creatures, ghosts, zombies, large abominations... all the good stuff. Their levels were all around 290, with some of the larger undead just around 300.

Looking beyond the undead lands, Jake saw a few watchtowers, likely to contain the undead. Further back were plains, wilderness, some forests, and even some cities. It was very much the same in both directions, though he did also spot another distinct region, and even from this distance, Jake felt a powerful curse lingering there.

One might wonder how Jake could see this many things. It wasn't because all these locations were bunched up or anything, but due to the peculiar layout of this world... because they sure as fuck weren't on a planet. There was absolutely zero curvature anywhere, and the land was surprisingly flat, with not a single mountain of any kind in sight. Even with massive planets, Jake could usually notice the ever-so-slight curvature if he ascended far enough, but here, there truly was none at all. A fact he shared with the party.

"Hm, so it's a bit like the land the Endless Empire knows as the Great Plains," Dina said, gladly sharing some more great multiversal knowledge. "Enormous landmasses just floating in space, the largest of which nearly matches the overall surface of a Great Planet, with the Heartlands of the Endless Empire placed primarily on these Great Plains. I have only seen some pictures from Grandpa, as getting to visit the Great Plains is quite difficult... though I don't think Jake would have any problems."

"Let us hope this place is not that big," the Fallen King commented with displeasure.

"Doesn't look like it is, based on what I've seen so far," Jake said, shaking his head. "Anyway, what's the plan?"

"Going by prior floors, if we want the event boss, we have to take the hardest path possible, which I would reckon is not teaming up with any of these factions," the Sword Saint said.

"Ree, ree," Sylphie added helpfully, making Jake nod.

"Yeah, not making any allies will also give us the most potential enemies to hunt."

"Before we make a final decision, we should become more familiar with the world," Dina said cautiously. "If these Twin Emperors are B-grades or above, we may be forced to at least act like we are allied with one of them."

Jake shook his head again. "I doubt they are. I think it's way more likely that at least one of them is the event boss. But you do have a point; learning more about this floor would be a good start."

So they went and did just that, heading toward one of the cities Jake had spotted. On the way, they learned a bit about what kind of races they were dealing with. Unsurprisingly, it was a mix of many different enlightened races, but it did surprise them to see that most were orcs of different kinds. Orcs weren't a rare race in the multiverse, but they were often looked down on compared to other enlightened races, primarily because they tended to be on the... simpler side. However, from the looks of it, the orcs in this world were a variant race of some kind.

With orcs also came a lot of goblins. Why these two were often grouped together, Jake had no idea, but a theory was that goblins tended to have strong mental stats, while orcs were more on the physical side, making the two races complement each other.

These two races made up over seventy percent of the enlightened, with the rest being a mixture of the usual dwarves, elves, humans, beastfolk, and all that.

Anyway, having not sided with anyone yet, they believed it would be possible to enter cities and study the place a bit, but... yeah, things didn't work out like that.

"Stop!" a guard said as the party approached a large stone city gate. "Identify yourselves immediately!"

Jake looked at the guard, who wore simple leather armor and wielded a halberd. He looked like a common low-level grunt, but his level said otherwise.

[Orc – lvl 284]

Then again, it was also entirely possible that the standard for fighters was just really high on this floor. The few enlightened Jake had seen on the way were also all at least mid-tier C-grade, even the damn farmers.

As usual, the most diplomatic person in their party stepped forward, and luckily, they had already discussed what they would do if they got into a situation like this. The Sword Saint smiled as he bowed politely to the orc. "Greetings, we are a but a group of adventurers who have just returned from fighting the nearby undead, and—"

Before he could say more, mana flashed beneath their feet as a magic circle appeared. Some goblin mages on the tall walls who had been listening in had stood and raised their staves the moment the old man mentioned fighting the undead.

"Bunch of fucking morons," the guard swore as he shook his head and looked at Jake and company with pity. "Either you are incompetent spies or even worse adventurers, walking up to a guard and outright admitting to a severe crime."

The Sword Saint admirably tried to save the situation by looking taken aback. "We... We were not aware we had broken any laws. Could you—"

"Save your words for the mayor," the guard said, and Jake noted the magic circle below them growing in intensity. "Now, try to stop acting stupid for just a second and surrender. Who knows, maybe the upper brass will be nice and spare you from execution. We could use some more war slaves."

So... yeah, negotiations broke down.

Jake wasn't even the first one to act. The Sword Saint simply nodded, and before the orc had a chance to open his mouth again, his head flew into the air. This clearly surprised the goblin mages on the wall, who prepared to activate the magic circle, but before they could, the Fallen King erupted with energy. A golden wave spread from his body, utterly dismantling the magic circle. Meanwhile, Jake drew his bow and Sylphie shot toward the wall like a bullet.

Siding with whatever Twin Emperor was in charge of this city definitely wasn't an option anymore. Especially after their group effectively leveled the place, killing everyone who didn't flee in terror from the five newcomers. Jake asked if he should pick off those who ran, but the group decided against it—which Jake honestly preferred, as he didn't like shooting a bunch of crafters who were just fleeing.

The city did have a mini-boss of sorts in the form of the mayor—a level 310 orc wearing heavy armor and carrying a battle hammer—who definitely did not look like some official who spent most of his time in the office. In fact, barely anyone they encountered looked like they belonged outside of a battlefield. Even the average citizens were C-grade and took to weapons without hesitation. The population of the city was also way lower than Jake had first assumed. It was large enough to house at least ten thousand, but only about eight hundred had lived there.

Killing the mayor was easy enough, and using records found in the city's rubble—as well as some captured survivors—they learned more about the Vast Plateau. There was a lot of boring history, but to summarize, two powerful, nearly peak C-grades had appeared less than a hundred years ago, calling themselves emperors after uniting a bunch of smaller factions. Smaller factions had already been enemies with the factions that the other emperor brought together, which made going to war quite easy for them.

From there, they'd constantly fought and created many battlefields. At first, only E-grades had fought with the excuse of wanting to preserve power, but soon, D-grades had joined in, and now there were barely any D-grades left outside of some crafters. Even low-tier C-grades were scarce, with the majority of them filling the battlefields.

At least a few billion had died within a single century, all concentrated on big battlefields. Battlefields that both emperors had made it illegal to enter, much less hunt undead within. Instead, they were treated more like wildlife preserves.

After listening to everything, Jake couldn't help but reach a conclusion. "They are cultivating these areas of curse energy and death—and working together to do so."

The others looked at him.

"Why?" Dina questioned. "What would the purpose of that even be?"

"I know, like... at least seven rituals that use curse energy in an area. I reckon that at least one of these Twin Emperors has something similar for the undead areas. As for why, I'm just gonna take a shot in the dark here and guess it's about trying to gain more power." Jake shrugged.

"The endless folly of those too untalented to progress without cheap short-cuts," the Fallen King said, scoffing.

Jake sighed. "Yeah, not a fan of it either, assuming I'm correct."

"Aren't alchemists from the Order of the Malefic Viper known to sometimes wipe out entire civilizations during their experiments just to try and get a level or two?" the Sword Saint said, being very judgmental towards poor alchemists just trying their best. He was entirely correct, sure, but still a bit judgmental.

"I wouldn't know anything about acting haphazardly, my actions ultimately ending in the destruction of a planet," Jake said to defend himself.

"Ree?" Sylphie asked with a tilted head.

Jake quickly shut the bird up. "We aren't talking about that one." Why had he decided to share all the things about Temlat with her, again?

"Anyway, going by Jake's theory, how would it function if we joined either faction when they are working together?" the Sword Saint asked to get the discussion back on track.

"Even if they are in symbiosis right now, it doesn't mean either isn't trying to reap all the rewards," Dina said with a frown. "It may be that they are both benefiting from the creation of these death- and curse-filled domains, and that our interference can tip the balance of power, resulting in the death of one Twin Emperor."

"Ree," Sylphie added, making a good point.

"The name Twin Emperors does indeed communicate they are connected to one another and not merely competitors," the Fallen King said. *"That they appeared at the same time is also highly suspicious."*

"So, what you're saying is..." Jake hinted.

"We already discussed not choosing a side, so let us indeed not. They attacked us first. We are now merely retaliating and defending ourselves as we march toward the Twin Emperor."

"Ree?"

"I am pretty sure using disproportionate force to pretty much slaughter an entire country or two would be considered a war crime," Jake commented. "Actually, never mind. Let's not think about that."

"To summarize, we're all in agreement we will be a third force who just fights everyone?" the Sword Saint asked clarifyingly.

"That is indeed the way to get the most experience," Jake agreed.

"In that case, let's not dally," the old man said, nodding. "Rather than ravage more cities, how about we check out one of the active battlefields instead?"

"You want us to just show up to an ongoing battle and put ourselves right in the middle to fight everyone at once?" the Fallen King asked.

"Precisely."

"See, we're all in agreement!" Jake grinned. "Now, let's go to war."

Chapter 33

Wartime

War...

War never changes...

Except for when a group of five extremely powerful beings decide to just fuck shit up. In cases like that, war would very much change, and not for the better. At least not for those already involved in the war.

Floating far above one of the smaller battlefields of the Vast Plateau, this group of five observed the ongoing fighting. There were only a few hundred on both sides at this point, primarily because most of the weaker C-grades were already dead. The fighting also didn't happen as one would usually expect from a war like this in the multiverse, which, for reference, was quite a bit different compared to wars on pre-system Earth.

Usually, based on what Jake had read, even if an all-out war did happen at the beginning of a conflict, it would often devolve into a standstill. The most powerful beings on both sides would be hesitant to enter the fray out of fear that they would be teamed up on by the most powerful people on the opposing side.

This resulted in the weaker C-grades fighting in a big skirmish, with the stronger ones standing back for the most part. Only when it was clear one side would win would the stronger people step in, and even then, it was done with caution.

To become a C-grade, one had to have walked far on one's Path. C-grades were not weak, even in the context of the multiverse, and only a scarce few among the enlightened races would ever manage to reach it. It was only natural that someone would be careful after making it that far and not want to die needlessly in some big war just because thirty people decided to attack them at once.

Due to all this, what usually happened in big wars after the slaughter of those on the weak side was that the strong ones would only partake in smaller skirmishes. If one side sent out three fighters, the other side would respond with three in kind. If one died, the side with a death would send out another. If it could be avoided, neither side sent out a fourth to get a numerical advantage because that would result in the other side doing the same, making it a four-versus-four.

If more were sent out, it could quickly become a five-versus-five, then six, seven... until suddenly everyone was fighting at once, and none of them wanted that. Big wars like that were simply horrible for the individual. As a C-grade, everyone had a strong sense of self-preservation, and entering a conflict where you could get unlucky and have a hundred people decide to attack you at once was not fun for anyone involved.

Even if one side did have a numerical advantage, such as having six hundred fighters while the other only had five hundred, the larger group wouldn't just rush in. Sure, they would more than likely win, but how many of them would die? Half? To the individual, the danger was simply too large, resulting in an all-out fight pretty much never happening.

This explained why war and individual battles during the war could last for extreme lengths of time. It was more akin to a sequence of duels between fighters from opposing factions, with neither side ever running out as they kept getting new fighters to join them. At least, this was what Jake had read as part of the explanation for why factions like the Risen and Holy Church could have ongoing battlefields for thousands of years. This entire structure of war was also far more beneficial, as it allowed those fighting to improve more and gain Records without risking just getting unlucky and dying during a massive skirmish.

All this had to be clarified to understand why the wars on this floor were... off. When Jake and company arrived at this first battlefield, expecting things to be pretty calm, with things proceeding as usual, they instead found around a thousand total C-grades in a massive skirmish, just trying to tear each other apart.

There was no structure, no caution, just reckless fighting. Jake was really taken aback until he felt something, and he wasn't the only one, either.

"Their souls are... polluted," the Fallen King noted.

"I sense a negative energy afflicting them, affecting their mental states," Dina added.

"It's a curse," Jake finally said. "And a pretty damn powerful one at that. I can't say for sure, but I get the feeling it's there to amplify hatred for the other empire. That would at least explain what we're seeing right now."

"The picture is coming together, huh?" the Sword Saint said. "This entire conflict is truly manufactured. But this does make me wonder... if these Twin Emperors want everyone to kill each other during these battle-fields, won't we just be helping them by interfering?"

"Isn't that the plan?" Jake grinned. "To let them do whatever they plan on doing and let them get as powerful as possible... to then have a proper damn fight to finish out Nevermore."

The old man smiled. "I just wanted to make sure we were all on the same page."

"Ree?" Sylphie asked.

Jake smiled. "Yeah, I think it's time to put an end to this war once and for all."

"By leaving no fighters alive on either side," the Fallen King agreed.

Dina nodded. "And then kill whoever is behind it all."

Without further ado, Jake pulled out his bow as the others also prepared to enter the battlefield.

The C-grades fighting were all around level 290 to 310, meaning the guard they'd faced had been on the weaker side of this world. At least, weak in the context of those who'd survived the Twin Emperors borderline wiping out the population of the Vast Plateau with their scheme.

Spells were flying, the air repeatedly exploding with magic. Melee fighters clashed as they flew through the sky, sometimes crashing into each other and spiraling in groups toward the ground. Whenever someone seemed to have a flash of clarity from the curse and tried to escape, they were hunted down. Jake watched all this as he nocked an arrow and concluded that without any interference, everyone would be dead within the next couple of hours.

Jake and company would cut that time down by a lot. Releasing an Arcane Powershot, Jake took down one C-grade before he even had a chance to react. The Sword Saint dove in from the side to pick off some of the ranged fighters, while the Fallen King and Sylphie dove straight into the middle of it all and unleashed their skills. Dina had the unfortunate job of watching out to ensure the two of them didn't mess up and get ganged up on.

Even as their party interfered, the two warring groups didn't team up or anything. Jake and the others just become more fighters of the enemy side for both factions. The entire situation was also so damn chaotic that even if some of the C-grades did notice Jake and company weren't part of either faction, they didn't exactly have the opportunity to voice this insight.

Thus the slaughter continued, but after ten or so minutes, the situation did change. Hundreds had died at this point, many of them easy kills due to their existing injuries. However, as numbers reduced, some stability did return to the situation, and the surviving C-grades had their level of bloodlust subside as more and more gained clarity.

More tight groups formed on both sides as everyone backed off a little, regrouping with their own factions. Jake and the others tried to incite more fighting, but soon enough, they noticed a clear target on their backs. Not necessarily because they were a third party interfering in the battle, but because of the small size of their group. In a battle where two groups had over a hundred each and a third group only had five, they would definitely stick out as the weaker prey, right?

Not in this case.

"Seems like the real fighting starts now," Jake said through the Golden Mark.

"Show them no quarter," the Sword Saint said without hesitation. *"Focus on the left group and get behind them."*

They all did as the Sword Saint said, their group retreating and circling around to get behind the group on the left, putting them between their party and the other faction. Sylphie helped by creating a wind tunnel, and while their movements weren't quite teleportation, they were nevertheless damn fast.

The moment they appeared there, they all attacked by sending arrows, crescent blades of water, and wind, along with golden shockwaves, into the army in front of them. Jake instantly knew what the Sword Saint wanted, as the opposing faction noticed their sworn enemies suddenly under attack and decided this was a great time to restart the battle.

"Avoid using boosting skills and do not tire yourself out—fight with longevity in mind," the Sword Saint reiterated, as they were very much taking this first battle as a trial session for the many more fights to come. *"Simply watch the fires burn across the river as we wait at leisure while the enemy labors."*

"For those who forgot, he is telling us to chill while the enemies tire themselves out before we attack and wipe them all out," Jake explained, as he already saw Sylphie looking confused from the old man talking like an old man.

Following the Sword Saint's elementary plan, one group was rapidly wiped out as they were attacked from both sides. When desperation set in, some did break completely free from the curse, but at that point, it was too late. Jake and company made sure not to advance too much during this fight, resulting in many from the other faction also dying. Those who managed to survive till the very end were also well and truly tired out, making them easy picking as Jake's party let loose and cleaned up the rest of the battlefield.

After they were done, they quickly moved on toward another battlefield. On the way, they ran into some smaller groups of soldiers and reinforcements heading to other battlefields spread throughout the Vast Plateau. One of them even had a map detailing a few of the closest battlefields. Through some extrapolation, they learned there were at least thirty active battlefields in total, with even more now abandoned areas filled with only undead and curse energy.

The Vast Plateau was truly vast, but as they traveled, Jake did notice how odd things were in regard to the placement of these battlefields. They weren't in a line, as one might expect from two warring factions with borders, but instead spread out across the Vast Plateau. Jake began to consider if they were maybe placed purposefully to set up some form of large magic circle, but he couldn't make that fit with any of the knowledge he had.

Things were weird until they reached the two-month mark on floor eighty. On one of the battlefields, where more curse and death energy than usual had already begun to appear, Jake questioned how it had happened so fast. He and Dina had already talked about it plenty during their travels and how it felt off, but after reaching this particular battlefield, they understood.

Jake landed on the ground and inspected the soil in the process of turning gray, and right as he did, he felt something from his boots. A natural treasure of some kind, hidden in the middle of the battlefield, pretty deep underground. With the help of Dina, they quickly dug it up. It was a sphere of interconnected bones.

Unsure what it was, Jake inspected the sphere, and surprisingly enough, it was the King who had some insight. *"This is a soul-sealing hex-trap created from collecting the area's buried ancient bones. Bones that are connected to the land. It creates a field that seals in the soul energy of those who die in a ruthless way... which often results in the birth of curses or undead in the land where one is deployed. Based on the runes on it, I believe it even serves to amplify the curse."*

"You have come across one before?" Jake asked.

"No, I learned about things like this from the witch on the World Council. And while this Totem Bone Sphere, as they are called, is not witch magic, it isn't far off. Whoever made this is a powerful witch doctor or shaman."

"Likely one of the Twin Emperors," Jake said with a frown. "Can any of you use Identify on it? Mine isn't doing anything."

As everyone shook their heads, the Fallen King added, *"It has protection against such things placed on it. In fact, it should have been hidden from most forms of detection. Something that doesn't seem to matter to you."*

Jake shrugged, not going to deny that one.

"What are we going to do with it?" Dina asked. "Destroy it now?"

"Hm," the Sword Saint hummed, and Jake felt everyone glance at him.

"I got nothing," Jake said with a shrug. "I could absorb the curse energy in the sphere with Eternal Hunger, but it doesn't really have much in it yet."

"I would reckon it has the function of absorbing all the energy in the domain," the Fallen King shared. *"Doing so will complete the item. In most cases, these totems are made to cultivate curse and death energy, likely to be used in some form of ritual at a later time."*

"In that case, we probably shouldn't mess with it," Jake said after thinking a bit. "Destroying it may mess up unlocking the event boss. Maybe a bit like how you needed the Demon Lord to have all its artifacts intact for the fight."

"It's possible, if not probable," the Sword Saint agreed. "Let us do that, then."

"Alright." Dina didn't argue as she put the sphere back underground, and they buried it again, trying to act as if they had never been there.

Knowing what was going on now helped a lot as they continued their crusade. Their objective was clear: end the fighting on every battlefield and complete all the preparations for the Twin Emperors to come and extract them. Or at least one of the Twin Emperors. They still needed to figure out what was up with them and how the two were connected. It could just be the same person acting like both, but that was something they had to confirm.

Perhaps by going to actually see one of the two leaders of the Vast Plateau.

On a particularly large battlefield at the five-month mark, Jake and company had to be careful, often retreating from and later reentering the fight. Each side had at least five commanders who were effectively mini-bosses around level 320, and that forced their party to be very careful.

While killing a single commander was fairly simple, killing several at the same time sure as hell wasn't.

And this is kind of what happened. Sylphie and the Fallen King messed up and got overwhelmed with enemies from all sides, forcing Dina to go all-out and use one of her trump cards to bail them out. While she succeeded, this did leave Dina in a weakened state for several days, prompting a decision about whether they should keep fighting or maybe take some time to recover.

Ultimately, they decided to recover, but to avoid wasting time, they agreed on at least still doing something productive. A job for Jake and the best bird.

"Getting to the capital shouldn't take more than a week, especially with Sylphie assisting you," the Sword Saint said as he looked at a map, showing this battlefield pretty close to one of the capitals. "Remember, the job is not about fighting, but getting a feeling for who or what one of these Twin Emperors is."

That's right... it was time to finally figure out the true identities of the Twin Emperors. Or at least one of them.

CHAPTER 34

TWIN EMPEROR IDENTIFIED

For the longest time, Jake had found Sylphie's version of stealth very endearing and silly despite it being utterly useless. She believed that by simply making a giant tornado and hiding within it, no one would notice anything was amiss and just ignore it. She thought the same when it came to hiding sound: Just make so much noise no one can hear anything, and you're good.

Well... it turns out Sylphie had kind of been correct all along? The problem had just been that Sylphie didn't use her stealth technique on a big enough scale.

If a small tornado was ripping apart an area, someone would notice it. However, if a giant gust of wind flew by, while people would surely notice it, few would instantly connect it to a small green hawk. Particularly when said small green hawk was merged with the wind itself, effectively making her a natural phenomenon. At the very least, it worked on this planet, as no one bothered Jake and Sylphie during their travels.

Jake could already imagine the horrors of Sylphie's stealth technique when she got even stronger. Giant hurricanes would wash across planets from her attempts to conceal herself.

Of course, Sylphie's stealth did have the issue of not really working when not traveling swiftly, as a giant gust of wind not moving or just flying in circles to create a tornado was definitely suspicious. The giant gust did have some unforeseen advantages, though, such as allowing Jake to ride alongside it.

Even with all of Jake's improvements to One Step, Thousand Miles, he was still not as fast as Sylphie, so having her adjust her speed to boost Jake was a big help. It allowed the two of them to travel across the Vast Plateau swiftly as they headed for the capital closest to the battlefield while the Sword Saint and Fallen King stayed back with Dina to protect her.

Jake didn't doubt the two of them would still mess a bit with the battlefields, but they would definitely show restraint. The reason the two hadn't come along for this scouting mission was partly because someone needed to stay with Dina and partly because they were both too slow. Plus, neither had good stealth skills, and if they did end up encountering combat during their travels, Jake and Sylphie were the two people in their party most suited to escaping.

Alright, maybe Dina was equal to Jake, as they both had trump-card escape skills, but Sylphie was second to none with her incredible speed and elusiveness. In either case, Jake was the king of stealth and was thus the best at trying to get a good look at this Twin Emperor.

Since Jake was the best at stealth, Sylphie sadly had to hang back when they got close to the capital. They found a small forest not far from the capital where Sylphie found a nice branch to sit on, and Jake continued toward his target. Who knows, maybe he could even manage to sneak into wherever the emperor lived and have a look around.

Setting off, Jake flew into the air with his stealth skill already active. He wanted to get some height first to get a good look at one of the two capital cities of the Vast Plateau, and when he did... honestly, he felt a bit disappointed.

It was so damn small.

Alright, it was still pretty big, probably large enough to house around fifty thousand, but compared to what Jake had come to expect from capital cities in the multiverse, it was pathetic. The fort portion of Haven was way bigger than this small capital, and when compared to some of the cities they had seen even on prior floors—especially those in the Neverending Journey Challenge Dungeon—it barely looked like a town.

However, as Jake scouted it from afar, he did notice one thing. Despite using Identify more than fifty times, he had yet to see a single individual below level 280. And there were a lot of people in the city, even if most of them were crafters. The weapon industry was definitely in full swing, as well as large alchemy labs and sites that worked on supplies for the war efforts. The city was clearly still underpopulated for its already-smallish size, but he reckoned a few thousand should be living there, which also truly attested to how many were already on the battlefields.

In the center of the capital was a large, burly tower, only about ten stories tall but damn wide. Jake wasn't even sure if he could call it a tower, as it pretty much had the shape of a cake. He didn't hold any doubt this would be where the Twin Emperor could be found, and not just because it was the largest central building in the capital, but due to the magical runes covering the entire thing.

Jake even felt an energy that was faintly reminiscent of the one in the bone spheres, making him certain this emperor was indeed involved.

Entering the city, Jake covertly made his way toward the large building. If the emperor was home, he wanted to avoid entering the building if he could. If the Fallen King was correct and they were dealing with a witch doctor or something similar, things could quickly get hairy if Jake entered. Casters like that were very similar to witches like Miranda and enjoyed their well-established magical domains a bit too much.

Luckily, he didn't enter before confirming the emperor was home. After circling the building a few times and sitting watch, he saw a figure at a window. There was a barrier that prevented observers from looking inside, but Jake didn't face many issues in Perception-checking it. Indeed, he saw the full form of one of the two floor bosses.

The Twin Emperor's frame was large and burly, and he stood nearly four and a half meters tall. He wore simple robes, with tattoos covering almost every piece of visible skin, and on his forehead was a small horn. He had the muscles of a warrior but the clothing and demeanor of a mage. His race was also a bit of a surprise, as Jake had fully expected to see an orc, considering they were the most commonly encountered race in the Vast Plateau. Not that he was overly surprised at seeing an ogre, as there had also been quite a lot of those here and there.

It was a bit risky, but Jake still decided to go for an Identify, partly to confirm he was indeed looking at the right boss. Sure enough, it was one of them.

[Twin Emperor – lvl 330]

Level 330 was honestly just about expected. The event boss on floor seventy-five had been level 325, so this one had to be stronger. One also had to remember that level wasn't everything. This Twin Emperor was clearly a powerful variant, making it incredibly strong for its level.

Not that this Twin Emperor was the event boss... because he definitely felt weaker than the event boss from five floors prior. In fact, Jake felt he could fight this boss in a one-versus-one, and even if it would be a damn difficult fight, Jake gave himself at least a sixty-forty chance. With Sylphie joining in, they had better than a three-to-one, and with the entire party, they could definitely do it.

Jake still felt certain this boss related to the event boss, though. At least his gut told him so. Moreover, when Jake had used Identify, he'd felt as if something was off. His Identify hadn't been detected by the Twin Emperor, but something had still interfered with it.

He did have a skill that messed with the bone sphere, so it wouldn't be odd if he could also hide his own status, Jake mentally noted.

Refocusing, Jake narrowed his eyes. This was far riskier than the Identify he had done before, but he was certain that a successful Identify would offer very valuable information. Primal Gaze partly activated as his eyes began to glow, and ever so vaguely, Jake felt as if he saw some kind of veil around the Twin Emperor. Something obscured his sight, making him see false information, almost like a shroud that was way shitter than Jake's own version.

Forcefully, Jake pierced the veil. The moment he did, the ogre boss noticed his presence, whipping his head around and peering out the window straight at where Jake was standing using stealth. Due to the nature of Unseen Hunter, the ogre now saw Jake very clearly as the two of them momentarily made eye contact.

Well, shit.

Jake didn't have time to hesitate. The entire cake-shaped tower lit up with runes as the ogre barged out his own window, breaking it in the process. When a staff appeared in his hand, Jake summoned his wings and quickly used One Step to try and get away, but he felt the space around him being suppressed.

Dodging to the side, Jake narrowly avoided a descending lightning bolt aimed straight at where he had been standing. A massive explosion from the impact sent him tumbling through the air as he continued trying to get away.

The ground itself began to warp beneath him, and then a giant hand of stone rose and tried to grab him. It didn't help when he realized that it wasn't truly space itself being suppressed, but the air actively working against him. Moreover, Jake felt as if his body was beginning to grow heavy as even more concepts came into play. Far more than Jake wanted to try and deal with.

Arcane Awakening activated at the stable 30% as Jake lifted his foot and stepped down. Despite half a dozen concepts and elemental magics closing in on Jake, he still felt everything around him stabilize as his foot found solid ground, allowing him to teleport safely, courtesy of the best boots in the multiverse.

He appeared over two kilometers away, avoiding all the attacks coming for him. Even if Jake kind of wanted to strike back, he avoided doing anything, as this was no time or place to fight. He was still in the capital city, and he felt auras beginning to spike all over. Even if it was nearly only crafters present, Jake didn't want to try and deal with a few thousand of them.

Fleeing, he dodged several attacks and felt the pressure on him lessen. The ogre behind him was preparing something big, and Jake sure as hell wasn't going to stay back to experience it.

Picking up speed, Jake quickly saw that the boss had stopped chasing, though he was still casting something. For a moment, he felt relieved—and then something impacted his Shroud of the Primordial, as well as his soul in general. Energy seeking to invade his soul had somehow appeared in his body. It wasn't a curse, nor was it death magic, but something odd Jake remembered seeing Miranda using.

A hex...

Luckily, the energy didn't seem capable of finding anywhere to settle due to Shroud obscuring his soul. With a rush of destructive arcane energy, Jake managed to get rid of the energy from the hex, purging himself while feeling very happy he had been the one to go and not Sylphie or any of the others, as they would have had a way harder time dealing with the high-level hex.

Far behind him in the capital, Jake saw a massive thunderstorm erupt as a roar of anger echoed out. Jake could only breathe a sigh of relief as he got further and further away. He didn't dare head straight to where Sylphie was hiding, so he sent her a quick message.

"We're bailing out of here. Fly back toward the party immediately, and keep a steady pace till I catch up."

"Ree," Sylphie responded, screeching telepathically into Jake's head.

Jake kept flying for a good while longer, as he did have some pursuers, but they quickly gave up. While still flying, Jake deactivated his boosting skill, happy he didn't have to use it above 30% so he could avoid the period of weakness. After reactivating his stealth skill, he sent a message to Sylphie for them to meet back up, then had a telepathic virtual meeting with the party.

"So, some good and some bad news," Jake told the four others. *"What do you want first?"*

"Bad news," the King responded without hesitation.

"I didn't manage to infiltrate the main building controlled by the Twin Emperor, and I ended up getting chased away when he noticed my presence. So, still not entirely sure exactly what his plans are, and I doubt I can try and sneak back in now."

"Alright, and what is the good news?" the Sword Saint asked.

"The Twin Emperor was level 330 and pretty strong on his own, which must mean the event boss is even stronger, so we'll have a good fight ahead of us!" Jake sent with a smile.

The Sword Saint sighed. *"And what else?"*

"Oh, yeah, and I figured out what's up with the Twin Emperor... or should I call him one part of the Twinhead Emperor," Jake said, referring to the successful Identify he'd managed to sneak through just as he was found.

[Left Twinhead Emperor – lvl 330]

Jake couldn't say he wasn't excited by what he'd seen... because what they were dealing with was an insanely rare variant of ogre. One he had seen quite a bit about, as one of the more powerful gods who once worked with the Order had been one and even authored the books Jake had read on the subject.

"Are you saying it's a...?" Dina began.

"Yep, we got a genuine Twinhead Ogre on our hands," Jake said with glee.

"What is this Twinhead Ogre you speak of?" the Sword Saint questioned.

"Oh, man, they are quite something..." Jake said as he began explaining this fascinating race.

Twinhead Ogres were as rare in the multiverse as they were interesting. For creatures to have more than one head wasn't actually that rare—see hydras as one example—but those heads were just natural parts of the main creature. They were more like extra arms or something. It wasn't as if every head was its own living entity.

A Twinhead Ogre legitimately had two heads and two minds. Mind you, they still shared the same Truesoul, but the rest of the soul was split in two. Each could have independent thoughts and act entirely on their own. This meant that one Twinhead Ogre could research two topics at the same time, and far more effectively than just about any other race. In combat,

they could also do two things at once, making them formidable foes...
when the two heads got along, that is.

Indeed, Twinhead Ogres also had quite the disadvantages. First of all,
as each head was its own, but they shared one body, there could be a lack
of unity, especially when it came to combat. They had to be in agreement,
or they could often fight very sloppily. Growth-wise, they also faced some
challenges. They were a bit like Jake and his Anomalous Soul in this
regard. Their souls were very different from those of usual creatures,
requiring more experience per level and making evolutions a lot harder,
resulting in most Twinhead Ogres never making it to B-grade despite
being naturally born C-grades.

The biggest downside of this race was, by far, the lack of independence
for each head and the Twinhead Ogre being two people forced to share
one body. This resulted in a phenomenon where many Twinhead Ogres
ended up actively plotting to take full control. They would work to
completely kill off their counterpart, making them mindless slaves no
different from a powerful Virtual Mind skill or even cutting off the head
entirely and evolving into a race with only one head.

Of course, some Twinhead Ogres also tried to find another solution...
which was what Jake thought this Twinhead Ogre was doing. He had
managed to split himself in two and was now working on a grand ritual,
perhaps with the purpose of making it a permanent thing, allowing the
two of them to exist independently.

To clarify, this was impossible.

They only had one Truesoul. Which also gave Jake another thought he
shared with the party.

*"If they are a split Twinhead Ogre, they will have to meet up once in a
while. Seeing as the Twinhead Ogre is level 330, they will probably have to
physically meet every month to a month and a half to maintain their split
state. Oh, and also, while the split doesn't halve their power and allows each
to maintain most of the main body, the combined version of the two will be
even more powerful than them separate, even if they fight together."*

"So we think the event boss of this floor is the merged Twinhead Ogre?"
the Sword Saint asked clarifyingly.

"Sure as hell fits the criteria," Jake answered. *"Now, killing just one of
them would result in the permanent deaths of both in their current state, so
that would be the easy way to beat this floor. To unlock the event boss, we
likely need them to merge, but I think the two of them are legitimately
competing in some way to kill the other and absorb their twin permanently."*

"*I assume that means—*"

"*Yep, Sylphie and I are headed to the other capital city to confirm... and this time, I'm not gonna give myself away too soon. I'll find some actual evidence for this theory.*"

CHAPTER 35

DIFFERENT POINTS OF VIEW (AKA THE LAZIEST CHAPTER TITLE POSSIBLE)

So, there were a few things to address.

First of all, the second Twin Emperor turned out to be quite different from the first one. Rather than carrying around a staff and wearing robes, he had durable metal armor and carried a massive two-handed sword on his back at all times. While Jake avoided the guy, he was confident that this second half of the Twin Emperor was a far more physical fighter.

Secondly, this entire war was indeed a plot by the Twinhead Ogre. In traditional Nevermore fashion, information was left out in the open within the main residence of the second Twinhead Emperor, which Jake had managed to successfully sneak into after the boss left the capital—likely to meet up with his other counterpart.

In the home of the boss, Jake found written records, as well as some books and even communications from the other Twin Emperor, where they discussed what they were doing. To summarize, the Twinhead Ogre wasn't native to the Vast Plateau; he had ended up there after his own homeworld was invaded, and he'd used an ancient teleportation circle to try and get away. After arriving on the Plateau, he'd quickly come to realize there was a severe lack of enemies that would allow him to continue progressing and reach B-grade.

Without evolving, the Twinhead Ogre believed he had a low chance of being able to leave the Plateau to explore the rest of the multiverse, so the two heads had hatched a plan of using all the enlightened life in the Vast Plateau to fuel their own evolution. At that time, they had clearly been unified in their goal, but when Jake read the notes of the Twin Emperor now, he saw that things had changed.

Jake had been off when he theorized the ritual was meant to permanently split them. That had never been the plan at all. However, after the split, the Twin Emperors had both experienced independence for the first time in their lives, and it turned out they both quite liked it. The warrior Twin Emperor, at least, suspected the mage variant also preferred the split state.

Researching more, Jake discovered that even if the warrior variant looked like a pure warrior, he was more akin to a death knight. He was capable of rather powerful death magic, and the bone spheres had been created back when the two of them were still merged as one body, using both of their powers.

Meanwhile, the mage variant was something called a hex shaman. He was capable of using shamanistic magic along with hexes, wherein curses were a sub-category. So, one head focused on physical combat and death magic, while the other focused on shamanistic magic and hexes. A pretty damn strong combo when combined, Jake would reckon.

The problem now was that the two of them didn't want to fully recombine, which was a bit of a problem if their party wanted to fight a recombined version. Jake even found evidence of the warrior making plans to use his death magic to "kill" off his counterpart when they did the grand ritual to re-merge, hopefully gaining enough Records to reach B-grade. At the same time, Jake didn't doubt the mage was making his own plans to get rid of the warrior in a similar fashion, which this warrior version already suspected.

So, yeah, things were a mess, which spelled problems for Jake and company. If the event boss was the re-merged version of the Twinhead Ogre, they couldn't make do with one of them "dying" during the re-merging, as that would undoubtedly weaken the final product. Something this Twin Emperor also fully recognized, but his desire to remain independent made the lower overall power worth it in his head.

Interestingly enough, Jake also found out that the two ogres recognized the presence of Jake and company. There were several correspondences related to their group and how a third party had appeared, but so far, the Twin Emperors did not seem overly concerned. In fact, they were almost thankful that their party sped up the process of killing everyone, doing such a good job on every battlefield by leaving no one alive. For some reason, the two ogres also felt the need to insult their party for not realizing they were just helping the ritual along, but Jake wasn't going to get angry about that. He would get even in time.

Jake ended up spending half a day or so going through all the information the warrior Twinhead Ogre had left spread throughout his home. Some of it was sealed away and hidden, sure, but Jake easily found everything using Sphere.

One could ask why all of these plans and correspondences between the Twin Emperors had been left all over the place and not destroyed once the warrior had memorized everything, but Jake wasn't going to question the flawless logic of a Nevermore floor. It hadn't made sense on any of the prior floors either, so why suddenly get all up in arms over this one?

He managed to sneak out of the second Twin Emperor's residence before anyone caught him, then moved to meet up with his other party members once more. Sylphie had already rejoined them after helping Jake get most of the way to this other capital, and the four of them were busy making a mess on more of the battlefields.

Timewise, they were still good. They still had a few months left to finish off this floor and defeat the re-merged Twinhead Ogre. The plan was to fight the strongest version of the Twinhead Ogre possible, and to do that, they reached a conclusion.

"*To summarize, we will first clear up all the battlefields to ensure all the Totem Bone Spheres are fully charged,*" the Sword Saint explained. "*Then we will allow the Twin Emperors to collect them, but before or perhaps in the middle of their ritual, we need to make the two of them realize that they need to merge with one another fully to stand a chance against the five of us. If all goes well, we will end up with a Twinhead Ogre fully put back together, further empowered by the ritual. It's risky, and we may be biting off more than we can chew, but this is the plan.*"

A simple plan where a lot could go wrong, with the end result potentially being an event boss far too powerful for them to beat. Yep, Jake was definitely going to enjoy this final floor, and especially what would happen over the next few months... because it was time to wipe out all the battlefields and get just a few more levels under his belt.

———

Azal cursed under his breath as he looked out at the vast plains in front of him. It did not get better when his party member, the Dungeon Engineer, shook his head as he opened his eyes, having finished his analysis.

"Nope, no way to do it in time," Casper said with a sigh. "This floor has two main bosses, from what I can sense, and in order to get the best reward, we need to do something with the two of them. Not just kill them both, but something more complicated... and time-consuming."

"The essence of death is powerful in this world... It's one suitable for us," the ghostly bride said as a few ghosts returned to her, having scouted their immediate surroundings. "However, it has an artificial feeling... as if it's cultivated. Do we need to finish this cultivation to ensure a perfect victory?"

"Right... I sense a lot of focus points where both death and curse energy are gathered. As you said, it's all happening in a rather artificial fashion, so probably something that's being done by one of those Twin Emperors." Casper shook his head again as he looked at Azal. "Sorry, boss, no way to do everything in time."

Azal couldn't fault the Dungeon Engineer. They had simply been too slow in passing the prior floors and even made some major mistakes along the way. Their attempts to do the event boss on floor seventy-five had been especially overambitious, resulting in the death of one of their comrades and Maltrax having to overuse a certain boosting skill, weakening her for more than a year afterward. Luckily, the Risen had sent a replacement from one of the other elite teams. This meant another team was crippled by losing a member, but there had simply been no other choice. Azal had been prioritized by the higher-ups; that was the end of it.

My score should still be acceptable in the eyes of the Blightfather, Azal thought. No, *hoped.* If not, he could potentially lose his title of Ghost King.

As he stood there considering the situation, his party kept discussing it.

"Can't we just kill these two Twin Emperors and quickly pass the floor that way?" Maltrax, the beastfolk Risen, asked.

"Look at the objective of the floor again," Casper said. "It says to end the conflict—something I doubt just killing one or both of the Twin Emperors will do. It would also just be too easy from a design perspective."

"Well, fuck," Maltrax cursed out loud. "What, then? We got a month and a bit left or something like that, right?"

"Right," Casper confirmed. "In my opinion, the best way to optimize points would probably be to hunt down at least one of these bosses. While it won't be as good as clearing the floor, hopefully it will give us a few achievements. We can also try and do a few bonus objectives, but yeah, the best thing is probably to just kill a Twin Emperor or two. I would assume that's also the best for levels."

"Let us do that, then," Azal said with determination. Even if he doubted he would be able to take the top spot of the Leaderboards as his Patron had hoped, he would, at the very least, do his best till the very end.

———

Jacob relaxed on the fourteenth City Floor, sitting and drinking tea with Bertram as he waited for more members of the Holy Church to come see him. His former bodyguard and current Guardian had a tentative look on his face as he looked at the teacup in front of him.

"You're really satisfied with this?" he asked after a bit.

"It was for the best," Jacob said with a sigh, having had a similar conversation before. "We can do more good here, helping those who have questions or are beginning to doubt if their Path needs improvement. Since most finish all the Challenge Dungeons on this floor, it's the best place to have these conversations."

Bertram just grunted, not entirely satisfied with the answer.

Jacob understood... Bertram was a fighter. However, Jacob wasn't. While the two of them were bound by the unique bond between a Guardian and an Augur, they were still two separate people with their own Truesouls. This meant they took up two spots in the Nevermore party, and that sadly made them burdens.

In the earlier floors, this wasn't really a problem, as Jacob's abilities as an Augur were highly valuable, allowing them to often skip many time-consuming steps. Back then, the true difficulty had been in pure navigation and figuring out the floors. Now, the difficulty was in the actual fights.

Bertram and Jacob could pull off some interesting moves, considering Bertram's near-immortality and ability to be resurrected repeatedly. He could use boosting skills far beyond where one would die and wield powerful weapons such as a Holy Sword to serve as a true pinnacle fighter for difficult fights.

The problem arose when every fight was a dangerous one. In his basic state, Bertram was only a good warrior. He was skilled for sure and considered an elite, but compared to the others they had in their party, Jacob and Bertram simply fell too far behind.

That was why it had been decided that Jacob and Bertram's Nevermore journey would end here, not going to floor seventy-one. Instead, they had been replaced by two others from the Holy Church. In fact, the Church had split up their entire party and made one with the five best prospects to go as far as they could during the final decade or so. It was the very best the Holy Church could muster for this early era of Nevermore, and hopefully it would be enough.

Meanwhile, Jacob would stay back and help guide people until this decade expired and it was time for him to leave. One could question why he didn't try and do some more floors to at least gain a few more levels, but to someone like Jacob, staying back on the City Floor was better even for that. He would gain more experience acting like an Augur for a decade compared to doing more floors.

Finally, and perhaps most importantly, the higher-ups believed it best Jacob didn't take more risks. On floor sixty-eight, he had triggered his One More Light skill, which had resurrected him after death. The skill gave him one charge per grade, and while he did have one more left since he hadn't died in D-grade, the Church believed it too risky for him to continue. His death back then had come when they pulled off one of their special strategies with Bertram, leaving Jacob defenseless against a regular monster no one had seen coming.

"Hey, at least I have some positive news," Jacob said with a smile. "I have ensured we will be able to go back to Earth when the Prima Guardian arrives. I didn't even have to act like this would be my compromise for not making a fuss over being told to stay on the City Floor."

"Oh?" Bertram said with surprise. "That is good news... I hope everyone is doing well back home."

"Based on what I heard, things are just fine," Jacob answered. "My father is even part of their World Council, running things in place of Jake having to actually do any work as a World Leader."

"Definitely for the best. Not the thing about your father, but that Jake isn't running things all on his own. Doubt that would end well."

"For sure," Jacob said with a look of nostalgia.

The two of them tended to avoid talking about Earth, as it was a sore subject for both of them. Jacob didn't like how he had been borderline fooled into leaving before Ell'Hakan had made his invasion, much less that the Holy Church had taken advantage of this invasion to force the Risen off the planet.

At least he had learned that the Holy Church had expected to be able to remain and still have some presence, even if it wouldn't be prominent or displayed openly. Efforts Miranda had managed to crush, as the planet was nearly entirely dark in the eyes of the Holy Church due to the removal of the people affiliated with them.

Perhaps for the best. No matter how involved Jacob got with the Holy Church, he still cared about his home planet and the people from it, and he genuinely hoped they were all doing well.

———

Carmen didn't like being forced to spend time with more people she didn't know, but at least the three of them were more skilled than their former party members. Plus, at least they were doing fun group activities.

Davion, their party leader, rushed forward, and the four others followed him onto the battlefield, where they became a machine of death. While clearing all of floor eighty would be a stretch, they sure as hell should be able to get in quite a few good fights.

Moving swiftly, Carmen took the frontal position as they were noticed by a group of enemies. A few dozen spells flew toward them, but Carmen just smiled and took the magic head-on. It didn't even manage to leave a mark on her body as she punched a particularly large fireball apart before continuing to pummel the mage who had cast it.

Two warriors attacked from behind, their blades hitting her back. The loud clang of metal hitting something tougher than itself sounded out as Carmen turned with a grin. She punched one of them in the throat before kicking the other in the stomach, sending him tumbling back into the two-handed blade of Davion, who cut him in two.

Flashing him a grin, Carmen turned to face more assaults. She took every hit without a care in the world, the level 300 foes far from capable of piercing her natural resistance. Especially the casters. Ah, but there were a few who could maybe nick her a bit here and there, so she could still have some fun.

Her three other party members also went hard. A shaman with a dozen or so summoned fire and earth elementals was practically a one-woman army, as she wielded her own staff to shoot out torrents of lava to burn her enemies. A caster that didn't really fit into the usual Valhal arche-type cast spirit magic to buff their party members up and act as a healer, while a third guy wielded a massive greatbow to shoot devastating arrows. He wasn't as good as Jake, but he was decent enough.

Their party had been shuffled up a bit after doing all the Challenge Dungeons, resulting in only Davion and Carmen continuing in the "elite" group. While Carmen hadn't been a fan of this shuffle initially, she had to recognize it was probably for the best, as there was no fucking way they would have made it to floor eighty with their old group.

Not that they would beat it... but at least Carmen would have a good time until the very end of Nevermore by punching her way through a few dozen active battlefields.

CHAPTER 36

LORD OF HUNGER

J ake stood back along with the three others as they allowed the Sword Saint to do his thing. More than seventy combatants remained, and despite being on opposing sides, they had teamed up to face this one swordsman. Nevertheless, the outcome was clear.

Rain fell from the sky, every droplet piercing their barriers and shields. The swordsman himself fought in a simplistic fashion as he moved swiftly between foes, never giving them any chance to surround him or catch him out in a vulnerable position.

Even when his sword swings didn't manage to leave injuries, the piercing rain did. These tens of thousands of small, piercing droplets fell every second, making them simply impossible to block. The water itself, even when blocked, also contained the concept of time, weighing and slowing down everyone as they grew more soaked. Moreover, Jake knew this was only the first part of the old man's mythical skill—an extremely powerful move for sure.

The only big downside was that to use this skill, the old man had to be fighting alone... not because it was a requirement, but because it would strike everything and everyone in the area indiscriminately.

When about sixty enemies remained, the Sword Saint used the next move. The rain began to slow down before stopping in mid-air while the old man floated backwards and took a stance, pointing the blade toward the ground and grasping it with both hands as he knelt. With a slow movement, he began to move the blade upwards, the floating droplets doing the same.

"Rain of Time: Reversal."

Instantly, he swung upwards, the raindrops following along. The ground below was torn up as every single droplet reversed in time and launched toward the sky, looking like the old man had just swung a blade dozens of kilometers long and wide.

Every single person caught in it was cut up, many of them ripped apart altogether by the powerful strike. Only about twenty of the most powerful C-grades remained, all having used powerful defensive skills or hidden items to survive.

It was the same skill the old man had already shown off quite a number of times before. It was the mythical skill he gained in D-grade that had downgraded to legendary when he evolved... A downgrade that had now been reversed, because the old man had upgraded it back to mythical once more. Thus, the skill was not finished, even after this move.

Rather than use the skill to restore a bit of the spent resources, he activated a second part. Pointing his blade toward the clouds above made of pure water, he spoke once more.

"Rain of Time: Thousand Blades Descent."

All of the rain that had fallen coalesced into blades far up in the sky as the Sword Saint swung down once more. Every single blade of water descended with his strike, and rather than simply flying straight down, they each aimed for the still-living combatants.

The poor twenty or so survivors tried to defend themselves but were unable to, as each was already injured. Limbs were sent flying as every single one of them was cut apart, and many of the blades of water were colored red with blood as they continued down and pierced the ground, penetrating the rocky sprawl for dozens of meters. The terrain itself began to look like Swiss cheese. Definitely not a good sight for anyone with trypophobia.

Breathing heavily, the old man sheathed his sword before flying back toward the group, looking pretty damn tired.

As he got closer, Jake couldn't help but yell, "Six hundred and thirty-seven!"

"What?" the Sword Saint responded as he reached them, looking quite confused.

"You said there were a thousand blades, but I only counted six hundred and thirty-seven," Jake said as he shook his head in disappointment. "That's just false advertising right there."

"Really?" the old man responded with a tired sigh.

"I call it as I see it." Jake shrugged and smirked.

"Don't you have a skill called One Step, Thousand Miles? I'm positively confident I have yet to see you ever travel even a hundred miles in a single step using that skill, much less a thousand."

"In my defense, I use the skill with a focus on quick activation over range... Plus, I didn't make that skill; it's a set upgrade path. You made that skill, so the name should at least be accurate. Also, all of my other skills do as advertised." After all, his arcane arrow skills were indeed made of arcane arrows.

"Do you not possess a skill called Sagacity of the Malefic Viper? That, too, is a lie, as I see no sage before me." It seemed the Fallen King had decided to team up with the old man to attack Jake.

"Of the Malefic Viper. He is the sage, not me," Jake said, deciding to change the subject, considering he was getting mercilessly attacked from two directions at once. Looking at the Sword Saint, he asked what they were all thinking. "Anyway, did you get the level?"

"I did indeed," the old man said, politely accepting the change of subject as he nodded.

The reason the old man had handled this small battlefield alone was for him to get one more level before the final fight with the Twinhead Ogre. He had been level 289 in his class, and with this level, had gotten a new skill selection.

A few of the others had also gotten over this breakpoint, but sadly for Jake, he was still a bit behind. Not to say he hadn't also made some good progress.

'DING!' Class: [Arcane Hunter of Horizon's Edge] has reached level 285 - Stat points allocated, +50 Free Points

...

'DING!' Class: [Arcane Hunter of Horizon's Edge] has reached level 287 - Stat points allocated, +50 Free Points
'DING!' Race: [Human (C)] has reached level 274 - Stat points allocated, +45 Free Points

This was for the entire floor, mind you. Getting three levels was good for sure, but he had gotten less than the others simply because this particular floor didn't suit his Path that well. Jake wasn't made for big wars or conflicts; he was instead far more specialized in hunting down powerful individuals. In truth, Jake's Path also wasn't super well-suited for group combat in general.

"Any update on the Twin Emperors?" Dina asked as the Sword Saint went off to the side to focus on his skill selection.

"They are collecting their bone spheres pretty quickly," Jake answered with a smile as he stopped thinking sad thoughts about his own relative lack of levels. "At least, I guess that's what they're doing when they go to all the different battlefields."

"Ree?" Sylphie inquired.

"Yeah, we should have time," Jake responded as he focused on the two Hunter's Marks he had placed on the bosses. "If they keep up this speed, collecting them all will take two weeks more at most."

In preparation for the final fight, they naturally needed to know where this ritual would be taking place. Finding this location had once more been assigned to Jake, as he was the scout of the party and, quite frankly, just the best at it.

He had marked one of the Twin Emperors and followed him to the two bosses' meeting point. It was in the middle of nowhere, but when Jake used a Pulse, he understood. A massive magic circle had been put there, hidden beneath the ground itself, likely buried using the earth-bending powers of the shaman Twin Emperor.

Watching the two of them meet up had been pretty damn boring, but he did notice something interesting. When the Twin Emperors were close to one another, both their bodies seemed to warp a bit, and as he had a Mark on them, he saw their Soulshapes shudder ever so slightly. Their very souls wanted to merge back together, but the two ogres did some simple-looking magic, stabilizing their souls, before exchanging some words Jake couldn't hear and then going home again.

As they left, Jake made sure to refresh his Hunter's Mark on both, partly to check how long the Marks would last and partly to keep track of the two ogres. Well, Jake turned out to be pretty lucky, as his Mark lasted more than an entire month, which coincidentally was also the time between the ogres meeting up. It was a bit annoying that he had to go re-Mark them every month, but luckily, he only had to do it a few times before the floor would be over. There hadn't been that many months left, after all.

Marking them turned out to be a great idea, as when they cleared one of the last few battlefields, both Twin Emperors started to make their move. They went to all the old and abandoned battlefields one by one, sometimes even returning to where the giant ritual circle was in between gathering a bunch.

By now, pretty much all the bone spheres had been gathered. Jake and company had also just cleared out the final active battlefield, which meant it was time for the next step in their plan.

"Let's make our way toward the ritual circle so we can begin to set things up there," the Sword Saint said with a nod.

"How far was it again?" the Fallen King questioned.

"Just four days with Sylphie assisting us."

"Ree!" Sylphie said, always happy to help, and the wind gathered around them.

The Sword Saint was a bit worse for wear after using his flashy and powerful mythical skill that Jake totally wasn't jealous of. He could only reverse rain and create a torrent of falling swords; how was that even impressive? Jake could stare at people really menacingly, which was definitely way cooler.

Flying toward the ritual site, the five of them spoke a bit and went over their plans once more. The Sword Saint also shared a bit about the new skill he had unlocked. It was a defensive one that allowed him to shift his location in space back a second or two while summoning a water clone where he had been standing prior, allowing him to dodge attacks...

So, yeah, a shittier version of Eternal Shadow. Jake's skill was definitely better there, especially considering the old man's skill was only of ancient rarity.

As expected, they arrived at the ritual site just under four days later. Jake released a Pulse to inspect the place, and as expected, he found over a hundred Totem Bone Spheres sealed beneath the ground at different focus points of the magic circle. Using his knowledge of ritual magic, he could also see that the two ogres needed just twenty more spheres, and they should be good to go.

"How much time left till we're kicked out of Nevermore?" Jake asked the Sword Saint, wanting to make sure they indeed had enough time.

"A bit less than a month," the Sword Saint answered. "As long as the Twin Emperors are as fast as you expected, we should have at least two weeks left when they get here. That should give us time for them to finish whatever preparations they need to begin the ritual."

"There aren't any further preparations, really," Jake said after he finished looking at the ritual circle. "It's fully complete already... has been for a long time. It just needed its batteries to get powered up."

"Hm." The Sword Saint frowned. "Do we still have time to—"

"Yeah, I already got it all planned out in my head." Jake grinned as he looked at the old man. "I will need your help, of course."

"Alright, then let's get to work." The Sword Saint nodded in agreement as the two of them went down toward the ritual circle that the Twin-head Ogre had totally forgotten to put a "don't touch" sign on.

Meanwhile, Dina began her preparations by spreading seeds throughout the surrounding plains. The Fallen King also made sure he had all his weird golden spheres for recovery. In truth, he and Sylphie didn't have many things to prepare, as they just needed to be in absolute peak condition when the Twinhead Ogre appeared... because if one thing was sure, it was that the following fight wouldn't be easy.

———

The two ogres arrived at the ritual site at approximately the same time. They spotted each other from afar and gave knowing looks before they began depositing the Totem Bone Spheres in their assigned spots. Getting everything in place only took about half an hour—somewhat quicker than usual, since they no longer needed to be careful and keep everything hidden.

In fact, they turned the soil over to unearth the entire formation, revealing the complex magic circle the two of them had carved into the ground before they had split into two. It was the last thing they'd done before splitting up. Their final joint project.

Now... now they would never work together again. As the final preparations were made, the two of them came together in the center of the circle. The place where they would absorb all the death and curse energy from the ritual to uplift their existence, hopefully getting enough Records to evolve to B-grade and finally get off the Vast Plateau.

"So, it has finally come to this," the Left Twin Emperor said as he stood there with his staff, staring at his counterpart. The person with whom he had once been one... and now wished to get rid of permanently.

"It's the only way," the Right Twin Emperor said, one hand already on the sword he rested upon his shoulder. "Neither of us wishes to become one again, and without unity, we would never be capable of evolving anyway."

There could only be one ending... and they both knew it. One of them had to perish, and each had a plan to rid themselves of the other. They also both knew what the other had planned, as the closer they both got to the end of this ordeal, the harder it became to hide their true intentions. So, rather than try and plan behind the other's back, everything was now out in the open.

One would use a cursed seal to remove the consciousness and free will of his former second half, while the other would simply kill part of their twin's soul. Both were cruel methods, but neither blamed the other... to do so would simply be too hypocritical.

Besides, neither of them truly hated the other. This was simply their fate. They had tasted the forbidden fruit of independence, and this was the price they had to pay if they wished to ever continue progressing. It would weaken the winner significantly compared to if they simply fully merged once more, but that was a sacrifice that had to be made.

"May the best one win," the Left Twin Emperor said as his aura began to spike.

"And the loser never forgotten," the Right Twin Emperor responded, also pushing his aura.

Their two presences clashed with one another as they entered a battle of wills. An actual fight would only result in destroying the surrounding magic circle while weakening the eventual winner, making pulling off the ritual more difficult.

Instead, they would battle it out with their souls. They were both already at an identical wavelength and power level, meaning neither had any innate advantage. The winner would instead be the one with the greater will to win and live on as his own entity—and likely also the one with the highest chances of evolving afterward.

The presences clashed and intertwined, yet neither got an advantage. Around them, the ritual began to activate as planned, empowering both of them at the same time with the power of curses and death. Everything would be decided soon; only one would remain. Their souls were already half-merged, the process no longer able to be stopped.

Yet, just then, something unplanned happened. Something unexpected.

Another aura entered the mix. A third presence made itself known, seemingly appearing out of nowhere as an unfamiliar yet recognizable energy covered the sky above. The energy of curses... but one far more powerful than anything their ritual was dealing with.

For a moment, the ogres paused their clash and looked up. A shadowy figure had appeared in the sky, floating and surrounded by rolling clouds of pure curse energy, staring down at them and the ritual circle with pure hunger.

"I knew I smelled something... delicious," the being said, their voice echoing.

The pure hunger intensified as the Twin Emperors used Identify at the same time, and their eyes opened wide when they saw the creature that had appeared.

[Lord of Hunger – lvl 345]

Neither knew how this had happened, and in their state of clashing souls and intertwined existences, they both knew what the other one was thinking. They had somehow attracted a powerful creature neither of them had known about... Perhaps they'd even had a hand in giving birth to it.

"A worthy feast," the being spoke once more as a shadowy hand was raised.

Both Twin Emperors felt the bone spheres begin to react. The creature was trying to absorb the curse energy within them, devouring everything they had worked for. What's more, they both also experienced pure blood-lust and knew that the being was not going to stop at simply reaping the fruits of their labor. As soon as it had eaten the spheres, they would be next.

As they were in the middle of the ritual circle already, and their state was that of being half-merged, the Twin Emperors faced a choice... and for the first time in a long time, neither held any doubt as to what the best decision would be. Stopping the merging could not be done, and what good was independence if they would die anyway?

Better to try and find another solution instead of dying to this cursed creature. And to do that, they would need to be at their most powerful state. With determination, their souls came together and restored unity, rebirthing the Twinhead Emperor.

CHAPTER 37

TWINHEAD EMPEROR

J ake deserved a goddamn award for his performance as the mysterious yet powerful Lord of Hunger. Ah, not those awards given for good acting, but those reserved for extremely shitty performances... because hot damn, had Jake felt embarrassed while saying his lines.

He could at least partly excuse how horrible it was by blaming sim-Jake a little. In order to really sell it, Jake had infused his body with curse energy and even sent it out of Eternal Hunger while mixing it with his presence. Shit, he'd gone so far as to summon his Eternal Shadow to overlap with his own body during the entire thing.

This did inadvertently result in Jake being affected by his own curse energy. No way around it. It wasn't much, but it was enough for Jake to feel like he could blame the remnants of cringe on sim-Jake. At least his party members were kind enough to not say anything during or after his speech.

Not that they had much to complain about... because their plan had worked. Without them even having to use either of their two backups in case Jake's acting had failed.

The ritual created by the Twinhead Emperor was in full swing as the curse and death energy exploded out of it. While over a hundred pillars of pure energy shot toward the sky, the Twin Emperors merged into one being, energy continuously infusing their body.

The energy pouring out of the many Totem Bone Spheres was made of impurities, as the Twinhead Ogre only absorbed the cleanest of energy and Records. More than ninety-nine percent of this energy would not be used by the ogre, as this ritual was never meant to raise their power, just their future potential. In all honesty, it was a damn impressive ritual, if also flawed in many ways, as it was rather forceful. Perhaps it would allow the Twinhead Ogre to reach B-grade, but just like someone absorbing a fragment of the Viper and instantly evolving a few grades, B-grade would be the end of the Twinhead Ogre's Path.

Well, if he ever did manage to evolve... Jake and company were going to make sure that wasn't gonna happen. As the ritual was winding down, a system message appeared before Jake and the others.

Event unlocked: Return of the Twinhead Emperor.
The culprits behind the war on the Vast Plateau were moments away from having their wish come true at the sacrifice of most enlightened beings on the Plateau. Their ritual was complete, everything ready, all factors accounted for... except for the appearance of five unknown entities.
Despite their prior plans, the Twin Emperors have decided to once more merge with one another, rebirthing the Twinhead Emperor in a state more powerful than ever. They viewed it as their only choice to face this threat, even if it ruined all they had been preparing for. Now, with all hopes of evolution squashed, they seek only their own survival and revenge on those who forced them into this state.
End the Path of the Twinhead Emperor once and for all, thus ending not only the conflict on the Vast Plateau but also the cause of it. Ensure that it may never happen again.
New Bonus Objective gained: Do not allow a single party member to be slain during the battle while ending the Twinhead Emperor for good.

The message was borderline identical to what they'd encountered on floor seventy-five with the event boss, except it now had an added bonus objective. Jake and company had completed all of the bonus objectives on this floor already, so to get a new one was a bit of a surprise... Plus, it communicated that the difficulty of this fight was high. The only other time Jake remembered seeing a bonus objective like that was during their fight with Minaga.

Jake stared down at the Twinhead Ogre as the ritual fully came to an end. The whole thing had only taken ten or so seconds, as the ritual had already been well underway by the time Jake appeared and interfered. As all the energy began to die down, the ritual kept humming with energy, and the two figures standing at the center turned into one.

The ogre had gotten slightly taller and was the same bundle of muscle as before. His armor had changed quite a bit, as it was now a mix of the two Twin Emperors' prior equipment. All the most important places were protected by metal, while the rest was just cloth. The only mostly visible flesh was on the ogre's arms, legs, and face, with his legs defended only by a kilt. Even the feet were wide open, as the boss wore some sandal-looking footwear.

As expected, the biggest change by far was what could be found above the neck... or necks, as it should be called now. Two heads rested side by side, each having the face of one of the Twin Emperors. The right side wielded a giant sword, and the left side a staff, matching the approach of their respective heads.

Using Identity, Jake confirmed the result.

[Twinhead Emperor – lvl 335]

Even if the ritual had not been done to gain more power, getting a few levels was still inevitable. In fact, Jake found it a bit lucky the boss had not risen further in level... because if the Twinhead Emperor had, this would have gotten even harder than it was already going to be.

The aura of the ogre had entirely transformed after the two had merged into one. Before, they had both been incomplete, but now, reunited, the Twinhead Ogre could show his full power once more. In pure power, it was by far the strongest creature Jake had ever faced in Nevermore, outside of the B-grade he had tried to fight in Minaga's Labyrinth.

Powerful for sure... but compared to a B-grade, this ogre was still manageable.

"**Lord of Hunger! You have forced me into this, so be prepared to face the consequences!**" one of the heads of the Twinhead Emperor yelled, infusing his voice with mana. Jake felt like this was his cue to continue their plan.

"**Consequences?**" Jake said, acting as much like a being born of a curse as he could. "**No, thank you... I'd rather not deal with you at all.**"

"**That is not your choice to—**"

Before the ogre could finish the sentence, the attacks arrived. A massive drill of wind descended from above as hundreds of spear-like roots shot up from underneath. At the same time, a thin, piercing blade of water shot at the Twinhead Emperor from one side, and a golden beam arrived from the other. Jake didn't use a direct attack, simply staring at the boss as his eyes glowed orange with Primal Gaze.

He felt a powerful impact on his soul, making him flinch in pain, but he still continued doing his part. A shadowy version of himself also flew out of his body, barreling down toward the ogre with a katar in hand while the real Jake prepared to use the cover of curse energy to fly upward.

The many attacks reached the Twinhead Emperor, and they momentarily froze. Right as they did, the eyes of one of the heads began to glow, and something entirely unexpected happened. The soul attack Jake had made was entirely taken on by only one of the heads, allowing the other one to control the body and energy fully.

Slamming his staff into the ground, the ogre crushed the roots and erupted the earth. Massive spikes hundreds of meters tall shot up all around him, weakening the attacks coming from the side, just as a barrier of swirling wind also appeared around the boss. The barrier did not look powerful enough to block the attack, but Jake understood when he saw the barrier slightly reflecting the trajectory of the drill of wind from above, making it crash into the golden beam from the Fallen King. At the same time, the sword in the right arm rose and blocked the Sword Saint's attack fully, the ogre's arm barely moving from the impact.

The only one unblocked was Jake's Eternal Shadow, but that was because the Twinhead Emperor had chosen an offensive option for that one. The glowing eyes of the ogre that had taken on the soul attack intensified as two burning beams blasted out. Rather than getting hit, the Eternal Shadow dodged the blow, and the beam turned in mid-air to strike from behind.

This one, the Eternal Shadow didn't even bother to dodge as it threw its weapon. It wasn't even close to hitting the ogre, yet it pierced through several layers of rock before embedding itself in the ground. The ogre's attack did hit, though. The Eternal Shadow dispersed into energy, making the ogre temporarily look confused.

They didn't have much time to ponder, though, as more attacks arrived. Jake's party—except Sylphie, who had been flying far up in the air —had all taken up hidden positions Jake had made using stable barriers of arcane mana around the ritual circle. Dina further helped to hide them using her nature magic. Now, they were all out of hiding and went for the boss.

As for where Jake, the Lord of Hunger, was? Well, he was already "dead," or at least gone, right? At least it looked like he had disappeared as the true Jake rapidly ascended, hidden by the remnant curse energy he had filled the sky with. He even felt that the Twinhead Emperor was no longer fully aware of him, allowing him to once more enter stealth while flying upwards. In his quiver on his back, an arrow was also being created.

While ascending, he turned parts of his attention to the battle below, hoping the other four could also handle their role until it was time for him to make his reentrance.

The Sword Saint went straight for the Twinhead Emperor, blade already in hand. He was the only true melee fighter of their party, and thus alone in close combat more often than not, at least when the boss in question didn't try to avoid fighting him directly. This was undoubtedly a risky role, but he was more than up for it.

Staring at the boss, Miyamoto knew the merged ogre was powerful. He did not have Jake's ability to judge others' power extremely accurately, but he had been in plenty of fights himself and had acceptable insight when measuring a foe... and this Emperor was powerful. Very powerful.

Due to that, he also didn't dare hold back, activating his boosting skill immediately. He would need it no matter what, and out of everyone, his was the one that could be used the longest. It was based on water and time, both concepts rather gentle in nature, though it did come at the sacrifice of its power being less explosive.

The Twinhead Emperor noticed him as he closed in, one head turning his way. He had approached from the right side, which, in retrospect, was perhaps not the best, as he found himself confronted with a massive sword. One that would usually be wielded in two hands, but the ogre wielded it with ease as he swung for the approaching swordsman.

Blocking was not an option. The Sword Saint momentarily delayed his step, allowing the blade to swing down in front of him, missing entirely. The blade struck the ground and released an explosion of death mana that washed over the old man, but he wasn't deterred. He went for a light slash, not wanting to overcommit to any attack.

Moving quickly, the ogre pulled back the arm the Sword Saint was going for, but a small cut was still left. Without waiting for a full response, the old man retreated slightly, which proved a good idea when the ogre ripped up the blade embedded in the ground, making it erupt and send black rot shards infused with death energy flying toward Miyamoto.

Deflecting those he couldn't dodge, he tried to launch a crescent blade of water to keep the ogre engaged and focused on him. However, the boss clearly wasn't taking him overly seriously yet. Miyamoto was, in effect, only fighting one of the heads, as the left one focused entirely on being prepared for the three other attacks.

Attacks that arrived soon after as Sylphie descended from above. She pierced down, aiming straight for the left head. Unfortunately, the ogre had been prepared. He raised his staff toward the sky and released a torrent of fire and rock, blasting upwards and lighting up the sky.

Right as the ogre did this, a blast of force arrived from the side, hitting the ogre in the arm and forcing the blast slightly off-course. This allowed Sylphie to penetrate the flames, but she was still forced to abandon full commitment at the very last second when a pillar of rock shot up toward her. Still, she managed to use all her momentum to launch a bullet of air that hit the ogre in the shoulder, drawing blood.

Both the Fallen King and Sylphie continued their many attacks while the Sword Saint stayed in melee range. So far, the ogre had yet to move, staying more or less still throughout the entire battle. Yet he was not really losing any ground at all, handling the three of them. It didn't help that the few minor wounds they did leave were healed within seconds, as the boss could even cast healing magic on himself.

Not that their party was struggling much, either. The Sword Saint used a primarily defensive style while engaging the right side of the ogre. He dodged all the blade swings and blasts of death magic as he left minor wound after minor wound. Sometimes, he was a bit too slow to fully dodge an attack, which was where Dina came in with her healing.

A status quo was established, and the Sword Saint believed things were progressing far better than expected. They were buying time for Jake to do his thing without expending many of their resources, and they still had "that" prepared for later, too.

Continuing his attacks, the Sword Saint began to gain more confidence, as the boss was not as dangerous as first believed. The ogre wasn't attacking much, but mostly defending, and when he did attack, it was to blast one of them away. It was almost as if the ogre was also buying time... but for what?

They would soon get their answer.

The Sword Saint tried to land a deep cut on the arm of the ogre, only to suddenly find a staff pointed at his head. Quickly, he dodged to the side as a bullet of air shot toward him, and before he could even raise his blade to block, a blade came swinging in from the side.

With alarm, Miyamoto was forced to use his newly gained evasion skill, replacing his body with a water clone. At the same time, he was sent back about five meters, where he still suffered from a shockwave of pure death energy the blade had released.

Stumbling, he didn't even have time to stabilize before a shard of stone struck him in the shoulder, sending him flying back and blood spurting out. To make matters worse, he also saw the Fallen King in distress; a massive lightning strike came down right where he was standing, and Sylphie had been entirely pushed back by two summoned snake-like creatures of fire chasing her.

In a matter of seconds, the ogre had entirely changed. His moves were coordinated, calculated, and perfectly in sync. Retreating, the Sword Saint felt Dina quickly heal him as he ripped out the rock shard, luckily not getting injured too badly despite being taken by surprise. As he created some distance, he heard the ogre speak once more.

"It took a bit," the right head said.

"A century apart was a long time," the left followed up.

"However, I do believe—"

"—I've gotten used to it—"

"—once more—"

"—by now."

That was when the Sword Saint realized why the ogre had seemed so off... The two of them had been living as separate entities for so long it had taken them time to truly synchronize. Frowning, Miyamoto realized they had missed a great opportunity to strike, and looking at the entirely changed demeanor of the Twinhead Emperor, he hoped it wasn't going to haunt them.

"How long?" he asked Jake.

"Ten seconds... Brace for impact," the hunter answered, the Sword Saint steeling himself. He and the rest of the party knew there was no time to hesitate.

Bending his legs, water condensed on Miyamoto's blade as he activated Rain Blade and charged forward. From a cloud of smoke also emerged the Fallen King, swinging two large, golden hammers on what looked like chains as he rapidly approached the boss. Sylphie also unleashed a blast of wind to push away the flame snakes, their entire party moving to ensure Jake would have his opening.

CHAPTER 38

EMPEROR VS. KING

The power of every being's soul varied widely. Levels were far from everything when it came to determining their fragility or susceptibility to manipulation, even if it was a factor. The Fallen King had encountered beings well into the 300s with incredibly malleable souls who fell to the slightest touch and crumbled before the slightest manipulation.

Those of the enlightened races had more powerful souls than the average beast. Unique Lifeforms were naturally in a league far beyond even these. Creatures with no true sapience had weak souls by default, though it was not necessarily a rule.

Making comparisons with anyone in the Fallen King's party had little meaning, as all of theirs—save for perhaps Sylphie—were not ordinary. Ordinary in that they weren't mutated in some way, either through a Bloodline or a Transcendent skill.

Variants of all races could appear with more powerful souls—even if they were not utter anomalies like his party—and the nature of their magic and affinities also played a huge role. Casters were naturally more resistant to soul magic, with the Willpower stat alone having a huge impact. All in all, there were many factors, but few set rules.

The only true rule was that the power of a soul was heavily related to how powerful the creature was... and if a creature happened to be a powerful variant with a Path that naturally resulted in a powerful soul, a high level, and a further mutated soul... they would become an absolute nightmare if the goal was to cause any soul damage to them.

This was the exact type of opponent they faced with the Twinhead

Emperor. Never before had the Fallen King seen such a powerful soul in another C-grade. Sure, Jake and the others had strong souls, but their real power lay in the quality of the Truesoul, not the pure quantity and overall power. This event boss was at a whole other level compared to them. It truly was as if they were fighting two souls in one body.

At the beginning of the fight, the oddly mutated soul of the Twinhead Emperor had been... off. It had been unstable, as if it didn't really fit fully together, and each segmented part of the soul was in conflict. However, everything now seemed to have snapped into place, as the Twinhead Emperor had one of the most stable and powerful souls the Fallen King could ever imagine for a C-grade without a Bloodline...

Besides his own, of course.

While buying time for the hunter to unleash his attack, the job of the four others was to keep the boss busy, but the Fallen King didn't plan on not also doing some damage of his own. Entering semi-close range, the Unique Lifeform summoned two hammers of golden energy and slammed them into the boss. The shaman side of the ogre raised his now glowing staff and blocked just as the warrior side swung his blade upwards, unleashing a dark wave of pure death energy to deter Sylphie.

This proved to be a mistake. While a torrent of wind-infused stone shards shot up from the ground toward the human swordsman, he didn't even hesitate and continued his charge. Right before he was struck, a powerful green barrier appeared around him, deflecting every single stone shard the man couldn't dodge. The swordsman managed to get close as the ogre swung his blade down once more, aiming to crush the swordsman.

The boss swung down with force the Fallen King wouldn't even dare to try and block, yet the swordsman merely met it with his own thin blade. Had the Fallen King not known this swordsman, he would have expected to see the small blade shatter and the man crushed, but instead, the large blade merely slid down the side of the small one and struck the ground, giving the swordsman a clear opening to slice his sword upwards.

Blood mixed with water flew into the air as swordsman cut halfway into the Twinhead Ogre's arm. Not because his blade wasn't sharp enough, but because he had to retreat when a beam of condensed death energy shot out from the eyes of the warrior ogre, launching him backward. Dina hurriedly came to his assistance.

Not wanting to be outdone, the Fallen King also got more serious. Swinging his golden hammers again, the shaman kept blocking, not getting distracted by his counterpart in the slightest. The Fallen King kept swinging, yet every hit was easily blocked, the shaman even finding time to shoot lightning bolts toward Sylphie in between blocks.

Until the Fallen King suddenly mixed things up, that is. A hammer flew for the shaman, and once more, he blocked. However, just before the hammerhead hit the staff, it unraveled into a net of chains that wrapped around the staff. Before the ogre had much time to react, the Fallen King made the side he was holding into a ball and shot it behind him with a massive wave of force.

The staff was yanked away, but the ogre kept a firm hold, which resulted in him getting lifted off his feet and forced to move for the very first time. With the staff disabled, Sylphie also finally found her opening. The green bullet flew down and past the outstretched arm holding the staff. Dozens of large, deep gashes were left across the left arm as the ogre groaned in pain, Sylphie turning in the air to do another fly-by.

Wanting to also attack again, the Fallen King prepared to strike, but he suddenly stopped himself. And just in time, too.

A lightning bolt came down right as the King was about to move, making the ground erupt and sending the Unique Lifeform floating backward while defending himself. Sylphie was more unfortunate, as a torrent of lightning went for her, forcing the bird to scatter her body to avoid taking too much damage.

On the other side of the ogre, the human swordsman had also been pushed back while fighting the large blade with the assistance of the dryad. During a temporary lull in the battle, the Twinhead Emperor scoffed loudly.

"I do not know who any of you are or why you are here... but I do know that you made the worst and final mistake of your lives when you forced me into this state," the two heads of the ogre said, speaking in perfect unison. The many tattoos across his body began to glow as he took a new stance and raised the staff into the air. **"I have seen enough... Now perish."**

With those words, the ogre slammed the staff into the ground and released a burst of magic before he disappeared. The Fallen King was taken by surprise, and a warning came through the Golden Mark right as he felt the reappearance of their foe's soul. *"Behi—"*

The Fallen King had barely raised his hands to block when he was struck in the side, the claws on one of his hands cracking from the impact of the large blade clad in death. Sliding across the ground, tearing it up in the process, the Unique Lifeform turned to face the ogre, who had fully shifted his focus to slaying him. Right as they were about to clash again, a message came.

"*Arrow incoming... Arriving in five...*"

The Fallen King blocked again and was sent flying even further. By now, his boosting skill was already fully active, as he was forced to face the full wrath of the boss alone. Magic and physical force both slammed into the Unique Lifeform, leaving him to fend for himself due to the magic the ogre had used just before he teleported.

The old swordsman found himself within a prison of stone, while the hawk far up in the air was surrounded by black clouds, impeding her movements. The dryad was trying to assist as best she could, but was significantly limited when a tornado of deathly wind whirled toward her, forcing her back. For now, he would simply have to handle the Twinhead Emperor on his own.

"*Four...*"

Raising both his glowing golden hands, the Fallen King faced the ogre as best he could, the large blade coming down with incredible force with every strike. Using his own golden weapons, the Unique Lifeform refused to back down and clashed with the ogre, who was clearly also using some type of buffing skill to make him significantly faster.

The King had parts of his natural armor ripped apart, as he simply couldn't block the attacks of what were effectively two people. His bark-like armor cracked and tore as strike after strike continuously forced him further back. He also landed his fair share of counterattacks, but the battle could only be described as one-sided.

"*Three...*"

Despite his party still struggling to assist him, one of the Fallen King's legs was entirely burned off by a powerful torrent of flames. The Unique Lifeform did everything he could, but his soul attacks proved useless against the effectively two-souled creature.

Finally, as the Fallen King found himself slowed by a blast of cold air mixed with electricity, he was no longer able to fully block when the Twin-head Emperor stabbed the large blade of death forward in a vertical position. Simply unable to resist, the Unique Lifeform was impaled, and the power of death spread throughout his body.

"**Now die,**" the two heads of the ogre said as the energy of death intensified even further.

"*Two...*"

As the Fallen King felt the energy invade his body... he scoffed.

His claws began glowing with intense light as he struck forward, clasping both of the ogre's heads. Piercing into their skin, the Fallen King taunted the boss.

"Do you believe I fear your energy of death? That my soul is so weak as to crumble before such a pathetic concept?"

The Twinhead Emperor did not use words to respond. Instead, all four eyes began glowing with power. Instantly, both golden claws had holes burned through them, and the Fallen King was struck by four beams straight at his mask.

"One..."

Despite the two sets of beams burning into his mask, the Fallen King was undeterred and refused to let go. His claws were damaged, yet they kept piercing deeper and deeper into flesh as destructive, soul-destroying force spread through each of them.

The ogre had already let go of his sword, which still impaled the Fallen King, and didn't even try to use magic as powerful impacts struck the already-damaged body of the Unique Lifeform over and over again. Rather, the Twinhead Emperor had resorted to punches. Partly because hitting with his staff was difficult at such close range, and partly because focusing on magic while having scorching golden force spreading through one's brain made it difficult.

Golden pressure also began to bear down on them as the Fallen King made sure they weren't moving a single step, even as his body was slowly torn further and further apart. The three others had just about broken out of their restraints by now and were making their way over... but not before something else finally arrived.

The Fallen King barely noticed the attack due to how fast it flew. At one moment, he felt the energy in the air above, and the next, it was there. The Twinhead Emperor was even less aware and only reacted right before he was struck. Instinctively, the Twinhead Ogre wanted to move the head that the arrow was coming for, but the Fallen King naturally wouldn't allow such an action, holding it firmly in place with a vise grip.

Looking on, he saw the deathly attack penetrate one of the Twinhead Emperor's skulls before continuing its descent through the ogre's body. However, right before it would exit out the other side, the entire arrow exploded within the body of the Twinhead Emperor.

This was the Fallen King's cue to let go and allow himself to get blasted away. The destructive arcane energies washed over him, but he felt as if none of it wanted to even harm him. No, it sought only to destroy the ogre. Observing the sheer power in that one arrow as he was sent flying, the Fallen King could barely believe it belonged to a mid-tier C-grade.

After flying backward for a few hundred meters and landing, the Fallen King finally allowed the damage he had sustained to affect him. He barely managed to keep himself upright, not even bothering to try and keep his dignity by floating. He only had one leg to stand on, and looking at his arms, they hung limply down at his sides, the energy he had channeled through them too much to handle.

"Are you alright?" the dryad quickly asked as he felt her soothing presence and plants surround him.

"This vessel will need to be rebuilt entirely," the Fallen King responded.

It was truly a mess, inside and out. In many ways, he had been lucky the ogres had decided to strike his mask. Perhaps they'd known destroying it would be the one way to ensure his destruction. Sadly for them, they were far from capable of doing such a thing. In fact, besides a few burn marks that could easily be washed off, not a single mark had been left on it. But then again, the same could not be said about the rest of his body. Alas, he had done his job for now and would adopt a more passive role... because he still had a role to play.

The strike unleashed by the hunter had been powerful beyond belief, but as he observed the flayed form of the Twinhead Emperor, he saw not only the vicious injuries inflicted upon him but also the soul. One part had been severely damaged.... yet the other remained stable, making it clear the fight was far from over.

———

Fuck, he's tough, Jake thought while flying down at top speed to rejoin the fight after his arrow struck true. He wasn't just talking about the Twinhead Emperor, but the Fallen King, who had handled the boss for a good while alone. He had been worried for a time, but the King had done damn well and allowed his arrow to land as well as it could.

The arrow had torn apart the left head of the ogre. Jake had deliberately aimed at the shaman version of the ogre, as he was the one best at healing. Right before his arrow struck, Jake had slightly manipulated its movements to ensure he struck true, the King helping immensely by making sure the boss couldn't move so much as an inch.

Below, the boss stood with one head nearly entirely destroyed and a huge hole in his belly from the following explosion. The damage was utterly immense, yet the ogre was far from down. To a C-grade, losing the head wasn't necessarily fatal, but it did nearly always result in the person losing control of their body, making them easy pickings. This meant that to most, losing the head was still a death sentence... but things were a bit different if you had two.

Despite taking tremendous damage, the ogre didn't leave a single opening for Sylphie and the Sword Saint, who tried to follow up. Stomping hard on the ground, the Twin Emperor made the ground erupt with blackened rock infused with death, seeking to protect himself by wrapping all the rock around him. At the same time, Jake detected odd movements of energy within the ogre. The Fallen King explained what was going on a second later.

"One soul is healing the other, sharing the damage," the Fallen King explained. *"Strike now, when we have the opening, and force them into desperation."*

No one had to be told that twice. Jake began shooting arrows while flying down, as Sylphie, the Sword Saint, and Dina also all went on the offensive. The shell of stone surrounding the ogre was quickly torn through, forcing the boss to defend himself as he retreated from the onslaught.

The left head was rapidly regenerating, and before it was even fully healed, Jake felt the presence of the shaman begin to reappear as elemental magic was unleashed. Seeing the ogre still fit for a fight was a bit discouraging, but Jake knew they had done some serious damage... and things were only about to get even better, as the Twin Emperor did something they had hoped would happen.

Retreating back to where the fight had begun, the Twin Emperor landed right in the center of where the ritual had taken place. Despite the ground being torn up several times over, along with every visual remnant of the circle itself, it was still there... and while the boss had absorbed much of the energy of the many bone spheres, some still remained. Not enough to raise the ogre's power, but enough to help rejuvenate him.

"That got dangerous for a moment," the Twin Emperor said as the mouth of the left head regenerated, speaking even if the top half of the skull was still healing. **"Sadly, you missed your opening!"**

Slamming his staff into the ground, the ogre reactivated the ritual one more time... Jake grinned at that and sent a message to the Sword Saint.

"Our turn. Go!"

CHAPTER 39

ONE TANKY BASTARD

From the very first moment Jake laid eyes on the ritual circle, he'd known there was no way the Twinhead Emperor would be capable of absorbing all the energy contained in the bone spheres. Each sphere held the death energy and curse energy of hundreds, if not over a thousand, dead C-grades alone. This wasn't even mentioning the uncountable D- and E-grades who had also senselessly fallen in the conflict created by the Twin Emperors.

Even if the boss had filtered much of the energy out to only absorb the pure Records, there was still a lot left over. This energy had all merged into the semi-intangible ritual circle, which remained mostly untouched despite all the physical destruction.

Now, the Twinhead Emperor was going to reclaim this energy as he stood in the center and raised his staff high. In their initial plans, they had expected the Twinhead Emperor to absorb the energy to help heal. This was still part of the boss's plan, but Jake realized they had once again underestimated their opponent.

As the Twinhead Emperor reactivated the ritual, two things happened at once. First, death energy began entering a set of new body runes to promote healing, and second, a massive rune was summoned in the air, drawing in all the curse energy.

"Those runes on his body... They are reversing the concept of death into pure life energy," Dina said, sounding a bit perplexed.

"Even better." Jake grinned... because, in this rare instance, underestimating the boss had worked to their advantage.

The boss had erected a barrier just around himself, as he couldn't cover the entire ritual circle. Just as the Twinhead Emperor began to absorb death energy and condense some curse magic, a raindrop fell upon the barrier. Soon, more began to fall all over the ritual circle, each drop containing the energy of time.

It took him a moment too long to notice something was off when Jake mentally activated their little trap. Before the two Twin Emperors had begun their ritual, Jake and the Sword Saint had spent a bit over a week doing some slight modifications to the ritual circle the boss had created. Very minor ones they had overlaid on the other ritual circle. Without power, it had been borderline undetectable, but now, it was getting fed plenty of time-affinity energy, which would be one fuel source.

The other? The power of pure hunger.

In the middle of the ritual circle, forgotten entirely by the boss, was a black piece of metal sticking out—a lone katar thrown by Jake's Eternal Shadow right at the beginning of the fight. Now, this katar suddenly began to hum with power as it became one with the ritual circle.

"What have you—"

The Twinhead Emperor didn't get further than that. He suddenly stopped, feeling the effects of the ritual. He had merged himself with it to absorb its energy... creating a direct connection between himself and anything inside said ritual. And now, there was a very hungry katar, further empowered by the concept of time, that was more than happy to tap into this delicious connection.

"YOU! Lord of Hunger!" the Twinhead Emperor roared, Jake grimacing as he continued to descend from above. He really didn't need to be reminded of that nickname.

Not that the ogre was wrong, as it was the energy of the Sin Curse that was suddenly overwhelming the entire ritual. It was so dominant that intangible and semi-translucent black tendrils rose from all over the circle and sought the Twinhead Emperor with pure hunger.

The tendrils began to latch onto the cursed rune above the ogre while also piercing the runes on his body, sucking out energy like leeches. Jake happily controlled it all as best he could, feeling the delight from the mythical weapon as it ate well from not only the ogre but all the remnant energy from the ritual itself.

Realizing he was not winning this fight for control, the Twinhead Emperor made a quick decision. The rune above him promptly exploded, releasing a black wave of energy that was mostly pulled in and absorbed by Eternal Hunger, but Dina did have to block the rest.

"Fine, have it your way," the ogre said with anger as he raised a foot and stomped hard.

Jake, flying above, saw cracks spread out from the Twinhead Emperor below. As dozens of them extended hundreds of kilometers in every direction, he stomped a second time.

The cracks instantly shook and fractured further. A massive earthquake shattered the terrain below, the sheer power enough to finally dismantle the entire ritual circle for good, dispelling all the tendrils. Giant masses of land began to rise, and others fell, the world looking like it had split open. Jake also sensed that Eternal was about to be buried deep beneath the ground, but with a mental command and some focus, it dispersed into black energy before reappearing within his Soulspace a few seconds later.

"Everyone okay?" Jake quickly asked, trying to check in with his party. Before he even got an answer, he pulled his bow back out.

"On me," the Sword Saint responded, Jake having already spotted them. In the chaos, the Twinhead Emperor had singled out the Sword Saint and was now engaging him in a one-on-one. The two of them were rapidly moving through the deep ravines, the old man clearly at a disadvantage but holding his own pretty well. His new skill was definitely being put to use, as water clones were destroyed in spades.

It did help when an arrow suddenly launched out from one of the ravine's walls, hitting the ogre in the side. A second arrow descended from above just before a third came from yet another unpredictable angle. The boss was already damaged quite a bit, which was part of why he was slowed down, but annoyingly so, he was still healing even if they had stopped the ritual. One thing was for sure, though... The boss was using up his energy damn fast.

Once the three others—except for perhaps the King, who was not in the best state—joined them, they should be able to—

"Elementals!" Dina suddenly yelled through the Golden Mark.

Jake cursed internally as he released a Pulse of Perception to check out the situation.

Just as she had said, elementals had begun to crawl out of the deep walls of the ravines. Jake counted a dozen of them, each more than ten meters tall and made of the ravine's earth. Using Identify, Jake cursed even more.

[Summoned Earth Elemental – lvl 320]

"Hunter, continue to assist the swordsman; the dryad and I shall deal with these elementals," the Fallen King said quickly.

"Ree!" Sylphie added as she swooped in from above the crevice, crashing into an elemental that was closing in on Dina.

The Fallen King also quickly made his way to the dryad, who knelt down and focused while protected.

Jake continued helping the Sword Saint while flying down. Every one of his arrows gave the Twinhead Emperor pause or forced him to take damage, giving the Sword Saint enough space to avoid being overwhelmed. The pressure on him was still intense, as the ogre used both staff and sword to try and take him down, but the elementals the shaman had summoned seemed to have taken a lot out of him, given that the staff's magic was limited. It also didn't help that the shaman's head wasn't fully healed from Jake's nice opening arrow.

The poison inside the Twinhead Emperor only got worse and worse with every arrow, the first one having naturally come with a nice payload. Annoyingly, his poison didn't work as well as he had hoped. The Heartrot Poison was very rooted in the concept of death, which the ogre had a high natural resistance to. The poison was still working, just not as well as Jake would have liked.

Even as Jake shot arrow after arrow, he felt a green aura spread from the deep crevice sheltering Dina as she finished with her magic. She, too, had made her preparations before the battle, which took the form of quite literally planting the seeds for a big upcoming spell... that she used now.

A deep thrumming sound came from beneath the ground everywhere as the ground suddenly erupted once more. Thick roots pierced out of the walls and floor of the deep valleys formed from the earthquake, quickly entangling all of the Summoned Earth Elementals at once. The Twinhead Emperor himself wasn't spared either; he suddenly found himself surrounded by thick roots that began to promptly sprout vines that whipped toward him, restraining both his arms.

Finally, the Sword Saint could get some distance... except he decided to use this chance to attack instead. Barely taking a step back, he raised his sword and took a stance, not allowing the many wounds marring his body to affect him. As he took a deep breath, his body exploded with power, and for a moment, his entire form reverted to his younger self as he stabbed.

"Glimpse of Spring: Erosion."

Entangled, the ogre couldn't fully respond. He tried to fire a beam from his eyes at the water stream, but the thin stream was too fast, and even as the eyebeam hit, it was simply sliced in two, and the stab continued forward into the chest of the Twinhead Ogre.

Jake saw the torrent of blood shoot out of the ogre's back as his own arrow rain also arrived, a dozen points piercing the arms and shoulders of the boss. In his chest, a hole big enough to pass a basketball through had opened from the Sword Saint's Glimpse of Spring, dripping with blood and water. Jake quickly charged another Arcane Powershot, aiming to hopefully take the boss down for good or at least blow up one of the heads again.

Yet right as Jake began to charge his Powershot, a sigh echoed in his ears, the ogre's aura changing once more. Below, the Sword Saint rapidly retreated as Dina sent yet another message.

"Watch out... I feel a powerful energy of death. Make distance."

Jake still kept flying down despite the warning but wouldn't go all the way. He saw the Sword Saint quickly make his way back toward Dina and the others, who were quickly finishing off the Summoned Earth Elementals, which were still entangled in dense and powerful roots.

Right then, the roots began to decay. It started with the ones surrounding the Twinhead Emperor but quickly spread from there, soon rotting the huge root network from within. A dark mist spread from the boss—one that gave Jake a powerful response from Sense of the Malefic Viper...

It was poison mist. A natural poison of pure death, born from decay, further infused with a powerful curse. The form of the Twinhead Emperor had turned gray within the dense mist as the ground itself began to lose all color, and with heavy steps, the ogre walked toward Dina and company. With every step, the mist grew stronger, the Twinhead Emperor walking with his thick blade over one shoulder.

Then the ogre suddenly sprinted toward Dina. The staff was gone... which was also when Jake noticed that the head of the shaman looked unconscious. His eyes were closed, and he didn't do anything. Jake was confused, but luckily his confusion didn't last long.

"One soul... is purely assisting the other," the Fallen King warned. *"We face only the warrior as of this moment, limiting the diversity of skill for power. A temporary empowered state. We should aim to buy time."*

The message was instant, courtesy of telepathy. Jake saw the Twinhead Emperor close in on his party, the Sword Saint having just made it back to them, pretty injured, along with the Fallen King. For them to enter this domain of death wouldn't be good, and in their injured states, they were simply too slow... so he made a split-second decision.

"Dina, focus on fixing up the two oldies. Sylphie, make sure the poison doesn't reach them... I'll keep the big guy busy." Jake focused while stepping down, pushing One Step to its limits. As a minor *fuck you* to the Fallen King, Jake also finally passed a barrier as he, with a single step, traveled more than a hundred miles. He appeared on the ground right between the charging ogre and his party members, who were still creating some good distance.

"You..." the Twinhead Emperor spoke. **"Deceitful rat. You are no Lord of Hunger!"**

"That," Jake said, getting into a stance with katars drawn, "we agree on."

The very next moment, the wave of pure, deathly mist washed over his body. Jake hid his smile as he took a deep breath through his nose, really experiencing the poison. To breathe a naturally born poison, mixed with curse energy like this... was actually surprisingly tasty.

Honestly, poison and curses... Yeah, it was quite an unlucky matchup for the Twinhead Emperor.

Jake charged toward his opponent, too, Arcane Awakening already fully activated. No matter how good the matchup, he could not afford to hold back in the slightest. The two of them clashed in the middle of the deep gorge, the large two-handed blade swinging with the intent of cutting Jake in two.

With a light jump, Jake dodged the blow by stepping down while just above the blade, double-jumping in the air to get behind the large ogre. The Twinhead Emperor quickly spun around, trying to backhand Jake, but Jake was faster. The fist of the ogre met an outstretched katar that pierced his flesh.

Groaning once more, the ogre continued his blow, sending Jake sliding back from the impact with his wrist hurting. Without pause, the Twinhead Emperor continued his attack, aggressively swinging while making sure to keep Jake close. The curse and poison were being subtly controlled throughout the fight to congregate around Jake and affect him more... which he truly didn't mind. In fact, he found it kind of nice to have increased resource regeneration from Palate working overtime, with even Eternal Hunger getting in a good dessert after the ritual.

Jake tried not to let this slip by fighting in an almost desperate fashion, constantly staying on the offensive. In truth, he was very much playing things safe, never overcommitting or going too far as he battled the far more powerful opponent. The punches alone were enough to send him flying, and he definitely didn't want to take a blade head-on like the Fallen

King had done a few dozen times, so he stuck to dodging and weaving in between the swings.

It ended up taking over a minute before the Twinhead Emperor noticed something was wrong. Jake had tried to fake being affected by the poison, but he simply couldn't do it convincingly enough while also staying fast enough to not lose a limb.

"**I understand now,**" the Twinhead Emperor said as he suddenly stopped attacking. "**You are the Lord of Hunger... or at least the one who pretended to be. I do not know what trickery you used or how you knew of that old forgotten legend, but you truthfully had me fooled.**"

Jake stared blankly at the boss after hearing those words. What the fuck kind of old forgotten legend was he talking about? Jake had just picked a generic name he thought sounded kinda cool and rolled with it. Well, not like he was going to complain about tapping into some old legend to sell the story more convincingly.

"**Perhaps you are our trial to reach beyond... A lesson by the multiverse for the two of us to realize our foolishness in trying to no longer stay as one,**" the ogre said with a thoughtful voice.

"You got it mixed up... You're our challenge to reach beyond," Jake shot back, happy to keep the boss talking for a moment.

"**I do not believe those two statements to be contradictory.**" The Twinhead Emperor shook his head—the head that was actually awake. "**But I do find it questionable of you five ... to have chosen a challenge you cannot hope to overcome.**"

As he said this, the poison mist began to fade as it flew toward the boss. The runes that had tried to absorb energy from the ritual earlier appeared again, sucking in all of the mist and infusing the ogre's body with energy.

Jake cursed under his breath as he once more saw the boss heal, even the hole in his chest visibly regenerating. Sure, he was using up his resources, but due to his soul mutation, the boss had way more than could be considered normal, and he was also absorbing energy from the environment at an unnatural pace.

It truly made for one tanky bastard that was ridiculously hard to put down for good. Jake just hoped he didn't have too many more tricks up his—

Slamming the two-handed blade into the ground, the Twinhead Emperor's body exploded with power as a pillar of black light fell upon him.

"Arise, cursed spirits of the fallen."
Oh, you gotta be bloody kidding me...

CHAPTER 40

INDEPENDENCE ACHIEVED

How many phases and different abilities can a single event boss have?

The Twinhead Emperor's answer to that was apparently just a "yes," as he always had more to show off. From what Jake and the others had gathered, the Twinhead Emperor primarily had the warrior move the body while the shaman handled magic and energy control. This also proved true as death magic was unleashed, except the shaman head wasn't even fully awake. Instead, the soul was wholly focused on controlling the magic, truly functioning as a second, extremely powerful Virtual Mind.

As for the magic itself... it was rather basic, yet incredibly strong. Clearly, the Twinhead Emperor had absorbed a shitload of death and curse energy into the blade from all the different battlefields and was now unleashing it upon their group. Usually, this wouldn't be that huge of a problem, as a bunch of undead filled with curse energy would just attack everything indiscriminately... except for one minor detail.

Jake and company had been the cause of many of their deaths, and clearly the target of their resentment.

From where the ogre had stabbed down his sword, a deep pitch-black pit opened up, and within seconds, Jake heard screams coming from beyond the grave. Spirits began to pour up from the hole all around the ogre, screeching with anguish and anger as the boss opened what looked like a portal to the underworld.

Gritting his teeth, Jake quickly pulled out his bow and shot an Arcane Powershot at the Twinhead Emperor, who was protected by the beam of death surrounding him. The arrow pierced through the death energy but was severely weakened by the time it hit the boss. Not letting up, Jake kept shooting and landed several arrows on the boss, who focused on protecting his heads while doing the summoning magic.

He continued loosing arrows until he was forced to stop when the summoned spirits began to close in on him. Checking them out, he saw their levels weren't super impressive, pretty much mirroring the soldiers they had killed on the battlefields.

[Cursed Battlefield Ghost – lvl 302]
[Cursed Battlefield Ghost – lvl 306]
[Cursed Battlefield Ghost – lvl 311]

Each of these spirits was a mix of black and white ethereal energies in a humanoid shape. Their eyes were hollow, and while they did look like the various enlightened races they had slain, many of them looked very disturbing. The beastfolk, who did not have a single trace of hair on their ghostly bodies, looked especially off.

Retreating, Jake focused on getting some distance. He counted around a hundred total ghosts already summoned, with a few still exiting the abyss every second or so, but it was clear the boss was running out of ghosts to summon. The ghosts weren't really dead individuals, but more the gathered energy of several victims. Most of the energy had also been absorbed by the bone spheres, and this felt more like the leftovers.

All of these ghosts were coming straight for Jake, seemingly ignoring his entire party. This proved pretty damn unwise when it soon started to rain. Jake responded by empowering the small stable arcane barrier covering his body to avoid being infected by the rainfall, as he knew what the Sword Saint was doing. At the same time, he also stopped retreating and instead circled around to begin taking potshots at the boss.

By now, the Twinhead Emperor was finished with his summoning. He stood back up and used his blade to block Jake's attacks. However, he didn't move, instead seeming to focus on controlling his legion of ghosts. When the boss felt the rain infused with time magic, he commanded his ghosts to spread out and head toward the rest of his party—something that would prove more difficult than he liked.

A few ghosts were flying away but were suddenly rebuffed and sent flying back toward the boss. A powerful wind swept through the battlefield, forming a tornado. Far up in the sky, Sylphie was flying in circles, making the tornado even stronger and effectively creating a barrier, forcing all the ghosts to stay within the somehow unaffected rainfall.

Turning to look at Jake, the Twinhead Emperor flashed a smile. **"Abandoned, huh? Or do they believe you are enough on your own? Very well. You can die first, then."**

Remember how Jake had suspected the ogre wasn't moving because he was too busy controlling the ghosts? Yeah, that went out the window when the Twinhead Emperor charged with his army of ghosts rapidly surrounding Jake. Wings sprouted on Jake's back as he tried to dodge as best as he could, but even he had his limits.

The ghosts were relatively limited in their methods of attack, but they were far from harmless. Every ghost could summon long, tangible, white claws to try and cut him, release blasts of pure death energy, and even just charge straight through his body, dealing significant damage in the process.

In order to create some space, Jake repeatedly released arcane explosions around himself, making the ghosts, at the very least, hesitate to charge through him. Still, he was not in a good spot. Several ghosts managed to land blows, with the Twinhead Emperor getting too close for comfort quite a few times. At least he was only capable of swinging his sword while also controlling the ghosts, but that was still a lot, considering the vast difference in stats between the ogre and Jake.

As things were starting to get a bit too hairy, Jake finally got the message he had been waiting for.

"Now."

Without hesitation, Jake's wings began to glow with energy. His entire body turned dark green, and in the blink of an eye, he disappeared. For a mere half a second, everything warped, and then Jake appeared a good fifty kilometers away, his wings burning away from using his escape skill—just in time to see the old man standing in a small hole in the tornado and executing his move.

"Rain of Time: Reversal."

The terrain was torn up, and the tornado began to unravel. All the ghosts were ripped up, some of them scattering from the attack alone, and even the Twinhead Emperor was caught in the mythical skill. Only a dozen or so ghosts died from the initial activation of the skill, but the Sword Saint quickly followed up.

"Rain of Time: Thousand Blades Descent."

Blades of rain collected in the sky above before rapidly descending toward the ogre and the many ghosts. There still weren't quite a thousand blades... but the old man had gotten closer this time around.

Nearly a thousand blades fell, each aimed at the ghosts and the Twin-head Emperor himself. Dozens more undead were slain as they were stabbed through, but a bit over a third still remained even after the mythical skill had been used. Partly because the Sword Saint had focused more than half of the falling blades on the big boss himself.

The Twinhead Emperor had hunkered down as all the blades came, trying to defend himself. Even so, he was still stabbed more than a hundred times, leaving his back even more damaged than before. He didn't really seem to bleed in his gray semi-undead form, and while the ogre did begin to heal once more, it was clear he didn't have much energy left in the tank.

Things got even worse, as Sylphie wasn't done doing her part either. The tornado had far from fully scattered, and now Sylphie regathered all of the wind and made it close around the many ghosts with the Twinhead Emperor still in the middle, creating a massive, cutting wind-grinder.

As even more ghosts were torn apart, the boss finally roared. A torrent of death energy erupted from him, and he stood back up with a furious look on his face. Swinging, he sent out a wave of pure death, creating a hole in the tornado that he quickly passed through, followed by the twenty or so surviving ghosts. Two did end up getting caught as the tornado reclosed, but he still had eighteen left.

Since the Sword Saint was the closest, the ogre quickly locked onto him. The old man was breathing heavily from his earlier injuries and using his mythical skill after Glimpse of Spring. Both he and the Fallen King were in pretty shitty states, to put it lightly.

The Sword Saint was far from ready to meet the ogre in combat when he roared and charged forward with ghosts flying alongside him. **"If you thought I would fall this easily, you are—"**

He didn't get further than that before his eyes opened wide. Jake smiled to himself when he saw Dina had decided it was her turn to show off a bit. A green aura exploded out from where the dryad was standing as her entire body began to transform. Her antlers grew, her dress changed, and she even grew a bit taller. It was naturally her ultimate boosting skill, showing Dina was done messing around.

The still-charging ogre suddenly found himself surrounded by thick, bark-covered vines as the ground erupted. At the same time, Dina's aura washed over both the boss and the many ghosts, the dryad purposefully controlling and amplifying it.

Slamming her staff into the ground, a massive tree formed from all the aura, seemingly taking root right on top of the boss. The ethereal summoned tree stood nearly ten kilometers tall, its thick trunk covering the Twinhead Ogre, the Sword Saint, and all the undead.

While the Sword Saint's injuries began to heal at a rapid pace, the experience was not the same for the undead. It turned out that infusing death with life resulted in a rather... explosive outcome.

The remaining ghosts screeched as they blew up one by one, the gray body of the Twinhead Ogre also beginning to rapidly break down. His skin cracked open as life mixed with death, yet Dina didn't let up. Her entire form began glowing brighter as the tree grew more and more tangible.

More roots also began to shoot up and stab at the ogre, further tearing apart his skin. He tried to resist but was quickly forced down on one knee when a vine wrapped around the neck of the sleeping head, thorns growing on it.

Without any hesitation, the Twinhead Emperor raised his sword, a look of sorrow flashing on his face. Without any further warning, Jake's vision temporarily turned black as the world was covered in darkness. Only a second later did he feel the shockwave and hear the sound of an explosion. Powerful death energy flew past him, forcing him to raise his arms and summon an arcane barrier to defend himself as he stared at the devastation.

In the distance, he saw the giant ethereal tree rotting from within, its leaves scattering like ash. Quickly looking over, he spotted Dina down on the ground, propping herself up on her elbows. Her transformation had been forcibly undone, blood flowing from every orifice due to the backlash. As Jake saw the worry in her eyes, he understood what she was afraid of.

Shifting his gaze, Jake spotted the Sword Saint being dragged away from the epicenter of the explosion by the Fallen King. One of the Unique Lifeform's arms was missing, and Jake saw what looked like black metal fragments sticking out of his frontal armor. The Sword Saint had a few black veins covering his body, but he was still alive and conscious. Only now, examining those black metal fragments, did Jake fully realize what the boss had done.

Fucker blew up his sword.

As the thick miasma of death began to finally fade, the true destruction was revealed. A large crater had formed where the Twinhead Ogre had blown up the sword, all life more than a kilometer around him entirely wiped out. Not a single trace of anything Dina had done remained, save for a few black leaves here and there.

In the middle of this crater was the Twinhead Emperor, standing tall. Yet his aura was different now, showing that his last attack had truly taken a lot out of him. His skin also no longer carried the aura of death; whatever boosting skill he had used was clearly over.

Jake was already flying over in case the boss attacked again so he could assist his party. Everyone besides himself and Sylphie were in pretty rough shape, and while Dina had taken some damage, she wasn't that bad off and could easily still take up a supporting role. It wasn't as if Jake and Sylphie were uninjured, either. Sylphie was doing the best, as she'd pulled off her assigned roles mainly using ranged attacks. Jake had taken a good beating when he was buying time earlier, but he was still more than fit for a fight.

Jake really hoped the Twinhead Emperor was not... but given how many damn tricks the ogre had already pulled out of his ass thus far, Jake wouldn't count on him being down for the count. At least he didn't have to wait long to be proven right.

Just as he arrived at his party, a few seconds after the miasma from the explosion had fully subsided, the boss spoke once more, offering some unexpected words. **"I... am sorry..."** the Twinhead Emperor said... No... only the warrior head was speaking. He was not speaking to anyone in Jake's party, either. Instead, he looked over at the second head, which began to open its eyes and wake up.

"I... failed... was too weak," the warrior said with a melancholic smile. **"I didn't think any of us would want it to end this way... but... you were always the stronger one of us... so let it be you."**

Now fully awake, the shaman head looked at his second half. The shaman closed his eyes for a second before nodding in understanding. **"Thank you."**

Jake was confused about what was going on as the head of the warrior suddenly went limp. Dead. That was when Jake understood, and the boss made everything absolutely clear mere moments later.

An ear-piercing roar sounded out from the ogre as his entire body exploded with power that made the ground below him crack. A staff appeared in his hand, and his voice echoed across the whole area, his aura soaring to a level it never had before.

"My second half... killed... I wanted solitude... independence... but not like this," the Twinhead Emperor, who had now been reduced to only one head, said. His energy kept surging as Jake felt the pressure on him intensify. **"But luckily, I shall not be alone for much longer..."**

"The second soul... merged fully into the first one..." the Fallen King said,

a clear sense of trepidation in his voice. *"It's unsustainable. Won't last for more than a minute or two... but during that time..."*

Jake and the others all understood... during this time, the Twinhead Emperor was in an even more empowered state. However, once it was over, the fight would end, as the sheer backlash of burning away half of your soul couldn't be healthy.

Jake didn't want the ogre to make the first move, even if he was empowered. He quickly responded by reaching out, his hand glowing dark green. While the other head had been alive, his death energy had helped to suppress much of Jake's poison. This had led to much of the death-affinity poison going dormant, but now that the warrior was gone, Jake could truly let it all loose.

It spread throughout the body of the ogre, and Jake felt it do significant damage... but the boss didn't seem to care in the slightest.

"You think your poison matters? I... am already half-dead and have no plans on lasting much longer. Soon, it all will be over. But fret not..." The Twinhead Emperor slammed his staff into the ground, and runes lit up all over his body, more intensely than ever before. **"You shall join my other half in the grave before my time is up."**

CHAPTER 41

WIND

Jake and his party were faced with a choice... run away and drag things out until the Twinhead Emperor's empowered state ended, or try and fight back while buying time. Directly confronting the boss was definitely not advised—something they were all in agreement with. Jake usually wasn't a fan of just running away, but if his party decided to do just that, he wouldn't object.

"We should retreat for now—fighting directly is too risky," the Sword Saint quickly said as he received some emergency healing from Dina. She couldn't restore his resources or cure fatigue, but she could get him back in temporary fighting condition... or at least well enough to launch one more good attack.

"I concur," the Fallen King instantly agreed.

"Me too—" Dina tried to say, but she was cut off by the boss.

"You wish to flee? To drag things out? You all seem to thoroughly misunderstand something." The Twinhead Emperor's staff began to light up. Jake felt the entire environment shift as the mana all around them took on the aura of the ogre. **"It's already far too late to run."**

Then Jake felt the pressure as his body grew far heavier. The ground all around them cracked and buckled, even the mana in the air itself getting pushed down. It wasn't suppression of aura or anything like that, but something far more tangible. *Gravity magic...*

A fucking complicated school of magic that was, needless to say, pretty damn strong. What's more, the shaman clearly wasn't done. He pointed his staff at Jake and the three others around him. A massive flamethrower flew out, unaffected by the increased gravity that weighed everything else down.

Reacting quickly, the group manifested barriers. One golden, one green, one of water, and one of stable arcane mana. As the flames washed over the four attempts to block the attack, each was burned through in moments. When the flame shattered the final barrier, all of them were sent scattering in four different directions to dodge the attack.

The Twinhead Emperor wanted to follow up, but just then, a blast of wind descended from above, making the staff's head smash into the ground and creating an explosion that sent the boss stumbling back. It was naturally Sylphie, who'd gone on the offensive.

Several more bullets of wind shot down, the boss raising a hand to block them with his own barrier of wind—only to then have an arrow strike him in the shoulder when Jake took the chance to launch an attack of his own.

A long, thin blade of water also struck the boss mere moments later, followed by a blast of force that pushed Jake's arrow further into the ogre's shoulder. These attacks were not done with the intent of dealing damage to the Twinhead Emperor, but trying to limit his mobility and disrupt his attacks at least a little bit. Plus, dealing damage should help hasten his demise.

Sadly, their attacks proved to have little effect. The ogre stomped down, making the ground erupt and release ten large boulders that flew up and, with a hand motion, condensed into small stones. Pointing his staff once more, the stones all began to glow molten, cracks forming all over them before he sent them flying toward the four non-birds in Sylphie's party.

Jake quickly reacted by shooting down three of the approaching boulders that were aiming for the Sword Saint and Fallen King. When he hit them, all three exploded, sending sharp obsidian shards flying everywhere. This gave them some early warning as to the nature of the attack, so when the remaining seven arrived, everyone had prepared by erecting barriers and gaining distance.

Even so, the Sword Saint failed to deflect all the obsidian shards. One tore straight through his stomach and another through his thigh, while the Fallen King had over a dozen join the black metal shards already sticking out of him.

Bobo, Dina's living armor, managed to block every single one of them while Jake dodged and prepared to continue his own counterattacks. He shot several arrows that were all sent flying by a blast of wind when the ogre swept his free hand upwards.

A large plate of earth was lifted and flipped over right on top of Jake and his party, but before it could crush them, a tree sprouted from the ground smashed into it, tearing it in two. Dina was back for a bit of action as she channeled mana into the otherwise dead ground, making it explode with life as hundreds of vines shot up.

However, the boss easily responded with a scoff. The gravity around him increased, crushing all the vines back into the ground. Raising his staff toward the sky, the shaman mumbled something silently and fired a single bolt of lightning upwards.

Once it got high enough, it exploded into a massive black thundercloud that instantly began rumbling. During this magic, Jake only managed to land a single arrow, as he found himself struggling with the increased gravity, but luckily, Unblemished Arrows made things easier by resisting some of the effects. The Sword Saint and Fallen King also shot their ranged attacks, but to little effect.

Someone who was luckily not struggling at all was the lightest and smallest person in their party of five. A barrage of wind blades fell upon the shaman, making him groan in pain while trying to use his staff to block. From the staff, he shot several large blasts of fire toward the hawk, trying to hit her, but Sylphie simply transformed her body into wind time and time again to avoid taking any noticeable damage.

Having realized her plants couldn't do much, Dina had also shifted her attention to helping Jake and Sylphie with buffs and defensive barriers whenever necessary. She was also still helping the two oldies recover, allowing the Fallen King to remain in action and land a barrage of golden beams and blasts of force, making the ogre stumble, and Sylphie to land another good attack, sending blood flying.

The problem was that the Twinhead Emperor didn't care about taking damage, simply tanking everything. He was fully on the offensive, and he quickly stopped bothering to deal with Sylphie and went after the slowest people in their party.

Dina was prepared, but she could only do so much. As fireballs began raining toward her, the ogre lifted a hand to condense cold energy. A massive spear of ice was summoned and thrown, Dina barely managing to make a tree shoot up and block in time. Meanwhile, Sylphie and Jake continued trying to attack the boss, but all they could do was slightly delay his casting at times.

Things were getting bad... and Dina knew it.

"Jake and Sylphie..."

"I got it," Jake assured her, giving her the go-ahead.

"Ree!" Sylphie also agreed.

Without further hesitation, Dina did her thing. Pushing herself, she once more entered her empowered form. Trees began shooting up all around her, each of them bending and surrounding herself and the Sword Saint and Fallen King. Just before the entire thing fully closed, the two of them sent out a final goodbye.

A large golden beam shot out toward the boss, hitting the ogre before he could react. For a moment, he stopped, and using Mark, Jake saw the Soulshape of the Twinhead Emperor temporarily look as if it was wrapped in golden chains. Not for long, but enough for the next attack to arrive. For the Sword Saint to exhaust the final energy he had.

"Glimpse of Spring: Erosion."

His second use of a Glimpse of Spring instantly made him cough up blood, but his attack was not weakened. The stream of water soared toward the head of the Twinhead Emperor, and Jake decided to also lend a hand by trying to use Gaze.

Sadly, even if the boss was frozen for a moment, the gravity magic in his immediate surroundings proved too strong, and their ability to stop the ogre too weak. He managed to jump right before he was struck. Combined with the gravity, the ogre managed to dodge a potentially fatal blow, but he couldn't avoid the attack entirely.

The beam of water struck him in the right knee, blasting off the entire leg beneath it. Landing on the ground again, the shaman used earth magic to quickly form a new temporary leg before turning toward his attackers.

With an enraged gaze, the boss looked toward Dina and the two with her but found a dense dome of wood had formed to protect them. He took out his anger by pointing his staff and unleashing a torrent of lightning upon it, along with a flamethrower from the staff. Taking advantage of this, Jake released a Powershot that struck the Twinhead Emperor in the arm, making him nearly drop his staff, while Sylphie did a quick fly-by and left a deep cut on his shoulder, the ogre barely avoiding a nasty neck wound.

The shaman's attacks had all washed over the wooden dome, but once the smoke cleared, the Twinhead Emperor grimaced as he saw a burnt formation that was rapidly mending itself.

Unfortunately for the boss, even in his empowered state, he couldn't pierce Dina's powerful defensive technique. At least not within a few seconds. While he could likely get through it within a minute, he couldn't do much with Jake and Sylphie actively attacking him. The problem with this technique was that Dina couldn't do anything else when using it, nor let anyone out. Something the shaman quickly realized, as he didn't bother attacking the dome again. Instead, he turned his attention to the two people remaining outside with him.

"And then there were two..."the Twinhead Emperor said as he regarded Sylphie, who had returned to the sky, and Jake standing a few hundred meters away, an arrow already nocked.

The ogre wasn't wrong when he said there were only two of them left... because Jake felt that the Sword Saint was practically unconscious, while the Fallen King could barely maintain himself with all the damage he had taken. Once the dome expired or was destroyed, and if the boss still lived, things wouldn't be good, and unless the Sword Saint wanted to take the massive risk of using his full Transcendence in his current state, the three of them had little other choice than using the escape tokens they still had saved from Minaga's Labyrinth... so things were up to Jake and Sylphie now.

"Well, you're down to just one," Jake said. "Heads, that is. At least ones that aren't just for decoration at this point." He was taunting the boss, trying to get an emotional reaction and drag out time with banter while charging his Arcane Powershot further.

The Twinhead Emperor didn't respond with words. Instead, he shot a flamethrower toward him, making Jake release the string of his bow. The Arcane Powershot pierced through the flames before finally being deflected by the staff. The ogre did not strike with explosive anger, but more a seething hatred as he proceeded to launch several more attacks.

Sylphie dove down and mimicked him, attacking plenty on her own. Erecting an ice barrier, the boss blocked the wind attacks while continuing to launch spells toward a quite frankly struggling Jake. Under normal circumstances, he would be able to dodge something like this... but the gravity magic was really fucking with his movements, making everything he did slower and more cumbersome.

Small cuts, frost burns, and seared flesh soon began to cover his body, but nothing lethal ever landed. Jake's senses were focused like never before as he kept track of every single shift of mana in the atmosphere, moving before the magic even manifested. As his read on the ogre got better, he even began to launch a few counterattacks here and there, especially when he chose to use Eternal Shadow to also dodge a big blow.

Throughout, Sylphie also kept attacking the Twinhead Emperor, avoiding all the lightning strikes he tried using to keep her in check. Her assistance was one of the reasons Jake could still manage dealing with the constant assault.

Seconds ticked by, and Jake saw the shaman's Soulshape seem to almost shrink in density. It was odd to describe, but Jake felt as if he could effectively see the soul slowly fall apart. With the poison and accumulated damage, the ogre would soon die no matter what happened... so all the hunter and the bird had to do was hold on.

Also, realizing he wasn't going to achieve his goal of revenge in time if things continued like this, the Twinhead Emperor made a decision.

Without any warning, the ogre suddenly flew over toward Jake, seemingly wanting to get in melee combat now. Jake naturally retreated as an answer, making sure not to get caught by any attack... which was when the shaman did something entirely unexpected. With a flick of his wrist, the staff he had been holding flew toward Jake, who dodged away, only for it to suddenly slam into the ground just beside him.

As it slammed down, the ground dented, and Jake felt the pressure instantly. He smashed straight into the ground from the gravity field suddenly increasing in power several times over. The ogre was still holding out a hand as it glowed with magic, holding down Jake and the staff.

"**Killing you in time... does not seem feasible,**" the ogre said while blood poured out of his mouth. He turned his head and raised his other hand toward Sylphie in the sky. "**But the odd elemental... I have experience killing elementals.**"

"Ree!" Sylphie responded while pushing down a dense wave of wind. The Twinhead Emperor looked at it as his hand began to glow with power. At the same time, his entire body shone, every single set of runes enveloping him in light. His body practically burned as his soul was set aflame, blood dripping from his eyes.

"**Wind, bend before my will!**"

Jake felt the sudden rush of power as the atmosphere changed. The blast of wind Sylphie had shot down toward the boss was somehow caught in his hand as if Sylphie had lost control of it. At the same time, the thunderclouds above suddenly became hyperactive, venting all of its lightning in mere moments. Sylphie dodged by spreading out her body into wind as she normally did.

But upon seeing the smile on the shaman's face, Jake got a bad feeling.

As the raised hand of the ogre slowly clenched into a fist, the sky above moved. Wind began to gather as a giant, spinning sphere of dense wind magic condensed. The stormcloud was already gone, scattered by the wind, as the sphere began to grow smaller.

Sylphie, who was caught within the sphere still in her pure wind form, shot out wind blades to cut it open, but all her magic was simply absorbed by the wind sphere. Jake saw her try to control the wind around her, but it looked as if it no longer responded to her.

The sphere kept growing smaller and smaller, further condensing the air. Sylphie struggled, and Jake tried to stand as he looked up. Then his eyes opened wide. Somehow, the wind was condensing so drastically that Sylphie was forcibly reentering her beast form.

Jake saw her struggle, the ogre grinning as his hand closed tighter and tighter. As Sylphie was entirely forced back into her physical hawk form, Jake saw something he never thought he would. The wind began to cut her, slicing through her feathers. Flashes of red appeared as blood was drawn, Sylphie having no way to escape or avoid the attacks.

Trying to help, Jake used Touch of the Malefic Viper to intensify the poison, exploded his Mark to try and deal some more damage, and even used Gaze... but all it did was make the boss pause for a fraction of a second, barely giving Sylphie any respite.

Everyone in their party knew what was going on, and Jake's mind temporarily blanked as he heard Dina say something through her Golden Mark. He heard her mention his name, but he could only stare as the small hawk struggled in vain, slowly getting sliced apart as the sphere of wind grew smaller and smaller, crushing her... killing her.

She... she did have the Phoenix Feather gifted to her, but it was risky to use... Maybe... No, he shouldn't tell her to, but... Jake didn't want to know what could happen if she didn't get out. He finally stopped doubting what had to be done and yelled through the Golden Mark, *"Sylphie, use your escape token!"* Nothing happened. *"Sylphie! Now!"*

Jake tried again, as did the others, but all they got in return was a rush of feelings from her. Fear... indignation... confusion...

Gritting his teeth, Jake resolved himself. He didn't have much after Valdemar, but he had regenerated some of that special energy over the last many years, and even if it wasn't his life in danger, he would—

Sylphie's desperate mix of emotions suddenly stopped... paused... and an overwhelming sense of fury rushed through the Golden Mark, washing away everything else. Then an ear-piercing screech echoed out... sounding almost scolding in nature.

———

As Sylphie found herself surrounded by the wind, forced into her physical form, and unable to fight back... she didn't understand what she had done wrong or why this was happening.

Sylphie fought well—or at least, she thought she did. She had done everything Uncle and the others had told her to do. Sylphie was really good at doing that! Maybe Sylphie was even the best at doing what she was told to do because Sylphie knew how important it was to listen.

She had learned that back when Uncle had to save herself, Mom, and Dad from the bad sun bird. Learned to listen to what her parents told her. When she left on adventure with him, her parents had told her to always listen to Uncle, because even if Uncle could be very dumb, he was still pretty smart sometimes.

So, she did what she was told. Even if Sylphie was her own hawk, she did what Uncle and her parents told her to do. That was just how things were and how they should be.

But... in the fight with the two-headed big bad ogre, things weren't as they should be. It was a super hard fight, but Sylphie had been in many super hard fights before, so it wasn't that. No, it was that something acted like it shouldn't. Things were wrong.

Just as Sylphie did as Uncle or her parents told her, the wind always did what Sylphie told it to do. That was how things were and how they should be. But now, against the big bad ogre... the wind stopped listening to her.

It ignored her, no matter how much Sylphie tried to tell it what to do.

The wind... *her* wind... attacked her from all sides. Trapped her, cut her, injured her. It closed in on her as she struggled but couldn't do anything.

Why wasn't the wind listening to her? Why did it do as the big bad ogre said? Why was what he wanted more important than what Sylphie asked?

That was just... wrong. Not how the world worked. The wind was supposed to listen to her. It was hers and not anyone else's.

For the wind to act like this, refusing to do anything she said, and even attacking her just because someone else told it to was just... just...

So rude!

Sylphie had always been nice and always asked the wind to help, and it had always listened... but now, it seemed like that wasn't enough anymore. It was rebelling, so she did as her mom had done when Sylphie acted up.

She got angry and channeled that anger toward the indignant wind, acting up like a rebellious child. If it didn't want to play nice, fine. No more niceties at all, and definitely no more asking politely if this was how the stupid wind was going to act!

From now on, Sylphie was going to make it *very* clear how the world was supposed to work and who was in charge here. Make it clear this was a world where the wind did exactly what Sylphie told it to do, without any complaint or talking back. To put it nicely, she was no longer making a request. Opening her beak, with the wind attacking her from all sides, the injuries rapidly accumulating, Sylphie focused on nothing else but screeching out her first direct command, leaving no room for disagreement.

"REE!"

And as her order came, the wind responded as it rightfully should when the Sylphian Hawk exerted her authority.

***Skill Upgraded*: [Sylph Wind Whispering (Legendary)] -->
[Sylphian Authority (Mythical)]**

CHAPTER 42

WINDS OF CHANGE

J ake stared at the sky as the spinning sphere of wind stopped in its tracks. The ogre's eyes opened wide. His clenching hand began to glow even brighter than before, but he couldn't close it any more, no matter how hard he tried. Instead, the opposite happened.

The Twinhead Emperor's fingers were forced apart when the shift happened. The sphere of wind scattered as Jake felt the atmosphere change entirely, and he saw the sky almost vibrate as the wind gathered from all around. Jake also felt the pressure from the ogre lessen, and he saw the clear look of shock on his face.

Clouds were torn apart far up in the sky and on the horizon as more and more wind blew toward Sylphie from all over the Vast Plateau. Every single iota of environmental wind mana no longer felt *environmental*. Instead, it had the clear aura of the hawk in the sky, who was gathering more power than Jake had ever seen her control before.

Then everything suddenly stopped.

The wind was still, and Jake saw the Twinhead Emperor stare as Sylphie beat her wings a single time, making it move once more.

A soft wind swept down, making Jake's clothes flap a bit as the attack descended. There were no fancy colors and no real sound; all that arrived was a stream of wind headed straight for the boss with speed rivaling Jake's fastest arrows.

Right before it hit, Jake saw the confusion and hint of fear on the Twinhead Emperor's face. **"Authority... How can—"**

Jake didn't hear the final words as the attack arrived. A pillar of wind descended upon the Twinhead Emperor, pushing Jake backward from the gusts that spilled over the sides of the constant stream.

While sliding back, Jake observed the ogre. Immediately, the skin of his face was cut, and he was forced to close his eyes and raise his arms to defend himself. The ogre's arms were sliced up next, skin and flesh tearing off from the sheer pressure and cutting nature of the wind. The boss tried to use some magic to summon a barrier of stone, but the mana didn't have the slightest chance to gather before it was blown away by the constant wind.

It was like a small, localized jetstream of pressurized and intense air, smashing down on the boss and the boss alone. What's more, it wasn't stopping and only seemed to grow stronger. The effect on the surroundings was the most impressive. The wind blew harmlessly past everything, not even cutting into the ground. The only one who felt the pressure was the ogre, whose leg and stump were already forced halfway into the ground, and the parts of his body that were hit directly by the wind stream weren't doing good.

Bones were showing on the Twinhead Emperor's arms, and barely any skin remained. It was death by a million cuts. The jetstream somehow only seemed to intensify with every passing second, shearing off more and more flesh.

"I... will... not... fall... alone!" the Twinhead Emperor roared loudly as his body exploded with a second wind of energy. He attempted to—

"REE!" Sylphie screeched with anger. The rising energy was smashed right back down, the stream of wind empowered as it took on a light green glow from being infused further with Sylphie's Sylphian concepts.

With a new, desperate roar, the boss tried to reach out toward his staff, only to find Jake holding onto it with a vise grip and a few chains of stable arcane mana. For a moment, Jake saw the Twinhead Ogre open an eye and glare at him in anger. Then the eye was hit by the wind, the pupil and eyeball cut apart.

The ogre's arms fell limply to his side soon after, no longer protecting him as the wind bore down fully on his face and body. His entire face was sheared off, and his torso began to suffer the same treatment, the second head that had belonged to the warrior already unrecognizable.

It didn't come as a surprise when Jake heard the system messages a second later, the seemingly impossible-to-finally-put-down boss finally succumbing to his countless injuries.

You have slain [Twinhead Emperor – lvl 335] – Bonus experience
earned for killing an enemy above your level*
"DING!" Class: [Arcane Hunter of Horizon's Edge] has reached
level 288 - Stat points allocated, +50 Free Points*
"DING!" Class: [Arcane Hunter of Horizon's Edge] has reached
level 289 - Stat points allocated, +50 Free Points*
"DING!" Race: [Human (C)] has reached level 275 - Stat points
allocated, +45 Free Points*

The attack didn't stop when the Twinhead Emperor's energy left his body, leaving it defenseless as the wind had a field day. Only a few seconds later did Sylphie stop. The jet stream subsided, and Jake felt the atmospheric wind return to normal, the little hawk no longer exerting control.

All that was left of the Twinhead Emperor was a ruined corpse, half of its flesh sheared right off the bones, with even these bones covered in thousands of small cuts. A dozen or so meters off to the side, Jake saw a door had popped into existence. This one led to the next city floor, making it clear the floor was now complete.

Looking up, Jake saw Sylphie descend, just gliding on the wind slowly. Without any hesitation, Jake flew up to her and sensed just how exhausted she was. It was not as if Jake was in peak condition himself, but from the looks of it, Sylphie was in an even worse state.

Once he reached her, he let the small hawk glide into his arms and caught her. Sylphie was covered in wounds all over and even missing a lot of her feathers, making Jake's heart hurt as he gave her a light squeeze.

"Ree?" Sylphie let out a low screech as she looked up at him.

Jake shook his head in response. "No, just relieved you're okay."

Floating down, Jake went toward the wooden dome. On the way, he saw the sheer devastation their battle had wrought. It looked like a natural disaster had hit the Vast Plateau. It wasn't unexpected, considering it had been a fight between powerful C-grades, but Jake still felt this one had been particularly rough... and it had definitely been a close call toward the end.

As Jake and Sylphie approached the wooden dome, it soon began to unravel. Once it did, Jake laid eyes on the Sword Saint leaning against a rock while the Fallen King sat on the ground, not able to stand easily due to the lack of an arm and a leg. Dina was the one who looked the best, but Jake knew her resources were quite spent. Who knew that healing wounds inflicted by intense death energy would be difficult?

Well, Jake did. That was why he liked to use it in his poisons. But Dina definitely also knew.

"Good job, team," Jake said as he saw them, flashing a smile. "You all look like shit."

"All the hair on the left side of your head is burnt off," the Sword Saint shot back, having recovered quite a lot from Dina's healing while in the dome, though it was clear the old man wasn't going to be fighting any time soon, as he looked barely able to lift a sword.

"I never argued I am not also in the category of people currently looking like shit." Jake grinned as he sat down with Sylphie, all of them taking a rest in silence. He reflected on the fight as he scratched Sylphie somewhere she wasn't injured, the bird happily using the space between his legs as a nest.

There were definitely things that could have gone better, and they had probably not prepared enough or spent enough time learning about the skills of the Twinhead Emperor before choosing to fight him. If they'd had a small bout with each of the Twin Emperors individually, they would have learned quite a lot, Jake reckoned. But they hadn't. Partly because they were pressured for time, and partly because they had overestimated themselves a bit.

In many areas, they'd also gotten lucky, and Jake estimated there had been a good chance one of them would have had to use their escape tokens if just one small thing had gone wrong. Luckily, nothing had, and when things had looked like they were about to take a turn for the worse, Sylphie had come through with... something. Jake still didn't know exactly what that something was, and he wasn't going to begin interrogating her here and now.

"I would set up a restoration circle, but..." Dina muttered as she frowned.

"Relax, dryad," the Fallen King said. *"There is no rush, so simply relax and recover."*

"Yeah," Jake said with a reassuring smile. "Everyone, just chug a potion when you can. I still got plenty."

The others nodded, and they all relaxed for the next hour, barely any words being exchanged during this time and most meditating. Everyone had consumed a potion at some point during the fight, with Jake himself taking his after the solo fight to buy time when the warrior head had taken full control.

As they rested, Jake also decided to finally check out the system messages he had received upon completing the floor... and things were a lot better than expected.

> **Eightieth floor completed. 16,000 Nevermore Points earned.**
> **Bonus Objective Completed: Do not allow a single party member to be slain during the battle. 30,000 Nevermore Points Earned.**
> **Grand Achievement earned: Slay the Twinhead Emperor after fully allowing the two Twin Emperors to merge in an exemplary manner, thus ending the conflict of the Vast Plateau for good. 100,000 Nevermore Points earned. Due to completing a Grand Achievement, you will receive a 10% multiplier to all Nevermore Points at the final calculation.**

First of all, that was a lot of Nevermore Points. Secondly, getting another 10% multiplier had not at all been expected. The only other event boss they had gotten a percentage bonus for was Minaga, and that had been a 25% multiplier. Jake did kind of feel like the Minaga reward had been a bit too much, but then again, that fight had been a lot harder overall.

Checking his Nevermore Points, Jake saw he had finally broken the two million mark and then some.

> **Current Nevermore Points: 2,120,950**

Besides the Nevermore Points that he and the others had just gotten, the rest of the floor had only awarded 21,000 more, coming from a few bonus objectives and achievements. This was a lot less than on other floors, but that was to be expected. It had been very similar to floor seventy-five and its event boss. All of the achievements and objectives more or less got boiled down into doing the event, resulting in a whole bunch of points from that alone.

Time passed, and with potions and Dina eventually setting up a restoration circle, they all quickly began to recover. The backlashes from boosting skills and overusing certain skills—such as the Sword Saint's Transcendence—would take a while longer to shake off, but after only a few hours, they could all move about just fine. Jake even had all his hair back.

The door leading to the city floor was not far away, but they weren't going to enter it yet... because while it would be nice to head there right away to relax on the city floor, they all knew there wouldn't actually be any relaxation going on. Not mentally, at least.

While the fighting was most certainly finished, there was still a bit of politics to manage and some important decisions to be made—one of which was figuring out the order of who they believed would end up with the most Nevermore Points, so they could have those with less fully finish Nevermore first.

This was all for the Leaderboards... because during this time in the World Wonder, they had confirmed how the rewards worked, and Jake did think parts of it were a bit dumb. But, as a quick summary, it mattered a lot *when* someone got on the Leaderboards... because just holding a spot for a mere moment would reward one the same as if they held it for thousands of years. There were potential rewards if one held a spot for the rest of the era, but all of that was way too far off for Jake to even think about.

Anyway, this all meant that their plan was to finish Nevermore one after another, having each person finish faster using time dilation... with Jake naturally being the last to go because, to the surprise of no one, he would definitely end up with the highest final evaluation. At least from their group... though Jake hoped he would just be the highest. Period.

But he had a feeling there were quite a few people who wouldn't like that much.

———

Ell'Hakan nodded, satisfied that they had managed to accomplish their goal—and just in time, too. The large beast lay dead before them, with the others now scattered, having lost their will to fight after the death of their leader, the last of the Mad Beast Kings.

As a door appeared nearby, he turned to his party members while skimming the floor completion notice.

Eighty-second floor completed. 16,400 Nevermore Points earned.

These two last floors had been done quickly, with little regard to bonus objectives or achievements, but the Nevermore Points gained had still been more than worth it. It was a bit sad they hadn't encountered more opportunities for Grand Achievements, because the one from floor eighty had most certainly been a welcome addition.

Grand Achievement earned: Make the Twin Emperors fully merge

**once more and bring harmony to their Path as the Twinhead
Emperor, ending the conflict of the Vast Plateau for good. 80,000
Nevermore Points earned. Due to completing a Grand Achievement,
you will receive a 10% multiplier to all Nevermore Points at the
final calculation.**

It had taken quite a bit of... Bloodline Therapy to get the two halves of
one whole to agree on things and merge once more, but it hadn't been
something he couldn't handle. Ell'Hakan just felt fortunate he hadn't had
to fight that monster, as he doubted they could have beaten the Twinhead
Emperor without having to resort to things he would prefer to avoid, and
even then, it wasn't an assured victory.

In fact, he doubted many could beat that boss... but he did see the
party of the Malefic's Chosen doing it. They had a lot of trump cards to
throw in, and Ell'Hakan knew not to underestimate the hidden cards of
someone who had managed to not only fight, but *defeat*, the absolute
monster that had been Valdemar's image in the Colosseum of Mortals.

"We must hurry and finish before too many others have a chance to do
so before us," the Saintess of the Holy Church reminded him as she stood
with his two remaining party members, one of their comrades sadly having
fallen during this final floor.

Ell'Hakan regarded the Saintess before nodding and walking to the
door with her. She had been far more helpful than he had ever expected,
truly earning her recognition as one of the ten most talented C-grades of
this generation in the Holy Church. He most certainly did not regret the
deal he had struck to get her and the Church as a whole on board to
support him.

Allowing the Holy Church to obtain his Bloodline was but a small
price to pay for their cooperation. Ah, but nothing would happen with the
Saintess; Ell'Hakan wouldn't want too much to do with her after Nevermore if he could avoid it. He liked people he could influence, and absolute
fanatics were quite difficult to sway in any way. He was also fully aware she
had no positive feelings toward him and had her own Path to walk.

Anyway, his decision to enter talks with the Holy Church had been
quite a good one, if he said so himself—especially when one considered
the further implications of their deal... because to obtain his Bloodline, he
naturally had to be alive, and for the best results, they wanted him to get as
strong as possible before he would pass on the Bloodline.

This naturally meant they had a vested interest in keeping him alive,
earning him quite a good ally... and a backup plan in case the winds of

change did not favor his current Patron and Yip of Yore failed in his grand plan.

Pushing down these thoughts, Ell'Hakan refocused, straightened his back, and walked through the door to the city floor. Soon, it would be time for his final score and placement on the Leaderboards to be revealed, and needless to say, he was more than confident in his placement... and not just on the two publicly known Leaderboards, but the third, hidden one.

The All-Star Leaderboards.

CHAPTER 43

THE FINAL STRETCH

To a C-grade, while fifty years wasn't considered a very long time, it was definitely still a significant part of their lives, especially for those from the new universe, who were all very young by multiversal standards. For many, it was even a majority of their lives, truly highlighting the pure momentum of the natives in a new universe.

For another group who had also been heavily involved in Nevermore, fifty years was but the blink of an eye. The gods who kept an eye on everything that was happening—either inside Nevermore themselves or outside and using messengers they sent in—hardly ever considered fifty-year period to be of any consequence. But when a new universe was integrated, things always got exciting.

The Records were flowing freely, as the system was more active than ever, throwing events and special happenings around everywhere—and not just for those in the new universe, even if the majority were for the newly integrated.

To the gods, this was a prime opportunity to grasp power for themselves and expand their factions... and Nevermore was a huge aspect of this. The Leaderboards were perhaps the best advertisement, not just for the groups with powerful people, but for the geniuses of the new era who had yet to fully integrate themselves with a faction.

Few would dare aim to recruit those who were in the top spots, and most of them were already in big factions anyway... but the ones who would have ranked in the top thousands were still more than worth it to recruit. For these geniuses who were close to the pinnacle, the best thing they could do personally was get closer to the peak while also aligning themselves with the factions capable of nurturing these other peak C-grades who did top the Leaderboards.

Perhaps luckiest of all weren't the newly integrated mortals or the gods who could now finally progress once more, but the young talents who had been born in other universes before the new integration and could now partake in the festivities. They had the advantage of growth before the integration and tended to be older, with far stabler foundations than the newly integrated Nevermore Attendees... yet no one expected any of them to actually take the top spot, at least not right away.

History had proven that it was always newly integrated people who disproportionally dominated the Era Leaderboards, at least in the beginning. Each era was a few billion years at minimum, so many records would be broken during that time, but it did happen on occasion that a record set in the initial stages held strong for an entire era. Yip of Yore was one such happening.

When he had done Nevermore back in the day, he had taken the top spot, with his rival at the time, Altius, taking the second spot. Over time, Altius had been pushed down to number four—still showing he had been an absolute pinnacle talent—but Yip had managed to maintain his rank, even as all the geniuses of an entire era competed with him, truly proving himself the pinnacle talent of the 92nd Era. He had been alive during the integration and set an unbeatable record... and now the question was whether that feat would repeat itself as the next generation began to appear on the Leaderboards.

"Any spoilers?" Minaga asked the Wyrmgod, who was sitting silently and watching a myriad of lifestreams and timers with the other gods.

"No," the Primordial said, shaking his head, "but I do believe most can infer some things."

"Alright, alright... thoughts from the room on how their factions did?" Minaga asked loudly, even calling out to the large gathering of gods observing from the back.

Yet it was the Blightfather who spoke up first. "Can't say I'm particularly disappointed or overjoyed. There were some pleasant surprises and some who underperformed, but that is all to be expected. Overall, while Nevermore is certainly an important step in the Paths of C-grades and an excellent recruitment tool to find worthwhile talents, it isn't that important in the grand scheme of things."

"While I will not disagree with your main point, we shouldn't downplay the most well-known World Wonder of the multiverse either, now, should we?" the Holy Mother countered. "Also, let us not pretend this iteration hasn't been a bit out of the ordinary... Our very presences in this room is proof of that."

Vilastromoz just sat back, once more seeing no reason to get involved when the two of them got into it. He also knew that the reason the Holy Mother wanted to put more emphasis on Nevermore was due to how well the Holy Church always did. They were the single largest faction in the multiverse and focused on working together, after all, so for them to be displayed prominently on the Leaderboards was only to be expected.

Overall, they were definitely the ones doing the best simply due to their sheer numbers, but if one looked at the factions with the highest average placement, they were far behind. This space was instead dominated by the most elite factions, such as the Order of the Malefic Viper and Court of Shadows. Ones that didn't solely care about making a big organization, but also every member being worthy.

Of course, even among the major factions, there was one that dominated here more than any other... A faction that was focused nearly entirely on combat: Valhal.

Valdemar also seemed pretty happy with how things had gone. Even if their average placements were high, they tended to not have anyone at the top either. It did happen from time to time, but their members didn't tend to focus enough on their professions or crafting in general to place that high.

As for the factions that did the absolute best, they were incredibly small and had very strict requirements. Organizations such as the Crimson Flame, led by Gwyndyr. Even that archer from Earth affiliated with him had done pretty well for herself. Not to the level of beating any of the true top contenders, but a respectable performance, a bit like Jake's brother from the Court of Shadows. Pretty good but not outstanding.

The discussion of how each faction would do quickly filled the hall as the gods talked openly, some even making subtle bets here and there. This was a rare chance for many of these representative gods to talk to a Primordial, which both parties were open to in this forum. Didn't hurt that it was primarily just them being rained with praise while bragging, but that was neither here nor there.

Talks continued for a while until the topic moved toward what most of them ultimately cared about. The most interesting part of this period in Nevermore. It was a time where, more likely than not, the top spots of the Leaderboards would be switched out several times a day as more and more pinnacle geniuses finished until finally, the dust would settle, and only one name would remain atop as the Era's Pinnacle.

And while there was much discussion about who could take the top ten and even top five slots in the end, there was no doubt only two people were truly in contention for the top two.

They were the most discussed Chosen of this generation, primarily because of the stuff one of them had pulled off recently and because their two gods had an open conflict:

Ell'Hakan, Chosen of Yip, the former Era's Pinnacle and top genius of the last era.

And naturally the absolutely most spoken of, the Harbinger of Primeval Origins, and Villy's own drinking buddy, Jake.

They would soon know who would take the top spot, as both were about to finish the World Wonder. It was certain one of them would finish before the other, potentially blocking the other from holding the Era's Pinnacle title for even a moment.

————

"We should quickly sort our order and get going," the Sword Saint suggested after they had been talking for a while. "Also to put additional pressure on other factions who may be dallying too much."

"It isn't like we will finish immediately either way," the Fallen King added. *"It will take some time, even with our respective time chambers. Does the Order of the Malefic Viper have some prepared already?"*

The final part was naturally addressed to Jake, who confidently shrugged. "I have no idea."

"No cause for concern in that area." The Sword Saint shook his head. "Someone affiliated with my Patron shall be there and have everything ready."

"That's convenient," Jake said, tilting his head. "Did Aeon contact you or something?"

"No, this was planned before I even entered Nevermore in the first place. Also, let me be clear—this isn't something specifically prepared for us. Others are also very much interested in the services of the best time mage one can find in C-grade."

Jake nodded. "Makes sense, I guess."

"Ree?" Sylphie asked.

"No, it's definitely faster to stay inside of Nevermore to take advantage of the compounding time dilation," the Sword Saint answered.

Sylphie had asked if it wouldn't be faster to go to Nevermore City— the entrance of Nevermore—and have someone above C-grade set up a time chamber there. One had to remember that even if they left Nevermore and the time expired out there, it would still count. But as the Sword Saint said, it was better to stay in Nevermore to double-dip on the time dilation.

Even if the C-grade in Nevermore could only manage, say, ten-to-one dilation inside of Nevermore, coupled with the natural dilation of Nevermore, one easily hit a 100x multiplier in Realtime. Or, well, the opposite of a multiplier, as more time would pass inside the chamber than outside.

"Now, let us proceed to decide our order... and as much as it annoys me, I reckon the bird and I are first, considering our performances in the Challenge Dungeons," the Fallen King said.

"We still need to decide the exact order," the Sword Saint said. "As in... how many points do each of you have, exactly?"

Jake perked up at hearing that. Each of them naturally had a lot of points, but if Sylphie had somehow ended up with more, it would be hilarious.

Spoiler.

It was hilarious.

"A measly, not even two thousand points is..." the King said, trying to make excuses.

"Ree."

"The sheer incompetence in design behind that ridiculous labyrinth..." the Fallen King said, shifting the blame.

"Ree."

"No, it was by far the worst of the Challenge Dungeons, of that there is no doubt," the Unique Lifeform said, now moved onto anger, before finally... acceptance. *"Let us not waste time on what has happened. Additionally, the hawk has gained more levels, which will add even more points at the end. So, move on to decide the winner between the dryad and swordsman."*

"Ree," Sylphie courteously agreed, and they did indeed move on.

Jake had kind of forgotten the extra points one would also get from levels and wondered how that worked. It was one of the reasons it was advised to be as close to level 200 as possible when one entered, even if one could compete on the Leaderboards as long as one was below 210. Anyway, he would definitely find out soon.

"There is no need to compare us," Dina said, shaking her head. "I think it's best he finishes first. With a 70% multiplier from the Challenge Dungeons, neither of us are getting on the top 10 Leaderboards for the era, but the Sword Saint does have a very good shot at the top 10 on the 93rd Universe Leaderboards."

"We should still decide," the Sword Saint said, smiling. "Even if we don't get top 10, reaching top 100 or top 250 is bound to also have certain rewards, and I want no enmity born from one of us blocking the other."

"I wouldn't—"

"1,952,976."

Dina was silent for a bit before muttering, "Fifty-eight thousand..."

"So, you got me beat," the old man said with another smile.

"No... no, you got more levels than me." Dina shook her head. "While I'm not sure about the details, I am sure that will add even more at the end, making you overtake me."

The two of them ended up agreeing on the old man going first after a bit more back and forth, which just left Jake.

"Anyone wanna know how many points I got?" he asked with a bright smile.

"I will assume so many that it would be shameful if you failed to reach the top spot of the Era and Universe Leaderboards," the Fallen King shot back.

"I wouldn't say shameful... but enough so that I would be disappointed if I didn't top at least one of them." Jake shrugged. "And I say that knowing full well that there is a good chance a certain orange fuck is already topping one, if not both of them already. Anyway, we're all good, right? Let's get moving and finally get done with Nevermore."

There were no complaints as everyone finally got up, and Dina dispelled the recovery circle. They all at least looked presentable now as they moved toward the door and the final city floor.

On the way, Dina threw Jake a few glances before finally asking, "Would... Would you really be disappointed if you didn't get the top spot? Do you expect to get it?" she asked a bit cautiously. "My grandfather said that to take the top spot isn't easy, and even if getting it doesn't necessarily mean one is the strongest of a generation... it won't be far off."

"I think I would be, yeah," Jake muttered. "I did my best here in Nevermore, and as you said, the spot is often reserved for the top of a generation, right?"

Dina nodded. "Yes."

"Well, then, I belong there." Jake shrugged as he grinned. "My goal has always been to be the very best like no one ever was."

"Ree?" Sylphie asked, still held by Jake since she was still very tired. Or, at the very least, pretended to still be very tired to get carried.

Jake shook his head while scratching her. "No, no, you're in the generation after mine, so you can be the very best of that one."

"Does that mean I am from the generation before you?" the Sword Saint asked with a raised eyebrow.

"Of course not," Jake said, sounding almost offended. "You're at least three generations before me, if not more."

"That... isn't how generations work in the multiverse," Dina said. "While a generation isn't a set time, in most instances, especially when talking about C-grades, one considers a single generation at least a few hundred years..."

"That sounds like something I will definitely ignore ever learning." Jake grinned as the five of them finally entered the door and went to the final city floor they would ever see.

It was... pretty basic and very empty, if Jake said so himself. Especially compared to City Floor Fourteen, where all the top teams did Challenge Dungeons. Still, the ones that were present were either those not competing on the Leaderboards—in other words, those who had entered while already above 210—or the absolute top teams. And most of those teams wouldn't be found just wandering about, as they were doing exactly what Jake and company were about to do.

Ignoring the system message welcoming them to the city floor, the five of them made their way to the location where the Sword Saint felt a gathering of powerful time energy. Jake also felt it, and using Pulse, he spotted the place the old man was talking about.

Reaching the area, they saw a large set of buildings that looked a bit like one of those motels where the doors opened directly from the outside into the rooms, except the doors, in this case, were heavy enchanted gates, and the rooms were lined-up boxes of metal.

"This the place?" Jake asked the Sword Saint as he read the sign above the fence surrounding the weird, motel-looking place... and it did not inspire confidence.

Time Chambers for Rent! Best Rates, Best Service, Best Performance!

"It is indeed," the old man said, nodding, and Jake chose to believe him as they walked inside. They had barely entered when Jake spotted an approaching figure, who raised a hand and waved.

"You're finally here! Damn, I was getting scared you fucked up and got stuck on floor seventy-five or something, as you didn't go to the city floor. A fellow follower of the glorious God of Time, too!"

Jake observed the man and used Identify, quickly being told what he already knew... This guy was strong.

[Hobgoblin – lvl 349 – Divine Blessing of Aeon Clok]

"Greetings," the Sword Saint said, bowing. "I do not believe I need to say why we're here?"

"Of course not." The hobgoblin shook his head. "Seeing as you're a follower of our god, I can even throw in a three percent discount! No, wait, with the Malefic's Chosen also here, I believe I can make it three-point-five percent! The true VIP treatment!"

"How generous..." Jake muttered.

"I know, right?" the hobgoblin said, still smiling. "Now, let's get you all settled, alright? I will naturally need payment upfront, as you'll all just pop right back to Nevermore City when the timer expires."

"Can I ask, has the Chosen of Yip of Yore also arrived here?" Jake asked.

"Yep, he already got here over a full day ago and will pop out soonish, I reckon," the peak C-grade explained.

"I see..." Jake muttered. "Say... would it be possible to pay a bit extra to maybe make his time dilation less effective than it maybe should be, allowing a certain other Chosen to finish first?"

As the hobgoblin looked at Jake for a moment, his smile faded entirely. "Are you asking me to divert from my own Path by maliciously breaking my business practices?"

"I would never ask that and simply made a tasteless hypothetical," Jake quickly backtracked as he smiled. "Anyway, five rooms, please."

"Oh, of course—you would never truly ask something preposterous like that," the hobgoblin said with a serious look before he went right back to smiling. "Now, follow me, and I'll show you to your rooms."

CHAPTER 44

THE CALM BEFORE THE
LEADERBOARDS

One by one, Jake and his party members entered their respective time chambers. They went in the order they had decided, so the Fallen King would finish first, then Sylphie, the Sword Saint, and Dina. Jake would be the last one to appear back in Nevermore City when his fifty years expired.

When Jake was the only one left, standing right in front of his own chamber, the hobgoblin threw him a glance. "So... you gonna win?"

"What?" Jake asked, a bit confused.

"Are you gonna beat Yip's Chosen on the Leaderboards? In my mind, it's pretty much down to you two for the top spot, given what I know. There are a few others who may also have a slight chance, but, eh... not really."

"Why do you care?" Jake questioned with a raised eyebrow.

"I am a gossip; what can I say? I just like those juicy—"

"There's bets on it, huh?" Jake interrupted.

"Really?" the hobgoblin said, trying to look surprised. "I would have never thought that! But say there truly is live betting going on regarding the finishing positions of all the different well-known Nevermore Attendees competing on the Leaderboards... Surely there would then be a lot to gain from betting on the top spot. Ah, by the way, I am talking about the Era Leaderboards here."

Jake, not really in that much of a hurry to start his own time chamber, had a thought. "Who's the top seed right now?"

"Ell'Hakan, and pretty convincingly, too, so if you beat him on the Era

Leaderboards, you should also top the universe one," the time mage said. "Followed by a demon prince, a young princess from the Regalflight, an elemental of some kind, and, of course, you. A few others in there, too, but I have my personal doubts about these individuals, and I tend to be pretty good at judging situations like these. The thing is, we don't know your Challenge Dungeon score, and while it can be assumed that it's good, seeing as you are also an alchemist and should do well even in those focused on crafting, there's still a lot of question marks. Especially after you didn't publish your results. Left many to believe you maybe actually did horribly and were embarrassed."

"That Chosen of Yip is really rated that highly, huh?" Jake muttered, ignoring the last part of what the time mage said. He did know he had gotten a good score from the Challenge Dungeons, but...

"He passed floor eighty-two and did pretty damn well throughout the World Wonder," the hobgoblin kept readily sharing. "Only one other group did eighty-two floors, with even the majority of the top groups not managing to complete floor eighty, and even if they did, it wasn't exactly with flying colors. Also, is it surprising for the Chosen of Yip to be rated highly? Based on what I saw when he came here, he is quite an unsettling entity... not that I wouldn't say the same about you."

"I see," Jake said while nodding, thinking to himself.

"So...?"

"What?" Jake asked, confused.

"You gonna beat him or not? If you tell me, and you're right, I'll waive the fee for using the time chambers entirely for your entire party."

"Didn't you make a big deal about offering a discount before...?"

"Alright, I'll even throw in... What do you want?" the time mage asked, seemingly not sure what to offer a Chosen.

Jake thought for a second, considering what he would do after Nevermore and what would be of use at that point... and one thing instantly popped up.

"Something for a time banana musa... eh, a Celerita Musa, ancient rarity," Jake said.

"Musa? I thought bananas grew on trees?"

"A lot of people do," Jake answered, having a very important conversation before it was time to have a multiversal competition on a few Leaderboards. "They're actually not trees, but a type of flowering plant that is often confused for one due to their size and large stem."

"Huh, you learn something new every day." The hobgoblin nodded, seeming genuinely interested. "You really are an alchemist. Either way, I got something I'm sure will be of use to your banana plant... so, what'll it be? You gonna take the top spot?"

"If I was the one betting, that is sure where I would place my money... because I wouldn't say Ell'Hakan's Challenge Dungeon run struck me as particularly impressive." Jake smirked and gave a knowing look.

The hobgoblin looked surprised for a moment before he smirked in kind. "I'll trust ya on this one. See ya around—I'll send someone with the stuff for your plant if you make me a rich goblin. Alright, an even richer goblin."

With those words, he shut the door to Jake's time chamber. Seconds later, Jake felt the magic circles activate as time distorted. While time would be warped, he would still need to sit there for at least a few days, giving him plenty of time to have fun. Thus, he pulled out his Puzzle Box of the Seeker, an item he had dearly missed playing with.

Before he immersed himself in the puzzles, he briefly reflected on recent happenings and what he had just learned. Jake had surprised himself a bit when he asked the hobgoblin about potentially messing with Ell'Hakan's time chamber to fuck him over on the Leaderboards, as that honestly wasn't like him. He had just wanted to fuck with the other Chosen, and title-blocking him seemed like a fun way to do that.

But... letting Ell'Hakan emerge on his throne for a small while before smashing him down would also be satisfying. Jake also had to admit one other thing... For a moment, he had considered the possibility he would *need* to finish first. That he wasn't the one with the top score. Jake knew he was strong—people kept telling him that—but it was still hard to imagine he would be the one to take the absolute top spot on the Leaderboards.

If Nevermore had been pure fighting, he would have been more confident. But it was so many other things, and Jake knew there were a myriad of different creatures and people in the multiverse who had their own unique advantages. In many ways, the words of the hobgoblin before he entered the chamber had calmed him. Hearing two groups had beaten two floors more than him wasn't nice, but it told him there wasn't some mega-outlier who had somehow managed to do ninety floors through having five Transcendences or some shit like that.

Again, Jake knew he was strong, but he had seen stronger C-grades. The face of the First Sage flashed in Jake's mind, as he was a major part of his doubt. Who could say someone like that absolute outlier couldn't have appeared again? The chances were really fucking low, but...

Shaking his head, Jake decided to dispel all thoughts about it and began to play with his Puzzle Box to pass the time. All that was left for him to do was wait for the final results to be published. He'd hated that after exams back in school, and sure as hell didn't like it more now.

Jake, immersed in his box to distract his mind, failed to grasp the irony of his thoughts... which he would only come to realize later. Because while he was afraid of some mega-outlier coming in and sweeping the board...

He didn't realize that in the eyes of others, he was that mega-outlier.

———

Nevermore City was busier than ever, even exceeding the time everyone went to enter the World Wonder. The massive city was housing guests from every faction, their many strongholds, and compounds filled with influential figures from all over the multiverse. Within many, even gods sat, covertly keeping an eye on everything that was happening.

Within the compound belonging to the Order of the Malefic Viper, Viridia was kneeling before another familiar-looking woman who stood beside two nearly identical copies of herself. It was one of the Witches of the Verdant Lagoon, sidelined by projections of her two sisters.

"The Malefic One informed us his Chosen will soon exit Nevermore," the sister with a physical avatar said. "There are also some others to keep an eye on, like the Malefic Dragonkin, but sadly for them, they are overshadowed by the presence of the Chosen."

"Will we proceed according to the Order's regular procedures?" Viridia asked, a bit unsure.

This wasn't her first time going to Nevermore because some highly talented member of the Order was doing the World Wonder, but as an S-grade, it was naturally her first time seeing a true Leaderboards competition like this. In preparations, she had read up on old procedures of the Order... but those had all been written during the Malefic One's absence. So, they very much emphasized not rocking the boat too much.

"I read those, and they are pathetic," the Verdant Witch spat. "Viridia, who are we? We are the Order of the Malefic Viper, loyal servants of the Malefic One. We are subservient or apprehensive toward no one but the Malefic One, and this is our chance to truly show the multiverse we are not afraid."

"Then..."

"Walk forward with pride," one of the other sisters said in a stern tone. "Stand alongside the other representatives with a straight back. You represent the Malefic Viper, a Primordial. Do not embarrass him, us, the Chosen, or yourself. Your job is not to prove you are worthy of that pride. Leave that up to the Malefic One and his Chosen and simply bask in the glory of their shadow."

Viridia listened intently before bowing deeper. "The will of the Malefic One shall be done."

"Good. Now go and show those uptight posers the Order of the Malefic Viper is not to be looked down upon or forgotten."

Standing up, Viridia nodded as she turned, determination in her eyes. As she walked through the compound, she gathered those who would walk alongside her. Among them were a few branch leaders and other S-grades, including Fairleigh, the patriarch of the Nalkar vampires. Something that usually wouldn't be possible.

There were a few reasons for this. The first one was that vampires still didn't have a good reputation in the wider multiverse and were often antagonized simply for existing. Among the influential factions, pretty much only the Order had any vampires, with the rest being solo or with smaller groups. Due to this, the Order usually didn't have vampires with them whenever they participated in any social happenings like this, as that would just be inviting trouble from those who still sought the extermination of the vampire race as a whole.

With the return of the Viper, this would change. No longer did they carry the same fear of making others angry by bringing one. The mere fact they dared bring a vampire was also a way to tell the rest of the multiverse that the Order would do whatever they wanted from now on, with the other factions not able to pressure them or tell them what they could and couldn't do. A show of force, so to speak, and a declaration that the Order was openly supporting the vampires.

Finally... Fairleigh had wanted to come. He had been incredibly embarrassed that he had been the one to welcome the Chosen and speak to him for a prolonged period when the Chosen was selling off items from the Treasure Hunt system event, all without the Nalkar Patriarch noticing who he was truly dealing with. He'd just thought Jake was some new recruit with a Blessing. The primary reason Fairleigh had even wanted to speak to the Chosen personally was his own personal interest in old vampire memorabilia. Now, he wanted to at least show his respect by showing up like this and being there to observe how the Chosen did in Nevermore.

"Are you nervous?" Viridia asked Fairleigh as they exited the compound and began making their way toward the central square.

They were a group of twelve total, most of them old and loyal members of the Order, while some were newer recruits brought along. Calling S-grades new recruits was a bit weird, but many had wanted a closer relationship with the Order and even joined after the Primordial's return.

"What worry could I possibly have, Hall Master?" the vampire patriarch asked with a relaxed smile. "This is the domain of the Wyrmgod, and none would dare insult two Primordials by making a move. I am just happy to finally walk in the light and not be hidden away like should I be ashamed of my heritage."

Viridia slowly nodded. Fairleigh was older than her, but as the Hall Master, she had seniority. Still, it felt odd that the vampire she remembered first seeing as a C-grade herself spoke so formally. "There truly is no need for shame. You are recognized by the Malefic One, and his recognition is worth more than that of every other faction combined. I know his Chosen also has no negative emotions toward your race, and from what I heard, there are even vampires living on his home planet."

Fairleigh smiled, and they kept walking in silence for a while longer before the central square entered sight. Compared to when the Chosen and others had entered, things were slightly different now. The entire square had expanded, and not just by a little. Some serious space magic had been used, so perfect it defied belief, quite literally stretching reality itself to make everything bigger.

This was all done to make space for the many stands and podiums reserved for the different factions who had proven themselves worthy of one. Behind these were large buildings placed in a massive ring around the central square, all with a view of the two Leaderboards from large terraces atop their roofs. These were reserved for the top factions only, with the Order of the Malefic Viper naturally having one of these reserved.

The Leaderboards themselves were currently hidden, both appearing entirely blank. This had been done when the Era Leaderboards unlocked, primarily to build up excitement about who would take the top spot. There was no doubt this was more than just a mere competition among young talents, but a large social happening involving pretty much all of the major factions of the multiverse.

Viridia led her group into the building belonging to them, and they soon stood on the rooftop. Quite a few curious gazes had landed on them, especially when they saw the vampire among them. The Risen were only a few rows away, and their representative was throwing some nasty looks, while the Holy Church was luckily on the other side of the square, placed as far away from the Risen as possible.

Looking over at the Risen, Viridia just smiled and nodded in greeting. The other representative clearly wasn't happy but still returned her greeting in kind, professional enough to know that being impolite would gain them nothing.

There were a few dozen of these buildings for top factions, with most of them having already arrived by now. Viridia had been to other social gatherings and was used to mostly being ignored... which was why she was surprised when they were soon visited by many guests who wanted to offer their greetings. And not just from small factions.

A few of the Dragonflights, the United Tribes, the Altmar Empire, demon factions, powerful warbands... factions Viridia usually felt looked down on the Order came to pay their respects and wish them a good performance for their Chosen.

One of the reasons why the larger factions had entire buildings was due to the length of this event. It would take weeks, at the very least, for all of the top performers of this first generation to be revealed. Probably even a few months. So this was also very much a time for political meetings, which the buildings could be used for. Viridia took this chance to meet with representatives left and right.

It also had to be noted that only mortals participated in this. Mixing gods with mortals simply wasn't feasible, and Viridia didn't doubt some gods didn't also have their own dealings, but the majority of the diplomatic work was left to the mortals.

Days turned to weeks, as they had naturally come in good time, and the Leaderboards had yet to be revealed. Finally, they got a warning in the form of a message projected into the sky above Nevermore City:

Leaderboards Reveal: 23:59:57

Viridia had gone to their rooftop in preparation as the timer slowly expired. As it reached zero... the sky and square filled with lights, and Viridia heard something she hadn't expected. Music began to blare from who-knows-where as a being appeared in the sky, hands spread out, and she felt the presence of a demi-god.

It was a figure she had read up on and whom she knew was associated with Nevermore. A powerful being that many feared as much as even the Primordials—not necessarily because of power, but the sheer damage this being could cause if pushed. Truly, a creature worthy of respect. Viridia and all the other mortals knelt before the demi-god they, in truth, knew had already stepped into divinity. Perhaps the only god capable of showing up as a mortal:

The All-God Legion.

CHAPTER 45

LEADERBOARDS

Lights danced in the sky as the music kept playing while the All-God Legion, better known as Minaga, walked down a pair of invisible stairs right above the two blank Leaderboards. He easily got the attention of everyone, and Viridia had to admit he was perhaps the best creature in the multiverse to do something like this... He was both a mortal, making his aura not overwhelming, and a divine being that could stand alongside the pinnacle all on his own. This offered him the possibility of absolute confidence.

"Welcome, welcome, welcome! What a great day for all of you to show up, and all just to come and see little me!?" Minaga's voice was projected throughout Nevermore City, reaching not just the square. "Oh, wait, I read that wrong... You're here for the Leaderboards, eh?"

Not a single person present let out the slightest laugh.

"Alright, alright, tough crowd. Everyone's so freaking serious, so let's just stop messing around and get right to it! The great Leaderboards reveal! Okay, I lied; we won't get right to it. One small intermission first, and I need to make a few clarifications, and as a preamble, I will share some stats!" Minaga summoned a floating screen above himself. "Firstly, I can happily announce the death rate for this year's Leaderboards-competition groups was 10.3% below the expected amount! That means only about 9.4 out of every 100 Nevermore Attendees competing on the Leaderboards ended up dying, compared to 10.1 out of every 100 last era."

Viridia looked up at the screen and saw the stats that represented, at the very least, millions of deaths. But it also meant that more than ten times the number of dead had come out of Nevermore, now more powerful than before and with a brighter future ahead of them. She also knew that the members of the Order tended to fare better in survival due to their far higher average power level.

"The Nevermore Points achieved by the average group is also 3.6% higher than the last era, sitting at a whopping 42.214! Pretty good, if I say so myself, and you can all be proud for fostering another great generation... especially now that we're getting to the juicy part."

Minaga smiled even more brightly as he dispelled the prior screen and showed a new one. It was just a single number, but Viridia instantly understood what it meant. *That's... impressive.*

"10.5%. That's how many more Nevermore Points the average in the top 1 percentile gained this time around compared to the last era. To clarify, this is the second-biggest jump between two eras ever seen, and compared to last time, there is no explanation besides one simple fact: even the average talent of this era vastly surpasses any we've ever seen prior."

For the first time, there was an actual crowd reaction as claps were heard. Viridia also joined in, along with the other S-grades around her. It was an applause for the next generation and what she believed was an outstanding performance. A generation the Chosen of the Order was a representative member of.

"Now, at the very tippity top we will soon see on the Leaderboards, the disparity is a bit harder to find, showing that those at the Pinnacle Tier, even in prior eras, are still not to be taken lightly," Minaga continued once the applause had fully died down. **"But fret not—the young talents are a little bit better, but within the margin of error."** Viridia heard some low discussion all around.

To see the average rise was a good sign.. but to see the top shift wasn't, especially after the last era. Yip of Yore had been an outlier who had been praised for surpassing all prior eras, and what he had grown into could only be described as a problem for many divine factions. The many factions had also long learned that many top geniuses would be very difficult to control unless they had an existing connection to a top faction.

Those from the new universe naturally didn't have any pre-existing connections, making them far more unpredictable. So, while seeing the average grow was good, many hoped to not see the top spot once more be taken by someone from the new universe... Something that would be difficult to achieve, seeing as quite a few of the top seeds were from the new universe.

"The following clarification is mainly for those who haven't really been paying attention to how the Leaderboards work... but the Leaderboards have naturally been open for quite a while; we just decided not to show them. In fact, they've been open for about a year, but we have naturally kept them hidden, as honestly, quite a few of you are utterly insufferable when it comes to wanting to show off. You are so desperate to have names from your factions shown on a list that is shifting every hour that it's honestly kind of sad. Seriously, how many people have been forced to cut their Nevermore journeys short halfway through for some insecure Holy Church, Risen Altmar Empire, or whatever, to use their lost futures as a brief marketing stunt? Anyway, so, yeah, to stop this pathetic display, we chose to hide the Leaderboards till now, when the rankings are at least semi-stable, and I am certain no one has anything against that, right? We allow people to at least see the Universe Leaderboard a bit in the beginning for you bastards to do your scouting or whatever, and even that's too much, in my opinion..."

Viridia stood and stared blankly, the entire square silent after the Unique Lifeform's rant. She couldn't help but look over, and she saw a Cardinal from the Holy Church clench his staff tight, holding in his anger after the All-God Legion had effectively insulted the entire Holy Church and even the Holy Mother herself. It wouldn't be an understatement to say Minaga had just insulted half of the peak factions with a single rant... and Viridia knew that out of nearly anyone in the multiverse, Minaga was perhaps the only one who could do just that without ever suffering any repercussions.

"Ah, I really needed to get that off my chest... Now to get back into it. So, as I said, the Leaderboards have been open for a while, and the listing has sure shifted a lot. For the Era Leaderboard alone, the top 100 has had a total of 351 names on it, quite a few more than usual. As for the top 10, we have had a total of 21 names there. Again, this is for the Era Leaderboard... but we naturally aren't going to address that first. Instead, let's keep it a bit more local and discuss the far more volatile Universe Leaderboard."

Having changed the topic away from insulting peak factions, Minaga shared some more stats. Waving his hand one more time, another screen appeared.

"I call this Leaderboard more volatile because it's been quite the

shuffle! People getting high spots only to be bonked down from the top 50 to below the top 100 within a day happened more than once! The higher average has resulted in far more than usual reaching the minimum Nevermore Points required for Pinnacle Tier to qualify them to even appear on the top 100. This has resulted in a whole new record of the most names ever appearing in not only the top 100, but even the top 10 of the Universe Leaderboards! An all-time record, too!"

The screen floating above Minaga began to fill with the stats of the Universe Leaderboard. Stats that made Viridia and many others raise an eyebrow.

"1084 have had their name appear in the top 100, with a whopping 76 in the top 10 at some point! That's a lot of people getting some sweet, sweet titles! However... there have only ever been three names at the very top. Two of which now still dominate the Leaderboards. Yes, Leaderboards, plural."

This was the first real hint about the actual people on the Leaderboards. No hints as to who they were, just that they were from the 93rd Universe, which instantly made Viridia think that the Chosen of the Malefic One had to be among these two. He had to be.

"Now, for some more interesting miscellaneous stats regarding the Challenge Dungeons and the thought process behind their designs..." Minaga began before smirking and stopping himself. "Relax, I'm just messing with you all. I guess it's time to get to the real meat of this entire thing."

With a snap, the screen with stats disappeared as Minaga paced back and forth up in the air.

"Some of you keen-eyed ones may have realized by now I am just dragging time out because I am waiting for something to happen. Or maybe you didn't realize anything and just assumed I like to ramble on—something you would be entirely correct about, but in this instance, I am also dragging out time purposefully, as we quite frankly started this entire thing at least a few minutes too early. You see, for suspense, we have delayed some arrivals of those who had already finished Nevermore, and we had to make sure everyone was done for maximum dramatic effect to put on a good show and all that. Also, relax. Their order of completion is still intact; we just delayed them teleporting to Nevermore City. With all that said... may the young talents descend!"

With these words, space began to move as Viridia felt the energy of the

Wyrmgod himself at play. All around the huge central square, figures began to appear in rapid succession, either on the stands or on top of the many buildings belonging to top factions.

Viridia quickly looked around, and on one of the buildings, she saw the swordsman who had entered with the Viper's Chosen appear, standing among followers of Aeon Clok. On another platform with followers of Stormild, she saw the hawk, and on a third belonging to the Pantheon of Life, the dryad. Finally, on their very own platform, a figure appeared, and Viridia was ready to bow when she saw it was not the Chosen but instead the Unique Lifeform.

She didn't have time to say anything to this Unique Lifeform before Minaga spoke once more.

"And now for the grand reveal... of one of the Leaderboards!"

Finally, the time had come. Space itself warped around the Universe Leaderboard, words appearing on it line-by-line before soon showing the top 10. At the same time, beams of white light descended from above, highlighting ten figures who were all standing spread around the square. It didn't take long to realize who was highlighted... it was naturally the ten top performers... and Viridia saw a real smug Cardinal over at the Holy Church building as two beams descended on them. This light began to change up in the air as projections of these ten figures appeared, allowing all to see them.

Ignoring everything else, Viridia finally gazed upon the Universe Leaderboard... and it didn't look right. It didn't look right at all.

"Two did better than anyone else... Please join me in applauding the performances of our runner-up, Wintermaul, along with our top dog, Ell'Hakan, Yip of Yore's Chosen!"

Viridia just stared at the Leaderboard... Things truly didn't make sense. *Where is he?*

Nevermore Leaderboards (C-grade): 93rd Universe.
1. Ell'Hakan – Pinnacle Tier
2. Wintermaul – Pinnacle Tier
3. Lopas – Pinnacle Tier
4. Holy Dawn Paladin – Pinnacle Tier
5. Arnold – Pinnacle Tier
6. Eastbound Monk – Pinnacle Tier
7. Disciple of Lucenti – Pinnacle Tier
8. Sword Saint – Pinnacle Tier
9. Immortal Faith – Pinnacle Tier

10. High Templar – Pinnacle Tier

Silence filled the entire square as everyone looked at the two large projections in the air highlighted more than the others. The two atop the Leaderboard. Soon, celebration erupted from several places, and nearly everyone did as Minaga said and gave a round of applause... except for those from the Order.

Viridia looked up and saw the figure of Yip's Chosen projected. He had a light smile on his face, not exactly looking smug, but not like his performance had come as a surprise either. He looked like someone who had just been told something he found rather obvious as he bowed a few times. Yet Viridia also saw something else... doubt and a bit of confusion that seemed to mirror her own.

The other highlighted figure was the one called Wintermaul. It was an ice elemental of some form, looking a bit like a mix between a yeti and a bear, but made entirely of ice. To see an elemental do so well was rare... which had to mean this particular elemental was truly outstanding.

Still... things were wrong, and as everyone else was celebrating and Minaga gave them time and space to do so, Viridia turned to the Unique Lifeform that had been part of the Chosen's party, throwing him a questioning gaze. One he instantly understood.

"I must say, I am pleasantly surprised to at least find myself in the top 100... and to see the small planet I now call home have not just one, but multiple individuals in the top 10..." the Fallen King said. *"To see the mechanic with relations to the void outperforming the swordsman does surprise me a smidgen, though. Alas, I can only say it's his fortune."*

Frowning, Viridia looked at the Unique Lifeform. "What happened in there? The Chosen..."

"Allow me to make a prediction... My fellow Unique Lifeform by the name of Minaga has been putting on an entire show, which was part of the reason I was held in a white void for a few minutes before I was teleported here."

"The All-God Legion is in charge of this Leaderboards reveal," Viridia said, nodding.

"Then it makes sense. From all I have learned about Minaga, he is a performer who enjoys making drama and putting on a show more than anything. So do not worry quite yet, and just enjoy the show as the suspense builds, and we await the grand reveal."

Viridia instantly realized what the Unique Lifeform was trying to say. She breathed a sigh of relief and did as he said, waiting for Minaga to continue. A few minutes passed as the celebrations died down, and the congratulations of the top 10 came to an end. Until the factions would host larger celebrations at a later time, that is.

"Once more, I want to congratulate all those who placed in the top 10 from the 93rd Universe. You all have done pretty well for yourselves, considering you've only been part of the multiverse for just a short amount of time... but what's perhaps even more impressive is that we still find four names from the Universe Leaderboard also present on the era one! Behold, our top 10 of this era... and the Era's Pinnacle!"

Space once more moved to reveal the second Leaderboard, and ten figures were highlighted again as projections appeared, four of these highlights repeated. Along with the highlight of the Era's Pinnacle... which had gone to the one most people had expected to see there, and the top seed according to all the gambling houses.

Nevermore Leaderboards (C-grade): 93rd Era.
1. Ell'Hakan – Era's Pinnacle.
2. Demon Prince of the Fourth Hell – Pinnacle Tier
3. Wintermaul – Pinnacle Tier
4. Aishalstromoz Regalflight – Pinnacle Tier
5. Ghost King Azal – Pinnacle Tier
6. Disciple of the Heartsoul Daolord – Pinnacle Tier
7. Lopas – Pinnacle Tier
8. Grimclaw Noxmane – Pinnacle Tier
9. Holy Dawn Paladin – Pinnacle Tier
10. Saintess of the Holy Church – Pinnacle Tier

———

Two beams once more highlighted the smug Holy Church, showing that they had impressively maintained two spots in the top 10. Only one of them was a repeat, as someone Viridia recognized as the Saintess—part of Ell'Hakan's group—was also highlighted.

The newcomers included a demon prince who had made some waves recently, currently shown standing with an arrogant sneer as he gazed toward where Ell'Hakan was standing. Next up was a princess of the Regalflight—the golden dragons—who nearly always had members toward the top due to the extremely high average power of those who managed to become golden dragons. She was standing with a neutral look in her humanoid form, but no matter what, she couldn't hide her innate pride.

Azal, the Ghost King, was also an expected figure. The same was true for the Disciple of the Heartsoul Daolord, a young girl looking no older than someone who had barely entered adulthood. Then there was Grim-claw Noxmane, a wolf from the United Tribes, who looked like a, well, large wolf.

The creature known as Lopas did strike Viridia as an odd one. This Lopas had appeared on both the Universe Leaderboard and the seventh spot of the Era Leaderboard, gaining the creature quite a bit of attention... which was why it was surprising to see the sloth-like creature's projection clearly sleeping in mid-air.

All of these top performers got a lot of praise, and even if the Church had two in the top 10, there was no doubt who had the most attention out of everyone. Ell'Hakan had repeated the feat of his Patron and claimed the very top spot, proving himself the Era's Pinnacle. Viridia clenched her fists as she threw a glance toward the Fallen King, who looked unbothered, just waiting.

"Truly an impressive display by everyone, and I will say... even if you do not find your name on the top 10, do not be discouraged. Top 100, or even top 1000, is also a feat to celebrate. Even if you don't find yourselves on any Leaderboards, do not for a second believe this is an evaluation of your entire Path and your potential. To many of you, this will be but a slight blip in your existence, and hopefully just a pleasant memory that may or may not have rewarded a sweet title. This is also a warning to the ones who did place well on the Leaderboards: Do not relax simply because you did well in one World Wonder. This is just a single step on your journey."

The words of the Unique Lifeform were both sobering and encouraging. It was likely something many of those who had either done better or worse than expected needed to hear. Putting too much stock in Nevermore wasn't wise, after all. Viridia herself hadn't done that well back in Nevermore, partly because of her Path as a witch not being the best for the World Wonder, yet out of her entire party, she was the only one who'd ever even reached A-grade.

After Minaga allowed the words to sink in a bit, he spoke once more.

"Just one more thing before we all go our separate ways... I'm

going to tell you all a bit about a personal grievance of mine. Trust me, it'll be relevant." Minaga began to pace back and forth. "I've been working with the Wyrmgod for quite a few eras now, working on floors, consulting on different projects, working on Challenge Dungeons... with my mainstay creation naturally being my labyrinth. Both the floors and the Challenge Dungeon."

The ramble seemed entirely irrelevant to everything else that was going on, yet as the All-God Legion began to talk, Viridia saw the Fallen King slump and let out an audible sigh as he let her know his thoughts.

"Here we go again..."

"I worked hard on this, and I try to make them pretty fair so people can't cheat, yet every single era, there are some individuals who find new ways to 'break' stuff, if you will. This is fine. It gives me data to fix the error for the next iteration. Except this time around, this bastard appeared who exploited the hell out of both my labyrinths without a single trace of shame, doing so in a fashion that I can't even fix for the next era. He even went as far as to set an all-time record in my Challenge Dungeon, and not even by a little, but by so much I felt like he did it only out of spite."

Viridia frowned as the Unique Lifeform gave her a small nod. A nod that made her smile when the Unique Lifeform continued, "And wouldn't you know it... that very same bastard is just about to come out of our precious World Wonder in... three... two... one..."

A beam of light descended right beside Viridia as she felt space warp... and a masked figure appeared, the Leaderboards all shifting in real-time.

CHAPTER 46

PEERLESS CONQUEROR OF NEVERMORE

Nobody liked being interrupted while having a good time, and Jake was no different. He had just been chilling with his Puzzle Box when he suddenly felt space shift around him, throwing him out of the space inside the box. For a brief moment, he saw his surroundings, and then the entire time chamber disappeared, and he found himself standing within an entirely white void reminiscent of those he had been tossed into after doing the Challenge Dungeons.

Just as he appeared, a screen popped up in front of him.

Nevermore Leaderboards Challenge successfully completed.
Initiating final calculations.

Jake read the message and nodded. *Bloody finally.*

He waited for more text to appear for a few seconds, but nothing was happening, making him impatiently tap his fingers and cross his arms.

"I swear, if this messes up any of our timing for finishing..."

"It won't," a voice suddenly said as a figure appeared behind him. "While in this space, time is paused, courtesy of the system."

Turning his head, Jake saw a familiar figure and smiled. "Didn't expect the big boss herself to handle these evaluations, too."

"Usually, she doesn't," Nevermore answered. "But in some rare cases, I do. Primarily for those who performed well enough for it to be warranted."

Jake smiled. "I guess that's a way of telling me I did well."

"You already know you did well," Nevermore said. "Now you just need to find out exactly how well."

The Bound God waved her hand, and a screen appeared off to the side, making Jake look over.

"Are you nervous?" Nevermore asked, clearly already knowing the results of everything.

"I feel like I shouldn't be, but a little bit of nervousness did manage to sneak in. Overall, I wouldn't say I was, though." Jake shrugged, pretty sure that was normal.

"Perhaps not for this... but I will give you a courtesy warning that once we are done here, you will be teleported into the Nevermore City square, surrounded by nearly every peak faction of the multiverse, with all eyes on you," she shared kindly. "Minaga is in charge of announcing the Leaderboards results, after all, making me relatively certain he won't just allow you to appear without at least a few comments."

"Okay," Jake said with a pause, "now I might be a little nervous..."

"Good. Now for the part you don't need to be as nervous about."

The screen began to fill with lines of text.

Nevermore Points Leaderboard Calculation:
71 levels gained (204 --> 275). Calculating rewards.
You've earned 7100 (100 per level gained) Nevermore Points.

Jake had to jump in here, as 100 points per level just seemed way too low and almost insulting... until he remembered how few points the lower floors gave, and with that in mind, maybe this wasn't so bad. Yeah, he also had to consider he had probably gained way fewer levels than some others, so the extra points per level being shit was—

You will receive an additional 35.5% (0.5% per level gained)
multiplier to all Nevermore Points.

Alright, never mind. Levels were still pretty damn fucking important, even for those with a lot of points. An extra multiplier per level gained had not been something Jake expected; that's for sure. He knew levels would give something, but a percentage multiplier seemed like a bit much. Not that he was going to say no to it, as it would help make his final number even bigger.

And looking at the next three lines, his number did end up being pretty darn big... with quite the impressive multiplier.

Current Nevermore Points: 2,128,050
Nevermore Points Multiplier: 185.5%
Total Nevermore Points Earned: 6,075,583

"Six million... That feels like a lot of points," Jake commented as he looked at Nevermore. "Is it a lot of points? Relatively speaking, I mean. I was definitely more confident before I was aware of the multiplier from levels gained. Why is that even so large?"

"Let me start with your final question. The multiplier is as such to even the odds a bit for monsters who are less favored in several of the Challenge Dungeons. Since they tend to gain more levels than the enlightened, this stage benefits them the most, more often than not."

"Makes sense, I guess. Say, since we are done... who got the most levels out of everyone?" Jake asked curiously, not at all expecting to actually get an answer.

"The record is 149 levels gained by a monster doing the entirety of C-grade in one go," she answered.

Jake's eyes opened wide. "How in the hell..."

"Through means that also result in this very same creature not ever being able to evolve to B-grade. Gaining a lot of levels through ways that destroy one's foundation is not particularly difficult. Or at least, so I've been told." A curious remark, given that the Bound God had been born effectively omnipotent within the World Wonder. "Also, no, this monster is not on any of the Leaderboards."

"Alright, who was the one who gained the most levels while also being on the Leaderboards?" Jake changed his question, surprised Nevermore was even sharing this much, which made it even more surprising when she answered this question, too.

"Someone you at the very least heard of. Ghost King Azal managed to gain a total of 112 levels during Nevermore, with more than a third of that earned during the final month." Nevermore sighed. "Only slightly beating out someone from the Holy Church who earned 108 through a similar trick."

"That was an option?" Jake asked after pausing. "How the hell did they do it?"

"Treasures bound to them they brought in from the outside. A final resort to try and bring honor to their organizations by sacrificing much of their foundations." Nevermore shook her head in disappointment.

"Damn," Jake muttered. "I guess this brings me back to my first question... Is six million Nevermore Points a lot?"

Nevermore smiled at him for a moment before a second screen appeared above the first. One with a number on it.

5,991,906

Jake took a second before pointing. "That's lower than mine."

"Brilliant observational skills, truly putting all your Perception to use." Nevermore shook her head. "This is the current record."

Hearing this, Jake grinned. "Fuck yeah... Totally knew I had him beat."

No matter how much Jake had tried to distract himself, he had been afraid that somehow, Ell'Hakan still had a higher score. Especially after that whole thing with levels also awarding points and multipliers... though, then again, you needed 10 race levels just to get 5% more, so maybe it wasn't that extreme.

Feeling happy, Jake looked at Nevermore as the Bound God shook her head and waved her hand again. A third screen appeared with yet another number on it.

5,705,821

Jake looked at it for a bit before scratching the back of his head. "Not sure what you're trying to tell me with that... Is it the tenth spot on the top 10 Leaderboards or something?"

"That's the score of Ell'Hakan, the one now holding the second place on the Leaderboards in this era."

"What?" Jake exclaimed, looking confused as he pointed to the first number that was more than a quarter of a million bigger. "Then that is...?"

"The score set by Yip of Yore last era... the man now holding the second place on the All-Time Leaderboard."

Jake didn't have time to say more. A giant slab dropped down from out of nowhere, smashing into the white floor and showing that Nevermore also had a flair for dramatics whenever she wanted. Words began to appear on the slab, revealing ten names from the bottom to the top. When Jake saw the full list, he did have to do a double-take, despite Nevermore having already confirmed what was going on.

Nevermore Leaderboards (C-Grade): All-Time
1. Jake Thayne
2. Yip of Yore

3. Monk
4. The Holy Son
5. Anonymous
6. Gwyndyr of the Crimson Flame
7. Anonymous
8. Aurustromoz, Dragon of Gold
9. Ell'Hakan
10. Ninth Hell Devil

———

He kept staring at it for a few more seconds as he let it sink fully in. His goal had been to beat Ell'Hakan... and, well, he had definitely done that. An impressive feat in its own right, seeing as he had managed to snag the number 8—now 9—spot on the All-Time Leaderboard. One thing did strike him as weird, though, as he looked at the Leaderboard.

"I recognize Gwyndyr, the Holy Son, and I also read about Aurustromoz, the Patriarch of the Regalflight... Is everyone on this Leaderboard still alive? Did every person with a top placement in prior eras really all become gods?"

"Yes," Nevermore answered. "But you got things a bit mixed up. They are on this particular Leaderboard because they are still alive. You lose your spot if you die, and another may rise and take your place. It happens more than you think, and the two who have been on the list the longest are the Holy Son and the Monk."

"Who is this Monk?"

"Someone that wished to be anonymous," the Bound God explained. "You can choose your own name on the Leaderboards—not just this one, but also the two outside. Which is something we should address right away... What do you want to be shown as? Do know there are some limits, and the name has to be associated with your Path and Records to be accepted. Also, if you wish to change your name at any point, you can return to Nevermore and request it."

Jake looked at the name currently displayed for a bit. He had gone by many things throughout the times... Chosen of the Malefic Viper was probably at the top of that list. Recently, he had been called the Harbinger of Primeval Origins quite a bit, and then there was, of course, the final option: the Primal Hunter. All of these were possible choices, and he kind of wanted to go with the final one... but not yet. For now, he would simply let it be.

"Jake Thayne is fine," he said, shaking his head. Others also tended to use their names, based on what he saw, and there was no need to break that pattern.

"As you will," Nevermore agreed with a nod. "In that case, allow me to be the first to formally congratulate you for your performance within the World Wonder. It has been a pleasure to have you visit."

Smiling, Jake nodded in acknowledgment. "It's been a long but pleasant stay. For the most part, anyway... You could do away with the water levels."

"I'll be sure to pass on your feedback. But before you go, two more things. Let's first get the easy one out of the way." With a single wave of her hand, Jake felt as if power rushed through his body. Everything tingled for a moment, Jake nearly feeling like he was using his boosting skill. Except he didn't, and quickly, everything returned to normal.

Jake raised a hand, opening it and closing it into a fist a few times. He realized what had happened and quickly checked his system messages as he grinned.

Titled gained: Peerless Conqueror of Nevermore
Peerless Conqueror of Nevermore – Throughout the ages, few have stood at the true pinnacle of an era. Even fewer have stood above even this at the true apex, dominating all eras prior. Attain first place on the All-Time Nevermore Leaderboards, proving yourself a Peerless Conqueror of Nevermore. Only one Nevermore Performance title can be held at a time. As a Peerless Conqueror of Nevermore, you are a master of dungeons, increasing stats gained from Dungeoneer and Dungeon Pioneer titles by 50%. +15% All Stats.

15% to all stats was... a lot. Coupled with the title he had gained from the Challenge Dungeons, he was up to a 20% bonus to all stats from Nevermore. He also noted the part about only being able to have one Nevermore Performance title at a time, which was apparently different from the Nevermore Dungeon titles.

Then there was the other effect of getting more stats from his Dungeoneer and Dungeon Pioneer titles. This effect was, currently, honestly kind of shit. Jake only got 65 stat points from his Dungeoneer XV title in the first place, and even with a 50% boost, that only became 97. However, it was the kind of title that would keep getting better the further Jake progressed. Maybe it sucked now, but if he managed to also max out his Dungeon Pioneer, it would give a respectable amount. In later grades, it would also keep adding more and more. Plus, with Jake's quite frankly ridiculous percentage amplifiers to stats, any raw base stats held immense value.

"That's a nice title right there." Jake grinned and looked at Nevermore. "Thanks."

"Do not thank me; you earned it through your own merit," the Bound God answered, returning his smile. "Now, the final thing before we say our farewells... There are no item rewards, as everything was put into the title and the items awarded from the Challenge Dungeons. Usually, those who perform really well do not really need any equipment either, just leading to lost work for crafters if we gave out such things. But there is still an extra exclusive reward I will offer you, granted by the system due to... unique circumstances."

Without any forewarning, a small bottle appeared, floating just within reach of Jake. Confused, Jake used Identify on it.

[Bottle of Restoration (Unique)] – Restores Primal Origin Energy. Must be consumed before fully leaving Nevermore.

Jake took a bit to realize what this item was... and he felt almost disappointed. Had the system just decided to officially name his Jake Juice?

"To clarify something, the description you see may not reflect any true names," Nevermore said.

"Oh, good." Jake sighed with relief. "Then there is still hope for it to be called Jake Juice."

"You know, that isn't even impossible. If that is the name the energy gets known by, and it becomes cemented in its Records, that will be the official name for any who see it."

"On second thought, maybe I shouldn't call it Jake Juice, though that would be extremely hilarious." Jake smiled as he took the bottle. He had to drink it now, so... "Bottoms up."

Drinking the liquid inside, Jake didn't really feel anything. It also just tasted like plain water, having no real taste. However, when he sought deep within himself, he felt it. The hidden "pool" of energy had just gotten a huge infusion, and even if it had gotten pretty damn big already after he had gained so many levels over the last decade, he now had more than even before his fight with Valdemar. A lot more, in fact.

"With this, I believe your journey through Nevermore has fully come to an end... at least for now. Though I have the feeling your next visit will be a bit more relaxed with none of the time pressure of competition." The Bound God gave a final smile.

"See you again," Jake said, nodding.

"Perhaps," Nevermore said. "Now, prepare yourself, as Minaga has prepared quite the stage for your arrival. Oh, and one more thing—would you be fine with your number one All-Time placement being shared?"

"Sure." Jake shrugged, not seeing the harm. He was already the top of the era; no need to avoid sharing he was the top of every era.

"Very well... I'm sure that will create some wonderful political turmoil."

Jake tried to say more, but before he could, the world warped around him as he was tossed out of Nevermore.

———

There was quite a lot to take in as Jake appeared in the central square. Instinctively, he quickly shot out a Pulse of Perception, only to get overwhelmed by how much information he had to sort through. There were so many goddamn people, many of which he knew. Then there were well over a hundred gods hidden all around, mixed with the crowd.

Jake stood atop the building belonging to the Order of the Malefic Viper, with Viridia right in front and the Fallen King beside him. Looking up, he saw Minaga dramatically float in the air, gazing down at him with a grin.

"Well, I guess we should redo a few things, seeing as things have... shuffled a bit." Minaga smiled.

Out of the corner of his eye, Jake spotted a fading beam of light that had been focused upon a building belonging to the Holy Church, and he saw the Saintess, who had been in a party with Ell'Hakan, glare daggers at him. It wasn't hard to notice who he had bumped down from the top 10.

"Join me in welcoming my personal bane, the one who ruined much of my confidence in dungeon design, and our new top dog of Nevermore... Jake Thayne!" Minaga announced loudly as music began playing.

Jake just stood there and stared, happy as hell he was wearing his mask, as everyone began clapping while staring at the giant projection of his visage in the sky.

"Oh, wait, I nearly forgot!" Minaga suddenly cut the music. **"I guess I failed to clarify what I meant by top dog... because I'm not**

just talking about this era. It's with pleasure I can announce that for the second era in a row, the All-Time record has been broken!"

Viridia stared at Jake, while the Fallen King looked unsurprised. Minaga started back up the music, louder than ever, as even more attention fell on Jake, now also from a shitload of gods...

Maybe I should also have just gone with Anonymous...

At least, Jake thought so for a moment... until he saw him across the square. An orange humanoid stared at Jake with a look of genuine shock, at least for a second, before Ell'Hakan managed to hide it. So, yeah, maybe this level of flexing hadn't been that bad of a call, as he could at least smack down the ego of that orange fuck with his own even larger, superior ego.

CHAPTER 47

SOMETHING WORTH CELEBRATING

Vilastromoz just leaned back and smiled, still within the streaming room that was now just showing the Nevermore City square and all of Minaga's antics. Well, one of Minaga's clones anyway, as the god was also still in the room with a god clone.

"Man, ain't that host the most handsome Unique Lifeform you've ever seen?" Minaga praised himself loudly. "His presentation skills are also just through the roof!" They were all waiting for the grand reveal... and it soon came when his clone announced the dramatic twist of one more person appearing.

To many of the mortals in the square, it was perhaps a surprise... but to the gods in the living room, they had just waited for this to happen. They had watched Jake and his party for the last many years, and they knew how well he had done. For him to not even reach the top 10 made it clear to everyone that he would appear at some point for a grand announcement.

Something he did... making Vilastromoz grin even more. The Wyrmgod and Minaga's clone both looked at him as Jake appeared and his performance was revealed.

"Congratulations," the Wyrmgod said with a slow nod. "A joyous occasion."

"Found a good one, huh?" the Blightfather said, acknowledging Jake's achievement.

"A fortunate and earned victory," the Holy Mother said, also showing her respects.

"Glad to see he did well," the Nature's Attendant added happily. "For little Dina to have been in the same party as the new champion of the All-

Time Leaderboards... it was a good decision to have her join him. Thank you, Vilas."

The Viper just smiled back at the second-in-command of the Pantheon of Life. "She pulled her weight; you have nothing to thank me for."

"But I do," his father-in-law insisted. "I expected him to do well, but this still exceeds it. The impact on her future will be felt for certain, and she has been granted a great boon. She was even on the top 100 of the Era's Leaderboards, doing far better than I thought possible."

The Viper shook his head. "Well, in either case, you shouldn't be thanking me, but Jake."

"I will make sure to." The god nodded as he turned to Artemis. "What say you? Shouldn't we have him visit the Pantheon of Life once he is available? I am certain Ygg will also want to see him. We should probably wait a little, though... Let things calm down a bit."

"My image already effectively extended an invitation within the Colosseum of Mortals, and I'm sure the Malefic One's Chosen is more than aware he has an open invitation standing," the archer god responded, sounding a bit more confident than before, having gotten quite used to being in the presence of so many far more powerful gods over the last nearly two decades.

"Well, he strikes me as the sort to easily forget things, so perhaps we should remind him," Nature's Attendant commented.

"I'll do it for you; no problem." Vilastromoz waved it off as he looked at Artemis and smiled. "I have a feeling he wants to visit anyway. I heard something about archery lessons."

Artemis averted her gaze as the Viper just grinned. This was fun, and he was feeling pretty damn good right now about how everything was going.

"Ya done talking? Finally! Anyway, bloody well knew he would do it." Valdemar grinned as he waved his hand. "And if it ain't a feat that calls for a proper celebration. Drinks are on me!"

A large keg appeared, and the god held it up and yelled toward all the observing gods, "Hey! Get over here already; grab a mug!"

Receiving a direct invitation from a Primordial was not something any of the many observing gods would ever refuse. Quite the opposite, as they reveled in the opportunity. Many gods went by and offered their congratulations to the Viper for how well his Chosen had done, which Vilastromoz gladly accepted.

Everyone got their mugs of ale one after another, and the Viper saw no reason not to accept, joining in on the festivities and grabbing a mug.

Raising a mug of his own, Valdemar infused his voice with energy and spoke loudly, **"To Jake Thayne and a new record!"**

With that, he downed the entire mug, joined by a few others, who only a second or two later stumbled back as the alcohol, brewed to be strong enough for a Primordial to get drunk, entered their system. Vilastromoz also had a taste, and he found it quite pleasant, even if it did carry too spicy of an aftertaste for the otherwise sweet initial impression.

For once, the Viper simply enjoyed the moment. There was cause for celebration, after all. Jake and the Viper both had things to celebrate... while a certain other pair of Chosen and Patron were probably feeling quite the opposite.

Jake defeating Ell'Hakan on the Leaderboards had most definitely been within their margin of error for the story the two were trying to spin. They would either lean into a story where Ell'Hakan beat Jake and thus began his comeback to defeat Jake or turn him to the "good side"...

Or they would embrace the other possible path where Jake won, in which case Ell'Hakan would remain the underdog... The problem was that Jake hadn't just beaten Ell'Hakan. He had beaten both of them. The announcement that Jake had also beaten Yip of Yore was a brilliant strategic move by Jake—certainly made entirely accidentally—as it helped undermine the god who sought to become the first slayer of a Primordial.

It was publicly known, at least among the gods, that Yip had held the top spot before. That he was the greatest genius of the multiverse, and for the top genius, what were truly his limits? As an unrivaled genius, it was only natural he would keep improving, perhaps to one day even become strong enough to slay the Malefic Viper. To slay the Primordial who had been hidden away for so long and was, in the eyes of many, the weakest of the twelve.

Now... now he was no longer the top genius. Jake had stolen that throne—that legend. Ell'Hakan was also troubled now, for he was no longer just the underdog fighting another Chosen genius; he was fighting the top genius. Was he even qualified anymore to challenge Jake? So much doubt had been sown with that one announcement.

And doubt was the biggest enemy of those two storytellers. They needed certainty and steadfast belief in the legend they tried to spin, not potential confusion and people questioning the validity and possibility of their claims.

All in all, Jake had performed damn well, and Vilastromoz definitely owed him a beer. Not just with regard to the stuff with Yip; the Viper also had to thank him for the personal rewards he got from having his Chosen be the new holder of the top spot on the All-Time Leaderboards.

———

Ell'Hakan held a stoic expression as the Unique Lifeform known as Minaga announced the arrival of the Viper's Chosen. This was not an unexpected turn of events, as he and his Patron had already discussed the possibility of the Viper's Chosen doing extremely well within Nevermore.

On a personal note, he did find it disappointing that he'd lost to the human. Ell'Hakan had done his utmost within the World Wonder, even beating the other Chosen in regard to how many floors he had completed. What was perhaps even more infuriating was that Ell'Hakan had genuinely started to believe he would take the top spot.

When he'd announced his Challenge Dungeons multiplier, none had surpassed him, only reached a tie. This had given him the false belief there was a good chance the Viper's Chosen hadn't surpassed him either. If he had, why wouldn't he have revealed it? Getting a 100% multiplier would have led to much prestige in its own right, so even if he had failed to take the Era's Pinnacle spot, he would have won at least a minor victory.

Due to this lack of an announcement, Ell'Hakan had proceeded with the assumption that the other Chosen had equaled his score at best. This had meant the next years after the Challenge Dungeons would be crucial. In order to get a leg up, he had even prepared a welcome party on the city floor after floor seventy-five to receive the Viper's Chosen and have him waste some time dealing with them while trying to sow discord within his group. However, Ell'Hakan never even heard of him appearing on the city floor, his rival having just skipped right past it to proceed to the next floor.

Even so, Ell'Hakan had just focused on himself and his own party. Sure, they'd ended up losing a member, but the one who'd died could only blame himself, and Ell'Hakan's Patron would handle any blowback from the god backing his fallen party member.

He had kept doing his utmost until the very end, where he'd at least had the foresight to make sure he would finish before the Viper's Chosen. There were only upsides to this; had he ultimately won, finishing first would've blocked the Chosen of the Malefic Viper. Meanwhile, if he lost, he would've at least still gotten the title. A title that was most certainly nothing to scoff at.

Era's Conqueror of Nevermore – You have done what few could

ever hope to achieve: proven yourself the pinnacle of an entire era. No matter how brief the achievement or how fleeting this position is, this accomplishment can never be taken away from you. Attain first place on the Era Nevermore Leaderboards, proving yourself an Era's Conqueror of Nevermore. Only one Nevermore Performance title can be held at a time. As an Era's Conqueror of Nevermore, you are a near-unrivaled expert in dungeons, increasing stats gained from Dungeoneer and Dungeon Pioneer titles by 40%. +10% All Stats.

It was a truly great title that Ell'Hakan was more than pleased to have achieved. He was fully aware that had he and the Viper's Chosen not shared a generation, he would truly have had no equal... but then again, perhaps he was only as powerful as he was because of the Primordial's Chosen. It helped Ell'Hakan push himself further and truly seek to be the pinnacle of this generation... no, this entire era.

All in due time.

As the light beam descended upon the newly arrived Chosen of the Malefic Viper, and Minaga announced how he had won, Ell'Hakan saw the Leaderboards shift, his own position falling one spot. Clenching his fists, he maintained his composure, even if the situation didn't particularly—

"I failed to clarify what I meant by top dog... because I'm not just talking about this era. It's with pleasure I can announce that for the second era in a row, the All-Time record has been broken!"

For a moment, Ell'Hakan let his expression drop as he stared toward the Chosen of the Malefic Viper in the distance. He briefly met the eyes of the other Chosen before regaining his wits.

This... was not part of the plan, and Ell'Hakan cursed internally, as he knew they would have to shift and adapt the narrative even more... potentially toward a direction Ell'Hakan was truly not a fan of.

———

Jake remained as composed as he could while the music blared and all eyes were on him. He wasn't sure what he was supposed to do or say. During the Chosen Ceremony, he'd at least had a game plan and been able to prepare himself, but now he was just thrown onto what was effectively a stage. Should he say something? Smile and wave?

It didn't get better when people started to actually fucking clap. Meanwhile, Viridia stood right behind him with her head slightly bowed and an incredibly happy grin on her face. Jake also saw Farleigh, the vampire patriarch. He wanted to say hi, but the situation didn't seem to allow it. The Fallen King noticed Jake's discomfort and sent him a quick mental message to assist.

"No need to act. Simply be. Remain stoic and reveal no emotion. Just maintain a straight back and forward-looking eyes to exude confidence. You are the Chosen of the Malefic Viper, and someone recognized as the most talented genius of this generation, if not the entire era. To you, this result is naught but a meeting of your expectations."

Jake took the words to heart as best he could, doing just that. He simply stood there and let everyone observe him as they clapped. It felt unnatural to him, but seemingly no one else thought so. Seconds passed, and with every moment, Jake really hoped something would happen... Maybe Valdemar could swoop down and kidnap him to try and force him to join Valhal? Yeah, that would definitely be preferable to his current situation.

Luckily, Minaga continued before things got too awkward.

"Alright, calm down, people. It's just someone breaking a record that has existed for a few billion years and beating every single other living being who has ever competed on the Nevermore Leaderboards. No big deal." Then Minaga turned a bit more serious.

"All jokes aside, the overall performance surpassing that of previous eras should only bring us joy. It's representative of the growing base of Records supporting every faction and individual through the continued expansion of the system. Represents progress on a wider scale. Jake Thayne is simply the one standing atop a new generation that will be the first to lead us into the 93rd Era. These C-grades you see before you represent the future of every faction. They represent possibilities of Paths never seen before and even more new Records to populate this multiverse.

"Finally, to the ones who do not find their names on a Leaderboard despite hoping so, do not see this as a failure you should take to heart. You were beaten by the strongest generation ever—one you are still a part of. The Path to godhood is no sprint, and to try and reach ultimate power is an endless trek. You are still in the early stages of walking that Path. So, if you believe what you did was a failure, don't. Become a success to show the multiverse what you are capable of, as it's your future that defines you... and if you ascend to

godhood, no one will give a damn that you did horribly in Nevermore while still a C-grade."

Minaga was surprisingly wholesome as he spoke some words of
encouragement to everyone, especially those who might be feeling dejected
after realizing they hadn't qualified for the Leaderboards. Looking at the
Fallen King, the Unique Lifeform sent him a quick answer. *"I got top 100
on the Universe Leaderboards and top 250 on the Era one."*

He didn't sound disappointed, so Jake just nodded as Minaga's presentation seemingly neared its end.

**"Anyway, time to wrap things up. Thank you all for coming to
this little ceremony of ours to celebrate the next generation and the
revelation of the Leaderboards. Quite an eventful one this time
around, eh? I hope you all enjoyed the show and will continue to
revel in all the amenities of Nevermore City during your stay.
Goodbye for—"**

Suddenly, Minaga stopped as his eyes went wide, and he yelled loudly,
"Wait! How is this even possible!? There was one more!?"

A beam of light descended from above, and Jake, along with many
others, looked over to see the new arrival...

Which was a Minaga clone wearing a funny hat and holding a sign
saying *Made you look* with a dumb grin on his face.

"Gets them every time," Minaga said, grinning as he bowed. "Too-
dle-oo!"

With that, Minaga disappeared along with all of the beams of light and
projected figures. Jake also felt much of the attention on him beginning to
fade, and he subtly breathed out a sigh of relief. Now that everything was
finally done with, Jake was just looking for a way to get out of there... until
the words of Viridia washed away all hope.

"Congratulations, truly," she sent. *"You have brought honor to the
Malefic One and the Order of the Malefic Viper, and I cannot even hope to
begin to express my gratitude. Now, are you ready to meet the others?"*

Jake looked at her and sent back, *"Meet the others?"*

*"Ah, you perhaps weren't aware. It's customary for all of the top
performers of the Leaderboards to have a get-together after the rankings have
settled down a bit."*

Jake then realized he was still not free, and that he would face one of
his most dreaded challenges: forced social interaction with strangers.

CHAPTER 48

A LITTLE GET-TOGETHER

If Jake was being perfectly honest, he had hoped to quickly bail and get out of Nevermore City as soon as it was convenient. He would first want to visit the Order and ensure everything was good there before making his way back to Earth, where he was certain quite a few changes had also taken place. After his Chosen Ceremony and all that had happened surrounding that, this was pretty much a given, and he hoped Miranda hadn't been too overwhelmed.

However, it appeared that was not an option, and Jake ended up following Viridia and the Fallen King to a large conference hall of sorts. When Viridia had said this after-party was for the top performers on the Leaderboards, she hadn't just meant those from the Era Leaderboard. In fact, those from the Universe one were far more interesting to have there due to their newness to the multiverse.

As Viridia explained telepathically while they walked over there, *"It has long been known the most effective way to forge an alliance and recruit new members is through first creating positive relations between a member of your faction and the one you want to recruit. While it may sound cynical, the objective is to effectively use friendship to convince someone to join a faction. This is especially true when it comes to those from the new universe, as they often have a difficult time relating to a large faction, while the bond between themselves and another individual is far from comprehensible."*

"To be clear, you are not actually expecting me to do any recruitment or alliance-forging, right?" Jake wanted to clarify this before he arrived at the conference hall.

"Not actively. Your mere performance will serve as a recruitment tool in

its own right, and many factions and unaffiliated individuals are already showing much interest. This is a time when the Malefic Viper is making his comeback to the multiverse, and your performance in Nevermore will be their first impression of him. They will see that only a few years after his return, he already has a Chosen who has proved himself a talent at the pinnacle, which is about as good of a showing as one can have."

"So... what am I even meant to do?" Jake asked, genuinely unsure. "I don't see it doing the Order much good for me to be in a room with Ell'Hakan alone. While we can't fight due to being in Nevermore City and all, there is a good chance we will enter a battle of words... and as much as I hate to admit it, I don't think that's a fight I'm gonna win."

Viridia was silent for a moment before answering, *"I cannot tell the Chosen what to do... but I would avoid getting into any squabbles needlessly. You have nothing to prove and only prestige to lose if you engage with the other Chosen. Let others handle Yip's Chosen, and simply try to learn about and maybe even get to know the other top performers, especially those from your universe. Information is scarce on them. It also won't hurt to get to know young talents from the other large factions, as there is a good chance you may encounter many of them in the future during your adventures. The system has a tendency to push talents together, either directly through system events or in subtler ways none can truly understand."*

"In other words, you're telling me to try and make friends?" Jake asked clarifyingly.

"You can view it like that. But more than that, you are there for them to try and make friends with you, as I am certain the majority will be more than happy to approach you. As the Order has not been in the best state for the last many eras, we have adopted a very neutral position in the multiverse, resulting in us having few enemies and allies. This lack of any strong relations means you become more approachable, as doing so won't lead to any political issues. So I believe it highly probable you will be sought out by most of the talents on the Era Leaderboard."

"That all sounds very logical and extremely annoying... but fine, I'll try to play nice," Jake finally relented.

At least he wouldn't be alone there. Using a Pulse, he spotted others also making their way toward the conference hall, including his Nevermore party members and quite a few familiar faces from Earth. Arnold was walking with his group of void-related lifeforms, and surprisingly, they were all headed toward the hall. He also saw Carmen heading there with some people from Valhal. So, yeah, he would have some pleasant company.

"Hey, who exactly will participate?" Jake asked. *"You said people toward the top of the Leaderboards, but I see a lot heading there. Like, a lot."*

"Top 250 on either Leaderboard. With the repeat of names between them, I expect no more than four hundred individuals to participate. Do also note that only you C-grades will take part. The rest of us will be busy in the interim, dealing with other political endeavors."

"Got it," Jake confirmed once more, and they soon reached the hall. It was just a large building, with the inside further spatially expanded. Jake looked at the Fallen King, who had been floating alongside them, and gave him a look. *"You got briefed on what's going on?"*

"The vampire gladly did so," the King answered.

"Thanks for getting him up to speed," Jake said as he looked at Farleigh, who'd quietly walked with them while apparently telling the King what was about to happen.

"It is the least I can do." He smiled and bowed. "I'm also uncertain if this information is useful, but I came to learn from an acquaintance of mine that this get-together will be hosted by a trusted person of the Wyrmgod of Nevermore."

Jake looked at the vampire before sighing. "Probably Minaga again..."

"That... I cannot rule out. But I do not believe it is." The vampire patriarch scratched the back of his head.

"Guess we'll see."

Standing before one of the entrances, Jake and the Fallen King were already beginning to gather a lot of attention on themselves. Especially Jake, but a Unique Lifeform also gathered interest in its own right. Seeing no reason to stand outside and get ogled, the two of them entered the large venue, while Viridia and Farleigh stayed outside, seeing them off.

Once inside, Jake scanned the area and found a nice empty spot for him to chill at. He threw the Fallen King a look, and the Unique Lifeform gave a small nod and followed. Luckily, it wasn't just the two of them for long, as a bird entered the hall and headed straight for Jake.

The Sword Saint soon entered, and then even more familiar faces made their appearance, including Arnold and Eron, who headed toward Jake and the others after only briefly looking around. Jake smiled when he saw Carmen waltz in, and she did not even think twice before splitting off from the others from Valhal to head their way.

Jake had barely said hello to her when he saw two more Earthlings walk in, neither of whom he'd really expected to see there: Maria, the fire archer blessed by Gwyndyr, and Jake's very own brother, Caleb. Waving them over, Jake soon had gathered quite the group... Indeed, when Casper arrived with a group of Risen, he quickly bailed to join the gathering of individuals with one thing in common:

They were all from Earth.

Jake, Sylphie, the Sword Saint, Carmen, the Fallen King, Caleb, Maria, Arnold, Casper, and Eron... ten people from a single planet in the new universe. Okay, the Fallen King kind of wasn't, but he had been revived on the planet, so Jake counted him. This gathering reminded Jake a bit of the get-together they'd had on Minaga's City Floor, just without Jacob and Bertram, with the setting also rather different.

Quite a lot of attention was garnered as their diverse group gathered. So many factions represented in one group was rare to see, and many were throwing them looks as if trying to spot the commonality.

Ell'Hakan had also entered and stood a good distance away with his own gathering of people. Jake just ignored him as he followed Viridia's advice, acting like the other Chosen didn't even exist. Which was quite easy as he did a bit of catch-up with old friends and family.

"Who in the hell did you scam to make it into the top 250?" Jake asked Caleb shortly after he arrived.

"You," Caleb said with a smile. "At least, I'm pretty sure that's why Umbra suddenly wanted me to join an even better team after the Challenge Dungeons to try and get more Nevermore Points."

"So, what you're saying is that you owe me big time?" Jake grinned.

"Sure, sure," his little brother said, waving him off. "I would say I'm also surprised to see you take the top spot, and Umbra sure seemed like she was, but honestly, I can't say I am."

"Glad to impress an ancient god and meet my little brother's expectations," Jake said jokingly.

After a brief talk with Caleb, Jake checked in with Maria, who had joined a group of followers from the Crimson Flame and apparently done quite well for herself in Nevermore. She did know she had primarily been chosen for her group because it required someone from the new universe, but she still believed she'd carried her weight.

She also recognized that her relations with Jake made Gwyndyr want to invest more in her. Even if they weren't close in any way, she was still the closest Gwyndyr had. Jake also learned that the reason everyone had gathered around him almost instantly wasn't just because they liked his company. They had borderline all been told to seek out Jake once in the conference hall, in large part to communicate that their faction already had an established bond with him. Bullshit politics that Casper confirmed to be true. Not that Jake particularly cared, and he felt many of them gladly used the excuse of wanting to forge a stronger bond with the top performer on the Leaderboards to chill with all the other Earthlings.

He also asked Eron some stuff, generally just catching up and getting a feel as to how others were doing. Carmen mainly complained about her party members disappointing her with how fragile they were while throwing in jabs about a certain Challenge Dungeon that may or may not have contained labyrinths. Besides that, they just shared stories of Nevermore and had a good time.

Arnold was just using their group as cover as he stood and fidgeted with a tablet, not engaging with anyone. Just as Jake expected of him.

All in all, things were chill for a while as the entire hall filled up, and due to the already pretty large group Jake was with, no one really bothered them quite yet. The fact that they hadn't officially started yet also helped, as people were still arriving.

Soon, there were just shy of four hundred people in the hall... and with that, a magic formation activated that sealed them off from all observers who wanted to spy on them. Jake instantly felt a few dozen observers disappear as it activated, most of whom were gods or high-level mortals, as far as he could tell.

Shortly after this formation activated, a stage rose in the middle of the hall and a figure appeared on top of it. Jake looked over and saw the newcomer, who was definitely not a C-grade.

"Welcome, everyone. It's my pleasure to have you all here, young talents of the multiverse. I will be your host today, and am present to ensure everything proceeds calmly and peacefully. I will also admit that it will be nice to make some new acquaintances I may come to know better in the future." The man was... probably A-grade.

"Now, I am not much for speeches, but let me still give a small one. One that can also serve as a small warning and food for thought. All of you have already proven yourselves, but do not forget Minaga's words. You may be exceptional now, but who is to say the same will be true in a few centuries or even just decades if you stop striving to improve? If it's worth anything... when I was in C-grade, I didn't even crack the top 1,000,000 on the Leaderboards, as far as I could tell. I was just a wyvern back then, trying my best to find my Path, teamed up with a ragtag band of others who also didn't have any trusted comrades. Compared to me back then... you all definitely have a better start on your Paths. Revel in that knowledge, but do not let your momentum and potential go to waste."

This presenter had shoulder-length silvery hair and a fair, almost androgynous appearance. He wore what looked like an expensive medieval shirt, pants, and boots, and looked entirely human outside of his eyes. Rather than pupils, it looked like he had spinning wheels of light in there. Again, could still be human, but Jake felt an aura he had gotten quite good at recognizing: that of a dragon.

As Jake looked at the dragon in human form, he also felt an odd sense of pressure. One he could easily resist... but it hit somewhere he hadn't ever felt being hit before. It wasn't that of grade suppression or even power, but one born of Records related to something Jake hadn't expected:

His Blessing.

An Identify quickly confirmed the reason, and Jake realized this was a first.

[Dragon of the Silverstorm Fissure – lvl ??? – True Blessing of the Wyrmgod]

Ignoring the overly long name, this was Jake's first time ever meeting the Chosen of another Primordial.

"Ah, where are my manners? A few of you seem to have already checked me out yourselves or realized who I am, but allow me to introduce myself: I am known as Silverstorm, Chosen of the Wyrmgod of Nevermore. Currently A-grade, but with hope I will reach S-grade soon. It's truly a pleasure to meet all of you."

Jake observed the man closely, and he didn't have a shadow of doubt in his mind: this Silverstorm was definitely already at the level of a weaker S-grade. Jake also felt that despite his gentle outward appearance and words... he was hiding quite the bloodlust. He was not someone who had reached his current level of power through making labyrinths and crafting, but through slaughter.

"Now, let me not delay things anymore. Enjoy, all of you."

With a clap of his hands, tables appeared all throughout the hall, containing food and beverages. A few dragonkin also entered the hall, and as Jake checked out a few, he saw they were all C-grades and all held Blessings of the Wyrmgod. Jake had expected them to join the get-together, but he soon realized... they were the catering staff.

The stage in the center also lowered into the ground, just fading into solid matter, as the Chosen of the Wyrmgod returned to ground level. Nearly instantly, he was swarmed by people from the different large factions, and Jake truly knew the dragon's pain. Living the life of a Primordial's Chosen wasn't easy.

"This is going to be so awkward," Carmen commented after a few seconds. "Who thought it was a good idea to throw a bunch of strangers into a conference hall? They could have at least set up a dueling ring in the middle or something."

"Doubt you would find many willing to fight you. All that would do is expose your skills in front of hundreds of potential future rivals." Caleb shook his head. "I sure wouldn't want to fight anyone here."

"I hate that you're probably right," Carmen eventually mumbled, annoyed. Turning to Jake, she threw him a look. "So, what's the supreme genius of our generation going to do?"

"I have absolutely no plans, and I'm currently in full survival mode," Jake answered, only half-joking.

"Just take it easy and deal with whoever approaches you," the Sword Saint advised. "You are the Chosen of the Malefic Viper and, as Carmen said, the top performer on the Leaderboards. It's only good etiquette they come to you and not the other way around."

Jake slowly nodded as he looked toward one of the tables right next to them. Reaching out, he sent out a string of mana and pulled a glass to him, not spilling a single drop. "Well, in preparation for that, I think I'm going to check out if they at least got some proper alcohol."

"Ree?" Sylphie asked.

"I feel like you shouldn't," Jake said, as Sylphie had asked if she could also have something to drink.

"Ree..." Sylphie screeched, dejected.

Jake took a swig of the drink he was holding, and as he felt it burn its way down his throat, he got an idea. "Alright, alright." He shook his head and, using a bit of mana manipulation, made a small bubble of the liquid float out of the glass and up toward Sylphie. "Have a taste."

Sylphie, with glee, opened her beak and consumed the bubble. Half a second later, she began flapping her wings rapidly while making screeching sounds. Having fully expected this result, Jake had erected a sound-sealing barrier around the two of them while Sylphie learned alcohol maybe wasn't for her.

Still smiling, Jake saw the Sword Saint motion, making him remove the barrier just as Sylphie calmed down.

"Approaching on your six," the old man said.

"I noticed, but kind of hoped he was gonna change his mind," Jake said while calming down dear Sylphie, as he had indeed seen the approaching man. Turning around to meet him, Jake saw the one he recognized as the Demon Prince of the Fourth Hell and third-place finisher on the Leaderboards, trailing only after himself and Ell'Hakan.

Guess it makes sense the number three approaches me first... though I don't hope it becomes a pattern.

Jake feared it would when he saw the elemental called Wintermaul throw a look toward Jake's group, seemingly checking out when they'd next be free...

This is going to be a long day...

CHAPTER 49

A PROPOSAL FROM THE HEART

Jake hadn't met many demons throughout his time in the multiverse. Even if they were a widespread and diverse race, he just hadn't really run into many of them outside of the occasional enemy here and there. Outside of dungeons, Irin was the only one he really knew, and she was practically an entirely different species compared to the Demon Prince of the Fourth Hell.

He had mostly ashen skin with what looked like crackling blue lines across it. As if he had more mana in his body than it could contain. On his forehead was what looked like an amethyst crystal merged with his flesh, veins spreading out from it. The elaborate blue robe he wore was clearly not of poor quality, and overall, he radiated the aura of a rich young master. However, he clearly also had the power to back up his demeanor. With him were four other demons who Jake guessed were from his party, meaning they'd all made it into the top 250.

Stopping in front of Jake, the Demon Prince smiled and reached out a hand. "A pleasure to make your acquaintance, Chosen of the Malefic One. Rather than waste your time, let me get straight to it: I have come with an inquiry that I hope you might entertain."

Jake didn't reach out and grab the other man's hand right away. "What kind of inquiry?"

Pulling back his hand, seemingly not at all offended, the Demon Prince smiled even more than before. "How you might benefit from assisting us in bringing about the second coming of the Cerulean Devil."

Yeah, Jake had no idea who the fuck that was.

This was far from the first time someone had walked up to Jake and dropped some kind of grand revelation while looking at him as if he should totally know what the fuck the other party was talking about. How in the hell—pun intended—would he know about some devil that he guessed, based on context clues, was dead?

Alright, think fast, Jake. Devil is the name demons give to their gods, so likely some dead devil who really liked a slightly off-blue color. Got it... and I guess it's pretty easy to figure out how he wants me to help.

Keeping his calm, with a great assist from the mask, Jake looked deep in thought for a second. "I wonder what the Demon Prince might have in mind."

The demon observed Jake's reaction for a moment before speaking. "I guess my name would make things a bit clearer. I am known as the Cerulean Demon, or the Demon Prince of the Fourth Hell. I have inherited a fragment of the Crystalized Cerulean Devil's Heart, and the Legacy of the once great ruler of the Fourth Hell." The Demon Prince motioned toward the crystal on his forehead. "None of this is a secret... nor is it a secret that the remaining fragments are not as potent as those that once were."

"Am I right to assume you are not asking the Chosen of the Malefic Viper, but what people call the Harbinger of Primeval Origins?" Jake asked clarifyingly, already certain about the answer.

"A bit of both, I believe, but that will depend on if you are willing to take up the task and how you would be able to accomplish it. In either case, we—no, I—require your unique talents to do something we believed impossible and that I have cause to believe you may be capable of."

"Let me take another guess—you want me to use my abilities on one of these Devil Heart Fragments to make it more powerful?"

"No... no, not quite; we may have our own methods to do that, even if they are likely more flawed than what you can accomplish." The Demon Prince shook his head. "What I want to ask of you is not to empower a fragment of the Crystalized Cerulean Devil's Heart... but to create an entirely new, fully formed Crystalized Cerulean Demon Lord's Heart using the Records of a fragment... My fragment."

Jake's eyes narrowed a bit. "You want to create a Demon Lord's Heart with the Records of this Cerulean Devil using that crystal in your forehead? That... sounds risky, to say the least."

"Of that, I am fully aware. Usually, I also wouldn't attempt such a thing, but this iteration of Nevermore has offered me a golden opportunity. I am certain you are aware of what this is." The Demon Prince summoned a familiar-looking item that Jake quickly Identified nearly on instinct.

[Crystalized Demon Lord Heart (Legendary)] – The crystallized heart of a Demon Lord. The immense energy contained within the crystal can be absorbed by any demon, allowing them insight into the heritage of Demon Lords. Grants demonic powers to any item it is fused with. Can be used in a limited number of alchemical products of a demonic nature.

"You, too, have one of these, yes?" the demon asked. "Or at least someone in your party does."

Jake nodded slowly. "I have one."

Smiling, the Demon Prince admired the heart. "A Crystalized Demon Lord Heart is usually created through a ritual using a Demon Lord, which inadvertently leads to some of the Records of this particular Demon Lord entering the crystalized heart. However, look at his heart. It's pure. Untouched. So brimming with power and Records pertaining to no particular Demon Lord. Now, imagine if all this energy was aligned with the Cerulean Devil. No, not just the energy of this heart... the energy of several hearts, fused together with my fragment into one!"

He radiated ambition as he spoke of his plan, and Jake was... not entirely averse to the idea. In fact, it sounded quite feasible as the demon went on, even if it remained incredibly risky. Moreover, based on what Jake had heard, he wouldn't even need to use his Jake Juice. Arcane energy should be more than good enough as long as he kept everything under control during the fusing process.

Jake also understood why the Demon Prince had approached him in particular. It truly hadn't just been due to his talents as the Harbinger of Primeval Origins—even if that certainly did play a part. It had as much to do with Jake being the Chosen of the Malefic Viper, and the greatest alchemist in the multiverse, in the eyes of many. Plus, as the Harbinger of Primeval Origins, he had already shown himself capable of similar feats before.

One also had to remember that the Demon Prince likely needed a C-grade to do the ritual. It was similar to how a B-grade blacksmith couldn't craft weapons for a C-grade, their Records simply not up to the task. So if the Demon Prince wanted to craft this heart to be usable by a C-grade, he would need another C-grade to craft it... and Jake likely looked like the best candidate to do just that.

As for why Jake would accept such a task? Perhaps a better question would be why he wouldn't. To do a ritual with several legendary hearts and a fragment likely of a rarity above even that was bound to reward a shitload of experience and Records. Plus, it would be a positive diplomatically. And, finally, he did, of course, expect some form of payment. All of this naturally assumed he would succeed.

"So, what say you?" the Demon Prince asked after a few seconds of Jake looking deep in thought.

"I'm tentatively interested, but I will need to think it over a bit," Jake said. "Assuming you don't want me to just try and wing whatever ritual you are planning, more likely than not killing you in the process."

"I would very much prefer an outcome that does not involve my death." The demon smiled, at least seeing the humor in Jake's response. "That was all I wanted to ask, and I will not take up any more of your time. Congratulations once more on your achievement, and I will be staying here in Nevermore City for a while after this ceremony. If you do accept the task, do be aware it's time-sensitive in nature, and I would much prefer it to happen before you depart from Nevermore City. I will make sure to have everything prepared ... and I will do anything in my power to fulfill any request you may have, should you succeed."

Jake simply nodded. "I will send a response with my decision before I leave the city."

"That is more than I could ask for," the Demon Prince said with a small bow as he backed away.

It was definitely an interesting proposition, even if Jake had a few doubts... many of which were dispelled by what his brother told him next. "If you are doubting whether you can trust that demon, you definitely can. The Cerulean Demon is part of an old Lineage of very proud demons, and they value verbal contracts nearly as much as written ones. It would quite literally hurt his Path if he went back on his word or tried to deceive you."

"You seem to know an awful lot about demons," Jake commented.

His little brother smiled. "What can I say? They are the best clients and wonderful assassins. Great work ethic all around, and they are one of the few races where the majority love paperwork."

"Huh," Jake muttered. Now that he was thinking about it, Irin did seem a bit too happy doing administrative tasks...

As Jake was thinking, he was already prepared for the next group of people to approach. The ice elemental, Wintermaul, who had seemingly been waiting for his chance, was just about to make his way over when someone else jumped ahead... Someone the C-grade ice elemental would definitely not raise an issue with.

The silver-haired Chosen of the Wyrmgod appeared only a few steps from Jake, space barely affected as he moved through it effortlessly. He looked at Jake as he took a step forward, and Jake's mind worked at high speeds, trying to figure out what he was supposed to do or say.

Villy had never coached him on how he should act around the other Chosen of high-level gods. Was he supposed to act like they were the gods they represented? Villy talked about that often being the case... but he was also a Chosen, so maybe he should just treat them how he wished to be treated? But then there was the issue of the grade disparity, so... yeah, fuck it, Jake would just act like usual.

Right as Jake was about to greet the other Chosen, the dragon named Silverstorm smiled brightly and reached out to grab Jake's hand faster than he could react.

"We meet at last!" the dragon said in a jovial tone. "I have been hoping to finally get a chance to thank you! Ah, and it sure was wonderful to see you take the top spot on the All-Time Leaderboards! I cannot hope to begin to express the debts of my gratitude, my fellow Chosen!"

Jake, completely confused, had no idea what the hell the guy was talking about. "Why would you want to thank me?"

Had Jake met the dragon before? Nope, definitely not. He would have remembered if he had. He was good at forgetting stuff in his spatial storage, but he tended to remember auras pretty damn well, and this definitely wasn't an aura he had experienced before.

"Oh... I guess you haven't been told," the dragon named Silverstorm said, still looking extremely happy to see Jake, even if he'd calmed down a bit. "You're the reason why I'm the newly selected Chosen of the Wyrmgod, and this little gathering is more or less my first big public appearance."

Once more, Jake had to search his memory to try and figure out when or how the hell he'd caused that to happen... but luckily, the dragon quickly saw through his confusion and elaborated.

"Let me clarify. I have carried the Divine Blessing of my Patron for a long time and was one of a dozen or so Chosen candidates, waiting for our Patron to choose one of us." Jake then felt space subtly sealing off around them. Clearly, the other Chosen only wanted Jake to hear the next part. "The thing is... and this part naturally shouldn't be shared... my Patron is not the best at picking his Chosen. That's not to say that he is bad when it comes to who he picks, as that would just be putting myself down needlessly. It's more to do with how and when he picks them."

"Now you got me curious... and I'm still waiting for why I am the reason you got chosen to be the Chosen," Jake commented.

"Getting to it," Silverstorm said. "You see, there are nearly always a few Chosen candidates picked, all of us working for our Patron and fulfilling our duties, such as handling the mortal affairs of Nevermore, gathering certain items that are required, recruiting more members, handling politics... All of the things we should not bother the Primordial with. We do all this to ensure our Patron can focus on the World Wonder itself, which has led to a minor problem. He can get a bit... engrossed in it."

Though Jake was beginning to understand, he wasn't sure what to feel...

"So, what tends to happen is that all of us candidates kind of end up staying as candidates while he works on the World Wonder... and by the time he decides it's time to make a selection, we are all dead to the endless march of time. That means the next batch of candidates will be picked and given Divine Blessings, as the Wyrmgod naturally doesn't want to pick someone as his Chosen without vetting them first, and the cycle continues. To a god who has lived for that long, even the life of an S-grade is short and forgettable, so perhaps this is all understandable. I also just don't think my Patron cares particularly much about having a Chosen compared to many of the other Primordials, on account of him not really having a faction. However, it seems that seeing an old acquaintance inspired my Patron to select a Chosen rather promptly this time around, with it ultimately being me who was chosen. So for that, I must truly thank you, even if you caused my Blessing simply by existing."

Remaining silent for a while, Jake still wasn't sure what to say or feel. But one thing was for sure: "I don't think you have anything to really thank me for. Doesn't look like he picked you as his Chosen without merit."

Silverstorm was powerful; of that, there was no doubt. As for that entire thing with the Wyrmgod being forgetful... Jake could totally see that happening. Duskleaf had talked so many times about massively long experiments, and as a dungeon engineer in charge of the most popular World Wonder in the multiverse, Jake didn't doubt the Primordial also kept busy. One could even say that Silverstorm had been unlucky to be born just before a new initiation, as that meant the Wyrmgod was even busier than usual. Now, though, it seemed Jake had somehow turned that misfortune into good luck.

"Even if you do not believe you did anything that requires my gratitude, you still have it," Silverstorm insisted. "Anyway, I didn't mean to be overwhelming; I just had to thank you. Oh, and the Wyrmgod did say that he may be interested in seeing if you could assist him in getting a lower-grade Chosen using your unique abilities at a later time. But, as I said before, the Primordial tends to work on pretty broad time scales, so don't think it will happen any time soon, if ever, unless you ascend to divinity."

"I still think it's unnecessary to thank me, but you're welcome about the entire Chosen thing, I guess," Jake said. "As for the other Chosen thing, I won't make any promises."

"No need for any rush or pressure. Just know that I owe you a favor that I will be sure to repay one day. Now, let me dispel this barrier, and let us show the multiverse how great of friends the two Chosen of Primordials are." Silverstorm smiled... Perhaps this had been part of his plans all along.

The barrier faded as Jake and Silverstorm shook hands, and the dragon gave the human a nod. "Thank you for taking the time, and congratulations once more. I hope you enjoy yourself the rest of the day."

With that, the Wyrmgod's Chosen left again and was promptly swarmed by interested parties, and almost like clockwork, Wintermaul was right there to also greet Jake. At least, that was what Jake thought he was there to do... until he noticed the elemental wasn't really that fixated on him. Instead, he was far more interested in Sylphie, from the looks of it.

Wintermaul had slightly changed his form even more and now looked like a human with extremely pale skin, wearing a fur coat of sorts. His body was still made of pure mana, and the subtle signs of ice and frost could still be seen here and there, but he could easily pass for a human from a distance. A human that was definitely also an ice mage.

"I greet thee, Chosen of the Malefic One, and I bring congratulations for your accomplishment," the ice elemental said to Jake as he came over with a small bow.

"A pleasure," Jake said, nodding. "I should congratulate you for your impressive performance as the top-scoring monster of the era."

"Your words bring me honor," the elemental said, very much going through the usual pleasantries. "If I may, would it be possible to speak to your companion?"

Jake already knew who the elemental was talking about, and he just shrugged. "Depends on if she wants to talk to you."

Sylphie was definitely interested, though, as she also stared at the ice elemental. They both seemed to evaluate something about each other before Wintermaul finally said, "The Sovereign of Ice greets the Sovereign of Wind."

"Ree," Sylphie responded.

The elemental nodded. "Your authority is strong indeed. Impressive."

Jake decided to just sit back for once and observe as the two of them communicated back and forth, seemingly discussing elemental magic stuff. It was nice that Jake wasn't the center of attention for once, especially after talking to the Demon Prince and Wyrmgod's Chosen. The other Chosen had been especially mentally taxing to deal with. So, to see the elemental and semi-elemental talk was a nice break, and he was happy Sylphie seemed to be making a new friend. Yep, definitely a good turn of—

"Your power truly makes you worthy, and I believe I too have proven myself worthy. Join hands with me—you as my empress, and I your emperor—and may our offspring be—"

And just like that, Jake was about to break the rule of no fighting in Nevermore City.

CHAPTER 50

AN UNEXPECTED ENCOUNTER

Jake took a second to process what the hell the elemental had just said, yet before he could even do that, he felt bloodlust radiate from behind him. This shook Jake back to reality as his own aura also unconsciously leaked, joining that of three others.

Carmen had been the first to stare daggers at the elemental, seemingly ready to pounce, but, to Jake's slight surprise, the Fallen King and Sword Saint also showed their clear displeasure, looking ready to assist Carmen should she attack.

However, before any of them could do or say anything, Sylphie proved that she didn't need anyone to stand up for her with a no-nonsense reply. "Ree."

The elemental was taken aback, partly by Sylphie's screech and partly by the four C-grades seemingly ready to turn him into slushed ice. Still, he managed to keep his head cool as he focused on Sylphie.

"Please do not take offense. It would be an honor for you to join hands with me. We are both holders of autho—"

"Ree."

"Such a reply is shortsighted and—"

"Ree."

After a pause, he asked, "What?"

"Ree, ree, ree... ree," Sylphie explained, perched on nothing in mid-air.

Surprisingly, Wintermaul looked deep in thought for a moment before he tried one last time. "I... I can change, or we can maybe find a solution..."

"Ree." Sylphie shook her head, making the poor ice elemental look dejected.

"Alas, it seems we are not meant to conjoin our Paths. I apologize if I overstepped... I did not mean to make anyone uncomfortable or make any enemies."

Turning to Jake, who was still looking at him with narrowed eyes, the elemental bowed. "I congratulate you on your brilliant accomplishment and shall take my leave before I make a further fool of myself."

With that, the elemental backed away. Jake, the Fallen King, the Sword Saint, and Carmen didn't let him leave their sight before he was far enough away.

"I swear, if not for those rules," Carmen muttered as she unclenched her fists.

"An uncalled-for proposal," the Sword Saint also said with a hidden anger in his voice.

"Such arrogance for an inferior being that dares approach one superior to himself," the Fallen King chimed in, clearly not being entirely honest with himself as he tried to hide his protective feelings toward the little hawk.

As for Jake... well, he briefly considered the possibility of marking Wintermaul and tracking him down in the 93rd Universe to have a "conversation" around boundaries and social etiquette, but that didn't appear to be necessary.

Sylphie had handled the situation surprisingly well, and while the knowledge did make Jake a bit uncomfortable, she clearly understood what the elemental had asked. Her response had also indicated that she'd genuinely considered the offer carefully before rejecting it. With brilliant Sylphie-level arguments, too.

"So... not to butt in, but I have no idea what Sylphie's screeches meant," Caleb muttered, having not yet learned to speak Sylphian Hawk. Perfectly understandable, as it took a bit to get used to the nuances of the complicated language.

"She just kindly explained to the ice elemental why they could never work out," Jake said, shaking his head.

"And that explanation was?"

"He's too cold, hard, and spiky to make a proper nest, and Sylphie only likes to sit in cozy and warm places, making them incompatible," Jake explained to his little brother. "Plus, he didn't even have any feathers. Which is apparently a deal-breaker to her."

"Ree," Sylphie confirmed with a firm screech.

"I... I see," Caleb said, looking at Sylphie and then back at Jake. "I guess that works."

"Sure as fuck hope it did," Carmen added in, throwing a final glare toward the elemental. "I don't hope for that icy bastard to try anything weird somewhere without a Primordial keeping watch. Then again, I do like crushed ice in my drinks."

"Him trying again would appear to be an unwise decision," Caleb agreed as he glanced at the four people who had been ready to start a major conflict over an elemental with absolutely no flirting game.

The atmosphere in their group had grown a bit tenser due to the elemental's visit, but it soon calmed down again when Jake gave Sylphie some well-deserved scratches for dealing with the situation well.

Even if Sylphie was more than fifty years old by now and was to many definitely an adult, Jake still thought she was too young to get into any committed relationships quite yet. Then again, to Jake, she would always be the fluffy little ball of feathers that would run away whenever he took out his cauldron, screeching bloody murder.

Once things were calmer, they spoke more internally, finally giving Jake a chance to catch up with his old buddy Casper. And it turned out his friend had a favor to ask.

"So, you know how the Prima Guardian is descending on Earth in a few years?"

"Still got a system notification hidden away somewhere about it," Jake said, nodding.

"Well, so do I, which is kind of the reason I'm asking. There is good reason to believe there will be some unique rewards from the event, and not participating would kind of suck, so could you maybe hook me and some others up with a way back to Earth? Just for the event." Casper seemed a bit nervous about making the request.

"Of course," Jake said. "Shit, if you want to stay afterward, that would also be fine. It's ruled by a council of sorts now, and there are already plenty of immigrants there, so no one would notice a bunch of Risen also settling there again."

"Thanks for the offer, but we're quite happy with what we got going on," Casper answered. "We have quite a nice hidden world set up by now on our floating piece of rock. New Yalsten, we call it. It will take some time, but with the root you gave me, I think we can regrow the tree again and turn it into a proper mystic realm."

"Fair enough," Jake said, nodding. "Guess I'll have to visit one day."

"One day." Casper smiled. "Right now, it's still very much closed off to outsiders. I could still get you in, but honestly, there isn't much going on there. Unless you want a lengthy lecture in Dungeon Engineering and the work that went into creating New Yalsten, that is."

"You know what? I think I'm good." Jake smiled back.

"To add, I will also be returning for the event," Eron suddenly said, having overheard their conversation. "For the same reasons, too."

"I also heard that some people from the Holy Church, including the Augur, will return," Maria added further. "Wouldn't be surprised if most people try to return to their native planets to reap some rewards."

Jake smiled again. "Sounds like we'll have quite the gathering." At this point, he kind of felt bad for this poor Prima Guardian. Imagine arriving on a planet only to be met with Jake and all the others standing there, ready to pounce... Definitely didn't sound like a fun time.

"Speaking of having quite the gathering," the Sword Saint said after a bit, "I believe I have a few people I should seek out. I sense two others who also carry the Blessing of my Patron, and it would be rude not to at least go say hi."

"Yeah, I think I should regroup with Azal, too," Casper said. "By the way, I asked if he wanted to speak to you directly, but he didn't seem keen on the idea." He shook his head. "He did something very dumb to try and get a higher spot on the Leaderboards, and I don't think he is feeling good about you pushing him out of the top 5."

Jake nodded as he remembered what Nevermore had said about Azal. He had been the one to gain the most levels out of everyone, but only by making a dumb sacrifice that would likely hurt his future. Jake was a bit too curious, though.

"What exactly did he do to gain so many levels?" he asked, knowing full well there was a good chance Casper couldn't or wouldn't respond.

Casper sighed. "I probably shouldn't share this, but fine. The weapon he carries around is a powerful mythical sword he made himself, and with it, he can absorb spirits and souls to increase its power and use them as resources for certain skills. However, at the end of Nevermore, he chose to do a pre-prepared ritual to absorb and destroy all of the spirits he had gathered—not just throughout Nevermore, but since he made the sword right after he evolved. Repairing the sword will be expensive as hell and take a long time, and his Records took quite the hit, but I think he can recover, though it won't be easy. He isn't a bad guy, and it does suck, but he cares way too much about the honor of the Risen and all that. At least he can take solace in having beaten every person from the Holy Church, even if I heard they did something similar. All in all, as I said... he did something dumb, in my opinion."

"I see," Jake said, the others having also listened intently.

What Azal had decided to do was similar to if Jake had done a ritual to absorb all the curse energy inside of Eternal Hunger. Well, alright, it would also require Jake to have a Path that revolved around curses far more, but if he did, absorbing all the curse energy to gain a lot of levels would technically have been possible. It would be stupid and lead to a shaky foundation and a limited, if not ruined future, but it would have been an option.

These thoughts also inadvertently made the face of a young half-elf pop into Jake's head. He shook his head to dispel the thoughts. What Azal had done wasn't even close to the same level as Temlat.

"Anyway, enjoy," Casper said, starting to leave a few seconds later to give Jake time to process what he'd said. "Oh, and I will now have to also share some details about you with Azal to make things fair. Like the fact that you are still walking about with the curse version of a nuclear bomb in the form of a katar."

"Fair enough; not exactly a secret." Jake smiled as he saw his old coworker and friend off. It was still a bit weird that Casper had turned into a pale undead, but alas, what can you do about it?

With Casper gone, Jake just took the time to observe the hall a bit using his sphere. Carmen and the Fallen King were talking, comparing whether his claws or her fists were tougher, and Eron and Arnold had somehow ended up standing and staring at a tablet together. The healer motioned and pointed at the screen, and Arnold gave short responses.

Meanwhile, Maria talked to Jake's brother, leaving just Jake and Sylphie, the bird enjoying the relaxing downtime. Elsewhere in the room, others had also gathered and talked, with a huge group around Ell'Hakan, pretty much as far away from Jake and the other Earthlings as possible. Silverstorm was with a woman with golden hair and horns, which he recognized as the princess from the Regalflight and fifth-place finisher. Together with the two of them was also the seventh-place finisher, the Disciple of Heartsoul Daolord, a young girl who looked barely in her teens, though she was definitely far older in reality. He had a good feeling he would get to talk to them later, and based on how they occasionally threw some glances his way, he even got the feeling they were talking with Silverstorm about him.

Jake had been a bit surprised Dina hadn't gone over to say hi yet, but he soon saw why, as she chatted with a few people he presumed to be members of the Pantheon of Life and United Tribes. More accurately, the wolf who'd taken the ninth spot on the Era Leaderboards, Grimclaw Noxmane. Jake did know that the United Tribes and Pantheon of Life had a close relationship, so it made sense she was doing a bit of politicking. He also saw the beast that reminded him a bit of the Great White Stag with this group, along with several other beasts and beastkin who had all placed highly.

Speaking of beasts, Jake had to look further before he found another person of interest. Lopas, the sloth-like beast—fourth-place finisher of the universe and eighth in the era—was currently sleeping under a table, having taken one of the tablecloths to cover himself.

Jake could only respect that. He was a sloth who knew what he wanted, and what he wanted was apparently to just be left alone and sleep. Jake also looked around a bit for the person known as Immortal Faith and the Eastbound Monk, but he wasn't sure what they looked like. The monk was probably part of the Dao Sect, though, with Immortal Faith... Well, that person could be part of pretty much any faction with gods in it. He had even considered if it was maybe Eron who had used that name, but that wasn't the case.

Finally, of all the factions Jake looked for, there was the Holy Church, the largest of them all. In their group alone, they had nearly forty people— one-tenth of the total number of people attending. While they hadn't ended up taking any of the absolute top spots on either the Era or Universe Leaderboards, they could still be said to have dominated it simply by the sheer number of people they had in the top 250.

Alongside their many allies who also stood nearby, with even Ell'Hakan standing not that far away, it was almost as if a line had been drawn down the middle of the conference hall. There definitely were cliques, with many of the fully neutral factions standing in between.

As Jake was standing there, just looking out at the room after taking another drink, he was approached by someone. He turned and looked, instantly seeing an appearance that didn't match what was in his sphere, and he also felt an aura he wouldn't ever fail to recognize.

"Greetings, Viper's Chosen, and congratulations on your performance," the young woman said as she got closer, raising a glass with a smile on her lips.

Jake narrowed his eyes. "Thank you, Miss...?" He kept calm, wondering what the hell this person was doing here. Everyone else was busy, and Jake made sure to keep some distance, trying to speak privately without any of the others involved.

"Does what you call me matter?" they responded, swirling the liquid in their glass. Jake realized that only he could hear what this person said, his own replies inaudible to everyone except them. "And no reason to act that suspicious. I have come with no ill intent, just curiosity about something."

Jake narrowed his eyes further as he stared at the young woman... the shapeshifted Eversmile. He couldn't understand why he had appeared here or how he had even done so. Then again, he had seemingly been able to hide his true identity even from the Wyrmgod inside of Nevermore...

"What are you curious about?" Jake asked... and the answer was not at all one he expected.

"Where did you get those boots?"

CHAPTER 51

MYSTERIOUS BOOTS & DRAGON
PRINCESSES

J ake had been so damn distracted by everything else going on that he
hadn't even noticed Eversmile before he was right there. Sure, he had
seen the figure approach, but his aura had been entirely hidden, and
with so many other notable presences filling the hall, he had managed
to blend in long enough to surprise Jake.

Yeah, this type of setting really wasn't for Jake, throwing him off this
game that much. And now this...

To say Jake was taken aback by the question would be an understatement. Especially when one considered who it came from. Eversmile wasn't
some insignificant figure, and Jake's mind began to work at high speeds as
he tried to give a noncommittal answer. One that could hopefully give him
at least some information to go off.

"Why are you asking?"

"Karma," Eversmile simply answered. "Now answer me."

Jake really wanted to tell the guy—or girl, as at this point, Jake had no
idea what the fuck Eversmile was—to just fuck off, but he felt like that
wouldn't be a good idea. Eversmile was just too eccentric and unpredictable. Plus, the true answer shouldn't be that suspicious.

"From the Challenge Dungeon made by the Viper," Jake answered
honestly.

"Hm? That could explain some of it, I presume," Eversmile said, seemingly deep in thought. "But not all of it. If these boots are indeed connected
to Vilastromoz, then it appears I will need to have a conversation with him."

By now, Jake himself was getting really curious. So he took a chance.

"Why the curiosity? Is it that odd to see boots given to a Chosen with powerful connections to their Patron?"

"You are fully aware there is something with those boots far more complicated than merely a connection to your Patron." The Primordial didn't even try to entertain what Jake said. "However, seeing as you have been cooperative and the Malefic Viper would likely gladly share the details of our future conversation with you, I shall give you an explanation."

Jake heard the sound of fingers snapping... and then the world around him seemed to twist and turn. He felt like the ground beneath him fell away, everything replaced with an empty space that made him feel as if he was deep underwater.

The only two things that remained were Eversmile and Jake himself. Then the strings appeared. Multicolored threads spread out from Jake and Eversmile, countless in number, but soon nearly all of them faded. However, a few strings still existed, and Jake saw them all connected to the boots on his feet. One of these threads led to Eversmile himself, while all the others simply disappeared into the vast emptiness of the space he was in.

"As you can see, there appears to be a powerful karmic connection between these boots and myself," Eversmile said, motioning toward the thread connecting them. "Despite that being the case, I cannot see any reason for why this would be... much less the cause of all these other threads."

Jake, floating in the odd space, took a moment to really get his bearings. Things were seriously freaky, especially since he also felt the conference room all around him through his sphere, making it certain he hadn't actually been transported anywhere. In the real world, he was just standing and staring into empty space while his mind and potential soul were somewhere entirely different. What made everything even worse was the distortion between these two things, as time seemed slowed in the real world and overly fast in this special state.

"What are these other karmic threads?" Jake asked, confused.

"This is the second conundrum," the god said as he reached out and touched one of the threads. "I do not know. They are obscured... No, they make no sense in the first place. As if they are misplaced within both space and time, leading to something that once was or never came to be. Some of the threads I do recognize, though."

As Eversmile began walking through the odd space, he tapped a karmic thread. "This one leads to the Malefic Viper. Unsurprising, based on what you said."

Jake slowly nodded. Yeah, that made sense.

Tapping a second thread, Eversmile spoke again. "And this... this is Valdemar."

That... was weird?

A third thread was tapped. "Blightfather."

Okay, definitely weird.

And a fourth. "Holy Mother."

Eversmile continued speaking while walking a circle around Jake, tapping thread after thread.

"Wyrmgod."

"Starseizing Titan."

"Rigoria."

"Yggdrasil."

"Stormild."

"Aeon."

Then he reached the last thread.

"Daofather. All twelve Primordials connected to a single pair of boots through karmic threads. And do not misunderstand: These are not weak connections. They are firm, old, and seemingly without any good reason to exist, as I cannot read their history or origin."

By now, Jake was more than a little confused. As he searched his brain for an explanation, he blurted out a potential cause without much thought. "These boots did once belong to the Viper himself. Like, he used them while he was a mortal..."

"Another potential reason, perhaps," Eversmile said as he thought deeply. "The connection to the Malefic Viper does appear more unique in nature than the others, so perhaps... No..."

Jake felt sidelined upon realizing that this entire thing hadn't been done by Eversmile simply out of the kindness of his heart or to help Jake. He had done it to try and make Jake spill more information, which had definitely worked. Perhaps it had also been done to spark Jake's curiosity and see if he truly didn't know.

However, even with all that, Jake wasn't going to say anything about the First Sage. Not just because that was private history between the Viper and his first master, but because Jake wasn't sure what he'd do with the implications of it all if the First Sage was somehow the cause. Hopefully, he would get some answers when they had their fateful meeting... He just needed a lot more profession levels to make that happen.

"Alas, information is lacking, and the best course of action would be to simply question Vilastromoz," Eversmile said after a bit.

"What's the current working theory?" Jake ended up asking, not really expecting an answer.

"That, as you said, the boots once belonged to the Malefic Viper, and they were infused with further Records in the process of becoming an item in one of the Challenge Dungeons created so many eras ago, leading to some sort of mutation caused directly by the system simply because of how much time passed before they were claimed. Some form of mutation that linked the boots to the Records associated with being a Primordial, thus also naturally forming a karmic connection with all who carry those same Records."

Jake was a bit surprised by Eversmile's straightforwardness.

"However, this is highly improbable, just the best theory till more is known," the Primordial finished as he threw Jake a final glance. "You have been of some assistance. Take this experience as a reward for your help. Oh, and I say this genuinely: congratulations on beating Yip of Yore on the All-Time Leaderboards. It's both an achievement worth recognition and something that has certainly turned this entire situation with him and the Malefic Viper far more... interesting."

With those words, the world around Jake collapsed again, and everything returned to normal in an instant. Jake found himself back in the hall, standing alone with a glass in his hand, no sign of Eversmile anywhere.

"Ree?" Sylphie chirped, confused, as Jake looked around on instinct.

"It was..." Jake began before stopping himself. "Eh, the woman that was just there. The one I talked with."

"Ree?" Sylphie asked, even more confused.

Jake just looked at the hawk with his own confusion before shaking his head. "Never mind. I blame the alcohol. See, this is why you shouldn't drink."

"Ree!" Sylphie definitely agreed, having already learned about the horribleness of alcohol.

Smiling, Jake hid his thoughts and considered what Sylphie had said. According to her, Jake had just been greeted by some woman who said congratulations before walking off into the crowd, with Sylphie seemingly finding the encounter so forgetful she couldn't even remember how the woman looked.

This was really odd, considering they had both just seen Eversmile's transformed form, and as C-grades, they both had near-perfect memories...

yet when Jake also tried to recall the transformed Eversmile, he just saw the "true" form of Eversmile instead.

I really don't want that dude as a straight-up enemy, Jake thought. *That would be fucking terrifying.* A shapeshifter with such skills could cause so much chaos without anyone even realizing it...

Deep in thought, Jake barely noticed when two people approached him.

Only when they were nearly upon him did he snap out of it and notice it was the princess from the Regalflight and the Disciple of the Heartsoul Daolord. Quite a few people noticed the two approaching Jake, as if several expected something interesting to potentially happen. The Demon Prince even threw Jake a smile from across the hall as he raised a glass.

Soon enough, the two arrived, and Jake turned to meet them. The princess was at the front, and Jake felt her aura easily from this close. He could definitely see how she had gotten such a high placement on the Leaderboards. She was powerful, and she had also gained a lot of levels, as one had to remember she wasn't a dragonkin, but a full-on dragon. Well, she soon would be... As a C-grade, she was still not fully mature yet, very much the same as Sylphie. Though, looking at her humanoid form, Jake definitely wouldn't describe her as immature.

"Greetings, Chosen of the Malefic One," the princess from the Regalflight said while doing a curtsy. Jake didn't even know people in the multiverse really did curtsies... "I congratulate you on your exemplary performance within Nevermore and can only begin to imagine the wonders you will show us in the future."

The Disciple of the Heartsoul Daolord simply smiled and nodded, not saying anything. Jake didn't take offense, though, as he responded with a nod of his own. "Pleasure to meet you both, and let's not pretend like the two of you didn't also do pretty darn well."

"Your words bring me honor," the princess said with a smile. "Allow me to properly introduce myself. I am Aishalstromoz Regalflight, daughter of the Dragon of Gold and Princess of the First Golden Palace. However, you are more than welcome to simply refer to me as Aisha, as my friends call me."

Lots of stuff in that one... and hey, Jake knew who this Dragon of Gold was. Aurustromoz, the current leader of the Regalflight—the most powerful of all the Dragonflights but also the fewest in number. Oh, and the eighth-place finisher on the All-Time Leaderboards, above even Ell'Hakan. To learn she was his daughter meant her father was an extremely powerful god, and from the looks of it, she was living up to her

Lineage. As for all that stuff about the First Golden Palace and all that... yeah, Jake had no idea, but it sounded impressive.

Moreover, Jake also kind of understood the implications of her requesting that he call her something only friends usually do. Not that he particularly cared, as he wasn't going to refer to her with some long title or her long name if he had an alternative.

"And you can also just call me Jake, Aisha," Jake said politely... his answer apparently coming as a surprise for some bloody reason, as the not-yet-fully-mature dragon blushed and turned her head slightly away...

"Al... alright, I shall... Jake..." Aisha said, stammering as she quickly worked to regain her composure. The volume at which she spoke his name would make even mice ask her to speak the hell up.

The Disciple from the Dao Sect just smiled, seemingly finding the situation amusing, as she still didn't say anything, which... Jake honestly found kind of weird. Something Aisha likely noticed and jumped on, as it was a great change of topic.

"Please do not be offended. As the disciple of the Heartsoul Daolord, I am sure you can understand why she isn't able to converse normally." The dragon princess's explanation... didn't explain jack-shit to Jake.

Luckily, Jake got an assist from Silverstorm, who had been observing their exchange and seemingly had information Jake didn't know. *The Heartsoul Daolord is a master of Willpower and making their will a reality. As the disciple of the Heartsoul Daolord, every word of hers is infused with the power to alter the world around her, making even a casual word effectively an attack. In fact, any way she communicates her intent toward the world will have such an effect.*

Jake listened intently... and he was pretty sure he remembered seeing something similar in a video game before the system, which instantly made Jake assume this Heartsoul Daolord was some old, bearded man living on an icy mountain.

Anyway, Jake nodded in understanding as he looked at the Disciple. "No worries—I wouldn't want you to speak and push me back with unrelenting force by accident."

The Disciple of the Daolord smiled and nodded, still not really communicating much. Actually, why wasn't she just using telepathy? The Fallen King couldn't speak, but he could still release his voice through soul magic stuff all around him, and as the Disciple of the Heartsoul Daolord, she should be able to do something similar. Soul was literally in the name.

Then again, Jake clearly had fuck-all idea how her Path worked, so he probably shouldn't ask a question that would just make him appear ignorant. He already felt uncomfortable enough as things were with all the attention on him, and embarrassing himself definitely wouldn't make things any better.

"Thank you for your understanding." Aisha bowed her head slightly. "Now... I will confess, I did not merely approach you to offer you my congratulations, but for more personal reasons."

Jake realized there was indeed something up, yet he nevertheless inquired further. "What could the princess of the Regalflight possibly need of me?"

She seemed a bit nervous as she explained, her volume a bit lower than usual, "I know you have had some interactions with both the Emberflight and the Azureflight, some of which haven't been the most positive... and I just want to ensure that there is no lingering resentment or negative sentiment between you and the Dragonflights."

"No worries. Truly," Jake said, trying to sound reassuring. "I'm not that petty as to be offended by something small. Besides, the guy from the Azureflight seemed to have learned his lesson directly from the Viper, as far as I remember."

"That he did." Aisha nodded, looking solemn. "It was an... unfortunate encounter. One we take full responsibility for."

"Again, don't worry," Jake said, waving her off. "I'm not going to hate an entire race or faction just because one of their members sucks. So relax. We just met, and thus far, you've made a positive first impression, so let's just say that balanced out all the prior negative encounters, and we're back to neutral."

He really didn't want a bunch of dragon tribes to think he bore a grudge. He liked dragons. Dragons were cool—simple as that.

Aisha smiled. "I... That would be great."

"Great. Then from here, let's create some positive encounters," Jake said, with the intent to be polite and create positive relations with the Dragonflights.

"That is... If the Chosen wants, then..." The dragonkin princess suddenly blushed and hid her face, while the Disciple of the Heartsoul Daolord shook her head and elbowed the dragon in the side as if telling her to get her head out of the gutter.

Turning toward Jake, the Disciple of the Daolord smiled and bowed as she finally spoke. **"Let us meet again."**

Jake felt an odd shift in the air as the Disciple dragged away the dragon who looked like she was about to overheat with how red she was. Jake sighed internally as they left. *That went well, I guess?*

CHAPTER 52

HEARTFELT CONVERSATIONS & HIDDEN AGENDAS

"You're a real smooth-talker, huh?" Jake heard from behind as Carmen walked up to stand beside him. "Sure trying to get that little dragon princess wrapped around your finger."

"Hm?" Jake said, not entirely sure what she was getting at. "No, I was trying to be polite. She just seemed a bit sheltered and nervous."

"Damn, you're dense at times." Carmen sighed. "Think about it. That little princess has definitely been praised and raised up her entire life, with every single male influence in her life being either a family member, someone trying to get in her pants, or people too fucking scared to try anything, as they know the kind of trouble they could get into for offending her. Then you come along, confident and unbothered by her status, treating her like an equal and being all nice, while she also knows her dad would probably be over the moon if she dragged you home with a ring on her finger."

Jake stared at Carmen for a while before shaking his head. "I think you're reading way too much into this."

"She definitely isn't," his brother said, backstabbing him by deciding to join her. "Let me put it in terms you can probably understand better. Imagine if it was you, before the system, as a young man. One day, you are asked to deliver something to some attractive millionaire model, who then proceeds to have a nice conversation with you, treating you incredibly friendly. All the while, Mom and Dad are hiding behind a bush ten meters away, giving you thumbs-ups, telling you to go get her."

"I... don't think that analogy works," Jake muttered.

"Kind of does," Carmen agreed. "Not really, but kind of, I guess.

Anyway, the point is, most women who view you as a potential partner will see you being nice as a green flag and potentially even the most mundane flirting in the world. Coupled with them being sheltered, with no idea how to act around the opposite sex, you get situations like this."

Jake looked at her and Caleb, who nodded in the background, and sighed. "So, what's the solution?"

"Fuck if I know." Carmen shrugged and smirked. "Not my problem either. Just trying to be helpful here so you are at least aware of what you're doing and don't get taken by surprise when you suddenly get a surprise proposal. In all honesty, I find your cluelessness and all the blushing fair maidens quite amusing."

"Ditto," Caleb seconded. "Also, it would be hilarious if you dragged a dragon home to Mom and Dad. Even more hilarious if you dragged a whole bunch of women home from all sorts of different races..."

"Are you hinting at wanting me to introduce someone to you? Damn, I'll have to tell Maja what you're up to while exploring the multiverse..." Jake gave his brother a faux-disappointed look.

"Alright, alright," Caleb said, raising his hands in surrender, "you just keep doing you. Anyway, I actually came to say that I'll have to do some politics of my own, so see you around. Oh, yeah, and I feel like I say this every time, but do come by Skyggen for a visit sometime, yeah?"

Jake nodded. "Okay." Yeah, he really should visit, especially after spending such a long time in Nevermore.

Caleb walked off, and Jake noted that Maria had also bailed somewhere. The others were busy on their own, though Carmen was still standing beside Jake.

"Don't you have to do some Valhal stuff?" Jake questioned her.

"I am doing Valhal stuff right now by standing next to you and chatting in full view of a bunch of major factions, including that orange fuck across the room," Carmen responded.

"Ah," Jake said as he smirked. "So you only bother to hang around me because it's work?"

"Not gonna lie—I am getting a bit annoyed at both you and Valhal at this point. One day, they're telling me to get closer to you; the next, they're telling me to stay as far away as I can, and now we're apparently back to them wanting to make it look like Valhal has a good relationship with you." Carmen shook her head. "Fucking politics."

"Amen," Jake agreed wholeheartedly before quickly putting up a barrier of stable arcane mana to keep their conversation private. "But if it's worth anything, I have a feeling they're not going to flip-flop more after I met Valdemar."

"Nah, definitely not." Carmen shrugged, and with the barrier up, she seemed a bit more open to sharing information. "Seems pretty keen on making you join Valhal at this point, and from what I heard, Ell'Hakan and Yip of Yore are fully aware of that, potentially even on board. I have no fucking idea what they're planning, but it definitely includes separating you from the Malefic Viper, one way or another."

Jake was a bit surprised as he looked at Carmen. "You seem awfully informed. Do they keep you up to date on things?"

"Apparently so." She casually continued, "Gudrun agrees with wanting a closer relationship between you and Valhal, and she seems to think the best way of doing that is through me. Pretty sure they want me to be a honeypot or something like that. Haven't directly asked me yet, but damn, have they hinted at it."

"I'm not sure how to respond to that," Jake said, scratching the back of his head.

"Now you're the one overthinking." Carmen grinned as she punched Jake in the shoulder. "Ain't no fucking way I'm going to be anyone's honeypot."

Jake felt a bit relieved as he nodded in response.

"Not that you can't have some honey once in a while," Carmen said flirtatiously. "Just don't get your dick stuck in the pot."

Chuckling, Jake shook his head. "Not gonna say no when offered."

"You know, I just realized how damn good I am at my job," Carmen said as she stared out of the transparent stable barrier of arcane mana. "Look at how damn well I showed the multiverse the great relationship between us, to the level of making that little dragon lady of yours jealous."

Jake had indeed spotted a certain dragon in human form throwing glances their way, with the Disciple of the Heartsoul Daolord trying to take her attention away from Jake and Carmen talking.

"Oh, well. I guess I should stop breaking the hearts of every young lady present." Carmen then threw Jake a deep look. "Hm, maybe it's the mask? Nah, definitely the dangerous and mysterious aura."

"Very funny," Jake said as he waved her off and dispelled the arcane barrier.

"Hey, it has its appeal." Carmen shrugged as she walked off. "See you around, Jake."

"Enjoy politicking," Jake said.

The Runemaiden gave him a middle finger before she decided to finally get back to some people from Valhal.

Returning to the others from the Earth group, Jake had an enjoyable chat with Eron and Arnold. Alright, mainly Arnold, as Eron preferred to listen, not really adding much and only ever chiming in when he asked some questions about certain concepts. The three of them ended up mainly discussing the House of the Architect as time passed slowly, the conversation quite enlightening.

By now, most of the people who really wanted to talk to Jake had. More did come by simply to congratulate him but without wanting anything in particular. People from the Altmar Empire, the United Tribes, and a few other factions, big and small, either invited or restated their offer for him to visit, and they were all very polite about it.

From these interactions, it did become clear that besides the titles Chosen of the Malefic Viper and Harbinger of Primeval Origins, Jake apparently now had a third title that made others both wary of him and interested in forging good relations. In other words, his prestige was building, and it was building at a far higher speed than that of his so-called rival.

Something this rival clearly knew... as it appeared Viridia's prediction had been slightly off. She had predicted that Ell'Hakan would keep a good distance from Jake throughout the get-together, avoiding any interactions with him. However, Jake soon saw him approach, not even walking with any of his cronies or people from other factions. He made his way over all alone, and as the person with the second-most interest placed on him in the whole event, his movements caught quite some attention. Since the entire get-together was also winding down at this point, far less interesting things were happening, making the Chosen's actions stand out even more.

Jake calmed himself down as he saw Ell'Hakan approach from behind. He quickly considered what the hell the other Chosen was planning, as he also realized the implications of his approach.

For him to seek out Jake was almost a sign of submission—a sign that he viewed Jake as someone with a higher status, making it only proper conduct for him to make the approach. What's more, for him to do so alone indicated he came as an individual and not someone representing any faction or gathering of factions.

When Ell'Hakan got within ten or so meters, Jake turned to meet him. Acting arrogant or haughty would gain Jake nothing. He had treated every other person who'd approached him so far politely, even those he didn't really know or wasn't a fan of, and treating Ell'Hakan differently or even antagonistically would only play into his story that they were fated rivals or something dumb like that.

Jake especially wanted to avoid looking like some arrogant young master. Arrogant young masters never won.

One could almost sense the tension in the room as Ell'Hakan did something Jake had not expected. He cupped his hands and slightly bowed toward Jake with a smile. "Greetings, Lord Thayne. I wish to congratulate you on being the new champion of the All-Time Leaderboards. It's truly an achievement worth recognition."

It took a lot from Jake to not just blurt out and ask what the hell the guy wanted, but he kept his cool. He couldn't let emotions control any of his actions, especially not in front of Ell'Hakan, who could read everything. Jake really didn't like being put in this situation, but he would have to manage as he evaluated things.

Ell'Hakan had clearly taken a more respectful stance. His choice of calling Jake "Lord Thayne" was definitely also deliberate. It communicated a closer relationship than merely using a title and remained polite in nature while also conveniently leaving out mentioning any relations to Jake's Patron. Just from this alone, and his earlier talk with Carmen, Jake had a guess as to what Ell'Hakan's goal was.

"Thank you," Jake said calmly, responding in kind yet failing to avoid taking at least a small dig at the other man. "I should also congratulate you on your placement as Era's Pinnacle. To hold such a title for even a moment is impressive."

Ell'Hakan smiled at Jake's response, as by now, quite a lot of attention had gathered on them. The conflict between Yip of Yore and the Malefic Viper was an undercurrent of the multiverse that all factions with influence of any kind knew about. It was a situation they closely monitored, and a social clash between their two Chosen had to be of significance.

"I did my best, and I guess I couldn't have done more than that," the other Chosen said with a sigh. "Still, I take pride in what I did accomplish, even if my performance ultimately only allowed me to enter the top 10 of the All-Time Leaderboards."

"All anyone can do is their best," Jake agreed noncommittally, trying to give Ell'Hakan as little ammunition to work with as possible while remaining polite and neutral.

"Isn't that the truth," Ell'Hakan said with a melancholic smile. Then, in a tone slightly louder than before, he added, "It's what we all strive to do. To do our best in any situation, with the power, resources, knowledge, and state of mind we have at that moment in time. Yet sometimes, even our best does not prove enough, as was proven on the Leaderboards this day. This... brings me to the past, where I also made decisions and did things that I, at the time, believed were my best course of action... but now, in retrospect, only bring me regret."

Jake had tried to not give Ell'Hakan ammunition... yet it seemed like he had done just that as the other Chosen continued, "My failure was to be found in the knowledge I had, forming the reason behind my actions. Assumptions created from nothing but my own biases and through sin by association... Something I now realize was a mistake, and the second reason I approached you here today, Lord Thayne." It was clear he wanted as many eyes on him as possible as he bowed.

"With my deepest sincerity, I apologize for past transgressions. I acted foolishly and committed sins I can only hope to be forgiven and strive to make up for." Speaking as much to the room as to Jake, he continued, "I invaded your planet, killed people close to you, and created chaos, believing I was doing the right thing. Believing I was freeing your world from a tyrant who wished to use the planet in the fashion we have seen the Order of the Malefic Viper use so many others. I was wrong and had jumped to conclusions, and now I realize you never acted on the orders of your Patron. I realize you are not the second coming of the Malefic Viper... You are Lord Thayne, your own person, through and through."

There were few times in Jake's life when he had been more glad he wore a mask than now, because his face did not look good. He had no idea what to say, as by all accounts, Ell'Hakan's words sounded honest. Moreover, Jake did not detect the slightest use of any Bloodline shenanigans—assuming Jake would even be able to detect it.

The only place it was maybe used was Ell'Hakan using it on himself, making his own words sound more emotional and sincere. Because damn, did he sound genuine in his apology. Thing is... Jake knew he was playing at something, and Jake desperately tried to figure out what that was so he could get out ahead of it before it was too late.

"In fact, I came to learn that despite your identity, Jake Thayne is far more than just the Chosen of the Malefic Viper. Harbinger of Primeval Origins and now the one holding the top spot of the All-Time Leaderboards are but two of your titles. Look at those you associate with, too. Your fellow natives, friends, blessed by more than half of all the Primordials."

Ell'Hakan no longer had his head bowed. He looked up with a smile on his face. "You are truly a one-of-a-kind existence. A Bloodline Patriarch, wielding more potential than possibly anyone the multiverse has ever seen, and for the longest time, I didn't realize that you weren't this special because you were the Chosen of the Malefic Viper... You would be you, regardless of which god had realized your excellence first."

His words were clearly praise, but they made Jake feel slimy, as he now had a really good idea of what he was trying to do.

"I say all this with the hope of making it clear... I never bore any animosity toward Lord Thayne. Only the Chosen of the Malefic Viper. The one friend I killed was also a follower of the Viper, making me believe he, too, was a fanatic who would only cause the multiverse harm." Ell'Hakan adopted a sad look. "Now I see he may have been innocent... and that knowledge truly gnaws at me.

"Alas, I hope we can look toward the future. I hope you will give me the opportunity to make up for the sins of my past and repay you, Jake Thayne, for the transgressions I have caused. I swear now that I will truly do my best to try and set things right."

Jake simply stared at the other Chosen for a bit, and just as he was about to open his mouth, Ell'Hakan bowed one more time.

"Please, take the time to consider my words... I do not need an answer here today. I merely wished to express my emotions and regret, as I hope to one day be forgiven. Regardless of your decision, know that I no longer hold any animosity toward you. Even if you can't forgive me, I, at the very least, hope that the next time we meet, it will not be as enemies. I truly do not want to fight you if it can be avoided."

Ell'Hakan did not leave more time to say anything, speaking loudly to the crowd and Jake alike, "Thank you for listening to my words so patiently today, Lord Thayne. May next we meet be an encounter we both look back upon and call fortunate."

With those words, Ell'Hakan bowed and was swiftly teleported away... leaving Jake with a final telepathic message.

"Do not think my words a mere ruse or deceit. I truly have nothing against the man known as Jake Thayne, only he who identifies as the Chosen of the Malefic Viper... and I have a feeling you perhaps are more of the prior than the latter. You do not need the Malefic Viper, but he desperately needs you to rebuild himself. I already know how thin your loyalty is and how little faith you have in your heart. This is not a sin, but merely recognizing your own worth. So, I implore you to rethink your position. Rethink if staying with a god such as the Malefic Viper is truly in your best interest in the long run.

Valhal, a reputable and respected faction, is also interested in having you join them, and if you choose to throw off the chains that is the failing Malefic Viper, I truly believe the War God himself would take you as his Chosen. I will not tell you what to do, just remind you of the many alternatives you have. You will thrive anywhere; you need no one. Can find a home anywhere. So why stay on a sinking ship?"

CHAPTER 53

TEMPORARY FAREWELLS

Jake wasn't sure if he should have said or done anything before Ell'Hakan left. It felt as if he had given the other Chosen the floor and allowed him to say and do whatever he wanted... but that didn't necessarily mean what Ell'Hakan had done was in his best interest.

As the saying goes, never interrupt an enemy when he is making a mistake.

Ell'Hakan was clearly under the impression that the relationship between Jake and Villy was on thin ice. That Jake was not satisfied with him as a Patron. That, or he at least believed Jake didn't hold any loyalty toward Villy... which he was kind of right about.

Jake didn't hold the kind of loyalty one would expect of a Chosen toward a Patron. He held no faith, and he wouldn't just do whatever the Viper told him to do. Ell'Hakan and Yip of Yore had already figured this out, from the looks of it, making their current strategy make a lot more sense.

Eversmile is likely involved in some way, too, Jake mentally noted as he considered the situation more deeply.

From this entire thing, coupled with what Carmen had said, Jake reached a conclusion... They had officially adopted a narrative that did not require them to kill Jake. This was likely a direction they had moved toward for a while, but only now did they state it outwardly and speak it into reality. The fact this had been done in front of a crowd that would quickly spread it to every major faction in the multiverse also wasn't a coincidence.

They wanted to show that they held no animosity toward Jake, just the

Malefic Viper. The way they framed it also wasn't entirely idiotic. Jake doubted it would be long before it was also common knowledge that Valhal was interested in recruiting Jake, potentially even offering him a similar position. All of this was to give Jake an escape.

Ultimately, this meant Jake staying with the Malefic Viper was framed as a choice. That Jake chose to stand on the side of an evil tyrant, despite having been given ample opportunity not to, giving them an excuse if they did somehow kill him. Perhaps they also bet on Jake's sense of self-preservation and wanted to clarify that should he choose to abandon the proverbial sinking ship, there would always be a lifeboat waiting.

Jake would guess the two spin doctors didn't really want to do this but felt forced into it. There was definitely pressure from many factions who would oppose Jake's death before they could make use of him. With his new achievement as the top performer of the All-Time Leaderboards, he had only grown further in fame and gained the interest of even more major factions.

This entire situation is messy... but not really that complicated, Jake thought. And it truly wasn't.

Yip of Yore wanted to kill the Malefic Viper to become a Primordial Slayer. This was the crux of it.

Ell'Hakan was helping Yip of Yore to do this, initially by trying to kill Jake.

Even if that had now changed, the core of what Ell'Hakan wanted to accomplish remained: to have the Malefic Viper lose his Chosen. Rather than losing his Chosen to death, however, he would lose him to choice, which would definitely also negatively affect the Viper... because if not even his Chosen believed he could win and stood behind him, did he really stand a chance?

Of course, Ell'Hakan and Yip had made one major mistake. Ell'Hakan had been right in saying one can truly only do their best, but the best one can do is limited by knowledge... and those two clearly had no idea Jake was a Heretic-Chosen, nor could they comprehend the concept behind a god and a mortal genuinely just being friends.

The large hall had fallen silent with Ell'Hakan's speech, and it took quite a few seconds before anyone made a sound after the Chosen left. All the focus was on Jake, and from the looks he got, many of them seemed to believe something positive had just happened to Jake. Which, in some ways, it had. Ell'Hakan had admitted to what he had done, and even if he had apologized... well, Jake wasn't obligated to forgive.

Not that he was going to say anything to anyone. The less he gave away, the better.

As Jake stood there, the Fallen King sent over a telepathic message.

"An apt strategy adopted by the Chosen of Yip. He has created a situation where he is no longer the aggressor, and many believe it would only make sense for you to forget and forgive whatever, in their minds, minor mistakes he's made. Everything ended up nicely being blamed on the Malefic Viper, and I wouldn't be surprised if the next time you have a public meeting, he will offer you some kind of compensation to make his actions also match his words."

"Honestly, he can do whatever the fuck he wants," Jake shot back. *"He killed Chris; that's unforgivable."*

"Yes... but in the eyes of others, he just killed a fanatic serving the Malefic One. An insignificant D-grade. Lives are not equal, and someone like you or Ell'Hakan could kill millions without anyone truly caring. In their eyes, your value exceeds that of countless weaklings."

Jake wasn't going to argue, as he knew the Fallen King was right. Shit, some would maybe even argue Jake had done more to Ell'Hakan than Ell'Hakan had ever done to Jake, simply by beating him on the Leaderboards and hurting his pride while killing several of his comrades during the "misunderstanding" that was his invasion.

The mood in the conference hall had shifted quite a lot after Ell'Hakan had done his thing, and his departure seemed to have marked the end for many others, too. Jake saw Wintermaul leave, only throwing a single glance toward Sylphie while departing. Jake threw one in return, making the ice elemental hurry out. The Holy Church didn't stick around much longer either, and Jake saw Carmen leave with a group from Valhal soon after. The same was true for Casper and Caleb, who went with their respective factions.

Before even arriving at this meeting, Jake had already been informed that they would be offered passage back to their home planets or wherever else they wanted to go, all facilitated by the Wyrmgod. In retrospect, this was probably a necessary service to not leave a bunch of mortals stranded on a floating disc in the middle of the emptiness of space.

Soon, as the hall was thinning out, the Sword Saint returned to their group, bringing along a certain dryad. Dina looked like she had some mixed emotions, and Jake understood why. Everyone from Earth but Sylphie and the Fallen King had tactfully departed, leaving their Nevermore party as the only ones left.

"The gang is all back together," Jake said, smiling as Dina rejoined them.

"Ree!" Sylphie screeched happily. Dina smiled at that, even if she couldn't quite hide her sadness.

They had spent the vast majority of the last fifty years together—a huge part of their lives, and likely the majority for all but the Sword Saint and maybe the Fallen King, in terms of pure life experience. In the beginning, Dina had been reserved and barely spoken to anyone but the old man. However, with time, she'd opened up a lot, happily discussed things, and shared her vast knowledge of the multiverse imparted to her as a high-level member of a large faction.

So Jake understood her emotions now that things were coming to an end and they would have to go their separate ways. Even if it wasn't a goodbye, no one knew when they would meet up again. Jake and company were all to return to their own universe, where she couldn't follow, and they likely had quite a few system events to go before their universe would open up fully.

Additionally, it wasn't as if Dina didn't also have her own things to deal with. She was the granddaughter of Nature's Attendant and held his Bloodline, giving her many responsibilities and limitations, and especially now that she had placed top 100 on the Era Leaderboards, the expectations had only risen further. Making friends while in a position like hers surely wasn't easy; Jake knew that pretty damn well, being the Chosen of the Malefic Viper. He was just a lot luckier, in that many of the people around him didn't really care overly much that he was a Chosen.

"I... I nearly forgot," Dina said as she looked at Jake. "Congratulations on the All-Time Leaderboards... and thank you for allowing me to accompany you during this time."

"Eh, I should also be thanking you for helping me even get the record," Jake said, waving her off with a smile. "Then again, we did all carry our own weight, so maybe we should all thank each other in some circlejerk of gratitude?"

"There is no need to openly display gratitude between equal partners; it's simply an implicit understanding," the Fallen King added, both ruining Jake's joke and being pretty on-point. There truly was no need for anyone to thank the others.

Dina smiled a bit. "Still... thank you."

Jake shook his head, not really bothering to argue about something this dumb. They'd had plenty of dumb arguments over the last half a century, and there was no reason to add another one to the list.

"Where are you headed from here?" the Sword Saint asked Dina, partly to change the subject.

"I'll be heading home with Grandpa. I was told there was a celebration back there for all those from the Pantheon who took part in Nevermore." She then turned to Jake. "Grandpa also said you should come visit once you find the time... but I think all of you would be welcome if you wanted to come by."

"Sounds like something worth considering," the Sword Saint said, nodding.

"Perhaps, but not before we have handled this Prima first," the Fallen King added.

"Not like we're in a rush." Jake shrugged as he looked at Dina. "Do tell Nature's Attendant and Artemis that I'll come by at some point after the Prima Guardian is dealt with and things calm down a bit. I doubt any visit I make will be a brief one."

"Ree!" even Sylphie agreed.

"Okay!" Dina smiled, happy they all seemed open to one day stopping by.

Their group was quiet for a while before the Sword Saint spoke once more. "I believe it's time we stop delaying needlessly."

"Yeah..." Dina said, her smile rapidly fading.

The Sword Saint shook his head as he reached over and put a hand on her head, rubbing her hair-like plants. "This is not a goodbye but a temporary farewell. It's been a pleasure spending the last few decades with you, Dina."

Jake just smiled as he saw Dina hesitate before seemingly thinking *screw it* and advancing to give the old man a hug. He returned it while still rubbing her hair. Jake already knew that of everyone in their group, she had definitely become the closest with the Sword Saint. Maybe because he also had those grandfather vibes.

Soon enough, the two of them stopped hugging and she said goodbye to the others. Sylphie got a few scratches before getting pulled into a hug, while the Fallen King and Jake both got more reserved goodbyes.

"We shall meet again, dryad," the Fallen King said, getting about as polite as he ever got.

Jake smiled. "Yep, see you around."

"Take care of yourself, alright?" the Sword Saint said as he gave her a final head pat.

"Ree!" Sylphie screeched, waving with one of her wings.

Dina nodded resolutely. "Farewell for now."

With that, she turned around and left, only looking back half a dozen times as the four from Earth remained in the conference hall that was rapidly emptying out.

"I shall head back to Earth now," the Sword Saint said after a brief pause.

"And I shall follow," the Fallen King concurred. *"Too many of the World Council have been gone for too long."*

"Can you take Sylphie with you?" Jake asked the two of them. "I'm gonna go visit that Demon Prince first and stop by a few other places before I also head back."

"Very well," the old man said, nodding. Sylphie didn't complain either; she flew over and landed on top of the Fallen King, who didn't even protest.

"In that case... see you all back home." Jake smiled as he turned to leave, heading for some of the people he had to visit before going to the Demon Prince. He wanted to finish all other business first in case something went wrong with that ritual and he had to flee Nevermore City. Not like that was going to happen... When did anything bad ever happen when people tried to do rituals that included ancient devils and Demon Lords?

———

Within a vast library, a being sat with legs crossed in mid-air while holding a large tome. All was still until suddenly a hole in space formed, and a figure appeared.

"He is annoying, isn't he?" the floating god said with a sigh as he put down the book he had been reading. "Way too unpredictable. Then again, that isn't only hurtful to us but to his dear Patron, too. Say, what was his mental state like during your grand apology?"

"Confusion overshadowed nearly every other emotion, as he seemed unsure what our goals were... at least in the beginning," Ell'Hakan answered, totally fine with not beating around the bush and getting straight into business. "However, he seemed to realize them about halfway through, at which point he suppressed his emotions for the most part. He isn't very good at it, though. He definitely isn't a fan of the change in narrative and still seems keen on getting personal revenge."

"Not anything we didn't expect," Yip of Yore said, nodding. "Say, what was his emotional response regarding you insinuating he should abandon his Patron?"

"Multifaceted, but thoroughly lacking in one vital emotion... There was no anger, an emotion I would very much expect from someone being told to abandon their god." Ell'Hakan smiled. "He also clearly didn't disagree with any of my assessments regarding his lacking loyalty towards the Malefic Viper, nor my insinuation he is entirely his own person. One thing is certain: Jake Thayne holds no faith in his heart toward the Malefic Viper, even if he does seem to have a generally positive view of the Primordial."

Yip of Yore nodded slowly. "That is likely what keeps him with the Order."

"That, and he would hurt his Path if he left," Ell'Hakan added.

"Hm? No, not particularly."

Ell'Hakan feigned surprise. "What do you mean it won't?"

"He just needs to become a heretic." Yip of Yore shrugged. "The system has plenty of safeguards if you choose to abandon a god. In fact, should the Malefic Viper die after he becomes a heretic, he may even become a Usurper. Hm, just imagining it is a bit exciting... to be a Usurper of a Primordial's Legacy."

"Perhaps it may even be put on the table as a potential advantage should he abandon the Malefic Viper," Ell'Hakan pointed out.

The god shook his head. "No, let some things remain unspoken. In fact, let us not focus too much on the Chosen of the Malefic Viper for now. Allow Valhal to handle him, and let's see if they manage to recruit him, as that would be the best outcome. Killing him at this point would only lead to far too many problems, and quite frankly, I find it uncertain if you would even be capable of slaying him."

"He is powerful, yes... but—"

"No buts," Yip of Yore interrupted. "His story is too strong right now. Too many are interested in his Path and where it will take him. As of this moment, he is the worst kind of opponent for you, as fate is on his side, so to say, making him far more difficult to deal with than otherwise. If you want to kill him for personal reasons, you need to do it under the proper conditions and framing."

"Very well," Ell'Hakan relented. "As you say, let Valhal handle recruiting him."

"In the meantime, you know what you have to do. Make your preparations for the Prima Guardian and ensure everything is in place. Even if things have gotten a bit annoying, we will continue as otherwise planned. You may believe this entire debacle was a major setback, but in truth, I do not view it as such. Instead, I see it as an opportunity." Yip of Yore stood up. "The Malefic Viper's prestige is getting more and more tied to his

Chosen, meaning should he lose him, the impact will be far grander. And let's be fair—if we set all the conditions right, the Chosen of the Malefic Viper will abandon him for greener pastures. You should know that better than anyone."

Ell'Hakan was taken aback. "What do you—"

"Don't think I am unaware of your backup plan with the Holy Church," Yip of Yore said, grinning. "I'm not angry about it or even disappointed. In fact, I'm elated that my Chosen is not some moron who would throw all his eggs in one basket."

It took Ell'Hakan a moment before he understood. "You're certain that—"

"Please, do you really think I would gamble everything on getting rid of some Chosen to weaken the Malefic Viper?" Yip of Yore said with a smile, interrupting again. "Any strategy so reliant on a single element like that is prone to failure... especially seeing as there's truly only one factor that matters in situations like these. One thing that will ultimately decide the victor."

Yip of Yore looked down at the mark left by the Malefic Viper's touch on his shoulder. He traced it with a finger, the mark disappearing wherever his finger touched before he allowed it to reappear again. "Power. And between me and that washed-up Primordial... well, I got a slight edge."

CHAPTER 54

HAVING A COLD ONE

Jake had a few places he wanted to stop by before heading back to Earth. He first went to a few of the factions that had congratulated him on his Leaderboard placement. He did this primarily to be polite and stuff, but this entire tour had also been done for one other reason: politics. Well, and optics... but it all fell under the same umbrella of political bullshit.

Before going to visit anyone else, he made his way back to the Order of the Malefic Viper and said hello to Viridia. He even met Draskil there, who seemed a bit annoyed at having failed to place in the top 250, but he was still nice enough to give Jake a congratulations for his achievement. The Malefic Dragonkin had done pretty okay in his own right, but he simply wasn't a crafter at all, leaving him pretty darn screwed when it came to some of the Challenge Dungeons, and while his party was alright, they had only reached floor seventy-five and not even done the event boss there.

Anyway, while meeting these two was nice, the one he had come to the Order compound to meet wasn't Viridia or Draskil, but a certain snake that he found sitting in a chair on a terrace overlooking the vastness of space beyond the ring that was Nevermore City. It was a sealed-off area, and Jake passed a barrier as he made his way there, ensuring no one could see or hear their ensuing conversation.

While approaching the terrace, Jake saw the ice bucket with bottles in it, making him smile. He walked onto the terrace, the god sitting in the lawn-chair not even turning to look as he raised a bottle. "Take a seat and grab a cold one."

Jake didn't need to be told twice. He took a bottle, popped off the cap, and sat down. Taking a big swig, he felt the sweet beer run down his throat as he breathed out, satisfied. "Some good stuff. Where's it from? Doesn't taste like any of Valdemar's; he tends to prefer making ale, I noticed."

"It's from my personal collection, and quite a good lager. Good enough for when there's cause for celebration." Villy turned and looked at Jake. "So, how does it feel to be the top performer of the All-Time Leaderboards?"

"Eh, not really any different than usual," Jake said, shrugging. "I just went from being the best to more people knowing I am the best. The title is nice, though."

"Titles are nice, and they certainly know now that you are quite an outlier. Moreso than before." The Viper smiled as he kept peering out into space. "You know, I'm just gonna be honest with you... I didn't think you would actually take the top spot. I had hoped for the top ten and maybe the top spot on the Era Leaderboards, but both you and Ell'Hakan did better than anyone estimated. If you hadn't been here, he would have had all the attention on him for sure."

"A bit hurt you didn't think I'd do it," Jake said, grinning, "though I will say it wasn't easy, and I did get kind of lucky with the Challenge Dungeons. I could straight-up cheese the hell out of one and did pretty damn well in nearly all the others."

"Luck is such a fickle word. You may think you got lucky, but you need the skills to create that luck for yourself. It's impossible to design any scenario where some will not have advantages, and your Bloodline can create advantages in many situations, making it incredibly hard to restrict unless you want to make the challenges themselves overly restricted." While explaining this, the Viper finished his first bottle and took out another from the ice bucket.

"I guess Ell'Hakan also had his advantages," Jake muttered before smiling. "Oh, well, who cares? I did it, and that's all that matters."

"True, true." Villy nodded, taking another swig before looking a bit more serious. "Good job in there. You did pretty damn well."

Jake smiled, also quickly finishing off his first bottle before taking another. "Glad to impress."

"After this, you will have even more eyes on you than before," the Viper said, still looking pretty serious. "Being my Chosen and a Bloodline Patriarch with an incredibly potent Bloodline that may or may not include your abilities as a Harbinger of Primeval Origins already makes you a person of interest. Now you have added on an extreme level of talent in combat, too, not to speak of the Records attained from topping the Leaderboards.

"Before, you were just a young talent they hoped to maybe make use of for your unique abilities... but now that has changed, at least somewhat. To all the divine factions, you were just a mortal who would die off in a relatively short amount of time, and all they really needed from you before this happened was for you to spread your Bloodline and maybe use your abilities related to Primeval Origins. Even if you never helped a specific faction with any of these things, they knew that the amount of help you could offer was limited by your lifespan. However, now... now you have introduced another factor they need to consider with some level of seriousness: the possibility of you becoming a god."

Jake looked at the snake god, confused, then tilted his head and explained, "Becoming a god was always the plan and definitely a possibility."

Shaking his head, the Viper chuckled. "It's the plan for most young geniuses, but words, hopes, and intentions are cheap. I am sure every single individual in that little party today fully intends to become a god, but statistically, it would be impressive if even a few of you attained immortality. That's why it was never really something the factions bothered to consider, as the chances were so low. This is no longer the case. Even if your chance is still incredibly low in their eyes, it's now high enough to consider seriously."

"Why am I feeling offended by that notion...?" Jake muttered.

"In their defense, they are acting on incomplete information. They are not fully aware of your Bloodline, though they do have a better idea now. At least Valdemar does, having seen your little fight in the Colosseum of Mortals. But we both know what happened in that arena is far from everything, and at this point, I'm just looking forward to what other surprises you are hiding."

"Speaking of incomplete information... a certain orange bastard approached me during the get-together," Jake said, quickly explaining what had happened with Ell'Hakan inside the conference hall. Due to the barrier made by the Wyrmgod, not even the Viper had been allowed to look inside, meaning their little encounter was a surprise to him.

After Jake was done talking, the Viper just shook his head. "I had not expected them to take such a direct approach. But yes, you are definitely right that they no longer view you as a target to kill but still one to separate from me. And in many ways, their approach is correct. You are gathering so much attention these days, and I'm getting so many benefits with you as my Chosen. In nearly all ways, that's good, but should you choose to abandon me as your Patron, Yip of Yore would be able to turn all my gains against me, turning your exceptionalism into a demerit for me."

"Damn, too bad that's not even an option," Jake said with a smile, now already on his third beer. "Say, if I wasn't bound by my weird Path and could bail at any time, would you be concerned?"

"Concerned about you abandoning me, or concerned about the effects of you abandoning me? The distinction is important."

"Bit of both, I guess?"

"I wouldn't really be concerned about you abandoning me, but the effects of my Chosen abandoning me would be annoying for sure," the Viper explained. "While I don't have your instincts, I get the feeling you aren't the type to jump ship just because there are rumors the boat is taking on water. You're more the type to shoot an arrow at whatever bastard tried damaging the hull."

Jake smiled, yet he did wonder... "Ell'Hakan and Yip of Yore are still clearly confident, though. I get the feeling those two aren't the types of people to act with this much confidence if they don't have a reason. Exactly how strong is Yip of Yore, actually? Thus far, I kind of got the impression he is a high-tier god who could jump to reach the top tier using his weird storytelling skills."

"Hm, I believe I told you he killed off an entire Pantheon shortly after ascending to godhood, right?"

"Yeah," Jake said, nodding. He did remember the Viper briefly mentioning that and the notoriety it had gained him as the top god of the last era.

"Well, I didn't include that this particular Pantheon included a Godking and a Godqueen. He slaughtered them both easily, and when others tried to hunt him down for revenge, he killed all those, too, including one surpassing the realm of the Godking. He is... well, before you were around, he was known as the biggest genius to ever appear in the multiverse, and as of this moment, he is a god no one can say with confidence they would be capable of killing without him at least being able to escape. All of this is to say that even without all his tricks, he would be considered a pinnacle god, and with them, I can understand why he would have the confidence to aim for the very top. Especially when his target is me, a Primordial who hadn't exactly been doing much for the last many eras. In many ways, he is a counter to someone like me, as much of my reputation is based on stories of old, and that's very much his domain."

Jake frowned a bit at the long answer, which left him with one question. "If he appeared right here, right now, would you be able to kill him?"

"That isn't a question worth considering," the Viper said, shaking his head. "I wouldn't even try."

"Would you be able to at least fight and beat him if he tried to kill you?"

"Now, isn't that the question of the era?" The Viper just smiled as he motioned for Jake to take another beer. "I will not answer, though. While it may sound silly to you, speaking things into existence and the concept of jinxing can begin to seem very real when you get to my level."

Jake was silent for a moment, then sighed. "Alright, alright. Anyway, was me staying silent good or bad during Yip's Chosen's speech?"

"I don't think it matters overly much," Villy said with a shrug. "He would have found a way to get his message out no matter what, and in some ways, it's good he gave you an official apology like that. It proves he was the original aggressor and the one who initiated an antagonistic relationship between you and him. That he is the one chasing you and not the other way around. It also helps further establish they are no longer interested in simply killing you. Ah, but do note that should a situation present itself where they could kill you without the backlash, they would definitely take it."

Jake shrugged. "Well, I would take the opportunity to kill him too if I got the chance."

"And I'm sure he is also well aware of that and will ensure he never puts himself in such a position... unless he wants to, that is. Because that is the one good excuse he can have to fight and kill you: that he was merely defending himself from the mad Chosen of the Malefic Viper. I'm sure he would spin some story as long as it has the fundamental truth that you attacked first behind it, likely even putting the blame on me entirely. Should he win, that is. If you kill him, who cares?"

Jake just nodded as he emptied out his current bottle and got another. "To change the topic, you said there would be more interest in me now from major factions... How exactly will that materialize? Will I get bothered more than before?"

"Surprisingly, no. They will likely leave you alone a lot more. I'm sure you kind of even noticed it today. While the young talents of different factions may have invited you to visit or wished to form positive relations, they will do so in a calmer and more casual tone from now on, and many of them did it out of personal interest to try and forge relations with the top of their generation."

"That's... good?" Jake said, a bit surprised. He had fully expected to be bothered more than before. That was kind of the norm he had gotten used to. Standing out more equals more attention, which equals more people coming up to bother him and trying to make him join their factions and stuff.

"I would say it is. What you mainly accomplished was proving that they are not really in a rush to get you. Even if you don't become a god, many of the factions now have high confidence you will at least reach A-grade, giving you a significantly increased lifespan and thus more time for them to, at minimum, borrow you for a few decades. Should you become a god, they also want to ensure they formed a good relationship with you before ascension, even if they did fail to recruit you. If you are the next Yip of Yore, that would definitely be in their best interest." The Viper sighed. "Though... Jake, I am truly sorry. I know the implications of this are disappointing."

"What?" Jake asked, confused.

"They won't stop, but there will be less now..."

"Yeah, not taking that bai—"

"Your beloved honeypots! Woe is yours, to no longer be chased by the young maidens hoping to ensnare the illustrious Chosen Harbinger of Primeval Origins. It's truly a disaster." The Viper looked at Jake with extreme pity. "But don't worry—I am sure some will still try and shoot their shot, even if it's not heavily suggested by their factions."

"You know? I think I'll survive," Jake said in a deadpan tone.

"Stay strong, my Chosen. Keep up that façade." Villy gave him a pat on the back.

"Oh, would you look at the time! I have an appointment I must attend!" Jake smiled at the Viper. "Gotta help that Cerulean Demon do a big ritual with some Heart Fragment of the Cerulean Devil or something."

"Hm? That sounds fun; tell me more," the Viper said, suddenly seeming interested, and Jake gladly shared the details he knew.

"Yep, definitely fun, and I would go for it," Villy said while nodding. "Even if you have to spend some of your unique energy, I still think it would be worth it. Not often you get a possibility like this, and making friends with demons is always nice. They are very reliable when they owe you. Oh, yeah, and the levels and Records would also be nice."

"Knew you would be on board... but what if it goes wrong? Pretty sure that Cerulean Demon will be fucked if the ritual fails, or worse, it backfires on him."

"Oh, yeah, if that happens, you need a backup plan," the Viper said, looking deep in thought for a second. "Alright, two things. First of all, have them sign a waiver. Secondly, have those movement skills ready, and should things go south, just run the fuck away and act like nothing ever happened."

Jake stared at the god for a while. "Good idea with the waiver."

"Yep," the snake god said, grinning. "Ah, but before you head there, stop by the Valhal compound and stay there for a little bit, yeah? And don't hide it when you go there; let all know you went to visit them. And do so after going to a few other factions. Gotta at least keep people guessing if you are considering your options."

"More politics?" Jake sighed. "Oh, well. See ya around; good talk."

"See you," the Viper said before following up with a message sent through something Jake had quite frankly missed... their divine connection. *"And good to have my very own personal livestream—with direct communication—back."*

CHAPTER 55

A DAY OF FORCED SOCIALIZATION
IN NEVERMORE CITY

J ake walked out of the terrace and through the Order compound while making sure to swipe a dozen or so beer bottles from the somehow endless ice bucket on the way out. He had a few places to visit before it was time to head back to Earth. As Villy had talked about, he at least needed to make it look like he was actively forging and maintaining relationships with other factions, especially Valhal. That was also why he would visit there last, as he planned on spending a few days in their compound. He needed a few days anyway, as he came to learn on his way out of the Order's base.

Two messages had been left for him. The first was from someone associated with Aeon Clok, who was to deliver a present after having won the bet on the final City Floor. Jake had honestly forgotten it, but now that he was reminded, he looked forward to seeing what the mage had that could help his time banana not-a-tree at home.

The second message was from the Cerulean Demon, saying where to find him and asking if Jake was still interested. If he was, he could look through an included disc that detailed the ritual and the preparation the demons had made, which was part of the reason he would need to spend a few days at Valhal's compound. He needed to look through it and familiarize himself with the ritual, and he may as well do that there.

Okay, there weren't really only two messages... there were actually a few dozen, but only two of them were actionable. The rest were just pleasantries and invitations for different things, most of which Jake planned on just entirely ignoring. And by ignoring, he meant having someone else send back a diplomatic message—a job that would likely fall to some poor administrative worker from the Order who would be all stressed out about responding for him. Oh, yeah, and he also told them to respond to the Demon Prince first and say he was interested and would come by within the week.

With all that done, Jake ventured outside and went to a small shop in Nevermore City that the first letter directed him toward. It turned out to be a small job on the outskirts of Nevermore City, far enough away that Jake had to use a teleporter to get there, as flying would simply take too long.

Before he even entered the shop, he saw it was buzzing with customers. So many that there was a line out the door, making Jake consider whether he should maybe come back later, but he didn't get that chance, as he got a telepathic message while he was considering his options.

"I have been expecting you, Chosen of the Malefic One. Please, come in through the back entrance." He sensed that the sender was inside the building, but sadly, he couldn't see them with his sphere, as the inside was spatially expanded, distorting everything.

Doing as asked, Jake snuck around back and through a small door. Once inside, everything expanded as expected, and Jake found himself standing in a pretty large workshop with a dozen hobgoblins working. None of them even looked up, as they were all deep in focus, but one hobgoblin did walk toward him from across the room.

"Welcome to our little shop, Chosen of the Malefic One. And congratulations on your performance... To think the new champion of the All-Time Leaderboards would visit my humble little shop..." The hobgoblin smiled and sighed.

Jake instinctively used Identify, confirming what he kind of already knew. This was another follower of Aeon Clok, and a B-grade one at that.

[Hobgoblin – lvl ??? – Greater Blessing of Aeon Clok]

The fact that all of the hobgoblins were working on watches of different kinds should definitely have been a clue.

"I got your invite and was told you had something for me," Jake said, not really super interested in sticking around longer than necessary.

"Of course, of course," the hobgoblin said, still smiling. "The young master said you helped him acquire quite the wealth, and we were even allowed to reward you from his own stash. Please, I hope this item can be of utmost assistance and suit your needs."

The hobgoblin waved his hand, and more than a dozen large plastic bags about the size of a human torso appeared and fell on the ground. Jake instantly realized what he was looking at as he used Identify on the contents of the bags through the clear plastic.

[Primed Manure of the Timeless Simiiform (Legendary)] — **Manure created by a powerful B-grade Timeless Simiiform variant, a monkey-like beast that infuses its manure with the concept of time to defeat its foes. This manure is infused with powerful time energy and has been primed for easy absorption by any plant with the time affinity by an outstanding crafter. Limited alchemical uses due to the priming.**

Honestly, what had Jake expected when he asked for something to help his banana musa? Also, he found it oddly coincidental that this manure came from a monkey, considering he had originally found the tree in the possession of a time-magic monkey.

"Is the Chosen satisfied?" the hobgoblin asked, a bit nervous as Jake didn't say anything.

"Hm? Oh, yeah, this is good." Jake nodded as he swooped up all the bags. "I do have a question, though. Is there some form of correlation between monkeys and time magic? This is not my first time encountering such a beast."

"Why are you... No, not in particular, based on what I know," the hobgoblin said, looking confused. "Maybe there is, and I'm just ignorant on the subject."

"I see." Jake nodded, assuming it was just a coincidence. "Thank you for the bags; I will make sure to put them to good use."

Jake turned around, prepared to leave the same way he came in, but the hobgoblin stopped him.

"Uhm, sir... this may be too much to ask, but would you honor us by fulfilling a simple request?" the hobgoblin asked, fidgeting a bit. Yeah, Jake really wasn't in the mood for more work, but before he could say anything, the hobgoblin continued, "Could you maybe leave through the front entrance?"

"I guess?" Jake said, not really thinking much of the weird request when he heard it. However, the hobgoblin grinned from ear to ear as if he had just won some massive prize.

"Right this way, my lord," the groveling time mage said as he motioned for Jake to go through the workshop.

Honestly, Jake had gotten a lot more bags than he expected, so he just did this small and insignificant favor, walking out through a door leading to the back and entering the store behind the counter along with the hobgoblin store owner.

Once they did, all eyes turned to them, and the attendant manning the counter backed away. The store was filled with customers who saw Jake and the hobgoblin... Okay, they mainly saw Jake, and damn, did he feel glad he had worn a mask for his little outing.

"Thank you once more for your visit, Chosen of the Malefic One," the hobgoblin said again as he led Jake out of the store, the sea of people opening a path for them.

Jake just followed along as he heard people murmur while they all looked at him. Once they were finally outside, the hobgoblin bowed one final time.

"Please feel free to come again, and we will gladly be of assistance once more."

Jake suppressed a sigh as he decided to just be nice by playing along and nodding. "I shall if I ever find the need."

With that, he turned and walked off, luckily with no one following him. Through his sphere, he saw a single tear run down the hobgoblin store owner's cheek as he smiled. Yeah, Jake was pretty damn sure he had just lost out on this transaction, even if he had been given a dozen bags of legendary manure... Maybe he should do advertisement jobs? Well, it wasn't like he needed any money...

Anyway, Jake hurried along with his day as he headed for his next destination. He wanted to avoid being on the streets as much as possible because, quite frankly, he attracted a bit too much attention. No one actually approached him, but nearly everyone couldn't help but gawk his way when he just wanted to casually pass by. Annoyingly, he couldn't just try and sneak around either, as he did want to be seen visiting all sorts of different places.

After the "shitty" shop visit, Jake decided to go to a small base belonging to the Altmar Empire. He only went there briefly to thank them for their congratulations and was naturally met by some high-ranking young talents from the faction with whom he briefly interacted. He did the same with a few other factions, including those he knew people in. He spent a few hours at both the Risen's base and the one belonging to the Court of Shadows, while he tried to be faster in those only filled with strangers. A bit surprisingly, many of the young talents from the factions had already left Nevermore City, so he couldn't meet many of them, but luckily, Casper and his little brother were still there.

He also avoided going to places like the Holy Church. The Dao Sect wasn't an option either, as they didn't really have a base, and Jake wasn't even sure Eron had stuck around. Needless to say, the void-related people such as Arnold didn't have some big base either, seeing as they were so rare, but he still tried to make it a point to visit everyone he knew who belonged to a major faction.

Soon, after many hours of way too much socializing and politicking, Jake finally reached his final destination: Valhal.

Luckily, there was a teleporter pretty much right outside the compound belonging to the mercenary war-fanatic faction. Speaking of their compound... yeah, it definitely put the Order's to shame. It was massive in size and included far more buildings. There was even a large arena smack in the middle of everything, not to mention the many personal residences spread around the outskirts, all sealed behind thick walls and magical circles. The amount of spatial expansion was also minimal, allowing Jake to get a good look at everything before he even entered using a Pulse of Perception.

The entrance was a large wooden gate with a single guard standing outside. Well, more than a guard; it was a greeter of some sort, and the guy instantly spotted Jake as he appeared at the teleporter that was pretty much only used by people who were visiting the compound.

Jake didn't doubt he sent some kind of message, as four presences appeared within only a few seconds. He recognized none of them, but from their auras, it was clear the man in the center was in charge. The man was two full heads taller than Jake and had a pretty slim build compared to the three around him, who were all bald, muscular dudes wearing fur and leather clothes. The man in charge wore a pretty nice robe. Jake felt the use of Identify on him, and he responded in kind by Identifying the man he felt pretty damn sure was S-grade.

[Human – lvl ??? – Divine Blessing of Olav the Wise]

"Apologies for the disrespect; I merely had to confirm," the man said as he cupped his hands and bowed. "Welcome, Lord Thayne. I am Olaf the Not-Yet-Wise, the current head of Valhal's presence in Nevermore City. Well, for mortal affairs, anyway. "

Jake instantly noted two things. First of all, poor guy, having that name. His god must really hate him. Secondly, they called him Lord Thayne and not any of his other titles. Jake felt like this wasn't merely coincidental, almost as if they would prefer to not call him the Chosen of the Malefic Viper.

"Glad you would have me," Jake answered politely, taking extra note of the many scouts who had an eye on him. He counted... about four hundred people?... with more than a dozen of those gods, not counting Villy, who had definitely enjoyed Jake's day of going around doing social stuff.

"We're never going to say no to an honored warrior who wants to visit." The man smiled as he motioned for Jake to come in with him. "Ah, I also believe the Runemaiden of the War God has been informed of your arrival. She should arrive shortly as long as she is not preoccupied."

"It's fine either way; I can go see her myself," Jake said, making the man named Olaf raise an eyebrow before just smiling and nodding.

"Naturally. The Runemaiden has her own residence in the northeastern section. However, I do believe she is coming either way, if for nothing else than to show you around the compound. The entire compound, outside of any private residences, will naturally be open to you, and you are free to enjoy any amenities as if you were already a part of Valhal."

Jake nodded and walked through the gates together with Olaf. It was only now that Jake fully entered the compound, and he felt the majority of observers being cut off by the defenses of Valhal. Soon, the remaining gods also cut off their connection, likely to avoid offending anyone they shouldn't offend, leaving Jake with only his usual scaled stalker.

Also, Jake didn't doubt that they'd had that conversation with so many onlookers entirely on purpose. Especially the last part about him being treated as if he was "already a part of Valhal."

It was as unsubtle as you could get without outright stating they wanted Jake to join. Jake also didn't rebuff the statement, likely making many assume he was, at the very least, considering it. That, or Jake truly sucked at reading between the lines, even if what was written between said lines was barely a font size smaller than the actual lines.

The latter definitely would've been a possibility if Jake hadn't had political stuff hammered into his head over and over so many damn times.

Soon, the words of Olaf were proven true as he saw Carmen approach from afar... and he was pretty sure she had been preoccupied when he arrived. Her two red fists and blood-splattered clothes, at least, indicated she had been busy.

———

Vilastromoz had indeed enjoyed Jake's day of socializing as he sat within the Order compound and relaxed. There was just something special about his Chosen going around trying to act all polite while feeling awkward, making others assume he was just prideful or haughty due to his reserved attitude. It had been fun in Nevermore, but it was even more fun now that Jake's awkwardness could have an actual impact on multiversal politics.

But, hey, at least Jake hadn't done too badly yet. The Viper had nearly expected him to accidentally propose to some young princess or something like that at this point, but sadly, that had yet to happen. Oh, well. He still had many chances.

As the Viper was just relaxing, a figure walked toward the room he was sitting in. He felt the aura of an unknown god but quickly saw this god's appearance, and before the other god could even open the door, the Viper made a small request. "Well, hello there. Hey, could you do me a favor and turn that smile upside down?"

The door opened, and the Viper saw the smiling visage of the unknown god whose identity was already fairly obvious.

"You already know that is not an option," the god... no, Eversmile... responded.

Vilastromoz nodded. "True, true. But always worth a shot. Now, why the impromptu visit?"

"I take it your Chosen didn't share anything about our brief interaction within the conference hall?" Eversmile asked.

Vilastromoz raised an eyebrow. "No, he didn't, but now you sure got me curious."

"No matter—I shall not waste time for either of us: What are those boots he is wearing?"

The Viper was a bit surprised by the question. However, he quickly understood and played dumb as he smiled. "Oh, yeah, I know. They look so old and unsightly on a Chosen. He should really get them fixed by a leatherworker or something, huh? I'll be sure to give him some proper leather-maintenance products the next time we meet."

CHAPTER 56

THE MYSTERY DEEPENS

Should Jake question why Carmen was half-covered in blood? Maybe. He didn't overly care, though, as he waved when he saw her come over. "Hello again."

"You got here faster than expected, huh? Didn't anyone wanna host you longer or what?" Jake saw his escort grimace at Carmen's curt tone. Even the poor S-grade threw Carmen a look, which she seemed to not notice or care about. As things should be.

"No, they all threw me out on the streets," Jake said with an exaggerated sigh. "I only came here because I accidentally started four or five wars due to my sheer political incompetence and reckoned Valhal would be on-brand as my next visit."

"Oh, so you're looking to hire us, eh?" Carmen smiled. "Not gonna be cheap. I hope those potions have been selling."

"If all else fails, I'll just have to take out a payday loan... or does Valhal do commissions on credit? I can pay back in installments."

"If the Chosen desires to hire any mercenari—" one of the three bald warriors began, but Carmen threw him a look, making him shut up.

"For fuck's sake," she muttered before looking back at Jake. "See what I'm working with here?"

Olaf also sighed at the warrior, who looked confused for a moment. It appeared he then had the situation explained to him telepathically, as he looked like he wanted to somehow make himself smaller. Quite a tough task for someone of his size.

"Oh, well, that killed the mood." Carmen shrugged. "Guess I should do that formal stuff. Welcome to the Nevermore Valhal Compound or whatever the official name is."

"Thanks for having me," Jake said, smiling. "Now, I feel like it's only polite to ask, but who did you just beat to death?"

"Hm? Oh, yeah, no. I was just having some light spars with some of the young ones who just got here and talked shit... and groups who already did Nevermore and didn't accomplish fuck-all," Carmen said with a scoff, clearly annoyed. "They were bitching about there being no one from Valhal on any of the top 10 Leaderboards; who the fuck gives them the right to talk? These are groups who didn't even hit the top 1000... They deserved a good lesson."

"I see." Jake nodded as he smiled teasingly. "Say, why didn't Valhal take any of the top spots?"

Carmen glared at him as she shook her head. "Because we had a few dead weights in the party, and the Challenge Dungeons were absolute shit. Seriously, they sucked ass, every single one of them. Test of Character only tested how much bullshit I could keep up with, Neverending Journey was like going back to my old retail job, Minaga's Labyrinth was just shitty equations and puzzles, House of the Architect was a bloody waste of time, and the only one with any promise, Colosseum of Mortals, was ruined by its idiotic rules."

"I would have thought you'd do decently in the Colosseum?" Jake questioned.

"See these?" Carmen asked, raising a hand. "Yeah, right now, I can catch a speartip or use my palm to deflect swords. In the Colosseum, I would lose a damn hand if anything sharp hit it. I had to go back to how I fought before, making me feel like I regressed, and ultimately I had to pick up some fist weapons and stuff... It sucked."

Jake slowly nodded. "Yeah... does sound like a bit of an oversight, honestly."

"Sure as hell does." Carmen sighed. "Anyway, wanna go show off in front of them or have a look around first?"

"Are you offering a tour of the compound?"

"I feel like Olaf here would get mad if I didn't," Carmen said, throwing the S-grade a smile.

"It does sound like I'm no longer needed here and am just getting in the way," Olaf said with a nod. "I will be in the central building if there is anything. Do not hesitate to come by."

"I'll keep that in mind," Jake responded as he saw Olaf leave, the man not even trying to hide his smile from Jake and Carmen's interactions. It was pretty understandable why, too. Jake and Carmen didn't make it a secret they were close, and if Olaf had been tasked with trying to make Jake feel welcome, it had to be a huge relief to see the two of them interact.

"Now, what do you wanna see first?" Carmen asked once the guy was gone, pulling out a washcloth and cleaning herself up a bit.

"Any recommendations?" Jake asked with a raised eyebrow.

"Just a few. First of all, we could go check out the arena and maybe even go for a bit of a spar if you're up for it and not afraid of me hurting your pride. Secondly, we could go check out some of the training facilities, as Valhal has some interesting ones, including an archery range where you can spatially expand the range itself. Third, we could visit my personal residence, where having another kind of spar is possible." Carmen gave him a knowing wink.

"You know what... I think I'll take the second one first," Jake responded. "A spatially expanding archery range sounds pretty damn cool."

"Right." Carmen smiled, shaking her head. "My place is this way." Jake looked at her weirdly as she stopped herself mid-step. "Wait, you're serious?"

Scratching the back of his head, Jake couldn't help but look toward where he thought this training area was. "We can go to your place after?"

Carmen looked at Jake incredulously for a bit before just shaking her head and smirking. "Fine, let's go play at the archery range... Man, are you a nerd sometimes."

"Maybe that's what it takes to reach the top of the Leaderboards," Jake said, trying to look deep in thought. "Arnold also placed pretty highly, you know."

"Man, fuck you..." Carmen sighed. "We're definitely also making a visit to the arena later."

"Does sound kind of fun," Jake agreed. He was genuinely interested in seeing just how strong Carmen had become.

He could feel her aura, and it was kind of... odd. It was incredibly stable, to the level of it being unnatural. Usually, people leaked energy all the time, but Carmen barely gave off anything. He knew part of the reason for this was her lack of mana, but even with stamina, one burned it all the time just moving around. Carmen surely did, too, but it seemed either far less wasteful than everyone else, or she had some way to hold everything internally somehow.

It had to have something to do with her unique Path as a Rune-maiden. A Path that definitely was powerful, as the presence she did leak

was unmistakably a top-tier one. So, a little visit to the arena to see just
how tough she had gotten sounded fun, and he wouldn't say no to
another kind of spar before or after either.

But first... archery range.

And, damn, was it everything Jake had hoped for.

"So I can just turn this knob and... wow," Jake muttered as he stood
with a control panel floating in front of him.

Turning a single knob, the target could move further away and come
closer again based on how he adjusted it. There were several other buttons,
too, some of which added different kinds of targets, or changed the nature
of the environmental mana, or even summoned projected creatures for
aiming practice.

What's more, it had different "modes" for everything from D- to A-
grade. Jake was currently in the B-grade version, where he could expand
the range to what looked like an entire planet away. The only limitation
was that Jake had to stay on the metal platform he was on, or everything
would return to normal.

Carmen stood with her arms crossed as she watched him playing with
the options. "You like it?"

"This is beyond my expectations," Jake muttered.

It felt as if he was in some sci-fi virtual space, but everything was real. The
spatial expansion was just insane, though it was done using some ingenious
means. By limiting what had to move within the expanded area, the space had
to be far less stable all around, while it also didn't have to house any living
beings. It also didn't really add any details when it expanded space, making it
far, far more efficient. Still had to take up a lot of energy, but definitely not as
much as one would expect... because Jake learned another interesting detail.

"Apparently, it was made by the Altmar Empire, and they made it by
first creating the largest possible archery range and then shrinking that
down, making any expansion far, far cheaper, as spatial shrinking is a lot
easier," Carmen shared. "Valhal has a few training grounds here and there
similar to this, though in many cases, they also just make custom dungeons
to practice within."

"I should definitely look into getting one of these myself," Jake said as
he pulled out his bow and shot a few arrows. As all of them hit, Jake tried
to expand the range a bit more before he took more shots.

"Is it just me, or are your arrows somehow accelerating the further
they fly?" Carmen asked with a frown.

Jake nodded. "Yep."

"That... doesn't make much sense."

"Nope," Jake agreed.

"But I guess it's pretty damn useful," Carmen muttered.

"Definitely is."

Jake ended up spending another three hours or so in the training hall, also seeing some of the other facilities. There were some things Jake had never even considered one might need, including what was effectively weight-lifting equipment.

Carmen explained that these weren't really to train but to become more aware of your own power and how you applied your different muscles while completing tasks. This area was also pretty damn busy, and Jake saw many members of Valhal engrossed in their practice.

While stats were the primary factor, the ability of each individual to apply those stats still mattered a lot. The difference between getting punched by someone who knew how to throw a punch and someone who didn't wasn't small, and with ethereal elements such as concepts also getting more and more mixed into every action one made, things got even more complicated.

Theoretically, Jake understood why someone might need machines like these... He just couldn't see why he, in particular, would need them. He already had a good grasp of his own power, and he felt as if he was pretty decent at using his body optimally.

It had to be noted that anyone who could reach C-grade already had a high understanding of themselves, and that the differences wouldn't be like those between a professional and an amateur. It was more like that of an athlete and a top athlete.

"Wanna give it a shot?" Carmen asked as they stood before what looked like a shoulder press machine.

"I guess," Jake said, shrugging as he took a seat.

"Remember, it's not about using your full power on this one, but all about efficiency," she reminded him.

Needless to say, a small crowd had gathered at this point upon seeing the Chosen of the Malefic Viper. They all looked on with interest as Jake grabbed the two handles and lifted up without really thinking much, making sure to engage the right back muscles by instinct. He did a few lifts, keeping a consistent pace before stopping.

"This does bring back memories of going to the gym before the system." Jake smiled as he got up. "Anyway, how did I do? Does it even have some way of measuring?"

Carmen just looked at Jake with a glare. "Alright, time to visit the arena."

"Why?" Jake asked, genuinely confused.

"Just... fuck you," Carmen muttered as he turned and saw that the machine did have a small display he hadn't seen before. And, well... 99.95% did seem like a good percentage, if Jake said so himself. The approving looks he got from all the surrounding observers also confirmed Jake was indeed a master lifter.

"Did I break a record or something?" Jake asked Carmen as they walked out.

"You broke my damn record," she said, shaking her head. "And by so little that it's annoying."

"Sorry?" Jake muttered.

"Just allow me at least one good punch in the arena, yeah?"

"Yeah... having seen some of the punches you've thrown in the past, not gonna make that promise," Jake said defensively as they approached the arena.

———

On the terrace, the Viper was still smiling as he teased the shapeshifter, not really paying much attention to Jake playing around at the Valhal compound.

Eversmile's visage changed as he returned to his "usual" form. He stared at the Viper with a level of seriousness the god rarely displayed. A look he had seen on his fellow Primordial several times before, and always in the same circumstances.

He's starving... starving to know what's going on, the Viper concluded, unable to resist broadening his smile even more. *The mystery is too intriguing for him to handle.*

Eversmile cared about studying karma more than anything else in the entire multiverse. The intrinsic web of connections formed between people, locations, objects, and anything that ever interacted with a soul. He wanted to explore every detail in an environment where details were infinite.

Over the years, as he'd uncovered more and more, the "big" mysteries had started to disappear, and most of the time, he was actively seeking out new scenarios through his own experiments to make new major discoveries. However, he was now faced with a new mystery: Jake wearing boots with a powerful and unusual connection to the Malefic Viper. Even if it wasn't necessarily that big of a mystery, it was still—

"You know exactly what I mean..." Eversmile said. "Why do those boots have a powerful karmic connection with every single Primordial, myself included?"

The Viper's smile instantly disappeared. "What?"

He... did not know that.

"What do you mean *what*?" Eversmile said, getting riled up. "You gave him those boots."

"The system did," Vilastromoz said, deep in thought. "Can you explain what you meant when you said those boots have a powerful karmic connection with all of you?"

"Exactly what I said. Those boots are connected to us, and I cannot discern the cause. My best theory right now is that this is due to your Records as a Primordial bleeding into them over time, which managed to form a karmic connection between the boots and anyone else with the title of Primordial. Boots, as equipment, represent the art of travel, progress, and shortening the distance between two destinations... It is theoretically possible for some of these concepts to have led to this, but I believe there is more behind it."

The Viper remained silent as he listened to Eversmile talk with a fervor he rarely displayed. He understood why, too... because he earnestly wasn't certain either. The boots were connected to him, yes... but also the First Sage. If it was him...

Deciding not to hesitate, the Viper waved his hand to summon a projection of a human man. "Do you recognize this person?"

It was naturally a projection of the First Sage. It was odd, but Vilas-tromoz had never shown him to even another Primordial. In fact, he hadn't thought overly much about his first and only master for many eras. It was only now that his name suddenly appeared so much... The Viper pretty much knew it had something to do with Jake. He definitely didn't believe that any random person would have been rewarded with the same boots. They had been given to Jake specifically.

Eversmile looked at the projection closely, studying every detail before shaking his head. "No, I do not. Why? Who is he?"

Vilastromoz smiled as he looked toward the sky. "You know... these days, I'm asking myself that more and more."

"Is he related to these boots?" the other Primordial pressed.

"More likely than not," Vilastromoz said with a nod as he dispelled the projection.

"Who is he? What's his name?" Eversmile was clearly intrigued by who this mysterious figure might be.

"I actually never learned his name, but he was known as the First Sage," the Viper responded with a nostalgic smile.

Eversmile just kept standing there, staring at the Viper oddly. It felt like an eternity passed before the Primordial asked again, "So? Are you going to tell me why those boots carry a karmic connection with all twelve of us Primordials?"

The Viper frowned before shaking his head at the rare Eversmile joke. "Very funny. Good one."

"Good one, what?" Eversmile asked, showing signs of genuine frustration.

"Wait... you're not fucking with me, are you?" Vilastromoz stood up and, without waiting for an answer, summoned the projection of First Sage again. "Do you know who this is?"

Eversmile looked at the projection... studying it closely once more as if it was his first time seeing it, then shook his head. "No, I do not. Why? Who is he?"

"The First Sage."

Silence returned as the seconds ticked by.

Eversmile suddenly furrowed his brows and got a serious look in his eyes. "This... We were discussing the boots and their karmic connection with every Primordial... but..."

Finally, he realized what was going on at about the same moment the Viper did. They stared at each other in realization, muttering the truth they had both realized in unison.

"Forbidden Knowledge."

This just left one grand question... Why the fuck was information about the First Sage considered Forbidden Knowledge? Actually, make that two grand questions... Why could Jake know about it?

CHAPTER 57

FORBIDDEN KNOWLEDGE

E versmile departed soon after, even more perplexed than when he arrived. This left Vilastromoz alone back on the terrace with his own thoughts, a deep frown marring his face. A lot of things weren't making any sense right now. For something to be Forbidden Knowledge was... not normal.

To clarify, for the system to hide information wasn't anything new at all. Restricted Knowledge was a relatively simple term, as it just referred to knowledge restricted by the system, as the name very obviously implied. It wasn't any big secret either, and everyone encountered it throughout their Paths. Hell, it was what restricted people from sharing information about the Nevermore Floors or Challenge Dungeons with those who had yet to do the World Wonder.

This Nevermore example also nicely showcased another aspect of Restricted Knowledge: it varied widely to whom knowledge was restricted. People like Jake could now talk openly about Nevermore with anyone else who had either done it or wasn't capable of doing it. In other words, anyone who had done the World Wonder, or anyone at B-grade or above, could speak and hear about the C-grade version of Nevermore.

Forbidden Knowledge was a step above Restricted Knowledge. It was knowledge one was incapable of sharing at all with anyone except others who also already knew... with it many times even being a truth only you knew. In many instances, it also restricted people from ever learning these truths to begin with, and simply being told Forbidden Knowledge was impossible.

Impossible for anyone but the Malefic Viper, that is. Because the concept of Forbidden Knowledge did not exist to him. He possessed the Bloodline of the Immortal Mind, which did nothing but give him perfect memory... which meant that he never forgot even that which was forbidden. Vilastromoz was likely the only one in the multiverse who could simply be told something that was considered Forbidden Knowledge and remember it.

This led to him being called the Keeper of Forbidden Knowledge by certain beings, especially the Void Gods. Unsurprising, considering that they knew more Forbidden Knowledge than even the Primordials, and Oras had gleaned many secrets he could now only share with the Malefic Viper. This led to the Viper safekeeping a lot of knowledge that many would consider useless... but could be highly valuable for someone seeking to use the system cleverly.

However, the thing that still made no sense about the First Sage was... he had not been Forbidden Knowledge before.

It wasn't as if no one knew about the First Sage before Jake became the Viper's Chosen. He had mentioned him to several people throughout the ages... yet this kind of response had never happened before. He had spoken for hours with his wife, and he even remembered referring to the First Sage a few times when he taught Sanguine back in the day, as the would-be creator of the vampire race had sought to create a Transcendent skill, and the First Sage was naturally an expert at that.

Back then, there hadn't ever been a problem, and while people had certainly been alarmed whenever the Viper spoke of this C-grade master of his, they could definitely remember their conversations. What had changed besides Jake making contact?

He had to get to the bottom of this to confirm something, which was when he remembered a certain someone. Vilastromoz had not shared anything about the First Sage with many... but his right-hand hydra had known about his existence for sure. Without delay, he had one of his avatars seek out Snappy within the hydra's own realm.

———

"Master! To what do I owe the—"

"Skip the pleasantries," the Malefic Viper interrupted, Snappy instantly realizing the Viper was being serious.

"What's the issue?" the Lord Protector of the Order of the Malefic Viper asked.

"Do you remember someone called the First Sage?" the Viper asked, closely studying the hydra.

For a few seconds, there was no reaction. "Did you just attempt to share Forbidden Knowledge?"

"Apparently, I did." Vilastromoz frowned even more than before as he clenched his fists. For Snappy to have forgotten... this was a lot more than something simply getting a new designation as Forbidden Knowledge.

The Malefic Viper knew only of one precedent where this could happen. Removing existing memories that were already ingrained in the Records of a Truesoul was something the system never did. To take away long-term memories could be damaging in far too many ways, as the risk of it hurting someone's Path was simply too high.

However, it could happen, just not by the system causing it. The only time he had ever encountered this was as an aftereffect of one of the most feared and powerful Transcendent Skills in the entire multiverse: Karmic Annihilation. Eversmile's Transcendence.

The ability to remove someone from existence. To kill them completely, erasing even their Records and all memories anyone would have ever had of them. Complete and utter death, in every sense of the word. It was such a powerful technique that even Eversmile would find himself affected, unaware of who he had used it on. He would know he had used it, but all memories of why and who would be gone, and that was naturally far from the only backlash he would suffer.

To summarize... he could delete someone and turn anything related to their existence into Forbidden Knowledge.

Only the Malefic Viper would remember.

This wasn't caused by Eversmile, though. The Viper would have felt if it was... but it was likely caused by something similar. A Transcendent Skill cast by someone else, and it wasn't hard to figure out who. The First Sage was the one behind this. He had made his own existence into Forbidden Knowledge, and the Viper had no idea why.

The First Sage was dead. He'd died in the First Era.

No ifs. No buts. He was dead.

Vilastromoz had refused to believe a being like him would simply die, and he had done all he could to confirm the death of his master until he finally had it confirmed by the system itself. Even now, the Viper did not doubt this fact.

He was dead... yet now he was sending echoes through time. For what purpose, the Viper truly couldn't comprehend, but... it had to have something to do with Jake, right?

———

Jake had no idea about anything the Viper was doing, as he was busy with quite the situation himself. Standing within an arena, Carmen stood opposite him, wearing her leather armor with a big grin on her face. The stands around them were absolutely filled to the brim with members of Valhal who wouldn't miss out on a fight between the Chosen of the Malefic Viper and the Runemaiden of Valdemar to save their lives.

By now, Jake was kind of regretting agreeing to this, but Carmen had insisted, and he did want to have a spar with her. He could do without the audience, though. Before they began, they also had to set some ground rules... because there was no way they would fight at full power.

"What do you say to no active or boosting skills?" Carmen asked. "No limited items either."

"No bow also seems like a good restriction," Jake said, generously adding a further handicap to himself.

"Dude, we're in a small arena; I would be impressed if using a bow was even feasible without any active skills to create distance," Carmen said in a deadpan tone.

Jake smiled. "You underestimate my bowmanship."

"Fine, no bow either, then."

Jake wasn't entirely bullshitting, either. Even if the arena was only about a hundred meters in diameter, Jake was still confident he could have used his bow quite nicely.

The two of them looked at each other for a moment as the crowd cheered loudly. Even Olaf had shown back up, acting as the judge and the one to make sure they didn't accidentally end up killing each other. Not that Jake thought that was an actual risk, but better safe than sorry.

"Are both combatants ready?" Olaf asked. "Remember, no active skills or boosting skills, limited items, and the Chosen is not allowed to use his bow."

"Ready," Carmen said, nodding as she bent her knees.

"Read—" Jake tried to say as Carmen shot forward, straight for him.

Fast.

Jake swayed to the side. The fist flew by him, the air vibrating from the blow. Carmen quickly pivoted and did a follow-up, but Jake backed away and dodged five more quick hits while retreating further and further back. The crowd cheered as his back was pushed up against the back wall of the arena.

Trying to take advantage, Carmen struck right for his stomach, and

Jake simply looked down as the blow landed. He felt all the air being pushed out of his body as he was smashed into the hard stone wall, a solid imprint of a fist on his stomach.

Carmen looked confused and took a step back as Jake got back up and smiled while wiping the blood from his lips. "You've gotten stronger for sure."

"Why didn't you dodge?" she asked, perplexed.

"Felt like you needed to at least get one hit in," Jake said in a calm tone as he spread his hands apart and a katar appeared in each. "Remember our last duel?"

"Yeah? I think I do?"

"Let's just say I expect a better performance out of myself this time around."

Jake still remembered their fight a long time ago. Back then, Jake—to put it nicely—hadn't had any idea how to fight in melee properly. He'd been pure instinct, which had served him well, but in front of a skilled fighter, he was in trouble on the offensive front.

However, all that was before Jake got lessons from his other self, who had spent years creating a proper melee-fighting method. It was before sim-Jake... and now Jake was more than eager to see the difference as he decided it was his turn to go on the offensive.

Stabbing forward, Carmen avoided the katar and tried to counter— something that had worked well for her before Jake's improvements—but Jake had expected it. He countered her counter, slightly deflecting her fist to the side as Eternal Hunger struck Carmen in the shoulder... and Jake felt like he had just struck solid metal.

As Carmen stumbled back, Jake's hand hurt from the impact. Even so, he didn't stop. He attacked again, this time trying to use his Blackpoint Nanoblade and its penetrative effect, which was a tad better than Eternal Hunger's.

However, Carmen was ready. She dodged to the side, throwing a punch that Jake also dodged. The two of them attacked half a dozen times each, both dodging all the blows of the other before Jake finally found an opening. The Blackpoint Nanoblade was slammed down into Carmen's thigh... only for it to once more fail to penetrate. It slid down the side of her leg, nearly throwing Jake off balance, and he barely managed to jump away.

"Damn, you're tough," Jake said as he landed. "It's like trying to attack Sandy."

"Did you just compare me to a giant space worm?" Carmen asked, sounding offended.

"A giant Cosmic Genesis Worm," Jake corrected. "A very important distinction."

Carmen didn't seem to care much about vermeology as she responded by attacking again, Jake gladly meeting her offense. The two of them rapidly moved through the arena, Jake dodging every attack from Carmen, while the vast majority of his own blows also missed. Those he did land barely seemed to do anything, and thus their battle saw little progress.

One thing became clear after a good while: Jake was faster than Carmen, but Carmen had more raw Strength. Durability-wise, Carmen also had a massive edge, and she likely also had more Endurance due to her stamina-only Path. However... in every other category, Jake had her handily beat. He simply had far more raw stats than her, and while hers being focused on only a few stats did allow her to keep up, the disparity was clear.

Without skills, though, Jake couldn't really show off many of his stats, allowing their fight to look relatively equal. Then again, even if Jake had been able to use skills, he probably wouldn't have done so, because one other thing was also pretty clear... This was a lot of fun.

Jake smiled as he and Carmen traded blows, the woman also enjoying the bout even if she failed to land any attacks. Several minutes passed, and despite little changing, the crowd and the combatants became fully engrossed in the fight as the two fighters got more and more accustomed to how the other one fought.

"Would you mind if I changed things up a bit?" Jake asked as they clashed for what felt like the hundredth time.

"Still no active skills," Carmen reminded him as she deflected a katar and tried to punch him in the chin.

"It won't be." Jake smiled as he dodged another attack and landed a solid kick, making Carmen slide backward.

Before she could fully stabilize, the area lit up as the ground below her exploded with destructive arcane energy. Jake didn't hesitate to continue his attack as Carmen lost her footing, slamming a katar into her stomach. As a follow-up, more than thirty bolts of destructive arcane mana popped into existence around him, which he promptly sent forward.

"No active skills," Olaf reminded him with a frown.

"It's not," Jake said with a smile, leaping forward to strike alongside his arcane bolts.

Even if his melee hits did little to nothing, Jake still believed his arcane energy should have some effect. At the very least, it should lower her durability somewhat and allow Jake to do some actual damage... That was what he hoped would happen, anyway.

It wasn't.

Attacking in tandem with all the exploding bolts, Jake expected an opening but instead just found Carmen grinning as she charged straight through them. A large explosion erupted as all the bolts went off, and through the explosion, Jake saw Carmen's form. Runes lit up wherever bare skin could be seen, and the arcane energy had done nothing... No, it had done something. Just not anything good from Jake's point of view.

With runes glowing intensely, Carmen suddenly sped up, flying through the explosion and appearing before Jake sooner than he had expected. He dodged her first blow, but she managed to barely grab onto his clothes, pull him in, and punch him in the chest, sending him flying back.

Jake stabilized in mid-air as he did a somersault and landed on the ground safely. "I thought no active skills."

"All passive," Carmen said, grinning as the runes on her body faded.

"A pretty damn overpowered one at that," Jake muttered.

"You find it strange the runes of a Runemaiden are powerful?" Carmen smirked. "Also... I think this makes it two hits."

"Aight, you got me," Jake said, also smiling. Though, in his defense, he had not seen that coming at all. He'd kind of expected Carmen to have high magic resistance, but what he had just seen was far above that. Those runes hadn't simply negated the mana; they had absorbed it and temporarily turned it into a burst of power.

It was like she had a Palate of the Malefic Viper skill... just against magic. This also explained why her aura felt so off and muted. She was absorbing energy at all times, making it look like there was less in her immediate vicinity.

"Let's see how you respond to this, though," Jake said as another dozen arcane bolts appeared around him, making Carmen scoff.

"Pretty sure you already saw the result once."

"Nah, I feel like this time will be different," Jake said as he charged once more, seemingly repeating his move from before.

Carmen likely suspected something was off but still charged in kind. Right as they clashed, the arcane bolts hit Carmen... and didn't explode. Instead, they struck her like hard crystals, throwing her slightly off balance and allowing Jake to put proper power into his blow as he stabbed her in the stomach.

The Runemaiden was blasted back from the impact, smashing into the back wall and making a nice human imprint. However, more than that... a small trickle of blood ran down her stomach, where his Blackpoint Nanoblade had barely managed to penetrate.

"So you *can* bleed," Jake said as Carmen pushed herself loose. He saw her wound was already healing, but he felt satisfied at having managed to do at least some damage. She really was ridiculously resilient, though Jake knew this resilience came with other drawbacks.

"What the hell were those bolts?" Carmen muttered.

"I'm sure you'll figure it out," Jake said as more appeared around him.

"Damn straight, I will." Carmen gritted her teeth as she kicked off the wall behind her, making a section of it collapse as she launched herself toward Jake.

CHAPTER 58

PILLOW TALK

"But it's actually just pure mana?" Carmen asked, still not entirely believing Jake's claims. "Definitely didn't feel like mana."

"Pure arcane mana," Jake corrected. "The stable variant, that is."

"Hm, the stabby ones did feel borderline identical to the exploding ones... though the exploding ones maybe felt a bit more aggressive in nature?" she pondered aloud.

"They are definitely more aggressive, hence why they wanna explode." Jake smiled teasingly as he turned his head and looked at Carmen, who was lying with her hands behind her pillow, staring at the ceiling.

The two of them were currently at Carmen's place in Nevermore City, inside one of the private residences available only to top members. As someone who had been able to attend the get-together for those who did well on the Leaderboards, Carmen was naturally viewed as a top member. Then again, even if she had done horribly, the mere fact she was a Rune-maiden of Valdemar was already enough to get her this designation.

Their duel in the arena had gone on for a few more minutes, but ultimately, there was little progress on either side. Jake could do some minor damage here and there, but Carmen self-healed quite well. At the same time, Carmen couldn't land any good hits on Jake. Finding a winner would have required them to keep going until one of them ran out of resources, and while Jake didn't doubt the crowd would have enjoyed that, he and Carmen couldn't be bothered.

Without any skills, their resources would have lasted for hours, and who really had the time for that? Sure, they could have switched over to using skills, but the arena spar wasn't a real fight, and if Jake was being honest, he didn't want to reveal his skills in front of a crowd.

After their fight, they had naturally both been a bit worked up and decided to go to Carmen's place to "compare notes" and "reflect on their battle." Which was definitely what they did. Definitely. Why else would they now both be lying naked in the bed?

"Maybe I should also work on getting an arcane affinity," Carmen muttered. "Then again, the only two people I know with one are you and Eron... Well, besides the gods and stuff."

"It isn't like arcane affinities are necessarily better either," Jake said, shrugging. "They just seem like that because the affinity naturally fits the person who made it extremely well. Look at Sylphie; she just has the 'basic' wind affinity, and I sure as hell wouldn't call that weak."

"Pretty sure she has more than just basic wind. I heard something about Sylphs being a thing, and I'm pretty sure she's related to those."

"Still just wind affinity." Jake shook his head as he sat up. "Maybe empowered a bit and of a certain flavor, but it's still wind magic."

"Hm, I guess you're right," Carmen relented as she looked deep in thought.

"Honestly, I'm more curious as to how exactly your level of durability even makes sense," Jake said as he leaned over and poked her arm. "Feels and looks like soft human skin, but it felt like striking metal whenever I hit it."

Carmen didn't even comment on his pokes as she also sat up. "I guess it's a mix between reacting to what is considered attacks and not attacks mixed with... what did you call it again? System fuckery? Yeah, that thing."

"Huh. Well, thank fuck for system fuckery, then. I assume this is also why you can move normally despite your durability and tough skin? I would assume it to be less flexible by default."

"Probably," Carmen semi-agreed as she opened and closed a fist. "It's pretty sweet, though. I used to be really careful when fighting, and I had to make sure not to take any hits... Now, I can take quite a beating without much struggle while giving plenty more back."

"That actually got me thinking... This Runemaiden stuff also empowered your internals, right?" Jake asked curiously.

"Yep, it's all-around," she said with a grin, "though some parts are more affected than others. My bones and skin more than anything else. So, pro tip: if you ever need to kill another Runemaiden, aim for the eyes. That's probably our biggest weakness."

"Thanks for the tip, but I was more thinking... how nerfed were you in our little spar? I remember you using a lot of boosting skills that took a heavy load on your body, and these must be a fuckload more powerful now, right?"

"You bet my boosting skills are a fuckload better now." Carmen grinned. "But I'm not gonna act like I would have had an advantage with boosting skills. Sure, mine may have been better than yours, but I'm not confident they would have allowed me to land anything decisive. Besides, you would also have had way stronger offense if that happened, and while I'm tough, I'm not invincible. Using boosting skills too much also negatively affects my durability; I learned that the hard way quite a few times in Nevermore."

"I see, I see." Jake nodded. "Say, is it okay for you to be sharing details about Runemaidens like this?"

"Who cares? Valdemar sure as fuck doesn't strike me as the sort of guy who would." Carmen shrugged, unbothered, before turning a bit more serious. "He does seriously want you to join Valhal, by the way. Gudrun is also entirely on board, and after your Leaderboards placement, I doubt anyone would dare protest."

"I know he's interested." Jake just smiled, not really touching on the subject further. Even if he trusted Carmen, he wouldn't share with her details about how his relationship with the Malefic Viper truly was. The fewer who knew about his status as a Heretic-Chosen, the better.

"Personally... I don't really think you should join," Carmen said after a few seconds.

"Hm?" Jake exclaimed, surprised.

"Think about it. If you join, you'll likely be made the Chosen of Valdemar, or at least someone with a higher position than me, which will make things really fucking awkward. Moreover... I wouldn't want the competition." She smiled during that last part.

"You're aiming to become Valdemar's Chosen?" Jake asked.

"Sure as fuck giving it a shot. I need to if I want to even try and keep up with all of you other damn monsters... Seriously, why the fuck are so many of the strongest people in this generation from Earth?"

"Not a clue." Jake smiled and shook his head, happy to at least know others shared those feelings.

"It's just weird," Carmen said with a sigh.

The two of them didn't say more for a while. After a bit, Jake took out the disc he had been handed by the Demon Prince, having decided to read it over. Carmen watched him take it out; he'd earlier explained to her that he planned on spending a few days in the Valhal compound, partly to study this disc.

Seemingly not wanting to disturb him, Carmen got dressed and went out into the courtyard of her personal residence to do some training. Jake got curious and decided to see how she was training before he fully immersed his mind in the disc.

He saw her take up a position in the middle of a small, open area, then close her eyes and take deep breaths. Then her eyes shot open as she punched forward, followed by several more strikes into thin air. She barely moved faster than a regular, pre-system human as she boxed with a seemingly invisible opponent, and she even dodged and weaved in between unseen blows. After about a minute, Jake realized something. The way she moved, dodged, struck... was similar to their spar. Not in terms of general moves, either; the entire flow was recognizable.

She's shadowboxing a version of me? Jake questioned as he looked at her practice a bit longer. Even from within the building, he could feel the odd energy surrounding Carmen and her intense and unbroken focus. She was entirely immersed in her imagined fight. Some pretty powerful concepts were also at play, and Jake even felt some faint energy come out of the ground beneath her. With a second inspection, he noticed that the huge magic circle spanning the entirety of Valhal's compound faintly responded, a small part of it active, seemingly facilitating and assisting in training like this.

It really is a peak faction for fighting fanatics, huh, Jake thought with a light smile. With things like this and the archery range, Jake was tempted to find out if he could join Valhal as an honorary member. Or, at the very least, blackmail Villy into giving him cool stuff like the archery range.

He really wanted an archery range.

Jake looked on only a bit more before he decided it was time to focus on his own matters. Delving into the disc, Jake began to study the ritual proposed by the Demon Prince, and his first impression was that it felt... kind of familiar? It definitely had many conceptual aspects in common with some of the rituals Jake had done before. There was also a lot of novelty to it, though, and it was a more complex ritual than anything Jake had ever done before. Besides maybe the one that had helped birth Vesperia, although that ritual had required several stages and whatnot, while this ritual would be a one-and-done.

He also saw that he would not be doing this ritual alone. Several C-grade demons would assist him, but Jake would be the main maestro. The conductor who controlled everything. It was a bit similar to the ritual he had done with Mystie and Hawkie to help hatch Sylphie. This one would require the other helpers to do quite a bit more than Hawkie and Jake had to back then, but everything would be at Jake's discretion.

In fact, Jake was pretty quickly beginning to understand why the Demon Prince had asked him. This ritual was not one created to be performed by a C-grade, especially not a mid-tier C-grade. Moreover, based on Jake's analysis, the person performing the ritual had to be within only a dozen or so levels of the Demon Prince, or it simply wouldn't work due to the disparity in quality. While each grade was a massive jump, each level within every grade was also a small step, and having someone atop the staircase trying to do this ritual wouldn't lead to any good results for the demon.

Coupled with the extreme requirements of the ritual master—the one in charge of the ritual—Jake could see how it would be difficult to find someone qualified. It was also easy to see, especially when factoring in his identity as the Harbinger of Primeval Origins, why Jake seemed like perhaps the Demon Prince's best choice in the multiverse. And while the process of creating creatures like Vesperia was a lot simpler than most probably expected, it still wasn't easy.

With all of this in mind, one ultimate question remained: did Jake have confidence in pulling off this proposed ritual?

Well, he would give it at least a fifty-fifty. It was definitely harder than anything he had ever done before, but he had also grown a lot stronger since he last did any major rituals—outside of the one with the Twinhead Ogre, but that was more fucking up an existing ritual circle.

Over these last fifty years, he had definitely progressed a lot when it came to ritualism. In addition, he specialized in Soul Ritualism, which this ritual definitely fell under. From his analysis, the primary bottleneck with this ritual also wasn't pure skill or the knowledge of the ritual master, but the insane minimum requirement of control and stats. There was *a lot* of powerful energy to keep track of at once, and some of this energy would be related to the Cerulean Devil. Most wouldn't even dare try and touch anything related to a god... but Jake didn't really care overly much.

One annoying thing did become clear, though.

I'll need to throw in some Jake Juice as a binding agent of sorts, he noted to himself. Not a lot of it, just enough to nudge things to merge together. Maybe other alchemists or ritual experts could find some way to make them merge without this method, but Jake sure as hell didn't know any. With what he was reading from the disc provided by the Demon Prince, the demons sure didn't have any set plans either, as they would "leave the merging process entirely at the Chosen's discretion."

A nice way of asking him to please figure out how to do it.

He already had a rough idea regarding what kind of approach he wanted to take after just checking over all the information once, but he still had to fully familiarize himself with the roles of his would-be assistants and get a comprehensive understanding of everything that would go down. At least one good enough so that he could handle everything that went wrong on the fly by following his instincts.

Jake did also have to consider the—

"Damn, you're deep; you've been at it for hours," Carmen said, interrupting Jake's train of thought.

He opened his eyes and stared into Carmen's, which were right in front of his face. "I'm focused." Without moving, he smiled. "And for the record, I did see you coming."

"Sure as hell didn't react."

"Why would I?" Jake kept smiling.

"Out of politeness?" Carmen shot back, leaning slightly closer. "Maybe I wanted something?"

"And what may you want?"

Carmen smiled deeply as she leaned in and whispered in his ear, "I want you to touch me... with Touch of the Malefic Viper." Jake's smile faded as the mood quickly died, and Carmen leaned back with a big grin on her face. "More specifically, I want to see if you can get through my defenses."

"I see you've upped your game when it comes to mental attacks," Jake said as he pushed her off the bed with a small shove.

She landed easily on her feet, still grinning. "Or maybe the target was just too susceptible to this particular kind of attack. Now, are you up for it?"

"Alright, but it isn't my fault if I melt a limb off," Jake said, sighing as he also finally got off the bed and got dressed.

"Eh, I can always get a new one." Carmen shrugged. "By the way, have you learned to pop out new limbs yet? I nearly could before my Runemaiden Ritual, but my body is a bit harder to heal now, mainly because of how damn resistant it is to pretty much all kinds of energies."

"I think I'm pretty close if I use a healing potion," Jake answered, "though I tend to avoid losing limbs in the first place. Also, can we talk about how little sense it makes that healing a damn hole in my chest seems easier than a severed hand? I know why it works like that with the Soul-shape and all, but still, it's weird, right?"

"Weird for sure, and no one else seems to think so." Carmen sighed as the two of them walked outside into the small courtyard.

"Truly indoctrinated by the power of system fuckery," Jake said, joining her in sighing. "Now, are you ready to have your arm melted off? I have been meaning to test my newly improved skills with acids using Touch, and this seems like a prime opportunity."

"Give it your worst," Carmen said as they both sat down with their legs crossed and she stretched out her arm.

Jake put both hands around her forearm as he looked at her. "Ready?"

"Already told you," she said, unbothered.

"Here we go, then," Jake said as he activated the skill.

Runes lit up all over Carmen's body as he did so, and he felt the sheer resistance as his hands began to glow dark green. A crackling sound echoed throughout the courtyard. Carmen grimaced, the runes shining brighter and brighter by the second as Jake kept pouring in the energy, her skin turning a shade darker.

Jake felt the resistance grow, but after an assuring look from Carmen, he kept going. Her arm was definitely being slowly affected as the runes absorbed more and more of the deadly energy, but Jake just kept on pushing harder and harder. He kept going for nearly half a minute until suddenly, he felt all the resistance disappear, and all the runes in her arm fractured.

"Oh shi—" Carmen tried to exclaim, cut off when something that should perhaps have been predictable happened.

Her entire arm exploded, launching Jake and Carmen away from each other, splattering blood all over both of them. Jake even had to react at the very last moment by using Eternal Shadow as bone fragments flew for him, each of them giving off an intense sense of danger. He got the feeling that each of them could have pierced pretty damn deep.

As the dust settled, Jake saw Carmen stand back up, missing her left arm at her shoulder, with cracks forming from her shoulder down her upper body. A bit of poison had even leaked in, but he felt it quickly being consumed, as only the runes on her body had been destroyed.

"You okay?" Jake asked, he himself uninjured due to Eternal Shadow taking the brunt of the explosion.

"I'm all right," Carmen said, grinning as she looked at her missing left arm. "Get it? All right."

"That joke was bad, and you should feel bad," Jake said, yet he nevertheless failed to hold himself back from smiling. "Did you at least learn something useful?"

"Not to let people with glowing hands touch me for too long at a time," Carmen said as she took out a health potion and consumed it while looking at her right arm. "Wanna try again? I kinda wanna see if I can actively resist it..."

Jake looked at her for a moment incredulously before just shrugging. "Sure. You even got two legs, and I have plenty of mana to spare."

"Glad to see we're on the same page." Carmen smiled, seeming almost excited at the prospect.

CHAPTER 59

TIME TO MAKE HISTORY

Spending time with Carmen was always eventful, and Jake thoroughly enjoyed it. Maybe it was because they were very much on the same wavelength, and both had a bit of a screw loose. Then again, which talented individual didn't have a bit of a screw loose? It was pretty much a requirement, in Jake's mind.

Carmen was just his type of weird. Both were driven, fighting maniacs and were willing to do dumb shit to try and progress. Their little experiment with infusing her with Touch of the Malefic Viper was a prime example of this. Through their brief experimentation, they discovered that the problem wasn't the amount of energy Jake infused, but that Carmen was sitting still while he did it.

If she moved around and punched, the energy would be dispersed faster than even Touch could infuse it. The arm had exploded simply due to an excess buildup of energy. Jake also had to admit that the entire experiment was quite beneficial to him. It was rare he had the chance to use Touch on people without them dying pretty quickly, and especially to use it on someone with such high resistance to the skill.

Overall, it was a great time for them both, even if Carmen ended up losing a few more limbs before they figured stuff out. While she recovered and trained by herself, Jake worked on the Demon Prince ritual, making sure no time was wasted.

Anyway, he and Carmen had spent four good days chilling in the Valhal compound before it was time for him to head toward the Demon Prince. He had considered staying a bit longer, but he had gotten quite excited about pulling off the ritual once he fully formed a plan in his mind.

Shit, he had even made a few minor changes to make the ritual suit his particular set of skills better.

When Carmen saw him off and he left the compound, Olaf was naturally also there, along with a few others who gave him knowing looks. In retrospect, maybe spending all his time alone with Carmen inside her private residence could lead to some unforeseen rumors. Not that it hurt Jake in any way, and besides, these rumors had been around ever since their meetup on Minaga's City Floor... They weren't exactly wrong, either.

"I guess I'll see you back on Earth," Jake said as they stood at the exit of the compound.

"If you remember to show up," Carmen teased him.

"Eh, I'm pretty damn sure someone will remind me if I don't," Jake played along. He hadn't missed a system event so far... but it had been kind of close a few times, hadn't it?

"Worst case, we'll just handle this Prima Guardian on our own," Carmen said with a shrug. "Shouldn't be that hard, though I do expect our Guardian to probably be the most powerful in the 93rd Universe. At least, that's what Valhal's intel indicates with how many Primas we killed."

"Let's hope so! That way, it can put up a good fight," Jake said, looking forward to the fight in... slightly less than two years now.

"For sure," Carmen agreed. "I'll probably be back on Earth before you, so see you there."

"See you," Jake said before offering his goodbyes to Olaf and those muscly dudes who always accompanied him. Then he headed off toward the Demon Prince. Even if he was looking forward to this ritual, he was also looking forward to getting back to Earth and seeing how things had changed there.

They had been in Nevermore for just about three years in Realtime with the time dilation, putting the intensity of the dilation at a factor of sixteen or so. It was not extreme, but also far from insignificant.

Jake also learned that he had been a bit misinformed regarding some things with Nevermore. Because one thing had kind of bothered him. When he initially heard about Nevermore, he'd been told that the time dilation would get stronger as one cleared more floors, but with how everyone seemed to finish so close to one another, he didn't really feel like that was the case.

Well, it turned out that it did exist... It was just really dialed down for those competing on the Leaderboards. So rather than it going from a factor of ten to twenty-five, the version he had done only went from fourteen to seventeen or something like that. Jake didn't know for certain, but he had a feeling this had something to do with the upcoming system events and whatnot, and to make sure that those who did badly wouldn't end up being late. Either way, for all the other versions of Nevermore, the difference would be way more noticeable.

Either way, as Jake made his way to the Demon Prince's place, he made sure to be seen leaving Valhal's compound. A few teleports later, he was at what looked more like a grand estate than a compound. It was a single large building with two smaller ones off to the side, with a tall wall surrounding it all. It somehow looked both more prestigious and less prestigious than the Valhal compound, and it definitely gave off a "rich people live here" impression.

Not that Jake should be talking, with his residence at the Order of the Malefic Viper and vast personal wealth.

The residents of this mansion clearly noticed Jake before he even fully arrived, as he found the Demon Prince walking toward the opening gate as he approached, ready to greet him. The demon looked elated upon seeing Jake, making him guess the demon hadn't necessarily believed he would actually show up.

"Welcome! I must say, I feared for a moment you would be preoccupied with more important matters and be unable to visit." Indeed, the Demon Prince wore a big smile, looking at Jake like he was a living, walking treasure.

"I said I would show up, didn't I?" Jake answered in a casual tone. "I'm a man of my word, and having looked over the ritual in detail, I must admit I find it an interesting challenge."

"Nevertheless, I know the Chosen is a busy man," the Demon Prince continued as he motioned for him to follow. "Please, this way. I'm sure you're curious to see the real thing after studying it."

Jake nodded and followed the Demon Prince into the large mansion... and down into the basement. Yeah, Jake felt like someone was pulling his leg. To have a demonic ritual take place in a large, creepy cellar was almost too on the nose, but nope, they were entirely serious. What's more, when he arrived in the main ritual chamber, he saw that everything had been drawn in blood, and the circle was indeed shaped like a pentagon with a pentagram in it.

The pentagon was drawn with equally long lines around the perimeter, with the expected star-shaped symbol formed in the middle by drawing lines between all the different opposing sides. The borders were also well-defined, resulting in a total of eleven sectioned-off areas.

Ten of these would each house a Demon Lord Heart, while the

Cerulean Devil would stand in the very center. The ritual looked complicated at first glance, but it was a lot simpler than it appeared. Simple didn't mean easy, though. Each of those Demon Lord Hearts contained intense power, and Jake would have to manipulate the energy of ten at once. And that wasn't even close to the hardest part. No, that came when he needed to use this energy.

In the center of the pentagon, the Demon Prince would be the focus of the entire ritual and also the one taking the biggest risk by far. Because when Jake gave him the signal, he would remove the crystal from his own forehead, as that gem was what Jake was supposed to infuse with energy. Removing that gem was akin to temporarily severing a part of his soul, and if Jake failed, the outcome wouldn't be good for the Demon Prince.

He'd end up with a broken Path that resulted in him never being able to level up again. Debilitating soul damage would be him getting lucky. The far more likely outcome was just death. On second thought, maybe death would be the preferable outcome to getting your soul fucked up...

"What do you think about the ritual?" the Cerulean Demon asked. "I worked on a lot of it myself with some of the best experts I could find in the field, and this was the best we could come up with. I will also admit it was made after we became aware of your existence, as you gave me and my clan hope to pull something like this off. The entire concept is based on an old ritual that was attempted a long time ago but has never once succeeded. I hope to make today a first, because someone like you has never existed."

Jake looked at the circle closely, making sure everything matched what the disc had said. It did, and Jake nodded as he looked at the demon, also finally doing a quick Identify.

[Demon – lvl 280]

"This ritual of yours indeed isn't feasible at all," Jake answered, watching the Demon Prince's smile quickly fade. "For anyone else but me, that is. But you already knew that."

"Yes," the Demon Prince readily admitted. "If rituals like these were possible with our current means, we would be doing them far more often. If we succeed for the very first time, the gains would be unimaginable. Perhaps it's foolish of me, but I'm willing to take this gamble and believe in you. Also, to clarify... my elders are very much against this, which is the primary reason we are doing it here in Nevermore City."

Jake slowly nodded, a few things making more sense now. He also wouldn't want some junior to pull off a massively risky ritual performed by some virtual stranger. It was peak gambling. As the demon said, however, the gains could be immense if Jake somehow succeeded.

He understood the mentality of the Demon Prince. It reminded Jake a bit of his own. The demon was willing to take massive risks for a small chance to grow stronger, and he was clearly not willing to just be another demon who would become an elite mortal. He was aiming for the peak, even if it killed him, and Jake could respect that. Jake could also respect that the higher-ups among the Demon Prince's clan wouldn't like this, so it was good he had come prepared.

"Speaking of lacking approval from your higher-ups..." Jake said as he waved his hand, and a piece of parchment appeared. A contract.

The Demon Prince quickly scanned it, unsurprised, and nodded. "A contract between two individuals... personal choice... knowledge of risk... karmic separation... This is a liability waiver and an agreement this ritual does not include either faction in any official capacity?"

"That is what I believe it says," Jake responded, having to fully admit he hadn't read the massive contract that thoroughly himself. Seriously, it was so overly long that it being written on a single piece of paper made no sense. However, he had been assured by the Viper this was what he needed, and from what Jake had read, the contract didn't include some joke clause. Because he could totally see the Viper including a joke clause.

"Well, this is also to be expected," the Demon Prince said as he, funnily enough, waved his own hand to summon a contract. "I will admit mine is a bit less thorough. I do not have the authority to declare that should any vengeance be sought due to the outcome of the ritual, the Fourth Hell will officially be declared an enemy of the Order of the Malefic Viper, and the two factions will be at war."

Jake just smiled. "Gotta be thorough."

"Indeed," the Demon Prince said as he made a small cut on his finger and pressed it against Jake's contract. There was no magic mumbo-jumbo or anything, but Jake did feel a tiny bit of energy being infused into the contract. "Now, my excitement and anxiety for what is to come next is beginning to overflow... Does the Chosen need any more preparation time? If not, I will go fetch the team."

"Give me an hour," Jake said as he looked at the ritual. "I will need to make some very minor adjustments to prime everything for my arcane affinity. It won't be invasive—more like an extra layer on top that will assist me and keep everything under control more easily."

"You do not have to explain yourself to me," the Demon Prince said.

"I'm already leaving my life in your hands, and if you wished me harm, I would have no recourse."

Quite the pressure, Jake mentally joked, nodding and then getting to work on the circle. The Demon Prince left to fetch the others who would assist him, leaving Jake to do his slight modifications. As he'd told the demon, he didn't need to do much, just add some strings of stable arcane mana here and there that more or less functioned like wires. This was one of the great things about his arcane affinity: he could easily mix it with other stuff without it ever interfering with anything. Meanwhile, with a slight mental command, he could activate the strings and use them to channel energy. He had even done something a bit similar with the Twin-head Emperor ritual, and that had worked out well.

Jake ended up taking a bit over an hour to get everything ready, with the Demon Prince having already returned with ten other demons by the time he was done.

"So these will be the ones assisting me during the ritual?" Jake asked as he went over.

"Indeed. All of them are highly skilled mages and ritualists who I'm sure will be of great help," the Demon Prince said proudly as Jake scanned them.

All the demons assisting him were between level 275 and 285. Jake's level 275 was actually on the lower end of the scale, but that didn't bother him particularly much. When it came to pure power, these demons were... okay at most. However, he could also feel a severe lack of bloodlust from most of them, making him believe they were all more crafters than fighters.

"Well, it's a pleasure to meet you all," Jake said as he looked at the ten clearly nervous demons, half of whom seemed to think this entire ritual was a horrible idea but were still going to do it because a Demon Prince ordered it. "Before we begin, I would personally advise you to shake off some of that nervousness. While your roles aren't the hardest, I would be very miffed if one of you ended up fucking shit up for the rest of us."

Jake said the last part in a slightly threatening tone, so he decided also to apply a bit of the carrot. "Meanwhile, if you all help make this a success, you will have been part of a ritual to do something likely never done before, all while working together with the Malefic Viper. Seeing as we're all smart people here, I hope I don't have to explain the significance of that. Oh, and dispel all thoughts of this ritual being impossible. It may be to you, but I don't see why that should make it impossible for me. I'm pretty good at doing what others believe impossible."

Were Jake's words extremely arrogant? Yes, definitely. But he also had to make it clear to the group that he was not there just to fuck around. Based on the feeling he got from the ten demons, his words did seem to have some effect. He wasn't wrong, either; he did have a history of pulling off seemingly impossible feats.

"Alright, everyone," Jake said encouragingly. "Get in position, and make sure you're in peak condition. Let's make history."

Everyone did as he said with resolute nods. He also exchanged gazes with the Demon Prince, who smiled and walked by him while patting him on the shoulder. "Let's make history indeed."

Jake took a deep breath, fully mentally prepared for the ritual. Everything was planned out, and surely... surely nothing unforeseen could go wrong when messing with the ancient fragment of a heart full of Records left by a powerful devil of the past, right?

CHAPTER 60

A COUPLE OF MAJOR OVERSIGHTS

This ritual was kind of unique in the sense that Jake didn't really ever do these with the intent of accomplishing something specific. Okay, he knew he wanted the ritual to push some creature toward a more powerful and "primal" Path, but he didn't go in with any knowledge of how exactly that would look. He pretty much just went with the flow and let things play out.

In this ritual, he was trying to amplify a very specific Origin.

The heart fragment, which was the centerpiece of the ritual, had belonged to a devil. A demon god. To return that to its Origin would be to return it to something closer to the Cerulean Devil. The Records of a god, especially a seemingly powerful one, would simply overshadow any related just to demons in general or anything like that.

Gazing at the ritual circle—which was really more of a ritual pentagon —Jake noted that everyone had gotten into position. The Demon Prince had purchased ten Crystalized Demon Lord Hearts from other Nevermore Attendees before he even approached Jake in the first place, and while Jake had considered whether adding his own would help, he'd quickly realized it wouldn't. The ritual was made for ten hearts, and Jake also knew numbers could have some weird conceptual significance.

"Everyone, get ready; we begin in sixty seconds," Jake spoke out to the basement as he felt the tension rise.

The Demon Prince sat with his legs crossed in the center of the large magic pentagram within the pentagon, and while he put up a good front, Jake saw his nervousness. Again, pretty understandable.

Seconds ticked by as all the demons did their own final preparations.

Everyone had a few potions at the ready, and all knew exactly what their roles were. The one doing the vast majority of the work was Jake, and in part, the Demon Prince, who had to endure the process of tearing his soul apart and hopefully reshaping it into something better.

"I leave my life and future in your hands, Chosen of the Malefic One," the Demon Prince sent Jake telepathically as he took a deep breath.

Jake didn't respond directly to him as he stood at the edge of the pentagon. "Ten seconds."

With the tension as high as ever, Jake said some final words of encouragement. "Keep calm, do your jobs, and all will be fine. Seven seconds."

Jake really wanted to say, "You don't have to believe in yourselves; just believe in me, who believes in you," but he had a feeling that would have made them too confused with only a few seconds left before shit went down.

"Five."

Taking a step forward, Jake stood at the control point of the ritual.

"Four."

Activating his energy, he linked up with the ritual.

"Three."

He felt all the hearts and the Demon Prince in the center.

"Two..."

Closing his eyes, Jake allowed his Perception to fully seep into the entire ritual circle as he raised his hands.

"One..."

Red light filled the basement as Jake poured in his energy and activated the ritual.

"Start."

As commanded, the first demon ritualist activated his section of the ritual, making the Crystalized Demon Lord Heart begin to crack and leak energy. Jake instantly took control of this leaked energy and forced it into the formation, storing it within.

With a mental command, he made another demon also activate her part when the second heart began to let out energy in a controlled manner. Once more, it was forced into the ritual circle as Jake kept track and made sure it didn't leave its designated area.

A few minutes later, a third heart was activated, followed by a fourth a few minutes later. As this kept going, the energy levels of the entire ritual and basement rose at an alarming speed, and all the while, Jake allowed none of the demonic energy to run rampant.

Soon, they reached the eighth heart, which was when Jake gave the

Demon Prince his cue. Without even a second of hesitation, the Demon Prince's body lit up with energy. All of the glowing veins on his body activated, and with determination, the gem embedded in his forehead was torn out to float upwards, barely connected to the demon through a thin red and blue string.

The lines drawn in the very center around the Demon Prince were also activated, their function a bit different than anywhere else. They were there to keep him alive long enough for Jake to do his thing, as he was very much under time pressure.

With another command, Jake strained himself to take hold of the demonic energy. He commanded it to move toward the center of the pentagram and the now floating cerulean gem. The gem didn't even resist in the slightest, greedily absorbing the energy from all the hearts.

Jake kept everything under control, even as the ninth and tenth hearts were activated. They weren't being drained too quickly or slowly; all the demon ritualists kept a steady pace as commanded, slowing down or speeding up whenever Jake told them to.

The Demon Prince sat with an empty look in his eyes as blood poured out of his forehead where the gem had been, looking almost catatonic. Yet Jake felt that the demon's consciousness was still strong, as the connection between the prince and the gem remained powerful.

So far, so good, Jake reassured himself, as things were proceeding as they should. He knew the demons were struggling, but they held on nicely. They all knew this was only possible due to Jake's monstrous level of control and Perception, as he made sure everything was as it should be.

Soon, it was time for the next part of the ritual. Jake poured in a bit of his own arcane energy. Not his Jake Juice quite yet, but just what he had initially believed he would be able to do when he originally saw the ritual. The arcane energy mixed with the demonic energy that ever so slightly entered the gem, carrying with it nothing more than Jake's intent.

Intent it listened to, as Jake felt something from the cerulean gem. He felt a sense of greed and hunger.

Good... it's there. Jake grinned to himself. Just as affinities had things they "wanted," many magic items like this also had some very fundamental sense of instinct. This gem naturally wanted to absorb more energy and grow, and now Jake had metaphorically kicked that instinct awake.

Suppressing a groan, Jake felt the gem begin trying to greedily drag the demonic energy out of the ritual circle, but he knew he couldn't allow that. If he did, he risked the gem exploding, or the Demon Prince being overwhelmed. He was already struggling, but Jake had to take his hat off to the Demon Prince. The guy was not considered a peak genius for nothing, as he managed to keep calm and do his part perfectly.

Minutes passed as the gem consumed more and more energy, its aura growing in intensity. Soon, the first heart was fully consumed, followed by a second and a third. The hearts were emptied out one after another, crumbling into dust, and soon the cerulean gem contained not only its own innate energies but the cumulative energy of ten Crystalized Demon Lord Hearts.

Had Jake stopped the ritual here, or had someone else been in charge, all they would have accomplished was infusing the cerulean gem with a fuckload of demonic energy, resulting in the body of the Demon Prince probably exploding if he tried to fully reabsorb it. He would definitely die; no doubt about it.

Yet the cerulean gem still hungered, and the Demon Prince was struggling more than ever. Now, all the other demon ritualists could do was look on with expectation, fear, and doubt. The ritual so far had all gone as planned, sure... but everything till now had also been the "easy" part that they all knew was theoretically possible.

Now, they were on the "making history" part as they explored all-new territory.

Jake then did what nobody else could, activating energy from deep within himself. A mere spark, a whisper at most. It traveled through the arcane strings he had laid down before, unaffected by all other energies. The strings rose and wrapped around the cerulean gem as the spark of Origin Energy entered it.

Nothing happened for a moment, and then a deep, thrumming noise erupted from the gem, sending out a wave of pure demonic energy that now carried a slightly off-blue color, ripping apart all of Jake's arcane threads in the process. A second wave came soon after, and Jake felt the changes within the gem. It began to not just house the energy from the Demon Lord Hearts... but entirely devour it to empower itself, turning quantity into quality. All to allow it to return to Origin... and this was when Jake noticed oversight number one with this entire ritual.

It was originally a damn heart.

A heart!

Not a fucking forehead gem.

So when the gem began to slowly warp and change, he detected the fear from the Demon Prince and the horror on the faces of all the demon ritualists. The cerulean gem... which would probably be called the Cerulean Devil Heart by now... grew in size, way too large to be on the forehead of the demon it had originally belonged to.

The horror on the faces of the observing demons only grew when, a moment later, Jake stepped down and teleported forward. Without a shred of hesitation, he grasped the growing gem in his hand, feeling it burn into his skin as he fought back the demonic energy. With his other hand, he quickly equipped a katar and stabbed the Demon Prince in his heart before promptly plunging the hand holding the crystal heart inside.

Jake tried to let go and pull his hand back out... but couldn't. He felt as if his hands had merged with the gem-like heart as it began trying to pull energy from him. Not just any energy, either. It wanted his Origin Energy, and not a little of it.

Yeah, no, Jake thought, quickly cutting that off as he resisted. For a moment, he considered just slicing off his own arm, especially when the flesh he had cut open to put his hand in began to close around his forearm due to the damn healing circle below them. However, before he had a chance to cut it off, the heart was complete.

It hadn't needed any more input or guidance from Jake. From the moment he had poured in the Origin Energy, it had known exactly what to do. Now, this was where the second major oversight of this ritual reared its ugly head.

Once the Cerulean Devil Heart was fully formed, it returned to the state it had once occupied. It obtained the Records of a being that was long dead yet had been a powerful devil back whenever they lived. Those Records were now everything that remained within the heart... and that wasn't something the Demon Prince could handle.

As the thrumming sound echoed out again, Jake finally recognized it as what it was: a heartbeat.

This Cerulean Devil Heart was still connected to the Demon Prince, even after it transformed. It was merged with his soul, through and through. For this ritual, he had temporarily separated it, but now, it had fully become part of him again. This had been what they wanted. The Demon Prince would now merge with the pure Records of the Cerulean Devil Heart. Merge with whatever had come to life within the heart. This part was not what they had wanted.

And, well, this situation reminded Jake a bit of the time he had chosen to also absorb an object containing overwhelming Records of a god. Except that god had still been alive, while this situation was entirely unique and of Jake's making.

As Jake was trying to figure out what the fuck to do, the third oversight made itself known. Due to holding the heart, he had somehow become part of this merging process, and through that connection, he felt the internal battle within the Soulspace. Usually, this space was an untouchable realm deep within the soul, but in this very moment, Jake was connected to the Demon Prince in a rather unique way. So, he closed his eyes and made a rash decision.

———

The Cerulean Demon. Demon Prince of the Fourth Hell. These were the titles the demon had made his name, with him primarily known as the Cerulean Demon. He had been privileged and talented enough to choose his own name, to try and communicate he was the second coming of the Cerulean Devil, the former master of the Fourth Hell and one of the most powerful devils the demon race had ever seen. It had been viewed as a tragedy when he died a few eras ago while exploring one of the more dangerous World Wonders of the multiverse.

Luckily, they had managed to retrieve his body and completed the ritual to create the fragments from his heart. The Cerulean Demon had been granted one of these fragments. When he had merged with it and the Legacy of the Cerulean Devil, he had believed himself a genius at the pinnacle of the multiverse. In some ways, he was. He had proven himself in Nevermore, and even if two people had beaten him, he wasn't particularly disappointed. In fact, the Chosen of the Malefic Viper had given him hope of truly being the second coming of the Cerulean Devil... and in some ways, hadn't he succeeded? Just not in the way he had hoped.

As the cerulean lightning struck him, he was blasted back within his own Soulspace, the pain nearly unimaginable. Rolling on the ground, the demon tried to stabilize as a claw swept up, tearing his body into several pieces.

He reappeared a moment later, a bit further away, as lightning struck down from above, obliterating his entire body in an instant. Right as he appeared again, his head was severed from his body, and then he was blasted apart once more. He barely had time to collect his thoughts and wonder how foolish his ambitions had truly been.

During the ritual, after separating the gem from himself, the Cerulean Demon had gone to his Soulspace to keep everything intact. He had resisted as the energy flooded into him, and in the sky, the energy had gathered around the gemstone floating there, representing the fragment in the real world.

The energy levels had spiked so high the Demon Prince had been certain it would explode and shatter his entire soul and body... but then something had appeared. He couldn't remember what it looked like, but something had entered the gem... and then it had begun evolving. It had grown, pulsed, begun to beat like a true heart, and the Demon Prince had been elated, especially when he felt his connection to it strengthening more than ever before as it fully merged back into him. He'd been happy and, for a moment, even believed they had truly succeeded.

Until the heart didn't stop growing.

From the heart had grown a torso, legs, arms, and a head, and then an entire creature had appeared. For a moment, the Demon Prince had believed the Cerulean Devil had come back to life, as this demonic creature looked just like the paintings he had seen. The same blue leathery skin, four horns, clawed hands, and powerful physique. Yet the eyes were different. Empty. When the Demon Prince saw those eyes, he knew that this was but an empty husk... a husk that still possessed the overwhelming Records of the Cerulean Devil.

A husk that was currently destroying him.

The Demon Prince tried to fight back, but he didn't stand a chance. He was powerful within his own Soulspace, for sure—his Records allowed him to display power far beyond what he could muster in the real world— yet before this Cerulean Devil husk, he was nothing but a plaything to be repeatedly destroyed as the creature learned about itself. Like a curious and destructive child, it tried to kill him in all the ways it could. The Demon Prince felt himself weakening. Felt himself dying, fearing what would come next.

His soul would die, and this creature would overwhelm his own Records. It would replace him and evolve into something truly monstrous. He just hoped that even if it was powerful, the Chosen of the Malefic One and the others could handle this creature... but he feared that what he evolved into would not remain a C-grade.

Foolish. He and this creature were both foolish. It would likely become an A- or S-grade that would never be able to level again, existing as naught but a being of destruction. A short-lived Path, as they were within Nevermore City, where some powerful being would snuff it out instantly. The expected outcome of a creature with no sapience running wild.

Meanwhile, the Demon Prince's own hubris had led to this. He had believed himself far more capable than he truly was, and now he couldn't even struggle anymore.

His body was destroyed within the Soulspace over and over again, and he reappeared slower and slower with every death. At the same time, the Cerulean Devil husk only grew in power. The end was near, and struggle was meaningless, as—

"Oi," a voice suddenly cut through the Soulspace. "The fuck you think you're doing?"

CHAPTER 61

DEMONIC SOULSPACE ADVENTURE: CERULEAN DEVIL EDITION

The creature stopped attacking just as the Demon Prince reanimated again, his form semi-transparent due to the significant soul damage he had taken. He looked over in horror and saw the Cerulean Devil stare directly at the newcomer who had entered his Soulspace. Stare directly at the Chosen of the Malefic Viper.

"Get out of here!" the Demon Prince yelled with all his remaining energy. He quickly understood what had happened. The Chosen had somehow projected his very own soul into the prince's, and should he die here, the Chosen risked potentially even dying himself, or at the very least taking severe soul damage. That couldn't happen. "You can still escape! Go!"

However... his warning was too late. Even as the final words left him, the creature disappeared, only to appear right behind the Chosen of the Malefic Viper.

"Oh," the Chosen said as he slowly turned and looked at the creature more closely, tapping its forehead with a finger. "Pretty empty in there, huh? All instinct."

The Demon Prince just stared, confused. The creature had appeared behind the Chosen, raised a claw, and then stopped. It looked as if it was... shaking. However, its eyes soon regained their fervor as it roared loudly, nearly dispersing the prince's body. Its claw swung down, and—

An arm flew into the air as the Chosen stood with one hand raised. The creature roared again when a palm smashed into its face, pushing it to the ground and making the entire Soulspace shudder from the impact. Without the Demon Prince even knowing how it happened, three more limbs flew into the air, and he saw the Chosen standing with a foot on the chest of the Cerulean Devil's husk.

A pillar of cerulean lightning descended and blew the Demon Prince even further away. He felt the pain in his chest as he saw the ground had been split apart, a large crater left where the bolt had struck. Quickly, he spotted the Cerulean Devil teleporting a good distance away, its limbs already fully regenerated. Moreover... it was still growing stronger.

"Feisty," the voice of the Chosen once more echoed as he walked out of the crater with calm steps, not a single mark on his body. He then suddenly turned and looked toward the Demon Prince. "Things didn't quite go as planned, huh?"

The demon just stared as the Cerulean Devil teleported closer to attack again... only to get blasted into the air by an unseen explosion. The Demon Prince couldn't even begin to comprehend what was going on. *What... is happening?*

Jake gave the Demon Prince another look after gently pushing the odd devil creature away, but he still didn't get any answer. He began to fear he had been too slow in entering the Soulspace of the demon, and that the prince had taken too much damage before his arrival. But the fact he had yelled out with warning indicated he wasn't in that horrible of a state.

"Are you okay?" Jake asked again. "Any permanent damage?"

Finally, the demon seemed to regain some semblance of calm. "I am fine for now... but that isn't important. The Cerulean Devil is—"

"Annoying," Jake cut him off as the creature appeared again, forcing Jake to slap it into the horizon once more to give him some more time to talk. He also couldn't help but get a look around, as this was the first Soulspace he had ever seen belonging to another person, and he knew this was an incredibly rare opportunity.

The Soulspace was the representation of the Truesoul every living being had within themselves. Jake's was a massive area filled mostly with barren land and plains with barely any grass on them. The demon's Soulspace honestly wasn't that much different, with the ground just a bit more barren. The arcane energies filling the sky in Jake's Soulspace had been replaced with rumbling, blueish thunderclouds. Well, he also didn't have a shadowy version chilling there or a drop of blood from a Primordial, but those were more bonus assets, in Jake's mind. Not like Jake had a rampaging blue devil husk in his, either.

"How are you—" the Demon Prince began, but Jake cut him off again.

"Doesn't matter right now. What matters is finishing this ritual."

The Cerulean Devil attacked again. Jake dodged a few times before yet again kicking the creature away. It was a bit annoying, but he had to hold back. He had felt some energy being consumed when he severed the limbs earlier, and he didn't want to waste anything if he could avoid it.

"What do you mean?" the demon asked. "This... this is the finished ritual."

"Alright, then we need to finish the post-ritual issues we are now facing." Jake sighed, noticing the Cerulean Devil was a bit slower at attacking this time. Probably for the best, as he really didn't want to fight that creature. There was no point in doing so.

Jake knew he could kill the Cerulean Devil if he wanted, but he also knew what that would mean. It would destroy the newly formed heart he had implanted in the Demon Prince, resulting in all their efforts being wasted and the Demon Prince getting crippled, as he would lose a part of himself.

If he let it be, the Demon Prince would die, and the creature he was fighting would manifest in the real world, which definitely wouldn't be good. Simply locking down the Cerulean Devil by sealing it in an arcane barrier also wouldn't work. Jake knew instinctively that the moment he left the Soulspace, his energies would leave with him. They had to, or a part of Jake would be forever embedded in the Soulspace of the Demon Prince, which would hurt him immensely.

No... Jake needed to do something else. The easiest solution would be for the Demon Prince to just kill the Cerulean Devil, but that definitely wasn't going to happen. The thing was pretty damn strong. Jake wasn't sure one could really equate the power of creatures within a Soulspace to grades in the real world, but this one would definitely be high. For context, it was stronger than the cursed chimera had been when Jake first got it.

After the curse had merged with sim-Jake, things had become a bit complicated, but that was neither here nor there.

"Does the Chosen have a plan?" the Demon Prince asked as he quickly arrived at Jake's side. "The creature manifested from the Records of the Cerulean Devil is way beyond my expectations and not something I can deal with."

"I'm well aware of that," Jake muttered as he considered his options.

In the real world, he saw himself still standing there with a hand around the heart, and the many demon ritualists around himself and the

Demon Prince, none of them doing anything. They all knew trying to interfere wouldn't do them any good. Jake also knew that with a single thought, he could exit the Soulspace, closing the opening he had entered through in the process and leaving the demon to his doom. This was probably the safest choice... but Jake really hated losing, and failing this ritual would definitely count as a loss.

As he was still considering ideas, the Cerulean Devil attacked again, this time having changed up its goal. Rather than target Jake, it went for the Demon Prince to snuff him out once and for all. Too bad Jake was standing right next to him.

An arcane barrier sprang up, blocking the attack of the devil as an explosion of electricity covered the Soulspace. Jake didn't even feel it tickle him as he raised both his hands and motioned. A bit of mana appeared, raising six barriers around the Cerulean Devil before Jake pressed them together, sealing the creature within a cube.

Using my energies is pretty fucking hard, Jake noticed as the Cerulean Devil struggled to break free. Moreover, he felt his arcane energy naturally disperse at an alarming rate, even though it was the stable variant. It simply didn't belong in the Soulspace and was naturally being destroyed by the entire space. Jake himself was also a target for constant destruction. He just didn't really notice it.

Slamming against the barriers in an attempt to break out, the Cerulean Devil began generating cracks. Jake looked on, thinking hard... and then he remembered something. He remembered sim-Jake and what he had done during his stay in his own Soulspace. He also remembered something else from his many conversations about devils and demons.

Turning to the Demon Prince, he didn't beat around the bush. "Are you willing to take a massive risk?"

"What do you require me to do?" the demon asked, clearly determined to do whatever Jake asked of him.

"Nothing—things just might not turn out how I hope."

"I already left my life in your hands. I will trust you till the very end."

"You're really piling on the pressure," Jake said, smirking. "But alright... begin Operation Absolute Submission."

Jake stepped down and appeared right in front of his own barrier. His hand shot forward, shattering the arcane energy like glass as he grasped the neck of the Cerulean Devil. Before it could even do anything, he threw it down into the ground, creating yet another crater.

A storm of lightning descended, but Jake raised a hand and snapped, dispelling all the lightning halfway to its target he stared down at the devil. "Pathetic."

The creature didn't understand his words, but its roar of anger suggested it could somewhat comprehend his intent. Rather than attack Jake, it flew straight for the demon prince, but before it could even move more than a few meters, Jake grabbed its ankle and yanked it back.

"We're not done," Jake muttered as he slammed the devil into the ground again. It got up instantly, only for Jake to stomp it in the face, embedding its head in the ground again. Struggling, the devil tried to attack with its claws but found itself unable to even pierce Jake's skin.

Jake quickly took hold of one of its wrists, then tossed the devil away yet again before teleporting over and catching the creature, only to slam it into the ground once more. None of what Jake was doing actually hurt the devil, as he didn't put much power in... but it did make the devil feel utterly powerless.

He knew this devil wasn't a real creature. It didn't have a soul or any kind of real consciousness. It was just a bundle of Records, acting on instinct to come alive. Like the nascent energies of an elemental forming, fighting the environment to become a living being. All it knew was that it had to kill the Demon Prince, and it would live.

It couldn't really learn, as it couldn't think. Not truly. But it could ever so slowly adapt, which had been shown by the creature kind of learning how to move and control itself. Perhaps it would awaken a true consciousness one day, but only at the cost of the Demon Prince's life.

In summary, it was a being that had only one goal: survival. Right now, survival meant consuming the Demon Prince and taking over his body. Jake was going to show the Cerulean Devil that this was no longer an option. He would show it that it only had one option if it wanted to live in any way.

Minutes passed as Jake threw the Cerulean Devil around. It fought back in the beginning, but soon, it only tried to defend itself. This self-defense slowly morphed into the Cerulean Devil barely trying, instead opting to do the only thing it could to survive:

Run.

However, even that was no option. Jake allowed it no escape as he kept beating it down over and over again. In the meantime, he also began to leak out tiny bits of his own aura, frightening the Cerulean Devil further.

When he thought it was about time, Jake looked over at the Demon Prince, who stared, shocked at everything that was happening, and sent a simple mental message. *"Offer the Cerulean Devil a contract to submit and live."*

For a few moments, the Demon Prince looked at him in confusion. Then his eyes suddenly lit up with clarity as he understood. Jake wouldn't even have considered this an option under usual circumstances, but he was dealing with demons right now.

They were creatures of contracts. Deals. Agreements. Even if the Cerulean Devil was only a husk, it was still bound by its Records as a devil, and once it agreed to a contract, it would be binding. As for its ability to even agree, Jake also knew there would be no problems there. Every creature innately understood contracts created through the system. Perhaps they did not understand its intricacies, but they could instinctively comprehend the intent. Naturally, the Cerulean Devil's instincts would never allow it to submit to the weaker Demon Prince... unless it viewed it as the only way to survive.

Jake upped the pressure as he watched the Demon Prince prepare. Rather than simply smashing the devil around, he fully restrained it by wrapping it up in arcane strings, conveniently allowing it to still move one of its arms a little.

"Enough... It's time to end this," Jake said, seeing the Demon Prince approach with the contract. He had been hesitant to do this, but now, for the first time, he fully unleashed his presence and let loose, activating maximum-intimidation mode.

———

The Demon Prince wasn't sure something like this would work as he quickly spun up a contract of absolute submission. He approached the devil who had just been bound by strings, a floating contract in front of him.

Even if the devil feared death... submitting and becoming part of the Demon Prince was practically akin to its death. Something truly extraordinary had to pressure it into fully submitting. As he was connected to the Cerulean Devil, he knew it was not at all ready to give up yet. Still, he chose to believe in the Chosen as he got within range of the Cerulean Devil, who looked ready to tear the contact apart... until everything stopped.

And then it descended. An aura unlike any he had ever experienced overtook his entire Soulspace and crushed everything beneath it. All emotions were replaced with fear; the Demon Prince could barely look over the Chosen of the Malefic Viper, who appeared much bigger than he truly was.

In the sky, the clouds scattered as an orangish glow fell over the Soulspace. Looking up, the Demon Prince saw two massive irises stare down at him. He had never felt smaller or more insignificant... and then he felt a slight tap on the contract as the Cerulean Devil placed its palm on it.

Just like that, the eyes disappeared, the pressure was gone, and everything returned to normal.

Casually, the Chosen said, "Well, that ended up working out somehow. See you on the other side."

And with that, he was gone, leaving only a frozen Demon Prince and Cerulean Devil behind.

————

Jake opened his eyes in the outside world as he disconnected from the Demon Prince's Soulspace, and he felt the slight gap he had entered through close for good. The heart he was grasping in his hand no longer had the same suction force, so he let go, instantly pulled out his hand, and jumped back. Blood splattered out, but the healing circle was still active, rapidly mending the wound. Not that Jake believed that was necessary.

"Lord Chosen, what—" one of the ritualists began.

"Just wait for it," Jake cut in with a smile, and as if on cue, a shockwave of energy erupted from the Demon Prince's body as he was enveloped in light. Within this light, which Jake could only look inside of using his Sphere of Perception, he saw the Demon Prince disappear for a few moments before reappearing shortly after, now a changed demon.

The light faded to reveal his form as he stood there with his eyes closed. The forehead gem was gone, and his body had grown a bit in bulk, but the most notable difference was the head. Ten horns circled his skull, each of them pointing toward the ceiling, almost as though he were wearing a crown... and definitely making helmets extremely difficult to wear.

Using Identify, Jake smiled.

[Cerulean Demon Lord – lvl 280]

All around them, nervous demon ritualists stared with apprehension. Jake also looked at the newly born Cerulean Demon Lord and asked a pretty important question: "Are congratulations in order, or did we just birth some mindless beast?"

Finally, the Demon Lord opened his eyes and breathed out, then threw a look at Jake that contained an odd mix of gratitude, respect, and fear. Yet he remained polite. "Thank you... I am still getting used to things."

Jake nodded as he felt the aura of the Demon Prince. It didn't really necessarily feel that much more powerful than before. Only a little. Which perhaps shouldn't have surprised Jake, as the Demon Prince had come in third on the Era's Leaderboards, only behind himself and Ell'Hakan. It wouldn't have made much sense if he had somehow jumped up in power from this ritual, as he was already close to how powerful one could be for his level. It wasn't like Jake had just given him a bunch of stat-increasing titles.

However, he had definitely changed. His Path had evolved, and his future prospects were now far brighter than before.

Then—a bit late, in Jake's opinion—the pentagon and pentagram finally broke fully apart, marking the end of the ritual for good. With it naturally came the sweet system notifications of levels gained.

CHAPTER 62

TIME TO HEAD HOME

Vilastromoz had a lot of thoughts bouncing around in his head. It seemed the mystery surrounding the First Sage was growing exponentially. However, he could always trust Jake to offer him a good distraction. He sat on the terrace in Nevermore City with his avatar, very much enjoying the show.

He had kept an eye on the entire ritual, as quite frankly, he viewed the Demon Prince and everyone involved with creating that ritual as complete morons. From their conversations, they had clearly believed they were the first ones ever to think up such a daring ritual and viewed themselves as truly innovative and bold.

For the Viper, this wasn't even among the first hundred rituals he had observed like that, each of them practically identical in nature. What they were doing wasn't complicated at all; it was just stupid. Half the rituals like this ended with the entire thing just blowing up, while the other half ended similarly to how this one had, with the demon in the center mutating into something unintended.

This ritual was different, though. Not in its design, but in that it had Jake in charge. His application of the special energy he possessed had led to the creation of a far more powerful catalyst for evolution, but that didn't solve the issue of that evolution not ending well for the Demon Prince. Honestly, the entire thought process behind what the Demon Prince of the Fourth Hell wanted to accomplish was flawed.

The whole point was for him to improve his Records, and to do that, he would have to absorb an item with superior Records. However, for him to consume an item with superior Records, he needed to have powerful enough Records to begin with. It was quite the conundrum, and to put it in the simplest terms possible, the Demon Prince had tried to swallow something too big for him to handle. Mortals simply weren't meant to handle the Records of a god, period.

Vilastromoz was also certain the higher-ups of the Fourth Hell knew this. Shit, the Viper himself had seen recordings of their own failed rituals in the past, so they knew this wasn't going to work. Yet they had allowed the Demon Prince to go ahead, even after he had proven himself on the Leaderboards. Had they done so to use him as a political tool? Had the Viper's Chosen messed up and gotten one of their young talents killed, they likely wouldn't have demanded compensation, but they could've tried to leverage it to request help from Jake or perhaps even the Viper himself in the future.

It was naturally also possible that they'd simply wanted to take the gamble and see if the Harbinger of Primeval Origins could do what was thought impossible. To lose a Demon Prince to figure this out wasn't that big of a price to pay. They could always nurture many more. Meanwhile, the possibilities if Jake was successful were nearly limitless and something even the devils of the Hells would care about.

This was the reality they now found themselves with. Jake had succeeded... No, he had gone beyond expectations and done something that the Viper honestly hadn't been a fan of, even if things had worked out.

"Did your Chosen just astral-project his own soul into the Soulspace of another?" the Wyrmgod suddenly asked as the Primordial appeared on the terrace.

"And here I thought you respected the rights to private property," the Viper said teasingly. "Not to mention your illegal spying on residents... Do we have a public-relations disaster on our hands here?"

"Nevermore City is still partly considered Nevermore and thus my domain," the Wyrmgod answered. "And even if I observed the situation, due to its peculiar nature, I still remain with questions. Did your Chosen truly astrally project into another Soulspace?"

"He sure did," the Viper said, shrugging. "Mind you, this is after I told him not to astrally project his soul around like that way back in the tutorial."

"Foolish and reckless," the Wyrmgod said before he frowned. "Wait, he astrally projected during the tutorial? Where to?"

"To the Order of the Malefic Viper, using his connection to me as my

Chosen," the Viper said casually. "I did send him back pretty quickly, though."

"That is... hm..." The other Primordial appeared to be deep in thought.

Jake doing these things was impressive, but neither was considered impossible. Astral projection was a pretty normal ability, and Jake's version was quite frankly shit. It was the riskiest version there was, and one no one ever really used unless they didn't know better. Projecting at such an early grade did indicate an extremely powerful and stable soul, though.

Likewise, entering the Soulspace of another was not considered impossible, just incredibly rare, and not something people often did or wanted to do. Very specific circumstances had to present themselves to make it possible. There were also certain skills that could make one interact with the Soulspace, though.

The Minotaur Mindchief Jake had encountered all the way back in E-grade was a creature that could touch upon the soul. The skill that D-grade had wasn't quite capable of entering a Soulspace, but with a skill evolution or two, perhaps it would be possible. The thing is, more often than not, there were no benefits to entering a Soulspace, only demerits.

Anyone would be stronger inside their own Soulspace than in the real world. The Soulspace was a representation of your Records and allowed you to have power based not on how strong you were, but how strong you could become. It was a simplification, but that was roughly how it worked.

With how Records functioned, outside of extraordinary cases, everyone would have more Records than their actual power presented. The only ones who didn't were those who had reached the end of their potential, and even they always had a bit more potential to pull on and would be at a significant advantage within their own Soulspace.

This was due to the second reason why it was stupid to enter someone else's Soulspace: the suppression. A Soulspace was one's domain, and anything foreign that did not belong there would be suppressed and pushed out or destroyed. So even if two people were equally powerful, if the fight suddenly switched to the Soulspace of either of them, that person would have an insurmountable homefield advantage and readily destroy their opponent.

The Soulspace could most easily be likened to the divine realm of a god. It was the domain of the person it belonged to, and within it, they would be far more powerful while everyone else would be suppressed. So, for the same reasons one wouldn't ever want to enter another's divine realms, it was inadvisable to enter other Soulspaces.

That is... unless one was so powerful that any such suppression in other domains proved meaningless. This was what Jake had effectively done. His soul was simply at another level, and even if he astrally projected into another Soulspace, he didn't really care about anything and did whatever he did in there.

The reason it was still risky, though, was that if the Demon Prince had died, Jake would have lost whatever he astrally projected for good. Which definitely wouldn't have been good.

"His soul is truly not normal, is it?" the Wyrmgod questioned after a good while.

"Nope," the Viper said, smiling.

"Do you expect the Hells to begin making their move soon? I know the Order has maintained a strong working relationship with them, even in your absence. We both know that his accomplishment is related to his Bloodline, and the Demon Prince will surely return to the Fourth Hell and report everything that happened in detail."

"Oh, without a doubt, they'll do something fun." Vilastromoz shook his head. "They owe Jake now—especially the Demon Prince, whom I'm sure will be given quite a lot of attention going forward."

"They will undoubtedly want to propagate his Lineage," the Wyrmgod agreed. "I am also thinking... has your Chosen considered the impact of what he has just done?"

"Not at all," Vilastromoz said with certainty as he grinned.

"I see. Either way, I am still interested at some point in the future when he has matured more into his powers," the Wyrmgod said as he turned to leave. "Before, I was unsure if he would even be open to the suggestion, but now that he's opened that door himself, my doubt has lessened significantly."

The Wyrmgod disappeared as Vilastromoz shook his head. Jake indeed didn't know the impact of what he had done. No, not the achievement itself or anything related to it. It was the mere fact he had even agreed to the ritual in the first place.

Before this, he had only ever done rituals for himself. Even if it ended up benefiting some factions, he hadn't been asked by them to do it. This time, he had effectively done a commission using his abilities as the Harbinger of Primeval Origins. He had shown the multiverse that was a possibility he would consider, which also communicated he could use the ability purposefully, with its limitations perhaps not as severe as first hinted at.

In summary, Jake had sent a message to all the major factions of the multiverse despite not knowing he had done so. Or maybe Jake had, and the Viper had underestimated his Chosen—and his ability to understand the multiverse's political landscape.

———

Jake had naturally not thought about this at all. He had just seen a really interesting and cool ritual and agreed to do it, never considering the wider implications of his actions. But was that really his fault? It was just everyone else reading too much into things and making them way more complicated than they had to be.

Still standing in the ritual chamber, he waited patiently as the newly born Cerulean Demon Lord regained his bearings. Jake could understand why it would take a while. He probably had a lot of system notifications to deal with, so Jake also took the chance to check out those he had gotten himself.

First up was an interesting one; he wasn't sure he had ever gotten an "experience gained" message that looked like that before.

You have successfully conducted a ritual leading to the creation of a Cerulean Demon Lord – A new kind of creation has been made. Bonus experience earned.

He'd had other notifications that talked about rituals, but not in this fashion. It was mainly the conducting part... probably because this was Jake's first group ritual where he had been in charge. He had feared this would hurt his experience gain, but seeing the next few messages, that didn't appear to be the case.

'DING!' Profession: [Heretic-Chosen Alchemist of the Malefic Viper] has reached level 263 - Stat points allocated, +35 Free Points

...

'DING!' Profession: [Heretic-Chosen Alchemist of the Malefic Viper] has reached level 267 - Stat points allocated, +35 Free Points

Five whole levels for a ritual that only took a couple of hours. That was damn efficient leveling, if Jake said so himself, and it put him even closer to level 300, which was the next milestone he really looked forward to, as that would mean meeting the First Sage directly.

He had naturally also gained a few race levels alongside the profession ones.

'DING!' Race: [Human (C)] has reached level 276 - Stat points allocated, +45 Free Points

...

'DING!' Race: [Human (C)] has reached level 278 - Stat points allocated, +45 Free Points

All in all, it had been quite a fruitful endeavor, and even if he'd had to spend a bit of his special Jake Juice, it was such a tiny amount that the levels he had just gained nearly made up for it. He almost wanted to see if he could do another ritual sometime soon, but he also got the feeling that wouldn't be smart. Not like it would reward even close to the same amount of levels, due to the uniqueness of this one. He also wasn't sure where to find ten legendary Demon Lord Hearts.

"My lord?" one of the demon ritualists asked after a while.

The Demon Prince took a moment to respond as he opened his eyes again and rolled his shoulders. Rather than respond to the demon, he looked at Jake instead. "My apologies. There are a lot of things to take in, and the metaphysical representation of the Cerulean Devil still remains within my Soulspace. It will take a while to fully absorb, but with the contract in place..." As he spoke, he looked deep in thought.

"I would reckon you got a pretty smooth ride for the next evolution or two." Jake shrugged with a smile. He would be like Jake and Sylphie, in that he didn't have things like race quests but would still be able to evolve as long as his class allowed it.

"That is likely," the newly born Demon Lord agreed. "My racial skills have mostly all changed, but my class remains the same. One thing is clear, though: I am a full-fledged Demon Lord now. With all the perks and downsides that come with that."

"Is that a good or a bad thing?" Jake questioned.

The Demon Prince just smiled. "Think of Demon Lords as being to demons what a True Royal is to an ectognamorph, albeit in an admittedly far less extreme fashion. It's viewed as a higher race of sorts, though it does also come with a certain set of expectations."

Jake nodded. "So, it's overall good. Got it."

"Good indeed." The Demon Prince shook his head with a smile as he looked at Jake seriously. "You have given me a boon I have no idea how to ever make up for. No, not just me; the entire Fourth Hell owes you. It may be late to ask, but what does the Chosen desire? I realize we failed to ever discuss payment for your work."

"Hm," Jake said, having totally not forgotten he should probably get paid. "How about this... You owe me one."

Jake truly didn't need anything. However, a favor could hold a lot of value in the future, especially if the Cerulean Demon Lord rose to power as one would expect of him. One had to remember he was in third place on the Era Leaderboards, and that was before his evolution. Now, Jake didn't doubt he would have done even better, though it was doubtful he would have beaten Ell'Hakan, much less Jake.

"Owing you is but a given." The Demon Lord shook his head as he considered for a moment before taking out an odd emblem of sorts. When he did so, Jake saw the alarm on the faces of the ritualists, but none of them said anything. "For now, take this."

"What is it?" Jake questioned before he accepted it.

"The crest of my clan. With it, you will be treated like an honored guest in at least the first four Hells. Moreover, if you ever find anything you desire from us, feel free to use it and contact us, and I swear on my Path that I shall do my utmost to assist you."

"I see," Jake said as he chose to accept the crest. Then he got an idea. "I may not find a need myself, but if I have a comrade who can benefit, would I be allowed to give it to them instead?"

"What you use it for will be at your sole discretion," the Demon Lord said. "I am well aware that chances are we have nothing to offer that the Chosen of the Malefic Viper cannot obtain himself, outside of particular things unique to the Hells or items that could only benefit demons."

"In that case, I may just find a use for it," Jake said, nodding. Yeah, chances were he was just going to hand it off to Irin or something. As the Demon Prince had said, Jake didn't really need anything they could offer, and even the unique alchemical ingredients the demons had a monopoly on, he could still just buy as part of the Order if push came to shove.

"Anyway, it was a pleasure doing this ritual with you all, even if things didn't exactly go to plan," Jake said after they exchanged a few more pleasantries. "Good job, everyone. I told you we would make history."

It seemed as if it was only when Jake said this that the ten demon ritualists who had assisted with the ritual truly realized what they had been a part of. Only now did they realize they had indeed been part of a ritual that may have been entirely one-of-a-kind, shaping the very history of the multiverse. It was no understatement to say that the Cerulean Demon

Lord was not the only one who'd had their entire future changed on this day.

Jake didn't say anything more as he allowed everything to sink in, and he exited the basement, the Demon Prince escorting him out. He didn't lead Jake out of the mansion itself, as he wanted to remain hidden for now, which Jake understood. The Demon Prince had changed quite a lot physically, going from being just about Jake's height to now being two full heads taller, and that wasn't even counting the horns. He looked a lot more like the Cerulean Devil; that was for sure. Especially the part where he had turned way more blue.

Walking out of the demon mansion, Jake felt pretty happy about how things had gone as he considered where to go next. That was when he realized this had been the last item on his Nevermore City bucket list... which meant there was really only one more thing left to do.

It's time to head home.

CHAPTER 63

POST-NEVERMORE STATUS

Leaving Nevermore felt oddly weird. Probably because he had spent fifty years of his life within the World Wonder. He had met many interesting figures, learned a lot about the multiverse, and bonded a lot with his party members. At least he felt a lot closer to the Sword Saint and Fallen King now than before. Rather than simply being comrades of convenience, he would say they could actually be considered friends now.

Dina was also someone Jake now considered a friend, and he knew she felt the same way, even if she was still a bit reserved. Of course, Jake couldn't compare to Sylphie when it came to making friends, as he was pretty sure all three of his other party members would gladly cause a war for her. Not to say Jake wouldn't also do that...

Anyway, the point was that Jake had made a lot of memories and bonds. Of course, Nevermore had also brought with it one other quite important thing. The primary reason he and nearly anyone else even went to Nevermore in the first place was its status as potentially the best place to level in the entire multiverse, and that was showing.

Fifty years was a long time, but Jake definitely wouldn't say that time had at all been wasted, and when he did something he hadn't for a while, it really made it obvious.

He pulled up his full status, tweaked things a bit, and compared it to before he had entered Nevermore.

Status
Name: Jake Thayne
Race: [Human (C) – 204 --> 278]

Class: [Arcane Hunter of Horizon's Edge – 203 --> 289]
Profession: [Heretic-Chosen Alchemist of the Malefic Viper – 206 --> 267]
Health Points (HP): 182,060/182,060
Mana Points (MP): 401,321/411,484
Stamina: 205,651/212,790

Stats
Strength: 8536 --> 26170
Agility: 12496 --> 34616
Endurance: 8911 --> 21279
Vitality: 8834 --> 18206
Toughness: 7389 --> 14488
Wisdom: 11181 --> 26335
Intelligence: 9276 --> 22425
Perception: 23246 --> 53661
Willpower: 9385 --> 23267
Free points: 0

Titles: [Forerunner of the New World], [Bloodline Patriarch], [Holder of a Primordial's True Blessing], [Dungeoneer XV], [Dungeon Pioneer VI], [Prodigious Slayer of the Mighty], [Kingslayer], [Nobility: Marquess], [Progenitor of the 93rd Universe], [Prodigious Arcanist], [Perfect Evolution (D-grade)], [Premier Treasure Hunter], [Myth Originator], [Progenitor of Myriad Paths], [Mythical Prodigy], [Perfect Evolution (C-grade)], [Nevermore Challenger All-star], [Peerless Conqueror of Nevermore]

Class Skills: [Superior Stealth Attack (Rare)], [Splitting Arcane Arrow Rain (Epic)], [Archery of Expanding Horizons (Epic)], [Bestial Hunter's Tracking (Epic)], [Piercing Cursed Arcane Fang (Epic)], [Avaricious Arcane Hunter's Arrows (Epic)], [Arcane Powershot (Ancient)], [Protean Arrow of Avaricious Horizons (Ancient)], [Steady Aim of the Apex Hunter (Ancient)], [Arcane Awakening (Ancient)], [One Step, Thousand Miles (Ancient)], [Fangs of Man (Ancient)], [Horizon-chasing Big Game Arcane Hunter (Ancient)], [Unblemished Arrows of the Horizon (Ancient)], [Mark of the Horizon-Chasing Arcane Hunter (Ancient)], [Penetrating Arcane Arrow of Horizon's Edge

(Ancient)], [Moment of the Primal Hunter (Legendary)], [Relentless Hunt of the Avaricious Arcane Hunter (Legendary)], [Arcane Supremacy (Legendary)], [Unseen Arcane Hunter (Legendary)], [Eternal Shadow of the Primal Hunter (Mythical)], [Primal Gaze of the Apex Hunter (Mythical)]

Profession Skills: [Path of the Heretic-Chosen (Unique)], [Grimoire of the Heretic-Chosen (Unique)], [Alchemist's Purification (Inferior)], [Alchemical Flame (Common)], [Brew Potion (Uncommon)], [Craft Elixir (Rare)], [Concoct Poison (Rare)], [Soul Ritualism of the Heretic-Chosen Alchemist (Ancient)], [Malefic Viper's Poison (Ancient)], [Arcane Curse Manifestation (Ancient)], [Blood of the Malefic Viper (Legendary)], [Sagacity of the Malefic Viper (Legendary)], [Sense of the Malefic Viper (Legendary)], [Wings of the Malefic Viper (Legendary)], [Touch of the Malefic Viper (Legendary)], [Legacy Teachings of the Heretic-Chosen Alchemist (Legendary)], [Palate of the Malefic Viper (Legendary)], [Pride of the Malefic Viper (Legendary)], [Scales of the Malefic Viper (Legendary)], [Fangs of the Malefic Viper (Legendary)], [Anomalous Soul of the Heretic-Chosen (Legendary)], [Core Manipulation of the Primal Hunter (Legendary)], [Chosen's Offering of the Malefic Viper (Legendary)]

Blessing: [True Blessing of the Malefic Viper (Blessing - True)]
Race Skills: [Endless Tongues of the Myriad Races (Unique)], [Legacy of Man (Unique)], [Wisdom of the Hunter (Unique)], [Identify (Rare)], [Serene Soul Meditation (Epic)], [Shroud of the Primordial (Divine)]
Bloodline: [Bloodline of the Primal Hunter (Bloodline Ability - Unique)]

————

As always, the entire status was long as hell. Alas, there were a lot of things to go through.

He hadn't actually gained that many skills during his time in Nevermore, but he had upgraded a few. The real standouts were definitely Unseen Hunter, Protean Arrow, and, naturally, Primal Gaze. The upgrade to his Hunter's Mark was also great, though that one had been a bit forced by the story page book.

When talking about new skills, Penetrating Arcane Arrow upped his overall damage output a lot, especially in combination with Protean Arrow. Out of every single skill he had upgraded or gained throughout Nevermore, though, the most impactful had to be the one he had obtained at level 230:

Arcane Supremacy.

It was the type of skill that worked in the background but offered incredible effects, making Jake far stronger in every aspect. It increased his overall damage and speed regarding everything arcane-related when in combat, and with his body even more attuned to arcane energy than before, he could keep his boosting skill active for far longer or charge Arcane Powershot more before his body gave out. To summarize, it was a force-amplifier of significant proportion.

Of course, skills were far from the only thing Jake had gained in Nevermore. No, the true growth was definitely to be seen in the stats department.

When he compared the stats of pre- and post-Nevermore Jake, the difference was stark, especially the extreme growth seen in his Strength, Agility, and, of course, Perception stats.

Early on, he had decided to put all his Free Points into Strength and Agility, doing a roughly equal split between the two, with a bit more going into Agility over Strength. He had kept this going throughout the World Wonder for the most part, which had led to the two of them increasing greatly.

Perception had comparatively fallen a bit behind, but Jake had at least tried to keep it up there, and it was the stat that had the biggest raw increase by quite a margin. He had primarily boosted his stat gain by licking the wonderful Void Marble he had been gifted by Oras, keeping his potential stats from items maxed out at all times. It had been a bit funny that Jake had crafted so many elixirs without drinking a single one himself, but hey, his party had demanded it, and who was he to deny Sylphie a tasty snack?

Anyway... Nevermore had taken Jake from barely in C-grade to now solidly in mid-tier C-grade, a bit over halfway to his next evolution. He had gone from being able to fight weaker variants in mid-tier C-grade to now feeling confident facing late-tier C-grades even if they were considered high-tier variants. Especially after the title he had gained from completing Nevermore atop the All-Time Leaderboards.

It wouldn't be that long before Jake would be able to kill a weak B-grade. He wasn't quite there yet, but he was getting close. He did reckon that finding worthy opponents in mid-tier C-grade would be borderline impossible, though, unless they were peak geniuses like himself, and even then, he wouldn't back down.

All in all... Nevermore took a long time, but it was more than worth it, Jake once more concluded as he quickly arrived at the Order compound in Nevermore City. There was more activity than usual due to all the visitors wanting to make friends with the Order after Jake's performance, but Jake didn't want to get involved in any of that.

Through his sphere, he did see Viridia busily talking with a group of important-looking people, making him not want to disturb her. So, he just headed straight for a teleporter placed within the heart of the compound. It was one powered by Nevermore itself, allowing anyone to easily travel between universes to set destinations. It could even pierce through most protections against teleportation, making it possible to go straight into the home bases of all the different factions. Jake knew a lot of thought had gone into who had these teleporters and who could use them, but he didn't really care much as he approached the teleportation room.

Two guards stood outside, merely bowing as they saw Jake enter. Walking up to the small stone platform with the teleportation circle on it, Jake stopped and smiled.

"You heading back with me?" he asked as he turned and looked at the snake god that had appeared.

"Might as well; no reason to keep this avatar here after you leave." Villy shrugged. "All it could lead to was someone finding out it was there, and I risk someone wanting to meet me if that happens."

Jake nodded. "Perfectly understandable." Being forced to meet with people was indeed horrible.

"Before we leave... I had a run-in with Eversmile. Talked about those boots of yours and how interesting he found them. Also talked about meeting with you."

"Yeah, he approached me during the forced get-together. Said that he'd go talk to you, so I didn't think to mention it." Jake shrugged. "Or maybe I wanted to let it be a surprise. I can be unpredictable like that. Also, not gonna lie; Eversmile seriously freaks me out. I prefer to avoid thinking and talking about him."

"That's fair; he is an acquired taste for sure," Villy said, nodding. "He was very interested in the First Sage."

The god gave Jake a weird look as he mentioned the First Sage, but Jake just chalked that up to the Viper still feeling weird in general about his first and only master.

"Can't fault him for feeling interested in that guy; the First Sage is pretty damn intriguing," Jake said with a nod. "Did you tell him about the First Sage?"

"Hm, you can say I did, but also didn't," Villy said, acting all mysterious. "Either way, you did good not mentioning him. In general, you shouldn't talk openly about the First Sage with anyone. In fact, don't talk about him at all—even me, unless I ask about something specific, alright?"

"Alright," Jake readily agreed, a bit surprised at the request. He got the feeling more was going on than the Viper let on... not that he had much to say, as he also kept some secrets regarding the First Sage from the Viper. And now Villy had just told him to keep keeping those secrets, so... things had kind of worked out on that front?

"Good. Now, let's head back," the snake god said with a relaxed smile.

Jake nodded, and side by side the two of them stepped onto the teleporter and returned to the Order of the Malefic Viper, Jake himself going there for a brief pitstop before it was back to Earth.

"Now, notice the polluted area and avoid it," Duskleaf said. "Applying your healing there would do more harm than good, so... Alright, good job."

Meira desperately tried to avoid the spear-wielding plant soldier as she healed the warrior of her makeshift practice party, who was already busy dealing with two plant soldiers himself.

The warrior regained the use of his arm due to Meira's healing and killed one of the plant soldiers, but Meira was still struggling to deal with her pursuer. She summoned barriers to keep it at bay, but it was a lot stronger than it looked, breaking them apart one by one, forcing her to just run away and dodge instead.

Suddenly, when Meira thought she had some space to cast another healing skill, she saw the plant soldier speed up out of the corner of her eye. It shot toward her, and as a brief moment of panic paralyzed her she was stabbed through the chest. She felt the weapon pierce her, and even if she had felt pain like this many times before, the pure killing intent in the blow made her freeze up, fearing death.

"Stop," Duskleaf said as he raised a hand.

All the plant soldiers withered in an instant as a green light fell over Meira, instantly healing her completely. Meanwhile, she kept breathing heavily with wide-open eyes. She felt the place in her chest where she had been stabbed as Duskleaf went over to help her calm down.

The members of her makeshift party simply stood there with empty eyes, as Duskleaf had also deactivated them. They were all homunculi—mere imitations of life—and only there for her practice.

"I... I panicked," Meira said in a disappointed tone.

"I know," Duskleaf responded in a comforting tone.

Meira clenched her fists, wanting to punch the ground. Again, she had lost her cool when things got rough. She had hesitated and frozen up for a split second when the spear attack had come, making her suffer a strike she now realized was entirely avoidable. The following killing intent had only sealed the deal, and Meira just still couldn't quite get used to it.

"Can we go again?" Meira asked with determination. She felt disappointed in herself and wanted to make up for her failure. No, she *had* to make up for it if she wanted to go. Because as she was now, Meira would just be a burden for any party she went to Nevermore with.

All this training was for her to prepare for the World Wonder or just become able to properly fight, and it had been going on for longer than she felt comfortable admitting. After she had evolved to C-grade, she had been very confident in herself and wanted to head straight for Nevermore. However, that was when her teacher—Duskleaf—had made her aware of just how lacking she was.

During her leveling in D-grade, she had done some dungeons and stuff to gain levels, but she had always done so in a pretty safe fashion. She'd never truly taken any massive risks and had been well-protected as a dedicated healer. However, she couldn't expect that in Nevermore, or if she ever got in any real fights.

The problem was that Meira had never really learned how to fight or deal with everything involved in fights. Especially not fights against superior foes. So, Duskleaf had set up this training to allow Meira to improve so she could one day head to Nevermore herself. She wasn't going to compete on the Leaderboards or anything like that—heck, she likely wouldn't go while still below level 210, disqualifying her—but she still wanted to at least pull her own weight when in there.

And to make that happen, she had to learn how to fight properly. As the Chosen of Duskleaf, she had to ensure that she didn't embarrass her master and Patron, and as she was right now, she definitely would. Even Duskleaf had learned how to fight in his youth, as even alchemists had to be able to defend themselves.

"We could go again," Duskleaf said, "but I have the feeling you would prefer to go prepare before Jake comes back."

"Lord Thayne is returning?" Meira asked, surprised.

"That's what I heard," he responded rather casually. "Apparently, he has been doing a really interesting ritual with a bunch of demons before coming back, and from what I heard, I will definitely need a word with him."

"Let's stop here for today," Meira quickly said as she took a brief look at herself. She was covered in dirt, grime, blood, and bits of flesh and liquids she wasn't quite sure about. Her clothes were also mostly torn, and her hair was an absolute mess. Moreover, she wasn't sure when she'd last taken a shower... Not like C-grades really needed showers or any cleaning they couldn't handle with magic, but Meira still liked the feeling of cleanliness after a bath or shower.

Without delay, she headed off from the training area and teleported back to Lord Thayne's residence to clean herself up and prepare for his return. Things were a bit messy there, and she wanted everything to look as it did when he'd left.

Teleporting back, she appeared on the lawn and—

"Oh, hey there," she heard, freezing up as she slowly turned her head and saw Lord Thayne, who had seemingly also just teleported there.

CHAPTER 64

YEARS OF CHANGE

"Oh, hey there," Jake said as he appeared at his residence and, less than a second later, saw Meira pop into existence. Seeing her, he couldn't help but instinctively say hello as he got a good look at her.

For Jake, fifty years of Nevermore had passed, but for Meira, only three or so had gone by since their last meeting. Yet when he looked at Meira, he was certain that of the two of them, she was the one who had changed the most during their time apart.

Her entire aura had undergone a frankly shocking transformation. It was more qualitative than quantitative in nature, and when Jake used Identify, he quickly understood why.

[High Elf – lvl 206 – True Blessing of Duskleaf]

The first thing to note was definitely the fact that Duskleaf now had a Chosen. He also couldn't help but stare a bit at the "Duskleaf" in the Identify message, as it seemed a bit... off? It was weird to explain, but probably not anything that mattered much. No, what mattered was that Meira had been given his True Blessing, and that wasn't even the only big thing that had changed.

Somehow, she had also become a high elf. Jake wasn't sure about the exact requirements for an elf evolving to a high elf—something the Altmar Empire did much to ensure—but he did know the most basic of things, such as the requirement for an elf to have had a Perfect Evolution in D-grade and in general have a powerful Path. While Meira had gotten a

Perfect Evolution back then, she definitely didn't meet all the other criteria for becoming a high elf. Of course, he quickly understood how she had done it anyway. Or, more accurately, who had done it for her, as this was definitely the work of Duskleaf.

Outwardly, she didn't look that much different, besides her eyes now having a deep golden color to them, and maybe her ears being a bit pointier than before. Her blonde hair now also looked a tad more golden blonde? It was hard to tell, honestly. People changing things like hair colors with evolutions was far from anything new. Shit, Carmen had changed hers from red to blonde at some point, Jake was pretty sure. Or maybe it had just been covered in so much blood during their first meeting that it had looked red?

Anyway, the thing about Meira that had changed the most was definitely the aura and overall demeanor she now exuded. And, of course, her power.

She was still far from being a peak genius who had a chance to compete on the Leaderboards, but now she would definitely be considered high-tier, at least if one evaluated her purely based on her current aura. With time, Jake believed she could grow and become far more powerful.

While it was true that Meira had been subpar until she reached C-grade, that was far from the end of her Path or something that truly determined how powerful she could one day become. Jake's own massive growth in stats during C-grade thus far was proof of just how fast she could potentially catch up to others who also had powerful Paths in prior grades.

She had even begun to improve her combat skills, based on the state of her clothing and the blood and gore still on her, which was great to see. That was one of the areas where Jake had been the most nervous for her, as he'd never gotten the feeling she was much of a fighter.

With Duskleaf teaching her, Jake didn't doubt her skills—at least her crafting ones—would catch up with time, and he genuinely believed Meira had a bright future ahead of herself if she kept working as hard as she clearly had been during his time in Nevermore.

It was almost hard to imagine that it hadn't even been more than a few years since she first appeared before him. Back then, she had barely dared speak, practically shaking at all times when in his presence. Meira had been utterly incapable of making her own decisions, and it wouldn't be an understatement to say she hadn't had a Path at all. At least none she could call her own. All she'd cared about was surviving another day, never looking toward the future.

Now, she seemed to have a purpose. Jake felt an odd sense of pride and happiness seeing Meira having come this far, and he hoped she would continue the Path she was on. Duskleaf was definitely to thank for a major part of her transformation, but Jake still felt glad he had been the impetus. Going from a slave to the Chosen of a god in around half a decade had to be some kind of record, right?

Jake had all these thoughts as he looked at Meira, who took a moment to gather herself before moving almost instinctively to bow.

"Welcome back, Lord Thayne," she said in a familiar tone that Jake chose to instantly take issue with.

"I don't think it's proper for my fellow Chosen to act this submissively," Jake said in a semi-joking tone.

Meira seemed to realize he was probably right, as she quickly straightened her back and stood properly upright, trying again once she'd gotten her bearings. "It's just... I did not expect you back this soon." She was still a bit nervous, though at least she didn't stumble over her words as much as she used to. What's more, she actually met his eyes and didn't look down. "And congratulations on your performance on the Leaderboards."

"Thank you... and I'm not even sure where to start when congratulating you," Jake said. "High elf, Chosen of Duskleaf, just reaching C-grade in general... Lots of things to celebrate there."

Meira smiled at Jake's words, looking as though she was about to offer another small bow, but then she stopped herself and only nodded. "I have done my best... but... Lord Thayne, would it be alright to speak in a bit? I want to return to my residence first to avoid dirtying the main building with my current state."

Jake wasn't sure why that was necessary. It wasn't like Jake ever bothered to clean up before entering the main building, and if she was afraid of spilling blood and gore inside, she should be able to quickly remove it all with some magic.

Alas, Jake wasn't going to argue with her. With a nod, he said, "Alright, see you in a bit. I'm looking forward to hearing all you've been up to over the last few years."

"And I to hear of your exploits," Meira said, hesitating for a moment before continuing. "Perhaps you should also contact Irin? Reika, Scarlett, and Bastilla are all in Nevermore right now, and Izil has headed back to the Altmar Empire for a bit and shouldn't return for a few months. It's just been me and Irin for a while now, and I'm sure she would also be elated upon learning of your return."

"Yeah, good idea, I should also tell her," Jake quickly agreed. This would also allow him to give Irin that token thing he had received from the Demon Prince before he forgot he had it. Because he would totally forget he had it.

"I will see you in a bit," Meira said, barely managing to stop herself from bowing yet again. She nodded and turned to leave, and as Jake looked after her, he couldn't help but speak up.

"Hey, Meira," Jake said. The high elf stopped mid-walk and turned to look at him, making him smile. "You're looking great. Keep up whatever you're doing."

Her eyes opened wide before she quickly whipped her head around and muttered in a small tone, "Tha.... thank you..." Then she hurried back to her own residence.

As Jake watched her leave with quick steps, he kept smiling and shook his head. Meira still had a lot to learn even if she had come far, and the first lesson was to get some more self-confidence, even around Jake.

Going toward the main mansion, Jake felt nostalgic at the sight. Everything looked the same as when he'd left, and even faint remnants of the ritual that had hatched Vesperia could be seen on one part of the large lawn.

When he got inside, he made his way to the couch and plopped down before he took out the Order Token. The item had been inactive during his stay in Nevermore, but now that he was back in the Order, it had been reactivated. While Jake took it out to contact Irin, he decided to do one other thing first.

Checking out the available lessons, he noticed quite an interesting trend. Lessons targeting early C-grades were nearly all gone, replaced by those catering to one subject and one subject only: Nevermore. Lectures about how to make good parties or combat-related stuff, workshops to learn teamwork, meet-ups for those looking for party members...

It wasn't that surprising. With a new version of Nevermore having just opened up, there was a rush to go there. Some wanted to compete on the Leaderboards to see if they could get a decent placement—decent in their cases being something like top 10,000 or even top 100,000. Because, yes, the Leaderboards gave titles to anyone who placed in the top 1,000,000. Of course, the title would be shit compared to those earned by Jake and the others who'd placed in the top 100 or even top 250, but they were still something any member of the Order would be proud to receive.

Others just wanted the experience, and if they had to visit Nevermore, no time was better than now. Even for those like Scarlett who couldn't compete on the Leaderboards, this was an opportunity to get at least a few levels in an efficient manner.

For mid- and high-tier C-grades, the lessons offered were more or less the same as usual, with a few additions talking about post-Nevermore planning and whatnot. From what Jake gathered, a lot were unsure what to do right after leaving Nevermore and needed a kick in the ass to get going toward a new goal, with courses like this helping with just that.

Jake wasn't interested in attending anything; he just wanted to see what was available. At least, he wasn't interested for now. Maybe in the near future, if he wanted to grind some alchemy before the Prima Guardian arrived, he would also attend a few lessons if they appealed to him.

Still sitting and fiddling with the Token, he finally decided to make contact with Irin. The Token had her contact information saved, and the second he dialed her, he got a response.

"Welcome back to the Order of the Malefic Viper, Lord Thayne, Conqueror of Nevermore," she said in a tone Jake couldn't place as either irony or genuine praise. Probably a mix of both.

"Thank you, Mistress Irinixis, Demon Who I'm Not Sure Has Even Been To Nevermore," Jake answered, choosing to take the joking approach.

"Mistress has a nice tone to it... but no, I have not been to Nevermore for a good while. The place just doesn't particularly appeal to what I do, and in all honesty, I would drag down any party I went with."

"Fair enough," Jake said. It made sense. Irin only had a profession and a race, having chosen to forego a class. Her race did offer some combat measures, but ultimately, she didn't have a Path suited for combat. Or, as Irin put it...

"You know I'm a lover, not a fighter. Also, I must say I'm flattered you contacted me this quickly after returning. You missed me?"

Maybe it was just Jake, but Irin seemed a bit more... straightforward than before. Then again, maybe it was just Jake. She had always been pretty aggressive and bold, so it wasn't like she was acting out of character. In either case, Jake was all fine with playing along a bit.

"I did contact you to invite you to visit, but now I'm doubting if I should. Here I was, wanting to give you a souvenir, and I feel like you're just teasing me," Jake said with a sad tone.

"Oh? Now, you got me curious, but please tell me it isn't the skull of a beast or something like that." She was clearly interested, though she didn't seem to take his words that seriously, likely thinking he was just continuing to joke around.

"Nothing that grand. Just this Crest thing I got from the Demon Prince of the Fourth Hell, who I recently helped in absorbing the Crystalized Devil Heart of some dead Cerulean Devil during a first-in-the-multiverse ritual, making him evolve into a Cerulean Demon Lord..."

A brief pause followed before Irin spoke.

"I'm coming over."

"See you in a bit." Jake grinned as the connection was cut and he leaned back on the sofa, waiting for her and Meira to arrive to get him all caught up on recent happenings.

———

Dina relaxed back at her own small residence on the small planet she usually lived on within the domain of the Pantheon of Life. She had a lot to meditate on as she soaked in the sun while reflecting on the last few decades.

She hadn't made many friends throughout her life, at least not before going to Nevermore. Part of the reason for this was just how busy she had always been, but another major reason was her lack of trust in others. Dina was the granddaughter of Nature's Attendant and had inherited a version of his Bloodline. This gave her a status she had never quite felt comfortable with and put a barrier between herself and her peers. Dina had still had some acquaintances, but she'd never known if those around her were interested in her status or who she was as a person.

When her grandfather had proposed the idea of entering Nevermore with the Chosen of the Malefic Viper, she had been less than keen on it. Especially because she'd heard what people were saying about the idea. While they'd tried to be sneaky, the area controlled by the Pantheon of Life was naturally filled with plants, and they gladly shared all the secrets and gossip people had been talking about, thinking she couldn't hear.

It was almost an open conspiracy that making her enter Nevermore with the Chosen was an attempt to forge a stronger connection with him. That was why Dina hadn't been keen, as she wasn't interested in that kind of thing. Yet she had allowed herself to be persuaded, as she truly couldn't say no to her grandfather, who'd seemed so excited at the idea.

So, with reluctance, she had joined his party... and she didn't regret that choice at all. While it had taken her a while to open up, she truly considered them all close friends now. Sure, the Fallen King was arrogant and not the nicest, but he was always respectful when it mattered and kept an extra eye on her during combat. Sylphie was the sweetest, and she didn't have a single negative thing to say about the bird. She quite honestly felt angry at the thought of anyone even thinking negative things about her.

The Sword Saint was probably the one she had gotten the closest to. Perhaps because he reminded her a bit of her grandfather. It was weird that despite being a C-grade, the swordsman truly felt like an ancient existence, but it likely had something to do with his Path and Transcendence. He had been the man who made sure Dina had initially managed to integrate with the group, and Dina would be very sad if they didn't get the chance to meet again relatively soon.

Finally, there was, of course, the Chosen of the Malefic Viper, Jake. And Jake was... odd. But not in a bad way. He was just always doing his own thing, and he always seemed to be looking forward, never back. His Path also confused her a bit. The Pantheon of Life had many hunters in it, Artemis being a prime example of this, yet in the eyes of the Pantheon, to be a hunter was to be the enlightened version of a predator who coexisted with and regulated the ecosystem. To be one with nature. And yet Jake didn't at all fit this mold, exemplified by one thing more than any other:

His utter lack of any nature affinity. No, his almost antagonistic relationship with the affinity.

The nature affinity was something Dina had come to associate with hunters, so to see Jake without it had confused her more than anything else. However, with time, she'd come to understand and reached a conclusion she wasn't quite sure if she should share with anyone.

Jake couldn't be one with nature. He didn't exist with it or even seem like he wanted to. He wasn't there to regulate some ecosystem or care about its continued existence. Jake's relationship with nature—no, perhaps the entire multiverse—was akin to what happened when people tried to interfere and assist an ecosystem by introducing some new creature that proved too strong for its environment.

He was like an invasive species. Too suitable for the ecosystem and nature to survive his presence, thus rejecting him. He was outside of nature, untethered by its natural laws. At least, this was Dina's theory on the matter.

In all honesty, Dina respected Jake a lot. He was incredibly strong, and whenever she was with him, she never felt like they could lose a fight. He always found a way to win, even when Dina feared they didn't stand a chance. As a person, she had also come to like him. Not in the way many members of the Pantheon of Life had hoped, but as a close friend, and she believed he felt the same way. At least, she hoped he did.

As Dina was absorbing the powerful life energy of the sun while reflecting, she suddenly felt two new presences appear. One of them was her grandfather, who had left only half a day before, while the other one was Artemis, whom Dina was a bit surprised to see there.

"Dina, how are you adjusting now that you're back home again?" her grandfather asked with mild concern in his voice.

"I'm fine." Dina smiled, happy to see him again so soon. While she enjoyed Nevermore, she had still missed spending time with her grandfather.

"Good, good," he said with a sense of relief, suddenly turning a bit more serious. "*She* wants to see you."

"Huh?" Dina asked with confusion.

"The Mother Tree has requested your presence," Artemis further clarified. "Requested all of ours."

Dina dispelled all other thoughts as she hurriedly stood up with a mix of confusion, anticipation, and a touch of fear. This would be her first time ever directly meeting her... meeting the Mother Tree.

"Please," Dina said.

Her grandfather nodded with a proud smile before the three of them teleported away.

CHAPTER 65

YGGDRASIL

The Mother Tree. Tree of Life. World Tree. Primordial of Life.
Yggdrasil, like the other Primordials, had many names she went by. Dina wasn't sure about the Primordial's true origin, but based on history, she had been a tree that had simply never stopped growing. The Great Planet Yggdrasil called her home had her roots piercing deeply toward the core, her crown towering above the planet. The entire tree stood more than a hundredth of the entire Great Planet's diameter tall, and there were legitimate concerns that even the Great Planet would one day prove too small.

Her crown was a vast network of planets, making the entire crown practically its own world. Within the crown, there were even subspaces housing large worlds and small galaxies. Countless beings resided there, and some even referred to it as its own universe. Which wasn't entirely incorrect... for it was all linked to the Divine Realm of Yggdrasil.

Most Divine Realms existed within the void. Hidden from all those who did not know where it was. However, some were able to directly absorb the realm into themselves and make it a part of their bodies. Yggdrasil was one such being—the Starseizing Titan was another notable example—making her a living divine realm, her body representing the growth of her realm and power. This had some benefits and disadvantages for sure, the biggest disadvantage being that should someone manage to fully destroy Yggdrasil's body, it would also spell the end for her. Not that many considered that a legitimate possibility.

Dina had naturally seen Yggdrasil many times before. It was impossible not to, and the planet she usually lived on was close enough to the Great

Planet that she could see the glowing green crown through space, like a massive star in the sky.

However, she had never interacted with the Primordial. Few people had, especially among mortals. The only notable one was her grandfather, Nature's Attendant, who acted as the right hand of Yggdrasil, dealing with everything that didn't directly pertain to her own realm.

As a tree, Yggdrasil did have some drawbacks that came with her Path, such as her inability to move. Even with her massive power, she could not move herself from the Great Planet she had taken root on... though Dina had heard some scary rumors that even if Yggdrasil couldn't move herself, she could move where she had taken root. The thought of an entire Great Planet being forcibly moved through space in any way was more than a little scary in its own right.

Either way, Yggdrasil's limitations meant she very much focused only on her own immediate domain and let Dina's grandfather handle all the multiversal politics on her behalf. In fact, he handled pretty much everything the Pantheon of Life did, Yggdrasil very rarely taking any actions herself. Yet there was never any doubt as to the true leader of the Pantheon of Life, as when Yggdrasil did make her presence known and directly got involved in a matter, she never hesitated to take decisive action.

To ask for someone to meet her directly wasn't something that happened often either. The only instances Dina knew of were whenever a new god arose within the Pantheon of Life, or when Yggdrasil decided to get a new Chosen. This matter was definitely not related to making Dina any kind of Chosen, though. If Dina would become the Chosen of anyone, it was her grandfather, and even if she wouldn't, the Chosen of Yggdrasil was still alive, last Dina heard.

This meant there was really only one thing this meeting could be about...

"Is... is this truly a matter important enough for the Mother Tree to get involved directly?" Dina asked as she traveled with her grandfather and Artemis. "I know Nevermore is important, but..."

"I talked to her after I returned," her grandfather said in a calm tone. "She was naturally interested, especially when I mentioned some matters related to the new leader of the All-Time Leaderboard. Even so, I was surprised when she said she wanted to see you directly. But don't worry—you're not in any trouble."

"I'm also surprised she asked for me," Artemis said, also sounding a tad concerned. "Is the reason she wants to see me related to... that?"

"To what?" Dina asked, having honestly been a bit confused as to why

Artemis was even here, or had been at Nevermore in the first place. Dina didn't really know Artemis that well, but her best guess had been that she was interested in seeing a hunter take the top spot on the Leaderboards. It wouldn't be weird for her to take an interest in Jake... but it appeared there was more to it, and she hadn't taken the kind of interest Dina expected.

Artemis looked at Dina before sighing. "What do you think of the Chosen of the Malefic Viper?"

"He's peculiar and definitely extremely powerful," Dina said after thinking for a time. "He was also a brilliant party member, and I wouldn't have done as well in Nevermore as I did without him."

"Not like that," Artemis said, waving her off. "What do you think of him as a potential partner or mate? I know you know there were intentions to pair the two of you up."

Dina was a bit taken aback by the question, and she saw how her grandfather also wasn't that happy with the question... though he did seem curious about her answer. She was afraid to disappoint him, but she wasn't going to lie.

"I don't have any thoughts toward him in that vein at all. I also don't believe he does toward me." She fully expected her grandfather and Artemis to be disappointed... and while her grandfather did let out a small sigh, Artemis reacted quite the opposite by grinning.

"Great, then you won't complain if I decide to pursue him," Artemis said, seemingly uninterested in hiding exactly what "that" was. "You know about my image in the Colosseum of Mortals and how those work, right?"

"I know," Dina confirmed with a nod.

"Well, my image and the Chosen got... let's just say... *involved* during his time in the Challenge Dungeon," Artemis said. "Very involved, if you catch my meaning."

"Wh... what?" Dina asked, her eyes opening wide.

"You know, I'm kinda glad Jake didn't mention it; very respectful of him," Artemis said with a smile. "Anyway, that's why I went to Nevermore to see him for myself, and... let's just say I hope he takes me up on my invitation for some archery lessons."

Dina calling herself shocked would be an understatement. Jake had slept with the image of Artemis within the Challenge Dungeon? The images had the full memories of the gods themselves, effectively just making them unlinked avatars... She had never heard about this happening before. Much less with someone like Artemis, who Dina knew was famous for rejecting every potential partner.

"What made you—"

"I think that's between me and him; wouldn't you agree?" Artemis threw Dina a glance, making a shiver run down her back.

She nodded slowly, dropping the subject yet still mentally mulling it over. Upon deeper reflection, wasn't this great? If Jake formed a closer connection to the Pantheon of Life, it would only benefit the faction, as far as Dina was concerned. For gods and mortals to pair up also wasn't that weird. In fact, it was practically the norm. Since two gods reproducing was simply too difficult and rare, it was normal for powerful mortals and gods to end up together with the goal of producing children, though it usually only happened when the mortal was S-grade.

Their group of three remained quiet until they finally reached their destination. On the way, Dina deeply considered the Jake-Artemis matter and only got more on board the more she thought about it. They had traveled this last part toward the base of the utterly massive tree on a wooden barge floating through space. Once they got closer, they entered the trunk through a hole, and the second they were inside, Dina felt the pressure fall upon her.

She saw Artemis buckle a bit while her grandfather remained unaffected. Dina also felt her legs shake, but she managed to remain upright without many issues. They kept floating forward for a few more minutes as Dina looked around what may as well have been a massive cavern. She saw rivers run within the walls, and a vine moved here or there, the life energy all around them nearly suffocating. Without Yggdrasil's presence, elementals or creatures would be born in the millions every single day simply due to the environment.

Soon enough, they reached a ledge, and once their barge docked they got off. Dina followed after her grandfather, who led them through a small hallway before they reached a small hole leading into a large, round chamber. There was a bit of furniture in the center, having grown out of the tree itself. To sit on this furniture would be like sitting on a part of Yggdrasil herself, making Dina feel a bit weird.

Even so, her grandfather and Artemis did not hesitate to sit, and her grandfather motioned for her to do the same. With apprehension, Dina sat down, trying to keep her composure. She and Artemis both suffered from the constant pressure, and while Dina found it a bit suffocating, she believed she would soon get used to it.

"You were right, Tonken," a voice suddenly echoed throughout the chamber. As Dina felt the attention on her, she lowered her head a bit. **"This is a first, child. You are the first C-grade to come here in many**

eras... and the first able to do so without a Bloodline or Transcendence allowing you to handle my presence."

"I will admit that this boon was not part of my initial intentions, and I view it as a happy accident," her grandfather answered with a smile.

"A happy accident indeed," the voice echoed again before it suddenly appeared much closer. "Tell me, child—what do you feel right now?"

Dina slowly lifted her head and saw a figure had appeared in front of her, sitting on a chair of wood. The woman looked a bit like Dina herself but didn't have things like antlers or flowers anywhere. She was nearly entirely green. She wore no clothes, with all the important parts covered with either her floor-length, grass-like hair or small natural growths coming out of her body. Dina naturally knew she was looking at Yggdrasil —or at least the dryad form she had momentarily adopted. As for her question...

"Ne... nervous..." Dina said, looking down again.

"Look up at me," the Primordial said, Dina not daring to not obey the command.

She lifted her head and looked forward, meeting the eyes of the dryad. She saw those endlessly deep green eyes, and she felt her consciousness waver for a moment before she had to avert her gaze.

"Intriguing. The soul does not appear mutated, yet it's clearly changed somehow..." Yggdrasil turned to her grandfather again. "And this is caused by the Chosen of the Malefic Viper?"

"Undoubtedly," Dina's grandfather confirmed.

"And she was simply in his presence for an extended period of time for this to happen?" Yggdrasil continued.

"Correct," her grandfather once more confirmed, Dina also instinctively nodding a bit.

"Hm," Yggdrasil sounded out before looking back at Dina. "That will be all. Keep up the good work. I look forward to hearing of your continued growth."

With those words, Dina disappeared from within the tree and found herself sitting back at her home a second later, as if she had never left in the first place.

———

While waiting for Meira and Irin, Jake played with his Cradle and checked in on the Soulflame progress. He still infused it with his arcane mana intermittently, but he kind of just had to leave it to do its own thing most of the time.

In the world within, the war of the Soulflames continued as they devoured one another constantly. Quite a few powerful Arcane Soulflames had been born by now, but none had reached the top tier yet. In fact, Jake had yet to see even a single pinnacle-tier Soulflame, much less a Supreme Soulflame, in all the time he had owned the mythical item. Checking its description, he had kind of hoped something had changed, but nope. He did take extra notice of one sentence, though.

"Only a single Soulflame can truly be born from the Cradle; the item is destroyed upon extraction, with all other Soulflames having become fuel for the chosen one."

Reading this, Jake began to think that maybe seeing a Supreme Soulflame wasn't even possible, and it could only be obtained upon extraction by further empowering a pinnacle-tier Soulflame. Or maybe he just had to wait long enough for one to actually appear.

This was definitely the most frustrating part of the Cradle of Soul's Kindling. Jake didn't truly have any control over when a useful Soulflame would be born. He couldn't exert any direct control over the internal world. The entire Cradle was more or less just Minaga exploiting the system a bit by making a method to gamble far more efficiently. But it was still gambling.

Jake could get lucky tomorrow, a powerful Arcane Soulflame appearing within the Cradle and devouring enough other Soulflames to become a Supreme one. However, he could also be so damn unlucky that he wouldn't see any Soulflame he considered worth extracting before ascending to godhood.

Of course, there was one option Jake could try: infusing some of his Jake Juice. However, Jake wasn't even sure that would help with anything. As mentioned, he had no control over the internal world, so if he sent in some of his special energy, he couldn't even ensure his arcane energy within the Cradle merged with it. It would seriously suck if he accidentally empowered a random ice-affinity Soulflame, wasting his time and energy while even risking bricking the Cradle in the process.

No... no, the best choice right now was to simply be patient. There were a lot more Arcane Soulflames within the Cradle now than any other affinity, and with time, they would only dominate more. It was impossible to make his arcane affinity the only affinity in the internal world, but to see so many Arcane Soulflames gave him hope. Plus, Jake believed himself to be a pretty lucky person, so it couldn't be that long before fortune smiled upon him and blessed him with a banger Soulflame, right?

Putting away the Cradle, he felt a new presence arrive on the lawn outside. Through his sphere, he saw it was Irin, who looked a bit flustered and in a hurry as she made her way to the main mansion. He also saw Meira heading over, no longer in her combat attire and having switched to less bloody and torn clothes. He still didn't think the change was necessary, but oh, well—who was he to police what kind of clothing people felt comfortable in, especially with his own tendency to wear a mask when around strangers?

Irin entered first, and Jake got up from the sofa and went to greet her.

"Hey, Irin," Jake said with a smile as she entered the living room. As usual, she wore clothing that left little to the imagination, and when she saw him, she had an almost hungry look in her eyes that she quickly suppressed.

"Good to have you back," she said, smiling in return.

"Good to be back," Jake concurred as he made sure to remember the Crest for once. Taking it out of his spatial storage, he tossed the item to Irin casually. "Catch."

Irin instinctively did so, then looked at the item Jake had thrown, her eyes opening wide. She looked almost afraid to be holding the Crest. "This... Do you even know what this is?"

"According to the Demon Prince, a Crest of some sort that will be useful if I decide to visit the Hells." Jake shrugged as a thought struck him. "Actually, that got me wondering... I know barely anything about these Hells."

"You... you said you helped the Demon Prince of the Fourth Hell with a ritual, not even knowing anything about the demon factions?" Irin asked, staring at him. "Tell me you at least signed a liability waiver before you did the ritual."

"Of course I did," Jake said in a serious tone.

For some reason, hearing Jake had the Demon Prince sign a waiver made Irin bite her lip before she licked it. She looked like she wanted to pounce on him then and there, but she quickly collected herself when she heard the door open as Meira arrived. Nevertheless, she continued talking. "Alright... I guess a brief lesson in the social and political climate of demon aristocracy is in order, along with a brief introduction to the Nine Hells."

CHAPTER 66

DEMON LORE GALORE

Before Irin had her chance to launch into a lengthy explanation about the demon race, Meira entered the living room. The high elf instantly spotted the succubus and smiled. "Irin! It's great you could come over so fast."

To Jake's surprise, Meira went over and hugged the succubus, who happily returned the gesture. After their brief hug, Meira joined Jake on one of the couches and Irin sat down on another. Jake noticed that the two of them made some small talk while being all smiles.

Okay, they have definitely gotten closer during my absence, Jake noted. It was honestly good to see that Meira had made some more friends. Jake also didn't doubt that Irin would gladly make friends with Meira, if only for pragmatic and selfish reasons, as surely it would only be beneficial to be friends with the Chosen of Duskleaf.

With everyone settled down, they finally got back to business.

The succubus looked at Jake and asked, "So, I'm just going to assume you aren't that aware of how the demon race as a whole works. Am I right to have this assumption?"

Jake slowly nodded. While he did know a bit, his knowledge was definitely limited, and a bit of repeated information had never killed anyone.

"Alright, let's start from the basics. While most demons you have encountered thus far were enlightened, there are far, far more types, with the majority being classified as monsters. The thing is, these are rather rare to find outside of certain specific areas, as they require demonic energy to be born, and the non-intelligent ones rarely, if ever, stray out of demonic lands. They tend to progress far slower outside, after all."

Jake nodded along, knowing this part already from some books he had read. Demonic beasts and monsters in that vein totally existed, and Jake kind of wanted to encounter one at some point. Alas, as Irin said, they were rare outside of demonic lands.

"Demonic lands can be found... well, pretty much anywhere. A few planets exist here and there that naturally possess the demonic affinity, and you can find certain sectors in every universe where it is the dominant affinity, making it a bit similar to the death affinity in that regard." She supplemented her explanation with projections of mana.

"However, the most well-known areas classified as demonic lands are no doubt the Nine Hells, also called the Nine Circles of Hell," she continued as the mana projection changed, showing nine layers stacked atop one another. "Do you know of the origin of the Nine Hells?"

"I'm going to assume they were created by the system," Jake said, making an educated guess.

"Yes and no. The history of the Nine Hells is a bit complicated, to say the least. The brief explanation is that, at first, it was artificially created by a group of nine devils to establish some form of safe haven and home base for all the demonic races by turning their respective divine realms into Hells, with every Hell symbolizing aspects of the devil's Path. With time, they began to be known as the Nine Circles of Hell, representing sin and whatnot. Not to be confused with Sin Curses... though curse magic is very much a staple among demons, so I can't really say there isn't any connection.

"Anyway, the Nine Hells exist in a separate dimension, accessible from all the universes far more easily than another universe, which is part of the reason why demonic summoning is such a prominent thing. The veil is incredibly thin, and even I have a treasure allowing me to enter the Nine Hells at any moment without much trouble."

This surprised Jake quite a bit. He knew snippets, and he knew how people could summon things from the "demonic realms," but he didn't know this was part of the reason. There were also the innate demonic racial skills related to summoning, so more likely than not, it wasn't that the demons had adapted to the Nine Hells, but that the Nine Hells had been created with demonkind in mind.

Looking at Meira, the high elf clearly already knew all this, making Jake feel a bit out of the loop as Irin continued her history lesson.

"These Nine Hells were expanded by more and more devils, forming a hierarchy was, until the integration of the Sixth Universe. I am not exactly clear on how or why it happened, but the system adopted the Nine Hells and made it into what it is today: a World Wonder. A quite unique one at that, as it's more or less its own separate universe filled solely with demonic energy and owned by the demonic races. And that concludes my brief history lesson on the Nine Hells and how they came to be."

"I see," Jake said, nodding. "That was very enlightening, and—"

"Oh, no, that was just the history part... Now we're on to the political climate of the Nine Hells." Irin smiled devilishly, not even giving Jake a break. "Each of the Nine Hells is ruled by a devil, family, or clan. These rulers of the Nine Hells are referred to as nobles, and status has a huge significance in demon culture. This is part of the reason I'm happy to be here right now, as merely working as your assistant of sorts has granted me quite a lot of respect among my peers."

"Well, glad to be of assistance." Jake smiled and shook his head. "And let me guess, the Cerulean Demon is part of the family that rules the Fourth Hell?"

"Correct," Irin confirmed. "The Fourth Hell is ruled by a powerful demon family that has controlled it for a long time, with the Cerulean Devil you mentioned being one of their most notable figures before his death. The Demon Prince you met is one of the most important figures in the younger generation, and he has a peak status among mortals. His title of prince also means his father is the current ruler of the Fourth Hell."

Jake nodded along, then asked curiously, "Are the Nine Hells ranked based on power? The Demon Prince said the Crest should allow one to be treated well in at least the four first Hells."

"Again, it's a bit more complicated than that," Irin said with a sigh. "Each of the Hells has a different environment. The Fourth Hell is filled with demonic lightning and wind, making it a suitable environment for those who have that kind of affinity. As each ruler of the Hells has held their throne for a long time, no one can really be sure who is the strongest anymore. There is some truth to it being ranked based on power, however, as none would dare argue against the ruler of the Ninth Hell being the strongest by a landslide."

"How would this ruler of the Ninth Hell square up against, let's say, a Primordial?" Jake wondered out loud.

"That..." Irin hesitated before steeling herself. "This is not meant to be taken the wrong way... but it very much depends. If the fight takes place within the Nine Hells, the ruler will have an advantage, while if the confrontation happens outside, the Primordial will have an edge. There is a story from a few eras ago about the ruler of the Ninth Hell and Eversmile getting into a contractual dispute. It ended in a fight where Eversmile had the advantage until they changed venue to the Nine Hells, at which point Eversmile chose to retreat."

"So, not a pushover—got it." Jake nodded as he seemed to get the gist of it. "What you are pretty much telling me is that the Crest I tossed to you earlier grants the person holding it the status of a demon that's part of the aristocracy within the Nine Hells, right?"

"More than that," Irin said in a serious tone. "It signifies you are an important and highly valued guest of the faction the Crest belongs to. These Crests are only ever given out by the respective leaders of the Hells, meaning should you do anything to someone holding a Crest, it will be viewed as a personal attack on them. It also means they take responsibility for the one they granted the Crest to."

"Surprised the Demon Prince said it was fine for me to hand it to someone else," Jake muttered.

"He probably expected you to hand it to an envoy. Someone acting as your agent if you didn't have anything you wanted yourself but perhaps needed something for your subordinates."

"I don't really have any subordinates..."

"A lot of people, me included, would vehemently disagree with that statement." The succubus just smiled and shook her head. "You may not officially make anyone your subordinate, but that doesn't mean they won't be subordinate to you."

Jake wanted to argue... but deep down, he knew it would be a waste of time, as Irin was most definitely correct.

"Anyway, you'll take the Crest, right?" Jake asked, wanting to change the subject. "I don't need it, and I reckon you can get something useful with it."

"If I'm being perfectly honest, I'm not even sure I dare use it," Irin said, sighing. "The amount of questions I will be bombarded with will be suffocating, and it will lead to a needless amount of rumors. It would have been better if you got a Crest from someone in the second circle of Hell."

"Let me guess, the circle of lust and home to many succubi?" It was another educated guess.

"And here I thought you didn't know anything about demons," Irin said, raising an eyebrow.

Jake smiled. "Just a really good guess." Honestly, guessing things based on memories of myths from Earth had a shocking level of accuracy, though the details did tend to, more often than not, be a bit off. Like... sure, Valhal had been some mythical realm of Nordic mythology before the system, meaning the halls of the fallen or something like that. In reality, it was called Valhal because Valdemar had literally called his faction Valdemar's Mead Hall in the early days, and with time, that name had been shortened to Valhal. Literally, Valdemar's Hall.

"But, yes, you're correct. It's the Hell run by a succubus, the strongest of my race, and is a land filled with illusions and dreams." Irin then added with a smirk, "A very popular holiday destination, too, in case you're interested."

Jake sighed. "At this point, I'm pretty sure I have standing invitations to visit half of the factions in the multiverse; I have no idea when I would even find the time."

"Hopefully, time will become an infinite resource." Irin smiled. "Besides, I'm sure you can learn to create avatars or something and just send those to visit all the places you neglected at some point."

"That feels pretty disrespectful," Jake muttered, not really keen on the idea. "But, back on topic... what the hell should I do with the Crest if you don't want it?"

"I said I wasn't certain I dared use it, not that I wasn't interested," Irin said with a smile. "Chances are that I'll just take my master along or go with a group to not stand out as much. Of course, you could also go with me, and we could stop by the second circle on the way back..."

"Tempting offer, but I think I'll pass," Jake said, really not having the time.

Irin smiled. "A pity."

"Anyway, enough about me and all this demon stuff... What have you two been up to during these last few years, and how have things changed around here?"

"Can't say I have much to report," Irin said, shrugging. "Things are very much as usual, outside of the rush for Nevermore and the many local celebrations recently taking place upon learning that the Chosen of the Malefic Viper topped the All-Time Leaderboard. Personally, I believe I have made good progress, but nothing too outstanding. At least not compared to the honored Chosen of Duskleaf, Grand Elder of the Order and disciple of the Malefic Viper."

"Irin..." Meira muttered, a bit embarrassed.

"Irin indeed!" Jake said in a stern tone. "How dare you joke around with the venerable Chosen of Duskleaf? You are lucky she is too merciful to have you whipped for such disrespect!"

"I am truly blessed, allowed to be in such company," Irin also continued to joke. "Though I wouldn't necessarily be opposed to a bit of whipping..."

Meira just glared daggers at them both before they stopped, and Jake waved it off. "Joking, joking. It's no lie; you're definitely the one who has undergone the most changes, so what have you been up to, Meira? And don't even try to downplay it, because you must have had quite an eventful period."

The high elf took a moment before she sighed. "Alright, yeah, quite a lot has happened. Shortly after you left for Nevermore..."

Meira proceeded to explain everything she had been up to over the last few years. How Duskleaf had continued to teach her, her leveling of her class and profession to get a Perfect Evolution to C-grade, and how the god had helped her become a high elf. Duskleaf had then blessed her with a True Blessing, making her his first Chosen in many, many years.

At this point, Irin added, a bit teasingly, how both Duskleaf and Meira had wanted to avoid any kind of celebration and how Meira had more or less hidden away for a while. Alas, such things could not be kept secret for long, and ultimately, an official notice had been sent out. Luckily, Duskleaf was already known as a bit of a recluse, so no one had questioned it when no big ceremony was held.

Continuing her story, Jake heard how she had returned to her home village, and when Jake heard about everything that had gone down there, he couldn't help but smile. He smiled not just at what she had done, but at the mere fact she had gone there. To want to take control of her home and help her family members was a selfish decision that had nothing to do with Jake or anyone else; it was something she had decided solely by herself.

This was one of the things Meira had needed to work on the most: being selfish. So to see her leverage her newly gained position was honestly great, in Jake's eyes. What she had done with her old clan was also good. She had effectively freed them all from slavery and made them part of her own faction of sorts.

Meira didn't talk that much about this, though, but more about how she had spent time with her family and how it had taken a bit for them to get used to what she had become. Luckily, her siblings were very accepting, but her mother had taken a little while.

Jake saw Meira's happiness as she explained helping out her family and clan. With it now being known Meira originally came from there, some people who wanted to get in her and Duskleaf's good graces had even moved there to improve the area further, with the clan members now all considered true members of the Order... which kind of got Jake thinking.

If Jake had revealed himself as the Chosen... couldn't he also have just freed Meira from being a slave the very day they met, declaring her an official member of the Order? Oh, he definitely could have, couldn't he?

Not that Jake regretted how he'd handled everything when he looked at Meira. He had no idea what would have happened to her if he had just freed her, but he seriously doubted she would be doing as well as she was now.

Meira continued with all her exploits, and it truly did sound like she had done more in three years than Jake had in fifty. Granted, she'd spent a bit of time in a time chamber reading a lot of books at one point, but it hadn't been that long.

After a while, the conversation shifted again as Irin and Meira began to ask Jake questions about his own time in Nevermore and everything that had happened there. Sadly, Jake couldn't really share that much due to the rules of Nevermore not allowing one to share specific details, but he could give an overview of some things.

As they were all talking, Jake suddenly felt something. The barrier around his personal residence had been reinforced by the Malefic Viper to ensure no one could peek inside or get in without Jake's permission, yet at this moment, Jake felt a small hole opening... at the hands of the Viper himself. Ah, but not for his own avatar to enter...

Jake turned his head and stared out the window. Irin and Meira also stopped their conversation when they noticed Jake's sudden inattention, turning just in time to see a massive worm fall down from the sky and land on his lawn with a big thump. Yet another Chosen had joined their little get-together.

CHAPTER 67

PLANTING SEEDS & SANDY'S RETURN

Within the largest tree of the multiverse, Artemis, Nature's Attendant, and the avatar of Yggdrasil remained even after Dina had been teleported away.

The Primordial seemed to be in thought for a moment before turning to Artemis. "Either you have made significant progress in a very short amount of time, or the aura of the Viper's Chosen has affected you despite the briefness of your encounter."

Artemis didn't even hesitate to agree. "Undoubtedly, though the effect is nothing compared to what Nature Attendant's granddaughter experienced."

"Even so, this proves it even works on gods," Yggdrasil continued. "Tell me, were you aware of the change taking place?"

"No." Artemis shook her head. "Only after I deeply inspected myself did I notice anything."

"I see," Yggdrasil said, nodding. "Any changes to your divine realm?"

Artemis once more shook her head. "None. I do not think there are any tangible changes in any form. It's more like a shift in perspective. It's not much different from how when I feel the aura of the Mother Tree, the auras of others just seem insignificant in comparison, even if they are more powerful than myself."

"Are you saying my aura is insignificant compared to the Viper's Chosen?" Yggdrasil asked in an amused, almost joking tone.

"That is..." Artemis said, taking the question entirely seriously. "In some aspects, yes. There is a sense of... superiority within his aura. One that naturally has to exist above any other, suppressing others not out of any desire or choice, but simply because it's expressing the rightful way of the world."

"His aura matched that of Valdemar's in pure quality," Nature's Attendant chimed in as he frowned a bit. "No... saying it matched Valdemar's isn't entirely accurate. It simply clashed with Valdemar's, not allowing it to gain any dominion where not allowed."

"And that which was not allowed to be imposed upon included Artemis," Yggdrasil said with a smile. "I am beginning to understand your interest in him."

"Does that mean—"

"You have my permission, but wait," the Primordial said. "Wait till he matures. Grows into something more sustainable than he is now. While attention is good, even the most rigorous of plants will wither if given too much."

"If he perishes, his Bloodline will disappear with him," Nature's Attendant added in a serious tone.

Yggdrasil just smiled. "If that happens, perhaps it's simply nature correcting itself. That, or he will be able to overcome even the natural balance. Either way... I look forward to seeing what he grows into. Ah, but feel free to continue planting the seeds for a budding future; it would be a shame for someone else to reap what we failed to sow."

With these words, the avatar Yggdrasil faded away, leaving Artemis and Nature's Attendant behind. The two of them didn't wait before they left the Mother Tree, both with quite some food for thought.

———

In the multiverse, countless Paths existed. The vast majority did have significant overlap, though, falling into either the camp of crafting or fighting. Extrapolated a bit to include monsters, this meant either being in charge of creating and rearing the next generation, leading their kin, or fighting. In fact, of all Paths in the multiverse, one thing was a near constant:

Fighting and killing.

Even those who focused on creation tended to leave a mountain of corpses in their wake. It was simply how the multiverse worked. Battle was the most simplistic form of displaying superiority over others. No matter how good of a crafter you were, what did it matter if others could simply rob you of your creations or kill you outright?

Yet some Paths didn't revolve around fighting. Jacob was one example of this. He was purely in the "creation" department. He helped shepherd people improving their Paths and was a leader and spiritual guide of sorts. One could almost say he was a crafter of other people.

But... on very, *very* rare occasions, there were those with Paths that had nothing to do with either creation or even fighting. Those who didn't particularly fit into any box, but were specialized in one extremely fringe direction.

One such example was the giant worm that had just fallen on Jake's lawn, ripping up the soil and making a real mess of things. Sandy had a Path that didn't require them to craft anything or fight. Sandy was specialized in doing one thing, and one thing only:

Eating.

And getting away with eating stuff that belonged to those who specialized in fighting.

This had resulted in Sandy being an utterly lopsided existence that, quite frankly, was borderline useless in battle. All the big worm could do was ram people or try and eat them, and based on all Jake knew, Sandy could only really eat those a lot weaker than themselves. The purpose of eating them wasn't to kill them, but to use them as "resources" within the worm's internal world.

Besides eating, all of Sandy's other abilities had gone into the art of escape and durability. While this kind of Path was rarely one that worked out well in the multiverse due to the lack of self-defense... well, Sandy seemed to be doing pretty well for themselves. Jake discovered this by using a quick Identify as he, Meira, and Irin walked outside to talk to the worm wiggling on the grass.

[Juvenile Cosmic Genesis Worm – lvl 242]

"Hey, Jake!" the worm yelled telepathically the moment Jake walked outside. *"Oh! Succubus and the elf are also here! Or should I call her a high elf now? Speaking of, why is it even called a high elf? Did she even get taller? Oh, wait, I ate this thing called a Highmountain-something, and that one was from a high mountain, so that name made sense... Oh, I know, maybe high elves originally come from big mountains? Hey, high elf that isn't actually that high, why are you called a high elf?"*

Meira just stared with a confused expression for a moment before muttering, "I... don't know exactly why we're called high elves... but it's probably to signify it's a higher race of sorts compared to usual elves?

While the stats aren't different compared to regular elves, we do have different racial skills."

"I guess that can make sense, too," Sandy said, readily accepting the answer that was frankly way more serious than Sandy's question deserved. *"Anyway! Jake! I heard you're back, and you are now an even bigger deal than before because you did some stuff on a Leaderboard!"*

"I am back indeed, and I did do stuff on a Leaderboard." Jake smiled, honestly happy to see Sandy again. The big worm was always interesting to be around, even if it did feel a bit weird talking to the giant mound of wiggling flesh on his lawn.

"That's great! Speaking of great, am I the only one who's starving?"

Jake sensed the expectant attention of the cosmic worm on him. However, before he could even say anything, Irin spoke up.

"I do believe we could all do with a snack, and while I'm not sure if Jake has anything you find appealing, I hope my offering can at least help please the Chosen of the Lord Protector."

With these words, she waved her hand to produce a bunch of lockboxes, making Jake throw her a look.

"Items given to me by the top brass in case I encountered the Chosen of the Lord Protector," she quickly clarified with a telepathic message as she smiled at him. Jake definitely noticed how she very heavily implied all this stuff was from her alone...

"Oh! That does smell good..." Sandy said happily. *"Just a second; I'm on a bit of a diet and have to watch what I eat, so I'll just have my dietitian take a look at things."* The worm wiggled a bit and floated into the air, then opened their mouth.

Space distorted as a man wearing an expensive-looking suit appeared.

"Wh—where am I!? What happened? Wh—"

"Oops, wrong guy!" Sandy said. They sucked the man back in before spitting out another suit-wearing man, this one far more put together.

"Does Lord Sandy require my services?" he asked the second he'd oriented himself.

"Yep! That stuff over there!" Sandy said.

The man somehow knew where Sandy had mentally pointed. Turning around, he spotted Jake and the others. His eyes opened wide as he bowed. "I greet the Chosen of the Malefic One, as well as the Chosen of the Grand Elder."

"Hey, there—don't mind us and attend to your matters," Jake quickly said, Meira nodding in agreement. With their approval, and while dealing with the pressure of being in the presence of three Chosen, the man went over to the offering and began to go through them with a clipboard. While that was interesting in its own right, Jake was more interested in what had happened before.

"Who was that first guy?" Jake asked, confused, as he turned to look at Sandy.

"Oh, that was just Tom."

"And who is Tom?"

"A guy I ate."

"Why did you eat Tom?"

"A better question is: why wouldn't I eat Tom?"

Jake just looked at Sandy and sighed. "You know what? Fair enough. Why do you need a dietitian anyway?"

"Eh, something about eating more quality over quantity and stuff like that. Basically about me not wasting time digesting stuff that isn't worth digesting."

"I see," Jake said, nodding. That made a lot of sense to him. It was probably like how he shouldn't waste his time hunting weaker prey. He could totally see Sandy only benefiting from certain kinds of natural treasures by now as they got stronger. There was definitely also a Records aspect to it.

No matter the case, Jake was sure the Lord Protector had this handled. The Boundless Hydra was very good at eating stuff himself, so Jake felt confident that if anyone was qualified to give Sandy advice on the Path of devouring, it was him.

With the dietitian hard at work, Jake changed the subject. "What are your plans regarding this Prima Guardian system event, by the way? Are you heading back to Earth with the rest of us?"

"Maybe?" Sandy responded. *"Not sure I should. The rules about the Prima thing said that beasts who consumed unique system-given stuff in the early days aren't allowed to fight against the big boss, only alongside it, and, well, I ate a lot of system-given stuff back then."*

"I... hadn't really thought of that," Jake muttered. "Then again, can you even fight? Say, what if you just help by doing stuff that isn't directly related to fighting, like helping people travel around faster or something? I doubt the system would force you to fight for the Prima Guardian, so indirect help may be allowed."

"Based on what I know of these system-event bosses, I believe Jake's assessment is correct," Irin chimed in. "Historically, in cases like these, the system-empowered entities won't be controlled or forced to do anything, but they may be punished if they choose to go against the event boss. It's also equally possible this Prima Guardian will have a unique ability to suppress anyone who consumed these system-provided items, making it nearly impossible for them to fight against the boss."

"Hm, if the succubus who brings me tasty snacks is right, I guess I should return," Sandy seemingly agreed after thinking a bit. *"Maybe I can even find some good stuff to eat in the 93rd Universe. I have heard people talking about how new universes tend to have a lot of tasty stuff in their infancy..."*

Jake suddenly had a thought. "Actually, can you even go? What about the people you ate? Will they be able to go to the 93rd Universe with you?"

"Good question that I already thought about all on my own! They totally can; I just can't let them out. Like, I already tried it once for funsies, kind of thinking that the person would go boom or something, but nope, they just won't come out no matter what I do. Ah, but don't worry... Tom can come out; he is from our universe."

"Good to know?" Jake muttered. "Did you eat Tom on Earth?"

"No? What a silly question; there's no way Tom would be from Earth!" Sandy wiggled in laughter.

Jake really wanted to ask more about Tom but stopped himself as he sighed. "In that case, will you return with me when I head back? I plan on going... actually, probably just later today. I don't think I have a lot I have to do at the Order; I mainly came by to say hi to these two."

He said the last part while motioning to Irin and Meira. Alright, he had not come specifically to see these two, but the people he knew in the Order. Seeing as everyone else was away, he only really had these two he wanted to check in on.

"You're leaving already?" Irin said in a downtrodden tone, with Meira not looking happy at the news either.

"Not like I won't come by once in a while." Jake smiled, shaking his head. "Things here in the Order are a lot more stable than places such as Earth. I feel like it's better I'm there. Also, I am more than a little curious to see how things have developed over the last three or so years. Finally... there are a few places I've been meaning to check out. Maybe even some places you can help me get to, Sandy."

"Sure, as long as I can eat everything there while you deal with all the things not wanting me to eat everything there," the gluttonous worm agreed. *"It'll be like in the old days!"*

Jake smiled. "Hopefully with less stress." While his adventure with Sandy had been fun, the circumstances in which they had happened hadn't been. He could definitely do without another invasion.

Shaking off the thought, the four of them kept speaking for a while before they moved things inside, which was when Jake saw just how much Sandy had improved their spatial abilities.

The giant worm, around a hundred meters long in total, rapidly shrank down at an incredible speed. In a mere moment, Sandy went from a giant worm to a small grub no larger than a guinea pig. Sandy proceeded to jump on Jake's shoulder, catching a ride as they all went inside to continue the conversation that Sandy had so rudely interrupted when they decided to drop in.

And with that, Sandy became yet another person willing to share their adventures over the last few years. Sandy gladly went into the details, though for some reason, their exploits were always framed around what was eaten rather than the enemies or the grand vistas they had seen while flying around with S-grades and gods alike.

Their catch-up chat continued for the rest of the day, but soon it was time. Jake had a planet to attend to, and much of the doubt he had about leaving Meira alone had been dispelled. He knew how dependent on him she had seemed, but now she truly had grown into her own person and had a status of her own. It genuinely made him happy, and he looked forward to what she would one day become.

As for Irin... well, she made it no secret that she planned on sticking as close to Jake as possible... for as long as possible... no matter the cost. Jake wasn't blind to the fact that he had also entirely altered her Path and future, and in retrospect, he should probably have cut her off a long time ago if he didn't plan on allowing her to stick with him going forward.

Not that Jake would have cut her off or denied her the chance to stick around, and he tended not to be a fan of dwelling on the past. In fact, doing so was pretty darn antithetical to his Path.

Jake headed off to the teleportation circle with a shrunken Sandy on his shoulder—after they ate the dietitian and the approved food, of course —and as they said their goodbyes, Jake caught the disappointment on both the women's faces. They had probably hoped he would stick around a bit longer.

He would definitely return even before the Prima Guardian to check in on things, but for now, he had quite a few places he wanted to visit once back on Earth... including a mountain with a certain wyvern he very much wanted payback on. Who knows, maybe it was even time to take a step for mankind and do a little moon trip...

CHAPTER 68

AN ALL-NEW HAVEN

J ake hadn't been back to his own universe for over three years, and if he was being perfectly honest, he wasn't looking forward to what Haven had become in his absence. He was afraid it had changed more than he liked, and he especially feared learning what had happened with his good old lodge. He was pretty sure Miranda or someone else had taken care of it during his absence to make sure it wasn't too horrible, but what if they had turned it into a tourist destination or something? Fuck, maybe someone had constructed a viewing deck overlooking it!

He could totally see that happening, especially with Miranda in Nevermore herself. Actually... who was even in charge of Haven right now? Lillian and Miranda were usually the ones doing everything, but neither of them were there. Maybe Hank? Jake sure as hell hoped it wasn't just some random person Arthur had put in charge.

These were just some of the thoughts Jake had as he went through the void. The only change he knew of for sure was the teleportation circle in Haven allowing him to teleport back there directly. Those snakes in Scarlett's former territory had improved their special magic circle significantly to the level where Jake could easily teleport to most regular teleportation circles back on Earth. As Jake understood it, it was a bit like a phone forwarding a call—with the call, in this case, being someone teleporting through the void with a shrunken-down cosmic worm on their shoulder.

A few seconds after stepping on the Order's teleporter, Jake was back on Earth, the void treating him nicely this time around, with no eldritch beings wanting a chat during his travel. He was actually a bit surprised to see that Sandy wasn't at all affected by the warping space despite using space magic on themselves, but he wasn't going to question how any of that worked.

"Home sweet home!" Sandy said with glee as they appeared within the large basement complex beneath Jake's lodge. Through his sphere, he naturally saw it all—namely, that nothing had really changed down there. Honestly, seeing it made him feel kind of bad when he remembered all the work Hank had gone through to make it, only for Jake to never really use the place.

The facilities are still pretty good, though... Considering I just need a cauldron to do alchemy, I should stay here more, Jake reckoned. Plus, there were some actual benefits to doing alchemy there due to the Pylon of Civilization—an oft-forgotten aspect of how cities on Earth now worked. It was also a tad more private, with no one able to contact him as easily.

Looking at the Pylon Jake owned, he saw it was still there yet had, as expected, changed slightly. It had grown denser and gathered more energy as he and especially Miranda had grown in power. Standing there, he also felt the slight increase in mana regeneration he benefited from within the borders of the Pylon. There was also that minor increase in experience earned for non-combat activities. However, Jake didn't even think that worked anymore. It had just been an early incentive to make people seek out cities for more than the safety they offered.

Shaking his head, Jake smiled at Sandy's happiness over being home. "Good to be back, indeed."

Making his way up to the lodge, he felt quite nostalgic. Especially when he entered the lodge itself. Everything looked as it had the day he left —even the bed he had dragged from the Tutorial Challenge Dungeon way back in the day. The rest of the furniture he'd dragged out was also mostly the same.

"Looking cozy," Sandy said, wiggling around. *"Not much to eat around here, though... except for that tree outside."*

"It's not a tree," Jake quickly corrected.

"It looks like a tree."

"But it's not."

"If it looks like a tree, smells like a tree, and sounds like a tree, it's a tree," Sandy insisted.

"You literally don't have eyes," Jake pointed out.

"And yet I can see it's a tree," Sandy said in a disappointed tone. *"Look, I can test if it also tastes like a tree, and—"*

"I'm going to give you a full lesson about the difference between a musa and a tree if you keep this up," Jake threatened.

"Oh, it's a musa? You should have just said that from the beginning!"
Sandy quickly stopped arguing as the two of them walked outside to the
clearing. Going down the steps from the porch, Jake took in the sights.
Everything here also looked very much the same. The trees had maybe
grown a little, and the grass was definitely due for mowing, but besides
that, things were serene, with no tourists in sight. No viewing decks overlooking the valley, either.

Jake purposefully held himself back from using a Pulse of Perception
to allow him to take in everything a little at a time. Looking at the banana
musa, he went over to it for a quick inspection. There were a few bananas
growing on it, and the magic circle Mystie had placed a long time ago had
faded with time. Size-wise, the musa was pretty much the same as it had
been the last time he saw it, though he did feel that it had grown at least a
little.

He considered the manure he had received and whether he should use
it right away, ultimately deciding to hold off, as it was definitely better to
have someone with gardener skills do it for improved effect. However, he
did do something incredibly smart.

Taking out all of the bags, he placed them near the musa. That way,
they would serve as visual reminders whenever he was there so he wouldn't
forget!

"That soil stinks," Sandy commented. *"Wait... it's not soil, is it? Did you
really just take out literal bags of poo?"*

"It's called manure and is a very common aspect of farming," Jake said
in defense of the bags, which he could see coming off as disgus—

"Can I have a little taste? Pretty please?" the worm asked in a pleading
tone while wiggling.

Jake looked at the worm for a moment before shaking his head. "Sorry,
it's for the musa. Maybe if there are some leftovers, but that will depend
on who I find to help spread it and what they say."

"Fine... Tom would have let me have some..."

Ignoring Sandy entirely, Jake went over to the small pond and water-
fall... and he felt something within it. Looking down into the water, he saw
a lot of small eels swimming around, making him smile at how serene it all
seemed... until he used Identify on one of them.

Yeah, that's a D-grade, Jake quickly confirmed. Actually... nearly all of
them were D-grades. Looking down at them, he saw a few stare back up at
him. He stood there for a few moments before just turning around,
shaking his head.

They didn't seem aggressive in the slightest, and using his sphere, he saw an underwater tunnel leading deep into the ground from the pond, likely connecting to the underworld of the planet. No need to complain about a bunch of nice eels guarding his little pond.

Jake checked out the exterior of the lodge a bit more before he decided it was time to head out into Haven proper. But before that...

"Hey, Sandy, do you have a good stealth skill?" Jake asked the cosmic worm. "I want to go explore a bit without attracting the attention of half the planet."

"Eh... kind of? It's not really a stealth skill, but I can disappear." Sandy wiggled around before suddenly popping out of existence. Yet as Jake felt a bit deeper, he sensed something was still there...

Before he could understand what Sandy had done, the worm popped back into existence. *"I can just enter Sandy's Sand World and hide there while putting an anchor on you, and don't worry—I can still feel and smell stuff while in there!"*

"Do I want to know what Sandy's Sand World is?" Jake questioned.

"According to people who claim to know a lot about space stuff, it's apparently what subspace is called or something like that... or was it what I called something called subspace? Either way, it's like space but different. Gotta be there to understand it."

Jake got the gist of their non-explanation. "Well, it works, so go hide in the sand, and let's explore."

The worm did as he asked, and they left Jake's lodge after he engaged his stealth skill. On the way out, he did notice the addition of more magical barriers designed to keep people out and stop them from peeping, so that was nice to see. The old sign telling people to keep out also remained.

Walking outside, Jake made his way into the city proper... and was more than pleasantly surprised by how little things had changed. Haven had always been a small, quaint place with tree houses and wooden structures spread relatively sparsely around the forested city. None of that had changed, and the natural vibe fully remained.

The areas with a few more buildings, such as a small street for shopping, were buzzing with activity as Jake walked through the non-paved roads of Haven. Looking toward some of the larger buildings, he saw even more activity inside. The building that had served as Miranda's home for the longest time was especially lively. It was more of a large office rather than a home, and since Jake's last visit, it had expanded both into the ground and onto nearby trees via a few satellite buildings.

When it came to the people, all that had really changed were the average levels. People had gotten stronger, especially those who lived in Haven. It had been considered a city for the elites for a long time, and that showed: Jake spotted more than a few C-grades, with most average folk in D-grade. Of course, there were also weaker residents, such as the family members of the strong people who'd settled there or the original residents of Haven. As far as Jake knew, it wasn't as if you got thrown out if you had a low level or anything like that.

Considering so many had left for Nevermore, the number of C-grades was honestly impressive, and based on all the statistics Jake had heard about how strong people from newly initiated planets usually became, Jake got the feeling Earth was well ahead of the curve.

Overall, the vibe of Haven was as great as usual. The population hadn't even expanded by much, which genuinely did surprise him, given all the people that had come to Earth due to his little Chosen ceremony. There was also the fact that an influx of people would have come once they all learned Jake was the Chosen... but it appeared Miranda had handled everything incredibly well.

Walking around a bit more in Haven, Jake just took everything in before he decided it was time to check out the other part of what many called Haven but he usually called the Fort. He had definitely expected that to expand quite a bit... but he really wasn't prepared for what he saw when he flew up over the treeline and looked in the direction of the Fort— or at least where he assumed the Fort should still be, somewhere in the middle of the massive bloody metropolis that had shot up.

Jake took a moment, wondering if he had really gone to the right place... but upon closer inspection, he did spot the dome that was Arnold's workshop. It was a bit off to the side and had a cleared area all around it, but it was still effectively surrounded by buildings, and not the small stone ones Jake had gotten used to.

When he called it a metropolis, he wasn't just talking about size but also representation. High-rises that looked straight out of huge pre-system cities shot up by the dozens, making a respectable skyline. Many of them even surpassed the pre-system height limits, with a lot of the architecture physically impossible if not for the system.

Looking below the high-rises, Jake saw apartment buildings and well-paved streets everywhere, but there was also stuff like flight lanes. It was far from as advanced as the world Temlat had come from within the Nevermore Challenge Dungeon, but it was clear that what had once been the Fort was developing fast into a proper megacity.

Luckily, Jake did see that a strip of plains had been designated as a no-build zone between the Fort and Haven itself, keeping the two of them pretty separate. Even so, the city's size exceeded Jake's wildest expectations.

The large plains that had once been there to make the Fort a better defensive position had served as premium space for the real-estate market's expansion. Outside of the large city center were suburbs, and while Jake didn't want to be a peeper, he saw more than his fair share of fully inhabited family homes.

There was still a tent camp, too, but what had once been one of the biggest areas of the Fort was now just a small district at most.

"It's gotten pretty big, huh?" Sandy said, apparently still able to talk to him from within Sandy's Sand World.

Jake just nodded as he kept looking out at the city. How in the actual fuck all this could be built in three years was beyond him. One thing was for sure: he had seriously underestimated the capabilities of builders and architects. He also had to consider that people had come representing major factions, and some of them maybe had some valuable skills to help. Oh, yeah, and the high-grade teachers who would be projected even from other universes to help teach the Earthlings.

Glancing around, he spotted more than a few notable buildings, including one he partly recognized, though it was now a few times larger than the last time he was there. A massive cathedral had been constructed near the city center, with a large garden in front, taking up quite a lot of space. The entire building looked overly fancy. When he looked a bit closer, he saw it had a total of twelve towers, with each building featuring a statue at the top. Statues Jake quickly recognized as representations of a certain twelve gods.

That's...

Finally, Jake decided to use a Pulse of Perception to get a proper look at things, focusing specifically on the cathedral. Instantly, he saw why the hell it was so large. Even with its massive size, it was filled to the brim. However, he also spotted two things that sent a shiver down his spine.

The first, Jake saw when he narrowed his eyes and barely looked through one of the windows. Standing on one of the cathedral's podiums was a recognizable figure that instantly gave him flashbacks to the worst parts of the Chosen Ceremony... Felix the sculptor.

[Human – lvl 286 – Divine Blessing of the Eternal Servant]

Ignoring how the fuck the man had leveled so fast, it looked like he had changed career tracks a bit, as he now looked more like a priest or a preacher. However, this part of what he saw wasn't what was truly night-mare-inducing... No, it was what was behind him.

Occupying center stage in the cathedral was a certain statue. One that made Jake seriously consider "accidentally" shooting an arrow at the building. But he feared that not even he would be able to easily break the monstrosity that was the mythical-rarity statue Felix had so proudly presented to Jake. It was the True Vision of the Malefic Viper's Chosen, and for some fucking reason, people were staring at it with reverence.

Yeah, I'm never going to visit that place, Jake swore to himself. He'd only ever go there to extract the Vision's Venom, and that was luckily only every ten years.

Shifting his attention elsewhere, Jake took in the many sights of the city. It pretty much had anything one would expect of a metropolis, including some form of floating train. If Jake had to give an estimate, he would definitely put the population in the double-digit millions, if not even more than that. By now, this had to be the largest city on Earth, or very close to it.

After looking around a little more, he decided to find someone who could actually tell him more about what had been going on over the last few years. Scouting a bit, he found the building that Miranda used to use when managing big-city stuff while at the Fort, though it had since been remodeled into a high-rise, so it really wasn't the same building anymore.

Anyhow, Jake used his Pulse to search through the building until he found someone near the top within an office larger than the others, so he assumed this person had to be among those in charge. Plus, when he got closer, Jake was actually surprised: He felt an aura that wasn't even all that weak.

"We should totally prank the guy," Sandy interjected when they were just outside the building.

"Not sure what that would accomplish," Jake muttered. "Outside of making him less willing to talk."

"So, pranking time it is!"

CHAPTER 69

THE DARK ONES AND HE WHO KNOWS

Holstred frowned as he read over the report in front of him. They would have to increase security personnel in certain districts if this development continued. Dissidence had been growing over the last few years, ever since he and the other slaves arrived. The natives had mostly been welcoming, but some weren't huge fans, especially of those who weren't humans.

When Ms. Wells was still on Earth, she'd kept everyone in check, but now that she had gone to Nevermore, a lot of annoying people had come out of the woodwork. Arthur was doing his best, and he had quelled much of the dissatisfaction on a more global scale, but in this city, his influence had little sway. This was a problem, as this was also the most multicultural and multiracial city on the entire planet. The majority of those brought to Earth from elsewhere had chosen to settle down here.

This had led to a lot of crime. Holstred wanted to say that the former slaves were innocent in this entire matter, but there was a lot of tension there, hidden under the surface. A lingering fear of the future and of what it would bring. Many of the freed slaves hadn't been sure what to do with themselves after finding themselves on an entirely new planet, making them lash out.

And then there was perhaps the biggest issue... Earth had many factions, some of which had been responsible for gifting the slaves to the Chosen of the Malefic Viper. Seeing a merchant proudly wearing the emblems of the same faction that had once slaughtered your family, ruined your home planet, and then enslaved and sold you off could be triggering, to say the least.

All of this is to say that when one has a melting pot, some of the individual ingredients sometimes have a problem properly mixing. Especially given how short a time it had been. Holstred believed many of these cultural issues would naturally fade within a few decades, but for now, they had to deal with the current situation at hand before it got worse.

While outright murders were rare, they did happen. With the system, everyone now had power, and there was a big disparity between individuals. Those more powerful could easily kill anyone who bothered them with little effort, which could be a recipe for disaster. Most would control themselves, but sometimes emotions ran too high, or someone truly vile decided to ignore the laws to take another life.

Holstred was the man Ms. Wells had entrusted to help uphold the law of Haven—a responsibility he had taken on with pride, and he had more than willingly sworn a Knight's Oath toward the woman, offering his unquestionable loyalty. Despite it effectively making her his master, it was far different than the forced servitude of a slave contract. It was his choice, and should she step onto a path deemed too evil, the oath would cease to be.

He'd been the Knight Commander on his own planet before they lost the war and he was enslaved, so he did have some experience in leadership. While he hadn't established any knight order, he had been put in charge of what Ms. Wells called a security force. With her and many of the other top brass absent, he had taken on even more work than simple security.

And he personally cared a lot about the security of Haven. His wife and child both lived in the city, and he wanted it to be the safest environment it could possibly be. Compared to many other areas of the multiverse, it was surely already considered very safe... but Holstred still wasn't satisfied, and thus he began to consider an action plan to address some of the ostensibly non-violent organizations that had begun to appear in opposition to certain races or people. Many of them were suspected of backing or inciting actual violence behind the scenes, but without proof, moving against them would only lead to more problems...

As Holstred was deep in thought, a magic token vibrated on the table, and then a woman's voice appeared, its tone exhausted. "Sir, he's here again... more insistent than usual..."

Holstred instantly knew who she was talking about. "Alright, alright. Just send him up."

Maybe this would be good for him. A brief respite from actual important matters. Because the man who was about to arrive was as far from important as he could possibly be.

522   ZOGARTH

Less than thirty seconds passed before the door to his office opened, and a man walked in with slightly disheveled hair. Once he saw Holstred, he smiled. "Honored Knight! Hard at work, as always! Truly a respectable figure. Even if you are surrounded by dark influences, you remain a light within the darkness, fighting off evil!"

"Hello, Greg—what can I do for you today?" Holstred asked, knowing what was about to come.

"I ask myself what can be done every single day, but before we ask what we can do, we need to understand what needs to be done, and for that to happen, we need to understand our situation and the world at large!" Greg said, more or less going on the same spiel as usual.

Holstred just leaned back as the man took the chance and summoned a whiteboard filled to the brim with... stuff.

"You remember where we left off last time, right?"

"Sure," Holstred just said, honestly not at all remembering the ramblings of the madman.

"Good! I knew you were reasonable... Anyway, as I said last, I believe I have finally cracked the code regarding the name Haven and the hidden meanings behind the Dome of Secrets, but that is not what is important right now. No, it's related to the news of the Chosen of the Dark Ones."

"Just so I'm sure, the Chosen of the Malefic One is still someone who has experienced the integration thousands of times before and is using his knowledge of all his prior lives to excel?" Holstred asked, hiding his amusement as best he could.

"Well, his status as a regressor is unquestionable, and his quest to force through what he considers an ideal future is as clear as day. But, no, this has to do with these so-called Leaderboards... or as they should be rightfully called, the Board of Leaders."

This could be amusing. Holstred nodded, trying to look serious.

"Think about it. This is their hidden list of members of the Dark Ones. Even the name is a clue... Nevermore. It's telling them they are to "never more" speak of the Board of Leaders they now belong to. Or are you truly trying to say it's a coincidence so many influential people are put on the same list like that? Preposterous!" Greg spoke with a level of certainty and confidence that Holstred could only find admirable.

It was good that Greg was ultimately harmless and more of a fun distraction. Somehow, the man had become convinced Holstred was someone who could be trusted, in part because he'd once been a slave and also because he had been a Knight Commander. Greg somehow had a skill that gave him a general sense as to what kind of Path others walked down, and knowing Holstred was a knight apparently meant he was a man of honor who could be trusted in the fight against the Dark Ones.

The man continued his lengthy rant about the secret leaders of the multiverse, the former Knight Commander nodding along almost automatically. About half an hour later, Greg's fervor finally died down as he took a deep breath, which also signified that Holstred should at least listen to his final words.

"So, do you see why we need to be extra cautious of any lines in magic circles longer than three and a half centimeters?"

"I do indeed, and I will be on the lookout," Holstred agreed in his usual serious tone.

"It's good to have allies fighting the good fight with me." Greg smiled as he took away the whiteboard. "I shall return and continue my... my..."

Greg's eyes went wide as he seemed to stare past Holstred. Holstred was confused and looked over his shoulder but saw nothing there. When he turned back to Greg, he saw the man already running towards a window.

"No! You shall never catch me alive!" Greg yelled loudly as he jumped through one of the windows, phasing right through it and using magic to take flight, breaking quite a few air-traffic rules in the process.

Holstred stared for a moment before he shook his head. "I hope he gets the help he needs."

———

Jake stood behind the guy in the chair that the man named Greg had referred to as a knight, quite confused. Sandy had tried to convince him to do some prank that included separating the entire space of the office from the rest of the world, but Jake had decided to just make a sneaky entrance. One where he would appear behind the man, taking him by complete surprise like some ninja in the night.

However, before he could pull that off, Greg entered. Jake wondered what the guy was here for and thought it would be fine to surprise two people at once... but once the guy started talking, Jake kind of forgot all about his plans. The words of Greg were just too... interesting.

It was like watching a trainwreck live. The entire thing only got more amusing when Jake fully realized he was the center of this entire conspiracy. Apparently, he had quite a few secret identities, hidden powers, and was a super mastermind villain beyond comprehension by mortal minds.

Which made sense, as Jake was actually a god—or at least had been a god at some point—according to Greg's very credible theories.

When the guy finished, Jake was even a bit sad. But... then, out of nowhere, the guy called Greg suddenly looked straight at Jake, screamed, and jumped out the damn window before flying away, leaving Jake standing there invisible as the knight muttered about hopes of Greg improving.

The confusion was very brief, though, as Jake instantly knew who was responsible. *"Sandy... what did you do?"*

"Wha!? Me!? Who says I did anything?" The cosmic worm had the guiltiest tone Jake had ever heard. *"Sheesh, what could I even have done? Revealed we were standing here all along, and told the guy the Dark Ones are always watching, and that the truth is more dangerous than he could possibly imagine? No, I would definitely never do that, ever. But if I did, it would be because a certain someone didn't want to do a fun prank, so I had to improvise."*

Jake stood there momentarily before sighing and walking around the table toward the door. He then opened it, his stealth skill ensuring the knight didn't even notice, and went to the other side before dispelling his stealth skill.

"Killjoy," Sandy sent, as they realized Jake wasn't even going to play their original prank anymore.

"Enough pranking for one day; I need this guy to actually give me some useful information and not be scared shitless or view me as some deranged lunatic, making him actually believe the words of that madman."

"Jake Thayne, Killer of All Joys."

Ignoring the cosmic worm, Jake raised his hand and knocked on the door.

On the other side, he saw the knight look up with a frown. "Who goes there?"

Jake could explain himself but decided to just open the door and walk in. The knight looked at Jake for a second before his eyes opened wide in realization. Scrambling, the man practically jumped over the table and knelt down in front of Jake, his head way too close to the ground.

"This lowly one greets the Chosen of the Malefic One," he said in a tone that held far more fear than any other emotion. This probably shouldn't have taken him by surprise, but it honestly did.

Jake knew Miranda had wanted to foster a view of him that was less negative than most initially adopted. That he was more of a protector of Earth who didn't get directly involved in matters and wasn't a symbol of fear, but one of stability and multiversal might, in that no one would dare attack a planet owned by the Chosen of the Malefic Viper.

Clearly, that hadn't worked super well. His reputation—or, more accurately, the reputation of the Malefic Viper—was just not that good. At least, not good if Jake didn't want to be treated as someone who would kill others just for looking at him wrong.

"No need to kneel," Jake said, trying to sound casual and relaxed. "In fact, you're just making this needlessly uncomfortable for both of us, so please stand."

Jake saw the man's hesitation, and finally the fear of refusing an order from the Chosen seemed to win out over his fear of what would happen if he stopped kneeling. The knight stood up with slow movements, though he still didn't dare look away from the floor.

"What's your name?" Jake asked, trying to get any kind of conversation going.

"I am known as Holstred, honored Chosen."

"Just call me Lord Thayne," Jake said, shaking his head. He wanted to ask the guy to just call him Jake, but that had literally never worked in any situations like this before, so he just defaulted to what he, more often than not, ended up settling on anyway.

"I... Very well, Lord Thayne," the guy answered, being quite receptive.

"Thank you," Jake said, relieved he wouldn't need a minute-long conversation to convince the guy to not call him some overly long or overly respectful title. "Now, I take it you work for Miranda?"

"That is correct, Lord Thayne. I am one of your former slaves who was employed by Ms. Wells to help with security within the city, with my responsibilities recently expanding due to her temporary absence." Holstred's answer was surprisingly detailed.

"I see... So, I assume you are aware of matters on the planet? I wish to learn the current status of Earth after my return and how things have developed in my absence."

"This... I am aware of current matters, but surely there are those more qualified—"

"No, you'll do," Jake said with a smile as he went around the table and sat behind it. "Now, take a seat and get me up to speed."

Holstred nodded, seeming to realize there was no reason to fight it. "If that is what Lord Thayne requests, then very well."

The man sat down and, despite his nervousness, began to go over everything that had happened on Earth over the last three years or so, including many things Jake doubted he could have learned from anyone who wasn't a former slave brought to the planet.

About ten minutes in, Sandy got bored and decided to just take off to who-knows-where, saying they'd be back later. Jake was only a tiny bit worried about what the giant space worm would be up to, but he didn't really want to invest any mental energy in worrying too much, as he had a lot of information to take in regarding the political climate of Earth and Haven in particular.

Besides, there was a limit to how much trouble Sandy could get into within such a short time, right?

———

Sandy and politics were two things that just didn't mix. The Big Boss Hydra had tried to make Sandy learn about politics, but Sandy didn't care. Neither did Sandy care super much about Earth, though they did want to go back and visit the dunes where they grew up. While Sandy had been effectively disowned for no longer being a Sand Worm, they knew this had mainly happened to give Sandy a good reason to leave and explore the rest of the multiverse with Jake.

And there sure were a lot of things to explore! And eat.

Mainly eat.

One place Sandy had quickly identified as worth exploring was a certain place in the big city. It had taken a while, as the tasties were hidden well... but Sandy had found them. Now, the only problem was just how to sneak into that big metal dome thing without getting discovered, which would make Jake mad and potentially take away snack privileges by reporting Sandy to the Big Boss Hydra...

CHAPTER 70

SCIENCE WORM & ROLLING WITH RICK

"You got stuck?" Jake asked.

"*I got stuck,*" Sandy confirmed.

"Really stuck?"

"*If I didn't want to break anything and make people mad kind of stuck.*"

"So really stuck." Jake sighed while staring at Sandy, now back at full size, lying on what looked like a giant mattress. Meanwhile, Arnold was busy operating some control panel as what looked like lasers shot over Sandy's thick skin here and there. Jake felt quite a few more devices at work, too, ninety percent of which lay beyond his understanding.

"*In my defense, he cheated,*" Sandy said, protecting themselves.

"You entered my workshop without permission and triggered the automatic defenses, then proceeded to escape those, forcing me to step in personally," Arnold said, not even looking up from the screen.

"*You still cheated.*"

"I only disrupted your application of personal spatial shrinkage, forcing you to expand within a limited space while jamming that frequency of space magic."

"*And how is that not cheating?*" Sandy kept complaining, wiggling a bit in annoyance and earning a glance from Arnold. Then the worm went completely still again so the scientist could continue his measurements. The big worm was practically on a massive scanner due to their crimes against Arnold.

From what Jake gathered, Sandy had smelled delicious stuff in Arnold's workshop, which, to be fair, there definitely was a lot of. Many of the treasures he'd cultivated also had powerful space mana within, especially the ones involved in projects he had going while in Nevermore. This naturally attracted the senses of a certain worm, who could detect these treasures despite all the defensive measures Arnold had deployed.

If Arnold hadn't been at home, Sandy would likely—no, definitely—have succeeded in wrecking the entire workshop by eating most of the power sources, thus ruining all ongoing projects. However, with Arnold there, he had deployed countermeasures that forced Sandy back to their full size, which was a problem when stuck within a heavily fortified tunnel. Together with a space-magic jammer of sorts, Sandy had gotten stuck, their only escape route involving the release of a lot of power to forcibly break free. Sandy totally could have done that and gotten away easily, but they would have broken things in the process for sure.

So, instead of breaking free, Sandy had deployed the strategy of negotiation. At least, that was what Sandy said. In reality, Jake highly suspected this entire arrangement was Arnold's idea. Sandy was undoubtedly an interesting creature, and Arnold seemed more than interested in researching the big space worm's abilities.

"Do you feel this?" Arnold asked as Jake felt some odd wave of energy move over Sandy.

"Not really. Like, I kind of felt it, but not very much," the worm responded. *"Hey, by the way, how did you even find me? Like... I was super hidden, I'm pretty sure, prepared to do a quick hit-and-run. Get in, get out, a quick second or two, but boom, you were there right away."*

Arnold didn't even seem to listen to what Sandy said beyond reporting the effects of the odd energy, making Jake take over.

"Sandy, he is quite literally blessed by a Void God known as the All-Seeing," Jake said with a smirk. "I'm pretty sure he's good at spotting people, even if they're super hidden."

"Bah. Don't tell me he is also one of those weirdoes with a lot of Perception?"

"Pretty sure he is," Jake said, smiling.

"I am," Arnold confirmed. "Now, tell me what kind of response this invokes."

A blast of energy struck Sandy in the side but seemed to disperse all throughout their skin, as if the impact was spread out evenly, resulting in no real effect. Jake looked on with interest.

"Nah, that didn't hurt me either," Sandy said in a happy tone.

"I see, I see," Arnold said, nodding as he pressed a button. When he did, Jake saw a drone fly into the room, carrying what looked like a large slab of metal. Sandy gleefully opened their mouth and sucked it in, drone and everything.

"Yummy!" the worm said happily. *"More of that later!"*

Jake threw Arnold a glance, and the man explained, "A piece of metal extracted from deep beneath the ground in a C-grade territory. So far, it has little purpose except its energy richness and ability to handle certain affinities well. I fused a large amount of it into the slab and found no further use for it."

"I thought Sandy was doing this as an apology?"

"Bit of both!" Sandy said. *"It's only fair that if I have to sit here for a while, I'm at least fed in the meantime!"*

"I see," Jake said, nodding before asking Arnold, "What are you using Sandy to research anyway?"

"Sub-space travel."

"Sandy's Sand World travel," the giant worm corrected.

Ignoring the worm, Jake continued, "What even is this sub-space thing? Some other dimension or layer of space?"

Jake considered how his own stealth skill worked and how that made him shift on the spectrum of Perception. This wasn't really the same, but Jake did know there were degrees to space and how stable or unstable it could be, as well as the presence of spatial layers.

"Rather than call it a different dimension or space, it's more accurate to say it interacts with another layer beneath stable space, contrary to all other spatial layers that are stacked on top of stable space," Arnold explained. "It changes the fundamental rules dictating the laws of time, distance, and speed by modifying them with a new conceptual factor that I call the sub-space affinity. This affinity is heavily connected to, but not to be confused with, the regular space affinity. It's instead something relatively unique I've found only some creatures or objects possess. It appears to have little to no active combat applications and is suited solely for travel over long distances without relying on teleportation."

"Isn't teleportation traveling through this sub-space?" Jake wondered.

"No." Arnold shook his head. "Teleportation is far more simplistic. It's merely shifting an entity's coordinates in space to an already-known location. To teleport, one must know where they're going, or at the very least have a strong general idea—for example, to teleport a set distance in a direction. Sub-space travel is far different, and a lot more sustainable for long-distance travel. It's also a requirement for exploration of unknown space, as teleporting there simply carries too much risk."

As Jake listened and nodded, he had another thought... Did his Wings of the Malefic Viper escape skill make him enter this sub-space thing? It stripped away nearly all other concepts by corroding them, including space, so if it melted all layers away, maybe it left only this sub-space? It was at least possible that was how it worked. Definitely something to experiment with.

"So, how long do you think this research project will take?" Jake asked as he saw Arnold walk over with what looked like an overly large camera to take a few pictures of Sandy.

"I do not know; there is simply too much to explore," the scientist said. "Before this, I used spacecraft with special material and magic circles, allowing it to enter subspace through the consumption of vast amounts of energy, but this... this Cosmic Genesis Worm is like a being born to live within sub-space. It's simply awe-inspiring that such a creature can exist."

"Well, Sandy belonging in Sandy's Sand World only makes sense, duh," the worm said smugly. *"And I am awe-inspiring, aren't I?"*

"Sure you are." Jake shook his head. "Anyway, are you fine with staying here for a while, Sandy?"

"That depends..."

"Throughout the last three years of Nevermore, vast amounts of resources have been collected," Arnold added.

"You heard the man! Why would I leave a nice buffet and a comfy bed?"

Jake just smiled and, after talking with the two of them a bit more, left the workshop so Arnold could continue to use Sandy for his experiments while Sandy happily lived the life of a living trash container, gobbling up all the valuable material Arnold had stocked up but no longer needed. He did wonder why the dietitian hadn't been spat out, but oh, well—he wasn't going to babysit a giant space worm and their eating habits.

He decided to take a bit of a trip around the city of Haven. Yes, it was a bit confusing that the metropolis once known as the Fort and the nice forest town were both called Haven, but what could Jake do about it? It wasn't like changing the name was easy either, as the system interface for cities called it all Haven.

Going back slightly, his talk with Holstred had been very enlightening, even if it had been cut short by Arnold's message that he had caught Sandy, and Sandy trying to play it off by saying Jake had told the damn worm to break in.

Either way, he and Holstred had gone over the most important parts. Earth was facing problems for sure, and the integration of the freed slaves would take some time, but honestly... things were way fucking better than he had feared.

Jake had half-expected to hear about some civil war having taken place, or at least a purge of some kind. However, things had been pretty damn peaceful, even if there were still issues. It was clear Miranda had done a banger job, and done much to help integrate the former slaves to make them feel like part of Earth.

That was also why Jake decided not to get involved in any of it.

Could he perhaps stand up and make some grand declaration telling everyone to play nice? Maybe, but he wasn't sure it would lead to genuine change. Jake also had to recognize that he was an idiot when it came to things like this. No, it was definitely better to not make any rash decisions and, at the very least, wait for Miranda to return. If she told him to do something, he would more than gladly step up and help, but doing so behind her back could easily fuck up things far more than it would help.

Walking around the city with his stealth skill active a bit longer, Jake remained impressed by how many things had developed. It was all incredibly similar to a pre-system city, but the touch of magic could also be seen everywhere. People bought stuff and instantly put it in their spatial bags or other such items. There were flight lanes above the usual streets, and the stores made ample use of different forms of magic to better show off products while defending their valuable stuff with barriers.

It's hard to imagine this was empty plains overrun by angry cows just a few years ago, Jake inwardly sighed to himself. The world was still changing at a rapid pace, no doubt about it.

Leaving the city, Jake returned to the "real" Haven. With Sandy preoccupied, Jake had a certain place he wanted to visit before he would take a bit of a solo journey.

Walking through a rocky tunnel, he felt the dense life mana from the cavern below. The walls were lined with shining moss and a few mushrooms here and there, all of them of high quality. He even spotted a few rare mushrooms.

Continuing, he soon reached his destination. A multicolored cavern filled with plants and life appeared before him, with a hole in the middle of it all. In the hole, one could find a metal disc leading to the dungeon known as the Undergrowth.

Few creatures lived in the cavern... but Jake instantly spotted a slightly familiar-looking figure. *Slightly* familiar... because while he recognized the patterns on its skin, the troll certainly hadn't been that big the last time he saw it.

[Undergrowth Cave Troll – lvl 112]

The troll that was still smaller than the troll in the dungeon had been busy weeding, as far as Jake could see. It hadn't noticed Jake, as he still had his stealth skill active, allowing him to silently admire its work. Going a bit deeper into the cavern, he soon saw the one he had been looking for: Rick.

Jake instantly knew he had evolved, even if his size hadn't changed in the slightest. His entire body had turned a slightly green color, with moss growing all over his back—something that didn't seem to bother him at all.

Currently, Rick was busy tending to a large blue plant that towered above any of the others. It looked a bit like a tulip, and Jake could feel it was a valuable herb. Using Identity, he did confirm it was an ancient-rarity natural treasure, and definitely one Rick had spent a lot of time cultivating.

Rick's new race had definitely helped with that.

[Troll Grove Keeper – lvl 227]

Jake decided to no longer sneak around as he revealed himself not far from Rick. The troll instantly noticed his presence and turned around to smile and wave.

"Hey, Rick," Jake said, smiling back. "It's been a while, huh? How are things going?"

Rick gave Jake a thumbs-up as he spread his arms to show off the cavern. Jake nodded, agreeing that it had become impressive. The cavern had even been expanded a bit, likely by the trolls themselves, to make more space for all their plants and flowers.

"Seems like things are indeed going well," Jake said, nodding proudly. He then heard the thundering steps of running trolls from behind him. Jake had, of course, already seen them coming and turned around with a smile to see two large Undergrowth Cave Trolls towering over him.

"You're all grown up," Jake said to two of them. One of them started clapping while the other reached out to poke him.

Rick roared lowly, stopping the troll from poking while looking a bit embarrassed. The troll in question then looked around before plucking a big flower and offering it to Jake, who gladly accepted the apology. Seeing the three trolls really brought a strong sense of nostalgia; he definitely didn't regret getting them out of the dungeon.

Jake decided to stay with the trolls for a little while, allowing Rick to show him around the large garden. While none of the trolls spoke, they did make sounds, and especially Rick was clearly intelligent. As for why they didn't speak, Jake had no idea. Maybe they just never had anyone to talk to and didn't need to learn?

While being shown around, Rick also made it clear he and his two kids sometimes went deeper into the ground through the tunnels. Using a Pulse, Jake saw a network of tunnels expanding downwards near-endlessly, much akin to the termite hive he had explored, except this expansion was entirely natural.

From the sounds of it and the shiny rocks Rick showed off, it became clear the three trolls pretty often delved deep to obtain natural resources and fight. Even if they were all working as troll gardeners, they were still combat-focused creatures who needed a bit of club-swinging once in a while.

After he and the trolls had chilled for a bit, Jake finally got down to business. "Hey, Rick, can you help me with a little something? I got some manure for the banana musa above, and I'm confident you would be better at using it than me."

Rick didn't even need to think before he nodded. Together, the two of them headed up to his lodge. When they got there, Rick instantly inspected the bags and the musa, with it pretty fast becoming clear to Jake that this wasn't the troll's first time seeing the banana plant. He had probably been the one taking care of it full-time while Jake wasn't there.

Jake also noticed how, despite Rick's large size, he never left any footprints when he walked. He didn't float above the ground, either; it was more like the grass he stood on was somehow able to hold all his weight. Not to say he was light... He just definitely had some skill to avoid trampling any plants he stood on.

With interest, Jake watched Rick at work. The troll unpacked the bags and began to mix the manure with the soil around the musa while infusing it with energy. He even saw the troll make a sound before spitting out a pretty damn big glob on the mixture that instantly seeped into it.

Don't question, just trust the professional, Jake told himself as he kept watching.

It didn't take more than half an hour for Rick to finish, making sure to use all the manure—something Sandy would definitely be disappointed with. Once everything was done, Jake could practically feel the banana musa suck in energy from the soil all around it. One had to remember that the original soil it grew in had been brought there by Jake when he stole the banana plant from that ancient temple thing from the time monkey way back in the day.

ZOGARTH

"Thanks for your hard work," Jake said, Rick just waving him off with a double thumbs-up.

"Will you help keep watch over it and make sure everything goes as it should?"

Rick naturally nodded in reassurance, making Jake feel pretty good about what the banana musa could grow into. Right now, it was an ancient-rarity musa, but if he could get it to legendary rarity, that would be pretty cool.

"It's been fun hanging out, but I think I'll have to head off now," Jake said. Rick didn't seem disappointed; he just nodded and extended a hand. Jake took it, and they briefly shook hands. Still smiling, he said his good-byes as he headed off, and Rick went back to his grove cavern.

It was good seeing the trolls, for sure, and it had been a fun reunion. Now, he planned on heading toward Skyggen to at least hang out there for a while until Sandy was done being experimented on by Arnold. On the way, he did plan on having one more reunion...

Though he doubted the frost wyvern would be as happy to see him as the trolls had.

CHAPTER 71

BLOOD ON THE ICE

Jake's first trip to Skyggen had taken quite a few days of constant travel. After the Ell'Hakan incident, he'd made the trip again a lot faster. Now that he had grown well into mid-tier C-grade, he was practically zooming across the landscape, the entire trip only taking a few hours at most, and that was partly due to him checking things out on his way.

Of course, Jake didn't count his one planned stop in the travel time. The giant mountain was still among the largest Jake had seen on Earth, towering extremely far into the sky and easily entering the aerial layers C-grades could occupy. One had to remember that C-grades and even D-grades, to some extent, were still restricted from entering the area designated as human lands. Jake was pretty damn certain this restriction would disappear with the arrival of the Prima Guardian, but for now, it was still in place.

Flying up the mountain, Jake rapidly felt the temperature drop. When he was there last, it had already been cold as hell, but now it was even worse. While it maybe wasn't quite needed yet, Jake covered his body in a faint layer of arcane mana to defend himself against the environment.

If it had been this cold the last time I was here, I wouldn't even have made it to the wyvern, Jake mentally noted.

Continuing upwards, elementals began to appear in great numbers. None of them were strong enough to pose any kind of threat, but he still Identified them.

[Ice Elemental – lvl 264]

[Snow Elemental – lvl 259]

Now, this did pose the great question of what the difference between a snow and an ice elemental was, outside of their difference in appearance. The snow elementals looked like badly built snowmen more than anything, while the ice elementals were partly see-through and a lot more angular. In fact, the main difference between the two was that one looked spiky and hard, while the other one looked round and soft.

Ignoring them just as they ignored Jake, he soon neared the peak of the mountain. Jake was looking forward to seeing if the wyvern was still there and had purposefully held back on using Pulse to avoid spoiling the reveal, but when he got closer and heard sounds of fighting, he couldn't help himself.

What he saw was a battle in the sky above the peak, with the expected wyvern in the midst of it. Jake had expected it to maybe be fighting ice elementals or monsters, which was why the opponents surprised him. It was a large group of humans, forty people in total. What's more, he saw many of them using a kind of familiar magic he hadn't seen since Yalsten, making him quickly realize who they were. They weren't humans... but vampires.

Members of the Noboru clan? Jake quickly assumed. He knew the Sword Saint had the divine artifact of Sanguine he'd received after the defeat of the Monarch of Blood, allowing him to turn others into vampires. He also knew that some had chosen this Path, and from the looks of it, they were doing pretty well for themselves.

As Jake kept watching, he decided to activate his stealth skill to get closer without them noticing him. Flying into the air, he soon saw the fight that was honestly quite intense. Concentrated blue beams of frost shot through the sky while layers upon layers of magic barriers tried to block the attacks. At the same time, over a dozen vampires attacked the wyvern from all sides, five of them carrying large chains as they tried to immobilize the creature.

Using Identify, he first focused on the wyvern.

[Northpeak Wyvern – lvl 271 – Greater Blessing of the Everfrost Dragon God]

Back when Jake first encountered the wyvern, it hadn't quite been in mid-tier C-grade yet, while now it most certainly was. It had definitely grown significantly stronger, and it had even snagged itself a Blessing. Or maybe it had always had the Blessing; he really had no way of knowing, as his Identify hadn't allowed him to see Blessings back then.

As for the vampires, Jake was also quite impressed when he saw their levels after just checking out a few.

[Vampire – lvl 255]
[Vampire – lvl 259]
[Vampire – lvl 253]

All of them were between level 250 and 260, as far as he could tell. This did raise some questions about how the hell they had leveled so fast without Nevermore... or, wait, had they leveled without Nevermore? Jake was one of the first people to enter in this generation, and also one of the first to go out, as far as he knew, but maybe it was possible they had gone anyway? If not for their entire allotted time, then just some of it.

Either way, they were all pretty damn strong as they fought the wyvern. Individually, none of them stood a chance, but fighting against forty opponents could be very difficult, especially for larger creatures who had more surface area to protect. For Jake, fighting more people wasn't as big of a problem as for someone like the wyvern.

Not to say that the vampires were winning, as Jake really couldn't tell who had the edge. After a minute or so of back and forth, he believed there was a turning of the tides when the wyvern unleashed its breath, hitting a party of five that had tried to flank it.

The five of them were blasted back, and healers and mages moved to help them. Jake was about to shake his head, as he assumed they must have taken too much damage to continue fighting, but to his surprise, the five of them came out of it with only severe frostbite and one of them losing an arm.

Vampires have high resistance to frost magic by default, Jake suddenly remembered. They were weaker to fire and, of course, as stereotypes would dictate, the sun affinity was also incredibly powerful against them. It wasn't as if they got weaker while in natural sunlight, but they did get stronger when there was no sun at all due to some passive skills from their race. This also resulted in their high resistance to all forms of frost magic.

The vampires had chosen their prey well, from a matchup perspective. They were resistant to the wyvern's attacks, while their primarily blood magic and physical attacks worked fine against the budding dragon.

Jake seriously considered what to do as he observed the battle. He had come to this mountain to have a reunion with the Northpeak Wyvern, but it was already preoccupied. Jake also didn't want to barge in and interrupt that fight, as that was just rude. After thinking for a while, Jake just lifted his legs and crossed them, sitting in mid-air as he decided to watch the battle unfold and then talk with the eventual winner. Not to attack them or anything, as that would also be boring, but just to talk. He was curious about both parties.

Focusing on the battle, it was clear the vampires had great coordination. With forty of them total, they had enough members to fill every role, with several healers and mages focusing solely on defense. A few mages also worked their offensive magic, and Jake even saw an archer in the group, along with two people wielding what looked like rifles.

The attacks rained down on the wyvern, few of them doing any damage since a layer of frost covered the large flying creature's body. Its eyes were glowing blue as it repeatedly unleashed magic, making the ground itself tremble as ice spikes shot up from below.

Choosing to have the entire battle in the air was an interesting decision by both parties. It allowed the vampires to attack from all sides, including below, while the wyvern got more space to dodge and unleash its magic. It was also clear that the wyvern had better maneuverability and experience fighting in the air compared to all the vampires.

Jake had his eyes on one party within the vampire raid team more than any other. It was led by a middle-aged man wielding an axe and a shield, while his party members broke the holy trinity entirely by being two women and two men who wielded different light weapons, including shortswords and daggers, with no healer or ranged attackers in sight.

These five were an absolute menace and accounted for the vast majority of the damage done. The leader was the highest-leveled person in the entire raid, and he proved that by repeatedly blocking the claws of the wyvern and creating openings for his party members to attack. They left several lacerations on the wyvern, cutting through the ice and drawing blood.

From afar, Jake heard the man yelling several things, though it made little sense to him. He just yelled out numbers and what Jake assumed to be code words that all the other raid members reacted to, and—

Oops, the first death.

A mage had been too slow to react when the wyvern dodged out of the way of a blow and, with a beat of its wing, sent a slicing blue wind toward him, cutting him in two. A web of cold, cutting winds had followed, freezing his body and turning it into thirty or so ice cubes.

Despite the death, the raid group didn't lose their cool, and a warrior even managed to use the opening to plunge a spear into the other wing of the wyvern. The five with chains also made their move but were rebuffed when the wyvern blasted away the raid leader.

As a rogue who believed she hadn't been spotted tried to attack using the perceived opening, the wyvern snapped its head around and chomped down. It ate the woman whole, and a second later, an explosion of blood erupted within the wyvern's mouth, as she seemed to have blown herself up.

Her death explosion allowed the warriors with chains to finally get their chance. They bound the wyvern's feet, disrupting its flight. Right as it became clear the wyvern was temporarily halted, a ritual spell was unleashed from eight mages combining their power, making a curtain of red light descend from above.

When this curtain cut through the sky, the immobile wyvern was struck, delivering a massive flesh wound to its side that nearly cut off one of its wings and went more than two meters into its mid-section, clearly doing a lot of internal damage.

"Good attack," Jake muttered to himself. "But they should have gone for the head."

The wyvern exploded with power as it roared loudly, releasing a freezing wave of energy that pushed all the melee fighters away. With its maw open, it unleashed a breath of gathered energy. A proper one this time around. The one Jake had been hit with during his first encounter had just been a casual one, similar to the earlier ones in this fight... but this breath carried clear intent to kill.

For a second, the world flashed a whitish blue. Then the breath destroyed all the barriers that tried to block it and hit the eight mages who had cast the ritual spell. They didn't even have a chance to fight back; their bodies were frozen and were blasted apart, and no amount of natural vampiric frost resistance was going to save them from this one.

Yelling loudly, the raid leader unleashed a large attack himself. His party members also launched a coordinated assault, but the wyvern's entire body was practically burning with power that blasted them away.

A blue wind began to revolve around the creature as a blizzard appeared in the sky, enveloping all the vampires. Without any warning, the wyvern flew to the side to flank the group, going for the backline.

"Good decision to try and split the group to ruin their coordination," Jake said in approval.

The only reason the vampire raid could even hold on was due to their numerical advantage and teamwork, so if the wyvern could address that, this fight would turn into a one-sided slaughter. The vampire side must've known this, as they moved to group up and take a defensive position, clearly aware that the wyvern was consuming a lot of mana with the summoned blizzard.

A barrage of large ice shards fell upon the grouped-up vampires as the wyvern flew over them. The harsh, cold winds of the blizzard also bore down on the vampires, who quickly summoned a large red barrier around themselves to ward off attacks.

Interestingly enough, the barrier did not seem to block out blood magic at all: The archer shot arrows made of blood toward the wyvern, while the two gun-wielding vampires also went fully on the offensive. While their attacks didn't do much damage, the three of them targeted one of the wyvern's wings, ripping holes in the thin flesh between the arms and body.

As the mages who weren't focused on the barrier also tried to attack, Jake saw faint cracks forming on the barrier from the wyvern's constant strikes. However, before it broke, the vampires made their move again. Over a dozen warriors were buffed up by some of the healers as they flew out, leaving reddish afterimages, all going for the wyvern at once.

Two of them were cut apart by cold winds before they even reached the creature, while a third was ripped in four by a claw. A fourth managed to stab the wyvern before his head was bitten off, while the remaining eight all landed their own attacks.

Several large cuts lined the wyvern as two warriors went together and wrapped a chain around its neck. The creature struggled, doing its best to shake off the eight warriors who were upon it while also dealing with ranged attacks and making sure those in the barrier of blood couldn't relax.

The situation was looking bleak for the wyvern. Jake saw a faint smile on the raid leader's face as he stood within the barrier, seemingly chan-neling some kind of buffing skill to those around him. The wyvern began tumbling toward the ground as another chain was wrapped around its wings, disrupting its flight.

As it tumbled toward the ground, it fell past the barrier of blood hiding all the less durable fighters... which was when the wyvern's eyes suddenly opened wide. Jake felt the mana in the air spike to unprecedented levels as energy welled up deep within the wyvern and was then unleashed.

For a moment, the world turned white. Pure cold washed over every-one, including Jake, who was quite a distance away. Even the mountain below was hit. When the light faded, Jake saw eight frozen statues falling down. The barrier of blood had been torn open, deep-freezing ten of the vampires within, and the rest didn't look that good either.

The raid leader made a quick decision, taking out an item and crushing it. A sphere surrounded the leader and all the remaining vampires as Jake felt space magic at work, and in a flash, the surviving vampires were whisked away to make their retreat.

"A good decision," Jake commented, as it was pretty certain the wyvern had won this fight. He couldn't exactly blame them, either, as he closely inspected the tired wyvern. "Damn, it already has a budding dragon's heart."

Dragons were known for their hearts, which were pretty much unrivaled organs when it came to magic. This wyvern had a budding dragon's heart in that it had mutated slightly to more closely resemble one—a pretty common occurrence for wyverns with the potential to become dragons, and likely even a prerequisite for the evolution.

The white flash had been the Northpeak Wyvern unleashing all the mana stored in the heart in one devastating attack. It had definitely been saving that one for a crucial moment.

Jake kept watching as the tired wyvern quickly flew down and caught all the falling statues of frozen vampires. With telekinesis, it carried them back toward the cave atop the mountain. Jake very curious about what it was doing with the bodies... Wait...

"Not dead yet?" Jake muttered. The vampires were frozen solid, with even their souls iced over as far as Jake could tell, but they weren't fully dead.

Flying closer, Jake wondered what the wyvern was planning to do with the frozen vampires. He decided to check out the cave, yet upon reaching it, he saw that a set of powerful magic barriers protected it, and while his stealth skill was good, he wasn't confident in getting through them without alerting the wyvern to his presence... so he stopped hiding, dispelled his stealth skill, and forced himself through the barrier.

Instantly, he felt the attention of the wyvern on him, but it didn't make any moves. It just stayed deep within the cave as Jake heard its voice echo forth.

"A mantis stalking a cicada is unaware of an oriole behind... Have you come to finish me in my weakened state?"

Yeah, Jake wasn't entirely certain what the hell that cicada thing was about, and he didn't even know what an oriole was, but he made an educated guess that the wyvern was shit-talking him for sitting back and waiting for his chance to strike.

"Relax," Jake said in a loud tone. "I'm just here for our reunion."

"Reunion?" the wyvern said, clearly confused, having likely fully expected Jake to be there with the intent to finish it off. This also explained the wyvern's strategic decision to blast its lone cavern entrance with a breath the second Jake showed up, leaving him with no space to dodge.

"You really don't remember me," Jake said, more to himself than the wyvern. "Guess I'll have to remind you and have a civil discussion about how rude it is to just blast people away with a breath when they come to talk."

CHAPTER 72

PRIMA PREPARATIONS & NORTHPEAK WYVERN

"It was far more powerful than our initial assessments," the middle-aged vampire said in a serious tone as he reported to the raid organizer. "I believe it possesses a Nascent Dragon's Heart, too, which is what ultimately led to our defeat. We may need to reconsider our approach or reach out for assistance."

"I see," the organizer said as she wrote in her report. "Did you get any indication of the beast's inclinations for the upcoming event?"

"Nothing concrete, but what little interaction we did have made it clear the wyvern is incredibly arrogant. I have a hard time seeing it submit even to a far more powerful being, and with its aggressive nature... I believe leaving it be is far too risky."

"Very well," the organizer said with a nod. "I will refer it to the upper brass. Now go to your team... I reckon they need you right now."

"Thank you," the middle-aged vampire said as he stood up. "But... once more, I must warn you. The wyvern is far more powerful than we believed, so make sure not to just send anyone to be slaughtered."

"It's fine; if worse comes to worst, the Patriarch has returned from Nevermore," the organizer said with a smile, making the vampire's eyes open wide at hearing his grandfather had returned.

"In that case, I can go rest with a peaceful mind," the vampire said as he left to rejoin what remained of his failed raid party. Losing so many people was a horrible experience... but it had to be done, even though he regretted the outcome.

Preparation for the Prima Guardian's arrival was already well underway, with the World Council having made a strategic plan. Based on the knowledge provided in the original system message regarding the event, it was clear that beasts who had consumed system-provided natural treasures had to either sit out the event or join the Prima's side.

Additionally, it was theorized that when the Prima Guardian event truly began, all protections of human lands would be lifted. Putting these together, it had been decided to address certain known powerful monsters living close to where humans lived, while also actively exploring the unknown zones of the planet.

One of the most powerful examples of a known powerful beast was the Northpeak Wyvern. It lived in between Skyggen, Haven, and two other smaller cities, all so close that the wyvern could reach them in a very short time if it decided to attack. To leave it unaddressed would be the same as leaving an enemy behind your own frontlines.

Originally, the vampires hadn't even gone to fight the wyvern but to try and reach some kind of compromise. Perhaps have the wyvern sign a system-bound contract making it agree not to fight for the Prima Guardian during the system event.

However, they hadn't even gotten that far before the beast attacked them, forcing the vampire squad to switch to plan B: simply killing it.

It was something they wanted to avoid when possible, but the Northpeak Wyvern had left them little choice. Plus, based on reports, this wyvern was incredibly aggressive toward anyone who entered its domain. It would kill without even asking any questions, so even if it wasn't going to ally with the Prima, getting rid of it was probably for the best, as keeping such a dangerous beast that couldn't even be talked to was simply too risky, especially given its power and proximity to human settlements.

Sadly, it seemed that even with their high assessment of the wyvern, they had underestimated it. His party had been one of the elite teams that hunted down these known high-level monsters, so they had genuinely believed it was a done deal and that there were few monsters they couldn't handle, at least on the ground. The Sky Whale was leading the assault on the underwater creatures to ensure there wouldn't be an invasion from the depths during the arrival of the Prima.

As with many others, the vampires had all gone to Nevermore but not stayed the full fifty years. They were all fully aware they were not competing for any kind of Leaderboard position, so they had only gone there for the leveling and stayed a couple of decades until they exhausted most of their potential after evolving to C-grade.

The middle-aged vampire had returned not even a month ago and had already disappointed himself and the family immensely. Alas, with the return of the Patriarch, they hopefully no longer had to hold any fear of these powerful creatures hidden across the planet.

Especially when one considered that his return would also mean the return of all those who had competed in the Leaderboards alongside him. With all those elite members of Earth, he had a bright view of the future and foresaw a less-than-bright future for the wyvern.

———

Jake walked through the icy cave but remained unbothered as he channeled arcane mana through his veins and protected himself with an outer layer of arcane energy. He saw the wyvern ahead of him within its cavern, in prime position to launch a breath at the entrance. Seeing this, Jake had already made a resolution.

If it dares attack, I kill it.

No arguments or discussions. Jake wanted to talk, sure, but he also wanted to remind it of how rude it was to use its breath on people without warning. If, even with this warning and the wyvern's wounded state, it still decided to attack, Jake would rule this particular beast a lost cause.

Luckily for the wyvern, it didn't attack even as Jake reached the entrance to the large, frosty cavern. Instead, it just raised its head and looked at him with wary eyes, seemingly considering if it should attack.

Jake just stood still as he observed the wyvern for a moment. It was pretty large, about nine meters in length, which, in retrospect, probably wasn't that large. Or maybe it was; Jake's only comparison was the Viper back in the day, and he knew sizes between wyverns, dragons, and pretty much all kinds of beasts could vary significantly.

Upon closer inspection, Jake also noticed that the wyvern's injuries weren't actually that bad. Sure, they weren't great, but the frost wyvern seemed to have a lot of Vitality based on how it was already healing. Likely assisted by some passive skill, allowing it to heal faster in a cold environment like this.

What was clear, though, was that it had spent a lot of energy. The half-baked dragon's heart in its chest had been entirely emptied of gas and would take a while to fully recover. Which made Jake wonder why it had unleashed all of the mana at once. Did it have to? Or was it to ensure the vampires became the living popsicles they currently were?

Off to the side of the cavern, he had already spotted all the frozen vampires, with the wyvern throwing glances toward them as if afraid Jake was going to try and rob it of its loot.

"So, you really don't remember me?" Jake finally asked.

"You do perhaps smell faintly familiar, but no, I do not remember any creature such as you," the wyvern said in a cautious tone.

"Oh, so you know how to speak normally?" Jake said, a bit surprised. What the wyvern had done before was more or less mana-speak, if one could call it that. It was sound produced solely through magic, not any physical movement of vocal cords or anything like that.

"What do you want?" the wyvern asked, not bothering with Jake's question or any kind of politeness.

"I told you already: I want to teach you about hospitality," Jake said with a smile. "The last time I came here, I did so with genuine curiosity. You see, this was my first time encountering a wyvern in the wild. Imagine my dismay when said wyvern proceeded to unleash a breath on me before I could even introduce myself, blasting me off the mountain. You really don't remember that or who I am?"

The wyvern was silent for a moment. "Do you have the slightest idea of how little that narrows it down?"

"Wow," Jake exclaimed. Was... was this frost wyvern just an asshole? So far, all information pointed to the answer being yes. "So you just attack anyone who comes here for no good reason?"

"No reason?" the wyvern huffed. "For an inferior creature to invade my domain is more than enough reason!"

"Inferior creature, huh," Jake said, his smile entirely fading. Instead of using words, he answered with actions by fully unleashing his aura upon the cavern, even going so far as to use Pride of the Malefic Viper a bit.

Instantly, the wyvern opened its mouth, seemingly to release a breath, but at the very last moment, it stopped itself and opened its eyes wide. It had felt Jake's killing intent the second it showed any indication of an attack, making it wisely hesitate.

"The only inferior creature I'm seeing here is you," Jake said as he stared down the wyvern. "And not just because you're a wannabe dragon. You're also a fucking idiot."

Jake's words were harsh and insulting, yet the wyvern did nothing but close its mouth and lower its head before the pressure.

"Do you have any idea about humans or the enlightened races in general?" Jake asked, making the wyvern hesitate. "Of course you fucking don't. Because if you did, you wouldn't have decided to kill a group that clearly came here and sought you out specifically. Much less flee back to this lair as if nothing happened afterward."

Based on the weapons that the raid party carried—and the fact they had shown up with a raid party in the first place—it was apparent to Jake that they had come here with the express purpose of hunting down the wyvern. Or at least being able to fight it if negotiations went south.

Seeing as they were also from the Sword Saint's clan and had failed in their raid, it also wasn't hard to see what would come next. They would send an even stronger party... or the old man himself. Even if the wyvern was pretty strong, even for its level, it wasn't peak-tier genius. Jake reckoned he could have killed this wyvern even if he were a lot lower in level than he was now, and the Sword Saint would also be able to slay it without any issues whatsoever.

In some ways, this realization was a bit disappointing, though it would also be kind of weird if some peak-genius wyvern appeared on a random mountain on Earth. The mere fact a wyvern with the potential to evolve into a dragon had been born there in the first place was already pretty damn impressive in its own right.

"Answer me—what do you think is going to happen now with that group of vampires who came to kill you?" Jake asked the wyvern.

It was silent for a moment before answering, "They will have learned to not attack my domain again... or report to their kin and come back with a stronger group for me to overcome."

"Let's assume it's the second one—because it's definitely the second one—what do you plan on doing when that happens? Keel over and die?"

"I shall defeat the—"

"Wrong," Jake said, cutting the wyvern off. "You die. If not with the next attack, the one after. The enlightened races operate like that. If you kill one member of their faction, they will keep coming back until they wipe you out, and the people who attacked you belong to a faction that contains at least one person I'm aware of who could easily kill you if he so desired."

"Do you belong to their faction?" the wyvern asked with a hint of nervousness, making Jake believe he was finally getting through to the dense lizard.

"No," Jake said, shaking his head. "Not directly." The wyvern was silent for a while before Jake sighed. "Seriously, you have a Greater Blessing and yet you are this clueless?"

"My Patron has never interacted with me outside of our first meeting..."

"Well, that sucks for you," Jake muttered. "Could have at least told you to not stay in the same place if you piss off people you shouldn't. Makes you a sitting duck."

"I must remain here," the wyvern said with a tone of certainty.

"Even if it means your death?" Jake questioned with a raised eyebrow.

"Leaving would be the end of my ambition," the beast said, once more not leaving anything up for interpretation. This made Jake frown a bit, but he soon realized something.

Jake had walked a lot on the mountain, and while his boots had certainly made him aware of natural treasures, he honestly filtered out the feeling most of the time when on stuff like mountains. All the random metals inside the rock registered, which wasn't particularly interesting. He did detect when a potent piece of metal entered his radar, but that had not appeared on this mountain.

However, now that he checked again, he did notice something peculiar. While there wasn't any particular piece of ore that registered as particularly valuable... there sure as hell was a lot of it. As in, the entire mountaintop was one big piece of metal with a thin layer of rock covering it, with a shitload of ice and snow stacked on top.

With this in mind, Jake quickly reached a conclusion: "You need this mountaintop to progress as you absorb the energies here?"

"Yes," the wyvern confirmed.

Jake also reached another conclusion as he scanned the room and found quite a few skeletons of different beasts encased in ice. "And you feed the mountain itself living creatures you capture in ice?"

The wyvern remained silent at that question, pretty much confirming that as a yes. It also helped that Jake faintly felt energy being drained out of the frozen vampires stashed off to the side of the cavern. With his sphere, he also saw what looked like the body of a large vulture hidden under some snow. It had died recently, from the looks of it.

"You plan on feeding those vampires to the mountain, too?" Jake continued questioning, though it was mostly rhetorical in nature.

Despite it taking a moment, the wyvern slowly confirmed, "I need it for the cold energy to keep increasing."

Jake now also knew why the mountaintop had gotten so much colder since his last visit. The wyvern was the direct cause. From what Jake quickly gathered, the metal around them was rather unique in that it wasn't just cold; it also actively absorbed all heat energy others expelled. Freezing people would keep them still, and they would passively fight back against the cold energy until they ran out of energy and died, giving plenty of nourishment to the metal.

"I'm not saying that's necessarily wrong of you, but capturing any enlightened like this isn't going to end well for you." Jake sighed. "With that in mind, release them."

"What?" the wyvern exclaimed. "I thought they were not part of your tribe?"

"I'm not part of theirs, but that doesn't mean they're not part of mine," Jake said, shaking his head. "They live within my domain, after all."

"How can they live in your domain if—"

"You seem to misunderstand," Jake interrupted with a smile. "You are also living within my domain. Everyone and everything on this planet is."

His words seemed to insult the wyvern, but with his aura bearing down on it, it didn't say anything as Jake continued. "Now, I'll give you an easy choice. Release those vampires and stop messing around with the enlightened species. Additionally, if people come here, don't just fucking attack them, but kindly ask them to leave if you really don't want them here. You can do that... or I'll kill you right here, right now. To make the decision easier for yourself, do me a favor and contact that Patron of yours."

"My Patron will not be plea—"

Jake sighed. "Just tell him the Chosen of the Malefic Viper demanded it of you."

It took a lot longer than Jake thought it should for the wyvern to finally reach out. Jake knew that anyone blessed could reach out at all times to their Patrons, though more often than not, they were just ignored or filtered out passively. He did hope that the Everfrost Dragon God would respond, though, as that would make things a lot simpler.

More than a dozen seconds passed, the wyvern clearly mentally preoccupied all the while. Its lizard face frowned and changed a lot during this time, probably partly due to dealing with a direct divine message and partly because of the nature of the message.

After what felt like half a minute, the wyvern finally looked at Jake, lowered its head to the ground, and spoke, "This lowly one begs for forgiveness and swears fealty to the Chosen of the Malefic One."

Jake stared at the wyvern that had an entirely changed demeanor, sighing internally.

Maybe I should have just gone with telling the wyvern to get divine customer support from the beginning, huh?

CHAPTER 73

RESULTS OF (UN)INTENTIONAL ASSISTANCE

Flexing status was always a great way to get a message across, but it only ever worked when the other party knew who you were. In all honesty, Jake had been surprised the wyvern didn't recognize him even after being blessed. It wasn't that he expected every single god to tell those they blessed about him... but wouldn't it make sense to at least mention the Malefic Viper if you bless a wyvern living not even a day's flight from the home base of his Chosen?

Well, it definitely would; there had just been one problem:

The wyvern was a hermit.

As in, it knew literally nobody. It also didn't know anything about the planet it was on or what was going on there. It had lived in its own little bubble, killing anything that dared try and approach it. It didn't even know about Nevermore. As Jake listened, he also realized that the damn dragon god that had blessed the wyvern was partly to blame.

That asshole dragon had told the wyvern to just dominate its own domain and keep absorbing energy there. They'd only ever had one meeting, speaking solely about making optimal use of the unique mountaintop.

However, now the beast definitely seemed to realize who Jake was, learning this information through what he assumed was a less funny Villy-style round of exposition. The beast kept its head low throughout, seemingly wanting to bury it in the snowy floor of the cavern every time it apologized, trying to excuse its own ignorance while groveling to Jake with promises.

"I had a severe lapse of judgment and can only wish to beg for forgiveness and make up for my transgressions through any form of assistance I can possibly provide," the wyvern said, definitely reading from a provided script.

Jake just stood back and let the poor wyvern get a talking-to. When he thought about it more, Jake kind of understood why the wyvern had acted like it did. Earth was a pretty fucked-up planet for it to be born on, and he was sure that in many other places, the wyvern would have been fine acting as it did. It would be the kind of creature the enlightened on the planet called a Beast King or something, and the mountain deemed a forbidden zone.

The problem for the wyvern was that Jake knew at least a dozen people who could kill it if they so desired, and when more people returned from Nevermore, that number would grow. Shit, based on the people he'd seen in Haven, he was confident a forty-man raid party capable of taking down the wyvern could be gathered there, not even mentioning if Skyggen got involved and sent a group of high-level assassins recently returned from Nevermore. Jake's brother alone could quickly kill the wyvern.

So... while the wyvern had indeed been a dick, it had acted pretty natural in the context of a normal planet, and as long as it was willing to correct its ways, Jake wasn't going to unilaterally kill it. Besides, with its level, it wouldn't even give him any experience.

Before the wyvern could begin to practically beg again, Jake decided to let it escape from limbo by saying, "Stop. You now seem to realize where your little mountain is located and why your actions up till now have been rather unwise?"

"Yes, Lord Chosen," the wyvern said, nodding enthusiastically. "My own foolishness and ignorance—"

"It's fine, as long as you know and will change your ways," Jake interrupted. "I can't have a wyvern living here causing trouble for people wanting to just pass by."

"I swear that I shall never attack another of the enlightened races again," the wyvern readily agreed.

"No need to go that far," Jake said, waving it off. "Just don't kill people randomly. If they attack you, go for it, but if they are just passing by or want to speak, don't automatically attack." Looking over at the frozen vampires and the burrowed dead vulture, he continued, "When it comes to feeding this mountain, I would advise you to stick with beasts, especially those around your own level of power. You will dilute the quality if you aim for quantity. Needless to say, those vampires also aren't going to stay here."

"Na... naturally," the wyvern said as its eyes glowed for a moment. Instantly, the ice started to melt, releasing the vampires from their icy imprisonment. As they quickly thawed, one thing also became pretty clear.

They heard everything... which means they were fully awake and aware despite being frozen, Jake thought. *Pretty fucking scary way to die, if I say so myself.* He noted the clarity in all their eyes, with a few of them even looking toward him with reverence and gratitude.

Jake waited patiently as the wyvern even removed some of the cold energy from around the vampires, allowing them to unfreeze faster while not letting the cold bother them as much. It didn't take long before the first one was fully free, and he didn't wait to bow despite it looking pretty damn painful, as his clothes and even skin had cracked in places.

"We thank the Chosen of the Malefic One for his assistance," the vampire said, the others following suit once unfrozen.

"The old man would have been mad at me if I just left you all here. Now get out of here; I'll handle the rest." Jake smiled as he saw the look of confusion on their faces before they recognized the old man Jake was talking about. At least they weren't offended, as they just thanked him once more before they left, supporting each other on the way. They didn't even address anything with the wyvern, seemingly trusting Jake to handle this issue without their input. He had kind of expected some calls for revenge, at the very least. Not that Jake would have helped them with that. If they wanted to kill the wyvern, they could go home, heal, and then come back for a rematch once they were stronger.

With the vampires gone, Jake returned his attention to the wyvern that had kept its head lowered, not even daring to look up. Sighing, Jake really wasn't sure what to do about the big lizard. He could literally see it shaking, and it definitely wasn't from the cold. Alas, he had already decided he wasn't going to give it more anxiety.

"I believe this concludes our business," Jake said, noting the look of surprise on the wyvern's face. Despite the entire conversation they'd just had, it definitely assumed he still wanted some kind of personal revenge. Which, to be fair, Jake originally had. The damn lizard had blasted him off a mountain, after all.

However, taking everything into account, he really wasn't in the mood. He also had to admit to himself that part of his reluctance was because he was dealing with a wyvern. No, not just a wyvern—the first wyvern he had seen in the wild. Killing it just for some slight born of ignorance would make Jake feel like he was bullying a teenager or something.

"Truly?" the wyvern asked, though it was clear it was also this Everfrost Dragon God behind the words.

"Truly... though I do have one thing I will demand as compensation," Jake said after thinking a bit.

"Anything," the wyvern insisted.

"What did you evolve from? I do not believe you were simply born a wyvern, so what were you before?"

This was something Jake was genuinely curious about. Mainly whether this wyvern had also once been a snake, or if it had become a wyvern from something else.

"The Chosen wants to know what creature I was born as?" the wyvern asked with a hint of confusion.

"Precisely. Just take it as satisfying my personal curiosity. Tell me how you became what you are today. The story of your life, if you will."

The wyvern was silent for a moment. "I was born as a creature called an iguana. I had lived on this mountain all of my life, simply surviving in the harsh environment. Back then, this was no snow-covered peak, even if it was cold at times. Then the system initiation arrived and everything changed. Day after day, the mountain grew taller as the world expanded beneath me. We all turned feral, killing each other and fighting for this odd energy far more sating than any food."

Jake listened along as the wyvern told its story. It was interesting to hear the perspective of a beast and how they'd experienced the integration compared to humans. The entire thing was definitely a lot rougher than getting tutorials. Unless you were thrown into a tutorial like Jake's, that is.

"I grew stronger and increased in size, fighting off all others at this peak. Some were also forced out when the temperature dropped too much, seeking further down the mountain. Yet I stayed until, one day, we were all drawn to this cavern. We fought, and I killed all of my kin before I finally consumed that which had brought me here. It was an odd plant, and after consuming it, the cold became a source of nourishment, not something to overcome. I do not know specifically why, but when I evolved to C-grade, I became a wyvern, and it was only then that I truly received a true self and realization of what I am."

The entire story wasn't overly long, and it did feel like the wyvern was almost talking about someone else. Which it kind of was, considering the final sentence. The wyvern hadn't had any true sapience before it became a wyvern, acting solely on instinct.

"And how did you obtain the budding dragon's heart?" Jake followed up. "A skill offering at some point?"

"Yes," the wyvern confirmed. "I selected it, and it warped my heart into what it is today. I am also fully aware that I need to upgrade it once more to have any chance of becoming a True Dragon in B-grade."

"I see, I see," Jake said, nodding. Yeah, that tracked. Based on all he'd read, if the wyvern failed to get the heart upgraded, it could only become a quasi-dragon in B-grade. Having heard the story, Jake looked toward the cavern exit. "This has been enlightening. I shall not bother you any more than this, and thank you for sharing your life story. I hope this experience has allowed you to wise up, and I look forward to seeing if Earth will one day birth a True Dragon."

"Once more, I thank the Chosen for his magnanimity." The wyvern bowed its head. "I shall endeavor to not cause you or anyone in your domain further trouble."

Jake just waved the wyvern off as he walked out of the cavern, at which point he felt a minor shift that made him glance back and use one final Identify that put a wry smile on his face.

[Northpeak Wyvern – lvl 271 – Divine Blessing of the Everfrost Dragon God]

I came here to scold the lizard and ended up getting it a free Blessing upgrade instead, Jake admonished himself jokingly as he made his way out of the cavern. His little pit stop for the wyvern hadn't turned out how he'd expected, but it had been rather eventful.

Turning to the horizon, he looked toward Skyggen and decided to continue his journey back to his family.

———

Thunder echoed in the skies as blue bolts descended upon the land, giving birth to elementals or simply killing anything they hit. These bolts carried the power to slay even S-grades easily, resulting in all but the most foolish or powerful avoiding clouds like these.

Below, the bare ground was filled with scorch marks and corpses, yet in the midst of everything, two figures were fighting. The rocky terrain, which had been molded and empowered by the onslaught of lightning for millions of years, was torn up with every clash.

One figure was a tall man, swinging a battleaxe and attempting to catch his opponent, a winged woman with more muscles than the warrior. She fought using her bare fists, deflecting her opponent's weapon as blue lightning enveloped both of them, sending out shockwaves with every clash.

Their fight continued for several minutes until the man suddenly appeared distracted. A fist struck him in the face, blowing off his entire head. He stumbled back before it rapidly regenerated.

"A cheap shot," the man said with a scowl as he used his horns to crack his neck.

"Not my fault you got distracted," the woman said with a smile as she looked toward the newcomer who had been the cause of the distraction. A suit-wearing devil had appeared, carrying a light smile on his face.

"Duchess, Duke, I apologize for interrupting your pastime, but his majesty requires your presence at the castle," the man said.

"We heading to war with the Fifth Hell again?" the duchess asked.

The duke scoffed. "No, you moron; it's related to Nevermore, isn't it?"

"Indeed it is," the suit-wearing devil confirmed to the two other devils.

"Has the princeling returned?" the duke asked with a frown.

"Oh, did the kid take the top spot?" the duchess asked. "If not, I don't see why we should bother being there."

"No, he got third, just behind the Chosen of Yip of Yore and the Chosen of the Malefic Viper, who took second and first, respectively," the suited devil answered. "The Chosen of the Malefic Viper also took the top spot on the All-Time Leaderboards."

"Impressive," the duke commented, "but I still fail to realize why His Majesty demands our return."

"It's related to the Chosen of the Malefic Viper... It would be easier to simply see it rather than me wasting my time explaining everything," the suited devil said mysteriously as he raised an eyebrow. "Besides, does His Majesty need a reason to recall you?"

The duke and duchess gave each other a look, both knowing that opposing the Devil King of the Fourth Hell wasn't a wise choice. With that in mind, they followed the third devil back to the castle nestled in the middle of the realm known as the Fourth Hell.

There, a massive mountain stood. Thunderclouds encircled the mountain in several layers, and unless one was welcomed, even gods would find it difficult to make their way through unscathed. Atop this mountain was the castle of the Fourth Devil King, leader of the Fourth Circle of Hell.

Arriving at the castle, the three devils made their way into a throne room that was already filled with other devils and high-ranking mortals who had been allowed there. All these mortals were kneeling under the pressure of the many divine beings, yet one remained standing in the center, speaking to the devil sitting on the throne.

The Devil King stopped speaking when he saw the duke, duchess, and suited devil arrive. "Good. All are here."

"We greet His Majesty," the three of them said, bowing, yet the duke couldn't help but throw glances at the mortal still standing. His aura felt familiar yet foreign, and there was something odd mixed in there...

The Devil King simply nodded as he returned his attention to the mortal. "Now, continue."

"Yes, Father," the mortal said, making the duke and the two other devils realize this was the Cerulean Demon—also known as the Prince of the Fourth Hell. "During the gathering of those who placed high on the Nevermore Leaderboards, I approached the Chosen of the Malefic One, and..."

The Demon Prince went on to explain everything that had happened. How he had approached the Chosen and gotten him to agree to help, and the entire ritual that followed, including everything that had gone wrong. Many devils or officials frowned or scoffed when the demon described the ritual. It was a foolish endeavor, no doubt about it, yet the results...

"And this Chosen entered your Soulspace?" the Devil King questioned.

"Yes, and suppressed the Records of the Cerulean Devil entirely," the Demon Prince explained, not hiding anything. "His presence overwhelmed everything, and it was only due to his assistance that I managed to become what I am now."

Silence roamed the hall as they observed the newly born Cerulean Demon Lord. The duke was confused about how all this had happened, even if he'd heard the explanation. He hadn't been particularly aware of this Chosen of the Malefic Viper before now, having only heard in passing that the Primordial had returned to the multiverse with a Chosen.

"Is that also why you remain standing now?" the Devil King followed up, his own aura spreading through the room. The duke felt the pressure but remained standing, as did the grand duke, the duchess, a few other of the top devils... and the Cerulean Demon Lord.

"I believe that to be the case," the Demon Prince answered truthfully.

"How amusing." The Devil King smiled, the show of emotion shocking many. "I also heard you gave him your personal Crest that I bestowed upon you?"

"Yes, Father. I seek forgiveness if that—"

"It was a wise decision," the Devil King interrupted.

"Thank you... though I fear the Chosen may not use it himself but send a representative or envoy," the Demon Prince said, somewhat nervous. "Perhaps even an ally of his."

"Even if it's so, treat whoever he sends as if they were my personal guest," the Devil King said after a brief pause. He then turned and looked at one of the devils in the crowd. "Begin preparations to send more of our young to the Order of the Malefic Viper. Additionally, contact the Second Hell and propose to them a joint venture to make use of their existing connections with the Order."

"It shall be done, Your Majesty," the devil said, bowing.

Turning back to his son, the Devil King observed him for a moment. "Let us also not waste time where unnecessary. A week from now, I shall appoint the Cerulean Demon Lord as my new Chosen and Crown Prince of the Fourth Hell."

Surprised expressions flashed across the faces of most in the room, yet the Demon Prince merely bowed. "It would be an honor."

CHAPTER 74

TO VISIT ONE'S PARENTS

Jake rarely felt nervous these days. He was the Chosen of the Malefic Viper, Harbinger of Primeval Origins, and now even the top performer on the Nevermore Leaderboards. Yet he couldn't deny his own trepidations before arriving at Skyggen.

There was no doubt that Jake was a pretty sucky son and now also uncle. Even before the system, he had been bad at calling home or visiting often enough, and with the initiation, he had become far worse. What made Jake feel even worse about everything was how he didn't really feel that bad for not visiting as often. The mere knowledge that they were doing well was enough for him.

The words his father had offered him before his last departure also helped a lot, having pretty much given Jake permission not to worry about them. There was also the fact that Caleb was with them at all times and would ensure they were kept safe alongside Maja and Adam—his wife and son, also known as Jake's sister-in-law and nephew.

Mixed in with his slight anxiety was a lot of excitement. The last time he saw Adam, he had just been a baby, while now he should be solidly out of the toddler years. He naturally also looked forward to seeing his parents and how they were doing.

Furthermore, he was determined to establish some way of contacting them this time around, if for nothing other than the ability to at least call home once in a while to check in on things. Though, rather than talking about some promotion or sharing a funny anecdote from that day, Jake would talk about how he had met some frost wyvern or helped create a Demon Lord.

Nearly at Skyggen, Jake decided to have a bit of fun and check the local defenses. He activated his stealth skill, wanting to see if he could sneak in without anyone noticing him. If he could, he would definitely have something to tease his brother about.

Sadly, the moment Jake made his floating arrival over the sprawl, he encountered one of the outer barriers covering the city that served as the headquarters of the Court of Shadows. It became pretty damn clear Jake couldn't sneak through without triggering it. There were over a dozen layers of barriers, most of which were only primed to be activated for defense against attacks. There were still three different ones designed for detection, though, as well as five, maybe six made to help hide the city.

"At least Caleb made sure the city is properly defended," Jake noted aloud, nodding. Haven also had defensive barriers, but far fewer than this. Instead, the city was primarily defended by two people: Arnold and Miranda. Both had placed down their own protective measures, and Jake knew that Arnold had launched a number of satellites to keep a lookout.

Entering through the barrier, Jake instantly knew he was detected. He could have taken the main entrance but decided it was more fun to fly down from above. That way, it would also be easier to find where his parents stayed—something he used a quick Pulse of Perception to discover.

As with most other cities on Earth, Skyggen had grown a lot over the last many years. Despite only really being a city for members of the Court and their family members, it looked surprisingly normal, especially the area where he spotted his family. It looked like the regular suburbs of old, with modern-looking houses on a closed-off street and big gardens. It didn't look very defended either, which Jake perfectly understood.

Caleb and Jake didn't want to keep their family in a cage with the justification that they were just protecting them. That would be insulting and unhealthy for everyone involved. No, Jake would rather make the entire planet a safe environment for not only his parents but everyone else. Despite never having spoken with his brother about this explicitly, he knew Caleb also felt the same way, which was why he had done things like this.

Flying toward the suburbs, Jake felt a few presences check him out, but the moment they realized who he was, they backed off, resulting in no one bothering him. He saw that his parents were currently both at one house, with his mother sitting in the back garden reading a book while his dad was in the house watching a projector—the system version of a TV. Assuming there weren't already normal TVs.

There probably were normal TVs, especially if Arnold could walk around with a tablet.

In the house next door, he saw Maja with three other women, as well as a group of seven kids. It wasn't hard to spot Adam, either. He bore an uncanny resemblance to a young Caleb, making Jake smile. The decision of where to go first wasn't hard, either, because there was no fucking way he was going to intrude on his nephew's playdate. Especially not with his current get-up, as he had a slight suspicion a masked, hooded man with glowing beastly eyes wouldn't be that popular with the kids.

Landing in front of his parents' house, Jake made his mask invisible, pulled down the hood, and tried to look as presentable as he could. Knocking on the door, he became a bit nervous when he saw his father get up and walk to the door before opening it.

Jake's dad froze for a moment when he saw Jake, who just stood there smiling. "Hey, Dad, I—"

"Debra, there's another of those alchemist salesmen at the door!" his dad yelled, surprising Jake.

"Again!?" he heard his mother yell from the other side of the house as she made her way over to the door.

For a moment, Jake's mind worked at high speed as he considered what had happened. Could karmic magic affect the memories of people, or was it—

"A fancy one from that snake club, too," his mother said as she walked over and smiled. "Doesn't he also seem oddly familiar, Robert?"

"He does look a bit like our younger son, doesn't he? I wonder what happened to our estranged older one; we haven't seen him in—"

"Ha, ha, very funny," Jake said in a dry tone. "Also, calling the Divine Order of a Primordial a snake club would definitely be considered heretical to most people."

"Ah, sorry, I'm just happy you finally found a club you wanted to join since getting you to join any when you were a kid was a real struggle..." Debra went outside and didn't waste any time before pulling him into a hug. "Welcome home."

"Thanks, Mom." Jake smiled as she practically dragged him inside. His father put a hand on his shoulder as they walked in, giving him an approving nod and a look that said it was good he had finally visited.

"Do you want anything to drink?" his mom asked. "We have coffee and... a lot of different teas. Actually, you may know this—how come tea is so popular now?"

"Tea was always popular," Jake argued. "But as for why it's popular in the multiverse in general... well, think about it. Tea is just dried pieces of herbs and can come in a variety of flavors and forms, allowing whoever is making the tea to aim for certain desired effects. Meanwhile, for coffee, it needs to come from coffee beans, right? Limits the variety."

"I see," his mom said, nodding. "So I take it you're big into tea now?"

"Not really; do you have any hot chocolate?" Jake asked with a grin.

"I'm sure I can find something," she answered with a smile and went into the kitchen. Jake looked after her, quickly using an Identify to confirm how she was doing.

[Human – lvl 144]

He also used one on his dad, confirming a similar level.

[Human – lvl 141]

Both had reached mid-tier D-grade and were on their way. Neither leveled fast at all, but they were still leveling, as far as Jake could tell. Actually, he was pretty sure that many would be jealous of his parents' ability to level despite neither of them being a fighter.

If this keeps up, they should at least reach C-grade at some point, Jake assured himself as he took a seat at the dining table with Robert, his father. The man didn't look a day older than his last visit and still looked a lot healthier than he had been before the system. All good things to see.

"I hear you've been quite busy," his dad said after a brief pause. "Something about you placing first on the best Leaderboards in Nevermore?"

Jake was surprised that his dad knew about all that, considering how disconnected they'd seemed from multiverse stuff the last time he visited. Still, if he was interested, Jake saw no reason not to answer. "Yeah, I managed to snag the top spot above everyone else."

"Very impressive, based on how I understand it," Robert said. "I won't act like I really understand how big of a deal it is, but Caleb seemed a lot more impressed than usual... so good job."

"Thanks," Jake said, smiling. "Say, where is Caleb?"

"At work," his mom answered as she came in carrying three mugs with hot chocolate, having made it a lot faster than Jake expected. "He is quite busy these days, and while he tried to take a small holiday after he returned from this Nevermore place, he was quickly dragged back to work. I guess his desk was full after more than three years of absence."

"Sucks to suck." Jake grinned, happy it wasn't him. In some ways, it was also good to have some one-on-one time with his parents.

"Don't bully your little brother for having a job," Robert scolded in jest before turning a lot more serious. "I know that to us, you've only been gone for a few years, but for you, it's been decades... Caleb was quite affected and stuck to Maja and Adam like a magnet the first day he was back. How are you doing?"

"I'm doing good," Jake said with a reassuring smile.

"No, you're not," his dad said with an exaggerated sigh. "Charity workers do good. You're doing well."

"Way to spoil the serious mood with grammatical pedantry." Jake shook his head. "And how do you know I didn't do good? I recently helped someone transform into a Demon Lord, and just on the way here, I talked sense into a murderous and ignorant wyvern on top of a mountain while freeing a group of vampires from the fate of dying as popsicles."

"The first one doesn't sound like it counts," Debra muttered.

"That's just your bias against demons born from media misrepresentation," Jake said in a matter-of-fact tone. "Most demons I've met have been pretty nice and chill."

"You're also part of what many call an evil snake club, with this Malefic Viper not striking me as a figure many would describe with the adjective good," his dad couldn't help but point out. "That may color your view a bit."

"Is it just me, or do you two seem more educated on matters of the multiverse than last time I was here?" Jake asked with a raised eyebrow.

"We didn't really have much of a choice, now, did we?" Debra asked while Jake took a sip of his hot chocolate, which, for the record, was superb.

"What do you mean?" Jake asked after another good sip.

"You had a ceremony or something announcing yourself to the world a few years ago, didn't you?" Robert chimed in again. "It isn't anything new for the parents of famous people to get some attention from the public, now, is it?"

Jake's smile faded. "Have people been bothering you because of me?"

"I wouldn't say that," his mom said, sighing. "It's more that there have been some odd types who've approached us, and sometimes it can be hard to judge who is there because of us or you. It isn't that big of a deal, though. We were already having similar issues because Caleb is the Judge of the Court of Shadows. Maja, too, and Caleb is doing a good job of making sure we aren't too bothered."

"I... see..." Jake muttered. "What kind of odd types have appeared?"

"Most people from these new factions who arrived are generally very polite," Debra answered. "There is this group of very weird people, though... What were they called again?"

"Primordial Church," Robert answered.

"That's right—the Primordial Church. There are these three in particular who are quite peculiar, though they don't seem dangerous or deceitful in the slightest. They're actually very straightforward about what they want, if a little pushy and overexcited."

"What is it they want?" Jake asked with some concern.

He had no idea why it had never crossed his mind that this could happen. Even if Jake had things like Shroud of the Primordial to hide him, people could still just do good old detective work to easily find out who his family was. Shit, the fact Caleb was Jake's brother was far from a secret, so all they really had to do was find Caleb's parents, and they would find Jake's.

"They just ask questions," Debra continued, shaking her head. "Their questions are just odd and kind of intrusive. They asked a lot about you, how and where you grew up, who you knew, what you were like when younger..."

"I think one of them mentioned something about writing a book?" Robert added. "Or a biography?"

"Are you sure? One of them tried to show me her poetry collection about Jake..." Debra muttered.

Jake stared at his parents as he scratched the back of his hand. "To clarify... you didn't actually tell them anything about me, right?"

"Not anything bad!" his mom quickly made clear, which didn't make Jake feel better. "But they were really polite and without any bad intentions, especially in the beginning."

His mom's words made a shiver run down his back. He knew enough about the Primordial Church to know they were fanatics, and he really hoped she hadn't told some embarrassing stories he could now look forward to having spread all throughout the multiverse.

"Don't worry—they didn't get much useful," Jake's dad tried to assure him. "And a lot of what they got was just nonsense that will make them laughingstocks with no creditability if they actually try to share it."

"I'm sure they will just ignore the outrageous things you said," Debra said with a sigh. "No one's going to believe any of that stuff you told them."

"What... what did he tell them?" Jake said, clenching his fists.

"As I said, nonsense," his dad replied, continuing to wave him off. "No one, not even people as unreasonable as them, is going to believe a five-year-old fought off a shark or that a ten-year-old became the world record holder for ultramarathons on accident just because he wanted to have a long run."

His dad laughed a bit at the last part, while Jake just had a look of horror. His father had no idea what he had done.

Jake looked up at them. "They are that unreasonable."

Robert looked confused and stopped laughing before shaking his head. "Even so, if they try to share it, no one will take them seriously."

"Dad... you don't understand these people," Jake said as he looked his father in the eye. "I accidentally showed a projection to a guy depicting a beer bottle and the words *danger noodle,* and the guy dedicated a significant portion of his life to creating a mythical-rarity statue..."

"Wait, are you talking about Felix, the High Priest in Haven?" Debra asked. "I heard he was a sculptor who gained your favor..."

"That's him, and the fact he is now a High Priest should tell you everything," Jake said with a serious look.

"They aren't actually going to write down and publish everything I said, right?" Robert said with a tinge of nervousness.

"Every. Single. Word," Jake assured him.

Silence hung in the room for several seconds before something vibrated on a small table in the corner of the room. Debra hurried over to it while Jake contemplated whether he should try and track down the members of the Primordial Church.

"Caleb is coming over," his mother said as she held the token with a smile. "He said he'll stop by and grab Maja and Adam on the way."

Jake wasn't surprised Caleb was coming, as someone had definitely reported to him that Jake had arrived, and he was happy to hear he was bringing Maja and Adam. Next door, he saw that Maja had definitely also been called by Caleb, as the other women were packing up and leaving while Maja herself got ready with Adam.

I'll deal with that damn Primordial Church later... For now, let's just try not to mess up my nephew's first impression of his uncle.

CHAPTER 75

QUALITY FAMILY TIME

J ake looked through the drawers, trying to find anything suitable as his mom stood at the door. He had never been a fan of his mom's tendency to buy clothes, as she had a horrible habit of not really remembering what size people were, but in this one instance, that came in handy. Jake quickly found a T-shirt and jeans that seemed about his size.

"I told you there would be something for you," Debra said in an almost proud tone.

"Not sure you should be bragging about buying things in the wrong size for Dad or Caleb." Jake smiled and shook his head before shooing her out of the room so he could change.

It probably shouldn't come as a surprise, but Jake didn't own any normal clothing. He had his armor, a few party outfits he used at the Order, and some more clothing that really didn't fit with a modern setting. With that in mind, Jake had decided to raid a drawer with clothing no one used, leading to his nicely fitting current outfit.

Glancing at a mirror in the room, Jake felt like he looked weird.

Since when did looking normal become weird, and looking weird become normal? Jake questioned. In the multiverse, people really just wore whatever, and finding people walking down the street in full plate armor, or armor obviously made from a dead beast, was considered entirely ordinary. Not to mention polymorphed monsters that didn't even need equipment with enchantments, making them wear even weirder stuff at times.

Jake still looked a bit off, though. He had undoubtedly changed physically after the system arrived and getting a few evolutions under his belt, but nothing was as notable as his eyes. While he hadn't exactly tested it, he was pretty sure they glowed in the dark now, or at least reflected light like the eyes of a cat, and if he tried to evaluate them objectively, they did make Jake look a bit... he wanted to say dangerous, but volatile was probably more accurate.

Wearing sunglasses was an option, but one Jake quickly dismissed. Firstly because wearing sunglasses inside makes you look like an idiot or a blind person, and secondly because his nephew would definitely end up seeing his eyes at some point anyway, so there was no need to hide them.

Exiting the room in his average outfit, he found his mom waiting on the other side. She looked at him from top to bottom, stopping when she reached his feet. "You're still wearing those old boots? According to Caleb, you should be doing pretty well for yourself, so couldn't you get some new ones? They certainly look like they have seen better days..."

"These are the best boots in the multiverse, and I will hear no objections to that statement," Jake said with a tone of utmost certainly. He wasn't really joking, either. Finding awesome, mythical-rarity boots like these wasn't exactly commonplace.

"Alright, not going to argue with you, but you should look into buying some product to treat the leather," Debra still insisted.

"I doubt it would work," Jake said, shaking his head. "They haven't changed appearance no matter what's happened to them."

"If you say so."

The two of them walked into the living room to wait for Caleb and Maja. Jake could already see them next door, preparing to leave.

"Look at him, not wearing dark clothes and looking all grim," Jake's dad said the moment Jake entered the living room. He had to admit that the blue T-shirt with what he was pretty sure was the logo of some company did make him look much less serious and grim than usual.

"I'll have you know cloaks and leather armor are quite fashionable," Jake said in his own defense as he took a seat at the dining table.

His dad didn't say anything but just looked at the projector that was playing what looked a lot like a TV show of some kind. Except it was clearly one made after the system arrived, making Jake look at it with interest. It was a show about a tailor struggling to find enough materials because a merchant union had recently moved in and increased the prices, but oh, wait, a new shop had just opened up on the street with a blacksmith who refused to back down to the evil merchant's demands...

"You look like it's your first time watching a TV show," his dad commented.

"It is my first time watching one produced after the system..." Jake said. "Not gonna lie, I didn't even know it was a thing."

Then again, all Paths were viable, so maybe stuff like this was too... though he had a hard time seeing how one could take acting to a particularly high grade. Like, what would the difference between a D-grade and a B-grade actor really be? Straight-up polymorphing into other people? That seemed more shapeshiftery, though...

"There aren't that many, but some people are trying to bring back a feeling of normalcy, and producing things like these is part of that," his mom added. "Not to say there isn't an entertainment industry—they just don't really do produced shows like this. A lot are recording and showing off spars or hunts, or creating lessons in certain professions and selling those."

"Interesting," Jake said. Recordings like these were pretty easy to make, and many were freely sold back in the Order, but most of the time it was done with the purpose of teaching and not entertainment. Sure, the teachers who were entertaining were also the ones who did best, but the primary objective was still to impart knowledge.

As Jake was watching the show, Maja, Caleb, and Adam finally arrived. He looked toward the door just before they knocked, and his mom got up with a smile. "You two just stay here while I go let them in."

"Alright." Jake nodded, his dad just letting out a low grunt.

In the entrance area, he saw Debra open the door and heard them greeting each other. It was pretty clear that they visited often, which really wasn't a surprise considering they were neighbors.

The four of them quickly made their way toward the living room, and Jake felt nervous but tried to look as non-intimidating and normal as he could. The first one to come into the living room was Maja, who smiled brightly when she saw Jake.

"Jake, so good to finally see you again!" she said as Jake got up and she came over for a light hug before pulling away. "It has been years! You really need to visit more often; I'm getting tired of hearing about your exploits second-hand from Caleb."

"I know, I know," Jake said apologetically as he looked over her shoulder and saw the three others enter. Caleb looked... calm. A lot calmer than he had in the get-together for all the people who'd placed on the Leaderboards. While he hadn't really shown it much then, Jake could really see now how tense he had been, and it was great to see him more relaxed.

Finally, he laid eyes on the newest addition to their family—at least if one talked about the humans in it. Adam looked as one would expect of a kid, and he stared at Jake with big eyes. He really reminded Jake of when Caleb was young.

"This is Uncle Jake," Maja said as she introduced Jake to his nephew. Caleb helped by pushing the little guy forward.

"Hey, there," Jake said with a smile as he squatted down.

As the kid stared at him for a moment, Jake felt a bit uncomfortable but tried not to let it show. After what felt like forever, Adam finally spoke. "Your eyes are weird."

"Adam, that's not nice," Maja said in a scolding tone, while Jake just chuckled and shook his head.

"My eyes are weird, aren't they?" Jake confirmed. "Why, don't you like them?"

"They're cool..." he muttered shyly, much to the relief of Jake.

Jake didn't really know how to deal with kids. It wasn't that he particularly disliked kids—only when they were annoying or disruptive—he just didn't really know how to act around them. It didn't help that he had zero experience with kids of any age. The system had surely also changed things, as based on what his mom had briefly mentioned before he went to grab some more normal clothes, kids seemed a lot smarter these days. Adam had been able to speak a lot earlier than usual, as an example, though physically he didn't seem older than Jake would expect.

"You might not remember Uncle Jake, as he was away just like Dad, but he visited when you were little," Maja said as she walked over to Adam.

Adam seemed interested in that as he stared up at Jake. "Does that mean you're super strong like Dad?"

Jake smiled, a bit taken aback. "I'm the strongest."

"Even stronger than Dad?" Adam asked with wide eyes.

Caleb's gaze bored into Jake as he stared at him with eyes that looked like they could kill, making Jake consider his answer carefully. "Your Dad and I don't fight, but we're both super strong. Strong people like us shouldn't fight without a good reason, right?"

That answer seemed to satisfy Adam's curiosity. Caleb threw Jake a thankful look. Jake got it. Flexing in front of his son would be a bit too much, and what kid didn't want to believe that their dad was the strongest in the world?

Anyway, with that, the introduction Jake had been so nervous about was over, with the kid seemingly not caring overly much the second his grandma brought out some treats. It was almost anticlimactic, but honestly... kids were probably a lot simpler than Jake believed, and they were definitely easily distracted.

Standing next to Caleb, he saw his brother's content smile. Jake sent him a telepathic message. *"How are you holding up?"*

Caleb threw him a look as he hid a sigh. *"It's been hard. I missed more than three of his most important years being away in Nevermore. What's more, for me, fifty passed... It's like I've been away an entire lifetime. It will take a bit to adapt before I really feel like I'm back. Adam will also need some time. I... I'm not even sure he recognized me when I walked through the door after I returned."*

Jake put a hand on Caleb's shoulder and gave it a light squeeze of encouragement. He wasn't going to pretend to understand how Caleb felt. To be away from your kid for so long had to be hard for both parties, and no one could pretend fifty years was a short time, even if Caleb could live for thousands at the very least as a C-grade. One had to remember all of them were still very young in a multiversal context, and he was pretty sure Caleb had spent less time than Jake in time dilation, meaning Nevermore had more likely than not been more than half of Caleb's entire life.

His brother threw him a thankful look, and the two of them just stood there and watched Adam talking with his mother as she unpacked a bag with some toys in it. Meanwhile, Jake and Caleb's dad looked at the projection of the TV show with one eye while keeping an eye on Adam with the other.

If one took a snapshot of this scene, they could almost be confused for an entirely normal family.

Maybe visiting home once in a while isn't all that bad...

———

The Sword Saint had done much to divest himself from the internal politics of the Noboru Clan. He had put distance between them, but no matter what he did, they still recognized him as their Patriarch, and he realized there was nothing he could do about that. Thus, he simply accepted the role. With that, he needed to, at the very least, understand the situation of the clan, if for nothing other than his role as a member of the World Council.

Upon his return from Nevermore, he was naturally swarmed by people who wanted to know of his exploits, and to update him on the happenings of the planet over the last few years. Something he gladly accepted. He heard all that had happened during his absence, and it genuinely surprised him.

He had half-expected *something* major to happen during this time, but everything had just been calm. What had happened instead was the rapid expansion of all human settlements, the development of technology, and the growth of the overall power of the planet. All the assistance their small rock floating through space received due to Jake was overwhelming, and while most of it was centralized in and around Haven, the Noboru Clan also benefited greatly, as it was well known that the Sword Saint was a comrade of the Chosen, and also someone carrying the Divine Blessing of Aeon, making him a person of interest in his own right.

The clan did have one issue, though.

Vampires.

In the multiverse, they were not a very popular race, and the Sword Saint understood why. The clan had been forced to set up an entire system to allow the vampires to exist there, and donations of blood were a requirement.

One had to remember the massive downside of vampirism after Sanguine's death, requiring them to consume life energy in the form of blood to regenerate their health. They had no other ways to truly regenerate it, and things like healing spells could only temporarily help. To make matters more complicated, the most effective blood was that of the race they'd been prior to turning into a vampire, or at least a similar one. In other words, others of the enlightened races.

Ah, and then there was the problem of vampires entering a blood frenzy if starved for too long or injured badly. All in all, vampires were an incredibly problematic race, and that was before one considered the fact that the Risen, Holy Church, and a few other factions openly had kill orders out on any vampire, wanting to wipe the race from the multiverse.

The Sword Saint was fully aware that the only reason they were accepted in any way on Earth was because of Jake and his identity as the Chosen of the Malefic Viper. The Order of the Malefic Viper was the only large faction that officially had vampires in it, and that was only possible because of the Primordial at the helm. The open support displayed for vampires had especially increased after the Order's bold decision to bring a vampire to the post-Nevermore political meetings. For the Viper's Chosen to also be accepting of vampires was only to be expected, and thus no one dared openly bother the clan.

Miyamoto also had to admit that vampires were powerful. For their level, they tended to be superior to humans in combat. This primarily stemmed from them only having either a class or a profession, and most of the vampires went with a class. Combined with their racial skills and the often-seen high level of synergy between their class and race, their high combat prowess wasn't that surprising.

While sitting in his own courtyard and meditating, the Sword Saint was interrupted by a person approaching his residence. Opening his eyes, he waved his hand to open the gates, revealing a familiar face. It was one of his many grandchildren, and one of those who had chosen to embrace vampirism.

"You looked disturbed," the Sword Saint said when he saw the look on his face.

"Greetings, Patriarch," his grandson said, bowing. "I apologize for the disturbance; however—"

He proceeded to explain that he had recently taken part in an attempted raid on a frost wyvern and that it had ended in their utter failure. But the most important part came at the end, as he explained the cause for urgency:

"The life tokens of those frozen are still intact, meaning the wyvern must have captured them. This may be presumptuous, but we have none capable of fighting this beast, so if the Patriarch would—"

"Very well," the Sword Saint agreed as he stood up, understanding the concern. "I shall head out immediately."

CHAPTER 76

ALL GOOD THINGS MUST COME TO AN END

Miyamoto felt the cold winds sweeping across his body as he trekked up the mountain. Many of the ice elementals noticed him, but none approached, and he soon reached the summit where this powerful beast known as the Northpeak Wyvern should reside.

Admittedly, an environment like this was far from favorable to him, as his water affinity was severely weakened due to the cold, but he was still confident. Its level more or less matched him, and while the vampire raid team had described the wyvern as powerful, the mere fact any of them had managed to return alive or injure the beast was proof that it shouldn't be a threat to him.

As described, he found the cavern atop the mountain, and within, he felt the presence of a monster. The last update he'd gotten before departing from Haven said that the captured vampires were still alive, but he feared things may have changed, as he only felt the presence of a single living being within.

If it was so, the least he could do was enact vengeance. The Prima Response Team, as the people in charge of preparing for the Prima Guardian's arrival called themselves, had designated this wyvern too dangerous to leave alive anyway, so someone would have to slay it. May as well be him.

Walking through the cavern, he was ready should it attack with a breath, as he had been informed the wyvern was extraordinarily aggressive and impossible to talk to, and the design of the cave made it a perfect choke point to—

"**Excuse me, can I help you with anything?**" a voice echoed through the cave.

The Sword Saint stopped and frowned. The tone did not carry the level of arrogance he had expected, but he wasn't going to let his guard down. Infusing his voice with energy, he said, "**I hope for your sake you can. A group of vampires recently fought you here, and I believe a number of them were captured alive.**"

"**That... that was all a misunderstanding that has been rectified,**" the wyvern responded in a meek tone, making the Sword Saint frown even more.

Usually, the data provided by members of his clan was extremely accurate, but the current situation certainly wasn't in line with his expectations. Had he somehow gotten the wrong mountain? No... no, that wouldn't make any sense.

"**I question your claims, but please enlighten me as to the nature of your rectification,**" he responded, not far from his goal.

"**It's... fine if you come to the big cavern to talk...**"

Continuing onward, he soon reached the inner cave, where he saw the large wyvern nested in the middle. He was ready to draw his sword but felt no aggression. In fact, he got a nervous impression from the wyvern.

"Gre... greetings," the wyvern said, seemingly trying really hard to be polite.

The Sword Saint didn't respond immediately; instead, he scanned the room and saw no immediate signs of any trapped vampires. "What happened to the vampires you captured?"

"They left," the wyvern responded quickly. "I, eh, I let them go, and they left a few days ago..."

Narrowing his eyes, Miyamoto placed one hand on the handle of his sword. "And why would you just let them go?"

"I saw the error of my ways?" the wyvern responded before seemingly nodding to itself as if to confirm the answer.

"Do excuse me if I question the validity of any creature changing their entire manner of acting so abruptly," the Sword Saint said skeptically as he looked directly at the wyvern. "Unless there is more than one Northpeak Wyvern, you are known for attacking indiscriminately any who dares set foot atop this mountain, and you mean to tell me that has suddenly changed within a couple of days?"

"Yes?" the wyvern responded, staring unblinkingly at the Sword Saint. "I, eh... learned my lesson and will no longer be a menace, but always talk first and not just attack."

"Forgive me for my continued skepticism, but what was the impetus for this change?"

"Impetus?" the wyvern asked, seemingly not understanding what the word meant.

"Reason. Cause. What event caused you to have such a sudden shift in behavior?" The Sword Saint hoped the wyvern had a satisfactory answer; if not, he wasn't averse to doing what he'd originally come to this mountain to do, even if the wyvern claimed it had suddenly wised up, as everything could easily just be a ruse to avoid powerful people actually slaying it. It would need a really good rea—

"The Chosen of the Malefic Viper visited, and—"

Yeah, alright, that'll do it.

———

More than two weeks passed with Jake doing almost fuck-all in the progress department. Instead, he spent all this time just relaxing with his family, doing a variety of activities. He watched pretty bad TV shows with his dad, went shopping with his mom, and talked with Maja while playing with Adam.

Caleb sadly still had to do a lot of work, but he tried to be home as much as possible. Alas, he was still the Judge of the Court of Shadows, and he had certain responsibilities he simply couldn't divvy out no matter how much he wanted to. Jake was sure happy he had managed to outsource all his responsibilities.

A lot of people would probably say Jake was wasting his time just relaxing with his family. He barely did any alchemy, and even then, only when Adam was sleeping—yes, children still had to sleep—or when everyone else was preoccupied. When he did do a bit of alchemy, he just made some potions and stuff, never focusing that much on the task.

Even so, Jake didn't regret this time in the slightest. He wasn't in some extreme rush to optimize every single second of his day, and in some ways, he even felt like a moment of downtime like this would be healthy for him in the long run, even from a progress perspective.

This time around, Jake didn't help Caleb with any kind of presence-resistance training either. Partly because Caleb didn't want to go with Jake and do it, taking them both away from quality family time. Jake wasn't complaining either, as he was totally fine not helping to train shadow assassins and instead learning all about what kids Adam's age played with after the system arrived.

Things had definitely changed for parents, and nearly all for the better. Things like sickness weren't really a thing anymore, and many of the usual woes of children were no longer a factor. Kids were also a lot more durable. Adam could climb a dozen meters up into a tree and just jump down without any issues, and while he was still pretty damn clumsy, he wasn't ever really hurt, even when he tripped and tumbled down a grassy hill. Instead, he asked to go again.

It definitely took a bit of getting used to. If Adam did end up injuring himself somehow, a simple healing spell or potion could instantly fix the problem. Still, Maja was very protective at times. As an example, she rejected Jake and Caleb's idea of putting Adam in a ball of stable arcane mana and throwing it around up in the sky, no matter how much the three of them begged her.

They ended up doing it anyway but got quite a scolding afterward, even if Adam had a great time.

He didn't speak to Villy at all during this time, remaining as disconnected as he could from that entire part of his life. It was a nice reprieve for sure, and he had formed some good memories. Hopefully, he had also given Adam some positive memories of his cool uncle.

Alas, all things have to come to an end. One day, when he was sitting with Adam and playing with stable arcane mana constructs, making whatever shape Adam wanted to see, he got the message he knew would eventually come.

It even happened a bit later than Jake expected—not that he was in any way complaining about that. During his entire visit, he had just been waiting for Sandy to contact him for them to begin their own little adventure. He had expected this to only take a few days, but as mentioned, it ended up taking more than two weeks, with Arnold definitely getting a lot of good data from the giant space worm.

In fact, from the sounds of it, when Jake talked to the worm later, Sandy had only left because the scientist had run out of snacks the worm's dietitian approved of. While the dietitian couldn't leave Sandy's stomach, he could check through the things Sandy ate and make the giant space worm spit out whatever wasn't part of the meal plan.

According to Sandy, even if they had left before the scientist would have liked, Arnold had been quite happy and talked about how he could combine the data provided by Sandy with what he had gathered—namely, from the spaceship Jake had been gifted during his Chosen Ceremony and what he already knew from researching the ruined ship he'd purchased during the Treasure Hunt auction.

Jake was already looking forward to what kind of spacecraft he would make, though it did sound like he was primarily working on improving his satellites before making any ships designed for travel. Plus, knowing Arnold, he would definitely want to do a lot of testing first to make sure he got things right the first time.

Finally... Jake already had a living spaceship by the name of Sandy.

"I'm wriggling to you now," Sandy had sent to Jake as they headed off from Haven, which also marked the end of his family visit. *"Should be there in a jiffy."*

"Are you sure wriggling is the right term? Not flying or teleporting?" Jake asked semi-jokingly.

"I'm the expert here, and the correct term is wriggling. What else would it be? I am wriggling, after all."

"Alright, alright... I'll be waiting," Jake said as he looked at his family, who had noticed his change in demeanor. They had just eaten dinner, and everyone sat in the lounging area on sofas, just talking.

"It's time for you to head off?" Caleb asked, having realized it pretty quickly.

"Yeah." Jake nodded with a sigh.

"Jake is leaving?" Adam asked, confused.

"Sorry, buddy—adventure calls." Jake smiled as he ruffled the little guy's hair.

"Where are you going?" his nephew kept asking.

Jake flashed a big smile as he pointed upwards. "To the moon."

Adam's eyes opened wide in amazement as Jake's mom scolded him. "You shouldn't just make up stories like that."

"I'm serious," Jake responded with a deadpan look. "I'm literally going to the moon."

"Are you going on a rocket ship?" Adam asked, incredibly invested.

"No, something even better," Jake said. "A big space worm."

Jake's mom once more threw him a look, but the gaze he returned made it clear he also wasn't joking with this one, making his dad chuckle. Adam looked a bit skeptical, though, which made Jake shake his head.

"You don't believe me?"

Adam didn't answer, but he did look at his mom as if he expected Maja to confirm if Jake was telling the truth.

"Well, if you don't believe me, I won't let you meet the big space worm," Jake said, acting offended as he crossed his arms.

"I wanna see..." Adam muttered, Jake taking the victory. It was not like he had much of a choice, because if he knew Sandy, the worm would have absolutely no sense of caution or forethought with how they would approach Jake. He was also sure Sandy would indeed arrive fast and have no issues finding him.

One had to remember that Jake carried around a weird rock-egg-thing Sandy had given him, which was apparently the result of the skill Sandy had gained upon receiving the True Blessing of the Boundless Hydra, better known as the Lord Protector of the Order of the Malefic Viper, and even better known as Snappy.

This weird item allowed Sandy to always be aware of where Jake was by tracking that odd item.

As Jake predicted, it didn't take long before Sandy arrived in a similarly predictable and chaotic manner. With little warning, a hundred-meter-long giant space worm fell from the sky, landing right in the middle of the road outside, barely missing any of the houses, though definitely doing plenty of damage to the pavement.

Jake's parents, along with Maja, were shocked. Adam, meanwhile, ran outside the house and saw the giant mass of wiggling flesh.

"Big worm!" Adam yelled as he ran forward, Maja going to grab him as they all exited the house.

"*Hello, little human!*" Sandy said in a cheerful tone. "*And other humans that are also little, but not as little! Also, did I stick that landing or not, eh?*"

"I am indeed surprised you didn't break anything... or, well, break more than you did," Jake said as he walked forward. "This is Sandy, every-one. A friend of mine and my travel companion for my upcoming adventure."

"*More than a travel companion! I am the very mode of transportation itself!*" Sandy said proudly.

"Are you gonna ride the big worm?" Adam asked with amazement.

"In a way?" Jake said.

"*I'm gonna eat him,*" Sandy said.

"That's not nice," Adam accurately pointed out.

"*It is if you have permission, and sometimes even if you don't have permission—just ask Tom,*" Sandy responded, addressing the accusations of non-niceness.

"Who's Tom?" Adam asked, a bit confused.

"*Tom is Tom,*" Sandy said, refusing to elaborate. "*Now, you ready to head off?*"

"Yeah, I'm good to go," Jake said, nodding, as Maja picked up Adam. Jake turned to his family. "It's been fun, and thanks for having me?"

"You remembered the token, right?" his mom asked in a concerned tone.

Jake flashed the communication token and nodded. The item allowed him to call them, or them to call him. It was pretty much a magic telephone and even had video calls in the form of projected images.

"Take care of yourself," Jake's dad said as Caleb gave him a nod.

Finally, Jake said his goodbyes to Adam, seeing that the kid was sad he was leaving. While it did suck to make him sad by leaving, it also made him feel a bit lucky that his nephew at least cared if he left.

"I'll bring you a moon rock; what do you say?" Jake said to Adam.

"Really?" he asked. "A big one?"

Jake grinned. "The biggest one your mom and dad will allow."

"Okay!" Adam said happily as Maja gave Jake a thankful look.

As he went over to Sandy, the giant worm floated into the air.

"See you, everyone," Jake said as the worm opened its mouth and sucked him in.

"Bye, humans related to Jake!" Sandy said as they turned toward the sky, wriggling, and propelled themselves forward with a final battle cry that no one had any idea how Sandy had learned.

"To infinity and beyond!"

———

As Jake flew off into the sky, Caleb stood alongside his wife and parents, staring up at him.

When the two of them shrank in the distance, Robert commented, "What an odd creature. I wonder how Jake even met and made friends with it."

"Oh, yeah, you might not know this, but that worm is the Chosen of the Boundless Hydra and probably one of the creatures with the highest status on the planet, definitely surpassing me," Caleb added.

The others remained quiet as they let it sink in. Finally, Debra commented, "It was a very polite giant space worm, though. Or maybe all space worms are just like that."

"Can't say I would know; I am not familiar with that many space worms," Caleb readily admitted.

"I just hope everything goes well... I don't think anyone has ever been to the moon after the system arrived," Maja commented.

"I'm sure he'll be fine," Caleb said. Genuinely, he was more concerned about the moon and whatever unfortunate creatures lived there than Jake.

————

The Primal Hunter continues in The Primal Hunter 13!

Thank you for reading The Primal Hunter 12

We hope you enjoyed it as much as we enjoyed bringing it to you. We just wanted to take a moment to encourage you to review the book. Follow this link: The Primal Hunter 12 to be directed to the book's Amazon product page to leave your review.

Every review helps further the author's reach and, ultimately, helps them continue writing fantastic books for us all to enjoy.

_____

Also in series:

The Primal Hunter 12
The Primal Hunter 13

———

Want to discuss our books with other readers and even the authors?
JOIN THE AETHON DISCORD!

Calling all LitRPG fans: be the first to discover groundbreaking new releases, access incredible deals, and participate in thrilling giveaways by subscribing to our exclusive LitRPG Newsletter.
https://aethonbooks.com/litrpg-newsletter/

Don't forget to follow us on socials to never miss a new release!

Facebook | Instagram | Twitter | Website

———

Looking for more great LitRPG?
Check out our new releases!

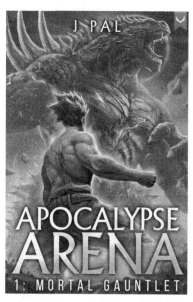

An action-packed apocalyptic LitRPG perfect for fans of Solo Leveling, Super Supportive, and Iron Prince! *The stronger his opponent, the harder he hits.* *Saving an innocent from a drug-crazed superhuman should've left Nil broken. Instead, it wins him the Nexus' attention. Nil is done feeling small and watching his family scrape by. He now has the opportunity to make a difference. Apocalypse Arena holds the key; where the multiverse's champions battle and keep the Scourge at bay. Pain, death, and heartbreak await all who run the gauntlets, but Nil has what it takes to grapple his way to the top. The multiverse is watching, and he'll be damned sure to give them a show. Perhaps even knock out a God.* ***Don't miss the start of an action-packed new Apocalypse LitRPG Adventure from bestselling author J Pal. Featuring a unique System that fuses LitRPG, Cultivation and super powers along with gladiator fights, battle royales and other combat games where death is always a possibility.*** It's perfect for fans of Solo Leveling, Super Supportive, and Iron Prince!

GET APOCALYPSE ARENA NOW!

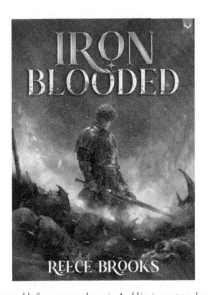

A new world of monsters and magic. A soldier in an eternal war. A champion rises. Thrust into a new world filled with monsters and magic, Will's life has become a war for survival. He has nothing more than a class called "soldier" and a strange leveling System he's never seen before. When he stumbles across a dying stranger, a mysterious questline activates. Now Will must head to the front lines where humanity wages war against a ruthless Goblin Horde. There he will join the standing Kadian Army and forge his name from the fires of legend. He'll have to face goblins, hordes of the undead, cultists, and demons from Hell. And that's just before breakfast... Enter a realm where humans battle monsters and the good die young in Iron Blooded, an epic new LitRPG Progression Fantasy. Featuring a focus on battles, leveling up, strategy, tactics, and political intrigue, it's perfect for fans of A Soldier's Life, Limitless Lands, and The Accidental Champion.

GET IRON BLOODED NOW!

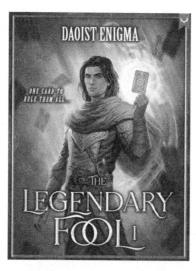

A LitRPG adventure featuring a card-based magic system utilizing soul cards perfect for fans of All the Skills. ONE CARD TO RULE THEM ALL. Thomas Lowe was destined for a life of mediocrity, working a dead-end job in rural America. But fate seemed to have other plans for him. One card changes everything. While he's gifted a power beyond imagination, he also unlocks a prophecy that puts him in the crosshairs of Ancient Clans and Noble Houses that have existed since the dawn of the first era. The name of the card is simple... [Card Name: The Fool] [Rank: Ephemeral/ Legendary-Unique] Join Thomas in this all new Deck-building LitRPG adventure from Daoist Enigma, author of Modern Patriarch. Featuring a unique card-based magic system utilizing soul cards, it's perfect for fans of All the Skills, A Summoner Awakens, and Card Mage.

GET THE LEGENDARY FOOL NOW!

———

For all our LitRPG books, visit our website.

Made in United States
Orlando, FL
26 July 2025

63292123R00350